REBECCA HANSEN CARRER

# Rain Shadow

*For Laurent, the fount of everything*

"*It is the proper destiny of every considerable stream in the West to become an irrigating ditch. It would seem the streams are willing. They go as far as they can, or dare, toward the tillable lands in their own boulder fenced gullies—but how much farther in the man-made waterways.*"

Mary Austin, *The Land of Little Rain*

This is a work of fiction based on real lives and events

Cover design and art direction: Randy Nickel
Cover photography:
  *City image:* courtesy Los Angeles Public Library Photo Collection
  *Aqueduct image:* courtesy Library of Congress

# AUTHOR'S NOTE

This story originated in an experience I shared during the late 1990s with many other people: being captivated by the television documentary *Cadillac Desert*, a four-part PBS series based on the book of the same name by the late Marc Reisner. The first part of the series, "Mulholland's Dream," explored the eventually violent confrontation between Los Angeles and the Owens Valley over water from the Owens River.

I remember wondering, as I watched the program, what it would be like to see your father get up from the kitchen table and go out with neighbors to commit what we'd today certainly call an act of terrorism. That question started me reading. Among the wonderful nonfiction works devoted to the subject or place, I'm especially appreciative of what I learned from Rebecca Fish Ewan's *A Land Between*, Margaret Leslie Davis's *Rivers in the Desert*, Abraham Hoffman's *Vision or Villainy*, William L. Kahrl's *Water and Power*, John Walton's *Western Times and Water Wars* and a remarkable first-person account, *The Enchanted Valley*, by Guy Chaffee Earl. For insights into writer Mary Austin, who appears prominently in this story, the superb biographies by Esther F. Lanigan and Augusta Fink were extremely helpful. And Catherine Mulholland's biography of her grandfather William was invaluable.

The Owens River drama has been the seed of fiction before, as well as of other arts. Mary Austin herself wrote about it in her 1917 novel *The Ford*. Many readers may know that Roman Polanski's 1974 neo-noir film *Chinatown* was loosely based on the conflict.

While *Rain Shadow* is a work of fiction, it is firmly based on actual characters and events. I've made some minor adjustments to timing, as in Mary Austin's stay in Carmel, while taking care to preserve the nature and significance of what really happened.

My heartfelt thanks to those who gave help and encouragement, including Richard Bray, Patrice Carrer, Randy Nickel, my father Hal Okholm and my husband Laurent Carrer.

# READER ENRICHMENTS

You'll find additional resources, including the original music score from the ebook, a map, and background information and images at http://www.rainshadownovel.com. There's also a "What Happened Next?" section and gallery of real historical characters.

*The Source*

He was poking his nose at me like other policemen used their nightsticks. Jab, jab. Leaning over the table toward me. Jab, jab, jab. Ridiculous.

All these years later I remember telling myself to find something laughable about him, and I'd sure enough found it. I made myself stare at his nose as he pointed it at me again, advancing until he was nearly shoving it into my face and I almost laughed. But as he got closer, either my pupils or nerve gave way, and I jerked against the metal chair, handcuffs clanging against the rungs.

"Tell me the truth, little missy, what were you doing up there on top of that dam?!"

He pulled back to assess the effect he was having on me. It was enough for my eyes to refocus, and what I was thinking then was that he looked like a wild boar, predatory dark discs on either side of the snout, the rolls of flesh that protruded over his tight white collar shaking with fury. But that wasn't helpful, because I suddenly realized it wasn't fury making his neck

— 1 —

*fat waggle. It was amusement and lip-smacking satisfaction. "Two-Gun Davis" was enjoying this.*

*The police chief had earned his moniker by waging a gun battle on the streets of Los Angeles against bootleggers and racketeers, who he'd publicly proclaimed should be "brought in dead, not alive." He was probably also behind a campaign of harassment against unions and political reformers, seeing little distinction apparently, and he'd warned his men that showing "the least mercy to criminals" would earn them a severe reprimand. Yet while brute force was Two Gun's preferred method of ensuring public order, he was not completely primeval. He was also modern in using statistics to figure crime trends and implementing the dragnet system of coordinated action to track down the most-wanted. This dual nature made him extremely effective and, to most people in the city, terrifying.*

*I was no exception, which is why, for a very long time, I've regarded that moment, when I sat stiff and mostly still as the beast sniffed and prodded, as one of my most courageous. Recently, however, I've realized it might have been the opposite: This may have been the point when I began to let fear whittle down my life. My victory in that airless room high up in the towering Hall of Justice was simply keeping the fear and anger locked inside. I was determined not to let the beast see it, and I mostly succeeded. In all the years since then, I've become even better at it.*

*Until this morning, when I heard something on the radio that made me feel as if I were back in that room, locked up with the beast again. As if my struggle to keep fear hidden that day and all I've done these many years hence to take my life far away from that place had achieved no purchase at all. Something that shook those old feelings up and right out onto my kitchen table. They're here, all around, filling up the space between the walls. If I dare open a window or the door, they'll explode into the street and fill up the whole valley.*

*It was the news that came after the weather forecast, cold and clear. A Stanford University lecturer, "an agitator" for the environment, as some folks around here called him, died last night in a head-on crash on an icy mountain road. His wife was driving. She and the couple's son escaped serious injury. A daughter did not. A fellow agitator, also in the car, died too.*

*The cause of the accident is known and understandable. When I was a newspaperwoman, I collected facts like these hundreds of times. It was* a snowy, treacherous night. A local man driving a pickup pulled into the opposite lane to pass. It was a bad decision; he didn't have enough time.

But plausible facts don't explain what happened. My brain, at 92 operating more reliably than my knees, prods me with two questions: Why should the life of this 24-year-old be ripped from its course? And why should this happen nearly 50 years after another man, also an agitator, met his death in a head-on crash on a mountain road? They not only had the same death, but the same enemy. Two Davids against one Goliath.

"Oh, for pity's sake, get ahold of yourself!" I scold aloud. Even before this shock I've been having trouble keeping my mind from constantly heading down some gopher hole. As my body has become less active, my brain has become more so. Sometimes it feels like one of those cradle toys where balls hung from strings swing left and right and left again, forever striking back at each other so the movement goes on and on. The toy, as I recall, illustrates some rational principle of Sir Isaac Newton, but watching it is irrationally dizzying, and having it inside one's head is exhausting.

To calm myself, I hobble over to the window and look out at the mountains. Light is beginning to reveal thick blankets of snow covering the peaks in the west. As the sun rises, the snowfields take on a pinkish glow, which deepens while I stand watching until it turns red…red as a rose, red as blood. Suddenly in my mind's eye I see the bloody crash, metal folded into flesh, glass shards floating down like snowflakes. Then that picture dissolves into the other crash, the one before: red staining the white fur of a little dog nestled against the man's crushed skull, growling and snapping at anyone who tries to approach.

Other pictures follow. Before I can stop it, my mind plays them like a newsreel in a movie theater:

There's a lake, and in it Paiute men, women and children struggle to swim against a strong headwind. As those ahead turn to shout to those behind, their phantom faces are torn by moonlight, their words whipped by gusts of moaning air that cloaks sound. From where the white men stand spread out along the shoreline, they hear nothing but their own jesting and hooping. Giddy, but still accurate with their rifles, they methodically pick off the swimmers one by one.

In a kitchen, a man fills his glass from a china pitcher, takes a long swallow, then places the glass by his plate. He rises from the supper table, looks back at his family from the screen door, strides across the yard and climbs into the passenger seat of a waiting Model T Ford. He has to hug his knees to his chest to keep his boots off of the crate of dynamite on the floor. Hours later the man returns home, a criminal in the eyes of the law and in his own.

On a dusty street, two brothers, rich, handsome and charming, looked up to as leaders all their lives, fall from grace in an afternoon. Some of their neighbors, even some who've lost a lifetime's savings because of them, testify on their behalf. Others curse and spit as the brothers are led off in foot irons to the state penitentiary.

At the bank of a river, a young boy huddles naked in the scrub brush, cradling his matted, shivering, whimpering dog. The boy's mother lies two miles downstream, impaled by a tree branch. His father is swept out to sea and washed up on a beach near the Mexican border. Hundreds of people have lost their lives under the onslaught of billions of gallons of water.

And then there's an airless room, where a young woman sits handcuffed and terrified, her spine going liquid against the rigid back of the chair as the beast noses forward again. She watches the nostrils of the snout open as if they were the organ spewing the words: "Tell me! You're in big trouble missy—people died! Tell me what you did!"

I shake my head sharply to clear the horrible pictures, and my eyes gradually refocus on the high snowfields. The sun has continued its ascent during my absence, and the red glow has faded back to pink and is now bleaching into blinding white. It hurts my eyes to look, but I don't close them.

I know all these dreadful things flow from the same source. I am looking at it.

PART I: 1904-1906

*The Valley*

Courtesy County of Inyo, Eastern California Museum

# Chapter 1

Another dead soldier. From the corner of his eye, Mulholland saw the arc of Eaton's arm and the flash of the bottle as it flew out along the same trajectory. Then a sharp pop and the bottle splintered into oblivion. Nothing remained but a few sparkling bits in front of a rock. Back to where you came from, thought Mulholland, sand made into glass, now sand again.

They had left a trail of "dead soldiers," empty whiskey bottles, across most of their now four-day journey from Los Angeles over the Mojave Desert. Only in the past few hours had Eaton, growing restless, started using them for target practice. They were passing through Red Rock Canyon, a vivid landscape of auburn, white, gray and sometimes green striped rock. The stripes, Mulholland knew, were the result of different types of sandstone and clay, laid down over millions of years in ancient river channels and floodplains, shaped and colored by earthquakes, volcanic activity and erosion. Repeated rivulets had worn away the softer layers faster, leaving them fluted and the overall cliff face uneven, with gaps and protrusions, like a badly made cake. Strange, he mused, a monument to the power of water, now bone dry. His companion seemed oblivious to the spectacle. Mulholland chomped with irritation on the cigar that habitually sprouted from his bushy handlebar mustache.

Still he admired the ease with which Eaton did it. Relaxing his long frame into the seat of the buckboard wagon as he swung his right arm gracefully back and up, fingers releasing the bottle, while the movement continued forward, the empty hand pointing to where the bottle seemed to hang in the air for just an instant, before the pistol swung up in the other hand and Eaton took his shot. Most of the time he was dead-on. Some of the credit no doubt owing to Eaton's new Belgian FN Model 1903 semi-automatic. A beauty of a beast, thought Mulholland, looking at how lightly Eaton's hand held the gun's walnut-checkered grip.

The man did everything with ease. Born with a silver spoon in his mouth to one of the city's leading families, Fred Eaton was a charter member of the Sons of the Golden West. His father, a Harvard-educated lawyer, had arrived with the first wave of gold rush fortune hunters, stayed to become one of the city's first district attorneys, had been much involved in Los Angeles civic improvement and was one of the founders of Pasadena, a city just to its north. Fred, fair-haired boy and pedigreed native son, joined the Los Angeles Water Company as an apprentice at age 15 and made his father proud a dozen years later by taking over the running of it. During a stint as city engineer, Fred later planned the community's sewer system. His father had not lived to see him elected mayor at the age of 43, an office he had held for just two years before becoming a private but ever-prominent citizen again.

Mulholland sniffed. He was about the same age as Eaton, in his late 40s, but his own history couldn't be more different. Arriving on a ship from Dublin at age 19, he had worked as a seaman, in lumber camps and in a dry goods store before heading to California in 1877. He and his brother had been so poor, they'd had to stow away on a westbound ship. But they'd been caught and put ashore at the Isthmus of Panama, and so had walked across it for more than 38 miles. In Los Angeles, he'd initially literally scratched a living from the dirt. His job had been to maintain one of the city's major irrigation ditches by clearing weeds, stones, brush and dead animals out of it.

Mulholland couldn't resent Eaton his privilege. He wore it so easily, like everything else, and he was good company, as able to savor one of Mulholland's raunchy yarns as a glass of fine wine. And Eaton had been generous to him, acting the mentor as Mulholland rose up the ranks in the city's water and power organization, eventually taking on Eaton's former position at its head.

He licked his lips for the thousandth time, but his tongue grated across rough, cracking skin. It was scorching hot and sucking dry this early September day. He wanted to be done with it. Even before reaching the Mojave, the trip had been brutal. Again and again they had painstakingly eased the two-mule team in and out of dry wash gulleys. At the Newhall Grade, a steep ascent up what Mulholland figured was about a 40-degree slope, they'd had to unpack their entire three-week supply of water, mule feed, bedrolls, beans, bacon, flour, sugar, coffee and whiskey. After leading the team to the top of the pass and tying the mules off, they'd gone back down and pushed the empty buckboard up, then repacked everything and moved on. The same tedious, sweaty process got them over the Tehachapi mountains, a dusty-brown range, folded and corrugated like cardboard.

Then down the other side to endless desert. Sometimes still and dead as the tomb it had become for the bleached skeletons of stage horses and the pioneers whose headstones they saw scattered along the trail. Sometimes screaming with wind as "dust devils," miniature tornadoes of sand, sprung out of nowhere, spiraling across the land and sending clumps of sagebrush bouncing witlessly in all directions. To climb out of this canyon, they'd have to unpack again and push over a 4,400-foot pass.

But they wouldn't have to go down the backside very far this time. After this they'd be on a plateau, where the desert floor rises up to meet the base of the Sierra Nevada range of mountains. Tonight they should reach Olancha, a small town sitting at an elevation of nearly 4,000 feet. Tonight they would have a proper dinner and savor a bottle of something other than whiskey.

Mulholland tugged his hat down on his forehead and looked out at the canyon floor dotted with tufts of brush and thick fingers of fuzzy cholla cactus. There God damned better be something on the other side besides a good meal and bottle of wine. He glanced again at Eaton, now dozing, chin on chest, crossed arms cradling another volunteer at arms, long legs stretched elegantly out over the front of the buckboard.

He'd taken the man's word for it that this trip through hell would be worth the making. He forced his eyes to seek the horizon, pupils contracting painfully against the glare. Holding his gaze steady, trying to peer through the liquidy heat-warped air to see…?

Mulholland jerked his head back and roared with laughter. We're like the fools in *A Thousand and One Nights* crawling our way across the desert toward an oasis that turns out to be a mirage! He looked over to see if he'd awakened his companion. Eaton was still snoozing peacefully. Mulholland tightened and released his aching shoulders. Perhaps it was not a mirage, he chewed his cigar contemplatively. The numerous ascents up steep grades had done more than break his back, they'd aroused his hopes. He and Eaton had covered well over 200 miles, and if they were to turn around right now and head back to the city, it would essentially be downhill all the way. Gravity alone would be enough to bring the water south.

Tossing the spent cigar butt, Mulholland snapped the reins to hasten the mules. He admired the animals for their sturdiness of body and character. The nature of a mule was marked by determination and persistence. Not unlike his own. I started out digging ditches and now here I am, he thought, looking down at his grimy, sunburned, strong and steady hands.

---

*I tear my eyes away from the glare of sun on snow and start some coffee. Then I go out to the front room to fetch pen and paper, return to the kitchen and sit at the table. I've a notion that by writing I might calm myself. The coffeemaker my grandnephew CK retrieved from a flea market, plunking it down on my table with a "Here auntie, it still works," gurgles and spurts, hissing steam like an old-time locomotive pulling into the train station…I remember gazing through a cloud of steam, vibrations coming up through my feet on the wooden slats of the platform as the immense engine approached, pulling a line of cars whose end I couldn't see or fathom… knowing I'd soon be climbing into one of those cars, leaving the station on my first journey, on my way to a place I'd never been…leaving my valley.*

*The valley I grew up in was not this desolate place. The valley I grew up in was described by inhabitants and visitors alike as a Garden of Eden. It was a magical place where the sun shone every day of my childhood—rain was a rare entertainment.*

*Technically that meant we lived in a desert. Yet here the gray of sand, sagebrush and chaparral was balanced by wide swaths of salt grass meadow, light green in summer and spring, golden in fall and winter. Pines, poplars, oaks, cottonwoods, water birch and willow trees grew in clusters. Marshes and sloughs here and there were thickly matted with reeds, rushes and cattails. Flowers peeked from beneath rock ledges, hid in briar thickets and, in their season, burst forth across fields. Fiery wild almond, red columbine, coral penstemon trumpets, orchids and tiger lilies, majestic blue lupine, fragrant pink tangles of wild rose, shy buttercups and spiky mauve checkerblooms. Songbirds of untold number and variety, eagles, hawks and prairie falcons hanging, tilting and soaring, casting shadows on earthbound creatures, waterfowl so thick, their wings rising in flight from the lake generated a roar audible from nearby mountaintops, scarlet-bellied golden trout, bighorn sheep, deer, coyotes, cougars and, my favorite, the ringtail cats all shared our little paradise.*

*This place of abundance was narrow, only five to ten miles wide, and hugged by mountains on both sides. To the west, soaring abruptly from the valley floor, was the mighty castle wall of the Sierra Nevada, its crenelated top dazzling with snow much of the year. To the east, a line of low mottled brown foothills fronted the grayish White-Inyo range, subdued mature sibling of the brash youngster to the west. Pa told us that Mt. Whitney, the tallest of the Sierra peaks at 14,505 feet, was the highest point of elevation in the country, except for Alaska. On the other side of the eastern mountains, the huge, scorching wasteland called Death Valley, 282 feet below sea level, was the lowest point. We sat between them.*

*From our house, nestled below a rocky creek in a clump of cottonwoods and aspens, the mountains were ever-present companions. They marked the boundaries of waking and sleeping, chores and play as surely as they marked the expanse of our physical world. They orchestrated the pageant of the day with perfect symmetry. Upon waking, we would look to the western wall, where a pink wash of light would be warming the Sierra peaks, sometimes turning their crests fiery red, before spreading* gradually down the ramparts toward the valley floor. You could tell the time of day and season of the year by how far it had reached, to this cliff or that outcropping of rock. Then the sun would finally clear the eastern ridge, in that instant taking all of the valley as its dominion. At night, the show played in reverse. As the sun dropped behind the western wall, shadows falling first on the rocks at the base of the Sierra would unfold across the valley floor before creeping up the eastern range, until all was dusky, save a rosy glow at the upper edge. Everyone on the ranch knew that when the shadow reached a certain point it was time to stop work, unhitch the horses, set the dogs to rounding up the cows and head home to supper.

The affection we felt for the mountains was reciprocated with extravagant gifts. The Sierra wall guaranteed the abundant sunshine. We were, my father explained, in the "rain shadow" of these mountains. Often of a summer, we would see black, threatening sky in the west, sometimes split by forks of lightning. Heavy clouds, sinking low with the moisture they carried, became trapped against the citadels of granite. We'd hear them roar in frustration at their inability to reach us until, giving up, they released their burden on the other side. On those few strange days when the thunderheads managed to break free of confinement, they expelled their rage over our valley.

Almost immediately, their fury would dissipate, and the irrepressible sunlight return. Numerous mountain canyons on the Sierra side, spaces long ago cut out of the rock mass by glaciers, would be filled with mist and garlanded with rainbows. The air all across the valley would turn sharp with the tangy scent of sagebrush.

Despite the infrequency of such events, our valley had plenty of water and rich soil, additional gifts from the Sierra. The snow crowns slowly melted and ran down from the lofty heights. Through steep, glacier-scoured canyons of polished rock rushed clear, cold streams with names like Oak Creek, Taboose Creek, Hogback and Little Pine. In years when the snow pack was heavy, the number of water courses multiplied, new rivulets carving small gulches, miniature canyons within the canyons, and fanning across rock faces. In summer these would dry up, leaving dusty gulleys in the earth and mineral stains on the rock as the only evidence of the season of excess. Tiny particles of rock and soil washed down the mountainsides, as they had for thousands of centuries, and were captured and held in the valley, forming large fans of alluvial soil, particularly at the northern end. Sierra melt soaked into the ground, creating numerous freshwater springs and occasional spongy patches where flowers and even small ferns grew.

Most of the runoff ended up in the Owens River. Fed by the numerous mountain streams, it ran the length of the Owens Valley, some 100 miles, before emptying into Owens Lake at the southern end. Viewed from above, when pausing on a trail winding up into the canyons, the band of grasses, willows and cottonwoods marking its banks formed a wavy green line.

On either side of the river were deeper green patches—more intense in color than the salt grass meadowlands—where water had been coaxed by irrigation ditches into fields of alfalfa, wheat, barley, oats and corn. The ditches themselves spread out like spidery veins on an old man's nose.

From the time I was old enough to notice until I left home as a young woman, the green patch-work carpet extended farther and farther from the river, pushing out across the valley floor. To us children, this transformation was one more thing that seemed magical, but, of course, every inch of land put to farming represented back-breaking work by somebody's parents.

No one ever complained though. On the contrary, people liked to talk about the ditches, and the steady advance of cultivatable land was a topic taken up again and again with inexhaustible enthusiasm. It was said that the soil was so rich here, all one needed do was add water, and crops would flourish. The possibility of rapidly increasing the acreage under cultivation—once irrigation on a far grander scale could be accomplished with the help of a hoped-for federal reclamation project—stirred the imaginations and ambitions of the farmers.

Mary Austin said they were fools, enchanted by dreams of riches and obsessed with covering every inch of brown with green, remaking the land, and themselves, in the process, but blind to its true nature and value.

Mary also said the blessing hastening down to our fields carried a curse. It had been so for the Paiutes, who had camped along the creeks and springs, and been first to use the snow melt for irrigation. They had planted fields with grass seeds and grass nuts, small tuberous roots that tasted like nuts. In fact, the name Paiute comes from "Pah-Utes," or "water Utes," and the Indian name for the valley was "water ditch." We kids found that very funny.

*She told us the Paiutes called Lone Pine Peak "Oppapago," which meant "The Weeper." "It's a sad, old rock," she said, "sitting apart from the rest of the peaks, head bowed like a rebozo-covered señora. Oppapago saw your good Christian granpappies shoot those Paiute in the lake. She cries for them, and for us."*

*Mary said some pretty strange things. We kids were embarrassed, but we laughed because this particular mountain did sometimes look like it was crying, dozens of rivulets streaming down its granite slabs, like wet cheeks.*

---

As it turned out, the only wine Eaton and Mulholland found in Olancha was the peppery, sweet red favored by the French and Basque sheepherders who passed through the small settlement on their way to and from summer pastures. Anchored at its dusty center by a tremendous cottonwood, soft-leaved like a willow but tall and stately, Olancha consisted of a livery, post office/general store, a hotel and not much else. The tiny town had sprouted with the discovery of a silver lode in the nearby Coso Range during the 1860s. When the silver market went bust in the next decade, Olancha survived by providing scant but essential municipal services to a cluster of cattle ranches.

The sole notable thing about it now was its location, a couple of miles south of a large body of water, a piece of sea long trapped by the land. Evaporation under the relentless sun had increased the salinity so that Owens Lake, cloudy green a hundred yards off shore, was milky white and crusty at the edge. The effect was eerie, like the gaze of an immense eye covered by cataract.

"Ooh-ee," whistled Eaton. "How long have I been snoozin? It's the God-damned Dead Sea!"

As the wagon descended toward the town, the harsh glare off of the lake from the dropping sun made the men raise a hand to shield their eyes. By the time they turned down Olancha's diminutive main street, the glare had subsided to a mauve glow. The hotel was empty, save a handful of locals in the saloon off of the parlor. Eaton, strikingly handsome with an even gaze and ready charm, was a man strangers easily warmed up to. He shook hands and stood drinks all around.

"The name's Fred Eaton, and this here's my friend Bill Mulholland. We're up here from the Tejon country for some fishing."

Mulholland said little. He drank freely of the local wine. Eaton took a swallow and decided to stick with the whiskey. They both downed a heaping bowl of mutton stew with bread and butter, then had another. Mulholland told a few jokes. They took turns quoting Shakespeare and Mark Twain. In this, Eaton, despite his upbringing, was no match for Mulholland, who loved the written word with the devotion of the self-taught. But after so many nights on the ground, the allure of a bed was irresistible. It wasn't long before they climbed the wobbly stairs to adjacent rooms.

The next day Mulholland stood clear-eyed, bareheaded, motionless in the chilly high-desert morning air. He had never felt better in his life. He stood staring at it, couldn't take his eyes off of it: If the lake had been the Dead Sea, then this was the land of milk and honey.

Earlier, moving their team and wagon quietly out of the little town before daybreak, the two men had rapidly covered the short distance to the lake. Reaching its northern shore, they had tied up the team and skirted the salt-encrusted rim by foot. Weaving their way around willows and cottonwoods, through tangles of grass, reeds, rushes, asters and marigolds for several miles, they had finally found it: the reason the brackish lake wasn't actually dead. Owens Lake hadn't dried up because its rate of evaporation was slowed by a strong influx of clear, pure, cold water from the Sierra snowpack, supplied in abundance by the Owens River.

Now, hiking along the river bank north of the lake, beneath a sky so thin and translucent it seemed lit like glass, the two men stepped over a half dozen rough cut irrigation ditches, diverting a bit of water in an easterly or westerly direction toward alfalfa fields and ranch houses. After a while they came to a well-tended canal, about four feet wide and six feet deep. A carefully lettered sign wedged in a pile of rocks announced "Owens River and Big Pine Canal" and listed the names of the ditch association's members: "Samuelsons, Allmons, Oliveras, Blacks, Kisperts, McGoverns, Springers, Cooks, Sextons, Gunns, Diaz."

"They're organized," said Eaton, "but stupid. There isn't a single reservoir, no place to store the overflow in wet years. When dry times come, they start fighting among themselves."

"Terrible waste," pronounced Mulholland, "It's not the Original Sin, but damn close."

---

*"Hazy, Haaaaaazy!"*

*I remember fancying I heard my brother's voice in my ear that night as I crouched in the dirt. It wasn't the wind but his voice I heard as I strained to keep the bouncing beam of a dime store flashlight aimed onto the fuse so I could light it, waiting for the moment I knew I would do it.*

*Chris was always teasing me for being a bit fuzzy, head in the clouds or off in some canyon of reverie. My middle name, Hazeltine, one of those legacy last names imposed on descendants, suited his purposes. But that night I wondered if he'd have thought better of it, even been surprised to see me there. If he'd still been alive, that is, and could have known I'd come to the end of my dreaming at last. That night I was taking action.*

*"Haaaaaazy!" he had called to me many years before, as I'd stepped down from the train on that first journey. It had been his voice calling me into the wider world as I'd placed my foot on the depot platform. Just as it had been his voice calling me out of the kitchen and into the yard all those mornings when, impatient with my dawdling, he'd needed help with the produce wagon.*

*From the age of 12, Chris was responsible for taking our ranch produce up-valley to the towns of Big Pine and Bishop, and down-valley to Lone Pine. Once a week he also made a two-day roundtrip to Cerro Gordo, where a zinc strike had recently revived the flagging silver mining town. I would watch, sleepy-eyed but fascinated as my blond, ruddy-faced brother cast a studied eye over the pile of potatoes on the barn floor, stretched out his hand and plucked out the largest and best-formed spuds. He'd turn them over in his palm, nod, then drop them into the bulging sack, tying it off when full and raking the rest into the corner of the barn. Pa had taught him to select only spuds of uniformly large size and good color for market, which Chris faithfully did. Those not meeting the standard would be boiled and fed to the hogs.*

*Task accomplished, Chris, who was already tall and strong, would hoist the sack onto the wagon bed, where a dozen others like it already rested beside big open baskets of onions, corn and cabbage, and slatted trays of small paper containers full of ripe blackberries. These were usually* harvested the afternoon before, packed in the wagon in the evening and covered with a wet cloth to keep them fresh until morning. To this bounty, Ma would have added fresh eggs, gathered before dawn.

Finally Chris would survey the wagon with satisfaction, glance to the west to see how late it was coming, then swing up into the wagon with a "Let's go Jessie!" His companion in commerce, our black-and-white border collie, would jump onto the seat next to him, tail thrashing with joy and impatience. I'd push her over and scramble up after, receiving a nibbly, excited kiss.

Jessie and I loved to go to the melon patch, the first destination for the wagon and the last step in Chris's meticulous preparation before heading off to town. I'd hop down into the tangle of vines, and he'd hand me his open knife so I could cut the stems of the ripe fruits, their hard shells laced with frosty dew. This was always done last so that when Chris arrived in town, the melons would still be fresh, cool and delicious. One by one, I'd hand them up to him where he stood in the wagon, watch him lean over to gently nestle them in a tarp between the baskets of potatoes. "That's enough," he'd say, holding his hand out for me to pop the knife shut and toss it over. He'd catch and pocket it in one smooth movement. "Thanks, see you at supper. Wear your bonnet!" he'd call over his shoulder as he and Jessie headed down the lane.

When he was well out of sight, I'd squat down again to where there were usually a couple of the best melons, which I'd surreptitiously freed from the vine but left where they lay. Often I'd hide them in the willows by the creek, so I could feast on them during the hot afternoon with my friends Juan, Emma and Rosie. But sometimes I'd take one to Mary. Untying the ribbons of the hated bonnet that hung down my back, I'd place the fruit inside, cradling the bundle to my belly, marching off through the fields toward Mary's house.

# Chapter 2

Mary Hunter Austin lived in a squat brown house on the edge of town with her husband Wallace and their daughter Ruth. The house, by the side of a musical little creek that ran down from Kearsarge Peak, and graced with a large willow tree, was the first home of her own for Mary since marrying a decade before. A series of business adventures had turned out badly for Wallace, forcing the young couple to relocate several times from town to town, renting rooms and, even once, being turned out of them.

She loved the house because it was hers and because it had a fine view of the Sierra, being situated at the end of the lane leading out of the village toward the rock face. Also, adjacent to the house, there was an untilled field that rose slightly as it reached west before ending at the slope of broken "talus" rock that marked the beginning of the Sierra. This field, which belonged to a neighbor, was not held in high esteem by the town. A succession of previous owners had attempted to cultivate it and failed, and the current owner had pronounced it unfit for crops or even firewood. In fact, the field was viewed with abhorrence by Mary's other neighbors, since, having begun to revert back to wildness, it had now become a breed-ing ground for wild seeds, which, born by the wind in season, invaded nearby gardens and fields.

Mary thought it a perfect place—that is, she thought it was perfectly what it was meant to be. She could be found there at all hours, attentive to its charms and observing its small changes. Mary watched fascinated to see nature's own bounty retake the once-cultivated land, sought out the stony patches where wild olives sprawled and rejoiced in how the leafless twigs of wild almond exploded into fire after just a few days of sun at the edge of winter, followed soon after by the clematis vine's flowery declaration of spring. In the late afternoon, she greeted a red-tailed hawk, who returned for two summers at a seemingly appointed hour every day in search of the jackrabbits, gophers and other burrowers who sought safety in the field's untended tangle. She liked it that way, marked by no order other than the natural one, her little bit of wilderness next door. To keep it with her, she had even gathered stones from the field to build her home's hearth. One by one, she had carted and laid them tenderly in place.

But the little brown house was not a scene of contentment. When Janey visited, she never knew what she would find there. Once she had heard Ruth Austin, who was her age but mentally backward, crying from yards away. Stepping onto the back porch, Janey had seen through the open window that the girl was tied to a chair. Mary was pacing to and fro, still in her nightgown, gesturing wildly, long, uncombed hair streaming out behind her, her homely face alive in silent conversation, deaf to her daughter's wailing. On another visit, Janey had found Ruth in the charge of Sally John, a Paiute who helped Mary with the housework. "Missus gone to Chinese town," Sally had reported, referring to the small back-street quarter where a handful of Orientals, come over to work on the railroads, had settled.

Sally had supplied the information without exclamation or interest. But there were plenty in the town of Independence and the broader valley community who would have been interested in this piece of news: Mary was a reliable source of scandal and frequent target for disapproving gossip among the good matrons.

For one thing, Mary had for several years worked as a teacher. Though women teachers were not uncommon in the West, the practice was still looked upon by many as suspicious and undermining to the foundations of society. It was the opinion of quite a few people in the town that Wallace Austin had been altogether too lenient allowing his wife to earn wages outside of the home, even though he himself was at the time county superintendent of schools and therefore in a position to oversee her activities. Worse, when Mary stopped teaching she began writing.

She had sold several of her stories to the *Overland Monthly* and *Out West*, two western periodicals, and her work had also begun to appear in well-known eastern magazines, including the *Atlantic Monthly*, *Cosmopolitan* and *St. Nicholas*. Just last year, she'd even gone so far as to publish a small book on, of all things, the land, weather, flora and fauna of the valley and surrounding Inyo County. What's more *The Land of Little Rain* had a whole chapter devoted to that blasted field!

Even if Mary Austin had confined her ambitions to being a housewife, she would have been the subject of gossip. For she was very odd: unattractive, with legs too short for her broad shoulders and bosom; face fleshy with a high forehead and thick lips set in a frown. Perhaps because

of these unhappy endowments, Mary's countenance had surrendered early
to gravity, with eyes, brows and lips all turning downward, and a chin that
would have been firm and resolute had it not been marred by jowls. Yet she
did not behave in the retiring, obliging way expected of homely women.
She was, on the contrary, bold in her opinions and too earnest in proffer-
ing them. She made people uncomfortable. Moreover she was seen as arrogant and selfish, more concerned with literary foolishness than with taking
care of her husband and child. It was said that she sat writing in bed while
Wallace made breakfast and fed the girl.

Those who might have been inclined to overlook these faults were
put off by Mary's erratic behavior. When she had first arrived in the valley,
Mary, who was a gifted cook, would occasionally show up on a neighbor's
doorstep with a fresh-baked pie or plate of cookies. But the next day, when
the poor soul attempted to return the favor, Mary would be distracted,
withdrawn, and unfriendly, her dress and hair unkempt, barely a word
to say at the door, if she answered the knock at all. And if, hearing Ruth's
wailing, a neighbor lady should be so bold as to enter the Austin house
while Mary was absent, attempting to soothe, feed and clean the child,
or tend to the piles of dirty dishes in the sink, Mary upon returning
would be cold and resentful.

Most disturbing, while Mary was invariably stiff and awkward with
her neighbors and with other townsfolk at church socials and community
events, she appeared to fraternize easily with her social inferiors. She was
always running off to the Indian campoodie, spent feast days in Las Ulvas,
the Mexican settlement at Lone Pine, and had been observed singing
around the campfire with sheepherders. Once she had caused a scandal
by baking a holiday cake for Li Bao, the Chinese laundryman, who had
proudly displayed it in the window of his shop for all to see. This, on top
of her advocacy of Higher Criticism, an unapproved method of closely
reading the scriptures, was too much for the congregation. Mary was "read
out" of the church, after which many of its upstanding members did their
best to ignore her, though they remained insatiably curious about all she
said and did.

Mary seemed amused rather than chastised by this ostracism.
Sunday mornings she would stride out across the fields, in long skirt and

broad brimmed hat, marching toward a canyon path. "A church is not the only place to seek God," she instructed Janey.

This was the strangest thing of all about Mary: her rapturous, even mystical adoration of the land. Everyone else in Owens Valley loved the land too, for its bounty, the wealth they could bring forth from its fields and mines, the cattle they could run over it, the sheep they could graze on it. But they simply couldn't understand writing a book about the trail a badger takes during the night to reach a water hole or how the colors of high-altitude flowers bleach in the sun, their beauty fading in a day. Above all, they found her reverence for that worthless field ridiculous and maddening.

While the indignant valley matrons clucked and pursed their lips, Thomas Rickey, the biggest rancher in the county and a man used to finding his own answers, grew curious. One day, Rickey stopped Mary in the street, her slender volume in his gnarled, bronzed hand.

"I bought it in San Francisco, ma'am," he replied in response to her exclamation at seeing him with the book which hadn't yet been stocked in the town's general store. Opening to the seventh chapter, he made a surprising request: "I was wondering if you might permit me to come out and stand on your porch so that I may see the field from your perspective. Shall we go there now?"

Rickey was accustomed to getting what he wanted without delay, and she, too shocked to but oblige, took the arm he extended. Together they proceeded down Main Street, Rickey tipping his hat to the townsfolk, who responded with the usual deference due the man, then gaped after the pair. Mary felt an odd thrill, looking up into the pale-blue eyes, framed by lines and permanently squinted from so many years on the range, feeling the corded forearm beneath her fingers as she hastened to keep up with Rickey's long gait. She thought how interesting that despite his great wealth and many sophisticated business ventures, the man still dressed in the rough garb of a cattleman. Yet he was cultured enough to have furnished the house at Long Valley, his immense spread at the northern end of the valley, with a Sargent and a Remington, and to have stocked an enviable library, to which, she now assumed, he would add her own modest work.

Thomas Rickey had picked up *The Land of Little Rain* out of curiosity, and been surprised by how much he liked it. He had read through it slowly, savoring a whiskey as he drank in words that hummed with the heat-scented air of the high desert, the shaded mystery of its canyons, the screech of a hawk tearing through brilliant blue. Other books that had moved him deeply, *Moby Dick*, *Great Expectations*, and Emerson's essay *Self-Reliance*, had taken him out of the world he knew, to other times, places and ideas. But Mrs. Austin's book captured his own world in a way that was completely familiar yet peculiar. Her words were simple, direct, muscular, not feminine. Yet they were also poetic as a sonnet. There was a cadence to the language that lulled him, so that the snap of the logs in the hearth had long ceased and the night was nearly over by the time he stood, stretched and retired to his bedchamber.

The next morning, Rickey awoke irritable, plagued by the uncomfortable sense he had missed something. This man who had started with just a few dollars in his pocket and built a ranching empire of more than a million acres was not known to overlook anything of importance. Whenever he came down from Long Valley into town the entire community bristled with attention. Folks drew near, hoping his good fortune would rub off on them. For days on end, Rickey's itinerary would be the subject of much speculation about what he was up to and whether it might afford some opportunity for others to "get into something" profitable too.

So when later that day, Rickey sought out Mary, his trajectory toward the little brown house was deeply perplexing to those observing it. What kind of business could he possibly be doing with that crazy Mrs. Austin? Heads craned to follow as the twosome turned off Main Street and headed down the lane to Mary's house. When Rickey handed her up onto the porch, Mary hesitated. "Would you like a bit of apple cake and coffee or some sherry?"

"Yes, that would be nice, any or all of it."

When she brought the tray out she found him sitting on the swing bench, looking out at the neighbor's field. He turned and accepted a cup with cream and sugar. They talked a bit then, he asking her about some of the things she'd written, about the virtues of buzzards, the wanderings of gold hunters and, finally, the field. She didn't talk much like most women, he thought approvingly, none of the usual nonsense. But Mary's nerves caused her to speak in such a hesitant and halting manner that Rickey found her conversation fell considerably short of the lyrical charms of her carefully wrought text.

In time, he stood up, tipped his hat, "Thank you ma'am. Good day." She watched him stride back the way they'd come. He never sought her out again.

Janey Bow, however, was Mary's faithful visitor. Whenever she could, Janey slipped away from the ranch, hoping Mary would consent to her tagging along on one of the woman's frequent rambles up into the canyons, what Mary called the "streets and alleys of the mountains." When this happened, Janey never knew what to expect, except that it would be interesting. Sometimes her guide would be silent the whole of the trek, looking intensely at this or that. More often she would instruct Janey to pay attention—to painted lizards scurrying in and out of rock crevices, to patterns in the sky traced by the sweep of hawks, to the elastic rebound of rabbits in flight and the dainty drinking etiquette of quails. She showed Janey how white gilias, called "evening snow" by the valley children, turned their pale petals to face the westering sun in the late afternoon, and how, at about the same time, if you listened well, you might hear the soft whoo-ooing of the burrowing owl stirring from its hummock for a night of hunting.

Usually somber, Mary could occasionally be gay and companionable. She had taught Janey to sing *canciones*, the traditional songs that swirled around the campfires and cook pots of the Mexican settlers, who made their homes mostly in nearby Lone Pine, where Mary had lived a few years before.

Several times she had taken Janey to see Seyavi, one of the most skilled basket makers in the Paiute campoodie. Janey had been mesmerized by the dance of the woman's nimble fingers, but Mary had pointed to the knotted fingers of an older woman tending the campfire.

"That's from a lifetime of unheralded artistry," she'd instructed Janey. "Many Indian women are blind at the end of their lives from spending hour after hour working reeds and pine needles, fine as lace, in the smoky huts."

On one of their visits, the expected welcome had not been forthcoming. On that day, Seyavi had sat silently in front of the wood and mud huts, which looked to Janey like giant wasp's nests, her blanket wrapped around her head and shoulders.

"Leave her alone," said Mary. "She chooses to be left alone. There are many men to cook for here and many children to care for. Sitting in her blanket is the only way a Paiute woman can have a moment of peace to herself. We must not disturb her." Though disappointed, Janey had found this piece of information as fascinating as everything else she had learned from Mary.

Still, Janey always held her breath as she approached the little brown house and gingerly placed her foot on the back porch. Would Mary be in a good temper today?

"There you are." The door cracked open a bit. "Ruth knew you were coming." Mary, who was in her walking skirt and boots, opened the door and inspected Janey Hazeltine Bow.

The brown overalls the girl was wearing were too short, revealing thin legs above scuffed boots. Equally scrawny arms projected from the rolled up sleeves of a faded red shirt. Above this awkward costume, however, Janey wasn't exactly homely: She had long honey-colored hair, its unruly waves tied messily in back with a ribbon. The brown face had a slightly scalloped chin, a small pink bow of a mouth and wide hazel-green eyes fringed with bronze lashes.

Mary looked down to where the girl hugged the melon-laden bonnet. "You need a proper hat for walking instead of that silly thing," she said disapprovingly. "Come in now and help me get her ready."

Ruth was perched on a chair eating pumpkin pie with her fingers. She held out sticky palms to Janey. "Patty cake!"

Janey caught her breath, as she always did at first sight of Ruth. The girl was startlingly lovely, delicate boned like her father but with her mother's full lips and intense brown eyes. She also had Mary's glossy chestnut hair. Ruth's creamy skin, for she was rarely allowed to play outside, was perfect and seemed lit from within.

"Patty cake, patty cake" sang Janey, slapping the outstretched sticky palms. They played the game for a moment, then Janey helped herself to a piece of the pie. Even food was intriguing at Mary's. In the Bow house children weren't allowed to eat pie except for after noon-day dinner.

Janey swung her feet back and forth, and put her nose up next to Ruth's. "Are you happy today?"

Ruth was clearly happy, though she never responded to such questions. You couldn't really have a conversation with her, at least not with words. But they communicated anyway. "Belle, Belle!" sang Ruth. Janey guessed that this morning Ruth had a special reason to be pleased: Mary apparently planned to drop the girl off for the morning with her neighbor up the lane, Mrs. Bellamy.

---

"She's headin this way again, with the little idiot in tow. You sure done gotten yerself set in her sights fer good."

Nellie Bellamy sighed and plucked at a spring of red hair, twisting it back with plump fingers behind an ear. She was more bothered by the mixed notes of exasperation and triumph in Frank's voice than by the prospect of another visit from Mary Austin. Her husband thought she was a fool to let Mary impose in this way again and again. Sometimes she felt he was right, but mostly she enjoyed these unexpected visits.

Peering out the window, Nellie saw a short, stout figure in skirt, boots and a wide-brim hat approaching from down the lane. Trailing a little behind, came a skinny girl in overalls carrying a bundle in what appeared to be a sunbonnet. To her side, holding one of the bonnet ties, came beautiful Ruth Austin, bareheaded like her companion, a ruffled dress flouncing as she skipped.

Nellie even felt a tad privileged to be the destination of this little parade. Special, like when the schoolteacher had called her to the front of the class to figure a sum or recite a poem. She had liked being singled out then and she liked being singled out now, maybe even trusted, by this strange neighbor whose behavior sometimes made her think of a hunted animal.

Like all the women in the valley, Nellie had, at first acquaintance, been well and truly shocked by Mary's comportment. But one day in town, Nellie had been standing in front of the general store, lingering for a moment in the shade of the awning before venturing out with her bundles into the furnace of a street, when she saw Mary approaching on the sidewalk, Ruth in hand. Something about the turn of Mary's thick neck and the tense manner in which she held her top-heavy torso made Nellie look closer. Above the sullen mouth were such extraordinary eyes, and in them Nellie saw something more than willfulness and arrogance. She's been so hurt, thought Nellie, so hurt and frustrated by her life's meager joys that she's gone sour as curdled milk. Her own throat had ached as she silently watched Mary pass by.

The next day, Nellie went by the Austin house with a jar of raspberry jam. She told Mary, who received her on the porch, that as she and Frank had no children of their own as yet, she would be glad of Ruth's company now and then. A ruckus from inside sent Mary in to see about Ruth, and Nellie followed, taking care not to notice the filthy floor or the child's soiled garments. Plucking a spoon from the sink, Nellie unscrewed the lid from the jam jar and offered Ruth a walloping, dripping portion of its contents. She laughed as the girl grabbed the spoon with both hands and licked it clean. Only then did she steal a glance at Mary, who was watching her with surprise, the walled fortress of her countenance lowering ever so slightly.

Mary made the next move, bringing by an apple pie, her daughter in tow, a week later. The pie was heavenly light, succulent and more flavorful than any Nellie and Frank had ever tasted. This was fortunate, as Frank barely complained when Mary returned a week later, this time with blackberry crumble, visiting with Nellie for but a few minutes before asking if she could leave Ruth awhile. The visits from Ruth had grown in frequency, however, and not every time were they sweetened by some of Mary's incomparable baking.

"Belle! Belle!" came Ruth's happy shout. Nellie emerged out onto the porch, smiling at the sound of her nickname, and the girl launched herself into the welcoming embrace.

"I've brought a pumpkin pie Mrs. Bellamy," stated Mary matter of factly. "And a melon, which is a gift from Janey."

"Mighty good of you Mrs. Austin. How are you this morning Janey? Thank you for the melon."

"I'm well ma'am," responded Janey, frowning at Mary's decision to pass along the gift she had carried through the fields, with nary a word to her about it. Sometimes Mary didn't seem to notice other people much.

"Expect to be gone a spell," Mary said. "Ruth had her breakfast."

Hmmm, thought Nellie, and I reckon nothing more than a piece of pie. "We'll be fine," she assured Mary, thinking about getting the child inside and some eggs, bacon and porridge into her. "It's so kind of you to bring Ruth by to keep me company."

---

A sweet breeze fanned Mary's face as she led Janey along the trail up the canyon through Onion Valley toward Kearsarge Pass. All across the fields to the border of town, where they had scrambled over the talus slope at the base of the mountains, the air had sat heavily, hot and still. But here on this first rock ledge was the familiar caress. A whispered welcome, thought Mary, though she knew it was caused by air currents sliding down the rock face.

Mary had no difficulty mingling poetic inspiration and scientific explanations. She had been the only woman at Blackburn College to major in science, despite her lifelong literary interests. Criticized by her mother for inconstancy of purpose, Mary had insisted that while she could teach herself English, she needed a laboratory to learn the scientific method. She refused, moreover, to view the two pursuits as incompatible or even separate. Drawn to the objectivity and careful observation of science, she had immediately perceived its application to writing. Now, as she walked her beloved mountain canyons, she felt she was not only in her own sort of laboratory but also in a cathedral. She went about her explorations with attention and reverence, a disciplined eye and an impassioned heart.

They climbed the slope, following a line of conifers marching upward like a pageant. After a while, they came upon a pinion pine hanging onto the edge of a rock shelf. At its base on the trail side was a sort of nest, made luxurious by a thick blanket of the tree's cast-off needles.

"We'll stop here for a rest," said Mary.

They sat side by side, gazing out at the valley and the blue arching vault above it. Globs of puffy white clouds were moving in from Death Valley in the east. They hung like scoops of vanilla ice cream in the hot blue sky, and Janey half-expected to see them melt, dripping sticky sweetness into puddles on the valley floor. She and her brother often played a game of seeing in the clouds fanciful shapes of flocks of sheep, men on horses, ships at sea, ghosts, warriors and angels. Janey's favorites were the oval clouds, shaped like fish without tails, which sometimes appeared over the Sierra. They came in schools, riding over the mountain crest like a parade of flying fish. Chris had shown her how to race the rippling shadows the fish clouds cast on the ground. Arms outstretched, they would run as fast as they could to try to get ahead of the liquid gray, but it almost always alluded them.

After some time, Mary said, "You can tell where you are by the plants that grow. This plant here, does it look familiar to you?"

"No…I don't think so. Except that it smells kind of like mahogany… it doesn't look like it though. It's much too big."

"You have a fine sense of smell, Janey, for this is indeed mahogany, though it is of the mountain variety." Mary leaned over and pulled a dark green leaf off of a tall bush and brought it close to breathe in the spicy fragrance. "Look," she instructed, holding it out on her flat palm. "Look how this leaf is large and just slightly curled under at its edges. The desert variety growing down below has tiny leaves, very tightly curled. What do you suppose accounts for the difference?"

"I, ah…don't know ma'am," Janey stammered under Mary's earnest scrutiny.

"Well, water, of course. The desert mahogany must conserve the scant water it receives, so it grows low to the ground and its leaves are very small. Small leaves offer less surface for evaporation, and the curling protects the underside, helping any moisture to remain there longer. But here at higher elevation, where there is less heat, the plant is free to stretch out its limbs and grow a bit taller. The leaves are not required to conserve moisture at all costs, so they may devote themselves to gathering the sunlight necessary to perform photosynthesis—you know what that is, don't you?"

Janey nodded, and she continued. "The leaf, therefore, takes a form well designed for sun exposure. The color is darker, to absorb light, whereas the desert variety is pale, to reflect it."

Mary let the leaf blow off her palm, watching it float and fall. "Water is the pertinent issue, since it is by the grace of water that most everything exists in this place. That is so for plants, animals, and equally for humans."

"Is that why Mr. Austin is always talking about building dams?"

Mary sighed. "Yes, he is, isn't he just…to anyone who will listen. And there are a good many who like to hear of nothing else."

When first married, Mary's husband had been involved in a private enterprise with his brother Frank, aimed at bringing large-scale irrigation to the valley. The enterprise had failed, and in the years since, while Wallace worked on and off at salaried positions, including superintendent of schools and, currently, federal register of lands, he had continued to involve himself in various business schemes. None had produced anything but debts for the struggling couple.

"This valley bewitches men," Mary stated it as if explaining another point of botany to her student.

"You mean there are witches here?" whispered Janey.

"No, here, it is the land and its myths that bewitch. Fables of treasure lost and found. Men look out at the eerie beauty, the timeless space and mystery of never-ending horizons, and believe. They hear the roar of water running down from the mountains and fall under its spell. Perfectly sensible men come here expecting to stay for just a few years, long enough to get into something and make their fortune, but when nothing comes of it year after year, they forget to leave. Tricked out of a proper sense of time, they go mad, becoming like the pocket hunters, going round in circles, searching endlessly for a vein of gold. But not as harmlessly, because unlike the gold seekers, these dreamers have families. Even when they must urgently take practical measures to secure the future of their loved ones, they continue dreaming on and on.

"Like this lichen here," Mary continued after a long pause. "It's just a little patch of green or rust. You wouldn't think it could wear down mountains, but it does. Over hundreds or thousands of years, it will break down the mighty rock into dust until finally there's a tiny pocket of soil where a little bit of grass or a flower might grow. Men who can't stop dreaming get ground into dust."

"But something grows from it, like you said?"

"Yes, but not what they planned."

"Are ladies bewitched too?"

"We haven't the time for it. The metronome of nature has been built into a woman's being. Men make their way in the world by endeavoring. Women aren't allowed to, so we make our way in the world by our charms, which are not of a durable nature. For most women, the passing of time is cruelly swift…little wonder we should be impatient of wasting it."

Janey didn't understand, but it didn't matter since she was used to strange talk from Mary. Distracted, she prodded inside her boot for an offending stone. Mary saw the thin, strong calf terminating in a slender ankle beneath the stocking. She stared at it resentfully.

"You should have no trouble bewitching boys with your charms someday," she commented. "The imbeciles insist on believing the slenderness of a girl's ankle is the measure of her value." Mary's own ankles were as unfashionably thick as her neck and waist.

"My most comely feature is these hands," she said, turning them to and fro in front of her, "and my arms are graceful, though no one, of course, may appreciate them save my husband." She didn't mention that for his regard, she no longer cared.

"But it will do you little good to have such a well-turned ankle," Mary lectured, "because you have far too much sense for the taste of the young men who will flock after you. Above a certain age, you may as well know, a young lady is not supposed to express her opinions or show the least curiosity about the world around her. She mustn't wander in the woods by herself. When taken walking by a young man, she must introduce into the conversation only subjects of interest to her partner, providing for him opportunities to display his intelligence, even if it be far inferior to her own…and if…"

Janey was still thinking about ankles. "My Pa bought my Ma a new pair of boots," she offered, "to keep her ankles from getting muddy when she's helping him scoop out the manure from the horse stall."

Mary stopped abruptly, her string of bitter thoughts broken by Janey's non sequitur. "Why dear child would she be doin that?" As Janey explained, Mary's tightly drawn features softened with curiosity and then, as the tale developed, opened with pure delight.

"Well, you know how cabbages round the valley were all poorly last year? Ours were too, until my Pa noticed that we had one or two that just poked up in the corral, must a been, he said, from the wind blowin some seeds in there. But them in the corral were growing strong while the others were so sickly. So Pa started thinkin maybe it was the manure. And so this year he and Ma shoveled up a wagon load and took it in buckets and spread it on the crops. And now they're all growing good and all the neighbors want to know why, but all my dad says is we've got good land."

Mary let out a peel of laughter. Janey looked at her, astonished. The sound was musical like the trill of a bird. Regaining her composure, Mary gazed out across the tapestry of fields and creeks below. "Your Pa's a clever man," she said, "different from some of the rest of those dreamers. He actually has his eyes open."

They retook the trail, and soon Mary was pointing out lupines, bitterbrush and the clever wild heliotropes, which she explained grow beneath the shelter of shrubs to protect themselves from foraging animals. She indicated a small water hole beneath a curve of rock and explained that a coyote had likely dug there, sniffing and pawing to release buried moisture. "Coyote are the true water witches."

The sun was reaching toward the west before Mary judged they had ranged far enough. They headed toward the sound of water to regain Oak Creek and followed the laughing cascade back down toward the valley. Where the creek met the talus slope at the edge of the valley, it spread out into a delta of smaller streams. Mary and Janey followed one of these into a hollow—an irresistible side trip on the way back home. Myriad seasons of high water had carried the soil here off to the lowlands, scouring out a depression in the land. A thick growth of sweetbriar at its edges made the hollow look solid from without, but inside it was open to the sky and light, the little stream emptying into a clear, cold pool. Mary and Janey made their way toward it, but stopped short at the sounds of splashing and shouting.

"Cold as hell!" yelled Eaton, as he shot his head up above the surface and whipped back a damp plume of hair.

"Witch's tit!" came the reply from half-submerged Mulholland.

Eaton flipped over, treading water. "A good soldier says I make it to that big willow first," he yelled, pointing to a tree on the bank.

Mulholland responded by drawing a deep breath, plunging his head down into the water and pushing off. He didn't let himself come up even when he felt his lungs near to explode, but kept pulling with his arms. At last he looked up, expecting to see the willow within another stroke's reach, but instead saw Eaton several yards ahead, already turning around to look at him triumphantly. Mulholland's determination had been little competition for Eaton's efficient form and streamlined movement through the water.

Nevertheless Mulholland's smile was quick, as he slapped Eaton on the shoulder. "Whiskey's on me tonight." Slipping and lurching on the slick rocks, they emerged naked, dripping and roaring with laughter at each other's gymnastics.

They made an odd sight. Mulholland's dark, wavy, thinning hair was going white at the temples, and his mustache was hanging heavily, dripping water. Nearly six-feet tall, with a wiry build and compact muscles, Mulholland was a physically powerful man, but next to Eaton's long, smooth musculature, he looked stunted and awkward. The whiteness of his body starkly contrasted with neck, hands and forearms, which were saddle-leather brown. His companion had a full blond-brown head of hair, was clean-shaven, except for a light two-day stubble, and his skin tone ranged from natural golden to coppery where most exposed to the elements.

Janey almost jumped as the men came out of the pool. A pinkish pendulum swung between the tall one's legs. She knew what it was. A ranch child, she'd seen horses, pigs, bulls, sheep and dogs with their member protruding, licking and rubbing at it, sniffing, chasing after and mounting females. On a ranch there was nothing private about the mating act, whether unsupervised or prompted by managed breeding. She'd witnessed folks hanging on corral posts, men, women and even youngsters, urging on a rutting stallion, giggles and lewd jokes flying round the fence, quieting down as the huge bullet of flesh found its target.

She glanced nervously over at Mary, who was standing still, mouth slightly open. Janey looked back at the naked men. She'd seen this before, an accidental glimpse of her father through the kitchen window as he eased into his Saturday night bath. And at the close of every other working day, her father and brother routinely stripped to the waist to stick their heads, hair plastered flat from sweating under a hat all day, beneath the cool flow of water from the yard pump. They'd scrub the grime from their chest and arms, and wash the stink from their furry armpits before heading inside to put on a clean shirt for supper. Sometimes, when there was a lot of plowing or harvesting to do on the ranch, there'd be an army of half-naked men in the yard, waiting their turn at the pump and passing round bottles of beer handed out by Janey's Ma.

Still, she'd never seen anything like the tall man. Janey turned toward Mary again, saw her mentor was also staring at that one, the one who reminded her of the statues from Greece she'd seen pictures of in *Young Folks* magazine. Her gaze swung back, as the god stretched out on his back over a flat rock. Skin glistening with water droplets, he raised his arms to the late afternoon sun. The other man with the big mustache, who looked older, was drying himself with his shirt. He dressed quickly, pulled a notebook and pencil out of his pack, then settled on a log, facing the pool. It looked to Janey like he was doing math sums.

Now the beautiful man bent one arm up behind his head. Closing his eyes and sighing deeply, he brought the other arm up and let its fingers drift lazily across his chest, stomach and thighs. Mesmerized, Janey jumped when she felt a tug at her hand. Mary had a panicky look on her face behind the finger she'd raised in front of her lips. "Shhhhhush," she exhaled, pulling Janey back through the tunnel of bushes, out of the hollow.

---

Her boots went slap, slap as she ran down the lane to the ranch. It was growing dark, and she knew she should have been home hours ago. She had missed helping Ma with the hoeing, and probably missed supper too. Guiltily, she realized she'd even forgotten about the melon she'd saved for her friends.

Janey slid under the fence and crept into the yard. She could see her mother turning up the oil lamp in the kitchen, glancing out the window just as Janey ducked behind the big oak. She opened the door of the milk-house and walked down the stone steps into its cool dampness. This cellar, built a dozen feet from the house, was basically a hole in the earth, excavated to about six feet, with a timbered, gabled roof rising about two feet above ground. Down the center of the room, ran a wooden conduit with a flow of fresh water, diverted from nearby Independence Creek and brought by force of gravity down a gentle grade to the Bow milkhouse. On either side of the little stream of cooling water were arranged long tables, roughly hewn from logs. On these tables sat a line of silver pails, their sides damp with condensation, each in a tin pan of water. Like moats around castles, the water protected the fresh milk, clotted on the top with yellow cream, from insects and rodents. Under the tables were stacked sacks of flour and bread, and paper-wrapped bundles of meat.

Occasionally Janey snuck into the milkhouse during the heat of the day to quench her thirst or slather a piece of bread with the thick, sweet cream. Now she sidled past the tables to the back of the cellar and a place in the timbers where she knew her mother had concealed fresh-baked oatmeal cookies in a bag tied with rope and hung with wire from a beam, out of reach to ants and children. But Janey's long legs had outgrown her mother's imagination, and climbing onto a rickety stool pulled from the corner, stretching on tippy-toes, she was able to get her hands around the sack. She untied the rope and dropped down on the stool to plunder its contents, shoving a handful of cookies into her mouth, chomping down into their dense sweetness. One after another she consumed all of the cookies in the sack, chewing more frantically and with less enjoyment, until her jaw ached.

Back out under the oak tree, Janey felt sick now as well as guilty. Would she be yelled at and punished when she went in? What would Ma say if she knew about this afternoon? The yard where Janey had played all her life felt unfamiliar, the branches of the trees twisting, pointing at her, the mountains to the west looming large and threatening. The empty windows of her own room above the kitchen dark and unwelcoming.

The screen door squealed her late arrival as she slid in. Ma turned around and pounced.

"There you are! You're just lucky, miss, your Pa is late too or you'd be havin no supper tonight. And I'm dishing it up late seeing as no one came to help me with the hoeing today. Why do you suppose that was?" Alice surveyed the girl, who looked a fright, as was usual after one of her adventure days, loose hair falling around the dirty face and poking every which way, along with twigs and burrs, out of her ponytail. The scrunched forehead showed concentration—she's really working up a good story this time, thought Alice Bow.

"None of that, no excuses. Your Pa will talk to you after supper. Now wash up and help me get this stew on the table."

Janey, relieved at the light reprimand, felt happiness returning as she worked beside her Ma. Pa, entering the kitchen tired and sore, though noting his wife's disapproving nod toward Janey, still opened his arms to give his daughter her usual bear hug. When they sat down, Janey's tummy ached, but she tried to eat. There was fresh-baked bread and butterscotch pudding to tempt her.

Chris was excited, telling his folks in an animated voice about the trip to Bishop and relating the everyday news of the valley he'd picked up from his customers. Later Ma seemed to have forgotten about the talk with Pa. They sat in the parlor all together, Pa reading aloud from *Out West* and a bit from *Harper's*. Ma pulling out her sewing basket to busy her fingers while she listened, smiling and nodding. Chris leafing through farm tools catalogs. The world had snapped back into place. Everything was right again. She was all right.

And when Janey climbed the stairs with her lamp and sat it upon the window sill, looking out to the dark yard and the tree's lace of black leaves against the graying sky, she felt ashamed recalling the turmoil she'd felt standing underneath it. The mountains that had looked down on her so critically and menacingly now regained their familiar benevolent aspect. Watching over her, their snowfields gleamed silver where touched with moonlight. My knights in armor, she mused.

Most evenings Janey took a book to bed, but tonight she lay quietly in the pool of light flooding through the window onto her quilt, trying not to think about the man on the rock and how he'd moved his hands. She pushed her toes down into the cool, smooth sheets. When the spot where her toes rested grew warm, she pushed them farther, onto the next patch of fresh linen, delighting in its fresh, cool newness.

She did this listening to the low hum of her parents' voices. Their words were indistinguishable but their tone constant, the warp and weft of their exchange weaving her net of sleep.

The moonlight shone down too on Mulholland and Eaton, huddled around a campfire. Despite the rapid onset of the high-desert night chill and Mulholland's wish to discharge his debt at the nearest saloon, the men opted to camp by the river, so as not to arouse local curiosity. They drank their own whiskey and cooked beans and bacon in a pot, while talking in animated but hushed tones about their plans.

Mulholland laid his plate on a rock and opened the notebook. "I figure it's about 400 cubic feet of water per second." He ran his fingers, split to form a V-shape, down his bushy mustache to his neck, pinching them together to pull at his Adam's apple. "And coming from an elevation of about 4,000 feet…"

Eaton had enough engineering experience to do his own math. Besides, he was the one who had first seen the possibilities during a fishing trip he'd taken with J.B. Lippincott, a friend who now worked for the US Reclamation Service. Created with the signing of the Federal Reclamation Act by President Teddy Roosevelt in 1902, the service's mandate was to extend settlement across the West by creating more cultivatable land through irrigation projects. The possibility of a Reclamation irrigation project in the Owens Valley was the subject of fevered anticipation for its inhabitants, who saw the opportunity to accelerate the steady but slow progress they had been making putting land under the plow.

"The key here," Eaton's excited voice rose, and he tamped it down to a whisper, "is Long Valley. It's the only place big enough to build a dam that will support large-scale irrigation, which Rickey doesn't favor. If we can get him to sell to us instead, we can not only stop the Reclamation project, but use the land to dam up our own reservoir."

"What do you know about Rickey?"

"Hell, he acts like a valley dignitary, but he's nothing but a scoundrel. Word is he got most of that land by running settlers off with hired guns. But he's smart, always sniffing out the honey pot and first to get his fingers in it. He'll sell if the pot is sweet enough."

"Good, but let's not approach him yet. Wait until we've got enough of the valley south of his spread in our pockets—that's the stick we need in case the sweetener isn't enough. You've got to do it Fred. You're a private citizen now, with no official relationship to the city. If they get even a sniff of who I am, we're done for. Come back up here and start buying water rights and land options. Do you think Lippincott will give you the maps drawn up by the Reclamation Service? What if we hire him as a consultant to help the city, uh, let's say, to help us explore methods of augmenting our water sources? What if we pay him a nice, fat fee?"

"Sure, he'll bite on that. And Jason might be able to help us in another way that would disguise who's doing the buying," Eaton's eyes twinkled, "while also sweetening the pot for Rickey."

Mulholland leaned forward with interest, as Eaton explained.

"Well, Rickey's an investor in one of the two power companies competing to build a hydroelectric power plant on upper Bishop Creek. The Reclamation Service is going to grant the right-of-ways they need across federal lands to only one of them. Say I convince Jason to hire me as a consultant to review the merit of those applications. I could go up to Owens Valley with a letter saying I'm authorized to act on behalf of the service. Most folks will naturally assume we're talking about the irrigation project, and I won't tell them any different." He winked at Mulholland. "Meanwhile I'll let Rickey know I'm ready to recommend that the service look favorably on his company's application—which should make him real cooperative."

"Good, but let's not jump the gun with Rickey. We need to wait until we have some of the other pieces in place."

"Agreed. Besides, it will take me some time to get with the bankers and put together the funds we need and…"

"No bankers. We'll raise it through a public bond offering."

"Now Bill, I figured you'd be financing the construction, and I'd put together a syndicate of investors for purchasing the land and water rights. That way…"

"No, no bankers, no investors." Mulholland's voice was a razor. "The city's lifeline cannot be dependent in any way on private interests."

Eaton retorted, "You think I don't have the city's interests at heart?!"

"I know you do Fred." Mulholland softened his voice and laid a hand lightly on Eaton's arm. "As a former mayor, of course you do. But what about 20, 30 years from now, hell 100 years from now? What about when you hand your business over to your sons, or to buyers? I won't allow the reins of the city's future to be held by…"

The pause was hardly more than a breath, but Eaton saw in the flickering light that Mulholland had reached out for his shotgun and was already spinning around to sweep the dark perimeter for the source of the sound he had just heard.

"Who is it? Call out and walk in here slow," Mulholland commanded, voice calm, finger ready on the trigger. Eaton crouched low and moved to retrieve his pistol, wondering how many were out there and which way to turn his back.

"Beg your pardon mister, I mean ya no harm," came a soft, shy voice. "Name's Debs."

The voice came from a dark spot in the shadows. It went on talking as a shape began to form. The self-announced Debs slowly approached the campfire. "Thought you might want to trade some a this here gold dust for that ther bacon smellin ser good…me and Georgina ain't had no fresh grub for months."

A small, bent man in a thin, filthy coat and ill-fitting hat appeared. He pushed the hat up on his head to let them see a face that was deeply lined and browned. The scant figure stood there in the frigid night, not coming all the way in, waiting and wiping his forehead.

Debs Yellman was an itinerant miner, a "pocket hunter," who worked alone, searching the hills for pockets of ore overlooked by the hordes of fortune seekers that had combed the land now for a half century since the first gold and silver strikes in the 1840s. He was pointing toward the trees from which he had emerged.

"Georgina, she's my mule, she makes herself satisfied with potato skins and will make a fine diner from bark pulled right off the tree…but she has the taste for finer things she do. Me, I wuddn't mind a sip a whiskey if ya got it."

"Come ahead," said Mulholland, laying his rifle aside.

Hours later the fortunate Debs shuffled back into the shadows the same way he had come, the pockets of his thin coat sagging with a half-pound of bacon and a small sack of hardtack biscuits. His hosts had been generous with their supper, whiskey and attention. For his part, the pocket hunter had answered every question put to him, quietly and thoroughly while chewing appreciatively on the contents of his bowl. This strange little man claimed to have been digging through the canyons and ranging over the ridges and flats of the eastern Sierra for more than two decades.

"Found myself one too, going on 12 year now, a thousand-dollar pocket. Took the Grand Tour, I did…seen the palace in London, even the queen rid by in a fine carriage. When my money was near gone, I came back here aimin to find me another pocket of gold. When I find the next one, I'm going back fer good…gonna wear one of them tall silk hats to the opera and ride in me own carriage with them thar footmen."

Eaton snorted, but flashed a smile to cover his amused contempt. Mulholland turned the conversation to more practical matters, questioning Debs closely about his methods.

The latter owned that the best way to find an untapped vein of gold was to look for an iron stain in a riverbed or gulley. Probably he didn't know why, though Mulholland did. Where there was no water, Debs still followed dry stream beds, weaving his way along winding mountain contours.

He was out alone, with nothing but the land and Georgina for company, for as many as nine months at a stretch, wandering a twisting course extending from the Truckee River far to the north all the way down to the Mojave Desert in the southeast. On these solitary quests, Debs traveled light. He took with him a frying pan, beans, flour, fat and coffee. To save himself the trouble of carrying a proper pot, he brewed his coffee in a rusty tin can, which, he advised, improved its flavor. The lack of personal items meant Debs and Georgina could carry more prospecting gear. Their working essentials included pick, gold pan, shovel and magnifying glass plus a small sluice box set up. Panning as he worked himself down a streambed, Debs's eyes would grow weary and red peering through the glass to read the rock fragments. But he and Georgina could rest a spell in a shady spot whenever they took a mind to, his head rising and falling on her soft belly. They might even pause for a few days if a spot looked promising before moving on to the next, always more promising spot.

The little man enjoyed the opportunity to talk, and clearly regarded himself as an expert in his chosen discipline. Technique mattered to Debs, and Mulholland approved of that. Eaton, meanwhile, was even more amused by Mulholland than by Debs. Gad, he's interviewing him like he was a damn Harvard-taught engineer! He chuckled to himself. Dammit if

Mulholland wasn't more at ease with the men on his work crews and even common laborers than he was with the city's business and social leaders. Still, it was a comportment Eaton knew had served Mulholland well, both as a foreman and superintendent—something, he suspected, could be useful if emulated. For Mulholland, though, the easy interchange with the deluded little miner was as effortless as breathing.

Debs Yellman was, in fact, telling the truth about striking it rich. Years ago he had found one of those pockets he was always looking for and made a lot of money, enough to sail on a ship from San Francisco to Southampton, England. Six months later, he was back, and the only thing he had to show for it were his stories about seeing the queen and three green canvas, leather-trimmed bags to carry his stores. Janey had heard the tale from Mary, who had befriended Debs, like so many of the region's oddest folk, sitting for hours listening to his stories.

One time, he had told Mary, he and Georgina had been making their way on a Monday, he figured it was, through the northwestern edge of the Mojave Desert, "ankle-deep in sand and scorpions," and on Thursday had made their way to a low ridge of the White Mountains, when a freak snow storm hit. Now they were knee-deep in heavy, wet snow, which came down so thickly they couldn't see more than a foot in front. Somehow, Debs said, they had reached a bunch of cedars that had been so bent by the wind that they formed a roof, making a shelter below. Exhausted, Debs had tied Georgina to a branch and crawled inside. In the morning, he woke to find that he had snuggled deep into the fleece of a bighorn sheep and, indeed, that the whole flock rested with him beneath the snow-laden boughs.

As Debs roused himself, the sheep moved away a little, to the edge of the tree cave, but didn't flee. He realized they were looking out in wonder at the sparkling white world that had appeared as the storm had passed. They remained that way until the leader stamped lightly, breaking the spell, and they moved out into the bright white landscape one by one.

Debs wasn't surprised that the sheep might just stand as such, enchanted at natural beauty. He saw little difference between all God's creatures, man and beast. Mary understood this about the pocket hunter, and was sorry for him. When Janey had asked her why Debs had come back from London she had replied softly.

"He knew somewhere deep inside that he didn't belong there, not in London, nor in any other civilized place. How do you suppose Debs might live in a fine house in London when he can't tolerate any place that isn't out of doors and he doesn't even notice weather? Sunshine or storm, it's all the same to him. Over time, he became part of the land, and in return it tolerates him more than it does most white men. He isn't of any more importance or bother to it than a jackrabbit or a gopher.

"Now the sensible thing for a body to do when they strike a small vein," Mary had lectured, "would have been to buy a business somewhere or a ranch and get out of these hills for good. But few do."

"Why?" Janey had asked.

"I suppose they go a little mad. Always thinking about the new life just waiting in the next pan. And all the time being out here so long alone making them thoroughly unsuited to any other kind of life."

But Eaton didn't know anything about Debs Yellman's fortune, good or bad. He saw only a little man spinning big tales, and he was impatient for him to leave. Damn if Mulholland wasn't still lapping it up like cream. Eaton couldn't stand watching anymore so he fixed his gaze on the fire.

As the sparks snapped, so did his temper. Bill Mulholland has no business telling me what I can and cannot do for this aqueduct, he thought. Hell, it was my idea from the start—and I was generous enough to bring it to him just at the moment when he's struggling to find water sources for the city. Hell, the guy's career would have washed up if I hadn't come riding to the rescue with a solution—and now this aqueduct will save his job and make his reputation. No, he has no business telling me what to do at all.

Eaton stood abruptly, towering over the other men. He'd waited long enough and now had careful thinking to do and plans to make. Saying goodnight, he retired to his tent, leaving Mulholland and the pocket hunter exchanging yarns.

# Chapter 3

Eaton scanned the platform as he stepped down from the first-class car. He spotted the glossy, decorated head instantly. Other eyes that turned to look at the tall woman as she advanced the length of the newly arrived train were struck by her powerful physical presence. This characteristic, recognizable in every member of the robust Eaton clan, was manifested here in a hypnotically swaying gait.

Helen walked like a lioness, her heavy dark gold mane looping around her ears, sweeping up under a feathered, jeweled hat and dropping into an intricately woven plait, cradled just below her shoulders in a fine silken net of pale blue. Eaton, who had bestowed his fairness and grace on his daughter, was immune to their effects, but he calculated Mulholland wouldn't be. Alighting behind him just in time to see Helen touch rosy lips to the cheek of his companion, Mulholland stopped, one foot on the platform, and gaped.

The two men had just completed a week and a half on the Owens River, taking calculations and charting and sketching the valley, river and proposed route for their project. Avoiding contact with the locals, they had camped the whole way, regaling themselves with trout for breakfast and dinner, finishing up their store of soldiers, and finally selling their buck-board and traveling by train to Carson City, then on to San Francisco. Now Mulholland would take another train from here south to Los Angeles while Eaton would stay a week or so with his daughter, who had been living in the northern California city the past few years following her marriage to a member of one of its most venerable families.

The length of the journey in their private compartment, Mulholland and Eaton had avoided matters of financing and ownership, but discussed every other detail of how they would build an aqueduct to bring the water of the Owens River to Los Angeles. With a flow of 400 cubic feet per second, the river would provide plenty of water to support the growth of the city, even if the current population of 200,000 doubled over the next 20 years. There were rivers closer to the city, like the Colorado or the Kern, but those would require pumps to lift the water thousands of feet. With the Owens River at about 4,000 feet above sea level, bringing it down to the city wouldn't require a single watt of pumping energy. Gravity would do the job.

The overall concept was that simple, but the details were daunting. Building the aqueduct would require a massive construction project stretching across the inferno of the Mojave Desert and cutting through the mountains. It was an engineering feat such as the world had never seen, which was exactly what Mulholland relished most about the idea. The power of nature combined with the power of the human mind and will.

Now stepping out of the stuffy compartment, blinking as if emerging from underground, Mulholland was struck by the reminder of another form of power.

"My daughter, Mrs. Helen Armstrong of Nob Hill, San Francisco. Helen, may I present Mr. William Mulholland of Los Angeles."

Eaton watched Helen focus her deeply blue eyes, a shade darker than the silk suit she wore, on Mulholland. A full-lipped smile began to rise, but she adjusted it down a notch. Helen had concluded from the looks of the man, and what she'd guessed from her father's telegram announcing their imminent arrival, that this Mr. Mulholland was of marginal importance.

"You might say that Bill, here, is following in my footsteps Helen. He's the current superintendent and chief engineer of the Los Angeles Department of Water and Power."

The smile receded a bit further but the voice was warm and practiced. "How charming to meet you."

Mulholland hadn't noticed the withdrawal, only the hand so gracefully offered, gloved in kid leather of dove silver. "It is a great pleasure, Mrs. Armstrong. I'd never have believed old Fred had such a daughter if I hadn't seen you in person."

Eaton was amused to see how little effort Helen was extending to make his friend feel comfortable. She allowed silence to hang heavily for a moment or two, then took Eaton's arm sweetly. "Come along with me father, Mr. Mulholland. Jeffers and Deacon will collect your bags."

A manservant and a chauffeur in well-starched uniforms emerged from where they had been standing discreetly behind a post and began stacking the bags that had been deposited next to Eaton and Mulholland by the train porters.

"Might as well just move mine down over to the other platform there," said Mulholland, waving off Helen's staff and gesturing to a station porter. "Train to Los Angeles leaves in half an hour."

Helen was pleased to hear it, as she had no desire to host this rough man. She accompanied her father and his friend graciously to the other platform and waited with them until it was time for Mulholland to board. As a native Angeleno, she couldn't help but be aware of the city's obsession with water, but the knowledge that her father had at one time held Mulholland's current responsibilities was mostly a source of embarrassment for her, only partly recompensed by his ascension to mayor several years later.

He had gained that lofty post just as she was introduced into society. It had been a heady season, she the incontestable queen of its festivities, golden and rosy in white organza, invited everywhere. Not just boys her age, but powerful, wealthy men were suddenly leaning forward to catch her every utterance, or hanging back, awkward and silly in her presence. It had all culminated with a big wedding, a honeymoon on the continent and the house on Nob Hill. At first, Helen had felt rightly pleased with all she had achieved. She had moved up in the world, as Los Angeles was regarded by just about everyone outside of it as a backwater compared to glittering San Francisco. Here she was aloft in this jewel of a city, so much like Paris. (Her father, jealous of the preeminence of her husband's family, infuriated her on her wedding day by remarking that her home to be had recently been just a hurly burly gateway to the Sierra gold fields and had no claim to take on European airs.)

Just two years later her father was no longer mayor, choosing not to run again or losing the support he needed to try. She had never understood what had happened. Maybe it had been the divorce from her pale, insipid mother, or too much indulgence in drink, but neither seemed sufficient explanation. For such a charming man, he often seemed to find himself at odds with people. Now he dabbled in businesses, she had no idea exactly what nor did she care. Her thoughts these days were absorbed by her own affairs.

For Helen had the disquieting feeling that her ascension was slowing. Something had changed since her marriage. On the arm of her husband, she still felt herself to be the object of envy and desire, but he was absent frequently, his ardor cool and attention wavering when present. At a ball where just a few years ago she would have felt a hundred eyes on her as she swirled around the floor, she now talked listlessly with other married women and waited impatiently for her husband or one of his friends to offer his hand. At a banquet where she would have once reigned supreme, talk and glances lapping about her in insistent ripples, she now sat mired in a still and tepid pool. Despite the latest couture and her new diamond collar, she would feel the eyes deserting her, drifting toward the other end of the table, where a young niece, freshly introduced into society, was heartbreakingly supple and fetching in a simple white dress.

Yet, she could still cast a spell over men such as Mulholland, older men and those on the middle rungs of commerce and society. The act of harvesting them was no longer thrilling, just reassuring.

All this she thought as she offered her hand again to Mulholland and helped her father wave him off on his journey. Then she laid the hand across Eaton's arm and began to steer him through the lobby, intending to take him across the street to the restaurant where she had ordered a sumptuous lunch. It hadn't been done so much to impress him as to entertain herself.

"Another time my lovely," he said. "I've had a change of plans."

She looked at him warily. "I don't understand."

Helen was now the one in tow, as her father loped to the ticket counter, Jeffers and Deacon lurching behind with his bags. Eaton asked for the departure time of the next train that would take him back to Carson City and on to the Owens Valley, and purchased a ticket.

"There's something I need to do back there."

"Really father!" she scolded. "Some explanation is in order I think. The Armstrongs are expecting you tonight, and we were planning to host you in our box at the opera."

"Please extend my regrets. I'll be back in a few days." He kissed her perfunctorily on the forehead, then swung up the steps of the train compartment.

A silly snob like her mother, he thought as he watched her wave from the platform. And she thinks she's bested us by becoming part of Nob Hill society. But Los Angeles won't be playing second fiddle to San Francisco much longer. And, in the process, Frederick Eaton is finally going to claim his due.

Although Mulholland was the more talented engineer, Eaton had been first to see this opportunity and he understood more clearly what it would mean. Thus when Mulholland delineated his projections on the city's probable requirements for Owens Valley water, Eaton smiled, nodded and kept quiet. Since his boyhood, he had seen the city's population increase five times over; it had doubled most recently in the space of just four years. Eaton knew Mulholland's estimates for population and water consumption, plotted based on the current rate of growth, were far too modest. Mulholland was saying the city would need 90 cubic feet per second of water per day by the end of the decade—Eaton was betting it would be two or three times that amount. He could see the day when there would be a million Angelenos, and all of them would come to the land of sunshine seeking a better life, including an interior bathroom with a flush toilet like the one in his own home and those of the city's other well-to-do households.

But this future would not occur without water. Situated in a basin surrounded on three sides by mountains and deserts, and on the fourth by ocean, the nascent metropolis was borrowing from the future to support its present growth, drilling wells to suck up groundwater that had taken tens of thousands of years to accumulate. How long the water would last, Eaton couldn't postulate, but he did know it would not be forever. Sooner or later lack of water would rein in the city's growth, and this, he knew, her ambitious citizens would not tolerate. They would do anything, pay anything to eliminate such limits.

Now, as the train pulled out of the station, he thought back on the sequence of events that had delivered him this opportunity of a lifetime.

A dozen years ago, in 1892, he had been introduced to Frank Austin, a young man who had come over from Hawaii with his brother Wallace to remake their family fortune in California. Frank had the business brains, Wallace the degree in engineering. They had an idea for an irrigation project to expand the agricultural production of the Owens Valley and export not only to the Nevada silver mining camps but to the growing city populations of Los Angeles and San Francisco. They had sought to get Eaton involved for his family's financial connections. He'd been intrigued, but finally passed on the deal, figuring that lack of transportation doomed the project to failure.

Potential markets for Owens Valley had always been restricted by lack of adequate transportation. For 20 years the valley had been served by the so-called "Slim Princess," the Carson & Colorado Railroad. Its track had been laid down with a narrow gauge, just three feet between the inner rails. This nonstandard design had been extolled by promoters as a way to reduce construction and maintenance costs, and increase economy and profit for a railroad envisioned as connecting the mining communities of southeastern California, Nevada and Colorado. This vision had never been fully realized, but the line did run from Keeler, at the eastern shore of Owens Lake, 300 miles north to Mound House near Carson City, Nevada. Apart from freight wagons, this was the only way to bring the valley's produce to external markets.

At Mound House, there was a sister line of the Virginia & Truckee Railroad, which connected to main lines reaching southward to Los Angeles and back over the Sierra to San Francisco. But because these tracks were built with standard-gauge widths, cars coming in from the Carson & Colorado could not run over them. Valley produce, therefore, had to be unpacked and transferred, making transport expensive and impractical for most purposes. And that, in Eaton's assessment, meant that the proposed Austin irrigation project was unlikely to be profitable.

When a few years ago a silver vein had been struck at Tonopah in eastern Nevada, followed almost immediately by a new bonanza at nearby Goldfield, he'd wondered if he had made a mistake. Mining towns mushroomed overnight, creating booming markets for Owens Valley produce. And a few years after that the narrow-gauge railroad line was extended to Tonopah, providing an alternative to overland routes.

Still, Eaton figured he had made the right choice. Without better transportation—across standard-gauge rails—agriculture in the valley would be forever hitched to the bust-and-boom cycles of the mining communities, when real fortune lay in the irrepressible growth trajectories of the cities. Confirmation of his wisdom came when he heard that the two brothers had failed to get their project off the ground, gone broke, and the younger had been turned out of a boarding house with his pregnant wife. He was now the registrar of the federal lands office in Owens Valley— another connection that might turn out to be convenient.

For the Austin business proposition had brought Eaton's attention to the Owens Valley, and in the hot, dry years of 1903 and 1904, with Los Angeles experiencing its first water crisis, his imagination returned there again and again. Eaton suddenly and uncharacteristically took a vacation, a camping and fishing trip to the Yosemite with J.B. Lippincott, a friend who worked as supervising engineer in California for the newly formed US Reclamation Service. Also along was Jacob Clausen, another Reclamation hydraulic engineer, with a talent for drawing. Jacob sketched the faces of the peaks and the changing countryside as they crossed over Tioga Pass and made their way down into a basin where they encountered the strange spectacle of Mono Lake.

This was a vast saline lake, punctured by weird protruding towers of limestone called "tufas." Reflected in the lake's still surface, huge cloud formations raced across the sky. The next day, the three men headed south, entering the Owens Valley on a morning when the air was so fragrant and pure, Eaton had felt he could eat it for breakfast. That had been a good thing too since they had run out of grub. Stopping in Bishop for supplies, Eaton caught his first glimpse of the river he now knew would make his fortune.

Clausen had innocently added to Eaton's interest. Normally earnest and quiet, the man had become vexed and outspoken over what he regard-ed as the wasteful irrigation methods of the local ranchers.

"They think that all they have to do round here to produce a crop is to pour water on the land, so they pour plenty of it! The town's cellars flood from the seepage coming out of the irrigation ditches. Yet come late spring and summer, the river sometimes goes dry for 50 miles above the lake. It just makes no sense what they're doing...there's land here they could easily be cultivating and it's let to lie bone dry while other places become swamps. They've got fields they can't even farm no more because there's so much alkali in the ground. I expect if you were to measure the groundwater plane, you'd find it near as tell just a couple feet from the surface."

The young engineer had gone on to single out the worst of the offenders: "Rickey Land and Cattle Company in Long Valley. To grow plenty of grass for their summer range, they drench the land with water— based on no systematic method or thought. The waste in evaporation is unfathomable."

Later, around the campfire, after everyone else had retired, Lippincott had let him in on why Clausen had been so passionate. The Reclamation Service was considering a massive irrigation project in the valley, which Clausen would likely head. Eaton had winked at Lippincott and whispered, "Don't be in too much of a hurry on that project...there might be a better use for the water—and one that might do you more good too."

Upon returning to Los Angeles, Eaton had gone to see Mulholland. His friend Mulholland, the city's present water and power chief, had recently completed a study of available means for meeting growing water demand, and the results had not been encouraging. His reaction, when told that the Owens Valley, 240 miles to the north, might be a saving grace, was skeptical. "You're a crazy son of a bitch."

Mulholland had listened, though, and whether it was the engineer in him or the desperate city administrator that got him up on a buckboard, headed across the Mojave, a few weeks later, Eaton didn't know. But that first morning in the valley, when Mulholland saw the river, he had looked at it with wonder, and then at Eaton with renewed respect. Something of the old days, when he had been Mulholland's mentor, had been revived.

Now Mulholland, he knew, was lost in the romance of the engineering challenge of building what would surely be the largest water project since Roman days. For the rest, Bill would seek to accomplish the thing in the most beneficial way possible for the city, beginning by presenting the plan to the Board of Water Commissioners and then seeking municipal funding. But the city moved slowly. And for once, Eaton was glad of it.

Eaton intended to obtain his own capital to finance the project. He would tap his banking contacts in New York, those he had refused to mobilize for the Austin project years ago. To hell with what Mulholland had said. If he could quickly put together a private syndicate to purchase the water and land rights necessary for the aqueduct, Mulholland would have no choice but to go along and buy water from them. They could sell the water to the city for a modest sum at first, then raise the price over time as the city continued to grow and its citizens to consume more and more water. In a place where progress was measured by population growth and land sales, Eaton had no doubt of it. To keep the water flowing, the city would have to pay him his due: millions, year after year after year— a steady flow of wealth into his pockets.

"Let Mulholland make history," he said to himself, chuckling. "I'll make a fortune."

But first, there was something he needed to do back in the valley.

---

The bell at the door tinkled, but W.A. Chalfant, who often wore an old felt fedora scrunched down over longish white curly hair even indoors, didn't look up. All day long the bell tinkled, heralding the comings and goings in the *Inyo Register* newspaper office he presided over, a small, cluttered shop smack in the middle of Bishop's dusty Main Street, next door to the butcher, across the street from the general store.

Chalfant's domain was a deep narrow room, reaching from the street front, where hazy sun streamed in through dirty windows, to the back, where it was darker and cool and the printing press stood. Above a wood plank floor littered with scraps of paper, ranged long wooden chests, which served as work tables, dozens of drawers along their sides, full of metal type, tools and ink. At the center of the room was a pot-bellied stove with a stove pipe running up through the ceiling. He had inherited this kingdom from his father, who had brought Owens Valley its first printing press some 30 years before.

"Hey there Mr. Chalfant, it's me, Bucky," came an oily voice from the direction of the doorway.

Chalfant peered up at him through bushy black eyebrows, keeping his head and shoulders hunched over his work. Bucky Porter, a skinny young man with a complexion as unattractive as his voice, came in and leaned against Chalfant's work table. He was the newspaper's sole reporter.

Chalfant didn't need much reporting, since more often than not his source of news was one of the townsfolk, dropping in to talk of some rumor or event. Or it might be a farmer or rancher come to town, stopping by after finishing his business for a howdy-do. In this way, Chalfant quickly heard just about everything going on up and down the valley, and a few "stringer" reporters on retainer in Los Angeles and San Francisco extended his reach beyond it.

Alas, truth be told, Bucky wasn't very good. In fact, when it came to writing and spelling, Chalfant liked to say he was about as capable as a cow in quicksand. He did have one sterling qualification for the job however, which kept him on Chalfant's payroll, Bucky Porter was as nosy as nosy could be.

"Whaddaya hear out there, Bucky?" Chalfant let his eyes drop back down to the article he was editing.

"Well, did ya know about them cabbages big as a bull's head the Bow kid brought to town this mornin? Everybody else is complaining 'bout how puny their cabbage patch be this year, but not the Bows. Kid says his Pa's spreadin manure to make them cabbages grow. They'se cart'in it over in buckets from the corral. Whaddaya think about that?!"

"Enthralling," Chalfant mumbled.

The doorbell tinkled again, and this time the voice was warm, deep and pleasing. Chalfant put his pen down and rose to greet Mark Watterson, a young man in his mid-twenties with an amiable disposition. Mark owned and managed the town bank, general store and several other businesses with his brother Wilfred. Striding toward the older man, Watterson clasped his hand and grinned. "I've come for a peek at the evening edition."

"Well, we've still got a few holes. Fearing I may have to write 'bout cabbages just to fill 'em," joked Chalfant. He gestured Porter toward the door. "Go out and get me some real news."

Watterson offered a cigar, then lit one himself, settling with one leg over the arm of a well-worn leather armchair against the wall opposite Chalfant. The editor pushed his rolled up shirt sleeves even further up into the green sleeve protector bands and sat back too.

"Have you heard anything more about the Reclamation project?" asked Watterson.

"Nothing yet. But you know how these government things move… like a snail climbin a greased log."

"Yeah, I know." Watterson sighed. "But there's so many folks here in the valley who could benefit from this project…and the produce they'll grow will be a boon to towns and cities all over the state."

"Wouldn't do the bank any harm either, financing all that growth," Chalfant smiled and winked.

"No, no harm at all." Watterson smiled back.

Mark took no offense, knowing the jab to be in jest. Chalfant and the Watterson family were the valley's most ardent champions, their two enterprises being the sinew that bound the valley's dispersed communities together. Moreover both of these profitable businesses had demonstrated a remarkable regard for the welfare of the community. The Wattersons, who held mortgages on a third of the valley's small ranches and farms, had the reputation of being scrupulous, fair and competent. They rarely refused a loan applicant and often allowed borrowers in financial difficulty to stretch out payment of their debts. Chalfant was known for using the power of the press to help his neighbors. Being of the same mind on such matters, the two men were easy with each other.

They sat talking and smoking companionably for some time in the growing heat of a valley morning, savoring the prospects for a prosperous and virtuous future.

---

Augusta Aames knew it was going to be a dreadful day the moment she opened the telegram and saw it was from William B. Matthews. Sitting up even straighter than was her habit, she scanned the page, refolded it and took it into her boss's office. The room she entered smelled of cigar smoke, but the desk was clean of the papers, files and ledgers that festooned the desks of most of the other men in the building.

Her boss, Mr. Mulholland, was rarely in his office or even in the building, which was why Augusta was allowed, in fact depended upon, to open all of his correspondence. Uncomfortable behind a desk and abhorring paperwork, Mulholland preferred to spend most of his time out across the city, amid his work crews and infrastructure. He had walked and inspected every mile of the water and sewer system. There was a widely told story that in Mulholland's early years, when he had been an employee of the Los Angeles Water Company, which was then a private business rather than a public agency, a city official had complained of the lack of adequate inventory records. Mulholland had responded by describing all of the pipes, gate valves and hydrants in the system, including their size, type and age, entirely from memory. The skeptical official had sent out a team of city engineers to spot check some 200 locations, and every one of them was exactly as Mulholland had said.

Mulholland was now at a meeting in the board room a floor above, and that alone, Augusta knew, would put him in a black mood. Her boss detested the politicians and insiders club of investors and boosters he had to deal with in his job as city water supervisor. Most of them, to his mind, were pinheads, without the simplest notion of the realities involved in supplying a city infrastructure. He'd had to fight hard to get them to approve modernizations, such as metering and other programs to reduce waste. They looked at him like dumb sheep when he argued that conserving forested mountainsides rather than cutting down trees was essential to delay the return of rainfall to the ocean and give it time to soak down into the subterranean aquifer. Yes, the city had to look for new water sources, but it was only prudent to also make the most of the water it already had.

He thought them a pack of fools, all except Eaton, which was why Augusta was so puzzled at the contents of the telegram. Mulholland not only tolerated but seemed to admire the former mayor. In fact, when Eaton had held that title, he could often be found at the end of the day in Mulholland's office—a refuge from the unceasing demands he faced in his far grander professional abode a few blocks away. The two friends would smoke cigars, drink scotch and guffaw at Mulholland's ribald stories. Augusta had even heard Mulholland quoting Shakespeare, playing Ophelia to Eaton's Hamlet. But Eaton's term as mayor had ended poorly, Augusta never fully knew why. The old friends who had built the city with Eaton's father and welcomed the son into their midst seemed to turn against him. Mulholland was the only one who had demonstrated steadfast loyalty. His public comments about Fred Eaton were always laudatory.

Augusta positioned the telegram front and center on Mulholland's immense desk of polished pitch-pine, avoiding the in-basket at the corner. She never put items of any import there, as her boss was fond of saying, "Leave a letter in the basket long enough and it will take care of itself." She placed his ashtray on top of the telegram to secure it from the breeze coming in through the open window.

Pursing her lips and running a hand absently over silver hair pulled back from her forehead into a twist at the nape of her neck, she returned to her desk in the large outer office, facing the desks of the other clerical staff, arranged around a bank of pine filing cabinets. Augusta turned her clear gray eyes to a pile of typing she intended to finish before lunch.

She was tapping steadily at her new Underwood No. 1 typewriter when Mulholland strode in and proceeded into his office without a word, slamming the door. He was not one to waste time on pleasantries, which Augusta didn't mind, being of a similar nature herself. Besides, he was just as abrupt with high-ranking officials as with her. Yet when inclined, her boss had a churlish sort of charm. Once he had brought her a handful of roses he had picked on a whim from the Mulholland house garden. Thrusting them into her hands he had growled, "Put them in water or they'll die."

Tap, tap-tap-tap, tap, tap-tap, she completed another line before expletives rang out. Mulholland burst from his office and slammed a piece of paper with his rough scribble onto her desk.

"Augusta, send this to Matthews. Now!"

"Yes, Mr. Mulholland," she emitted her habitual reply as his office door slammed shut again.

William B. Matthews was the city attorney, and at this moment he happened to be in New York on municipal business. The contents of his brief message, so cryptic to her, had obviously been meaningful to Mulholland:

EATON HERE TALKING TO BANKERS -(STOP)- SOMETHING TO DO WITH CITY WATER -(STOP)- ARE YOU AWARE

Mulholland's reply had been even more brief:

STOP HIM

Over the next few days, Augusta tiptoed around the office, as Mulholland, uncharacteristically present, glowered, stomped and hovered, asking if there had been word from Matthews yet. Finally, another telegram arrived:

ACCOMPLISHED

The storm in Mulholland's eyes calmed then, but his mood remained jumpy and irritable. Even so, much to Augusta's relief, her boss resumed his habit of being out in the field much of the time. A week or so later, Matthews strode into the office.

"Good morning my dear Miss Aames," he said, hat in hand. The man was more dapper in a well-cut suit with plaid necktie than his position as city attorney might prescribe. Medium-brown hair, parted in the middle and a full, neatly trimmed beard and mustache of the same hue framed dark, intense eyes.

"Oh, thank goodness Mr. Matthews. I thought you'd never get back! He's been very anxious to see you!"

"Is he…"

"Out at present, I'm afraid. Shall I fetch you directly when he returns?"

"That would be most appreciated. Thank you Miss Aames," replied Matthews, heading off to his own office.

About an hour and 20 minutes later, Mulholland was back and, upon hearing of Matthews's arrival, demanded to see him immediately. Behind Mulholland's closed door, the lawyer recounted the events of the previous two weeks.

After receiving Mulholland's telegram, it had taken the city attorney less than a day of working through his financial contacts to confirm that Eaton was attempting to line up backing for purchasing water rights and land options in the Owens Valley. Mulholland's telegram had said only STOP HIM, but Matthews had needed no explanation. He knew why. Although Mulholland had been an employee of the private Los Angeles Water Company that had supplied the city prior to the creation of a municipal agency in 1901, he was violently opposed to letting control over the water ever revert back into private hands. Matthews shared this view, having witnessed the agonizing years of lawsuits, political discord and bond electioneering required to bring about the birth of the Los Angeles Department of Water and Power. Then once the voters had approved the bond measure, it had fallen largely to Matthews to sell the bonds. He and the city treasurer had spent two harried months back East, away from their homes and families, to accomplish the task.

Matthews was surprised that Fred Eaton, a former city engineer and mayor, was attempting such a maneuver. The man was a bit of a puzzle. He'd been one of the bright rising stars of the city, but then, in his last months in office, his star had seemed to fizzle. There had been the divorce, certainly, but that didn't explain how Eaton had seemed to fade from view, didn't account for the lack of public statements of appreciation at his departure.

There was no time to waste figuring the psychology and motives behind Eaton's duplicity; Matthews needed a plan to stop him. He started by having a few cautious conversations with financial contacts. Could the city dissuade them from participating in Eaton's venture? But while he was gratified to see that the city's leverage could exert a certain amount of pressure on some banks and private financiers, he came away from these meetings convinced that he would never be able to sway enough of them to prevent Eaton from recruiting the capital he required.

Another approach was required, and soon an idea began to form. The city had contacts in the US Department of Interior, the father agency for the Reclamation Service. Perhaps he could get Frederick Haynes Newell, director of the service, to look into the matter. He'd gathered, from third-hand accounts of Eaton's prospectus, that the man was assuring potential investors that the service would step away from its plans for the reclamation project in the Owens Valley when made aware of the city's proposed aqueduct. Matthews guessed Eaton was probably basing this assertion on informal talks with his pal J.B. Lippincott, a regional engineer for the service, and had not yet secured formal approval from Lippincott's superiors in Washington DC. Would they not look less favorably on the project if they knew they were being asked to step aside for a private endeavor rather than a public one?

"I contacted Director Newell and found, as I had suspected, that he was completely unaware of these shenanigans." A sly, widening smile revealed the thin lips normally obscured by Matthews's facial hair.

There had been telegrams back and forth with Matthews, setting off a flurry of discussions and meetings in Washington and regional offices. The long and short of it was that the word had come down to Lippincott, and then to Eaton: The only circumstance under which the service would consider canceling the reclamation project was if the aqueduct to Los Angeles were one hundred percent publicly funded and managed.

Mulholland whooped with satisfaction and drew deeply on his cigar. "That must have wiped that Cheshire cat smile off Fred's lips!"

"We'll see tomorrow. He's back in town, and I've asked him to come in. I spoke to him by telephone about an hour ago. He sounds, shall we say, *accommodating*."

"Good, because we need him to go back up to the valley. He's still the best one to buy up the rights, the only one who can get this done fast and quiet."

"There's something more," said Matthews. "Eaton has apparently already made one transaction. There's a ranch up there, a place called Long Valley—I heard he bought it with his own money."

"That bastard!" roared Mulholland, jumping out of his chair. He whirled around the room, then came back and kicked the chair. It spun on its rollers and careened into the wall with a crash. In the outer office, the typing and filing girls looked up with a start, but August set them back to their business with a slight shake of her head and a look that said "that's none of your concern now" before returning her eyes to her own work.

"All smiles and sweet adieus when he showed me to the train, and all the time he was fixing to hornswoggle me!" Mulholland's tanned countenance was brick red. "Must a gone back down there before headin East." He swung around and looked at the lawyer. "How in the hell did he get Rickey to sell?"

Matthews said nothing, just raised his eyebrows. His interrogator was in a better position to answer that question than he was.

Mulholland knew it too. No one understood Eaton better than he. Chair retrieved, he slumped back into it and reached for a fresh cigar to give himself time to calm down, to think. He bit off the end, lit and puffed the flame, then sat, forcing himself to inhale and exhale in long drafts. After some minutes of silent smoking, he chuckled, twirling the cigar between two fingers. "He could charm the tits off a tart! Smart as a steel trap too, that one."

Matthews saw it was time to get on with business. "Is it going to be a problem?" he asked.

"Reckon not." Mulholland was leaning back in this chair, arms crossed, eyes flashing above a bitter smile. "He'll sell it. We need it, those

20,000 acres include 20 square miles of nice level flatland. Only place in the valley fit to build a large reservoir. We need it, and he'll sell it. Work out fine for everybody. Fred'll have his money, and we'll have a place to store our water—city-owned water."

# Chapter 4

Lace of the gods. Mary was looking straight up at the filigree of dark leaves against deep blue twilight sky. Every leaf swayed independently in the warm evening breeze, creating a moving pattern that rolled across her eyes in a panorama as the buggy moved forward beneath them. Tilting her head back farther still, Mary breathed in mystery and spirit, and held it in her bosom for a few seconds before releasing it in a sigh.

She looked down at her lap, where slender, lovely hands clutched a black crocheted bag over a blue brocade dress—a frozen reflection, she thought, of the pattern above her. Ahead, as the buggy advanced through the tunnel of cottonwoods, she could see a sparkle of lights like a glittering ball gown, she heard a snatch of music. A little thrill of anticipation awoke in her stomach, and swelled into an ache of longing in her chest. She glanced over at her husband, and the ache dropped into her gut and hardened into stone.

I am a disappointed woman, she pronounced the judgment on herself woefully. Her eyes were on the lights ahead. If they knew how bitterly disappointed I am, they would think even less of me than they presently do. What is worse than being odd is to be ridiculous. I can just hear them thinking: look at her, longing to be the belle of the ball at 35, when she was, no doubt, a wall flower even at 15!

I was never popular. I wasn't pretty, didn't bother to be coy, and was all too serious-minded. The things I found fascinating, other children found a bore. Boys don't like a girl who becomes wild with emotion at the song of a lark, quotes Mr. Thoreau, knows where to find obsidian arrow points and wants to talk about botany and Beethoven. They thought I was excited because of them. That's when I'd see that self-satisfied smirk, like they knew I wanted something from them, but weren't going to give it to me. As if any of them could have ever given me what I wanted, what I want.

She glanced again at Wallace, who was driving the horses contentedly, whistling to the snatches of fiddle music floating toward them. Tall and slender with slightly bowed posture, he had thick, wavy brown hair, brown eyes behind wire-rim spectacles, clear, pale skin, a crooked smile and a quiet, almost scholarly disposition.

Once she had thought he would give her what she wanted: make the world open its deep, beating heart to her. There was another night, she remembered, when the two of them had ridden like this to a dance, his thigh so nearly against hers that she had felt the heat of it through her dress—a dress of white, all ribbons and bows, a dress a girl wears when she wants something to happen. Wallace had proposed that night, and after accepting, she had lifted her lips for the engagement kiss.

She had read about romantic relations, and was nervous but so very disposed to it. But nothing happened. His lips were kind, soft and gone in a moment. She had waited during the drive home, but he didn't touch her until they said goodnight, and then, just a touch of the lips, nothing more. Mary consoled herself with the thought that once they were married…

But on their wedding night, he touched her just long enough it seemed to complete his duty, then rolled off of her, kissed her cheek and turned in the bed, a slight movement of his back soon showing he had fallen asleep. Mary lay on her side, her nightdress still bunched about her waist, legs tucked up, the place between them throbbing. Touching the ache, her fingers felt sticky. In the morning, having slept nary at all, she crept out of bed and down to the kitchen to wash at the sink pump. Locating a towel had necessitated a search through the stacked boxes of their belongings. Dully she realized this was the day she had looked forward to for months, the first day of being a wife, of unpacking her boxes and setting up her own home. In the dream Mary had pictured herself as Sleeping Beauty or Snow White, joyful and radiant from the long-awaited kiss of love, happy ever after.

Wallace had touched her in bed again several nights later. This time it was only her heart that bled. This time she lay thinking afterward, I must endeavor to make myself more worthy of my husband's ardor. For months Mary exerted herself, resolved to look prettier, speak more sweetly, act more agreeably. She tried so very hard for so very, very long. Finally, one day she realized nothing was going to happen, ever. Her marriage had been a grievous error.

I should have waited for a great man, an extraordinary man, a man of genius, she was thinking now. Ma and my brother were in such a rush to see me married off, one less mouth to feed. They thought I had done well to get Wallace.

Wallace Austin and his brother Frank had grown up in Hawaii, sons of a wealthy sugar planter. When their father's plantation foundered, they had come to the mainland to remake the family fortune. Wallace was so different from the other men of Mary's acquaintance. A graduate of the University of California at Berkeley, he had refined literary tastes and read poetry aloud with feeling and nuance. Mary had persuaded herself this signified greatness. Surely such a man was not ordinary and would never choose an ordinary woman like the rest of them here in the valley to be his bride. The proof came when he chose her. How well vindicated she had felt at last for all those years of separateness and shame. It had all been but preparation for this new life of happiness.

Wallace's wedding gift had seemed to corroborate her hopes. It was the one exquisite surprise of their life together. The night before the modest ceremony and reception he presented her with a small silver box wrapped in silver netting. She'd peeled the delicate casing back and released the scrollwork latch. Inside the little treasure chest, nestled in a bed of white satin brocade, was a silver, pearl-handled writing pen engraved with her initials. Surprise, rapture, recognition had surged in her. She had felt giddy and, something new: thoroughly, entirely satisfied for the first time in her life.

The feeling had bloomed in her heart until her wedding night, and for weeks after that she had struggled to coax it faintly back to life. She had failed, though she knew the failure was not her own. Regretfully and bitterly, Mary came to the conclusion that Wallace had been reaching far beyond his nature with the precious nuptial gift. He was a painfully ordinary man, with no courage and no abiding intellectual curiosity. She knew now that this man had garnered every ounce of greatness within himself to make this single down payment on the rest of her life as his wife, year after dreary year stretching into her lost future. No, the precious pen hadn't been a promise.

Of course Wallace had tried to please her. Efforts made in the name of matrimonial happiness hadn't been all one-sided. But his attempts toward her were as fumbling and ineffectual as they were with his business ventures. He's always fixin to get into something, but never thinks it through. Never prepares by putting something by to build a strong foundation. Starts out with enthusiasm, but there are always insurmountable problems, always reasons why everything comes to naught. Sitting on the boarding house steps after the irrigation project failure, sick and pregnant, turned out for nonpayment, Wallace off somewhere chasing down another scheme, leaving her to fend for herself, Mary had seen how it was going to be.

Never mind. She had promised herself she would give birth to the smartest child in the world, and for months this dream replaced the old disappointed one. The new baby was indeed exceptional, but in a way neither Mary or Wallace had dared hoped for: Ruth was beautiful from the day she was born, and became more so as she grew. But she was a difficult infant, crying incessantly, and by the time she was two years old, it had been clear something was wrong. The fretful sounds she made were unlike those of other children beginning to speak; her restless uncoordinated movements were unlike those of other children trying to walk. Ruth's temper tantrums increased in duration and frequency. Finally, the family doctor confirmed Mary's darkest fear: her lovely daughter was mentally retarded. The irony of it cut sharp and deep as a cactus thorn.

Mary was sinking into her sodden thoughts when Wallace pulled the team up next to a dozen others and tied the reins to a fence post. He smiled over at her, and she began to feel a bit cheered in spite of herself. Festive, exuberant voices called to and fro as people unpacked their wagons of food baskets and blankets.

Children scampered off with their playmates, joining games underway beneath trees hung with lanterns. In the clearing, a band played next to a large wooden dance floor. Jumping, giggling little girls stopped momentarily to gaze at the swirl of men in pale, open-necked shirts turning and turning with bright, full-skirted women. Boys ducked under bushes and chased each other out into the darkness, darting back now and then to swipe a chicken leg or hunk of cornbread from the long tables set with supper. Eventually they would all drop, exhausted, onto mattresses spread out just behind the chairs where the old folks visited, gossiped and watched the comings and goings.

Mary yearned to be one of these wild boys, to be having such pure fun. But fun, she had learned, was something not to be expected by females after a certain age. Anyway, even as a child, she had rarely been invited to join such games. Had she ever been so lighthearted as these lively, loose-limbed children?

Wallace interrupted her reverie, which had again turned sodden. He was asking her to dance, although she knew he disliked dancing and did it poorly. "Why don't you get something to eat," she suggested. Then, lying: "I'll be along in a minute."

His hand held hers briefly before he turned gratefully toward the tables. But instead of taking up a plate, he moved beyond the tables to where about a dozen men gathered under a big oak were drinking and talking enthusiastically. The topic of conversation—finally the long-await-ed federal irrigation project was getting underway—elevated their mood and the amplitude of their speech. Clearly, it wouldn't be long now before the dam would be built and the valley flourish like never before. For some months running, that man Eaton had been visiting around the valley, offering folks good money for the water rights and land the Reclamation Service needed to start work in the northern part of the valley.

"John Shepherd won't say exactly how much he got paid for his water rights, but it was 'bout half again what he figures they'se worth."

"Lou McGovern said the same. Reckon he got near two hundred dol-lars for water rights and an option on that bottom pasture land."

"Like taking candy from a baby," spoke up Early Blackmann. "He come by after supper t'other day and sitting there on my porch with the Missus's lemonade we done us a deal all right. He said $120, and I just put my head back and took a good long sip and said $175. And, don't you know, the damn fool went for it without a blink."

"Blackie, when are they gonna start building the dam?" asked Rory Cartwright.

"No idea. These government reclamation folks don't tell ya nothin. But who cares, they'se buyin the land and water rights ain't they? So it canna be too long now."

"Could be a year before they break ground on the dam, and another one at least before we can start increasing irrigation," cautioned Lou Albers. "This isn't like building an irrigation ditch, this is big, and these big government projects take their time."

"Never mind," insisted Blackmann. "Mark my words, we'd all be mighty smart to start clearin more field and investing in one of them new iron plows with changeable parts."

"Denton Lacey is fixin to get one. He says…" ventured Rory.

"Well, hello there Wallace." Chalfant, who was as usual doing more listening than talking, made room for Austin to join the group.

"Hey there, most of you know Austin here manages the federal land office. He had a meeting with Eaton." All eyes turned to the newcomer as talk quieted down.

"Can you give us any information about the irrigation project Wallace?" asked Chalfant.

"I don't have any as yet to give you," Wallace demurred. "They haven't disclosed the particulars, at least not to the land office. They had their own Reclamation Service maps and just needed to look at deeds and such. They're probably not ready to talk about the project until they're sure they'll be able to purchase the properties, rights and easements they need."

"Hell, they ain't gonna have no problem with that if they keep handin out greenbacks like they been doin," chortled Blackmann.

"Heard tell that Eaton fella is lookin to settle on a ranch hisself," remarked Barney Leito, who owned land along Bishop Creek, north of Blackmann's property.

"Told me it's his life-long dream," snorted Stu McQueeney, a man with a small ranch and a big mouth. The whole group hooted in laughter at the picture of city-bred Eaton in his well-tailored clothes running cattle.

"Man's got more money than brains," pronounced Frank Bellamy. "But that don't mean we ought not to oblige him!"

Mary had watched Wallace approach the cluster of men tentatively, with an air both awkward and hopeful. A reflection, she realized irritably, of how she felt. Observing him, she felt even worse. Chalfant was kind, though, to welcome Wallace like that. Always extending a hand and lending an ear. A useful comportment for a newspaper man, she reflected, but it also bespoke of his character.

Now she looked away from the huddle of men and cast her eyes about the dance floor. There were Earnest and Tess Beaton, a dull rancher and his pretentious wife. Tess, like many of the other middle-aged women, seemed to be exploding out of the bodice of her overly ruffled dress. The corset she relied on to imitate the youthful wasp-waisted style of popular dress, pushed her ample flesh up under her bust, amplifying her cleavage while giving her an armor-like flat front. Mary, who never resorted to rigid forms, partly because her thick waist would have responded too little to make the discomfort worthwhile, noted smugly that Tess danced stiffly and was out of breath after one turn about the floor.

Carl Fredeker, owner of the creamery, was dancing stiffly too, but so enthusiastically did he pump the arm of Jocelyn Mayfield, the petite, shy schoolteacher, that Mary liked him for it. Janey's father, Ben Bow, had no false airs, but a natural grace in dancing. With clear affection, he embraced the girl's mother Alice, looking youthful in the red dress she always wore on such occasions, white-blond hair perfectly woven into a gleaming chignon.

Wilfred Watterson, president of the bank and eldest son of one of the valley's leading families, was waltzing with Mrs. Kinsley. His own wife, being something of an invalid, rarely attended community events. The pair waltzed with self-assurance and ease, her with arched back and right hand holding out the skirt of her gown. As if they were at Covent Garden, Mary silently snickered. Mark Watterson was leading Katie Matlick out of the circle of lights, no doubt for a walk by the pond. Katie was the sort of girl young men sought out for moonlit walks, red-gold hair tumbling down her neck in ringlets, the requisite wasp-narrow waist, as well as finely shaped ankles just visible as she raised the hem of her lemony cloud of a dress to descend the single step from the dancing platform to the ground.

Mary knew her face had set into its customary frown, which she took pains to correct now, lest anyone watching get the impression she was pining here on the sidelines, a wallflower still. Out of the corner of her eye, Mary saw Janey waving to her from across the dancers. Mary acknowledged the girl with a reserved nod. Wouldn't do to have her come over here and me be seen talking with a little girl all night.

Oh, thought Mary, how much more at ease I felt the night of the fiesta in Las Uvas. There, all the smiles were friendly. The soft, plump bodies of the uncorseted Mexican women moved naturally, alluringly in loose white blouses and embroidered skirts. These women with warm, dark eyes wore their sex gently yet proudly, bellies bringing forth a new baby every year or two, breasts heavy with the nurturing. Mary loved to listen to the soft, musical speech cascading back and forth between the men and women as they joked, teased, scolded and flirted. With plenty of wine down their gullets, they would begin to sing about love, their fields and homes, children, exile and loss. They'd sing the Mexican national anthem, "America" and the *"Marseillaise,"* which had been taught them by the French shepherds tending flocks here, so far from home. The night of the fiesta, she had sung with them too and feasted on chicken with chili, tamales and corncake with a pungent sauce of chili, tomato, onion, cheese and olives. Pulling the pins from her hair, she had let it fall, incurring not a single disapproving look from her fellow revelers, elated to feel her treasured locks flowing freely around her hips. For some reason, that memory made her think of the tall, fair man she'd seen swimming naked in the river, the one Janey hadn't been able to take her eyes off of.

"May I have the pleasure of this dance Mrs. Austin?"

It was Wilfred Watterson, bowing slightly, extending his hand.

Mary colored at the robust male presence interrupting her earthy thoughts. Though surprised to be the object of such attention, she managed a shy "With pleasure, Mr. Watterson."

Stepping into his arms, she felt one sure hand capture the small of her back while the other rose to cradle her own hand. The warmth of his touch thawed her reserve, and she was soon whirling and twirling with pleasure. Being inside his arms, she was inside the music. Her mind settled and calmed as her feet moved to wherever he wanted them to go.

Her partner was someone she knew but slightly, yet had observed rather attentively from afar. He was, in her estimation, a man of upright character, careful habits, strong convictions, quick actions and a tendency to a high-strung temperament, which he generally kept under good regulation. His face, looking down at her, had clean-cut, symmetrical features.

Wilfred was the eldest child in a prominent family that had initially made its fortune in the valley from sheep ranching. As students, he and his brother Mark had dominated school sports and graduated with glorious approbation. The enterprise-minded brothers opened a mercantile, from which they provided valley folk with hardware, stoves, farm machinery, plumbing goods and harnesses as well as fine imported china and cut glassware. They went on to found and operate the valley's first bank, Wilfred as president and Mark as treasurer. Wilfred had also been first in the valley to own an automobile, a gleaming white Stanley Steamer.

"Tell me, Mrs. Austin, what have you heard about the land and water purchases that have been going on these recent days? As your husband is federal lands register, I imagine you've some insight into the matter."

"He discloses little of his work to me, Mr. Watterson, and I rarely prompt him to do so, as I have even less interest in it."

"Of course." He smiled. "But this development is of extraordinary interest to us all, wouldn't you agree Mrs. Austin?" He didn't wait for her answer, but continued, "This valley is beautiful to be sure, but nothing like it could be someday. With extensive irrigation, we could double our agricultural output, and the town would grow apace. Perhaps we'll even build a lending library where your book will be prominently displayed Mrs. Austin!"

Mary was amused. Even the gifted Wattersons weren't immune to the valley curse. She looked steadily into his eager eyes and spoke quietly but clearly.

"Beauty, Mr. Watterson, whether in the land or a woman, has a power that makes men want to master it. But I find that few men are up to the task."

Her partner stiffened a bit then, and she sensed his relief when, at the end of the tune, he guided her back to where she had stood. "Thank you for a most enjoyable dance and a most interesting conversation Mrs. Austin."

Mary sighed. Why had she not replied more agreeably. It had been lovely, after all, to be dancing, and now here she was, back on the sideline, alone again.

On the other side of the dance floor, under the dusky trees, Janey stood apart from a knot of little girls playing at waltzing. She watched as

Mr. Watterson relinquished Mary's hand and walked away toward the cluster of men at the end of the supper tables. She saw Mary's eyes follow his retreat from a countenance that looked thoughtful, then tired. Mary hesitated, looking for her husband in the group Watterson had just joined. Then, apparently decided, she turned, strode to the buffet, wrapped a handful of cornbread in her shawl and headed out, alone, away from lights, music and neighbors. No one noticed except Janey, but she was not surprised by anything Mary did.

*I wish CK could have known my valley then. I wish he could have run under oak canopies braided with lights and slept on blankets in a heap of friends. But my grandnephew was not fortunate enough to have enjoyed such a simple childhood.*

*I begin to realize I'm putting some of this down on paper for him. This is selfish, I suppose, this urge to explain myself, but there's little time and only CK left to understand. Also there's the possibility that learning more about what happened might even help him. Heaven knows, he needs help, though most folks would laugh at the notion. Born to a life of privilege, CK could do anything, be anyone he wanted. But he's always had trouble fitting into the world my brother Chris forged. Not as much trouble as his father, who died an unhappy alcoholic, but never much ease either.*

*It seems to me that very early in life we know the difference between those who fit in and those who don't. First we notice it in other children. There are always a few who hang back, never get picked first. CK was a child like that, even though he'd been endowed with Chris's robust good looks. But this little fair-haired boy was pudgy and habitually wore a somber expression. He was too shy to speak up and make friends. He was always invited to birthday parties though—most likely in hopes he'd show up with an expensive present.*

*Later, as we grow, we start seeing the difference among adults too. I always knew Mary Austin said and did odd and amazing things, but it took quite awhile before I noticed how other adults reacted to her.*

*Our magic days of wandering up and down canyons had almost come to an end when it struck me that Mary wasn't liked by most valley folk, and that she knew this and it hurt her. I had always found it easy to be liked, easy to be included in any game or group I chose to join, so it was strange to think that what was effortless for me—the girl who tagged along asking questions—was a struggle for her. And this person I looked up to and listened to, I also began feeling just a little bit sorry for her.*

Mary was at a disadvantage, having exchanged her sturdy walking shoes tonight for less substantial footing. Still, such a practiced trekker moved easily over the rough terrain. The moon, on the rise now, calmed and charmed her. And she, quiet and observant, was accepted by the desert and its small, skittering inhabitants. A rustle to her left, and something dove under a sheep skull, the bones bare and bleached of all color, gleaming in the moonlight among all the gray forms of rock and tumbleweed. She could hear a prowling band of coyotes moving garrulously along in the scrub. It never failed to amaze her what great talkers they were and how varied the notes of their conversations.

The outline of one of the beasts now appeared on top of a rock up ahead. Suddenly the coyote dropped down, crouching under the rock, startled, not by her but by the luminous orb peaking over the cliff edge. She watched it peer suspiciously at the rising shape until, released from the mountain, the moon was revealed, nearly full and penetratingly bright.

She'd seen this strange behavior before, written about it, in fact, in her book. How amusing that wild creatures were not more accustomed to the variable states of this constant companion to their nocturnal wanderings. How odd that they should be caught unprepared as its shape narrowed or spread, its hue shifting from lemon to pearl, its surface clear or cloud covered, uncertain therefore as to its identity. Perhaps, she considered, it is only we humans who retain a general notion of something despite such changes as it may undergo in particulars of shape, color and location. Perhaps to this coyote, the moon was not the same thing rising night after night.

She was pondering what it would be like to go out each night into a world full of new things when she understood, from the odor of burning sage, that she was nearing her destination. Mary headed toward where she knew the flock would be bedded down, where the gentle, hairy man who tended them would have made his campfire. Closer, as she neared the place, the perfume of sage became overpowering, mixed with that of garlicky venison stew. The drowsy yewing of the flock accompanied a lonely harmonica. It was the shepherd Matias, and she, fingering the bounty in her shawl, was sure of his welcome.

Sometime later, her lips greased with the fragrant stew, her eyes serenely following the popping play of flames, Mary spoke with her friend about the miles he had traveled with the flock and what had transpired in the valley during his absence. Though Matias and his kind were solitary creatures, shy and usually taciturn, they loved to gossip among each other and with a few trusted souls like Mary. It was, she thought, their way of staying connected to a sense of home.

Mary offered what news she could, telling of the hubbub among the valley folk caused by the man from the Reclamation Service spreading cash around for water rights and land options. Matias, stirring the fire to coax more warmth from the embers, asked quietly, "Is it certain to be a dam then?"

Mary was startled by the question. She waited for Matias, still poking at the embers, to continue.

"Debs Yellman come by my camp other day. Said he'd been crossing paths with that feller, the tall, good looker, and he recognized 'em. Seen 'em before 'bout six month ago with another shorter feller with a mustache. He done come upon them two camping along the river, and Debs asked 'em for some food and whiskey, of which they was most obliging. But before he made hisself known, he stood listenin fer a time in the tree cover, so as not to come unawares upon cattle rustlers or bandits. Said he heard 'em talking about the water, and seemed like they had a notion to be foolin the people round here and takin the water someplace else."

Mary suddenly felt the cold night air pressing in around the campfire. She was remembering the statuesque man she and Janey had spied bathing with his companion in the hollow. The sight of him had taken her breath away, but what made her hold it tight in her chest now was a strong sense of misgiving. She knew Debs, though many of the valley folk regarded him as a crazy fool, was clear-headed and that he never lied, fabricated a story or exaggerated its meaning. If Matias was recounting his words faithfully, and she felt certain he was, something was indeed very wrong.

Wallace left the party while the band continued to play and the discussion about irrigation was still underway. He walked quietly past the tables that had now given up most of their bounty, behind the elders, some still gossiping, some napping and snoring, between them and the mattresses where the drowsy voices of children losing the battle to stay awake could be heard here and there, to the fence post where the wagons and buggies were hitched. He untied his horse and led her down the path a hundred yards or so before stepping up onto the floorboard of the rig. Wallace preferred not to attract attention, and, as was normally the case with him, he did not.

He hadn't needed to ask for Mary because he knew she was gone. He hadn't seen her go, but he had known it soon afterward as he'd scanned the edges of the dance floor and found no heavy busted short woman with luxuriant hair and a frown. There was no point in looking for her further in the gaggles of women talking round the tables. Mary would never be among them.

Wallace sighed at the certainty of it. As pleasant as tonight had been, caught up in the general excitement surrounding the reclamation project, he knew he and Mary would always be apart from the others, mired at the margins of society. Though he felt himself to be liked and respected, as a former school superintendent and now in his poorly paid but respectable position as register of the federal lands office, the townsfolk would never understand his marriage. If they even suspected how unperturbed he was at his wife walking away from society into the desert night, how calmly he would gather his daughter from Mrs. Parker, who had taken on this charge, being she said, "too old to dance," how he would return to the house and, after putting Ruth down, go to bed alone, leaving the latch up for Mary's return whenever that was, if they even suspected this, they would be aghast, scandalized and, most certainly, would despise him.

The night events proceeded precisely as he had envisioned, but the next morning he woke, not to Ruth's usual wailing, but to the smell of apple muffins in the oven and bacon and coffee on the stove. Entering the kitchen in shirttails, suspenders hanging, he saw his daughter merrily licking a gooey spatula, which Mary, still in her blue dress from the night before, but now open at the neck, was extending from one hand while tending a sizzling frying pan with the other. She glanced around and smiled, her long, loosened hair, moving like a fringed curtain.

"Good morning Wallace. You were resting so soundly I feared to wake you and so slept in the parlor," she explained. He nodded, sitting down at the table.

As she pointed the spatula in the direction of the front room, Ruth's extended tongue tracked it like a hunter's gun following a bird in flight. Regaining her target, the little girl licked it clean.

Mary took the spatula away, and for a moment Ruth stared at where it had been. She started to whimper, but then noticing Wallace at last, flung herself wildly toward him, "Pa, Pa!" sending the highchair she had long outgrown rocking precariously.

"Whoa there little lady," he scooted his chair closer to hers, put his face up to kiss the sticky lips and stroked her silky hair. "Good morning to you!"

"Song, song!" she trilled, and he obliged with "She'll be Comin Around the Mountain," getting up and marching around the table as he sang.

Mary transferred the bacon from pan to platter, then leaned down to withdraw a tin of puffy, golden muffins from the oven. She brought them nestled in a basket, covered with a towel, to the table, along with two steaming cups of black coffee. Ruth immediately reached for a strip of bacon and joyously shoved it inside her mouth. Wallace moved the platter away, then placed two strips on the girl's plate.

"Here you go honey lamb."

He felt fine, almost quite fine indeed. The first bite of Mary's muffin was heaven, as always, fumes of butter and apple filling up his nasal passages as the incomparable taste awakened his tongue. What did it matter that the floor underfoot was dirty, Mary was sitting across from him and their beautiful daughter, and she was smiling, though, he now took notice, somewhat nervously. He could see she was fixing to have a conversation about something. Probably she wanted him to take care of Ruth today so as to free her for writing or wandering. He looked at his girl, who was now eating her way into the middle of a muffin, and felt fine about the prospect, almost quite fine.

"Wallace, I want to speak with you about that man from the Reclamation Service."

"The service?"

"That man who came by to see you at the lands office, the one you've been helping with maps and deeds."

"Oh, Fred Eaton. Why?"

"Are you quite certain he is who he claims to be?"

"I fail to understand your meaning my dear. What possible reason would the man have to misrepresent himself?"

She ignored his question. "Are you quite certain he is pursuing this program of purchases for the reclamation project?"

"Of course, only a large federal project would put forth such a quantity of capital my dear."

"But couldn't there be another large project, for something other than irrigation here in the valley?"

"I can't think what you mean Mary." He shook his head, exasperated, as his wife took off on one of her frequent flights of fancy. No telling what had set her off or where she was heading.

"Wallace, listen to me," Mary's voice sharpened. "Last night, Matias told me that Debs Yellman…"

"Oh, for heaven's sake Mary, that French sheepherder gossips like an old woman. And that broken down pocket hunter has a name for telling tall tales…"

"Name…name…Wait a minute…Wallace…" Mary's eyes widened. "What did you say his name is?"

"What, Debs Yellman?"

"No, the man from Reclamation!" Mary sprung from her chair and began pacing rapidly back and forth across the kitchen, hands flying to her head, grabbing, wrenching and knotting the heavy mane of hair, then letting it go to clutch at her apron. "Stupid, stupid, stupid," she muttered.

She turned, pointing, glaring at him. "You didn't even remember his name!"

Wallace stared. Something he had forgotten…his thoughts flitted about trying to find…anxiety rising, dread descending.

"Back when you and Frank were promoting your own irrigation project, what was the name of that man who came up from Los Angeles to talk about financing? What was the name of that man who said no, the one who refused to invest?"

Wallace felt the sunny kitchen darkening. Ruth was jabbering at something, but Mary's words cut through the din, painfully clear at last.

"It was Fred Eaton, wasn't it? Fred Eaton, you fool!"

---

The next day, talk about the irrigation project had reached a feverish pitch. It was Sunday, and after church small circles of men hung back from their families, whispering in excitement. Christopher Bow peeled away from one huddle, where he had been leaning in to hear, and bounded after his father and mother, who had finished saying their goodbyes to the preacher and were heading toward the wagon.

"Pa, did ya hear?"

Ben winked at Alice. "Hear what, son?"

"Pshaw, you know, about the irrigation project. It's finally happenin Pa! They're handin out cash for options to buy land and water rights."

"Oh that," conceded Ben, grinning now. "Alice, didn't we hear a little somethin 'bout that last night?"

"Would have been difficult not to hear it, way some folks were carrying on."

Alice smiled at her son as her husband handed her up into the wagon. She shaded her eyes from the late morning sun and began looking around to locate Janey, a habitual chore. There was her daughter, talking with Juan and Emma about 50 yards away, under a big cottonwood. The Mexican children were in overalls, barefoot; their families weren't members of the church, but attended their own services Saturday evenings at the small Catholic chapel.

Waving, she caught Janey's eye and motioned her to come, and to put on her bonnet. Janey waved goodbye to her friends and launched herself across the church yard, obeying the first command, ignoring the second. Alice noticed that her daughter's hated Sunday dress of white eyelet over pale blue was already too short, revealing long skinny legs pumping comically below the scalloped hem as she ran to the wagon.

"Hop up here with me, and put your bonnet on. We have to get on home now, Aunt Maggie's coming for Sunday supper." She was speaking about Ben's sister, the unmarried school mistress of Bishop Academy, the best high school in the valley.

"Here she is, lookin like a little fairytale princess," Ben teased.

"Awh, Pa!" protested Janey. She slid next to Alice, who smelled so good on Sunday, like roses and violets, she thought. Janey glanced up, from under her bonnet rim, at her mother. Alice's own bonnet was secured with a wide ribbon, tied in a faultless bow at one ear. Beneath this practical adornment, was thick, straight fair hair, the same color as Chris's, pulled neatly back, glowing skin, clear blue eyes. Nothing about her was vain or extravagant, but everything about her was remarkable. Janey, looking down at her own brown hands and ragged fingernails, knew she would never look like that.

Ben snapped Barlow's reins and they started moving out of the yard, maneuvering around other wagons doing the same. As they started down the lane that curved around the side of the church, Chris, in front beside him, pointed to where Wilfred and Mark Watterson, Willie Chalfant and Wallace Austin stood, talking intently, at the back of the building. Had Chris been granted a closer view of the scene he might have noticed that Austin's face was ashen as he kept pushing his glasses back up on his sweaty nose.

"Look, Pa, see, they know something big is happening. They're probably figuring right now how to turn this opportunity into a fortune. Pa, this could mean big things for us too."

Chris's eyes pranced back and forth from the group of men to his father. The wagon moved on down the lane, and soon the men were obscured behind a line of poplars. He turned back to his father.

Seeing Chris was about to re-launch himself on the topic, Ben replied in his calm, even manner, "They're not buying land near us, Chris. The dam site will be in the north valley, that's where folks are being paid those big sums. And what does it matter anyway, because we aren't interested in selling. You know that."

"Ain't talkin 'bout sellin, Pa, talkin 'bout expandin. Those manure-grown cabbages are the biggest in the valley and folks at market are buying them first, before the Laceys', the Cartwrights', before anybody's. You was saying other day we should try putting it on other crops. There's no tellin what we could do, and now with irrigation, we could plant double the acreage."

"Every other ranch in the valley will be doubling theirs too. There'll be 20 times more produce to sell than folks will have the notion or means to buy."

"Not if we sell outside the valley."

"You're already taking a full wagon load over to Cerro Gordo. And we just started shippin on that new line to Tonopah."

"But suppose we could ship our fruit and vegetables direct to Los Angeles too?" Chris's voice deepened as he related the big news. "I heard it's not only the dam soon to be constructed, but they're finally ready to convert the railroad line too!"

Now Ben looked at his son with genuine curiosity. This was interesting. Valley folk had recently felt cause to hope for a solution to their transportation woes. The Southern Pacific Railroad, which had acquired the Carson & Colorado "Slim Princess" in 1900 and built the extension to Tonopah, had begun converting the nonstandard narrow gauge track along this extension to standard gauge. It was rumored that the entire line would be converted, all the way south down to Keeler at the north shore of Owens Lake. Now it seemed Chris had heard that this work was about to get underway. If this were true, markets for Owens Valley produce would expand a hundred fold—and the reclamation project would provide the means to expand the cultivatable land as well.

"You sure about that?"

"That's what folks are sayin."

"I sure do hope they know what they're talking about." Ben let out a low whistle, which swung up an octave, then blended into a melody, "Foggy Dew." Chris joined in, and so did Janey, the best whistler in the family. Alice sang the words, her hands running over her knees as if she were playing the parlor piano.

They had done justice to several other popular tunes by the time they arrived home. Ben and Chris headed out to the barn to unhitch Barlow and check on the other horses. Alice and Janey went inside to put Sunday dinner on the table.

Alice had made a fricassee of lamb the evening before, and now she quickly sifted, stirred, rolled and cut large circles of biscuit, arranging them on top of the stew pot, which she slid into the oven. On the sideboard were a perfectly formed chocolate cake and cherry pie, which she had baked in the early morning before church. Aunt Maggie, when she arrived, was carrying molasses cookies bought from the general store.

Janey, eyeing these as she laid the place settings around the table, considered that her Ma's homemade sweets were far better than the one's from the store. And although they didn't taste as wonderful as Mary's, they were more reliably available. Days even weeks would go by and then, poof, like a fairy with a magic wand, Mary would make delectable sweets appear. Janey's Ma, on the other hand, brought forth a steady stream of breads, pies, cookies, cakes and cobblers to feed her family.

Ben, coming in to sit at table with his family, also eyed the sideboard of delights. He smiled at his sister, happy to have her with them, but his eyes lingered on his wife. He was thinking, for the hundredth time, of how much she did for them, never seeming to tire of it. Alice was, as she liked to say to him, born to be a ranch wife and mother. Ben felt such contentment as he looked around the table. It's a very fortunate thing, he rejoiced silently, to know exactly where on this earth you belong.

---

At eight o'clock Monday morning the sun was already blasting through the front windows of the *Inyo Register* office. Chalfant drew his two visitors toward the back for coolness and privacy.

"How could Austin not have recognized him?" asked Wilfred Watterson. "He almost went into business with the man!"

"Goes to show a college degree doesn't mean you're smart," commented his brother Mark.

"If the man's name is Fred Eaton, and he does hail from Los Angeles, then that sure is damn peculiar," said Chalfant. "They had a mayor name of Eaton some years back. Of course, it could be someone else."

"Even if it is the same fellow, he could still be working for Reclamation, couldn't he?" ventured Wilfred.

"Maybe," answered Chalfant, frowning. "Look, the whole valley is laughing at him, thinking he's a prime fool for paying top dollar." He looked hard at his companions and lowered his voice. "I can tell you one thing: If this is the same Eaton, he's no fool."

"You think he has another reason for spending so freely?" Wilfred was drumming the toes of his Italian-made shoes against a table leg.

"I don't know, but we'll soon find out," responded Chalfant. "I know someone who works for Reclamation, fella by the name of Clausen. I'll see if he knows anything about this. Meantime, keep it under your hats. We've got to stay as calm as skunks in the moonlight. If they are up to something, let's just let 'em keep on thinking they've got us fooled."

---

The Wattersons took Chalfant's advice and got on with their morning's business at the bank. It was unusually busy for the beginning of the working week.

Glancing down occasionally from his desk in the mezzanine overlooking the bank floor, Wilfred observed at least a half dozen of his neighbors, mostly ranchers and their wives, making deposits at the teller window. He guessed that these were payments received for water rights and land options. A couple of times, he went down, greeting his customers in his usual cordial manner. In both cases, his neighbors responded politely, but their overall manner was reserved. Not of a mind to chat this morning. Understandable, thought Wilfred. Some folk don't like to show when good fortune comes their way.

At a little past two in the afternoon, he was signing letters, when he saw something strange from the corner of his eye. A fidgety young man in a gray suit was standing beside the desk of Mr. Hirsch, the assistant manager. Hirsch was not to be seen, and Wilfred was about to proceed downstairs to ask the young gentleman if he could be of assistance, when he saw Hirsch return, carrying a safe deposit box. The assistant manager motioned to the young man to accompany him into the curtained booth. Hirsch then came out and went back to his desk.

From where he sat, Wilfred could see about six inches of the customer's feet and lower legs beneath the curtain. He chuckled. The fellow didn't seem able to stand still, he kept jumping around as if requiring a trip to the outhouse. A few moments later, the man poked his head out of the curtain, scanned the room and left in haste.

Wilfred wasn't chuckling anymore. On a hunch, he leapt down the stairs to Hirsch's desk.

"Who was that man?"

"Who, sir?" responded Hirsch.

"The one who just snuck out of the booth!"

"Oh dear, I told him to return the key to me," said Hirsch, looking over at the booth, where the curtain was closed as if still occupied.

"Where's his form?"

"Here, sir, here it is. Everything is in order." Hirsch primly held up the bank's security box access form.

Watterson scanned the form, his eye stopping at the name and address lines. Harry Lelande, Los Angeles, California.

"It was his own box he opened?"

"No, the box belonged to a Mr. Frederick Eaton, also of the city of Los Angeles. Mr. Lelande gave me this letter," said Hirsch, offering up another piece of paper. "It's from Mr. Eaton, giving Mr. Lelande permission to examine and remove the contents of his box."

Wilfred was out the door and down the street before Hirsch could close his mouth. He stood at the corner, anxiously scanning the street and sidewalks…nothing. All of a sudden Wilfred saw Lelande coming out of the US Post Office. He forced himself to move toward the young man slowly, forced his breath to slow.

"Hello there. I'm sorry Mr. Lelande, sir, but there's a small formality we forgot to carry out at the bank. Just another form to sign. Won't take a minute."

Lelande looked uncomfortable, but came along as Watterson led him back up the street, into the bank and up the stairs to his office, where he closed the door. Mark slipped in, curious. Wilfred made a gesture indicating his brother should lock the door, then fixed a cold-eyed smile on the young man.

"I want the deeds you took out of that box Mr. Lelande."

Lelande, eyes wide, croaked, "I don't know what you mean. These, sir, are private papers, just business papers."

"Take your jacket and pants off."

"What?! I don't understand."

"You heard me, take them off."

"You can't do that! This is a bank…"

"Wilfred, what are you doing?!" Mark was as startled as Lelande. He had never heard his brother use that steely tone of voice with a customer before, and he had certainly never heard him make such an outrageous demand of one.

"You'll find out," was Wilfred's curt reply.

Lelande rose shakily, heading toward the door he didn't know was locked. "I really must be leaving…"

"Stop right there!" barked Wilfred, reaching for his desk drawer. Lelande turned and gaped. So did Mark. Wilfred was pointing a small pistol at the clerk. It was a Colt Pocket Hammerless with a silver plated finish and ivory handle. Its size and handsomeness belied the deadly power of the weapon.

"Please come back," Wilfred said sternly, "and take off your clothes."

This time the terrified man did as he was bid, struggling to release his arms from his jacket, unbutton his braces and push his trousers to the floor. He stood, skinny frame trembling, in boxer shorts and undershirt.

"Step out of those…throw them over there." He pointed to Mark, "Take a look in the pockets."

Mark searched, but found no deeds. There was a business card, however. Mr. Harry Lelande, General Clerk, Office of the City Attorney, city of Los Angeles. Now Mark was beginning to understand. He felt sweat popping out on his neck as he handed the card to his brother.

"All right, now, put your clothes back on, mister city clerk. We're going to take a little walk over to your hotel room," said Wilfred. "Just going to go in there nice and friendly like three old buddies, you understand? And to make sure, I'll just keep this," he waved the pistol, "in here." He put the hand holding the pistol in his jacket pocket.

When they got to the room, Wilfred tied Lelande to a chair, using the man's own suspenders, while he and his brother went through the suitcase and searched the bedding and chest of drawers. Nothing. Wilfred turned, frustrated and furious, on the clerk.

"Tell us the truth, Lelande, or by God I'll pistol whip it out of you!" He was yelling now and brandishing the weapon. "I want the deeds you took from that box. They aren't for any irrigation project in the valley are they? Because you don't work for the Reclamation Service, you work for Los Angeles. And so does that scoundrel Eaton!"

Lelande hid his agonized countenance by looking down at the floor.

"Eaton didn't pay all that money because he's stupid, did he? He paid it because he's very, very smart."

The eyes rose now, a slight gleam of triumph amidst misery. "I can't give you the deeds because I don't have them anymore. As to what they are for, I have no knowledge of that. My instructions were simply to retrieve and relay them, which I did. My task is finished."

And then Wilfred knew what had happened: The damn clerk had mailed them. He'd been so worried about what would happen if anyone found out that he hadn't even taken the time to go back to his hotel, he'd gone straight to the post office, and that alone confirmed Watterson's suspicions. The man had just finished dispatching the documents when Wilfred had spotted him, a minute too late.

The brothers sank down, side by side, on the bed, Wilfred repocketing the pistol.

"What does that mean if the city has bought land and water rights here?" asked Mark. "Why do they want them?"

"I don't know" was his brother's miserable reply.

---

Janey Bow fit the bars of lead between the lines of metal letters in the second-page story for the evening edition of the *Inyo Register*. Chalfant didn't object to the girl's presence. She could spell, so he occasionally even allowed her to set headlines into type. She'd insinuated herself into the office during long summer days when, exiled from home and playmates to spend a fortnight with her Aunt Maggie, the child had been desperate for diversion.

Margaret Bow was gentle and kind but, never having married, knew little of how to occupy children outside of the classroom. As a woman of learning, however, she was friendly with the editor of the town's leading newspaper. One day, dropping in to say hello with her niece in tow, Margaret had gotten a notion it would be educational for Janey to spend a bit of time here.

Chalfant, who ran the *Register* on a shoestring, hadn't objected. He'd accept help from almost any quarter. And for her part, Janey had taken to the idea right away. She was fascinated by the long rows of metal characters, like game board pieces, and the process of putting them in lines with the lead bar spacers. She loved the ink smell, heavy, like a doused campfire, which hung in the room like smoke long after the press run. She also adored Chalfant for all the interesting things he knew, the patience he showed her and his jolly face, which made up for his often stale breath.

The bell at the door tinkled. Jane looked up to see Wilfred and Mark Watterson. She, like everyone in the valley, knew who they were. Usually they had friendly faces for all, but today they looked upset. Chalfant noting their countenances, motioned them toward the back of the room. Janey knew it was so she wouldn't hear what they said, but she did.

"You were right, must be the same Eaton from Los Angeles because he sent a city clerk to clean out his safe deposit box. That's pretty good evidence he's not working for Reclamation isn't it?"

"Yes, I would say it is," said Chalfant thoughtfully. "And I would say we can assume that Los Angeles has some alternative purpose for Owens Valley water. But that means the Reclamation Service would have to be willing to relinquish its plans for building the dam, unless these purposes are complementary. In any case, the service has to know what's going on. I've telegraphed Clausen, so let's find out what he has to say before speculating any further."

Wilfred nodded, Chalfant's steady voice and clear thinking making him feel slightly less miserable. At the hotel, when it had been evident nothing more could be gotten from Lelande, the brothers had let him go. The frightened man collected his belongings from where they had been thrown during the search and was out the door and down to the stage station in under five minutes.

The brothers had continued to sit forlornly on the bed. Then, as he began to fully comprehend the danger the deeds might represent, Mark had urged Wilfred to break into the post office outgoing mail box.

"I'm ashamed to say I considered it," admitted Wilfred to Chalfant, "but came to my senses."

"Good thing that," Chalfant said, nodding. "There are better ways to discover the truth. We'll get the facts from Clausen. Of all the service engineers, he's the most friendly to the valley." Chalfant inclined his head to the front room, where Janey was still working on the type frame.

"Never underestimate the power of the press."

Yes, Chalfant's line of reasoning always made sense, thought Wilfred. "Let us know when you hear from Clausen," he requested. "And see if you can get him here. Dinner at the old house Saturday, six o'clock. Let's have Austin there too and anyone else you think can help."

---

The senior Mr. Watterson's home, called "the old house" by his offspring, was a gracious, rambling stone and wood structure, which, despite having been gradually added onto over the years, retained pleasing proportions. Iron lanterns set on either side of a broad stone step curved up to the entrance, welcoming the dinner guests and beckoning them into the warmly lit interior.

Mary Austin, crossing the threshold with Wallace, found herself on a stone floor covered by an immense Mexican rug of geometric design and flaming color. Glancing about as a maid helped her out of her cloak, Mary saw a hand-fitted wood ceiling in a generously sized room furnished with roughly hewn oak and pine chairs and chests, deeply burnished by years of oiling and use. On the far wall, was a magnificent tapestry in faded hues of red and gold, antique European, she thought. The design of chevaliers and their ladies fair possessed a certain animation, as soft light cast by dozens of candles in a massive iron chandelier played across it.

Mary felt conspicuous and dowdy amidst such splendor in her blue brocade dress. But immediately her hand was taken by Wilfred Watterson, and she and Wallace received a hearty, sincere greeting from Mark as well.

The other guests welcomed by the younger Wattersons, acting as hosts for the evening, numbered 26, including the Chalfants and representatives of the valley's most prominent ranching, mining and mercantile families. In testament to the popularity of Wilfred and the respect in which he was held, it had required but a few days to bring this distinguished group together. In addition, there were the three Watterson sisters, Mary, Isabel and Elizabeth.

Jacob Clausen, Chalfant's acquaintance in the Reclamation Service stood at the back of the hall, glancing at the youngest, Elizabeth, as he conversed with William Watterson, fountainhead of the family and master of the estate. William's eyes twinkled as he listened to Clausen's words and noticed the latter's inclination. He's takin to her like a bear to a honey tree, the old man thought, chuckling, his own hand resting comfortably at the waist of his wife, Eliza, regal in Irish lace. She too noticed how Clausen's eyes kept wandering back to Elizabeth. Ah, lovely youth, she sighed.

Wilfred led their guests into the salon and offered them sherry. Not long afterward, dinner was announced. Despite the size and improbable composition of the party, the atmosphere around the table was as congenial as the beautiful home. No business talk was allowed until after the meal, Eliza let it be known with mock solemnity, lest her guests be distracted from the bounty of her table. Bountiful it was—breaded oysters, roast pheasant with yams, apples and sauerkraut, burnt-sugar corn and chilies, spinach soufflé and Delmonico potatoes, French Bordeaux wine. Despite the urgency of the night's purpose, the diners could naught but relax and enjoy such plenty, and so they did, their conversation remaining cordial and lively throughout the several courses.

The seed of this contentment, posited Mary, was in the singular personalities of Wilfred's parents. William was a courtly man of quiet strength, tempered spirit and modest learning. Eliza was warm, unpretentious and extremely intelligent. As a couple, they had a similarity of appearance not uncharacteristic in people long married, perhaps due to initial attraction to one's own kind combined with common purpose and experience over the course of many years. They both had thick white hair, his somewhat roughly shorn and longer than fashion, hers drawn back into a generous braid, wrapped and secured with an agate comb. The faces below were bronzed from years spent following their flocks and living on the land when they had first emigrated from the Isle of Man, come into this country and married. Their eyes were very light, perhaps for the same reason, though his tended to gray and hers to green. They both had strong hands, his were gnarled, bunched and scarred; hers slender, with bony fingers, widening at the knuckles and fingertips, unadorned save a thick gold wedding band.

Elizabeth, she supposed, was a radiant picture of what her mother must have looked like thirty years before. Dark, thick hair, caught back by a pale green ribbon, deep blue-green eyes both kind and enticing, translucent skin and a strong, slender, full-breasted body. During dinner, Mary noted, the young woman was respectful and reserved, attentive, observant and occasionally well-spoken. When Mary, in her persona as former schoolteacher, praised a careful comment Elizabeth had contributed to a discussion of Longfellow, the young woman accepted it graciously, smiled fondly at her father and saying that while she had done her best in school, her real education had come from the nights spent by the fire in her father's library.

"Would you like to see it after dinner Mrs. Austin?" offered William.

"I would indeed, sir, with the greatest pleasure."

Still, Mary was of two minds when, at the close of dinner, the women in the party were invited to retire to the parlor for coffee and the senior Mr. Watterson offered her his arm to instead lead her to the library. She disliked the custom of dismissing womenfolk, and knew that the other men, left to the pleasures of their brandy and cigars, would also, at last, take up the business of the evening: what was known and what to do about the scoundrel Eaton. She wanted very much to be a party to this discussion and not to have to rely on Wallace's ill-remembered account later.

Even so, Mary's heart leapt as she was led into what was reputed to be the finest library in the valley, superior, she had heard, even to that of Mr. Rickey. An hour later, she was sitting by the fire at old Mr. Watterson's knee, conversing in an ardent but quiet manner about poets and the natural world, a sense of deep satisfaction rarely felt in her life filling her up to the brim.

Eliza entered and, touching her shoulder gently, offered a buttery honey-almond cake along with a look of such fondness and understanding that Mary snatched up the cake, swallowed it in two bites and, licking the last succulent crumbs from her lips, exclaimed, "I've been so terribly hungry!"

The old couple watched her kindly, then Joseph reached for his wife's hand, saying to Mary, "The library's really her doing, you know. She's the one with the superior mind and devotion to books."

"Now, William," Eliza demurred. She floated to a divan and took up one of the volumes stacked on the adjacent table. A few minutes later, Mary, from her nest near the fire, observed how Elizabeth also entered the room quietly and gracefully, sitting close and leaning against her mother's shoulder to read with her. Oh how Mary wanted to snuggle up to Eliza too.

Her relationship with her own mother had not been of this type. Susanna Hunter had been more attached to her son's happiness and prospects than to her daughter's. She had been embarrassed by Mary's oddities, unable to see the rare talents and fine mind they signified. Mary's long-festering hurt made her rebellious, and her refusal to sacrifice her own opportunities for those of her brother as well as to accept the constraints of what Susanna regarded as proper for a woman of her limited charms widened the gulf between mother and daughter even more.

The end had come when Mary's own daughter Ruth was very small. When it became clear that Ruth was abnormal, Susanna had dug the knife into Mary with the accusation: "What did you do to bring such disaster upon yourself and your husband?" Mary had ordered the woman out of her house and had not spoken to her since. As far as she knew, her mother had moved in with her brother and his wife, off somewhere to the west in the Kern Valley. Eliza Watterson would never have done such a thing to Elizabeth, Mary knew. She will love and accept Elizabeth's offspring as genuinely and effortlessly as she does her beloved girl.

"Come sit with us Mary," offered Elizabeth, extending a soft hand, having observed that her father had drifted off to sleep in the big, old carved armchair.

"Yes, do come dear," joined in Eliza. And there, beside the two lovely, fortunate women Mary remained for the rest of the blessed evening, having forgotten about the discussion now long underway among the men in the dining room.

Wallace, in the midst of it, was feeling as deeply satisfied as his wife. Here he sat in this fine home, sipping a rare claret in the company of distinguished, accomplished men. Nostalgia washed over him, along with the glow of the wine, for his father's home, in the early years when theirs had been one of the finest plantations in the Hawaiian Islands and the governor had been a frequent guest at their table. This, he thought, was what I was born to and meant for, what my life should be again.

Wilfred had thought to broach the subject of the evening gently at first. He started by recounting the episode at the bank, emphasizing its humorous aspects.

"There I was, waving my pistol at this half-naked city clerk…His eyes bulging out of his head in terror, and he's about ready to either fly out of that room or foul his drawers…"

His audience roared with laughter as Mark play-acted the panicked Lelande clutching at his privates and stumbling about knock-kneed.

"We didn't find anything, neither on the man nor in his hotel room," continued Wilfred. He made an effort to keep his voice calm. "We're fairly sure the scoundrel had taken deeds for land and water rights from Eaton's safe deposit box, and that he mailed them, probably to someone in Los Angeles, just before we nabbed him."

"Did he tell you what for?" asked Gus Kispert, owner of a large ranch in Big Pine.

"No, he said he didn't know, was just doin what he'd been told. Said he hadn't even looked at the names on the deeds before mailing the lot."

"I may be able to answer the question," ventured Jacob Clausen in a low but clearly audible voice. The young hydraulic engineer had visited the valley numerous times to perform measurement and mapping tasks for the Reclamation Service. Seeking out Chalfant for local information, he had developed a warm relationship with the older man. Clausen had also come to love the valley during these sojourns, and had emerged as the service's most enthusiastic proponent for the irrigation project. Now he was appalled by what he had learned, probing about in his own organization over the days since receiving Chalfant's telegram.

"As you may have guessed," he began, "the city has designs on Owens River water. I believe they mean to take it by building an aqueduct with an intake point somewhere in the south valley."

Despite the roaring fire in the hearth, the temperature in the now silent room seemed to Mark Watterson to have dropped thirty degrees. He looked to his brother Wilfred, as usual, for a signal.

The latter was saying nothing. Wilfred had suspected for days it would be something like this, but hearing it stated, straight out and plainly by this Reclamation engineer was still stunning. He tried to breathe and think.

Clausen let the other shoe fall: "And I believe they are trying to convince the service to support their scheme by abandoning the irrigation project."

Voices erupted all about now. Glasses and fists came down on the table. The men were on their feet.

"They can't do that! They can't interfere with a federal project!"

"There's laws ain't there?! Lotsa families depend on that water!"

"Bastards! Think they own the whole of California! They can't get away with that!"

Wilfred looked around at the mayhem, and his head cleared suddenly. His voice rang out above the din, "Calm down, sit down gentlemen. Let's hear the rest of what Mr. Clausen has to say." He motioned for everyone to return to their seats.

Clausen waited until they were quiet, then he said, "I think you are all quite correct: They will not get away with it. There is some legal precedent however. About five years ago, following a couple of years of drought, the California Supreme Court recognized the claims of the city of Los Angeles to the groundwater flows of the Los Angeles River basin, which run below the San Fernando Valley, north of the city. Since then, the city has been attempting to enforce its rights by suing San Fernando ranchers and farmers to prevent them from drilling wells. The prospect of an agricultural community without access to water has caused land values there to plummet."

There was silence. Clausen knew every man in the room was imagining the prospects for Owens Valley should it face the same misfortune. He hastened to dispel the gloom. "The plan for the Owens River, I believe, is to bring the water down to the San Fernando Valley in order to enhance the flows of the Los Angeles River. It is preposterous, of course, but the city might take the position that it has the right to seize our water in order to protect its native water source." He paused, then said firmly, "This is a specious argument, and one that no court in the country would uphold."

There were nods and grunts of agreement all around. Clausen leaned forward in his chair, elbows on knees, hands clasped.

"That's it for the legal aspect. Now let's talk about their tactics and how to stop them." Clausen swept his eyes around the room, gathering his audience in.

"First of all, I can tell you that Fred Eaton is not purchasing water rights for Reclamation," stated Clausen. "I inquired of the director, and received an unequivocal denial."

"But you said Eaton had authorization from the service, didn't you Austin?" broke in Chalfant.

"Yes, he showed me a letter from J.B. Lippincott," replied Wallace.

"And that letter said Eaton was authorized to purchase land options and water rights for the irrigation project?" asked Clausen.

"Well, ah-hum," Wallace cleared his throat. "I didn't actually read the letter. He just showed it to me." He looked down at his hands, gripping the stem of the crystal glass. "Ah-hum, I just assumed."

Chalfant stared at him incredulously. "You're the register of federal lands, and you *just assumed?*"

Wilfred was just as shocked, but knew unity was critical. "Of course he did. No one had any reason to suspect anything different at that time."

Clausen continued in a calm, steady tone. "I suspect that had Mr. Austin looked at the letter he would have seen that it did authorize Eaton to represent the service, but for an entirely different purpose. Lippincott apparently hired Eaton as a consultant to investigate two competing applications for federal right-of-way permits. The Owens River Water and Power Company and the Nevada Power Mining and Milling Company both want to build a hydroelectric plant on upper Bishop Creek, and they've both submitted applications for the right-of-ways they need to do it. Eaton was acting as a consultant to help the service investigate the merits of these applications and recommend for one or the other. I believe he deliberately used this as a pretext to cloak his activities here in the valley and to excuse them should anyone inquire too closely."

"Which no one did," said Chalfant, exasperated. "Knowing of his association with Lippincott, everyone just assumed Eaton was involved with the irrigation project."

"There's more to this consulting deal than just a decoy," explained Clausen. "Eaton has submitted his report to the service, and he's recommending that the right-of-way be granted to Nevada Power. Now this is a conclusion that completely defies logic. Owens River Water and Power clearly is the better qualified and situated of the two applicants—truly, there is so little contest based on any factual comparison of the two companies that it is indefensible that public funds were wasted on consulting to begin with."

"That's nothing new." Chalfant shrugged.

"No, but this is," continued Clausen, his eyes now resting on Wilfred Watterson. "I suspect that if you had been successful apprehending those deeds from the city clerk, you would have found among them a deed for the sale of Long Valley."

Stillness iced over the room again. Cigars froze halfway to open mouths. Guts, rumbling with sumptuous fare, twisted and pinched. Derrieres inched forward to the edge of seats. They waited.

"Thomas Rickey, as you know, has long opposed the irrigation project. His attitude is not remarkable. In the service we usually expect the big cattle ranches to put up some resistance to anything that encourages the spread—or as they see it, the encroachment—of small family ranches and farms. But here's something that is remarkable: Rickey is a financial partner in Nevada Power."

"Wheeeew-eee" came a low, rising whistle from Jack Gunney, a man with a reputation as a clever businessman, who was an investor in the Cerro Gordo mine. "The go-ahead to build that power plant is worth millions. They'll be generating electricity for Tonopah, Goldfield and every new Nevada mother lode for a hundred years. Rickey is an octopus, and every one of them greedy, winding arms a his is a rattlesnake!"

But it was Chalfant who was first to see that Rickey had won much more with this deal than just an expansion of his already large fortune.

"That's not all," he pronounced grimly. "With one stoke of the pen, Rickey's not only ensured himself a new bonanza, he's also stopped the irrigation project. It can't go forward without that dam site in Long Valley. That's the frosting on Rickey's cake. And that's what, sure as shootin, Los Angeles wants too."

"God Almighty!" exclaimed Wilfred. This was far worse than anything he had expected to hear tonight. "How could this have happened so quickly, with so little warning?" he stammered.

"What do we do about it? We can't just let it happen." Mark looked to him, to Chalfant, then to Clausen. "What do we do?"

"There's one thing I think you should do right away," responded Clausen. "Try to block Eaton from purchasing water rights and land options in the south valley."

"Most of the folks he's been throwing money at are in the north, John Shepherd, Lou McGovern, Early Blackman and such," observed Wilfred.

"Exactly," said Clausen. "Lands that would be needed if Reclamation were to go ahead and build the dam and reservoir. But the game's up now, and they know it, so there's no reason anymore for Eaton to pretend he's buying land for the reclamation project. If I'm not mistaken, he's going to be shifting his focus south soon, if he hasn't already. They'll need land and water rights farther south too if they're going to build an aqueduct. And because the south land is the most barren in the valley—and not much good for cultivation *without reclamation*—he's probably also figuring he'll get it on the cheap. If you can talk to folks down there and convince them not to sell, or at least to hold out for high prices, we might be able to stop this. No city, and most certainly not Los Angeles, has bottomless pockets."

As the engineer spoke, hope began to bubble up through worry. Chalfant looked at Wilfred Watterson, whose clenched hands had turned to fists. "Your bank has lent money to most of the folks in this valley at one time or the other. They'll listen to you. But you'll have to do it careful-ly. If we don't keep this quiet for the time being, we run the risk of causing a panic, and that could work in Eaton's favor. Some folks might sell just to get out before their farms dry up."

The others nodded, as did Clausen, who continued, "Meanwhile, I will attack on another front by bringing this matter to the attention of Frederick Newell, the director of the Reclamation Service. It runs counter to the founding principles with which President Theodore Roosevelt signed the service into existence just a few years ago." The engineer's eyes glowed with pride as he quoted the charter from memory: "to extend opportu-nities for communities of self-reliant family farms by making more land habitable through irrigation." He stopped with a sheepish smile, realizing he had been preaching.

"At the very least," said Clausen, getting back to tactics, "there is the question of the propriety of Lippincott's involvement in this skullduggery and the blemish it may bring to the reputation of the service. As the first director, Newell will not want to see his organization tarnished, I'm quite sure," Clausen concluded. Then, looking over at Wallace Austin, he added, "Mr. Austin, it might also be advisable for you to write a letter to your superior, the commissioner of the General Land Office in Washington, and perhaps send a copy to the secretary of the interior."

"Yes, certainly I shall." Wallace nodded, basking in the approving looks and "Good man!" with pat on the back he received from Wilfred Watterson.

"For my part, I believe I shall have a word with Congressman Smith," said Watterson, referring to the representative to Washington for Inyo County. He winked at Clausen. "If the administrative branch needs a little push in our direction, the legislative branch may supply the muscle."

"There's another source of muscle," offered Chalfant. "The press. I know we want to keep this quiet, but my colleagues on the Los Angeles papers may have information we need and might be encouraged to divulge it, especially if we play to the rivalry between the *Times* and the *Examiner*." His smile was crafty and knowing. "Otis and Hearst, the publishers, will do anything to hang each other."

---

The next time Janey stepped onto the back porch of the little brown house, she held her breath as usual, wondering what she would find. This time it was a surprise indeed: Through the open window she saw Wallace Austin at the table, writing, and seated next to him, leaning toward him, hand alighting delicate as a dove on his shoulder, was Mary. They were talking softly, as Mary, other arm outstretched, fed slices of apple to Ruth.

It was a strange scene to Janey's eye, as she rarely encountered Wallace during her morning visits to the house and had never seen Mary display affection for her husband. She backed off of the porch and returned home, where Alice, surprised to see her, was well pleased to have help sowing early sweet peas in the east field.

At noon, damp and tired, they sank into the shaded grass below a big oak and shared Alice's lunch of bread, cheese and cherries. Then they played cat's cradle with the leather string that had tied off the bag of provisions. Finally rising to resume her chore, Alice reached out for her daughter, gave her a squeeze and a little pat on the fanny, and urged, "It's so hot honey. Go ahead, find your friends and have a swim."

Janey returned the embrace, then was off at a run.

"Don't go in the water right away," cautioned Alice, "or you'll be havin a bellyache!"

That evening before supper, Alice combed out Janey's tangled hair, sighing at the browned, freckled complexion of her daughter.

A sunbonnet unworn was of little help. Oh well, she reflected, this one is never going to be a debutante!

At table, Janey began eating with appetite, but was soon having trouble keeping her eyes open. Alice chose to overlook the elbow on the table propping the sleepy girl's head up. Field work, sun and water—she'll sleep well tonight.

Chris, on the other hand, could barely stay in his chair. In recent weeks, each time he'd headed off to town, wagon chock-full of ranch produce, he'd returned home, head chock-full of dreams, rumors and worries.

"Some folks sayin the irrigation project is comin, and some folks sayin it's not. It's the damnedest thing…"

"Chris, mend your language, you're at the supper table," his mother corrected him.

"…Sorry Ma." He put down his fork, picked it up again, tapped against the side of his plate, put it down again to scratch at the white fuzz on his sunburned chin. "Just don't figure why Reclamation is being so secretive. You'd suppose they'd be making a big announcement in the newspaper! And folks here in the valley are acting mighty strange too. Tongues are waggin about who's selling what to that fella from the service, but most a the ones doin the sellin are keepin doggone quiet about it."

"Yes, that does seem strange," agreed Ben. "But, on the other hand, son, we don't really know if it is or isn't. There's never been a government irrigation project in the valley before, so we don't know how folks are likely to behave or what to expect, do we?"

"No, I reckon you're right Pa. Just wish I knew what was gonna happen."

"We'll know when it happens," concluded Alice lightly. "More potatoes, Ben? Chris? Sleepyhead?"

Chris shook his head emphatically. "Ma, that's not the way to get ahead, just waiting!"

"Chris, whatever happens is fine," said Ben. "Sure, it would be nice to expand, but the ranch is already doing well. We have a good life here, you'll have a good life when your Ma and I are gone. Federal programs aren't going to change that."

"It's not enough…for me," Chris muttered to his plate.

"Son, are you speaking to me or to your steak?"

"To you." Chris looked up, eyes earnest, lips trembling with strain, knowing he ought not to say it, but unable to stop himself. "Pa, you know I love the ranch, and I'm grateful for all the confidence you put in me… But I don't plan on spending my life growin and haulin ranch produce."

"I see," said Ben evenly. "What do you plan on doing then?"

"Don't know, something bigger…I can do more Pa!"

"Big isn't always the way, Chris," Alice said softly. "Your Pa's built one of the finest small ranches in the valley, and you ought to be proud you've helped him."

"No need, Alice." Ben patted her hand. "Chris knows all that. He's said himself, many times, folks buy Bow produce first. Besides," he winked, "what could be bigger than those manure-fed cabbages?!"

Chris was in no state to be made fun of, and he hurled back the joke as he came out of his seat and shoved back the chair. "Ah, Pa, they'se just darn, stinkin cabbages!"

Alice was on her feet too now, hand locked on Chris's arm. "That's enough young man, more than enough!" She dragged the chair back to table with the other hand, and then pulled him back onto it. Ben had not moved. Janey, confused from her half-slumber, looked up from under her eyelashes at her father. She hardly recognized the drawn face. His mouth was making a slight movement, as if he were still chewing, but she didn't think he was.

"It's all right Janey," said Alice noticing her alarm. Then she turned to Chris, whose arm she still grasped. Her voice was firm yet still affectionate. "Peace in the family is more important than any of this," she pronounced, her adamant eyes spearing each of them, one after another, then moving back to hook and hold Chris. "I will have you apologize to your father, young man, this instant!"

Alice had her way, and rewarded them with clotted cream over warm peach cobbler. After the meal, Ben lifted his drowsy daughter into his arms and carried her upstairs to her room. He didn't return to the parlor to read aloud, but went out by the kitchen door to the yard. Alice joined him to look up at the moonlit peaks and the sky, speckled and glimmery like the skin of a trout. She took his arm, but said nothing. Such things weren't worth talking about. Leave them behind, like a pit in the road, and get on with life.

---

*I was raised to think optimistically. Both my parents were of that bent of mind. They believed that if they worked hard and lived a decent life, their efforts would be rewarded.*

*This view was widely shared by our neighbors. In fact, it would not be too fanciful to say that the valley was a natural cradle of optimism. Perhaps it was the reliability of sunshine and water that buoyed the spirit, and the abundance of uncultivated land, waiting to be irrigated and put under the plow, that engendered expectations of good fortune. Or perhaps the pure sweetness of the air filled the lungs and veins with inspiration.*

*Whatever it was, I grew up with the assumption that this positive state of mind was normal. And I assumed this despite frequent exposure to quite a different sensibility.*

*I won't say that Mary Austin was a pessimist. She was more of a realist, as she looked at the world with sharp, unblinking eyes. Mary once told me that after one of our rare thunderstorms, she had hiked up into a favorite canyon and seen a mother bobcat nosing through the fallen rock and branches of her ruined lair, licking the limp bodies of her drowned kittens. She included this sad episode in her book about the valley, along with her careful observation of the stages cattle go through when dying of thirst in the desert, a process that can take days. She recounted how the fear in their eyes when they first lie down, stretching out their long necks, is ultimately replaced by only intolerable weariness. The scavenger birds, Mary said, may tease the poor beasts, even alight upon their bodies, but will never sink a beak or talon into flesh until the last breath has passed. These "loathsome watchers," as she called them, do not eat live prey. All of this she reported in prose that was lyrical but not in the least sentimental.*

*Mary also wrote about the wonderful things she observed: how the towers of milkweed were bejeweled in summer by red and gold beetles, and how on warm mornings, white butterflies twinkled like sprinklings of fairy dust across the fields. She made me see beauty I would otherwise have walked by. It was my own tendency to focus on these delights rather than the other. My mentor was never so biased; she saw in the real, both brutal and beautiful, the workings of a greater, purposeful spirit.*

*Unfortunately for Mary, this perception of spirit did not make her a contented person. Looking back now, I think her habit of keen perception and untinted observation may have brought her a good portion of misery. For she was the first to get an inkling when things were going wrong, despite the optimistic assurances of everyone around her.*

# Chapter 5

With the evening edition of the *Register* in the hands of his hawkers and paperboys, Chalfant was taking his rest, leaning back against the bench on the sidewalk in front of his office. Gazing up at the Sierra wall, he watched a wispy cloud, as light as the smoke he exhaled, float across the silhouetted peaks. Lowering his gaze, he saw Wilfred and Mark Watterson coming down the darkening street toward him.

"Evening Willie." Wilfred tipped his hat. "You sent word you wanted to see us?"

"Evening boys. Thought you might want to hear some good news."

"We sure need that," said Mark, as the brothers settled on either side of Chalfant, accepting the cigars he offered. Wilfred bit off and lit his, puffing nervously.

"Austin's letter to his boss in Washington worked like a charm. Talked to Clausen by telephone today. The service is convening a panel to review the Owens irrigation project. They will submit their report and recommendations to the secretary of the interior."

"Hooooray!" Mark slapped his thigh. Wilfred exhaled slowly and nodded, smiling at Chalfant, waiting to hear the rest.

"Now here's the best part," the editor continued with a smirk, "Clausen said he and some of the other service engineers refused to serve on the panel if Lippincott was seated on it. So the director decided to keep him off the panel and call him as a witness. He'll have his say, but he'll also have to answer a lot of questions about what he's been up to with Fred Eaton."

"Hooray indeed!" Wilfred slapping Chalfant and Mark across the shoulders. "Calls for a toast. Gentlemen, it's on me," he suggested, pointing his cigar toward the saloon.

"Best have it here." Chalfant pointed over his shoulder toward the *Register* office. "We still want to keep this quiet. This is a good start, but we have a ways to go before we can really claim victory."

They filed inside, and Chalfant liberated his best scotch whiskey from its hiding place in a file cabinet, pouring three doubles. He handed the brothers each a glass, then took a piece of paper from the worktable.

"Here's my editorial for tomorrow morning's paper," said Chalfant. He took a long swallow, then read the piece, which discussed the formation of the Reclamation Service panel and called for an outcome of strong intervention:

**There is but one hope for the future of Owens Valley, and that is in government protection by the control of the water. Under the circumstances, we feel that it would be but simple justice for the government to specially interest itself in our behalf.**

The Wattersons voiced their approval and optimism, but Chalfant demurred. "I'd be foolin ya if I said I'm not a little worried about the panel. It won't convene for nearly a month. Between now and then, there's no law sayin Eaton can't continue spreadin cash around thick as manure. What are you hearin from your customers, anything?"

"Not much, never known folks to be so closed mouthed," replied Wilfred. "All this rumor and speculating isn't good for the community. It's divisive and upsetting to folks." Then he raised his glass to them both. "Thank goodness the panel will finally bring it all out onto the table."

"Does Austin know?" asked Mark, "about the panel, I mean? Does he know that his letter caused a big stir?"

"Not yet," answered Chalfant, "but I'm fixin to go by the land office tomorrow."

"Tell him 'thanks' for me, will you?" Mark tilted his head back to feel the last warm drop of whiskey run down his throat.

"Yes, tell him for me as well," agreed Wilfred. "That was a fine piece of work he did."

"Outta the way!" shouted the motorist.

The driver, looking like an insect in his driving goggles, was steering straight at him. Jacob Clausen scooted away from the black Ford within an inch of being run down, weaving his way across San Francisco's busy Market Street through cable cars, horse-drawn buggies and carts, bicyclists and pedestrians. Lurching for the sidewalk, he stood fuming and sweating in the late-July heat. Automobiles were few and far between, yet their owners acted like they owned the streets. Clausen pulled a crisp linen handkerchief from his pants pocket and blotted his forehead. To be fair, he reflected, the novelty of the machines did tend to attract gawkers, who like as not did their gawking smack in the middle of the street.

He headed south toward the new US courthouse and post office, which housed federal agencies, including the US Reclamation Service, on her second floor. The chaotic exuberance of the business district was soon replaced by the sights, sounds and smells of working-class immigrant neighborhoods.

There had been a rash of controversy when the site for the building, at the corner of Seventh and Mission streets, more than a mile from the city center, was chosen back in 1891. Its selection had been prompted by the high price of central property and the low budget allocated by the United States Congress. Many of the city's fine, industrious citizens had been appalled, but Jacob had always liked the idea of situating federal services among the homes and shops of the country's newest arrivals. Since the beautiful Italianate building had been completed a year ago, Jacob had taken the opportunity, when he wasn't out at local field offices, to walk to work, purchasing a strudel from the Koblentz bakery to enjoy on the way.

Clausen was munching the last of his pastry as he crossed the street beneath the building's imposing facade. Inspired by Renaissance palaces, the structure was ornamented with Florentine-style horizontally striped stonework, arched windows, carved pediments and bronze entry lanterns. The interior was even more opulent than the exterior. Clausen's steps sounded on rare, exquisite Carrera and yellow Siena marble. To his left, as he proceeded through the U-shaped space, opened an interior courtyard ornamented with geometrically patterned bricks glazed in red, white and blue. He looked up and winked at one of the hundred pink-tongued lion heads carved along the cornice at the top of the courtyard walls.

The panel meeting to review the Owens Valley irrigation project was to take place in a conference room on the third floor. Clausen took the stairs at a fast clip. He was on the panel and would also serve as its initial presenter. He had prepared long into the night to ensure that he would be able to clearly and concisely lay out the particulars not only to his fellow panel members, but to the press and other spectators at this open meeting.

An hour later, Clausen was well-satisfied with his efforts. The panel had been appreciative and the audience attentive. He felt confident he had successfully conveyed the indubitable merits of the Owens Valley reclamation project.

Next, J.B. Lippincott was led into the room and seated as a witness. The tall, lanky man, who had been a cowboy on the range before training in engineering, was given the opportunity to make a brief statement before answering questions from the panel.

"I agree with Mr. Clausen that there is a good project in the Owens Valley worth our careful consideration. I do, however, also believe that, as civil servants, it is our duty to consider whether or not the water of the Owens River would be more valuable if used in Los Angeles, the home of more than 200,000 energetic, prosperous and cultured people, rather than in a remote valley of about 250 farms. In addition, we must question the very feasibility of a large-scale irrigation project in the Owens Valley now that Mr. Eaton, presumably on behalf of the city of Los Angeles, has acquired an option to purchase the only land suitable for the requisite dam site."

Looking around at his fellow panel members, Clausen saw that many were not pleased with Lippincott's little speech. Not surprising, thought Clausen, since Lippincott had himself made it possible for Eaton to weasel his way into the valley. It was also rumored that he had essentially bribed Rickey to sell the Long Valley ranch, including the dam site, by promising to cooperate with the rancher's own hydroelectric business venture.

The questions flung at Lippincott following his statement revealed the extent of suspicion and ill feeling toward the man. One panel member wanted to know if Lippincott had indeed been paid as a consultant to the city of Los Angeles. Lippincott responded that yes, he had been hired to gather data and compile a report on possible water resources, and that he had submitted a report the previous May—a report that, he emphasized, did not mention the Owens Valley.

"No, but it did point to Owens by default," Clausen interjected, "as your statements pertaining to all other possibilities were uniformly pessimistic. Did you not conclude that, apart from the Owens River, there is little water available in Southern California adequate to support the future growth of Los Angeles?"

"Yes, that was my conclusion."

Another engineer asked whether, as supervising engineer for the Reclamation Service in California, Lippincott might not have rendered better service had he not been distracted with such outside projects.

"I prepared the report outside of my regular office hours sir."

Another member asked whether Lippincott knew Mr. Eaton had been misrepresenting himself as a government agent to the people of Owens Valley, to which Lippincott replied: "I know nothing of Mr. Eaton's general statements, and I do not consider that I am responsible for them. Mr. Eaton, however, is a friend whom I have known for many, many years."

Pressed about whether or not Eaton had been carrying a letter of authorization, Lippincott insisted that he had authorized Eaton in writing to act as an agent of the service, but only for the purpose of investigating the power plant applications.

The questioner then read aloud from a letter to the General Lands Commissioner from Wallace Austin, register of federal lands in Owens Valley. The letter complained that it had been generally understood by the people of the valley that Eaton was securing valuable water and land rights for the benefit of the government, but that there was now "a rapidly growing conviction" that Eaton was acting in his own interests and in those of the city of Los Angeles. Austin concluded his letter with the dire warning that should the government abandon the Owens Valley reclamation project, it would not only destroy the valley's prospects and cause severe losses to its people, but damage the service as well.

"Such abandonment at this time will make it appear that the expensive surveys and measurements of the past two years have all been made in the interests of a band of Los Angeles speculators, and it will result in bringing the United States Reclamation Service into disrepute."

That had been a powerful, sobering note upon which to end the morning session, thought Clausen. He and his colleagues on the panel were savoring a lunch of corn beef sandwiches and beer at Mickey's Pub. It's going the right way, he assured himself.

The afternoon session veered in a different direction, however. Director Newell announced to the group that Senator Frank P. Flint, the senior US senator from California and former governor of the state, had asked if he might speak before the panel. Clausen had absolutely no idea why, and he suspected neither did Newell, but of course it had been impossible to refuse. Clausen did know that the gray-bearded, hooded-eyed man who rose to the podium was often criticized as being too partial to business interests. He listened to Flint with a sinking heart.

"The question now is, is it in the public service to supply the water to great municipal and suburban interests rather than to a mere local interest?"

Clausen winced. Senator Flint went on to deliver a ringing endorsement and defense of Lippincott.

"I know he is above any wrong action. He has the confidence and respect of all who know him, and his integrity and faithfulness to this trust, I think, cannot be questioned."

Newell thanked Flint and escorted him out of the conference room as the panel tried to regroup. Clausen suggested they spend the rest of the afternoon reviewing the Owens Valley reports and maps prepared by the service, hoping to refocus attention on the virtues of the irrigation project. Enthusiasm for the task was wavering, however, and the discussion was desultory.

As he trudged home that evening, Clausen's spirits were low, and his mood was little improved by the cheerful bustle of people heading home from work, being welcomed by the savory smells emanating from neighborhood shops and the open windows of the flats above them. Yes, he was forced to admit it had been an unsatisfactory day. No matter, he reassured himself, tomorrow we'll be in closed-door session to discuss what we heard and write our report and recommendations. Tomorrow I'll put this back on course.

Mulholland had hat in hand and was walking out the door of his office when W.B. Matthews hastily entered the reception room and slapped his hand down on the immaculate desk of Miss Aames, who had long since gone home.

"That's it! The panel made its report, and it's very much to our advantage!"

Mulholland motioned the lawyer back into his office and shut the door. "What was their conclusion?"

"Oh, in typical bureaucratic fashion, they didn't come to any conclusion. The report acknowledges that the Owens Valley irrigation project appears to be attractive, but deserves further study and investigation." Matthews smiled knowingly. "And it notes that the project could be rendered infeasible if it were no longer possible to build a dam in Long Valley as a result of our purchasing that ranch."

Mulholland leaned back in his chair, nodding and smiling. "That's it then."

"Essentially. They've put the irrigation project into suspension for the time being, which gives us more time."

"We don't need any more time." Mulholland's eyes twinkled as he pulled a piece of paper from his jacket pocket. "Received this telegram from Eaton about two hours ago." He handed it to Matthews, who read:

THE LAST STAKE IS DRIVEN -(STOP)- ALL NECESSARY RIGHTS AND
OPTIONS PURCHASED

"Congratulations!"

"Thank you." Mulholland spun his hat around his index finger and took a mock bow. He was thinking that his instincts about Eaton had been right. The man had double-crossed him, sure, and maybe he would never quite trust his former mentor as he had before, but they were back on track now, doing what had to be done to achieve their shared dream. "What's the next step?" he asked the lawyer.

"We have to make a formal request to Secretary of the Interior Ethan Hitchcock," replied Matthews. "The panel's report stipulates that the Reclamation Service should refuse any demand from us that they abandon the irrigation project in favor of our aqueduct. That directive has to come from the secretary of the interior. Just a formality, a way for the service to cover its ass. With Eaton holding the option to buy Long Valley, Hitchcock really has little choice; he'll have to issue the directive."

Mulholland puffed on his cigar thoughtfully. Perhaps Eaton's errant act of betrayal would actually turn out to be of service. It was time to let go of resentment. He turned to Matthews and wagged the cigar tip at him. "Now let's hope the voters of Los Angeles will be so easily convinced. Next order of business: We have a bond election to win."

Matthews nodded. "It's unfortunate that we've had so much rainfall this year. Would have been a might easier to push a bond through back in '99 after two years of drought. In this new 20th century, folks are losing their fears of those dry times."

"Perhaps we can reawaken them," said Mulholland. "Suppose we furnish the *Times* with some new facts that we have heretofore kept secret from the public lest we create a panic."

"And what might those secrets be?" asked Matthews, a glint of conspiratorial enjoyment in his fine dark eyes.

"The fact that municipal water supplies are precariously low. At the rate the current supply is being consumed, the city not only won't be able to support more growth, it could even run dry."

"And what if someone questions the veracity of these facts?" probed Matthews.

"They may ask any questions they want, but they can't prove anything different, as the Department of Water and Power is the sole source of hydrological information."

"Ahh, I see, the water nightmare is come upon us," said Matthews in an amused voice.

"This is no joking matter, W.B., and I'm not conjuring up some phantom of the night," said Mulholland sternly. "We may be forecasting dire consequences ahead of probability, but we are not in any way misleading the public. Groundwater in the San Fernando Valley is the principal source of the Los Angeles River. The water table is dropping from overuse there and in other agricultural areas. Damn it, man, we've got more than two thousand artesian wells drawing up water!"

Matthews picked up the trajectory of Mulholland's thinking. "The San Fernando Valley situation may actually be turned to our advantage in this," mused a chastened Matthews. "Most of the lawsuits we brought during the drought to prevent the ranchers from drilling groundwater are still open. That might be interpreted as proof of our continued concern for the inadequacy of the municipal supply."

Mulholland nodded approvingly and continued with his argument. "If Los Angeles does not secure an abundant water supply, this nightmare will become a reality before many years have passed. Indeed, I am quite convinced we shall face outright water famine. To avoid this dreaded outcome, we must consider that most human beings are ill-inclined to take wise action for the future. They act only when there is an immediate threat. Therefore, we shall give them one." He blew out a string of smoke rings.

"Yes, I agree. But there is a problem we must anticipate," warned Matthews. "These lawsuits have driven the value of acreage in San Fernando into the dirt. Some of our city's leading citizens have in recent months purchased land there at a very good price indeed—acting, it must be said, on privileged information about the prospective aqueduct. When the news breaks that the aqueduct has become reality, and that its terminus will be the San Fernando Valley, land prices there will soar. These speculators stand to make an ungodly profit. There are those who will point the finger at us, accuse us of collusion."

"A tempest in a teapot," Mulholland assured his colleague. "There is no end to the political squabbling in this city. Yet there is one thing on which everyone finds himself in perfect agreement: the need for water to fuel the growth of this city. Everything else will eventually wash away down the sewer."

---

**TITANIC PROJECT TO GIVE CITY A RIVER**
*Thirty Thousand Inches of Water
to be Brought to Los Angeles*

**The Times announces this morning the most important
movement for the development of Los Angeles in all the city's
history—Options Secured on Forty Miles of River Frontage**

**in Inyo County—Magnificent Stream to be Conveyed to the Southland in Conduit Two-Hundred and Forty Miles Long— Stupendous Deal Closed.**

The *Los Angeles Times* broke the story the next day. Matthews had previously secured "gentlemen's agreements" from the editors of the city's newspapers by which, in return for staying mum about aqueduct rumors until the necessary land and water rights had been secured, all would be given the opportunity to release the story on the same day. Breaching this faith, the *Times* scooped its rivals, setting off a fury of catch-up stories and angry recriminations.

---

Chalfant was first in the Owens Valley to know. He received the news at eight o'clock in the morning in the form of a telegram, from a stringer reporter in Los Angeles, delivered by young Jemmie Shaw from the post office. Immediately Chalfant sent Bucky Porter down to the bank to fetch the Wattersons.

"There won't be any news other than this here news today" he told Porter grimly.

Before the Wattersons arrived, some 20 minutes later, Jemmie was back with another telegram for Chalfant, this one from Jacob Clausen, telling him of the disappointing outcome of the Reclamation Service panel on the Owens Valley project. He handed one of the messages to Wilfred and the other to Mark, who sullenly read and then exchanged them, eyes wide and mouths tense.

"What now?" asked Mark.

"We fight!" responded his brother.

"Yes, and the first order of battle is a special edition of the *Inyo Register*," said Chalfant. "Folks need to hear the news from us, not from some passerby with a Los Angeles paper under his arm."

The brothers chain-smoked and made suggestions, Chalfant reading out headlines and copy as he composed them.

### LOS ANGELES PLOTS DESTRUCTION
*Would Take Owens River, Lay Lands Waste, Ruin People, Homes, and Communities*

Chalfant's story on the "greatest water steal on record" accused "Judas B. Lippincott" of perfidy in trying to set the government "to despoiling the very lands it was supposed to reclaim." The article also included and rebuffed the city's most outlandish statements from the *Times* article: "This new water supply, immense and unfailing, will make Los Angeles forge ahead by leaps and bounds, assuring her future for a century." And, in regard to the Owens Valley: "The price paid for many of the ranches is three or four times what the owners ever expected to sell them for. Everybody in the valley has money, and everyone is happy."

In under two hours, the *Inyo Register* special edition had been written, typeset and printed. As hawkers took up their positions and began to call out the news, normal activity on Main Street, full of wagons and buckboards of families come into town to do their Saturday shopping, hesitated, then halted. Men pulled their horses and mule teams up short, jumping to the ground to exchange a penny for a paper, reading in stunned silence or aloud to their wives to quiet the incessant "What is it? What's happening?" Looking up, they saw neighbors doing the same. Like magnetized metal fragments, the men moved together into bristling forms, where the heat of their combined outrage rose until the street became a boiling cauldron of dust and anger.

"It's gettin pretty chaotic out there, someone had better head on out and have a word," said Chalfant. "You up to it?" He looked at Wilfred, who nodded silently.

"Now that we got 'em riled up, we need to channel that anger to organized action," continued Chalfant. "Let's call for a community meeting in the town hall, after church tomorrow. That'll give us time to form a plan."

He held the door open, and the three men stood on the sidewalk. Wilfred spoke tentatively. "My fellow citizens…" He repeated the phrase more loudly this time.

"We're going to need a cow bell or a tin can we can beat on to get their attention," said Chalfant.

Turning to go back inside the office, he stopped agog at the sight of Fred Eaton coming out of the Bishop Creek Hotel down the street. Bag in hand, the man was heading toward a team of horses tied next to an unhitched buggy. John Burkhardt, the hotel manager, stood glowering, feet planted, arms crossed. Eaton got the message, and began doing his own harnessing. "Damn that Otis," he silently cursed the editor of the *Times*. Eaton had been caught unawares by the premature article in the Los Angeles paper; he'd planned to be out of the valley before the news broke.

Wilfred and Mark turned to look where Chalfant was staring, and suddenly someone in the turbulent crowd also caught sight of Eaton.

"There he is, that's the man that stole our water, get him!"

Heads turned in unison, and a roar rose up as bodies surged toward Eaton.

"Tar and feather 'em!"

"Ride 'em out of town on a rail!"

"Hell, lynch him from that tree!"

Eaton stood, eyes level, looking calmly at his opponents, but he was on the balls of his feet, ready to move in any direction, one hand resting lightly on the pistol in his pocket.

A shot rang out. It was Chalfant, shotgun pointing up to the sky. The roar quieted down as Sheriff Collins, hastily alerted by Mark to the trouble brewing, came up the sidewalk behind Chalfant, hand on holster.

"All right now folks, let's move back and give this gentleman some room to git in his buggy." He spat a wad of tobacco on the ground to emphasize the word "git." It sizzled in the hot dust, an ugly blob of oozing red.

"That ain't no gentleman!"

"He's a thief and a liar!"

"Man's as crooked as a snake in a cactus patch!"

"A lackey for Los Angeles!"

"Well then," the sheriff said acidly, "he better git back there then."

Eaton hoisted himself up into the buggy to a chorus of catcalls and hisses, and snapped the reins. He drove slowly and deliberately out of town, skewered by the eyes of the now silent townsfolk.

Wilfred Watterson seized the moment to trumpet the call:

"My friends, join with your neighbors to stop these scoundrels! Community meeting, Bishop town hall, tomorrow, 2pm. Let everyone know. With unity, we shall surely win!"

Perspiration poured down her back as people poured into the room.
Mary, standing with Wallace by a long table set along a side wall,
observed with morbid satisfaction the distressed and subdued attitudes
of her neighbors, these hale and hearty ranchers and righteous matrons,
as they entered, standing just inside the doorway, looking about for what
to do next.

The Watterson brothers and Chalfant were doing their best to greet
folks and steer them over to the table where Mary, Wallace, Elizabeth
Watterson and Bucky Porter were helping them read and sign the Citizen's
Petition, to be submitted to the US Secretary of Interior. The document
began:

> We, the people of the Owens Valley, in mass meetings
> assembled, respectfully and earnestly petition that a thorough
> investigation be made of the proceedings of
> the Reclamation Service officers in connection with
> The Owens Valley Project. We believe that the officers of
> the Reclamation Service are, and have been, using their
> services to acquire the water rights of this valley for the
> City of Los Angeles instead of for the reclamation of arid lands.
> If this is accomplished, it will mean the eventual ruination of
> this beautiful valley and conversion of the same into a barren
> waste of desert.

Above the petition table, tacked to a cork board on the wall, was a
copy of a letter written by Mary's husband Wallace Austin, to be sent by
post the next morning to Washington DC. It was addressed to President
Theodore Roosevelt.

> I am register of the United States Land Office in Owens
> Valley, California. In behalf of the people of this district, I wish
> to protest against the proposed abandonment of the Owens
> River Project. The whole outrageous scheme is now made
> plain. Mr. Lippincott while drawing a large salary from the
> Government was employed by the City of Los Angeles, be-
> traying the government by turning this important project over
> to the city. Will you in justice to the Owens River Project, and

to the people of this district, see that this matter is thoroughly investigated. In the interests of fairness and of the honor of the Reclamation Service, I appeal to you not to abandon the Owens River Project.

Next to Wallace's letter, was an article Mary herself had just completed and which, she had received word from the *San Francisco Chronicle*, would be printed the following week. Mary noted with pride how her document, the last to be viewed by new arrivals before taking their seats, seemed to be having a stirring effect, causing many folk to nod in agreement, slap their hats against their thighs or raise a salute with their fist.

Every considerable city in the state is or is about to be confronted by a water problem. But what is to be gained by the commonwealth if it robs Peter to pay Paul? Is all this worthwhile in order that Los Angeles should be just so big?...It is worthwhile for other cities to consider that as this case proceeds their own water problems are likely to be shaped by it more or less. Shall the question of domestic water in California be determined by craft and graft and bitterness and long-drawn wasteful struggles, or conducted with rightness and dignity to an equal conclusion?

Mary had been reluctant at first to write the article. She had a bad feeling about the fight with Los Angeles. But she believed in the power of the pen, so she'd written the article, at Chalfant's suggestion, to raise the import of the issue above this single valley's fortune and enlist allies beyond its borders. She was also preparing an article for *Out West*, a periodical that had already published some of her stories, and had sent off a letter yesterday to its editor Charles Lummis. In fact, she hoped to pay him a visit in Los Angeles.

A soft touch to her hand brought Mary's thoughts back to the crowded, noisy room. Nellie Bellamy was saying "Thank you," and coming up behind her, Frank Bellamy was looking at Mary, for the first time in their acquaintance, with some amount of interest and respect.

Janey Bow ran up to her. "Good evening ma'am!" The girl was bouncing on her toes from excitement with the big meeting, though Mary suspected she had little idea why. Chris Bow clearly did. His expression was grave as he nodded to her and collected his sister, leading her to a chair, so his parents could read and sign the petition.

Even old Mr. and Mrs. Parker, who rarely attended social events, were there. Lesta Parker, upon reading Stephen's letter to the president, squeezed his arm and confided, "I believe I oughta write a letter to that there Mr. Roosevelt too!"

The petition form and chairs filled in, the meeting began. Wilfred Watterson rose to welcome his neighbors and deliver a rousing call for unity and action. Chalfant and several others spoke words aimed at bolstering morale. Nevertheless, at times the meeting veered into unruly and raucous discourse.

Mary paid scant attention to the particulars; she was distracted by self-consciousness. Throughout the evening, she felt the eyes of many of the valley folk upon her, but not in the usual way. Tonight some of the men who had been most dismissive, some of the matrons who had been most disapproving kept glancing at her. Most wore baffled expressions, some a little respectful, but in all of these faces the old animosity and certitude had softened. She was, after all, now the lesser of threats.

---

Within ten days of the *Times* story, property prices in the San Fernando Valley had jumped 500 percent.

Henry Loewenthal, editor of the *Los Angeles Examiner*, still seething at being scooped the first day, saw the opportunity to out-scoop and embarrass the rival paper, which had continued to print laudatory articles, gushing with praise for the aqueduct and stoking fears of drought should the bond measure not pass. Loewenthal sent a reporter to the courthouse in the San Fernando Valley. When the man returned, the editor could hardly believe his eyes: The speculators hadn't even bothered to conceal their names. The next day, the *Examiner*, ran the front-page headline:

**SCANDAL OF THE CENTURY!**

The article that followed exposed the enormous profiteering going on in the name of municipal water. The story boldly listed the names of some of the city's wealthiest and most influential citizens as members of a land syndicate that had gobbled up some 16,000 acres of San Fernando Valley property, now worth many times the purchase price. The names included, railroad tycoons Edward Harriman and Henry Huntington, street railway developer Moses Sherman—who sat on the Los Angeles Board of Water Commissioners—and Harrison Gray Otis, publisher of the very same *Los Angeles Times* that was so enthusiastically and unremittingly promoting the aqueduct!

Loewenthal's accompanying editorial implied that Moses, as a member of the board, had leaked details of the aqueduct project to his cohorts, who, it seemed, "have been let in on this deal months ago, purchased arid lands, and are in haste to have them made valuable by this water project."

Otis countered with a story in the *Times* that cast the *Examiner*, one of a growing chain of newspapers owned by his enemy William Randolph Hearst, as a "yellow atrocity" with malevolent intentions. "The insane desire of the *Examiner* to discredit certain citizens of Los Angeles has at last led it into the open as a vicious enemy of the city's welfare."

Brushing aside the charge of profiteering, the *Times* extolled the benefits to all of taking water from the Owens Valley for irrigation in the San Fernando Valley: "Go to the whole length and breadth of the San Fernando Valley these dry August days. Shut your eyes and picture this same scene after a big river of water has been spread over every acre. The San Fernando Valley can be converted into a veritable Garden of Eden. Vast areas of land, devoted now to grazing and grain, will be converted into orchards and gardens, the peer of any in the world."

---

"We've got them now!"

Chalfant had to raise his voice so the Wattersons and Wallace Austin, gathered round him at the back of the *Inyo Register* office, could hear above the din coming from the front of the room. Ever since the meeting, the number of folks dropping in throughout the day had increased. About a dozen men, ranchers and shopkeepers generally gathered near the windows to exchange news and complain to each other, in some cases quite loudly, about the valley's plight.

Chris Bow was there a couple of times a week, and Chalfant was glad of it, since the lad might bring Janey, leaving her for an hour or two while he saw to business so she could help with typesetting or clean up.

Still, Chalfant was sorry to see the usually amiable Bow boy in such a grim and agitated temper. And despite the need for united action and shared purpose, he sometimes wished his neighbors would all go home and stop adding hot air to the already steamy little room.

Today, however, Chalfant had good news to impart to his neighbors, beginning with the other leaders of the cause. He threw a stack of newspapers on a small table near the printing press.

For days the *Los Angeles Times* had been waxing eloquent in story after story about the glorious aqueduct, and Chalfant had winced this morning as he read through the package of papers mailed to him by one of his stringer reporters in the city. But Chalfant had also exulted because he knew *Times* editor Harrison Gray Otis was running away at the bit and the mouth. Otis had revealed far more about the plans for Owens Valley water than Eaton and the city officials he was in collusion with would have wanted.

"Here, listen to this," he said, grabbing up one of the sheets and reading: "The cable that has held the San Fernando Valley vassal for ten centuries to the arid demon is about to be severed by the magic scimitar of modern engineering skill." Chalfant threw the paper down in disgust and triumph.

"They've shown their hand, and it's a cheating hand. Hell will freeze over before the government is going to allow them to drain the Owens Valley just to pour the same water a couple of hundred miles away onto the San Fernando Valley! This isn't about a city wanting water, it's about speculators who've bought up land in San Fernando wanting profit! Otis—he's the publisher of this piece of bull crap—he's now revealed their secret. So there's no more hiding behind the smoke screen of civic good."

"It's almost unfathomable that they would try such a naked ploy!" Wilfred exclaimed.

"Well, I don't think they thought they were going to be stripped naked before the world like that—at least not until it was too late to stop them. Otis is like a bull in a china shop. He's gonna print what he wants come hell or high water. He says any newspaper that publishes objective writing is 'weak and vacillating.'"

"Well they know that about him down there, so they musta had some plan to rein him in. Luckily for us something went wrong. Whaddaya suppose happened?" asked Mark gleefully.

"I don't know, maybe they didn't give him a big enough piece of the pie. Or maybe they didn't count on Loewenthal asking some sharp questions. He's the editor at the *Examiner*, a rival paper, part of the Hearst chain, and he's an acquaintance of mine. Here…" Chalfant riffled through the fan of papers, pulled out one and poked it with his index finger. "Look here. Loewenthal not only exposed the land syndicate making 500-times profit in San Fernando, he's also revealed the profit made by a certain Mr. Frederick Eaton of Los Angeles." Chalfant read:

### FORMER MAYOR HAS GOLDEN KEY
***Since May, the former mayor has been busy getting these options and at the same time getting rich***

Wilfred whistled. "And everyone here in the valley called him a fool…some fool! Eaton didn't care how much he had to pay for land and water rights up here because he was getting reimbursed and then some!"

"I suspect they paid off Lippincott as well," said Wallace. "I don't see how the Secretary of Interior could refuse our requests for an investigation now. Once that's underway, he'll be exposed too."

"Yes, I think their sordid little scheme is unraveling thread by thread," said Chalfant with satisfaction. "And there will be ever more hands pulling it apart. Loewenthal won't stop. He's a good newspaperman, and he tells me he's put his best men on it. Besides, Hearst wouldn't let him stop even if he had the notion. I told you, Hearst hates Otis, and the feeling is mutual. The valley is not going to have to fight on alone."

He smiled broadly at his little army and held up a printed proof of the next edition. "And here's our battle cry." The headline screamed:
### NOT ONE DROP FOR IRRIGATION!

---

William Mulholland was sizing up the man who sat, on the other side of the desk, sizing him up. The eyes that looked back at him from behind spectacles were no doubt intelligent. The man's posture indicated he would wait for a reply to his question. Mulholland rather liked the fellow, but he sure didn't like his line of inquiry.

Henry Loewenthal was asking him to clear up "some details about the great aqueduct endeavor." These details, the *Examiner* editor was suggesting, involved the possibility of graft, not only involving the land syndicate but also involving the profiteering of former mayor Fred Eaton. Mulholland glanced at Matthews, who on hearing of the meeting, had insisted on attending.

He then looked squarely at Loewenthal and replied: "The choice of the San Fernando Valley for the terminus of the aqueduct has nothing to do with land speculation. It is the logical place since water deposited there will naturally drain into the aquifer that replenishes the Los Angeles River. Now, in regard to former mayor Eaton, the claims that he is improperly benefiting from his recent labors for the city are false and slanderous. I can tell you, there isn't a straighter man in money matters on God's footstool. I know that he never made a dirty dollar in his life and never will."

"It is to be expected that you would think well of the former mayor," remarked Loewenthal. "He was of considerable help to you, I understand, in the development of your career leading to your ascension to this office."

Mulholland peered at the man, who was evidently no fool. He had once heard it said that there are three kinds of men: Those who build the world, those who write about it and those who sit by and watch. No doubt, of course, about which category Mulholland claimed for himself, but he had always had great respect for writers. He had taught himself engineering from books, and his own dreams of glory, dreams he was now on the cusp of fulfilling, had drawn inspiration from the great works of fiction and adventure. He had, as he was oft to say, little regard for men who didn't read books.

"Mr. Loewenthal, you are correct to stipulate my admiration and debt of gratitude for Fred Eaton. I think you may understand me when I tell you that a man like Eaton, people can't comprehend his character. Because few people have a character like his, his whole soul, a big man."

Mulholland paused. He could see Loewenthal was a might non-plussed by such a personal, heartfelt defense of Eaton. The editor, he thought, despite muckraking proclivities, was finding his response cred-ible. And he almost believed himself too. He continued, "The results of this deal have been extremely favorable to the city and, I would say, only modest and just for Eaton."

Loewenthal felt the superintendent was being forthright, but pressed for details. "Eaton claims he has been paid only ten dollars a day plus expenses for his efforts."

"That corresponds with our records," replied Matthews.

"But isn't it true that in order to obtain a necessary reservoir site in the Owens Valley, the city must purchase the Long Valley ranch from Eaton, who currently holds an option on said property? How much is that going to cost taxpayers?"

Mulholland and Matthews exchanged a quick look. How did the editor know? Had he a source of information on the water and power company board?

"We have an understanding with Mr. Eaton that we expect will require an outlay of no more than $400,000 for Long Valley," answered Mulholland.

"An understanding...and what if he doesn't agree to sell?"

The man was getting on Mulholland's nerves now, prodding at a small, ugly mole of doubt in his overall certainty about what he was doing and how it was all going to go. Nip it out, he told himself. "As I said, Mr. Eaton and I have enjoyed a long association based on mutual respect and trust. These matters are all under good advisement."

Mulholland folded his hands over his chest and looked out the window. Matthews rose, signaling Loewenthal that the interview was over. The editor slid his notebook and pen into his jacket pocket. Mulholland turned to shake his hand, and Matthews retrieved his hat from the stand near the door. Loewenthal nodded at Miss Aames and strode out of the office.

"You've made friends with that bloodhound but have not, I suspect, put him off the scent," said Matthews to Mulholland's profile. The chief had gone back to gazing out the window. Matthews joined him, leaning against the sill to look down at the bustling street. He let his thoughts flow with the movement of people and vehicles. He had an idea.

"What if some of our city's leaders were to invite Mr. Hearst down for a meeting?" he suggested. Mulholland looked up at the lawyer's gleaming brown eyes. He nodded his interest, and Matthews went on.

"He wants to be president," said Matthews, referring to the newspaper tycoon, now a congressman as well, whose dream of ascending to the highest office in the land was well-known. "Presumably he would value the backing of some of our finest citizens?"

---

On September 2nd, William Randolph Hearst rode his private railroad car from San Francisco to Los Angeles. Henry Loewenthal, informed only that his boss was coming down for a business meeting, was astounded when, late in the afternoon, Hearst barged into his office.

"Help them along with the bond issue. That's our public policy from here on. That's it."

"But sir…"

"Stand aside."

Loewenthal watched, horrified, as Hearst, crisply suited despite the late summer heat, a black pearl and diamond stickpin securing his cravat, sat down at his editor's messy desk. Hearst plucked up a fountain pen and bent to the task of writing. Some minutes later, he raised his head, fixed a pair of reddened, pouchy eyes on Loewenthal and barked: "Here, print this editorial endorsing the aqueduct on the front page of tomorrow's morning edition."

When Hearst was gone, Loewenthal endured the humiliation of taking the copy out to his production editor, then rounding up the team of reporters he had assigned to the aqueduct scandal and reassigning them to other stories. After that he retreated to his office, closed the door and sank down on the divan by the open window.

Loewenthal had always known Hearst to be mercurial and tempestuous, but until now he had believed the man to be truly interested in good journalism and to take great pride in the achievements of his papers. All the editors in the Hearst chain were aware, of course, that their boss had been bitten by the presidential bug, but, Loewenthal surmised, they would be as surprised as he that Hearst now seemed willing to subordinate everything else for a shot at the highest office in the land.

Feeling jumpy and exhausted, he let his eyes rest on the map of the United States pinned to the opposite wall. Usually Loewenthal found this map comforting, reassuring as a depiction of the steady progress of civilization westward and the tremendous breadth and abundance of this young, intrepid nation.

But now he looked with a jaundiced eye on the star in the lower left-hand corner of the map. Our shining city, this "City of Angels," he thought bitterly. What does it matter if Hearst ripped the rug right out from under my exposé of a monstrous scandal? Do the citizens of this city really care? They not only tolerate scandal, but appear to have a genuine appetite for it. There is a spirit of lawlessness that prevails here, he reflected, which I have never seen anywhere else.

Loewenthal's eyes slid across the map. Maybe it's time to go back east, he thought, sighing and shutting his eyes against the tension in his head that had become a hammering ache.

# Chapter 6

The next morning, the *Examiner* came out with a strong endorsement of the aqueduct project, along with Hearst's convoluted justification for why the paper had switched its position. Loewenthal couldn't bring himself to read the editorial, but on each of the four days left before the bond election, the *Examiner* joined the tribe of Los Angeles newspapers beating the drums of civic glory and drought hysteria.

Mulholland's term "water nightmare" appeared in all the papers, as well as his prediction: "If Los Angeles runs out of water for one week, the city within a year will lose at least half of its present population."

"Should the bonds not pass," proclaimed the *Los Angeles Herald*, "building will stop and workers will have to leave the city!"

"The flow of the Los Angeles River has dropped to less than 34 million gallons per day in a city that consumes more than 38 million gallons on a hot day," the now-docile *Examiner* quoted Mulholland's dire figures without checking them.

Citizens joined in the cause. The *Times* society page editor covered a tea party given by socialite Mrs. Jefferson Chase Bixby for the city's leading matrons. Mrs. Bixby greeted her guests in high-fashion couture, but abandoned her jewels to wear instead a simple gold filigree chain with a crystal vial holding, she claimed, an ounce of Owens River water.

The ladies were delighted to receive their own necklaces, tied with a gold ribbon to the handles of their teacups. After huge quantities of tea, reputedly made from Owens River water, as well as cake, scones and gossip had been consumed, the stellar assembly stood for a photograph, which was seen in the newspaper by women all over the city. Overnight, passing the aqueduct bond became not just civic-minded but fashionable.

The weather made its contribution as well, with temperatures, which had blasted to over 100 degrees in late August, holding stubbornly high through the beginning of September. The *Times* printed Mulholland's warning: "Whenever a hot spell like this comes, the Los Angeles River is in itself entirely insufficient for the needs of the city. This illustrates better than anything else could the absolute necessity for securing a source of water supply elsewhere. We must have it."

And so they did. On September 7, 1905 the aqueduct bond measure passed with a margin of 14 to 1.

In the midst of the hurly-burly, with the *Examiner* tamed, there was no one to notice the coincidence of events. No one pointed out that on the same morning the *Examiner* had reversed its position on the aqueduct, the first advertisement for individual lots of one to five acres in the San Fernando Valley had appeared in the *Times*, showing a picture of a pretty little cottage surrounded by fruit trees, shrubs and flowers.

The syndicate had in mind more than one way to gain a massive return on its investment: initially irrigation with Owens River water would make San Fernando fields highly productive and profitable. Gradually, as the city's population grew, these fields could be broken up into small lots for even more profitable sale to homeowners wanting their own little piece of paradise—subdivisions as far as the eye could see.

---

Augusta Aames, hard-hatted and high-heeled, held tightly to foreman Davis's arm as he guided her over the muddy concrete floor, strewn with pipes and debris, toward her objective. Mulholland was at the far end of the facility, inspecting a new water filtration gallery.

For the better part of three weeks, he'd been out and back to this site where the work teams had been encountering a spate of unexpected problems. Then about a week ago, Mulholland had been standing, not too far from where he was now, talking to a workman, when a huge concrete block fell off of a derrick, killing the man and just missing the chief.

Across the tight-knit department, there was grief, but not shock. The men who did this work knew it was dangerous. During the recent building of the Buena Vista pumping station, they'd labored round the clock, with three-man teams lowered 112 feet down to the bottom of a shaft, where they dug with picks and shovels in a space less than a foot per man in diameter.

Augusta knew the risks borne by his crews were never far from Mulholland's mind, and that this was one of the reasons he constantly railed against water wasters. She also knew her boss made a point of going wherever he sent his work teams, and thus was often in the same tight, hazardous spots, though he brushed off concerns, whether expressed by her or his family. Referring to the incident of the falling block, Mulholland simply said, "My time had not come."

Given this general predilection toward being on-site and the troubles at this particular facility, Augusta was not surprised that Mulholland had declined to remain in the office today awaiting the outcome of the bond election. When the news came in, she had wanted to make sure he received it immediately, and therefore had appointed herself messenger.

"Mr. Mulholland," called her escort, "Your secretary is here to see you sir."

"Why Miss Aames!" Mulholland turned, surprised to see her thin, straight, skirted form in these environs. "Have you suddenly gotten an itch to see the water works?" he teased.

She was sure he had guessed the motivation for her mission, so she simply waited, holding back the information she knew he would pretend not to be anxiously awaiting. She could tease too.

"Well, sir, it did seem like a fine day for an outing."

"I see, well there Davis, perhaps we should show Miss Aames around, and up and down," he suggested, grinning.

"There'll be no need for that Mr. Mulholland." Augusta put a stop to such nonsense. "Just thought you would like to know sir that the bond measure passed by a wide margin."

Mulholland nodded, a smile tweaking the corners of his mustache and then broadening across his cheekbones.

"Hey, sir, that's great!" Davis stepped forward to shake his hand.

Mulholland pumped it vigorously and slapped the fellow on the back.

"I want six teams of surveyors out between here and Owens Valley in the next 15 days, and I'll be relying on you to head up one of the crews."

"Thank you sir!" Davis beamed. Then, turning to Augusta. asked, "Shall I take you back now ma'am?"

"I'll take her. You go back to work." Waving off the young man, Mulholland offered his arm.

"A great victory, and a sound endorsement from the citizenry, Mr. Mulholland. How do you feel sir?" She ventured a question she quite expected her boss to brush off.

But Mulholland turned her to him, placed a hand at her waist and began waltzing her in circles. "Let me tell you how I feel: I'm intoxicated, drunk with delight. I want to whoop and yell like a kid!"

"Goodness me!" was all the astonished woman could manage.

"Now Miss Aames, I want you to do something very important for me. I want you to send a formal invitation asking Fred Eaton to dine at my home next week. Check with my wife about days and times. Tell her I want it to be a very, very nice evening for a very good friend."

---

Much of the evening was very nice indeed. Mulholland awaited his friend's arrival on the deep front porch that ran across two sides of his home. The large Queen Anne style house on a corner lot had a mirror-image set of graceful curving entry stairs, one on Sixth Street leading up to the portico entrance, the other on Cummings Street, leading up to a slender-columned gallery. Mulholland had designed the house himself, making full use of the engineering opportunities available in the newer balloon framing construction methods, while eschewing the excesses this license had led to in many other abodes for the well to do. Mulholland's house had the signature gables and turrets of the style, but they had been executed with restraint, and the building displayed a balanced, pleasing sense of proportion in both structure and ornament.

When Eaton pulled up in front of the house in his bright red Stanley Steamer touring car, Mulholland thought, yes, he's certainly feeling his wild oats since the divorce. But he came down to inspect the shining, spurting machine and greet his friend with a hearty handshake and back slap. "We did it!"

"Yes, we sure did, congratulations to us!" Eaton, elegant in evening dress beneath his trench coat, was smiling broadly, and on this beautiful early September evening, in the mood to celebrate. He was so near his goal, his fingers were twitching inside his gloves.

Aperitifs and dinner progressed with good cheer all around. Mulholland's wife Lillie and his three sons and two daughters knew Eaton quite well and, like everyone else, found him charming.

Mulholland was pleased to see it, as it would serve his purposes for Eaton to feel as comfortable and at home as possible. Still he winced at the lively interchanges between Eaton and Lucille, his youngest daughter. Though only seven, the girl was already impetuous, daring and socially confident. While the other children were in awe of their father and observed the strict rules of comportment he prescribed, Lucille was a rebel. Glancing slyly at Eaton, she posed the forbidden question.

"Why didn't you want to keep your wife?"

And Eaton, damn him, had encouraged her, answering back without missing a beat. "Because she wasn't as gorgeous as you little miss!"

"Enough of that now." Mulholland looked sternly at Lucille, but she just smiled, took a bite of buttered bread and daintily touched her Irish linen and lace napkin to plump, red lips. Rose and Perry, the oldest of the Mulholland brood, at 14 and 13 respectively, both cast disapproving looks at their little sister. Richard and Thomas continued eating, as young boys will, without regard for the conversation. They'd all been instructed by their mother to avoid any mention of the Eaton divorce, an unfit topic for children anyway.

The meal ended without further incident, and Mulholland led Eaton into his large, book-filled study. He poured brandies and offered his friend a cigar. For some time they sat silently, breathing in the fragrance of these temporal rewards and savoring the glow of achievement.

They had done it. Their plan—begun with a trail of "dead soldiers" across the blazing Mojave Desert almost a year ago to the day—was accomplished.

Mulholland wagged his cigar at Eaton. "I'm going to send at least six crews of surveyors out, and I want to get one up to Long Valley to chart the reservoir site. So let's finish up our business Fred."

"Fine," said Eaton pleasantly. "The price is one million dollars."

Mulholland started to laugh, sure his friend was joking, but Eaton's countenance was mirthless and his eyes steely and steady. Mulholland was shocked to see he'd meant it, but figured the million was just an initial bargaining position to be negotiated down. Sure, Fred loved the game of business, so Mulholland told himself to keep his temper and let the man play his hand out.

"Now, Bill, you've said many times that I was the only person who could have made those deals in Owens Valley without arousing suspicion. I did it." Eaton raised hands, one with his drink, the other with his smoke, as if taking a bow. "And now you can build your aqueduct. The city owes me a fair return on my efforts."

"Fair, certainly," said Mulholland. He paused and blew out a long, leisurely plume of smoke. "Look Fred, I've been the first to defend you against accusations that you've profited too handsomely from actions performed on behalf of the city. I've described your compensation as modest and just, but you know and I know we've paid you over $100,000 in commissions for land and water rights transactions up there."

"That's a pitiful sum, and you know it Bill! I lost a fortune when you prevented me from financing the Owens Valley purchases with private capital. So now I'm asking for only a fraction of what that whole deal would have brought me. The city needs Long Valley, and if you won't buy it from me for a fair price, I know private financiers who are just waiting to do so."

"After everything we've accomplished together these last weeks, you would put the city's future in the hands of a bunch of greedy New York bankers?!" The game was becoming tedious and Mulholland angry. Apparently Eaton had learned nothing from his mistake, and he wasn't even remorseful!

"I won't be doing anything of the sort. You will, if you don't agree to my reasonable price."

"Reasonable you say! You're mad as a hatter!" Mulholland jumped to his feet, glowering.

Eaton did the same, looking down from his taller height. "And you're a tight-fisted, cheating bastard!"

The muscles in Mulholland's face and neck twitched, as he strained every fiber of psychological muscle to stop his Irish temper from exploding. Slowly he unclenched his fist around the now limp cigar, reached for his brandy and gestured at Eaton. "Surely we old friends can sit down here and find a compromise."

Eaton relaxed, sunk back down into his chair and let the usual expression of charm and ease return to his countenance. Mulholland didn't believe it.

"Of course we can, Bill."

"How about $450,000?"

Eaton looked at him, smiling stiffly for a long time, then he said: "For that price I will sell you half the land."

"Including the reservoir site?"

"No, I will keep that. If you want all of the land, including the reservoir site, the price is still one million. But I will sell you half the land along with enough water rights and easements so that you can build a small dam, enough to help you regulate the flow down the aqueduct. You're planning to build reservoirs in San Fernando and other places south of Owens anyway. That should be enough."

"You know very well those won't be enough. They'll help with managing the flows to local communities down below, but they won't be enough to regulate the overall flow efficiently. We need a larger dam and a massive reservoir at the source to ensure a steady water supply to the city in times of shortage and drought."

Eaton said nothing. Of course he knew this. Eventually the city would have to purchase all of Long Valley. If he held firm, Mulholland would have to meet his price.

Mulholland glared at Eaton. He would like to knock the man to the ground. But he daren't come away from this meeting with nothing. The City Council might well balk at the project if they thought the necessary reservoir site was in question. Bond approval or not, they could still refuse to release the funds. But if he accepted the compromise, he could honestly say he had secured the rights to build a reservoir in Long Valley—none of those nincompoops would know it was too small.

Eventually, Mulholland figured, Eaton would grow tired of holding onto the rest of the ranch—after all, what real use would it be to this city boy?—and he would sell it. There was time. It would be years before he would actually need to build the Long Valley reservoir anyway. Right now he had to clear away this obstacle and get on with the real work of building the aqueduct. He forced a thin smile onto his lips.

"All right, you have a deal Fred. Half the ranch for $450,000." Mulholland leaned forward and extended his hand. Eaton took it, and they shook briefly. They both sat back stiffly and downed their brandies.

Mulholland pulled a folded sheet of paper from his jacket pocket, opened it and spoke quietly. "Just so we understand each other, Matthews has provided me with a few facts. Long Valley has about 5,000 head of cattle and at least 100 horses and mules, also farm equipment. All that's worth a few hundred thousand."

Eaton nodded, said nothing.

"Therefore, with the payment we have just agreed to make for $450,000 and the $100,000 in commissions the city paid you previously, you will have gained in cash or kind somewhere north of three quarters of a million dollars from this venture." Mulholland's eyes bored into Eaton's. "According to this, your total cash outlay to purchase the options and rights you transferred to the city amounted to no more than fifteen thousand."

Eaton didn't flinch, still saying nothing.

"That's quite a profit."

"It's much less than I deserve, Bill—that's the God's honest truth. The Owens River is an unmatched source of clear, pure, abundant water for Los Angeles. Without me, you would never have conceived the possibility of bringing it here. The city still owes me."

"I think we've concluded our business," said Mulholland coldly.

When Eaton had gone, saying a cordial but hurried goodnight to Lillie, Mulholland returned to his study. He stood at the bow window, staring out to the street. Then he said under his breath, "I'll buy it over his dead body."

Mulholland was not to know for a very long time how prescient these words would prove to be.

This same night another dinner was taking place in the private dining room of the Bishop Creek Hotel. Wilfred Watterson had taken the room to welcome a special guest and friend to their fight: Sylvester C. Smith, US Congressman for Inyo County.

The name, if not the man, was familiar to everyone at the table. Smith had served several terms as a state senator before winning the election that had sent him recently to Washington. Chalfant also knew him well as editor of the *Kern County Echo*, published out of Bakersfield, California. Smith, a native Iowan, who had gone west as a young man to follow opportunity, managed the paper between stints of practicing law and pursuing agricultural ventures.

At the moment, the congressman, in late middle age but still robust of constitution and ruddy of complexion, was listening to Chalfant recount recent developments in Los Angeles. Seated with them at table were Mark Watterson, Wallace Austin, rancher Gus Kispert and Percy Murphy, a businessman with mining interests as well as a share in the Owens River Water and Power Company. That enterprise had lost out on the opportunity to build a hydroelectric plant on upper Bishop Creek when Fred Eaton had recommended the Reclamation Service grant the necessary federal right-of-ways to Thomas Rickey's Nevada Power Mining and Milling Company.

"They got to Hearst," Chalfant was saying, "and he told Loewenthal, the editor of the *Examiner*, to stand down. Heard it from Loewenthal himself. Hearst just bullied his way in and told him to support the bond, and that was that. Even wrote the next day's editorial with his own hand!"

Chalfant shook his head in mock wonder. "Goes to show, some things are evidently even more important to Hearst than destroying Otis!"

"Support in a bid for the presidency perhaps?" suggested Murphy with a snort.

"Most likely," replied Chalfant. "With all opposition vanquished in the city, the bond, of course, passed easily. And the city has filed a formal notice of appropriation for Owens River water with the Department of Interior. That's the bad news.

"Now here's the good news: I've heard from Jacob Clausen." Chalfant smiled and raised his glass of wine. "He's an engineer in Reclamation supportive of our cause," the editor explained to Smith. "Clausen says

Secretary of the Interior Hitchcock has flatly refused to approve the request without a thorough investigation. Let me see if I can remember, he said Hitchcock has announced that's he's determined to get to the bottom of the matter and to ascertain the exact facts in the case, whatever they may be."

He lifted his glass to Wallace. "Appears no small amount of credit goes to you, Austin, as Hitchcock was given a copy of your letter to the president, and he was very disturbed by what he read."

"Aaaaay!" There were shouts of glee, and everyone now toasted Austin, who smiled modestly, blinking with pleasure at the thought of how his wife would receive the news.

"That's not all, the talk at Reclamation is that Hitchcock has put Lippincott on notice he'll have to come to Washington for a private interview—more like a private grilling, I suspect! He's been given no orders yet about when he'll have to go. Most likely, Clausen thinks, after the investigation is completed, which could be as much as six months."

"Who's gonna do the investigatin?" asked Mark Watterson.

It was Austin who answered. "I've received word from Washington to expect a fellow out of Sheridan, Wyoming, name of O'Fallon. He's been one of the department's top investigators for years, a 'troubleshooter,' you might say. Before that he had a very good reputation as an Indian agent. I'll let you know when he arrives. We'll all have a chance to give him the facts as we know them."

"Excellent, excellent news," said Wilfred, lifting his fork, feeling better able to tackle his barely eaten meal now that his stomach was no longer in knots.

"Yes, very promising indeed gentlemen," agreed Congressman Smith, who had already finished his. "Of course it must be said that the findings of this investigation will go one of two ways. If that way is not our way, and Hitchcock makes his decision based on the report, it will be too late to alter the course of events. Therefore, I believe we must have a contingency plan—a compromise position if you will—to offer only if absolutely necessary."

Smith looked round the table. "I can see, gentlemen, that you have little enthusiasm for the idea, but hear me out. If there is a chance the investigator will produce evidence and recommendations fully supporting the valley's claims, then not a word of this proposal need ever be spoken. But if it appears that the results are less categorically in our favor, or in any way prejudiced toward the claims of the city, then we must be prepared to offer a third, middle course."

Smith's plan was simple and had the attractive qualities of appearing utterly reasonable in concept and generous in spirit: The Owens Valley would acknowledge Los Angeles's need for an additional domestic water supply and undertake to supply it from the Owens River. But because the Owens flow was far in excess of the domestic consumption requirements of the city's population, it made no sense to use the surplus for agriculture in the San Fernando Valley. The Owens Valley had its own agricultural interests and clearly a prior and superior claim to water usage for that purpose. Therefore, the Reclamation project should go forward in the valley, and the surplus water, after the valley's agricultural needs had been met, could be diverted to Los Angeles, for domestic use only.

"I know Secretary Hitchcock to be a fair-minded man, and I feel sure this is a compromise he will welcome if it comes to that," Smith tried again to reassure them.

Chalfant nodded. "If it does come to this, it's a position that would play well in the press. Imagine a headline: The valley is perfectly willing to accommodate need, but not greed!"

The rest of the men listened glumly, the words "if it comes to that" reverberating in their heads. They knew Hitchcock was right: It was wise to have another plan. As they rose and left the room, clasping hands farewell, everyone was hoping Smith's plan would stay
in the congressman's proverbial back pocket, and never see light of day.

---

It was well into the fall when O'Fallon appeared in the valley and took up a brief residence at the Bishop Creek Hotel. Bishop townsfolk flung open their doors to the tall, taciturn stranger, offering him no end of hospitality, most of which he graciously begged off. They anxiously watched him going to and fro, visiting the mayor's office, bank, newspaper and general store and riding out to speak with ranchers.

O'Fallon returned twice more during the winter of 1906, once with Jacob Clausen, who toured the investigator up and down the river while providing detailed explanations of the valley's geology, flora, fauna and history of settlement and development. The young engineer also happily accompanied O'Fallon to interview the elder Mr. Watterson, who had, he assured O'Fallon, "the best observation and insight in the valley" and, he kept this to himself, a most lovely and spirited youngest daughter, the beguiling Elizabeth.

For the valley folk, the fact of this Washington-mandated investigation was reassuring, but the process was slow and frustrating. O'Fallon kept his observations to himself, and not even valley leaders like Chalfant had an inkling of the outcome of his report—only that, according to Clausen, it would be submitted in early spring. In the meantime, Chalfant did his best to keep optimism high through the occasional article rehashing all the reasons why the cause was just, but valley folk, like Chris Bow, who scoured these writings for a glimmer of news, closed their papers more frustrated every day.

The process was equally shuttered and annoying to Angelenos. Mulholland, anxious to send a full complement of surveyor crews into the Mojave, was forced to content himself with sending just two advance teams as he awaited the end of the investigation. Attempts to judge which way the wind was blowing, and to put in a good word for J.B. Lippincott, were made by various highly placed politicians, including the governor of California, but were politely rebuffed by Hitchcock.

Finally word came that O'Fallon had submitted his report to the secretary of the interior, yet still no details were forthcoming about its conclusions. The weeks dragged on and then, for a time, everybody stopped thinking about the report…

On April 18, 1906 at about five o'clock in the morning, people in the Owens Valley, in Los Angeles, and in many other parts of the state felt the earth tremble. To many of these folks, long accustomed to living atop a restless land, the experience was unremarkable. They regarded the event as ordinary seismic wobbling. But soon, as news flew across the few telegraph circuits remaining in operation for a short time, it became tragically clear the tremor had been anything but ordinary. San Francisco had suffered an immense seismic upheaval, and large swaths of the city had been leveled by partially or completely collapsing buildings. Fires, lit by broken gas mains, had set many neighborhoods ablaze and were raging out of control, as broken water mains left survivors little to fight them with.

Mulholland, hearing the news, thought first of Helen Armstrong, Fred Eaton's elegant daughter. Had she survived? Most of the mansions on Nob Hill had reportedly fallen to the ground or gone up in smoke. At best, he supposed, she might be wandering the treacherous streets, cluttered with dangerous debris, begging shelter with the lesser mortals of the city.

In former times, Mulholland knew, he would have sought out Fred immediately and offered what help he could—hell, the two of them might well have set out by buckboard if necessary to find and save the beautiful Helen! But these were different days. Though he had tried several times to urge his old friend to reconsider the Long Valley deal, Fred had held obstinately to his million-dollar price for the reservoir site. And with each of Mulholland's attempts to bring him to reason, Fred had seemed to become ever more obstinate and embittered. Damn him to hell for his muleheadedness!

And damn him too for his foolishness. Several months ago Eaton had left the city, he said, "for good and all," and moved up to the Owens Valley, to Long Valley, where, it seemed, he was now determined to enact a crackpot dream of becoming a cattle baron. With him he had taken his new bride, Alice Slosson, a woman half his age and formerly Matthews's secretary! It was a scandal even Mulholland hadn't expected of the mercurial Eaton, despite the many occasions when he had witnessed his former friend flirting with the young lady.

Odd, mused Mulholland, that Eaton, the native son of Los Angeles, had chosen to take himself away from her at just this moment. While certainly no one would have wished disaster on a sister city, the destruction of San Francisco virtually ensured the ascendancy of Los Angeles as the leading urban center of the West—something that had been much within Eaton's aspirations until recently. Now he appeared to have transferred those ambitions to a cattle spread in the upper Owens Valley. Might he become a liability up there?

# Chapter 7

His fingers embraced hers, and he looked down at the small hand that had seemed lost to him forever just a couple of weeks ago amidst shifting floors and shaking walls. Yet now he held it in the terra firma of his own palm and thanked God for that privilege. Jacob Clausen and Elizabeth Watterson sat close together in Willie Chalfant's parlor, the young man lifting his teacup on his left so as not to let go of his newly engaged fiancée. He was recounting the harrowing aftermath of the earthquake to Chalfant and his wife and daughter.

Clausen had been tossed awake and thrust out of his bed by the rolling movement. The wood-frame boarding house on Sacramento Street where he rented a room initially survived the minute-long quake. Unhurt except for bruises, Clausen helped other boarders out onto the street, where he stood trying to breath and see through the heavy cloud of dust. The street, rolled and buckled, was unrecognizable. Next door, a three-story home leaned over its folded foundation at a 45-degree angle to the street.

Shouting and screaming penetrated his confusion, and Clausen rushed to join two men trying to climb a huge pile of broken masonry. They looked like burlesque players in blackface, eyes huge and white in dust-covered faces. For the next few hours, the trio dug through plaster, bricks, wood and sheared, twisted metal to reach calling, sobbing, moaning survivors. Other ad-hoc teams of rescuers formed, joined and split off, trying to respond to overwhelmingly urgent needs all about them.

At some point in the morning, he and another man were carrying an injured woman on an improvised stretcher when the earth pitched again and they fell to their knees, nearly dropping their charge. Clausen was overtaken by nausea as the buildings still standing waved in the dirty air above him. They squatted over the injured woman, trying to shield her from falling bricks and glass, knowing they were lucky to have been in the center of the street when the aftershock hit. One group of rescuers hadn't been so fortunate; they had been extracting a young boy from the rubble when an adjacent building collapsed on them.

When the shaking stopped, Clausen and his partner stumbled back onto their feet and made their way over to a makeshift hospital where neighborhood women were doing what they could to tend to the injured. They sat the stretcher down, then returned wearily to their task.

Before much time passed following the aftershock, a contingent of soldiers arrived. One of the soldiers, working alongside Clausen, said he'd seen people up on Market Street, rummaging through the ruins of jewelry stores, looking for melted gold and silver. He said stones from the great dome of City Hall had fallen to the street, leaving a bird cage of steel.

"What about the post office?" asked Clausen about the federal building that also housed his Reclamation Service office. "Is she gone?"

"No she's still standing, but pretty bad inside. There's walls, some of those with mosaic pictures especially, that fell right into the middle of the rooms. Some doorways and ceilings are down too. Even those rock-hard marble floors got split."

"But she stands!"

"Yessir, she does indeed."

Jacob, grateful now to be sitting in the pleasant, orderly Chalfant parlor, recounted how he had felt more hopeful upon learning that his beloved federal building had survived. After that he had worked with renewed energy, especially when they began to see smoke rising above the broken buildings down the street toward the Bay and to smell the approaching fires.

"Oh how dreadful! People must have been panicking!" said Elizabeth, drawing her hand to her mouth.

"Some were," answered Clausen, squeezing her arm, "but it was odd the calm comportment others maintained. On the street, there were groups of women standing here and there in their coats and hats, just watching as the fire drew nearer. Across the street from my boardinghouse a group of old men brought out chairs and sat on a piece of sidewalk, talking and watching as if they were socializing on a Sunday afternoon. As the air got hotter and smoke thicker, they just picked up their chairs and moved up the street a block. And then another block, and another block after that."

Clausen had stayed in the city, camping in the street, as the firestorms were finally subdued over the next few days. He'd then joined his fellow Reclamation Service engineers and other government workers in pitching tents and putting up temporary cottages to shelter those, like himself, who had lost their abodes.

He was still there a month after the quake when William Randolph Hearst organized several performances by Sarah Bernhardt to raise the spirits of his fellow San Franciscans. Clausen attended one of the plays, given in an open air theater at the University of California at Berkeley, just across the bay from the fallen city. Miss Bernhardt had been divine, of course, but mostly he marveled at her toughness of spirit—before coming to California, Bernhardt had toured the intemperate boom towns of New Mexico and Texas. There, the great tragic actress, celebrated by the intelligentsia and royalty of Europe, had played under tents and from wagons, in exchange for gold.

During all the weeks he forced himself to stay, Clausen had been itching to get to Owens Valley, to Elizabeth. The disaster, he now told the Chaffeys, smiling devotedly at his darling girl, had shaken sense into his head. No more hesitation, Clausen had resolved that as soon as he could extract himself from the city, he would go to the Owens Valley and ask for Elizabeth's hand in marriage. Joseph Watterson, as relieved as his daughter when Clausen turned up, had promptly given his consent. And now here they were, safe and with a shared future, a blissful dream Clausen had doubted in those terrifying moments on Sacramento Street.

The young Miss Chalfant watched the couple wistfully. So romantic that he had come running from the disaster to claim his true love! Elizabeth gave the girl a warm, kind smile, which, as Jacob wrapped his arm around her waist and squeezed her to him, expanded into radiance.

"I came for her, but I wanted to talk to you as well," Clausen was saying to Chalfant. "I've some information. It's nothing but word of mouth," he warned, as Chalfant leaned forward.

"The Reclamation Service is in as much disarray as everything else up there, but I think what I've heard is reliable. O'Fallon's report is not favorable to Lippincott. He apparently views the man's conduct as indefensible, bringing discredit to the service and deserving of severest condemnation. He's recommending Lippincott be removed forthwith. I believe that Hitchcock may act on this recommendation; I've heard Lippincott has been summoned to Washington."

"Terrific! That's unequivocal!" Chalfant clapped his hands together.

"Unfortunately, O'Fallon's conclusions in regard to the Reclamation project are less so. He acknowledges the city's need for the water, but says that the valley should be given a fair price for land and water rights—more than what Eaton paid."

"No, no, no…that's not what we were hoping to hear," said Chalfant, shaking his head and glancing anxiously at his wife.

"There's more." Clausen held up his free hand. "O'Fallon has recommended that the government establish an impartial arbitrator to ensure fair prices for the valley. But word in the service is that Hitchcock isn't inclined that way; he doesn't want to become embroiled in managing a complicated process like that. And it now appears that your Congressman Smith has come forward with an alternative proposal that could save him from the necessity. It's a compromise deal, and Hitchcock seems to find it imminently reasonable and fair."

"I know about the Smith plan. We discussed it with the congressman here in the valley some months ago. We had all hoped it wouldn't be necessary."

"Certainly, I understand that sentiment. But if it's a way to keep your homes and businesses—and, while you give away some of your water, you retain ownership of it."

"Yes, ownership is the fundamental issue. You say Smith is actively promoting the idea with Hitchcock? When will we know?"

"I believe the decision will be made very soon, within a week or two, and perhaps less than that."

---

Word of mouth on the O'Fallon report and its reverberations reached Los Angeles even quicker than Clausen had been able to bring it to the valley. Matthews picked up the telephone and told Augusta Aames to find Mulholland wherever he was. About an hour later, the chief returned his call.

"The Smith proposal has Hitchcock smitten because it gives the appearance of being fair to all parties," explained the lawyer. "I'm sorry to say I think we're going to have to consider it. If we don't, the city is going to be seen as greedy and unreasonable."

There was silence on the line. "Mulholland?" prompted Matthews.

"Tell them we're willing to compromise, damn it! Tell them anything you like for now. Then pack your bags, W.B., we're going to Washington… and make sure Senator Flint knows we're on our way."

---

Ethan A. Hitchcock pulled a sheet of paper from an open folder and held it up. He sniffed, put it down, picked up the next sheet, put it down. Soon he closed the folder, bringing his elbows onto the desk and the tips of his fingers together like a church steeple. On them he rested a determined chin, above which were arranged temperate lips, a well groomed silver mustache, high cheekbones, intelligent brown eyes and bushy dark eyebrows. The curly silver hair that framed the attractive assemblage had receded, leaving a partly bald pate, though the skin here, as across his entire countenance, glowed with robust good health.

He had promised to get to the bottom of the Reclamation Service controversy surrounding the Owens River. Having made good on that promise, he didn't much like what he'd found. In addition to O'Fallon's report, the folder contained copies of correspondence between Newell, director of the service, and J.B. Lippincott, the service's supervising engineer in California. Some of the letters contained statements from Lippincott clearly biased toward the interests of Los Angeles. But many consisted of defensive and, to Hitchcock's thinking, confused, unconvincing justifications for why Lippincott's extracurricular consulting work for the city was not being conducted in detriment to his position with the service.

The man is talented, no doubt, but sloppy in his professional comportment, and circular and self-serving in his thinking, concluded Hitchcock. He sighed and ran a hand over the smooth place at the top of his head. Well, let's clean this up.

Hitchcock pressed the buzzer for his secretary, who appeared at his door a moment later.

"Send in Mr. Lippincott please Miss Cassidy."

"Yes sir." She turned back toward the outer office. "Mr. Lippincott, he will see you now."

The man who entered was tall, lean and lanky. He had a prominent forehead, Roman nose, dark mustache and dark, thinning hair with white wings over the ears.

"Secretary Hitchcock, sir."

"Please sit down Mr. Lippincott. I have asked you here as the final step in my investigation into the Owens River controversy. I take it you are familiar with the report submitted by Investigator O'Fallon?"

"Yes, sir, I am."

"Then you know it is highly critical of your actions in this affair."

"Sir, I feel I must…"

"There are just a few more questions I wish to pose to you Mr. Lippincott, and I expect direct and truthful answers."

Lippincott closed his mouth, waited.

"On the first matter, that of the proposed Reclamation Service irrigation project in the Owens Valley versus the proposed aqueduct to the city of Los Angeles, I have gathered from your correspondence to Director Newell and the transcript of your testimony at the Reclamation panel that you look favorably on the diversion of Owens River water to the city for domestic and municipal purposes."

"Yes sir, I believe it is clear that the greatest public necessity is to be found in the use of the water in Southern California. And may I say that should the service aid in this enterprise, it is an endeavor that will be considered a marked public service."

Hitchcock ignored the ploy to political vanity. "And once the needs of Los Angeles for domestic and municipal water are met, do you think it would be a public service for us to allow the city to remove even more water from the Owens Valley?"

Lippincott didn't answer directly, falling back instead on what he had found to be a reassuring line of argument. "Well, of course sir, the proposed intake for the aqueduct is far south of most of the farms and ranches in the valley. The city has no intention of taking all the water, only of diverting unused flows."

"I see. In that case," began Hitchcock, lifting a corner of the folder on his desk, "the proposal of Congressman Smith, with which I am sure you are also familiar, should satisfy all interests should it not?"

Lippincott looked down at his long legs ending in the boots he'd just had shined for this meeting. He recrossed his ankles.

"Perhaps" was all he said.

"I would say it certainly shall." Hitchcock waited. When Lippincott did not reply, he moved on.

"Now, on the second matter, which is your comportment as an employee of the US Government. Your replies to Director Newell here," he tapped an index finger smartly on the folder, "are full of excuses for why you have persisted, despite numerous requests to desist, with consulting engagements throughout your tenure as a Reclamation Service supervising engineer. Why have you not put an end to this activity?"

"Sir, when I accepted a regular commission with the Reclamation Service I informed Director Newell that the value of my private business was such that I could ill afford to sacrifice it entirely, particularly because the compensation that could be offered by the service was so much less than the value of my private business."

"Indeed, I understand your reluctance in this matter, as it is common knowledge that you have been paid very large fees for consultation work. This is particularly true of your consulting engagement with the city of Los Angeles, where your fee seems to have been more than half your annual salary from the service."

"I am paid well because of the effectiveness of my work and because my name has developed a commercial value."

"Do you not consider that some of the commercial value your private clients ascribe to your name is attributable to your position in the Reclamation Service?"

"Perhaps some small portion of it," Lippincott admitted.

"Mr. Lippincott!" Hitchcock leaned forward and peered at the man sternly.

"Yes, yes I reckon."

"Then you have been making private gain from public office, and I insist you stop it."

"Sir, if I appear insubordinate in persisting in this work for Los Angeles, I did it believing it was a duty I ought to perform and an important public service. My conscience is perfectly clear. Moreover in future if I am prevented from doing any private work, my ability to provide for my future and that of my family will be severely reduced. That will make the retention of my position in the service difficult."

"Then you must choose, Mr. Lippincott. You may cut all ties with your current consulting clients and agree to take on no more, in which case I will allow you to stay in the service. If you cannot take these measures, you may return to your private practice without any further hindrance or benefit from the US Government."

Hitchcock sat back, but his eyes remained locked on Lippincott. He waited a long moment, then asked, "Do you rightly understand me?"

"Yes sir."

"I will grant you a fortnight to make your choice Mr. Lippincott. That is all. Good day."

Hitchcock reached for the buzzer so that Miss Cassidy would come in and usher the man out. He did not get up as Lippincott rose and left. He wished him gone, this man whose mind ranged like a child's drawing back and forth over the lines. Sadly, mused Hitchcock, he seems not even to see the lines.

## Chapter 8

At her feet was a moving tapestry of gold and green, ruffling at the touch of a flirty breeze redolent of sea and herbs. Kneeling down and plunging her hands into the luxuriant ankle-deep flowers, she was submerged in a vast field of California poppies, stretching west as far as she could see until it met a band of blue. A woman kneeling next to her pointed to a soft gray shape near the faint horizon line where sea became sky: Catalina Island, she said, about 20 miles offshore. One could take a boat there, to the perfect harbor of Avalon Bay, where there was a fine hotel and a dance pavilion in the middle of town, she said. It was Mary Austin's first view of the Pacific Ocean.

Mary and some two dozen other passengers of the Pacific Electric Railway were strewn out across the field in front of the brightly painted trolley car that had stopped to let its riders alight. Behind the Big Red Car, as the trolley was affectionately known to Angelenos, rose rugged brown foothills, their base marked at intervals by tall white poles strung with cable. The poles, shaped like an upside down letter L, curved around the hills, growing smaller and closer together in the distance as they reached back toward Los Angeles, a corner of which was visible to the southwest. They had enjoyed views of the city—its checkerboard of streets, a few soaring buildings, including the square arrow-like tower of city hall, poking the sky—at various points in their journey as the trolley had raced along at more than 40 miles per hour!

Their embarkation point at Fourth and Main streets, had been just a few blocks from the modest Hayward Hotel on South Spring Street, where Mary had checked in the evening before after a long train journey. Walking to the trolley this morning, she had been invigorated and charmed by the smell of sea air and the sight of blue and amber mountains as she looked from the street to the north and east through the canyons formed by the buildings.

On her way, she happened to pass the glamorous new Alexandria Hotel, which had just opened to much fanfare. Inaugural guests, according to the newspapers, had included Enrico Caruso, the great Italian tenor who was the star of the Metropolitan Opera in New York. Mary well remembered a phonograph recording of Caruso's *"No Pagliaccio non son"* that had regaled them during dessert the wonderful evening she and Wallace had dined alongside other leaders of the valley's cause at the Watterson home. Happy in the memory and feeling a bit cosmopolitan herself on this sunny morning, she braved the opportunity to enter the hotel briefly, walking across the elaborately carved wood lobby and peeking up at the stained glass dome of its Palm Court dining room.

But afterward, back on the bustling street, gorged with street cars, buggies, men and women on bicycles and the occasional loudly honking automobile, she felt the utter noise and constant activity wearing on her nerves, accustomed as she was to rural life. She tilted her head upward to see the top of the 13-story Continental Building, the city's first "skyscraper." There, the plain facade became encrusted with neoclassical decoration. Her head began to ache, so Mary tucked it back up under the rim of her bonnet, like a turtle retracting from the touch of a finger, and walked on. She was glad when the trolley arrived and she could step up, pay her 15 cent fare and escape into its cool, protected interior.

Now, glancing over at the wedge of city in the distance, Mary marveled at the proximity of frenzied streets and enchanted field. How had a city of such size and ambition come to be in this place of breathtaking natural beauty? She looked around at the Angelenos and wondered how they had come to be here. Many had, no doubt, been enticed from their homes in the East or Midwest by the prospect of gold, or were offspring of those who had come for the gold but stayed for other allurements. Here they were, laughing and smiling as the conductor called, rising up from this sea of floating flowers as if they had grown here from seed. Hands hidden in immense, untidy bouquets of poppies, they made their way back to the trolley, suited business men in starch collars, cravats and bowler hats, working men in corduroy trousers and jackets, women in wide, stiff collars over hugely puffed sleeves. A few children scampered ahead of the adults, holding out straw hats brimming with poppies for the approval of the jolly conductor.

The Big Red Car resumed its journey, climbing toward Altadena, a town to the north, beyond Pasadena, which sat more than 1,300 feet above sea level. Mary left the trolley much sooner, as her destination, El Alisal, the home of *Out West* magazine editor Charles Lummis, was only about a third of the way. Lummis's wife Eve had sent a carriage to meet Mary. Soon she arrived, leaning out from the vehicle to catch a glimpse of the house through a large grove of sycamore trees that surrounded it and were the source of its name.

Mary's anticipation had been stoked by an article she had read in *Good Housekeeping* magazine describing "one of the most remarkable and interesting homes in the West," as well as by frequent mentions of it by Lummis himself in his *Out West* editorial column. The house, a work in progress for nearly a decade already, was being built of stones from the arroyo, a rocky, often dry gulch extending from Los Angeles to Pasadena. Lummis was also incorporating old telephone poles purchased from the Santa Fe Railroad and myriad other salvaged materials and artifacts. Even in this unfinished state, the place had become a gathering place for artists, writers, composers and other luminaries, including Jack London, Will Rogers, Clarence Darrow, John Philip Sousa and John Muir. It had also received numerous dignitaries, not the least of which was President Teddy Roosevelt, who had been a classmate of Lummis at Harvard University.

With such preparation, Mary found El Alisal at first sight to be somewhat disappointing. The walls of the house, consisting of a two-story, south-facing center structure with single-story wings on either side, appeared to be constructed entirely of roughly fitted stones. At the far end of the western wing was a tall, round tower, which looked to Mary like a medieval castle turret from an illustration in the book *Ivanhoe*. Next to it, incongruously, extended an arched wall holding a large brass bell, which looked like belfries she'd seen in photographs of the California missions. This wall terminated in a chimney even taller than the belfry. All across this odd facade were gently arched openings for wood framed windows, some tall and narrow and others wide, some with diamond-shaped leading and stain glass and others quite simple, their placement, to Mary's eye, without rational plan. The building sat hugging the ground; there was no front stoop at all to mark the entry, just a similarly arched wood-framed portal with a pair of heavy doors.

Mary, dismounting and taking her small carpetbag, stood puzzled, looking at the doors. They were made of weather-beaten, rough-hewn boards bound together with huge iron bolts and embellished with a grid of iron studs. And they were secured by a rusty iron padlock, which, Mary would later be informed, was 150 years old, having been recovered, along with the door's bolts and hinges, from a derelict mission.

For the moment, however, it was simply a locked door, barring her way and offering no welcome. Mary hesitated, flustered, not knowing what to do until the driver, turning the carriage around, noticed her predicament. He gestured toward a path around the eastern side of the house.

She picked up her bag and followed the path, which led to a lovely courtyard, embraced on three sides by the house. At the center of the courtyard was an immense, leafy sycamore and beneath it a large round fountain. On one side of the court a pillared portico, offering shade from the sunny courtyard, was furnished with narrow benches and rocking chairs. Rising from one of these and advancing, hand outstretched to welcome her, was a tall, dark-haired woman with a countenance too strong of feature to be comely. She had a majestic form, however, clad in a dark blue skirt and soft white blouse adorned with a coral and turquoise studded silver broach at the collar. To Mary's astonishment, the woman introduced herself, not as Eve Lummis, but as Charles's former wife Dorothea.

"Don't bother yourself Mrs. Austin, we're all friends here," she said, smiling at Mary's bewilderment. "Eve has taken the children on a shopping excursion, but will return this evening. Do come along now, I'll show you the house, and your room." Dorothea took her arm companionably, leading her inside.

Stepping through double doors, they entered a square room, designed, Dorothea explained, around the traditional Spanish "zaguan," or entry hall, but serving here as a sort of living room. Mary gaped. It was like no room in any house she had ever seen. Blushing for her own lack of manners, she could not but gaze around her in wonder. The walls and floors were completely plain natural gray cement, yet the room was flooded in color from Indian rugs, blankets and clusters of striped wicker baskets adorning every surface and corner. On the walls were numerous paintings, ceramic tiles and strings of beads as well as cupboards displaying primitive pottery and sculptures. Some did not, Mary thought, look American Indian. Overhead, a rough planked ceiling was supported by exposed beams of huge round logs.

"Charles, as you may know Mrs. Austin, has put his own hand to the building of this house. He has little enough assistance. Each summer he brings two Indian boys out from Isleta Pueblo in New Mexico to help him. Most of them are among those he liberated from the Albuquerque Indian School—have you heard of that scandal Mrs. Austin? These poor children were being forcibly removed to the school from their villages, sometimes kidnapped from their families, and when one child's father came to assure himself of his son's well-being, he was beaten and run off of the school grounds like a dog! Charles helped the pueblo bring suit against the government, paying for the attorney with his own funds."

"Very admirable indeed," said Mary, overwhelmed by the nature and quantity of the information being divulged during this rapid tour.

Opening a door to an adjoining room, Dorothea pointed to a four poster bed, the wood studded with heavy brass bolts, the top fringed with buckskin curtains.

"He's made most of the furniture himself as well," she said, "except for this," her finger now tapping the fireplace mantle, which was carved with a bas-relief design. "The dance of the Navajos," explained Dorothea. She mentioned the name of the sculptor, Gutzon Borglum, as if Mary should know it, but she did not.

They proceeded upstairs. All the doors they passed by and through were unique, of different woods and decorative designs. One had a panel embedded with a wooden idol, which her guide said was made by the Incas in Peru a thousand years ago. Lummis had retrieved it, along with numerous other relics now in the house during an expedition there with the famous archaeologist Adolph Bandelier. As Dorothea opened the door to the room Mary would occupy for her few days' stay, she nodded toward the end of the hall.

"That's Charles's study. If he's not out plastering or cutting wood, he'll be in there. Shall this suit you Mrs. Austin?"

Mary replied that she was very well pleased with her accommodations, and Dorothea left her to refresh herself from the toil of the journey.

"The festivities begin at eight."

---

Mary's room was similar to the bedroom she had viewed downstairs except that it was smaller and the cement walls had a soft rose hue. She sat a few moments on the wooden bed covered with an Indian rug of cream, gray and rose, trying to calm nerves jangled by the strange surroundings. She poured water from a painted terracotta pitcher into a matching basin, unbuttoned and rolled down the bodice of her dress, and pressed a dampened cloth to her neck and face.

Then she placed her bag onto the bed, opened it and withdrew two flat packages wrapped in brown paper. Her heart began racing again as she contemplated the purpose of her visit. These were two stories she intended to submit to Lummis for publication in *Out West*. He had already published several pieces of her work in the magazine, and she thought these were at least as worthy as those. Her second errand was to request his intervention on behalf of the Owens Valley with his old friend, the president of the United States. It was widely known that the friendship begun in college had continued to the present day. Lummis, it was said, had helped the new president prepare his first address to congress, and Roosevelt had sought the advice of Lummis on conservation, irrigation and Indian affairs. He had even introduced Lummis once as "editor of the only magazine I have time to read."

Next Mary withdrew from the deep bag her blue brocade dress and began preparing for dinner. Who would be there, she wondered nervously?

She unpinned her long chestnut hair to brush out the dust of the journey, then resecured it. She was in the blue dress attaching small sapphire earrings to her ears when someone knocked gently on her door.

"Yes, please enter," responded Mary.

The head that poked through Mary's door was striking: Almond eyes of deep blue were set with perfect symmetry in a long oval face ending in full lips and a firm, slightly impudent chin. This perfection was crowned by a mass of curly dark blond hair, fastened up carelessly behind and left to float in sunlit clouds around the face. The body the face was attached to was equally charming, being tall, shapely and graceful of movement. It was embraced and flattered by a simple cotton dress, with a natural collar, long cuffed sleeves and soft pleating above and below the waistband. The fabric, which clung to the torso and swung at the ankles, had a modern, abstract design of large flowers in vibrant hues of orange, blue and violet.

"Hello, you've just arrived?!" The beautiful lips moved to issue forth a voice that was also well-rounded, melodic and charming.

"Yes, I'm Mary Austin. I arrived this afternoon."

"Pardon the intrusion Mrs. Austin, I'm Nora May French. I know who you are. In fact, I've been waiting to meet you. My friend George Stirling told me about you."

Mary was startled at the mention of Stirling, a poet with whom she had recently enjoyed a pleasant correspondence.

"I'm pleased to make your acquaintance, Miss French?" Mary extended her hand. There was a question about marital status in her voice. "Is Mr. Stirling here?"

"No, but he told me you might be. I suppose Lummis mentioned your visit to him."

"Oh, I should have so dearly loved to meet Mr. Stirling. He was very kind to send me a very complimentary note on the occasion of the publication of my little book."

"Yes, I've read *The Land of Little Rain* and liked it so very, very much too. And I've so enjoyed your sketches of Indian and Mexican village life too."

Mary, pleased and remembering her manners, asked Miss French to be seated in one of the two buckskin-covered chairs facing the window, and when her visitor had done so, settled onto the other. During this time she was thinking, who is this girl? She appeared to be quite young, perhaps in her early twenties, yet extremely well read and well spoken. Nora May French…Nora May French…yes! Mary now recalled reading some of the girl's poems in *Out West*. A fellow author! Mary looked at the young gorgeous creature amazed. Never had she thought that such melancholy poems came from the hand of someone so fresh and lovely. Yet the burden of sorrow in French's verses was lightened by notes of whimsy and a sense of beguilement with the beauty of nature, which Mary certainly appreciated and shared.

"Miss French, please allow me to tell you how much I admire your poetry. I am honored that my own humble work has been privileged to appear on the same pages as your excellent verses."

"Oh those," French waved a graceful hand. "They're not much. My best work, I think, is *The Spanish Girl*. It's a cycle of 22 poems," she shrugged and smiled, "about love, of course. Love that ends badly."

"I should like very much to read it."

"Shall I give you a copy tonight after dinner? At such length it may, in any event, relieve insomnia!" Mary nodded, and French continued. "Now, have you met Lummis yet?"

"No, I've seen only the former Mrs. Lummis. The current Mrs. Lummis, I was told, had taken her children on a shopping excursion, and I haven't the least notion of the whereabouts of her husband."

French, noting Mary's unspoken puzzlement, said: "Yes, Dorothea is something of an adjunct member of Lummis's new family. She has her own life too. She's a physician, and a very successful one. Still I think she shall all her life suffer from a bruised and broken heart. You see, Dorothea and Charles were still married when he went to New Mexico to recover from an illness. While staying at Isleta pueblo, he met Eve—she was the daughter of a trader there—and decided he must have a divorce from Dorothea to marry her. This was a long, long time ago…more than a dozen years. Now Eve is the mother of three of his children, yet he's still a danger to every woman around." She glanced at Mary, thinking to direct a warning to her new friend, but deciding, based on the woman's appearance, such an advisory would be unnecessary.

Instead she leaned toward Mary and whispered behind her hand, "Lummis told me he has made record in his diary of every one of his hundreds of affairs, but they are encoded so that neither Eve nor anyone else may comprehend them!"

Mary blushed and thought to change the subject. "This house is quite marvelous, is it not? It might almost serve as a museum it is so full of artifacts and artistry. The carved mantel in the Lummis bedroom is particularly fine."

"Oh, he doesn't sleep there," French remained fixed on the personal. "He makes his bedroom in the tower and he climbs up by way of the attic in his study! When you enter that room, make note of the narrow opening behind his desk, not much more than a hole really!" she giggled.

How very extraordinary, thought Mary. But the wonders of the evening were just beginning.

---

The two women descended the staircase into what appeared to Mary to be half fiesta, half Mad Hatter's tea party. Lummis, Miss French informed Mary, called these evening events "noises." Quite apt, murmured Mary.

"That's Pancho Amate," said French, pointing out a lean, balding man in suit and tie strumming a guitar. "He's from Andalusia, Spain, and currently the resident troubadour and groundskeeper."

The musician was apparently undisturbed that the dozen or so people talking and laughing in groups seemed indifferent to the exotic melodies emanating from his instrument. All the party goers became attentive, however, when the self-proclaimed "Don Carlos" entered the room. Lummis was a short man who walked in a tall manner that conveyed robust good health and absolute self-confidence. He was attired incongruously in what Mary took to be an Indian ceremonial costume of beaded and fringed white deerskin topped off by a soiled old sombrero, which he removed and swept to his side in a flourish as he bent into a deep bow.

"*Señores, señoras y señoritas, mi casa es su casa.* Welcome everyone to El Alisal!"

The removal of the hat revealed a tangle of long curly gray hair receding from a prominent forehead. Lummis had a large, pointed nose on a face that was otherwise small-featured.

Entering just behind him was a doe-like woman in a white gown covered with loosely worked black lace. She had fine features and a calm bearing. Her dark brown hair was braided and twisted into a crown shape at the top of her head.

"Eve Lummis," Miss French whispered as she grasped Mary's elbow and stepped forward to introduce her to their hosts.

"Charmed Mrs. Austin," said Lummis, "How delightful to make your acquaintance at last in the flesh." He surveyed her in manner that indicated he was anything but charmed by the flesh he saw before him. Eve took Mary in hand.

"Come now Mrs. Austin, you will have plenty of time to talk to Charles in the days ahead. There are people here who insist on the privilege of knowing you."

She nodded to Nora, whom Lummis was now addressing in a much warmer manner, and led Mary toward a middle-aged man in evening dress.

"Frederick, I want you to meet Mrs. Mary Austin, a celebrated author. Mrs. Austin, may I present Frederick Hodge. Mr. Hodge is an anthropologist, archaeologist and historian. He has recently left his position at the Smithsonian Institution to join the Bureau of American Ethnology. And now, if I may divulge your good news, Frederick: He has been conscripted to edit a great multivolume book of photographs on the North American Indian by the imminent Mr. Edward S. Curtis."

Mary took the gentleman's extended hand and pumped it with unmasked enthusiasm. She could scarcely believe she was standing in the presence of such an eminent scholar. Eve left them "to join heads over Indian matters" and moved on to see to other guests.

At Mary's prompting, Hodge described the project, whose purpose was to document the traditional life of the North American tribes before that way of life disappeared forever. The project was expected to comprise some 1,500 photographs to be published in 20 volumes, as well as recordings of Indian language and music.

"My goodness, such an undertaking!" exclaimed Mary.

"Yes, and it is at the behest and through the financial benevolence of Mr. J.P. Morgan that it will be done," said Hodge solemnly. Then he smiled and winked at Mary. "You see, Mrs. Austin, now that the great industrialists have plundered the country of its riches, they are in position to plow some of this treasure back into this land."

"On the subject of preservation," he continued, "I am sure you are familiar with the efforts of our host, Mr. Lummis, to preserve our California missions as well as to restore the Camino Real that once linked them like beads in a necklace. He is quite right, in my estimation, that we shall deserve the contempt of our descendants if we allow these noble structures to fall into piles of adobe rubble."

She nodded in warmly felt agreement, and they continued their animated conversation until a gong sounded announcing the hour for dining. The courtly Mr. Hodge offered Mary his arm when it was time to proceed into the dining room, which was a long, baronial hall with a fireplace at one end. "Gather around me! Who can weld iron—or friends—without me?" was the inscription carved into the mantle. Another wall held a cupboard of Mexican painted pottery, and in a corner of the room was a stack of antique rifles. Overhead, homemade chandeliers, consisting of electric lights mounted in upside-down Indian baskets fringed with buckskin, cast a soft light.

They made their way to the table, where Mary was disappointed to see that she and Hodge were to be seated quite far apart. Mary's place was between two gentlemen she did not know, but with whom she attempted shyly to make polite conversation as the first course, a traditional Spanish potato omelet, called a "tortilla," was served.

To her right was a robust gentleman of late middle age, who introduced himself as David Starr Jordan. Mary inhaled sharply. Her dinner partner was the president of Stanford University, established at Palo Alto, south of San Francisco just 15 years before. A distinguished scientist, he was, she soon learned, also a founding director of the Sierra Club, an organization created by naturalist John Muir to conserve and protect the mountains which he called "the range of light," and which she held so dear to her heart.

Once this common interest had been found, Mary found herself talking with ease about her solitary sojourns into the canyons. For his part, Jordan told her of his own jaunts around the northern California seacoast and attested to his infatuation with the small town of Carmel: "Of all the indentations on the coast of California, Mrs. Austin, the most picturesque and most charming is the little bay of Carmelo. You must see it someday."

To her left was a younger man, Henry Loewenthal, editor of the *Los Angeles Examiner*. He asked Mary how she had made her journey to El Alisal, so she ventured to describe the adventure of the trolley ride and the thrill of picking poppies in a golden field while gazing out to the ocean.

"Do you realize, Mrs. Austin, that the Big Red Car you rode up here is part of an urban revolution? Modern transportation methods make it possible to weave into one harmonious unit a much larger area of habitation and industry than ever before! Henry Huntington is building a system of transportation that will link downtown Los Angeles with new communities east, north and west of the city. As the railroad's advertisements say, Angelenos may now sleep in the woods and have an office in the city. You can board with your bicycle, Mrs. Austin, in Pasadena and, disembarking at Main Street, travel the rest of the way efficiently by power of your own locomotion to an office on Spring Street, arriving at your desk in less than an hour from when you departed. It is really quite an unprecedented manner of urban living, and through it we may not only avoid the teeming centers and crowded tenements of eastern cities, but encourage a happier and more healthful way of life."

Mary replied carefully. "I agree, Mr. Loewenthal, that living in the fresh air of the countryside is benevolent to the city's inhabitants. But must such salubrity be achieved at the expense of the destruction of another countryside of equal or greater qualities?"

Loewenthal looked at her closely. "Are you speaking, Mrs. Austin, of the Owens Valley?"

"Indeed I am, for that is my home. I left it but two days ago."

"I see. But certainly the aqueduct does not mean destruction for you and your neighbors, Mrs. Austin. I have interviewed Mr. Mulholland, the superintendent of water and power here, and he has given assurance of the city's intention to take the water below most of the valley's ranches and orchards, and to take only what is required for domestic and municipal use."

"I have read your newspaper, Mr. Loewenthal. The editor of our own *Inyo Register*, Mr. W.A. Chalfant, with whom I believe you are acquainted, receives it by post. In fact, we were quite pleased with a series of articles you published last year before the bond election investigating the connection between the aqueduct project and land purchases in the San Fernando Valley. I must say we were dismayed when those stopped and the paper suddenly joined the cause of the aqueduct and began promoting the measure."

"Yes, it was a change of policy," said Loewenthal, shifting in his seat and taking a sip of wine, "directed from, shall we say, the highest levels." He liked this homely, articulate woman, so he turned and looked frankly into her eyes.

"It was not, I assure you my dear Mrs. Austin, a decision for which I have any liking."

He turned then to respond to a question from Miss French, who was seated to his left. Mary noticed that the pretty poetess was drawing the eyes of most of the men across the table. As the meal progressed, and eating and polite conversation were supplanted by heavy drinking, ribald jokes and the singing of Spanish ballads, the girl's force of attraction seemed to increase, particularly when she stood and recited, at the urging of Lummis, one of her poems. Mary, meanwhile, found it difficult to converse as the mood became raucous and loud, and she grew silent and withdrawn.

Suddenly Eve Lummis was calling out her name, and all faces were turning toward her.

"Mrs. Austin, we would be ever so delighted if you would add a little spice to our stew of entertainments!"

Mortified, Mary pressed her napkin to her trembling lips and rose, terribly conscious of her dowdy appearance among this sparkling company. Her mind cast about for a proper subject, something from Homer or Shakespeare perhaps, for recitation. Then she changed her mind and began to speak the words of a Paiute love song, which she herself had translated from the native language.

Finished, she sat as whoops of approval rang out. They clapped and clapped, and called "More! More!" As she obliged them, Mary felt herself glowing in the warmth of approval and admiration. The rest of the evening passed very enjoyably indeed.

Late in the morning the day after, with most of the household emptied of guests save she and Miss French, Mary received a summons to the Lummis study. She smiled to herself upon entering the room, as her eyes couldn't help but search for the hole to the attic that led to the master's secret lair in the tower.

The editor stood by his desk. He was attired in a worn and faded green corduroy suit, a white shirt with lacings up the front and a red Navajo sash. Lummis removed his ever-present sombrero, revealing sweaty, matted hair, wiped his forehead with the back of his hand and motioned for Mary to sit down. She did so, thinking it was odd that such formidable romantic appetites and adventures should be attributed to such a funny, little man. Still, there was something commanding and even charming about the way his eyes and limbs danced about with unbridled energy.

"Good morning my dear child!" said Lummis in an avuncular tone, though he couldn't have been more than a decade older than Mary. "Did you enjoy our little festivities last night?! Have you been out of doors? A marvelous, marvelous day in front of us!"

Mary replied that yes, she had enjoyed herself last night and, indeed, had taken a turn about the courtyard this morning. She had even ventured out into the several acres of woodland surrounding the house, accompanied, though not through her own invitation, by two long-haired, barefoot savages: Lummis's children, the boy Amado and his older sister Turbesé.

Lummis noticed that she held two packages in her lap. "Are those new manuscripts for me?"

"Yes sir. They are additional sketches of life in the Paiute campoodie."

"Very good." He reached out his hand to accept them. "You are an accomplished and accurate recorder of native life, but you must resist the tendency to allow mysticism to seep into your writings. To record Indian spiritualism is not to surrender to it."

Mary said nothing, as she wanted no disagreement with Lummis to jeopardize the publication of her work.

"There are also two poems."

"Yes, that is the place to put such feeling!"

She felt he was about to dismiss her, so she asked timidly: "May I make a request of you sir?"

"Certainly, my dear. What may I do for you?"

"It's about the aqueduct to the Owens River, Mr. Lummis. As you are a friend and trusted advisor of the president, I wondered if you might venture a word in our favor?"

Lummis looked at her with an expression of slight irritation. He sat down at his desk, placing the wrapped manuscripts atop a pile of papers. "What would you have me say?"

"Only to beg President Roosevelt's support for the compromise offered by Congressman Smith. He has proposed an equitable agreement by which all parties, the valley and the city, would share the water according to their needs."

"I see. Well, I am sorry to inform you my dear that at present my entreaties could not but harm your cause. As you may know, I have lately taken up the case against federal Indian agent Charles Burton, who caused a number of Hopi men at Oraibi pueblo to cut their hair in an effort at forced assimilation. Male Hopi grow their hair long in back as a symbol of the falling rain for which they pray. Taking into consideration that Hopi prayers are always embodied within some material object, one can see the gravity of Burton's act.

"Furthermore," he said, warming to his topic, "the Hopi liken their hair to the silken hairs that grow from ears of corn. Therefore, it is considered improper to cut hair during the growing season, for to do so is tantamount to a request that the corn stop growing."

Lummis paused his lecture, blinked and sighed rather petulantly. "Since I have embarked on this cause, which Dorothea says I have taken too far in rhetoric and disregard for Mr. Burton and federal Indian policies, I have become persona non grata at the White House."

Mary was sorely disappointed, but felt there was nothing to be done. She thanked Lummis for his hospitality and for encouraging her work, and rose to take her leave. Her hand was on the door handle when she heard him speak.

"Mrs. Austin, I must tell you that you have talent and industry and a certain kind of knowledge, but little gift."

Mary felt she had been hit from behind with Zeus's thunderbolt, but when she turned and gaped at him, Lummis was seated casually at his desk, his expression revealing no recognition of the blow he had just delivered.

He smiled. "Good day my dear."

Outside the door, Mary pressed her back against the wall and felt her heart constrict as if she were pinned through it like a butterfly in a display box. At the sound of footsteps coming up the stairs, she thought to flee down the hall to hide in her room, but Nora May French's warm voice reached out to hold and soothe her.

"Whatever he may have said to you in there, pay it no mind Mrs. Austin. The world will be reading *The Land of Little Rain* long after his writings are forgotten."

The girl took her hand and gave it a little squeeze. Mary's returned the pressure as they walked together to Mary's room. There they sat companionably on the bed. French reached out and stroked a finger down the side of Mary's face.

"You have gorgeous hair! Such a rich color!"

Looking at Nora, fresh and fetching in a white open-neck shirt tucked into a belted wide skirt, crossed legs encased in reddish leather boots, Mary could hardly believe her to be sincere, yet clearly she was. This beautiful creature, who dazzled without effort, had offered the compliment most naturally and spontaneously. Mary smiled her thanks.

"What did you think of my *oeuvre majeur*?" asked Nora. She had given Mary a copy of *The Spanish Girl*, which Mary had stayed up much of the night reading by lamplight. She had finished it just prior to receiving her summons from Lummis. In Nora's words, which celebrated passion but were deeply skeptical of conventional married love, Mary had felt the agitation of a kindred spirit. Now a remembered stanza rang vindication in Mary's soul, still stinging from Lummis's belittlement of her person and talent:

> Swift, swift, to drink my freedom at its flood,
> I ran with flying feet and lips apart
> But love was wilder than leaping blood—
> Ah, louder than the beating of my heart

Mary reached out her hand and placed it on Nora's arm. "I think you have a talent with the potential to equal that of your George Stirling, and Jack London as well."

The eyes of the poetess sparkled, but embarrassed by such abundant praise, she changed the subject. "I'm going to move to San Francisco soon. This arroyo arts society is all well and good, but San Francisco is where the best writers and artists in the West are."

"Even after the earthquake and fire?"

"Well, things are getting better there faster than you might think. And one can always remove from the city to the coast for some relief. People have started to gather at Carmel—George and his wife have a place there."

She looked at Mary, "Will you visit me?"

Mary returned her friendly, eager gaze, feeling thrilled and hopeless at the same moment. She said, "Perhaps."

---

At midnight the air remained thick, steamy and still. Rivulets of perspiration ran beneath Hitchcock's crisp starched collar as he rode through the quiet streets in the hansom cab that had arrived, along with the president's summons, to bring him to the White House. Impetuous, immoderate man, thought Hitchcock.

In truth, he held a good opinion of his boss, Theodore Roosevelt, who at 42 was the youngest man in history to lead the nation, yet not without some misgivings. Hitchcock had been appointed to his post by Roosevelt's predecessor, President William McKinley, with the mandate to root up the culture of fraud and scandal that had plagued federal lands programs for decades. When McKinley was assassinated by an anarchist at the Pan-American Exhibit in Buffalo, New York, and Vice President Roosevelt ascended to the highest office in the land, the new president kept Hitchcock on. The secretary of the interior had been glad to stay. Like most of his countrymen, he had been swept up in Teddy's exuberant optimism, rousing oratory and prodigious energy. Yet he often worried that this man, who had been described by one newspaper as a "steam engine in trousers," possessed an ego that led him to rash acts and an appetite for power as insatiable and infectious as his zest for life.

Hitchcock put his mind and countenance under good governance and into a more favorable state as he walked through the gleaming white entrance hall of the new White House executive offices. Completed just two years before, they were situated to the west of the main building.

The removal of the offices of government to a separate location had fulfilled a dual purpose in Teddy's massive renovation campaign: It had allowed for the construction of a modern facility with all the efficiencies required by a 20th century president. The original building had then been renovated to better suit the comforts and convenience of a president with a wife and six children, to remove the Victorian decor Teddy felt detracted from the original federalist design and to expand opportunities for entertaining and hosting social and cultural events.

Roosevelt's secretary, William "Stonewall" Loeb, Jr., met Hitchcock outside of the president's office, and led him inside. Hitchcock entered a room of forest green walls with white wainscoting, furnished with dark wood furniture upholstered in the same forest green, sitting on a crimson and pastel blue oriental rug. A small painting of Abraham Lincoln hung alone above the white mantled hearth, where a fire was roaring.

There were already three others besides the president in the room. Gifford Pinchot stood near the hearth talking with Charles Walcott. "Gif," director of the newly created United States Forest Service, was the president's hunting and fishing partner. Tall and thin, with a patrician bearing and perfect composure, he was also the more mercurial Roosevelt's "right hand man" or, as some would have it, his "Richelieu." Walcott was a mild, studious paleontologist and member of the National Academy of Sciences, more comfortable with fossils than with politics. Still, as director of the US Geological Survey, he oversaw the US Reclamation Service and reported directly to Hitchcock himself. The subject of tonight's meeting, Hitchcock could now assume, was the Owens River controversy. Also in the room was Frank Flint, the senator from Southern California. Congressman Smith was conspicuously absent. An itch of concern prickled the damp skin of Hitchcock's neck.

President Roosevelt greeted him with a peremptory nod and waved them all to be seated. Hitchcock could see he was in a churlish, combative mood.

"Senator Flint came to see me this evening, laying before me the case for the Los Angeles Aqueduct. It was such a fine presentation." He nodded to the senator. "I thought we might all benefit from hearing it."

"Are we expecting Congressman Smith to arrive, Mr. President?" asked Hitchcock. "As author of the compromise proposal…"

"No, everyone who should be here is here," snapped Roosevelt. That troublesome Hitchcock, he was thinking. God knows he's a patriotic, sincere and painstaking man, but he fought Gif tooth and nail over grazing leases and commercial concessions in the national parks, and now he has a spur up his butt about Los Angeles. Roosevelt motioned for Flint to begin.

"Gentlemen, I have it on good authority that while Los Angeles city officials have tentatively accepted the Smith proposal, they did so only under the most extreme duress. It is our view, in fact, that this so-called compromise would be nothing short of a disaster for the soon-to-be great city of Los Angeles. This plan, by prohibiting the city from using aqueduct water for irrigation, allowing only domestic and municipal purposes, could mean that a homeowner hosing down his garden would be in violation of the law!"

"Come, come…" Hitchcock thought it a specious and ridiculous argument.

"Patience Mr. Secretary," Flint waved him off. "It could also mean that after domestic and municipal needs were met, surplus water would have to be dumped into the ocean. Such an act would be in violation of the Constitution of the great State of California, which forbids such inefficient usage."

"There's a simple solution to this dilemma," said Hitchcock. "Los Angeles can take only what they need and leave the rest in the Owens Valley, where it is certainly needed for reclamation."

Flint was ready with his response; he had been well prepared in a lengthy meeting with Mulholland and Matthews.

"It would be to their great peril, sir, and to that of the nation as well, if they did. After dearly paying for these water rights, if the city were to leave water unused year after year, the doctrine of appropriative rights could be invoked. Use it or lose it. Indeed, should the water not be sufficiently consumed by Los Angeles, the Owens Valley might well lay legal claim to it again. This would not be in the nation's interest. Verily, unless Los Angeles is given clear and incontestable rights to the water, the growth of our largest western city will be choked off at just this moment in time, when our other great western city lays in near-ruins, and we therefore most need it to thrive."

"Bully! Well said senator!" Roosevelt turned to Pinchot. "What do you think Gif?"

"I have no objection to letting Los Angles use the water left over after domestic and municipal requirements for irrigation."

"Charles?"

"I think there is little choice but to allow it," replied Walcott. "Certainly it would be most unseemly for a great metropolis to be forced to haggle in court against a tiny backcountry valley for every additional drop of water it needs."

"Hitchcock?"

Hitchcock saw he was outnumbered, but felt he had to try. "Allowing Los Angeles to use surplus water for irrigation is playing into the hands of a syndicate of land speculators. What can possibly be our justification for delivering up Owens River water to agriculture in the San Fernando Valley while depriving the Owens Valley farmers, who have prior and local claim, from the same benefits?"

"You have put your finger on the problem, Hitchcock," replied Roosevelt, "and I believe I have mine on the answer. Los Angeles must have full and free rights to use the water in any way it sees fit, including for irrigation, but it must be prevented from reselling water to private interests outside of the city. Senator Flint will place such a prohibition into his bill, putting us ahead of the game."

Roosevelt, pleased with himself, surveyed the nodding heads. He glowered at the only still one, on Hitchcock's erect shoulders. "So there is no confusion on this matter, I shall draft a letter to you right now Hitchcock. Loeb, take this down," he said to his secretary, silently present in the back of the room.

Hitchcock sat in silence as Roosevelt dictated the letter. It included an acknowledgment that a few settlers in the Owens Valley might be disadvantaged, but stated that the water "is a hundred or a thousand fold more important to the state and more valuable to the people as a whole if used by the city than if used by the people of Owens Valley."

When finished, Loeb handed the letter to the president, who read it, then looked cheerily about the room again. "Well, then, we are all agreed!" He held the letter out to Hitchcock, who came forward to take it. Roosevelt then snatched another letter from the pile atop his desk and offered it to Hitchcock as well. "Please be so good as to reply to this fine lady from Owens Valley and explain to her the rational and rightful basis of our decision."

Arriving home in the early hours of the morning, Hitchcock felt agitated and far from being able to surrender to sleep. A fire had been laid for the morning in his office hearth. He set and stoked it now to warm the chilly room. Pouring himself a stiff whiskey, Hitchcock settled in an armchair and glanced at the second letter handed him by the president. Addressed to President Theodore Roosevelt, Washington DC, it began "Dear Friend:" and ended "Yours Unto Eternity, Mrs. Lesta B. Parker."

Mrs. Parker described herself as an "old resident, raised in the valley." She and her husband had bought themselves a home and were "paying for it in hard labor and economy." She complained that "a man named Eaton and a few more equally low, sneaking, rich men want to get a controlling interest of the water, and they're telling folks to stay and starve or git! Where if we keep the water in the valley it won't be only three more years until the ranch will pay for itself."

Mrs. Parker asked President Roosevelt to intervene: "Is there no way to stop this thievering? As you have proven to be the president for the people and not the rich, please help the people of Owens Valley! I appeal to you in the name of the Flag, the Glorious Stars and Stripes."

Hitchcock sighed and folded the letter. The woman's confidence that her president would ride to her rescue was not only spectacularly naive but emblematic of a widely held misconception of Roosevelt. Teddy's "Square Deal" motto had promised that average citizens would get equal attention and due from the government. That, combined with Roosevelt's trust-busting activities against the big railroad tycoons, had given him an image as "friend to the little man." But Hitchcock knew Roosevelt was anything but a champion of little farmers on little patches of land. He was a Progressive, interested in efficiency, modernity and growth. In deciding for Los Angeles against the Owens Valley, the president had enacted a phrase he used often in his speeches—"the greatest good for the greatest number"—but had also shown his leaning toward a Spencerian "survival of the fittest." Teddy liked winners.

It was to be expected of a man who during the war with the Spanish in Cuba had led the charge up Kettle Hill and frequently referred to the

Battle of San Juan Hill as "the great day of my life." Hitchcock kept to himself attitudes that would have been anathema to this man. Though he had himself served with distinction against the Seminole Indians and in the occupation of Texas in the war with Mexico, Hitchcock felt the actions of his country too often veered toward arrogance and presumptive aggression. We profess to hold dear such grand egalitarian principles about the rights of man, he reflected sullenly, yet we bend at every occasion to our basest nature and allow the strong always to prevail over the weak.

He took up a pen and began writing a reply to Mrs. Parker. It was a futile and even cruel exercise, he knew, but it would be just like Teddy to press his advantage and ask to see the reply. So Hitchcock set about the detestable task of convincing a desperate woman who had pleaded for help in the name of "the Glorious Stars and Stripes" to sacrifice her family and lifelong beloved valley home on the altar of progress while rallying in good cheer round the flag.

Five days later, a bill sponsored by Senator Flint, granting Los Angeles all right-of-ways across federal lands necessary to build the aqueduct and including other provisions that put an end to the hopes of a Reclamation Service irrigation project in the Owens Valley, was passed by the congress and signed by the president.

---

*I've often thought that what distinguishes adults from children is that they know the world can change. Most of us manage to approach our maturity with an as yet unexamined core of certitude that what we are experiencing is the way the world is and will continue to be. A few of us even travel the full course of our lives without that core being shaken loose. Some less lucky souls encounter something when we are still very young that makes certainty drop out of our being. We've all seen these little adults, with their wary countenances above tender bodies. I saw them everywhere after the dam break, in all the towns in the flood path.*

*But I had learned that the world could change long before that.*

---

Mary had taken to the air. She watched the city spread out below her as she rode the funicular railway called "Angels Flight." The white tram car carrying Mary from Third and Hill Streets up to the terminus at Olive Street in the fashionable neighborhood of Bunker Hill was named "Sinai," for some inexplicable reason. The other white car, attached to the same cable and working in tandem to descend as its twin went up, was named "Olivet," which made a bit more sense.

The ride, which had cost a penny, was in Mary's opinion, suitable only for city folk who hadn't the legs for climbing. She, feeling the loss of her canyon rambles, had first ascended of her own two feet the adjacent 123 steps, then walked down again, before paying the fare and riding up.

Still it was an amusing way to spend a morning, and Mary was allowing herself some amusement. In the days since her visit to El Alisal, she had spent most of the time holed up in her hotel room laboring diligently on writing projects. She did not intend to submit this new work to Lummis, whose low opinion of her talent had been delivered with such a lack of cordiality. Perhaps, she thought, he'd been unkind because he knew she was not a woman to be trifled with, like that Nora. Though the girl had been very nice, she clearly was used to receiving the attentions of literary men, and probably not above using her allurements to secure their assistance.

Mary would indulge in no such dalliance. She would focus on the *Atlantic Monthly* instead. One of the premiere publications for the eastern intelligentsia, the magazine had featured work by Mark Twain and Henry James. It had also printed a few of her stories. Now she was determined to make a greater mark and gain the full recognition she felt was her due.

As was her habit, Mary attached so much passion to her task as to work herself into a frenzy. Yesterday, exhausted and reasonably satisfied with what she had produced, she had decided to take a short holiday before returning to Owens Valley. So today she was at Angels Flight and tomorrow she planned to visit Venice of America, a new seaside resort town built to resemble its namesake, complete with canals and singing gondoliers. She would go there on that marvelous Big Red Car for a fare of less than 50 cents.

After descending again to Hill Street, Mary walked a block to Broadway and began strolling down the street. She was becoming accustomed to the noise and pace of the city, even to succumb just a bit to its pulsing charm. With some delight, she paused her ramble to gawk at a patrol of a dozen bicycle-mounted policemen wheeling down the street.

Then she heard the newspaper hawker's cry: "Read all about it: President Roosevelt gives Owens Water to Los Angeles!"

Mary, wincing under the words, made haste to buy a copy of the *Times*, reading the cover story right there on the sidewalk, insensible to passersby jostling to get around her. The headline crowed:

**THE VICTORY OF LOS ANGELES IS COMPLETE**

The article described the passage of the Flint bill, which had been signed immediately by the president. "Owens River is ours," it boasted, "and our business now is to hustle and bring it here and make Los Angeles the garden spot of the earth and the home of a million contented people."

An accompanying article ridiculed the furor in Owens Valley:

**OWENS VALLEY PEOPLE GOING OFF**
**AS HALF-COCK**

The ill feeling in the valley was "ridiculous," said the article. The author poked fun at the hysterical reactions of country folk, but it also included some conciliatory quotes from Superintendent Mulholland saying that the flow of the Owens River was robust enough to provide plenty of water for both the valley and the city.

Mary's pressed her lips together, turned on her heel and began marching toward city hall. She thought it possible she would find Charles Lummis there, as in addition to all of his other activities, he had recently been named city librarian and was currently supervising the removal of large numbers of books from the library's inadequate quarters in city hall to the Homer Laughlin Annex building a block or so away. During dinner at El Alisal, Lummis had extolled his guests with comic tales of teetering stacks of books clogging city hall staircases and overflowing its attic and basement.

At her brisk pace, Mary arrived at the imposing Romanesque building within minutes and walked through one of the three portal arches that marked its entry. Inquiring at the information desk, she was pleased to learn her hunch had not led her astray. The clerk directed her to a stairway that would take her to an area in the basement where she might find Lummis.

He was there, in his habitual green corduroy trousers and white shirt, rolled up sleeves revealing muscular forearms. He had removed the sash and sombrero. These would certainly not have been conducive to his current activity, which appeared to consist of squeezing between tall stacks of books while writing furiously in a notebook. He was hanging halfway up a stack when she called out. He beamed, sweeping an arm around him as if to say, "Well here you see me, and is it not funny?!"

She wasn't smiling, though, so Lummis climbed down reluctantly to greet the dour Mrs. Austin.

"Have you seen the paper?" She held it out.

"Yes, I believe I did see something before descending into this Hades. I'm sorry my dear, it appears any further efforts we might make on the valley's behalf would be in vain."

"I want you to obtain an appointment for me with Superintendent Mulholland."

He stood silent, uncomprehending. Did the woman mean to shoot the man?!

"I simply want to talk to him, and see his face when he talks to me. Let him think I come to him in my capacity as a writer for *Out West*. You can arrange that can you not?"

Lummis nodded slowly. "I can try..."

"Please do so then, for this afternoon."

---

"I wish I could see Hitchcock's face when he finds out I've resigned and am now assistant chief engineer on the aqueduct—and making twice the money the service was paying me to boot!"

J.B. Lippincott raised his glass to William Mulholland, who had just hired him, and his new boss raised his, with a toast:

May the saints protect ye
An' sorrow neglect ye,
An' bad luck to the one
That doesn't respect ye!

"Here, here," agreed W.B. Matthews.

"I heard the president really rubbed Hitchcock's face in it, dictating the letter right there and then in front of him!" Lippincott chortled, then his expression became more serious. "Is that provision Roosevelt put in about not letting you sell the water outside of the city going to be a problem?"

"Not in the least," replied Mulholland, refilling the glasses. "The city has its own prohibitions, which have already forced us to make a plan for getting around that one."

He handed a replenished glass to Matthews. "Explain it to him W.B." Mulholland held out the other glass to Lippincott, then took his own and settled back in his desk chair.

"The Los Angeles city charter prohibits taking on a total municipal debt of more than 15 percent of the city's assessed value," said Matthews. "At the current valuation, the debt ceiling will be too low for us to issue the additional bonds we'll eventually need to complete the aqueduct. But suppose we expand the city and thereby increase its assessed value…"

Lippincott was quick to see: "The San Fernando Valley. You're going to annex it."

Matthews nodded. "It will have to happen sometime in the next few years. And that's another reason why it makes good sense to place the terminus of the aqueduct there. We achieve a higher valuation to pay for the water, a superb underground reservoir to store it and legitimization for using the water for agriculture in San Fernando or any other purpose we want. Three birds with one stone."

Lippincott, immensely impressed, watched Mulholland, who, with head back and feet up on his desk, was taking long, appreciative puffs on his cigar. The chief looked back at him and waggled the cigar.

"Bring the water to the city or bring the city to the water." Mulholland was well pleased. The road was now cleared for the job ahead—an engineering feat that would number among the greatest ever achieved in the history of the world!

There was a discrete knock on the door, and Mulholland barked, "Come!"

Miss Aames poked her neat silver head in and said, "It's that Mrs. Austin sir, the reporter for *Out West*. Just a brief interview. You remember, Mr. Lummis called about it earlier."

"Show her in," instructed Mulholland. "You gentlemen, take a seat outside and keep Augusta company. We have plans to make. I want to get all the survey crews out in the field within the week."

They rose and stood aside as Miss Aames showed a squat, homely woman in, then followed the secretary out. Mulholland rose, extended his hand to Mrs. Austin and asked her to please sit down.

"Well, you journalists have been banging down these doors all day. I've had to put most of them off until the morrow, but Lummis said you were to be seen today as you're leaving town soon."

"Yes, thank you for seeing me, Superintendent Mulholland, at such short notice. But I must avow my real purpose for pushing to the head of the line."

Mulholland looked at the heavy-faced woman with a thick chignon of shining chestnut hair. Her eyes locked on his with an intensity that was quite presumptuous. He was intrigued.

"I have, in truth, written a number of stories and sketches that have appeared in *Out West*, but I have come to you today not as a writer, but as a citizen of the Owens Valley."

"So that's it." He sat back, disappointed, then launched into his well-refined monologue of reassurance and obfuscation.

She said not a word to prevent him from continuing on at his leisure and remained attentive, her eyes never leaving his face. Mulholland grew weary with it, wanting to get on with the work to be done with his colleagues. He finished up in the usual way:

"So you see, Mrs. Austin, it is absurd to think that Los Angeles will ever grow to the extent that we should need all the water the Owens River supplies. Even in years of drought, there will be plenty of water for the city and the valley."

Mary Austin was thinking that from the moment this man had seen the Owens River, the outcome had been written in stone. He was possessed, she could see, of a formidable will, fueled by absolute belief in the rightness of his purpose. The polar opposite of Wallace. Here was a man to be reckoned with, a man who knew how to bend the world to his liking, and, as she had been with the cattle baron Rickey, she was attracted by his strength. She also hated him for the insulting way he churned out flimsy

assurances, then sat back with that self-satisfied smirk expecting her to
lap them up like cream.

Her eyes were fixed like those of a raptor and her voice bright, hard
and calm as she pronounced her truth: "It is not absurd, Mr. Mulholland,
it is inevitable. You will grow and grow and take more and more water.
You will never stop until you own the entire river and all of the land.
My beautiful valley will be utter desolation."

Mulholland sat still, confounded as to what to say, how to deflect
or even soften the peal of her words that now reverberated in the silence.
He was struck by a realization of her person, of the intelligence behind her
furious, unblinking gaze. He had underestimated her, fooled by her
dowdy, unattractive appearance. But now he was taken by something like
admiration as the woman rose and, without extending her hand, spoke the
words "Good day Mr. Mulholland!" like a pronouncement.

He hastened to open the door and watched, mouth agape, as
she marched out of the outer office and into the hall. Matthews and
Lippincott were perched on Aames's desk. While the secretary's countenance was as proper as ever, they were sniggering. He decided to put them
in their place.

"By God, that woman is the only one who has brains enough to see
where this is going."

The president of the United States says it's all right for a city somewhere
she doesn't even know to take the water in the river she's swum in just
about every day this summer with Juan, Emma and Rosie. Janey thought
about what the grownups were saying, but it just didn't make sense to her.
How could they take the river someplace else?

Pa explained that the river would still be here, but they would take
some of its water. Would she still be able to go swimming? Janey asked.
Of course, he said, they aren't going to take all of the water, just the extra.
How much of it is extra? Janey asked. Pa didn't know, said it depended on
how much snow fell in the mountains each winter.

"We'll be sharing the water with Los Angeles," he explained, "like
all the ditch associations in the valley share the water now. In wet years,
there's plenty to spare for everyone, and in dry years we all have to be good
neighbors and take just what we need. I expect that Los Angeles will be a

good neighbor, and everything will be just fine. At least it's decided and we can finally stop all this political wrangling and get back to normal life."

Valley folk did just that. There was incredulity at the president's decision, and disappointment and bitterness for the lost fight, but these were submerged beneath the native pragmatism and optimism that swelled forth again. The Wattersons and other members of the ditch associations were preparing to enter into discussions, at the invitation of Los Angeles City Attorney W.B. Matthews, to guarantee each ditch would have its required quantity of water. Chalfant was printing articles about the numbers of working men that would be hired to build the aqueduct. Alice Bow said that if President Roosevelt believed it was the right decision, it probably was. Chris Bow said those working crews were going to need to eat, and someone was going to get rich supplying them.

Soon Janey grew dreadfully tired of hearing them talk about it, at home, in the newspaper office, in the general store. She was bored. She'd been bored a lot over the past few weeks, with Mary away in that city that was going to take the water. Janey didn't understand why Mary had gone there to that bad city. But now Mary had come back, Chalfant had said so, and Janey was headed toward the Austin's with a sack of fresh corn ears, which she had just pulled away from their crackling, tasseled stalks in the Bow field.

At the little brown house, Janey saw traveling trunks, a carpetbag and several pasteboard boxes huddled on the front stoop. Maybe Mary was still unpacking from her trip. Janey went round back to the kitchen door as usual. It was open, so she poked her head inside, where she saw Ruth sitting on the floor, licking the frosting from the large wedge of chocolate cake she held in her hands. When the girl saw Janey, she cooed and held out the lump of cake to her visitor.

"Hello, hello," sang Janey. "No, that's yours. You eat it. I'll get my own." Ruth complied, and Janey rose, deposited her sack on the table and located the cake on the flour-dusted sideboard, next to the sticky bowls and spoons with which Mary had brought forth this miracle. She cut a generous slice, took it in both hands and maneuvered it into her mouth. Ummmm, there was a dark, heady charge of chocolate and a buttery, cinnamony taste too. Janey looked up appreciatively to where she heard someone, Mary, she guessed, moving about on the second floor landing. She joined Ruth on the floor to await her.

When Mary appeared, Janey saw she was indeed still unpacking from her journey, since she was yet wearing a traveling costume, including hat and gloves, and carrying a satchel in each hand.

"Welcome back Mrs. Austin!" called Janey, wondering if Mary would be of a temper to walk up into the hills today. Probably not, she thought, as Mary scowled at her and, saying nothing, proceeded down the hall to the front door, which she opened and shut again. She reappeared in the hallway with her hands empty, and came into the kitchen.

"Hello Janey, what are you doing here?"

"I heard you were returned. Brought you some fresh corn ma'am." She stood and pointed to the sack. Mary looked at her with such a sad expression, Janey thought she must not like corn. Maybe she should have brought blackberries.

"I'm not back, Janey. I'm just here to pack up. Ruth and I will be leaving soon."

"Where are you going?" Janey whined at the thought of more weeks of boredom.

"We're going away, far away. I am going to live in Carmel, at the seaside. And Ruth is going to live at a school in Santa Clara."

"When are you coming back?"

"We are not coming back. We are never coming back."

Janey's eyes widened and she felt a glob of cake and frosting in her throat. A hard swallow to get it down brought tears to her eyes. She looked at Ruth, still happily chewing her cake.

"Why?"

"Because there's nothing here to stay for anymore," stated Mary.

"Nothing?" echoed Janey. What could Mary mean? The valley, the mountains, the animals, the flowers, the birds, the little brown house and the field next door, they were all still here. Even the river was still here.

Mary looked at her young companion of so many walks, and her countenance softened. "You're too young now, Janey, but remember my advice: As soon as you're old enough, leave this valley. Do not waste your life here."

"Leave? Me?" Janey was fighting back tears of confusion. But then she thought: Maybe Mary was just talking oddly again. Maybe she was having one of her strange spells and would be in a better mood tomorrow. Janey thought she should take her leave and began moving toward the door. But she was so confused, she couldn't help but turn back to ask timidly: "But what about Mr. Austin? Is he leaving too?"

"I haven't the slightest notion. They're shutting the federal lands office down because of the aqueduct, so he's out of a job again. He talks about a possible opportunity with a potash and chemical company in Death Valley. What does it matter, he will fail at that too."

The girl gasped, her open mouth quivering, eyes uncomprehending. She felt a quiver of apprehension and looked down at Ruth.

"Why does she have to live at a school? You aren't going to leave her alone there are you?"

"That's none of your business little miss. Now I think it's time you went home."

Janey reached out a hand to stroke Ruth's silky hair, and the other girl smiled up at her. Janey knelt and hugged her, pressing chocolate crumbs and squirming limbs against her chest.

"Bye, bye Ruth. Be a good girl at school. Be sure to do everything the teacher tells you and all your lessons so you get top marks on your report card." She wasn't sure what kind of school would give Ruth top marks. She hadn't ever thought about Ruth going to school.

Janey rose, turned again to the door, mumbled goodbye to Mary, then descended slowly down the steps to the yard. She didn't know that Mary watched her make her way across the yard and down the lane, trying to commit to memory the thick wheat-colored braid bouncing between narrow shoulders, the straight back in faded brown overalls and red shirt, the long, skinny legs that quickly took the girl beyond a line of oaks, out of Mary's sight.

When Janey next returned to the little brown house it was empty.

*The Ditch*

Courtesy Los Angeles Public Library Photo Collection

## Chapter 9

The metal bit chattered and slid until it found a small depression in the rock to bite into. Erratic sideways motion resolved into a forward tug, which reverberated up the man's arms and across his back. He leaned into his forward leg, teeth grinding, as if they, and not the air hammer drill, were assaulting the wall of three-billion-year-old granite and basalt. The cut, driven by over 1500 blows per second from the bit of the electric drill, was continually washed clear by a jet of water delivered through the drill stem, splattering the man with a fine spray of sticky clay. He had to cut in more than five feet before he would stop, take a quick breather and start the next hole.

Denny Fisher felt the pounding through every inch of his muscular 5-foot, 4-inch frame. The task was punishing, but would have been impossible if he'd had to hold the steel gun, which weighed nearly 150 lbs. The Leyner air drill, however, was mounted in a cradle attached to a horizontal steel bar at the front of a drilling carriage, a flatbed rail car that moved along tracks on the tunnel floor as the point of assault advanced in increments. The tunnel bar supported the drill's weight and also helped position it to make each in the series of cuts required to mount the explosives that would rip out the next section of rock.

He glanced to his right as he felt the drill at the other end of the tunnel bar go quiet. Crew boss Jed Brecken had already finished his first cut hole and was shouting at Fisher to adjust his angle. "Hey Fishboy, cut in more!" Brecken voice was muffled by the din of Fisher's drill, but his hand signals conveyed to the other man the needed angle adjustment.

Two precisely placed pairs of "cut holes" were critical to efficient blasting. They were drilled about four feet apart, in a square, and at an angle so that their ends nearly met at a common center. Next would come a group of "black holes" around the side and top of the cut hole square, toward the outside walls of the tunnel. Last, four "lifters" would be drilled at equal intervals at the bottom of the tunnel. Fuses would be set so that these holes fired in the same sequence: first the cut holes, to blow a wedge out from the center of the wall; then the black holes, to break the rest of the rock face down to the center cut; and last the lifters, to throw the rock debris, "muck," as the crews called it, back into the tunnel, away from the newly cleaved rock surface.

Fisher corrected his angle and completed the cut, then leaned back against the carriage rail, drew a deep breath and grinned across at his crew boss, who was doing the same. Breathing the air in the tunnel wasn't too bad; big electric air blowers were brought in after each blast to clear the smoke. Still, the two men were covered in soot that had stuck to their clay-misted skin, the whites of their eyes gleaming in stark contrast. Fisher knew he looked the more ridiculous, with his small frame, matted mop of hair and protruding ears.

A minute later, Brecken was back at work on his second cut hole, and Fisher followed his lead. For the first couple of years they had been hacking at "the beast," as they characterized the solid granite core of the mountain range. They had drilled, loaded and fired a single round of holes during each eight-hour period. In recent months, they'd run three eight-hour shifts around the clock. But now each crew was often doing twice the work, in overlapping shifts extending as long as 12 hours.

When all holes were drilled and charges set, the two men rode the carriage away from the wall, and Brecken knelt on the tunnel floor to activate the detonator. "Let's light up our little Christmas tree," he said, then plunged the handle. With each of the three pops of explosion, Brecken nodded his head and gestured his hands like a symphony conductor. Black smoke billowed toward them. Brecken and Fisher turned their backs on it as two other crew members, Chess Dorman and Big Joey, the towering 240-lb. tunneler they called "beast slayer," brought the big blowers forward and started them up. The smoke began to disperse. Dorman, Big Joey, Powderface Kelly, Goose and a half dozen other "muckers" took up tools and headed deeper into the tunnel. Brecken and Fisher followed them to inspect how much they had wounded the beast this time.

"Not too shabby" was Brecken's assessment. The well-set blast had thrown the rock debris into oddly neat piles, which the muckers began shoveling into a couple of boxcars hooked to a small electric locomotive. The crew boss lounged against the tunnel wall, rolled and lit a cigarette, offered his tobacco pouch to Fisher.

"Get the next round just right, Fishboy, and we might just bust another record. Leave those yodelers in our dust!" the crew boss boasted, referring to a Swiss team at work on the Lichtberg Tunnel through the Alps. Brecken's team had repeatedly broken world records for hard-rock tunneling, including besting the US Bureau of Reclamation's top speed at the Gunnison Tunnel in Colorado. The Gunnison, 5.8 miles in length, had been inaugurated a few years before as "the longest irrigation tunnel in the world." This one, the Elizabeth Tunnel, was a bit shorter, at about 5 miles, but arguably a more difficult prospect. It was being bored through granite 250 feet below Elizabeth Mountain, which embraced at its base a small water-filled crater called Elizabeth Lake. When completed, it would enable the Los Angeles Aqueduct to traverse the Sierra Madre, whose 6,000-foot peaks posed the greatest obstacle to the project.

"Pshaw," responded Fisher, "I just wanna feel them bonus greenbacks in my pocket." His eyes gleamed. "Saw a little lady in Mojave I'm liken to spend 'em on."

Brecken regarded Fisher quizzically. "I know you've got a day off comin Fishboy, but don't go and drown yourself in a tank of whiskey will ya?" The smaller man's nickname came not only from his diminutive frame and boyish crop of hair, but his prodigious capacity for drink.

In Brecken's view, Chief Engineer Mulholland's idea of paying tunneling crews a bonus for every foot dug beyond their day's quota had been pure genius. The result was a well-motivated crew that acted as a solid unit and had no tolerance for loafers. But he wished his men would keep more of their hard-earned money instead of drinking, gambling and whoring it away in Mojave, the nearest town, if you could call it that. He'd heard it remarked, and it seemed to be true, that half the gamblers in the West had moved to Mojave to relieve the workers of their pay checks.

Still, the important thing was that the bonus system had proved to be a powerful incentive. In driving tunnels, Brecken well knew, the biggest obstacle to speed was getting rid of the rock debris from the blasts. Elizabeth Tunnel was too narrow for the steam-powered shovels in use elsewhere on the aqueduct, and the mucking machine they'd tried in the beginning was forever breaking down. Then Mulholland had introduced the bonus system and extended it not only to the blasters but to the muckers as well. Traditionally the lowest paid men on tunneling crews, muckers were particularly susceptible to the lure of "40 cents more per extra foot."

"Most important thing is to beat Aston." Brecken's eyes glittered as he made a stabbing motion in the air with his cigarette. While Brecken's crew was working from Antelope Valley on the north side of the Sierra Madre southward, another crew had started from San Francisquito Canyon in the south and was working northward. That crew, led by W.C. Aston, had also broken its share of speed records. Mulholland had pitted the two teams against each other: Whichever broke through to the other team's side first would win a large additional bonus—and the glory.

Brecken took the competition against Aston, a university educated field engineer in his 40s, personally. At 24, the young crew chief had only two years of engineering training, but was already more experienced, having led men in mine construction projects across Colorado, New Mexico and Wyoming. He'd been hand-picked by Mulholland for what the chief considered to be the toughest job on the aqueduct. While Aston's crew was tearing through softer rock of banded granite, Brecken and his boys were encountering mostly solid granite, and the area where they were drilling was prone to cave-ins and flooding as they hit large pockets of water-saturated sand and gravel. To counter these challenges, they'd been forced to spend time timbering the sides of the tunnel. In places, they'd even driven overlapping steel rails ahead of the drilling line. And with all that, they were still neck in neck with the southern crew.

"Let's go," said Brecken, moving toward the drilling carriage. Just as he leapt up onto the flatbed, there came a thunderous swoosh in the tunnel behind them. Turning toward it, he saw a massive wall of water descending upon them.

"Cave in!" yelled Brecken, diving from the flatbed for one of the remaining piles of rock debris. Perched on top of it, he held on fiercely as water laden with granite and debris ripped by him, knocking him free but for a single hand hold. He pulled himself back toward the rock pile and scrambled atop again as the water slammed against the blasting wall and sloshed back, nearly knocking him off again. He spotted Goose flailing in the turbulence and reached out, grabbing the man by the collar and pulling him to safety.

"Boss, I got Fishboy and Dorman! Let's get outta here!" Big Joey was standing neck deep in water, one hand each grasping a struggling mate. Watching Joey plow through the drink, dragging his cargo toward the tunnel entrance, Brecken saw that the water level was already receding, now chest-high on the huge miner.

"Come on, we can walk out now!" Brecken shouted to Goose. "Do it now before any more wall comes down!" He pushed tall, skinny Goose ahead of him, looking around for the other men. Powderface Kelly was clinging to a small outcropping on the opposite wall. He'd found a good handhold, though he was shaking violently.

Brecken pushed through the swirling water to reach him. He grinned at the terrified man, "Hey Kelly, can't ya hear it? The mess bell is ringing! Let's go get some grub!"

It was a pitiful joke, but enough to do the trick. Kelly extended a boot, feeling for the tunnel floor. When he found it, he let go his grip, grabbed Brecken's extended arm and shouted back, "I don't know which is worse, bein buried alive in here or eatin that worm-infested grub!"

They made their way to the entrance, emerging dripping, faces and arms scratched bloody. Goose was retching water, but no one was injured. Most had lost their hats. Dorman's trousers, which had been tucked into knee-high boots, were filled with muck, weighing down his suspenders. He stripped them off. Brecken went over to his rucksack, stashed by a large boulder near the entrance and pulled out a flask of whiskey, passing it around to his men.

"Go on, get yourselves cleaned up and go on to the mess tent. You don't want to miss lunch," he joked, winking at Kelly.

"Ain't ya comin?" asked Fisher.

"Going back in" was the reply. "Wanna set the next round."

"But you'll be drillin knee-deep in water!"

"Yeah!"

"You're a crazy bastard to be sure!" Fisher was shaking his head, but he picked up his helmet and followed Brecken, smiling in spite of himself.

The guy was insane, but he was a hell of a boss: determined, fearless and fair. He asked a lot from you, but always drove himself longer and harder, seeming to possess limitless energy. Hell, Brecken was almost as much of a legend on the aqueduct as Mulholland! Once when a cave-in had cost the crew days, he had worked five straight shifts, eating meals up to his waist in mud and exiting the tunnel for only brief periods, to take a crap or grab some shut-eye.

Fisher hadn't actually been here to witness that feat, but he'd read about it, in a dime novel loaned by a mate when they were hammering rails on the Santa Fe railroad. The chance to meet Brecken, even more than the lure of steady work, was why he'd signed up on the aqueduct. And here he was, side by side with the guy and, as a member of a tunnel crew, held in higher esteem at the camp than men who dug the open canals out in the desert.

Maybe they'll write a book about me, Fisher thought. The cave-in had provided him with his own tale of daring-do, which in any case ought to be good for a few free drinks and a nice, long lay with a certain lady once he finally got to Mojave.

"A strange sort of graveyard," mused Chris Bow, as his chauffeured limousine sped past the bleached skeleton of a mule. It was surrounded, as if on some festive funereal dais, by vibrant purple, white and yellow blossoms. Early spring rains had produced a carpet of verbena and primrose across wide swaths of the desert.

Skeletons of man, beast and wagon were common sights as one traversed the vast expanse. For Chris Bow, racing to and fro between the aqueduct's 40 work camps, they prompted little of the sense of mystery and mortality stirred in so many other crossers' hearts. Except for the new dead beasts: Here and there the limo passed huge metal carcasses, slumped and desolate, their caterpillar-like legs half-buried in the sand.

In the early days of construction, Mulholland had purchased 28 steam-powered tractors from a manufacturing company in Northern California. The chief said these machines with tracks looped around their wheels looked like caterpillars. They'd be just the thing for hauling heavy equipment for the aqueduct. At the time, Chris had been thrilled to know he was part of such a modern, forward-thinking endeavor.

But the tractors, which had performed well in the peaty farmlands of the Sacramento River Delta, were unsuited to the desert, where blowing sand clogged their clanking gears, and operators, unfamiliar with the new machines, wore them into the ground. They constantly needed fixing, and the bills for repair, Chris heard, had amounted to as much again as the original cost of the tractors.

As a businessman, Chris realized this was unsustainable, but the solution Mulholland had come up with was to replace the machines with 1,500 mules! This seemed to Chris like a huge step backward. More than 50 of the damned beasts had to be rigged together to haul a single section of the immense steel pipes needed in key parts of the aqueduct. To drive them, Mulholland had hired the most experienced drivers, "muleskinners," in western vernacular, he could find. Preeminent among this weathered, crusty aristocracy was the notorious "Whistling Dick," who had made his reputation in Death Valley hauling massive loads of borax, a naturally occurring mineral from the West's evaporated seasonal lakes, much in demand from eastern manufacturers of detergents and other products.

"It's the 20th century damn it!" fumed Chris. But the truth was, he'd lately been feeling the desert overtaking him as well. Three years in, and

Chris was losing some of the enthusiasm and optimism that had propelled him to take on the challenge of feeding the aqueduct's 5,000-man workforce. At the start, he'd been absolutely confident that it was just a matter of breaking down the requirements, developing a rational plan to meet them and implementing modern equipment and methods.

Initially, this approach had worked. He and his men had quickly set up cooking operations at every work camp and even built slaughterhouses at Mojave to supply them with fresh meat. There was nowhere else in the world, Chris had boasted, where a working man could start and end his shift with a bounty of thick sirloin steak and eggs, roast beef, fricasseed veal, succulent meat pies, cream of tomato soup, corn fritters, spaghetti, fried potatoes, apricot pie, cakes and the like—dining on freshly starched linen tablecloths—all for the price of 25 cents a meal. The *Los Angeles Times* had run a feature article on the youthful entrepreneur, pronouncing the fare he supplied "fit for a king of the realm." Chris's operations were efficient, clean, modern and, at first, extremely profitable.

Soon, however, the desert conditions had begun taking their toll, finding every vulnerable chink in his machinery, as they had with the tractors. It had proved impossible to keep meat, vegetables and dairy products cold in the relentless heat that beat down on the land from June through November. Though Chris employed a fleet of automobiles rather than wagons to transport the food as quickly as possible, it was often spoiled and infested with insects by the time it arrived at the camps farthest away from Mojave. Gradually, he'd been forced to pare down the menu for some camps and seasons to the hardiest staples like beans, biscuits and hot cakes.

Workers were grumbling, but the worst part was that the operation was losing money, even with the cutbacks. In his original bid, Chris hadn't thought to include a margin for inflation. Now, with the price of flour and other foodstuffs rising, he was in trouble. So today he was on his way to the Jawbone Division Headquarters to see Assistant Chief Engineer J.B. Lippincott to get approval for increasing the meal charge by a nickel.

Chris winced as he thought how much his Pa would disapprove of delivering less value for more money. Hell, Pa never had to manage an operation the size of this one, he reassured himself. Pa was still running just a couple of wagons, manned by hired hands now, to sell ranch produce at Owens Valley towns and nearby mining camps. That's easy, thought Chris. This is so much bigger, and in something this big, there's always gonna be some problems. He tried to talk confidence into himself, but his gut seized as he saw the land rising up ahead, and the camp, nestled among boulders and fir trees, begin to take shape. It was a makeshift village of tents and low-roofed wooden structures, built to be disassembled and moved.

"This is it, today, right now," Chris steeled himself for the fight. "I've got to win the increase or I fail. I'm not going to fail!"

# Chapter 10

J.B. Lippincott stabbed at line after line of calculations, checking his numbers, then made a final jab with his pencil at the quotient, 0.962, and marked it with two thick lines of lead. "We're saving nearly a buck a barrel!" he announced to himself.

"Did you want something Mr. Lippincott?" His aid, Davey Plough, stuck his head in through the half-open door.

"No, nothing. Err…yes, where is Mulholland? I want to get this report to him tonight!"

"I'll find out sir," responded Plough, retracting his head back into the outer office and, obeying a curt gesture from Lippincott, closing the door. The outer room, bustling with engineers and clerks, was always noisy.

Lippincott returned to his figures. They were saving almost a dollar a barrel in concrete, and the aqueduct, he estimated, would require more than a million barrels of the stuff to line its tunnels and canals. "Whew-ew," he let out a whistle. By the end of this, I'll have saved the city nearly a million bucks! That should be worth a hefty completion bonus.

It had been his idea to save money on concrete by making it from a mixture of ordinary cement and cement they made themselves from naturally occurring local deposits of tufa, a volcanic ash with a pumice-like texture. Like the weird limestone tufa towers protruding from Mono Lake that had so fascinated him during the Yosemite camping trip years ago with Eaton and Clausen, the volcanic tufa deposits near the aqueduct's charted course were evidence of the young, restless nature of the eastern

Sierra region. That trip had also been the first time he'd glimpsed the Owens River.

The day he had seen the Owens River had been a red-letter one for him and for the city of Los Angeles, Lippincott reflected. If he'd never gotten involved in the aqueduct project, it would probably be running behind schedule and budget by now. Adding tufa cement to the concrete mixture not only reduced the amount of cement that had to be purchased from outside suppliers, it also improved the quality of construction. While concrete made in this way didn't harden as rapidly as the normal mixture, and thus had to be kept in tension between forms longer, it continued to harden and gain strength long after the normal mixture had reached its zenith. Within days, Lippincott's tests showed, the tufa concrete surpassed the normal mixture in tensile strength. A slab that could support 20 lbs. three days after being laid down would support 155 lbs. in three months, and 300 lbs. in six months. And the higher the percentage of tufa in the mixture, the stronger and more impervious to water the concrete became.

He, J.B. Lippincott, had found a way to save the city a million dollars and make a building material equal to that used by the Romans in construction that had endured for a thousand years. He planned to publish his findings in the *Journal of the American Society of Civil Engineers*, to make sure he received proper credit. The other invaluable contribution he'd made to the aqueduct was often credited to Mulholland. But it had been he, and not the chief, who had come up with the idea of offering tunnel crews bonuses for pushing beyond their daily quotas. The incentive had lit a fire under the men and made all the difference at the Elizabeth Tunnel. Initially, progress on this critical linchpin had lagged expectations, averaging only five feet per day, but with the implementation of the bonus system, the average had soared to more than twice that.

Lippincott gazed out the window at the steep slope, where they were in the process of laying 8,000 feet of welded steel pipe. In the other direction, an empty expanse of flatland opened up below the camp, with a thread of road running across it to the east. That's been the way of it, he thought. Mulholland had achieved the status of a legend, extolled in the papers as an engineering genius. But more often than not, when confronted by a building problem, Mulholland would simply squat down in the sand and sketch a solution—leaving it to Lippincott to figure out how to implement it!

A cloud of dust was being kicked up far out on the eastern end of the road. Lippincott's frown deepened. There was only one man who arrived with that calling card: Chris Bow was on his way, barreling across the desert in his huge black limo, to needle the city out of more money.

Despite his ostentatious transportation, Bow was, in Lippincott's estimation, a nice enough young man. But a kid of not even 25 years of age was just too inexperienced to have charge of such a big operation— this was a decision of Mulholland's he judged to be a serious mistake. A job this size should be in the hands of a professional, which it had been at first. Mulholland had originally hired Joe Delavan, youngest son of the founder of the Delavan clothing store chain, who had won acclaim for himself by managing relief efforts following the San Francisco earthquake. The Bow kid, son of a small-time Owens Valley rancher, had somehow gotten Delavan to hire him as a sort of right-hand man, presumably for his knowledge of the region.

But when just a month before construction was to start, Delavan had fallen ill, Mulholland ought to have canceled the contract and hired another company. Instead he had allowed himself to be convinced by Bow's enthusiasm and youthful energy: "Delavan taught me everything I need to know. I promise you, sir, I can do it. I won't let you down!" In response to Lippincott's protestations, Mulholland had replied, "A young man needs his chance. Hell, if no one had seen fit to give me mine, I'd still be clearing ditches!" And that had been the end of it.

The kid, even Lippincott had to admit, had come out of the gate fast and in good form. Anxious to prove worthy, he had knocked himself out, working round the clock seemingly, to establish cook camps and food transportation systems. At first the grub had been good and plentiful, but over the months, it began to deteriorate. Lippincott had experienced the downhill slide personally, as all construction managers, including him and even the chief, ate in the same food lines as the rank-and-file workers—a Mulholland decision he did agree with. The men could complain, but they couldn't say they were being asked to put up with anything their leaders weren't putting up with too.

Lippincott went back to his work, figuring he had just enough time to wrap up the report before Bow arrived. And, indeed, he was putting the completed document aside when Davey Plough knocked on the door and stuck his head in.

"Mr. Bow is here sir."

"Send him in." Lippincott rose and took two long-legged strides to greet his visitor at the door.

"Nice to see you Chris." He gestured to the window. "In fact, I've been seein ya for the past five miles. That big Mitchell limo of yours sure kicks up a lotta dust!"

Chris Bow returned Lippincott's handshake in the same warm manner it had been offered, but bristled slightly at the jab. "Can't do nothin about the state of the roads can I? And I need a fast car to cover all the miles between camps."

Lippincott thought the young man seemed less self-assured and more testy than in the past. He motioned him to a chair and leaned against the front of his desk. It was a casual, friendly pose, with arms and legs crossed, but it positioned him several heads above his seated guest.

"I gotta tell ya Chris, barreling around in that fancy car with a chauffeur is one of the reasons the men are so prickly. It don't sit well with a fella who's just found a maggot in his oatmeal."

"I told you before, we're implementing new packaging methods for food transport, which should improve freshness. And I'm not the only one being driven around in a big car. Mulholland has a car and driver too."

"Yeah, but it's a Stanley Steamer, not a limousine, and when he gets out of it, it's usually to get down in the dirt with the crews. Where they go, he goes. What they eat, he eats. Hell, you don't even eat your own food!"

"That's not true. I do eat it, I just don't have time to do it sitting at a mess hall table chewing the fat for an hour with the crews."

"Might be time well spent."

Chris drew a breath and gathered his courage. He looked his inter-rogator straight in the eyes. "Look J.B., I didn't come here to discuss my eating habits or transportation arrangements. I submitted a proposal for an increase in the per-meal fee going on three weeks now. Do you have an answer for me?"

Lippincott uncrossed his arms and legs, then walked slowly around his desk, seating himself behind it. He reached into a drawer and pretended to look through the files, withdrew a random sheet of paper, pretended to consult it and returned it to its folder. Then he leaned back in his chair, stroked his handlebar mustache, regarding Bow for a long minute. Finally he said, "Mulholland approved it."

Relief pumped through Chris's veins. He was surprised; the assistant chief engineer's attitude had seemed to bode ill. But here it was, approved. That worry, at least, fading.

He stood up and extended his hand to the unsmiling Lippincott. "Thank you J.B. Mulholland won't be sorry, and neither will you. That's all I need to see this project through."

Lippincott accepted the hand without rising fully from his chair. "I hope so. Use it wisely, and not just to balance your books. If the men don't see some improvement in their grub soon, there's gonna be trouble."

"I understand, I'll fix it," Chris responded sincerely. "I'm off to Mojave right now, where I'm making improvements at the slaughterhouse, and I'll be going back there every couple a weeks to check on progress." He rolled his eyes, pretending annoyance. "Won't be long before I'll be collecting my little sister at the train depot. She's coming for a visit during her spring holiday from school."

"You're lettin your sister come to Mojave?!" exclaimed Lippincott, who had expressly denied his wife and children the opportunity to visit him at that pustule of industry and infamy, which was, sadly, the closest thing to a town within reach of many of the aqueduct work camps.

"She'll be all right, she'll be fine," Bow reassured him. "She's staying at the Harvey House, and you know how careful they watch over their waitresses—curfews and rules like as if they were schoolmarms!"

*It was my first adventure since Mary left.*

It had been eight years since I'd walked away from the little brown house, coming home to Ma in a blur of teary confusion. She'd been shocked to hear Mary was fixing to just up and leave her husband like that, wondering if I'd rightly understood Mrs. Austin's intention. But soon the facts of the matter were evident for all to see in the empty house, the desperate but resigned sorrow of Mr. Austin and, soon, his flight from us as well. The scandal was a long-lasting feast for the gluttonous gossips of the valley.

Ma didn't hold to chewing over the misfortunes of others. And, I think, her sympathy for that family torn asunder was balanced by a sense of relief for her own. "Just as well," she said, as it was high time I stopped gallivanting around, getting strange notions into my head, and started learning to be a young lady.

I tried best I could, spending more time helping Ma with chores. She knew a lot, just like Mary, and I started asking her more questions. But Ma wasn't inclined to talk about all the things she saw or thought about; she was content to go about her work and, I think, to have me as a companion.

It wasn't as if I were trapped at the ranch. I still spent some afternoons with my friends—Juan helped me improve my riding. And whenever Pa or Chris was heading up to Bishop, or my aunt invited me to stay a spell, I spent time helping Mr. Chalfant at the Register office. But I missed the heady sense of freedom and anticipation of discovery I'd felt on those jaunts up the canyon trails with Mary, and I was shy of going to the Paiute campoodie on my own.

Mary left, then Chris left. He got hired on by the company that was to provide food for the aqueduct workers. Though not so abrupt, his was a strange leaving too. My Pa's mouth went thin when Chris told us about the job, but he patted his son on the back. Later when I asked him if he was sad, he owned that he was, but that since he'd always wished his own father had been more encouraging of his dreams, he aimed to do better by Chris. My Ma was quiet for days, but she said she was proud of him.

I don't recall how I reacted to the news Chris was leaving, but I do recall how unsettled and lonely I was when he was no longer in the room next to mine, no longer clomping down the stairs every morning, no longer calling me out to the yard to help with the wagon. It's a very odd feeling, being the sole child left at home with your parents. Even though Chris was quite a bit older than me, we'd been a twosome in our own way. We were two and our parents were two, and now it was just me with them. I felt lonely when we sat down to eat, and I felt lonely when, tramping across a field, I'd spot a shadow gliding on the ground ahead and look up to see the flying fish clouds had returned. There was no one to race the fish with anymore, and, besides, it wasn't the kind of thing a young lady ought do.

At least I knew where my brother was, and he'd made the occasional visit home. There'd been no word from Mary, not about where she'd gone nor about how Ruth was faring at the school.

I knew where my brother was, and now he had finally invited me to make a visit. I had wrangled this invitation from him after learning that a school friend had secured a job at the Harvey House in Mojave, where Chris's operations were headquartered. I prepared for that visit, my first journey by train, for weeks, pleading with Ma to make me a new dress, even convincing Mr. Chalfant to let me try writing an article about the aqueduct. I bored Rosie and Emma with my imaginings, as I could think and talk of nothing else, and the night before I couldn't sleep at all.

Suddenly, the weeks of anticipation were over. Finally, Ma and Pa were taking me in the buckboard to the new depot platform for the Southern Pacific Railroad at Owenyo in the south valley. We were standing together watching the great steam engine approach, feeling it rumble through our feet, hugging goodbye in a cloud of steam.

Then I was on the train, feeling the car clunk and bump forward, waving to the pair of parents left behind on the platform, on my way to rejoin my other half. The music of the train—the clunking now replaced by a constant sound like wagon wheels, but so much faster and louder—excited my anticipation, but also lulled me like a cup of chamomile tea so that I was able to sit still, watching out the window as familiar sights were succeeded by landscapes I'd never before seen, waiting to arrive at a place I'd tried to imagine but really couldn't.

I realized how inadequate my imaginings had been the instant I stepped down from the train, aided by a gentleman who carried my bags, into the blast of sun and sound that was Mojave depot. The loud chugging of the train had been as a lullaby compared to the clanging, screaming contest being waged by what must have been about a dozen different pianos *and scratchy phonograph records. As we stood there, getting our bearings amidst the swarm of bodies on the platform, the cacophony was punctuated by eruptions of tinny, mirthless female laughter and harsh, angry male shouting—I thought I even heard gunshots. Faintly there came the familiar refrain, curling like a waft of smoke through the thick, hot, noisy air: "Hazy, Haaazy, here…over here!"*

As Chris Bow stood waiting for the arrival of the train from Owenyo, he scarcely heard the din and dither coming from behind him. He'd become well accustomed to the noise, dust and confusion of Mojave. A block to the east of the station, the town's Main Street was bisected by side streets full of enterprises of a dubious nature: saloons, dance halls, whorehouses and gambling parlors. Main Street itself was as respectable as could be under the circumstances of a boom town that had recently swelled to several times its original size to meet the demand for services created almost overnight by the aqueduct project. The single-story wooden structures fronting the thoroughfare included a general merchandise store, a bank and several boarding houses and flea-bag hotels. The only clean, well-run hostelry was the Harvey House, with a lunch room, dining room, hotel and staff dormitories.

The irreproachable reputation of the Harvey House was the reason he'd been able to convince his parents to allow Janey, who had been most unreasonable in begging for the privilege, to make this visit. He'd also been able to obtain permission from the Fred Harvey Company for his sister to stay in the dormitory with Lesley Cartwright, a school friend, a couple of years older than Janey, who was working in Mojave as a Harvey Girl, a member of the company's corps of well-trained, spotlessly attired waitresses.

Noise from the town's revelers muffled even the sharp whistle of the approaching train. Probably it had been a mistake to have Janey arrive the day after the aqueduct's payday, when the town really roared. But hell, when would have been any better? As far as Chris could see, any day of the year there was always one crew drunk, one crew sobering up and one crew working.

The locomotive arriving at the station was pulling a mix of passenger and freight cars. It had traveled the "Jawbone Branch" of the railway,

recently built from Mojave up to Owenyo at the lower end of the
Owens Valley by the Southern Pacific Company. Mojave depot also
served intercontinental trains traveling from Chicago and Kansas City to
the West Coast, including the Santa Fe Railway's celebrated California
Limited, which featured a luxurious dining car with meal service by the
Fred Harvey Company.

Chris couldn't help chuckling to himself whenever he saw this train
coming south from Owens Valley. The valley folk had been up in arms at
the prospect of the aqueduct. Yet without it, the valley might never have
gained what it most needed: a standard gauge rail line connecting it to
urban markets. The Southern Pacific had built the link for the aqueduct to
move equipment and supplies to construction sites, but the new line was
also moving tremendous quantities of produce from Owens Valley farms
and ranches. And with far less cost than the old narrow-gauge line to
Carson City, where it had been necessary to unpack the freight and repack
it onto standard-gauge trains headed to Los Angeles.

Travelers began disembarking from the two passenger cars. People
who'd been waiting on the platform and porters with carts rushed forward, making it difficult to catch a glimpse of Janey. Then he saw her,
standing next to a man, a businessman from the looks of him, who was
holding her cases. Chris called out, but she didn't hear him at first through
the noise, then he saw her head cock and turn toward him. He shot out his
arm and waved, moving forward. The man, seeing him, turned and bowed
to Janey, "Good day miss," placing her bags at her feet, then tipping his
hat to Chris.

"Thank you sir." She gave the gentleman a shy smile, but her eyes
were on her brother.

"Hello Haaaazy!" Chris teased, catching her up in his arms and
swinging her back and forth like a pendulum.

"Don't call me that!" she protested, wrinkling her nose and straightening her dress as he sat her down. But she smiled and reached up to hug
his neck and give him a peck on the side of his mouth.

He held her away to examine his catch. This was the first time he'd
ever seen Janey outside of the valley, and she didn't look the same. It wasn't
only that she was crisp and neat in a new dress with a fitted bodice and
waist that showed off her slender figure and made her look nearly grown

up. Chris had been home every couple of months since he'd started his business, enough to observe the normal changes in a girl approaching 16. But, somehow, away from home, standing here on this jangling platform, he really saw her as she now was.

Glowing cheeks, shining hair, clear, bright eyes—it was a picture that contrasted sharply with most of the females he saw these days: whores who were gay until you glimpsed them at a moment when they weren't playing for attention or effect, and then they just looked worn out. There were some married women about, most coming into town from nearby ranches, and some wives of aqueduct workers, lured by the modest homes the city had built in an attempt to create stable communities to counterbalance the influence of the bawdy boom towns. These women, carrying bundles and herding unruly children, seemed almost as worn out as the whores. Such a hard country it was on the ladies.

"Can we ride to the hotel in your limousine?" Janey was asking. She'd been thrilled and fascinated ever since he'd told her of his motor car and driver.

"No need. The Harvey House is right in here." He indicated the depot building behind them.

"But I want to see the town!" she objected, watching the stream of people leaving the platform and walking east toward Main Street. Others were being shepherded into the two-story depot building. It was a handsome structure of brown wood slats, with doors and windows trimmed a warm rust-red.

"Let's get you in." Seeing her disappointment, he added, "I'll walk you up and down Main Street tomorrow."

Taking her wrist and looking at her intently, he said in a stern voice: "Janey, you're never to walk on Main Street or any other street in this town without an escort, not even with Lesley or another Harvey Girl, do you understand? And never, ever talk to any stakemen!"

She nodded solemnly. He supposed she'd had the same lecture from Pa and Ma. "Good, and after our little tour tomorrow, you can ride in the limo with me to Jawbone Canyon and see the construction." Picking up her bags in one hand and taking her elbow with the other, he steered her toward the Harvey House entrance.

"Jawbone Canyon," she said, delighted, letting herself be brought along. "Why is it called that?"

"Ah, I'll explain it to you later."

"What are stakemen?"

"I'll explain that to you later too. This way," he said, opening the door and ushering her inside.

Chris followed her in and watched, amused, as Janey stood gaping. This was not only the first time she'd ridden a train, but would also be the first time she'd stay in a hotel. In fact, the Mojave Harvey House was a modest establishment compared to some of the other Harvey properties, such as the lavish Alvarado Hotel in Albuquerque, New Mexico or the El Tovar at Grand Canyon. Nevertheless, it was well-appointed and impeccable, as the company enforced the same standard of excellence across its entire enterprise. As Chris guided her across the gleaming wood floor toward the equally well-polished reception desk, Janey, glancing to her right, saw that the lobby opened up to a room where passengers were taking seats around a large counter shaped like a hollow oval ring. Several young women stood inside the ring, like soldiers at attention. They were wearing black dresses and white aprons, and held coffee pots. To the left was another room with a dozen or more tables, each covered with a white cloth, and here too a cadre of young women stood at attention as passengers seated themselves, only these waitresses were dressed differently, in white dresses with black collars.

"Welcome to the Harvey House, sir," said the bow-tied, suited man at the desk. "I'm Mr. Davies. May I help you?"

"Hello Mr. Davies. May I see Mrs. Thomas please? The name's Christopher Bow. She's expecting us."

"Certainly. If you and the young lady would like to be seated here," said the man, gesturing to a cluster of chairs and divans. "I will bring her to you. Katherine, please offer our guests some refreshment."

A young woman emerged from the back office with a tray. She served Chris coffee from a china pot and offered Janey cool lemonade from a cut-glass pitcher.

As they sipped their drinks, Chris leaned toward his sister and whispered, "This place is really keen! Before Fred Harvey, the best train travelers could hope for was canned beans, rancid bacon and week-old coffee served by some bartender. He changed all that, starting with his first café in Topeka Kansas. Now he's got a Harvey House every hundred miles or so across the entire Santa Fe line, and service on the trains too. Every single place serving fresh food with clean linen and polished silverware!"

"Do you know Mr. Harvey then, Chris?" his sister asked.

"No, the great man died in 1901, but I know his son, Byron—he runs the company now and he's the one who said it would be all right for you to stay here. Imagine that, Janey, inheriting this kind of business from your father, and the funds to keep building it out all across the West!"

Chris rose to his feet as Mr. Davies returned with Mrs. Thomas. Behind her stood Lesley Cartwright, Janey's school friend. She was the same round-faced girl he'd known in Owens Valley, but with newly acquired poise and dignity in her starched black uniform, with her light-brown hair pulled back from her face in the Gibson style, secured with a black hairnet. The girl's blue eyes danced with glee at the arrival of her friend, but she stood straight, awaiting the pleasure of Mrs. Thomas, hands folded gracefully at the front of her gleaming white apron.

"Mr. Bow, may I present Mrs. Thomas," said the manager, who then nodded to Chris and returned to the front desk.

"Wonderful to make your acquaintance Mrs. Thomas." Chris took the woman's extended hand briefly. "This is my sister Janey, of whom I believe Mr. Harvey forewarned you." He winked at Janey.

"Yes indeed, the young journalist!" Mrs. Thomas, who was tall and thin, and wore spectacles, had a warm and ready smile, which she focused on the nervous girl. "I understand that you'll be writing an article on the aqueduct for the Owens Valley newspaper."

"Thank you ma'am, but I'm not a real reporter. I just help a little at the *Register*, the *Inyo Register* is the name of our newspaper. Mr. Chalfant, he's the editor, said I might try to write a little story if I have the notion. Most likely he'll choose not to publish it." She dropped her eyes. "I've never written an article before, just fixed the spelling in some."

"Well, that's a good start, my dear. And you're certain to find plenty to write about here," replied Mrs. Thomas. Smiling at Chris, she added, "Not the least being the impressive business of your brother in feeding all those aqueduct workers! We're in the same business, in a manner of speaking, are we not Mr. Bow?"

"Indeed, ma'am, we surely are. And may I extend my personal appreciation for your willingness to accommodate my sister here in the Harvey House dormitory during her stay. Knowing that she'll be under your watchful eye is a source of great reassurance to me and to our parents."

"Ah, yes, although you, young lady, may not be so appreciative. Many of our girls say we're much stricter in our rules than ever their own parents would be."

Janey wasn't sure how to respond, so she dropped her eyes, trying to imitate the composure her friend Lesley was demonstrating. Mrs. Thomas now moved aside and motioned the other girl forward.

"I've excused Lesley from her normal serving duties this afternoon that she may help Janey get settled."

"Thank you ma'am," responded Chris. Then, with a grandiose air, he entreated her, "May I beg your permission also for Lesley to join my sister and me in the dining room this evening?"

Mrs. Thomas was surprised. "It's rather unusual, Mr. Bow, for Harvey Girls to sit as guests in the dining room."

"Perhaps just this once," Chris plied her with a winning smile, "it might be possible to make an exception? I've extolled the wonders of Harvey House dining to such a degree that my sister is greatly anticipating the experience and," he lowered his voice to a confidential level, "a little nervous. I believe she would be greatly eased by having her friend join us."

"Very well," Mrs. Thomas assented. "Lesley, you may join the Bows in the dining room tonight. As always, whether in service or in public, you are to dress and behave with proper comportment."

"Yes ma'am," responded Lesley, her eyes lit with excitement.

"All right then, take Miss Bow up to your room, and do help her with her cases."

Lesley stepped forward and took one of Janey's bags, then turned toward the main staircase, motioning her friend to follow. Janey, carrying the other case, was surprised when Lesley walked behind the main staircase to a small hall leading to another, more modest set of stairs. They climbed these to the second-floor staff area, where Lesley opened the door of a pleasant, well-lit room with two twin beds. Once inside, the older girl's composure dissolved, and the two friends hugged and giggled, and twirled round and round to the jumble of music and voices streaming in through the half-open windows.

"You'll get used to it," advised Lesley, throwing herself down on one of the beds, pulling Janey with her. "It goes on all night, but in time you hardly even hear it."

Janey took her word for it. Perched on the bed, she gazed around the nicely furnished room.

"That's Karen's," said Lesley, pointing to the other bed. "She's bunking with another girl whose roommate went home for a visit. Every six months you get a free ticket home, with free meals the whole way!"

"Then you like it here?"

"Sure, I do. Mrs. Thomas is strict, but she's fair. As long as you follow all the rules—and there's plenty of them—you come out fine. No jewelry, no makeup, no chewing gum, no staying out after 11 o'clock curfew. Spill a tiny drop of coffee on your apron and you gotta change it for a clean one."

"You don't mind being a waitress?" Janey asked. Waitressing was generally regarded in the West as a lowly occupation. Among the wage-earning positions open to women, it was even below domestic service and factory work in status.

"I'm not a waitress, I'm a Harvey Girl, and that's different," Lesley corrected her. "You have to be well-educated to get hired. Most of the girls here graduated from high school; there's a few who just went through eighth grade, but they're real smart too. And you have to be able to speak properly with the customers, no jokin or loose talk, and they're supposed to act proper with us too. Mrs. Thomas says being a Harvey Girl is a profession, like a school teacher or a nurse, and deserves respect."

Janey thought about her friend Rosie, who had applied to be a Harvey Girl too. She'd been turned down, the reply to her application saying only that there currently weren't any openings. But that hadn't been the real reason. Lesley had let Janey know in one of her letters that all the Harvey Girls were White.

"Do you like living on your own here, away from your family?" asked Janey.

"Love it! I'm independent, and I have my own money, which I can spend as I like! By the time I get married and have a home of my own, I'll have a whole pile of money saved!"

"You want to get married?"

"Of course, someday. Lots of the Harvey Girls from Kansas City, Chicago or back east signed up to come west so they can meet a real cowboy! Lots of 'em end up getting married and staying out here. For me it's different, since I'm from here already, like you. But believe you me, Janey, there's a lot more different and interesting men here in Mojave than you'll ever see walking down Main Street in Bishop. Don't you want to get married?"

"I'm too young," Janey replied, then switched to a more diverting subject. "What's Main Street here like?" she tilted her head toward the open windows. "Chris told me I wasn't to go walking there without a man to escort me—not even if I was with you."

"Oh, it's not that bad as long as you don't go down one of the side streets—that's where all the drunks and gamblers are, and the floozies who work in the bars and flophouses."

Janey nodded, pretending to share Lesley's sophistication. The two friends talked and talked until the sun was angling in sharply through the west-facing windows. The evening was approaching; it was time to dress for dinner.

Opening her suitcase, Janey unpacked her new party dress, designed and sewn by her Ma. It was of a soft voile fabric in a vibrant turquoise. At the high waist, the material gathered softly into pleats forming the bodice and extending down into the swirl of skirt. A satin collar of the same turquoise hue was embroidered with yellow and orange flowers, and a sprinkling of flowers also adorned the sleeves just above the fitted wrists. She was self-conscious and excited as she pulled the garment up onto her shoulders.

"Oooh, that's such beautiful work," said Lesley, watching as Janey pulled her arms through, then reaching out to finger the embroidery on one sleeve. She buttoned up her friend, and the two stood admiring the effect in the mirror.

"Put your hair up, use those," suggested Lesley, pointing to a bowl of pins and combs on the dressing table. "I'll help you as soon as I'm dressed."

Janey sat down and tried to secure her heavy tendrils, but they escaped her hands. No matter how many times Ma had shown her how to do it, step by step, she'd never been able to imitate the flawless chignon of her mother.

"Here, let me." Lesley came up behind her, and Janey gulped. The older girl looked like she had sprung from the pages of a magazine. She wore a tunic of crisp white fabric with a pattern of raised black squares, caught with a wide black belt at her waist and fitted over her hips. Where the tunic ended, at mid-thigh level, there extended a long, slim black skirt, just short enough to reveal a glimpse of Lesley's black stockinged ankle.

"What do you think?" Lesley asked, twirling around so Janey could see the flat-pleated back.

"It's very smart," said Janey, who immediately felt both young and old-fashioned in her soft, flowery garb. She'd never liked girlish dresses anyway, but had given in to Ma's preference. How was she to have known what kind of clothes to wear? This was what she should have had, if she'd only known. This was the kind of dress, sleek and grown up, she would never object to wearing.

"Never mind, once I've finished your hair, you'll look just like a princess," Lesley reassured her, not noticing how Janey flinched at the teasing phrase her Pa so often used.

---

The Harvey House dining room, its white table cloths gleaming with silver settings and glassware, was abuzz with activity and conversation as Chris Bow led the two girls in on either arm. Janey noticed that Lesley in her fitted outfit appeared taller and slimmer than she actually was, but had trouble walking in the tight skirt. Her brother looked equally modern and sharp in a charcoal gray three-piece suit, a white shirt with a high, stiff turned-out collar with rounded edges and a narrow tie of crimson and black stripes.

Looking about the room, however, Janey felt less self-conscious of her own appearance. There were a handful of other diners in modern, stylish garb, but the majority wore more ordinary attire, such as she was accustomed to seeing in the Owens Valley. Most of the women, she imagined them to be rancher's wives, wore simple frocks in navy, white or beige, and straw hats adorned by faded ribbons. She thought fondly of how her own Ma would have shone like a jewel in the room, and felt a surge of gratitude to her mother for her efforts to help her do the same. In truth, Janey felt pretty for the first time in her life. And she was thrilled at her circumstances. She had never dined in a hotel and never sat at a table with none but other young folks at her side!

Chris helped Janey peruse the menu, as ordering was also a new experience for her. "Here, these bluepoint oysters are shipped in from North Carolina, and the lobsters from Boston…au gratin means with melted cheese on top…the whitefish is from the Great Lakes…this sirloin steak comes from Texas, and au jus means there's a sauce to dip it in… edam cheese is from Holland…and the peach preserves," he said, winking at the girls, "are from Lone Pine in our own Owens Valley!"

Janey finally settled on roast pork with mashed apples and sweet potatoes. Chris ordered the steak with French fried potatoes, and Lesley said she'd have the chicken fricassee. While they waited to be served by Carrie, a Harvey Girl who was clearly tickled to find her pal Lesley at her table, Chris explained how the Fred Harvey Company was able to offer these delights in such an out-of-the-way place as Mojave. Lesley, who must have known much of what he related, nevertheless listened raptly to the handsome, confident young man Janey's brother had become.

"Fred Harvey was a genius to realize that by partnering with the Santa Fe Railway he could use their ice cars to deliver fresh, fancy food practically anywhere in the country! And it's not only that he thought of bringing seafood from the East and steak from Texas, but he also figured out how to use local produce efficiently. Before Harvey, the railroads used to serve eggs shipped from New York preserved in lime! Now both the in-train service and Harvey Houses along the line serve fresh eggs from local ranches. Genius!"

"The company must make a lot of money," remarked Janey.

"Not always," explained Chris, "but by advertising 'Meals by Fred Harvey,' the Santa Fe Railway is making so much income from ticket sales it can afford to subsidize some of the operations, like the Hopi House gift shop at Grand Canyon. So overall," he concluded, surveying the dining room appreciatively, "this a very profitable partnership for both parties."

Carrie soon brought their meals, which all agreed were delicious. The coffee that followed was equally good, and Chris savored his with an enormous piece of apple pie. Lesley was happy to reveal her own bit of Harvey mystique. "The coffee beans are a special blend from France, and we make it with the same bottled spring water all over the line, so the taste is never changed by local water flavors. Every Harvey House has a full-time baker, and he bakes all day long—has to, since we serve our pies cut into quarters, not eighths like everywhere else!" she said proudly.

Late into the night, the taste of the coffee and the few sips of his port wine Chris had allowed her, continued to play on Janey's tongue as she lay in the twin bed next to Lesley's. The window was closed to the cold desert wind, but its thin pane of glass did little to shut out the music and noise from Main Street, which never ceased the whole night long and became even louder in the wee hours. Accustomed as she was to quiet rural nights, Janey found it impossible to sleep. It wasn't just the noise outside; her own pulse also pounded in her ear whenever she lay on her side in the position she preferred for sleeping. And her limbs refused to relax and sink into the mattress as they usually did when sleep was about to overtake her; tonight they flitted like butterflies and buzzed like bees. She didn't care. Janey turned over on her back and lay gazing out the window at the moon, pushing her toes into the cool corners of her sheets, anticipating another day full of new things she had never done before, a day that would take her onto Main Street, Mojave, and into Jawbone Canyon.

---

Of all the amazing things Janey saw on her tour of Mojave with Chris the next morning, the most amazing was a tin of tomatoes.

It was an ordinary tin, like any one could see on the shelves of a general store. But this tin was held in the hand of a man who did some-thing quite out of the ordinary with it: He stabbed its top with a penknife, seesawing the blade back and forth to open a rough gash. Then he leaned over a drunken man lying propped up against a rail in the dusty street, tipped back the fellow's head and poured the bright orange gloppy con-tents directly into the slack mouth. "Chew, you bastard!" he barked at the drunkard, whose shirt was now stained with tomato juice as well as vomit. "Swallow!"

Satisfied that his patient wouldn't choke, the man stood back and smiled sheepishly at Chris and Janey, who had witnessed the scene from a few feet away.

"Sorry you had to see this miss. Nothing to worry about. Just one of our stakemen enjoying too much of his stake." He bowed slightly to Janey and, extending a hand to Chris, introduced himself. "I'm Doctor Taylor."

Chris introduced them, then queried Taylor about his unorthodox treatment of the drunkard.

"I don't know why it works," the physician admitted, "but it's the best and fastest cure for inebriation I know, so I always carry a few cans with me."

They said goodbye to their new acquaintance and continued down the sidewalk. Chris squeezed her arm and mused aloud, "I wonder how many cans of tomatoes they could go through in San Francisco's honky-tonk district? That's one way to sell produce even I hadn't thought of!"

After that, there wasn't much that could shock Janey, but there was much to interest her in the colorful, clattering streets. For one thing, there were so many people about. "Is it a holiday today?" she asked her brother. The only time she had ever been among so many people was the Bishop Independence Day celebration.

"Nope. Always like this." Chris wove her through the tide of male oncomers, mostly workers, but also tradesmen and dandies, who tipped their hats and stood aside to watch the young lady pass. Janey was wearing a split riding skirt and a wide-brimmed hat, at Chris's instruction. With long honeyed hair plaited loosely down her back and eyes bright with excitement, the girl was an arresting sight. Unaccustomed to attracting such attention, she tightened her grip on Chris and avoided looking at the sun-browned, unshaven faces, already sweaty under an unseasonably hot sun at barely nine in the morning.

Occasionally she spotted a woman on one of the wagons rolling through a cloud of dust in the street or being escorted down the sidewalk and through a door in the long, low rows of buildings that fronted it. Most looked old, their clothes faded, their hair going gray. The young and pretty women could be seen on the side streets that led from Main Street, a block or two to the east. As they approached these intersections, the pandemonium grew louder and louder.

"Don't look down there," Chris warned as they passed. "Nothin of interest for a respectable young lady."

But Janey couldn't help peeking. She'd never known folks to play music, sing and yell like that in the middle of the morning. And she'd never seen women dressed like those she saw clustered out in front of one establishment, with brightly made up faces and brilliantly colored satin dresses dipping low at the bodice. Bright flocks of ladies were leaning casually against rickety buildings, talking and laughing, skirts hitched up high on legs covered in black stockings like fishing nets—and they were smoking cigarettes!

Janey wanted to ask Chris about them, but she didn't dare. So as they made their way back to the Harvey House, she asked instead, "What is a stakeman?"

"It's just a name for some of the men working on the aqueduct," explained Chris. "A lot of these guys work for weeks or months at a time, saving up their pay until they have a 'stake,' as they call it. You know, like a man might save up enough money to stake himself to buying some land or opening a little business or something. But most of these guys never get that far. They save up just enough of a stake to have a good time here in Mojave or somewhere like it, and then they blow the whole thing in a few days or a few weeks. So then they have to sign up on a work crew again and start over. Some of them keep doing it again and again, never getting ahead, never with anything to show for their work. That's why they're called stakemen."

"When do they stop?" asked Janey.

"They don't. When they're too old and tired to do the hard work, they take easier, lower paying jobs, if they can get them. Or they find work sweeping up at some saloon just for pennies and board. The lucky ones stay strong and keep working until they just drop dead someday."

He glanced down at her worried face. "Hey, sis, that's not for you to worry about. You're going to ride in a limousine!"

If her morning's stroll down Main Street had been bizarre and wonderful, the rest of the day lived up to its debut. Perched on the edge of the Mitchell Limousine's plump back-seat cushion, she was racing ahead, faster than she'd ever gone, faster than when she'd borrowed a ride on Mr. Chalfant's bicycle, faster even than the train!

They were headed north on a gravel road that roughly paralleled the railroad tracks Janey had arrived on. So far, they had experienced little wind, and the dustless air was crystal clear. As Janey gazed out the window, the scant features of the desert stood out sharply to her eyes against the delicately hued landscape. The ground was the color, she thought, of a cube of sugar dipped in Pa's coffee. But in places it was spattered, as if from the brush of a wayward painter, with intense patches of color, which was why, she supposed, they called that red flower Indian paintbrush. There were also vast expanses of yellow from blooming brittle bush, and lavender Mojave asters poked out from creosote scrub. The landscape was punctuated with round barrel cactus, fuzzy fingers of cholla and, at the side of the road, there appeared at regular intervals, tall wooden poles strung with a daisy chain of electrical wire.

All these sights entered the frame of her window at the front, traveled swiftly across it and disappeared at the back. A moving picture, she thought, and wondered if it was anything like the moving picture show her brother had seen in Los Angeles and described to the family at length. She started to ask him, but Chris was already explaining about the poles.

"These had to be built before the real work could even get started," he explained. "The city built nearly 500 miles of roads and more than 200 miles each of electricity and telephone lines."

Numbers, which seeded, rooted and bloomed in Chris's head, floated through hers like the fluff of a dandelion. She was better at keeping mental pictures of what she saw. Janey lifted her eyes to the deep bluish hills far out across the desert. Their contour unfurled like a ribbon across the paler edge of the sky. It still being morning, heat distortion had not arisen yet to warp visibility, and Janey's eyes could pick out the woolly clusters of scrub brush and dark gashes of canyons on the rock faces.

Half the distance between the towns of Mojave and Indian Wells lay the particular canyon of their destination. Chris explained that it had been christened "Jawbone" by workers who thought its steep, deeply eroded sandstone cliffs had the shape of a jutting lower jaw. The name had gained notoriety when the work began: Here at an elevation of 2,400 feet above the floor of the Mojave Desert, the aqueduct had to pass up, down and under exceptionally rugged terrain, and the crews building it to endure extreme conditions, with temperatures below freezing in the winter and soaring above 120-degrees Fahrenheit in the summer. Chris explained that, apart from Elizabeth Tunnel—which Janey would also have the privilege of seeing during her visit—the work at Jawbone Canyon was the toughest on the aqueduct.

"They're building a huge siphon there, which basically means a pipeline constructed so that atmospheric pressure and gravity force water to flow uphill. In siphon construction, the velocity of the water flow is affected by the diameter of the pipe, so by tapering the dimension smaller, you increase pressure enough to push the water upward. The Jawbone siphon will take water up the slope more than 850 feet. To build it, they have to haul dozens of sections of pipe, some as big as 15 feet in diameter, about four miles up the canyon—and each one of those sections of pipe weighs more than 25 tons!"

"How do they do that?" asked Janey, turning toward him.

"First they tried with tractors, not like farm tractors, but this new kind they call caterpillars, owing to they've got these wheels with big loops around them. Kinda makes them look like caterpillars when they're moving…you keep your eyes open and you'll see a couple of them, broken down and just left out here to die, like the skeletons of animals."

Janey turned back quickly to the window, eyes scanning the terrain. Chris continued his explanation. "But now, instead of repairing those tractors, they're hauling the pipe using mules. Makes no sense to me. They need a team of 52 mules just to get one section of pipe up the canyon."

"So many mules?!" Janey couldn't picture it. Even on the big wagons that hauled loads of borax from Keeler, she'd never seen more than eight hitched to a wagon.

"You'll see," said Chris, puffing up a bit with pride at the sheer force and audacity of the endeavor, despite the inglorious mules. "If you're lucky, you'll get to see Whistling Dick driving them. Best muleskinner in the West. When they went to hire him for the aqueduct they asked him how many mules he could handle, and do you know what he answered? 'I can drive 'em as far as I can see 'em!'"

Another hour or so later, Chris announced their imminent arrival. "That's Cinco, up there, Jawbone Division Headquarters." He pointed to a cluster of buildings nestled among large boulders and a few scraggly pine trees on the low slope of mountains rising abruptly ahead of them. To Janey, it looked like a toy village. On the flatland below it there were circular shapes, which also looked like toys, though Janey guessed they must be the immense pipes Chris had talked about.

"Such a long way out here," murmured Janey.

"Sure, and I'm out here every week. Tomorrow we'll be down south of Mojave at the Antelope Valley Division, where they're tunneling right under the mountains. You can see why I need this big car, and Rex here."

His sister nodded, smiling at the back of the chauffeur's head and gazing with awe at her brother. Ma and Pa would hardly believe it if they could see how grown up and important Chris had become.

---

Arriving at Cinco, Janey could see that the toy village was actually a group of low wood-frame buildings with pitched roofs and rows of canvas tents extending across and up the slope. The circular shapes were far from toys. Indeed they were immense; the dozen or so workmen moving around and inside of them were less than half their height.

Rex turned off the engine, exited and, placing his cap on his head, opened the rear door to help Janey out of the automobile. As she stepped out, she was sad to see that the car's glossy black surface was now clouded with a thick film of dirt.

"Here you are young miss," Rex said with a slight snap of head and shoulders. "Welcome to the Jawbone."

"Oh thank you!"

Where's the cliff that looks like a jaw?" she asked Chris as he guided her up some rough steps that had been cut into the slope and secured with split logs.

"You'll see it in just a bit. We have to go up there by wagon. It's too steep for the Mitchell."

He led her to the largest of the buildings, and they stepped onto its deep shaded porch. It was cool there, and the air smelled wonderfully of pine and bacon. Janey took a deep breath and looked around. From here she could see that there were several men on top of one of the pipes; they appeared to be securing metal lines to them. There were a few men moving between the small white tents on the slope.

"This time of day it's pretty quiet here at headquarters. Most everyone's either working up in the canyon or sleeping here in their tents. Except my kitchen staff, of course," Chris laughed, "they're cooking meals for about a thousand hungry men!"

"There are a thousand men here?!"

"Well, several hundred anyway, depending on the time of year and what's needing to be done," Chris answered. "Now, over here," he continued, indicating a larger tent, "that's the mess, and over there's the division store—both my operations. The post office is the building next to it, and on the other side, that's the medical service. All of these wood structures were designed to be portable, so we can pick them up and put them back up somewhere else when this phase of the job is done. Jawbone is only one of 11 divisions in the whole of the aqueduct."

Chris hooked a thumb toward the door and shade-drawn windows behind them. "I need to go in there to arrange for our trip up the canyon, so you might as well come along and get a look at it. Then you'll wait here just a bit while I check on my cook staff."

The large rectangular room they entered had a flat, low ceiling below its pitched roof. Sunlight streamed in through panes along the long wall immediately to the right of the doorway. These windows, with their northerly exposure, were unshaded and most were open. On the narrow back wall hung an immense map, which had been annotated with circles, arrows and numbers. The southern wall was solid except for two doors with name plates.

There were a half dozen desks arranged in front of the windows, though only three of them were currently occupied. One of the occupants, a young man with sandy hair and a deeply tanned, smiling face, rose to greet them, extending his hand to Chris.

"Back again so soon Bow?" he asked. "Did ya bring my filet mignon?"

"Oh, no, I forgot!" Chris played along, "Next time?"

"Well, fine, but I want a case of champagne with it then."

"Why not?!" joked Chris. "Hey Plough, I want you to meet my little sister. Janey, this rascal is Davey Plough, or as we like to call him, 'Sir Indispensable.'"

"My pleasure Miss Bow." Davey extended his hand, palm up, and when Janey tentatively placed hers on top of it, he bent his head and pretended to kiss it. She was deeply embarrassed and jumped back slightly.

"Hold on there Sir Indispensable." Chris snatched Janey's hand away in pretended prudery. "Watch it or you might become more dispensable than I thought!"

"You can't blame me, Bow. Who would have guessed you'd have such a lovely sister."

Janey's face flamed, and she turned it hurriedly away, pretending to be interested in something outside the window. No one ever made a fuss over her like this at home.

"Here sis, have a seat." Chris steered her into a chair. "Plough, can you have a couple of horses saddled for us to take into the canyon? I want to show Janey what they're doing up there."

"Sure. Hey there, George!" he called to another young man seated at a desk, "ask Blakely to get Mister and…," he examined Janey.

"She's a good rider," Chris answered the unspoken question.

"…and Crosshatch ready for Mr. Bow and his sister here."

"Thanks Plough. Hey, is Whistling Dick up there on the ridge today?" asked Chris.

"Yeah, he and Corgie each took up a section already this morning, and they'll be comin back for another. Be careful on your way up cause you don't wanna get caught on the downside of 52 mules and one awful ornery skinner."

The clerk continued, his voice low now, "Speakin of ornery, Chris, some of the stakemen found weevils in their pie last night. Raised a bit of a ruckus."

"Damn. I'm gonna fix all that, I just need…"

"There was a sign up in front of the mess tent this mornin, said 'Don't make fun of the butter—you'll be old and smelly yourself some day!' Whaddaya think of that?"

Chris fumed and was trying to think of something to say about it when one of the inner doors opened and a tall man with a Roman nose and handlebar mustache emerged. Seeing Chris, he started toward him, face stern, but then, noticing Janey, slowed his stride and softened his expression.

"Well, well, I see that Miss Bow has arrived. Welcome young lady."

Janey rose to take his extended hand, and Chris made the formal introduction. J.B. Lippincott expressed himself pleased as punch about her visit.

"We need intelligent folk from Owens Valley to witness the work we're doing for the benefit of all and take the word back to their neighbors. Chris tells me you even do some work at the *Inyo Register*? Perhaps you'll write an article about us?"

"Oh, mostly I just help out Mr. Chalfant, the editor." She looked down, shyly. "But he did say as he might consider printing a small story if I were to write about something…" her voice trailed off. She hadn't the slightest idea what that something might be.

---

The obvious subject came barreling down the canyon at them when they were halfway up the steep, rutted road to the work site. Chris had been listening and heard the commotion early enough to grab Janey's reins and pull her horse onto the edge of the road, where it opened out slightly into a somewhat wider surface. He held the horses steady, and she held her breath, as suddenly, around the bend in the road above them, came a phalanx of mules, snorting and clattering, their hooves sending gravel flying.

The mule team passed so quickly and was down the hill, disappearing around another bend, that Janey, trying to count the 52 beasts, saw them largely as a blur. They had been pulling a huge wagon with immense wheels, unlike any wagon Janey had ever seen, and atop it, snapping the reins and emitting shrill whistles, had perched a gray-haired man in a big, shapeless hat with long side flaps that drooped down over his ears. He had looked to her like a gnome in a fairytale.

"Oh my, is that…?!"

"That's him, Whistling Dick," confirmed Chris. "Once we get up there, we'll have a chance to see better—he takes the trip up a lot slower than the trip down."

Chris returned the reins to her, and Janey directed Crosshatch, a bay gelding, to follow her brother, who rode a roan stallion, back onto the road. Janey's horse was gentle but spirited, and proved sure-footed and at ease on the steep grade.

Now that the danger of finding oneself flattened by the battalion of mules and wagon the size of a barn had passed, Janey was also at ease. She was not unaccustomed to steep trails. After Mary's abrupt departure, Janey had felt the loss of their mountain rambles keenly. Fed up with her moping, Ma and Pa had agreed that she might be allowed to go riding with her friend Juan, who was then 14, and his younger sisters Emma and Rosie. The girls rode Andalusians with elaborately hand-tooled Mexican saddles. Their brother, showing off, rode practically bareback, with just a blanket between him and his mount, Serrano, an Appaloosa stallion. Juan used a bridle, but no bit, and guided the horse mostly through touch, a hand on its neck, fingers entwined in its swirling mane, soft commands and entreaties whispered in its ear.

Janey later thought of Juan's thin, strong fingers, braiding themselves through the stallion's mane, when she saw Whistling Dick driving his army of mules up the canyon toward where she and Chris perched on a flat-topped boulder, awaited his second coming. On this trip up canyon, Dick held three jerk lines in his hands, and played them with the swiftness and sensitivity of a fiddler. One of the lines, Chris explained, controlled the mules harnessed six abreast in eight rows from the front of the wagon forward. Another line controlled a row in front of that. This row had only two mules, in the second and fifth positions. The third line controlled the head row, again with two mules, but this time harnessed closer together in the third and fourth positions. The immense wagon carrying the giant pipe section was actually two flat-bed wagons—each outfitted with steel wheels and tires two-feet wide—driven in tandem. Dick's nimble fingers never rested for an instant, tugging here, releasing there, holding down or pulling up. It was as if, Janey mused, he were playing some kind of immense musical instrument. This strange symphony of snorting, hawing mules and creaking, groaning rig, its tires crunching over rough ground, was punctuated by the muleskinner's high-pitched whistles.

After the contraption had gone by, they watched it make its way farther up the canyon while they ate the sandwiches Chris had supplied from the mess tent. Then they descended from the rock and remounted their horses to follow the trail up to where the pipe section was now being removed from the wagon and pulled into position. Soon an army of welders would descend onto the pipe to transform it into an airtight piece of the siphon.

They climbed higher, to a vantage point that allowed them to see a stretch of the siphon traversing a broad expanse of flatland below. Chris pointed out that in such areas the pipe was mounted on piers several feet above the ground to protect it from the flash floods that periodically swept through these washes. Janey said it looked like a giant snake or a garden hose used by a giant to water his begonias! Chris ignored her silly remark.

---

But the gaggle of Harvey Girls camped on and around Janey's bed that evening did not. They hooted and clapped when she repeated her description of the giant siphon "hose" and Whistling Dick "playing" his immense "instrument." Janey was amazed and flattered at the effect her little story was having on her audience, until Lesley leaned over to whisper, "Hey dunce, don't you know why they're laughing? Because it sounds like you're talking about a man's private part!"

Janey sank back against the headboard, face burning, as the talk and laughter swirled around her. The other meaning of her words had simply never occurred to her, which was an even greater source of mortification than the using of them. If she'd been sophisticated like these girls, she could have told the same story with a knowing wink, letting them think she had deliberately chosen the words to entertain them. Instead, it was obvious to everyone that she was a country bumpkin and still a child.

She had been alone in the room that evening after dinner, sitting on the bed, trying to figure out how to start writing a newspaper article, when Lesley had burst in the door with the other girls. "Janey, this here is Katie Poling, Melissa Shaw and Nora McCally," Lesley had made the introductions before flopping down on her own bed. "Helen and Amy will be comin too in a minute. They went to fetch the cookies Helen's Ma just sent."

"Hello."

"Hi there!"

"Meet any dashing young engineers out on the Jawbone today, honey?"

"I'm just flat after that last shift!"

"Get off your feet girl."

"So you're Christopher Bow's sister!"

"Watch out! She's on the make!"

"Am not! Just the same, he's a dilly of a guy!"

Janey had said hello, then watched fascinated as the older girls, teasing each other and laughing, had removed their plain black shoes and settled on her bed and Lesley's in black-stockinged feet. Katie was fine-boned with delicate features surrounded by a halo of curly brown hair. Melissa was a short, thick-waisted blonde with a square, freckled face. Nora, the girl who had asked about Chris, was strikingly handsome with thick, glossy dark-brown hair, deep-blue eyes and perfectly symmetrical features.

Soon two others arrived, wearing nightdresses and carrying a large tin of cookies. Both were dark haired. Helen, the tallest, moved like a tomboy and had huge brown eyes. Amy had a pointy chin, narrow eyes and thin lips, but her skin was like porcelain. She looked like the china doll old Li Bao, the laundryman, had once given to Mary's daughter Ruth.

"Tell us about your trip to the Jawbone!" Helen prompted.

So Janey had tried to tell the story, but had succeeded only in embarrassing herself. Now Lesley, perhaps to give her friend time to recover, suggested to the others, "You better change out of your uniforms!" As those girls still in their work attire groaned and left the room, she explained to Janey, "We have to purchase our own uniforms and keep them starched and spotless."

"I see," Janey replied. "They're very fine. You all look like ladies-in-waiting to Queen Victoria."

"Oh, la ti da! I'm a lady of the royal court!" Amy Winterhouse curtsied and twirled, holding out her uniform like a gown before leaving to change out of it.

When everyone had returned and Helen had rationed out the cookies, the subject turned, as it usually did in the evenings, to men.

"Tell us about your brother Janey," asked Nora.

"Yes, how is it he came to have that big company of his, being such a young man and all?" Melissa wanted to know.

"Oh, he used to haul and sell most of the produce from our ranch," explained Janey, "since he was about 12. When we found out the aqueduct was goin through, he told my Pa somebody had to feed the workers. My Pa was too busy with the ranch, so Chris got himself hired on by the company that was gonna do it, and then when the man that owned the company was ailing, he just started doing it himself."

"Ah, a man of vision and guts!" said Helen.

"Just my cup a tea," agreed Nora, stretching out luxuriously along one side of the bed. Janey noticed that she still had on her black stockings and appeared to still be wearing all of her undergarments beneath her nightgown.

"There aren't many like that around these parts," complained Katie. "Plenty a stakemen roamin the streets, but most of thems to stay well away from. They got no future…Now the trainmen," she signed. "That's another story. Some a them are just fine, and they've got secure employment!"

"Hey, there's a couple a fine fellas right here in Harvey House," piped up Melissa. "Arnold Garney is keen! He's the baker here," she explained to Janey.

"What about the chef?" countered Amy, dreamy-eyed at the thought of burly Francis Dodge with his deep voice, fiery eyes and deft fingers in the kitchen.

"We're not supposed to step out with other Harvey House employees. There's a strict rule, though some find ways to bend it," Helen explained to Janey. "But railmen are okay, so are aqueduct engineers, clerks and foremen, but they're usually out at the camps."

"While we're on the subject of foremen," Lesley, who had been munching cookies, spoke up, "you might be interested to know that our little Janey here is going to the Elizabeth Tunnel tomorrow. Her brother is taking her to see the north crew."

"Oh, my goodness, you're going to see Brecken!"

"What I wouldn't give for a nice long gander at him!"

"Not fair! You've all seen him already! He ain't never even come to town the past six months since I been here."

"Jed Brecken," Helen addressed herself to Janey's uncomprehending countenance, "is boss of one of the crews drilling the Elizabeth Tunnel, the toughest job on the aqueduct!"

"Here," said Lesley, reaching under her pillow and withdrawing a small dog-eared paperbound volume. She tossed it over to Janey just as the curfew bell sounded. "Read this and you'll be sure to have sweet dreams!"

The visitors started trouping out. Janey noticed Nora whispering in a quick, urgent tone to Melissa. When the door closed, Lesley smiled knowingly.

"I'll bet she's sneaking out again tonight. She's got a sweetheart!"

"But you said they lock the doors after curfew. How will she get back in?"

"Like Helen told ya, there are ways." Lesley didn't elaborate. She turned out the lamp on the table between them, and the two friends fell to talking about home, with Janey recounting this and that news of the valley and people they both knew, until Lesley's responses slowed and ceased. In the silence, the racket from outside was amplified. Janey settled herself on her back, preparing for a third long night of sleeplessness. Sometime later, feeling stiff, she turned onto one side and was surprised to see light bordering the window blinds. Lesley, who was working the breakfast shift, had already departed, leaving a smartly made bed and a lingering fragrance of lavender soap.

---

Chris was to be delayed that morning, having business at one of his slaughterhouses outside of town. So after eating breakfast in the dormitory kitchen, Janey returned to Lesley's room and settled down again to try to start her article about Jawbone Canyon. Again she found it difficult to start. After half an hour or so of fidgeting, she picked up the small volume Lesley had given her.

It was a dime novel in the "Pluck and Luck: Complete Stories of Adventure" series, with the title *Down the Shaft; or The Hidden Adventures of the King of Tunnelers*. On the brown paper cover, printed in black and red ink, there was an illustration of a broad-shouldered young man, legs astride, muscles bulging, drilling into a rock wall with a huge gun-like object. In the foreground, near the man's boots, was an open box of dynamite. In the background, men with shovels scooped up mounds of loose rock. Behind them, in the far background, a black oval suggested the tunnel entrance, through which a sliver of a moon shone like a silver dagger.

Janey opened the book and read the first sentence: "The largest water construction project since Roman days is a mighty river of steel and concrete that will stretch hundreds of miles across the most unforgiving desert in North America and drop deep below its soaring mountain peaks. To achieve this historic feat, the Los Angeles Aqueduct has turned to Jed Brecken to lead his team of modern-day heroes of the Wild West as they blast through solid granite at breakneck speeds!"

She flipped through the pages. Pa had always told her to be skeptical of what she read in dime novels. "They're not worth the paper they're printed on," he had advised. The writer of this story would have her believe that this Brecken fellow and his crew faced constant danger as they bored through the mountains, setting world records for speed. There were cave-ins, floods, explosives that misfired and even practical jokes verging on sabotage from a rival crew of tunnelers boring through from the other direction. Probably not true, Janey thought. Still, it was exciting reading, especially with the prospect of today's trip to the Elizabeth Tunnel—she had never dreamed she'd ever actually see, perhaps even meet, a hero from a novel in person.

Later when she was in Chris's big limousine, riding south out of Mojave toward the Elizabeth Tunnel, she asked her brother about Brecken.

"Dime novels need to have a hero," he replied absently, his mind still on the morning's visit to the slaughterhouse and the plan he was working on to transport more of the fresh meat via rail in ice-box cars.

"The girls at the Harvey House are all in love with him," said Janey.

Chris watched her then and answered thoughtfully. "Jed Brecken isn't a hero, Janey. He's just a young man shouldering a lot of responsibility. He's got a good head, a strong back, and he's a born leader. Also to his credit, he's not one of those fellas who spends his extra time and money in Mojave saloons and gambling houses. In fact, he's not been known to go to town much at all, mostly stays out for weeks and weeks in the work camp. Probably that more than anything else is why the girls are crazy for him."

"Is the job they're doing in that tunnel as dangerous as it said in the book?"

"Sometimes, not usually though. You can't build something this grand, Janey, something that's never been tried before, without brave men taking risks. But there have been very few deaths so far—not compared to other projects of this size. On that aqueduct they're building in New York, in the Catskill Mountains, why they've lost hundreds of men already, and they're not near done yet."

Janey felt a thrill of excitement at these words, then chided herself for it. Chris had changed the subject; he was asking about their parents. "Does Pa ever say anything about my business or about my not staying on to work the ranch with him?"

"Naw, you know Pa, he doesn't let things like that worry him." She felt a twinge at having to lie. Chris's decisions had been a deep disappointment to their father and still caused him considerable pain, she imagined, though he never owned that it did. But soon, Jane forgot about all that, losing herself in the desert panorama again.

When a few minutes later, Chris nudged her and pointed to their destination, just ahead, she could hardly contain her anticipation. But as the limousine arrived at Elizabeth Division headquarters, Janey saw that Chris was alarmed.

"Something's wrong." He pointed up the slope, where a crowd of men had gathered. "That's the entrance to the tunnel." Then to Rex, his driver, "Wait here with Janey. I'm going up there to see what it is."

Janey watched from the window as Chris walked up the slope to the knot of men. A few fellows at the edge turned around and spoke with him. In a moment he was back at the Mitchell.

"There was a cave-in, late last night. Most of the crew got out, but some are still in there. It's Jed Brecken's crew."

He gave Janey a half-smile. "Well, sis, I guess you're going to find out what's behind the dime novel heroics. I've got some business I need to take care of over at the mess tent, so I'm going to find you someplace where you can watch the rescue effort without getting in the way." He noted her worried countenance. "Don't worry, they'll get them out."

The place he found for her, to Janey's annoyance, was with a group of about a dozen women and children seated on camp chairs and blankets under a small stand of scraggly pine trees.

"Mrs. Daley," Chris addressed a large-framed woman with curly russet hair, holding a toddler on her lap, "could I impose on you to look after my sister Janey here awhile?"

"Of course Mr. Bow. Now Miss Bow, you just have a seat right here next to me—Pearl, you go sit on the blanket with your sister."

A sprite of a girl, maybe five years old, jumped down from the camp chair she had been perched on and onto the back of another girl, a bit older, who was sprawled on her stomach reading a book.

"Yeeeeoh! Maaaa, get her off a me!"

"Now, now you young'uns, show some proper manners in front of this young lady!"

Chris tipped his hat and walked off toward the large tents at the center of the camp. Janey took the offered seat gingerly.

"I'm Dolly Daley," said the matron, who had a youthful air despite her large brood. "Them two is Pearl and Myrtle," she indicated the girls, who were still eyeing each other suspiciously, "and I've got my Tom-Tom right here." The boy smiled and gurgled as she bounced him up and down on her knees.

"Janey Bow ma'am."

"Come to visit your brother, have you Miss Bow?"

"Yes ma'am."

"Where do you two hail from, if you don't mind my asking?"

"From near Independence," replied Janey. Seeing Mrs. Daley's blank look, she added, "It's a small town in the Owens Valley."

"Oh, I see. I would never have guessed Mr. Bow comes from there." The woman smiled at Janey. "He seems like such a city boy."

Janey didn't know how to respond to that. She thought maybe Mrs. Daley and the rest of the women here had always lived out in rough camps like this. There wasn't one among them as pretty and polished as Ma. On the other hand, they didn't seem as worn and faded as the handful of respectable women she'd seen in Mojave.

"Are they going to get them out?" asked Janey.

"Of course, dear. They always do," her companion assured her. "See Mrs. Kelly over there?" She pointed to a tall, gaunt woman seated a few chairs over. Next to her, his arm around her shoulders, stood a boy about 11 or 12 years-old. "Her husband's down there too, and she ain't lookin worried."

Looking at how the woman was clutching her son with one hand and skirt with another, Janey wasn't so sure, but she smiled up at Mrs. Daley, who continued to converse in a lighthearted tone. "Her husband's called 'Powderface Kelly,' owing to all the mountains he's blasted through with dynamite powder! Couple of other men on the crew, Chess Dorman and Goose, they got out when it blew, and they said it didn't look to them like there was any water this time. So, likely they'se just trapped in a pocket with plenty of air until they git dug out. Besides, Powderface is with Jed Brecken in there, and Brecken always brings his men out. There's Chief Mulholland here too—there he is, up there on the slope—and he ain't gonna let nothin bad happen."

She pointed to a man in an olive canvas jacket, trousers stuffed into high boots. He had a gray handlebar mustache and mostly gray hair under a low cap with a visor.

"Yes-sir-y, that's the great man himself, Mr. William Mulholland," Mrs. Daley continued. "He come down here right quick from Olancha Division soon as he heard about the cave-in. He been pacing in front a that tunnel fer the whole time I been here!"

Janey peered at the figure, who was striding back and forth with a bent, tense posture. Two other figures joined him—one appeared to be that doctor she and Chris had seen feeding stewed tomatoes to the drunkard yesterday in Mojave.

"That's my husband Tommy," Mrs. Daley pointed to the third man. "He's superintendent of this here Elizabeth Division."

Several more men joined the small group. Mulholland squatted at their feet and sketched something in the sand. Then he rose, clapped a hand on Daley's arm and moved off with the others toward a corral area where several wagons were sitting. Daley turned and walked down the slope toward the women.

The girls hopped up and danced forward to greet their father, who hugged and tickled them for a minute. "Go back and sit down now, there's work to be done," he said, patting them away. Looking quizzically at Janey for a moment, he turned to his wife and said in a low voice: "Rescue crew's been diggin near six hours now, and nothin, so the chief's decided to drill a shaft down into the tunnel, about 2,000 feet from the entrance, where they was drilling before the cave-in."

"Oh Dear Lord, couldn't that cause another collapse?" whispered Mrs. Daley.

"Could, but we don't think so, seein as they were driving those steel rods ahead as they went. Anyway, it's a chance we gotta take. We don't know how much air they got. Mulholland's already headed out there, and I'm going now with the rest of the equipment we need. Can ya inform Mrs. Kelly and the rest a the ladies?"

"Of course, dear, of course I will. They'll be fine. Don't you worry. We'll just wait here together for the good news."

Mr. Daley departed on a wagon with about a half-dozen men, the crowd at the tunnel entrance, turning in unison to watch them go. Soon the wagon was out of site, and the watchers began milling about again.

Suddenly there was a bright clanging from the center of the camp. A white-aproned and hatted figure was holding a triangle of metal out and striking it with a circling motion from the inside with a metal rod that flashed in the sun as it struck. The crowd began dissolving, with men moving off in small groups toward the mess tent. Janey turned and saw Chris coming from the tent toward them, followed by two other aproned men carrying large trays.

"I thought you might want to have your lunch here," explained Chris to Mrs. Daley.

"How thoughtful of you Mr. Bow," she responded with a warm smile, eyeing the sandwiches, cakes and lemonade, "but you and your staff oughtn't to be servin us. I know you've got more than your usual mouths to feed since they pulled in so many work crews from the desert to help with this rescue, so leave them trays with us and git on back to servin the men in the mess. We'll serve ourselves, won't we, Miss Janey? You can help me, and that'll give you a chance to make the acquaintance of the rest a the ladies."

Chris agreed, quickly figuring it might not do his business any harm either to put a feminine face on it, through the administrations of his sister. The food service wasn't held in high esteem at the moment, but if the wives of some of the workers could be brought to think better of it by associating with this nice young girl...perhaps that would calm things down. Wives, after all, had a powerful influence on their men.

There was just a smattering of families at each division camp, though Mulholland had tried to encourage more to come, offering small cabins for workers and larger ones for foremen, engineers and supervisors. He had ordered communal bathhouses built for female camp residents and recruited schoolmarms to teach in tented schoolhouses. To the many skeptics on the Los Angeles Board of Water and Power, the chief preached the wisdom of the investment, as having families to go to at shift's end kept men from dissipations, and the presence of women and children in the camp had a stabilizing effect on the entire workforce.

Janey, though she went forward graciously with Mrs. Daley, was quite put out with her brother. She had hoped he would take her with him to where they were drilling the new shaft or, at least, into the tunnel to observe the rescue efforts. Then she might have had something to write about that Mr. Chalfant would be willing to print in the *Inyo Register*.

Relinquishing her hopes of the day, she eventually relaxed and began paying attention to her task and the women to whom she was being introduced. They were simply dressed and simply spoken—much like the ranch wives of Owens Valley, much like her Ma. As the sun hung high in the pale afternoon sky, they spoke quietly among themselves, and she, accepted into their midst, heard much that the men, more taciturn by nature and guarded in their expressions, would not have relayed to a stranger.

A good deal of the talk was about Mr. Mulholland. Some of it was critical, like the story Mrs. Cora Brown told. During a previous cave-in, trapped tunnel workers had been supplied with hard-boiled eggs rolled down to them through a pipe. Mulholland had joked that they should be charged for the privilege! But not everyone in the camp had seen the humor of it. "He's always lookin to his own purse strings," Cora said bitterly.

Had Chris overheard this, he'd have recognized the bitterness was as much a reflection of bad feeling about the higher prices his operation was now charging for food as resentment about Mulholland. But Janey had no such perspective. So Mulholland was, after all, the monster some folks in the valley said he was.

"Oh, pshaw, that's nothin but a tall tale," Mrs. Daley dismissed it. "Everyone knows Mulholland would rather spend his day shoveling muck out of a tunnel than doing cost figures in an office. Besides, you seen how concerned he is about them workers, and all he's doin to help get 'em out."

Indeed, many of the women had nothing but good things to say about the chief, like how Mulholland worked beside his men and how he was infallible when it came to knowing every inch of the aqueduct's course. "My husband says he never carries even a notebook with 'em, but anywhere from Owens Lake to Los Angeles, you can ask him to show you the line of the aqueduct and tell you the exact elevation of the land there, and he can tell ya," Liz Pursey informed Janey.

Christina LeMark told how Mulholland was apt to visit the family cottages of an evening to roughhouse with the children and deliver a stack of books he thought they ought to read. "He even gave me advice about the correct method of diapering my young-uns!"

"Now that's a right engineering challenge!" squeaked Betsy Draker, her words dissolving into laughter, which the others joined with loud peals of merriment. It was a momentary release of tension from the strain of the long hours of wait and worry, subsiding quickly as the watch continued.

The sun was beginning its afternoon descent by the time Tommy Daley returned with Mulholland, the doctor and several other men. While the others walked to the tunnel entrance, Daley came over to the women, who watched his approach nervously. Was it good news?

"The shaft worked—they're alive, they're fine, and they're just where Mulholland thought they'd be. Now we've got a way to get fresh air and food down to 'em until the rescue team digs through, and they're very close now. Shouldn't be more than another hour."

Whoops of relief and joy greeted this wonderful news, the women and children all on their feet, dancing and embracing. Janey watched the release of emotion and how it was followed by a visible effort to regain the calm that had carried them through the difficult day. It wasn't over yet, the men weren't out yet. Custom and decorum called for the families to be seated once again and await the final act of the drama, staying out of the way of the rescuers.

"Can I go up there with you?" Janey asked when Chris joined them. "Please, I need to see what's happening for my newspaper story!"

"Okay, but stay close to me."

He tucked Janey's arm under his and led her up the slope and around the edge of the crowd to a place on the side where she was removed from the activity but had a clear view of it. From here, Janey was able to observe Mulholland, who stood waiting, pulling on his mustache and talking with the doctor. When he turned his head at an angle to her, she could see that his skin was deeply lined and leathery like an old pocket hunter or sheepherder.

A shout rang out from inside the tunnel. Mulholland and everyone else turned to see: Two men from the rescue team came running, yelling, "We've got them! They're coming out now!"

"Hooray! Hooray!" rejoiced the onlookers, pushing forward in a unified reflex of embrace. Janey turned to see the women and children streaming toward them.

"Stand back, stand back!" Mulholland and Daley restrained the crowd. "Give them room to breathe! After all those hours down there, they need to breath fresh air!" yelled the doctor.

And then they were out. Two rescuers emerged from the tunnel entrance holding the first of the freed workers between them.

"Kelly!" shrieked Mrs. Kelly, recognizing her man, though his "Powderface" was disguised by a mask of dark grime, which quickly transferred onto her face as she covered him with kisses.

Two more workers were carried out, and another after that. Men rushed forward from the crowd to help the rescuers and call encouragements to their chums.

Next a mountain of a man appeared, covered head to foot in grime, walking on his own. It was Big Joey. "Hoorah, the beast slayer!" came the shouts from his welcomers.

And then the crowd went wild, clapping and whistling and hollering, as a tall young man emerged, walking easily but, like the others, his face, hands and clothing caked with grime. Mulholland came forward and placed his two hands on the man's broad shoulders. The rescued worker returned the rough embrace, and Janey saw him wink one of the eyes that gleamed white through his black mask.

"Musta been that last Hail Mary you said, Chief, that did it!"

Everyone laughed in relief then, and Mulholland moved on to congratulate the others. Dr. Taylor approached the man who had made the joke, but his attentions were waved off. "See to my crew first, will ya please doc."

Someone brought him a jug of water. The man said thanks and placed it on the ground near his feet, but he didn't partake of it. Legs astride, hands on knees, he leaned over at the waist, holding that position for a few moments. Then he drew a deep breath and rose, his eyes floating upward, and from where Janey stood they seemed to be draining the blue of the late afternoon sky right into their orbs. It was her first look at Jed Brecken.

---

"Stop yer fussin er else!" Big Joey grabbed the chair and held it over his head. A plate smashed against his chest, sending globs of baked beans dribbling down his overalls. The huge man swung the chair at the opponent who had launched the bean assault, knocking him and three other men down.

"Come and git me, you bastards, all a ya at once!" Big Joey picked up another chair, as two pals of the felled men advanced on him. Joey knocked them down too. Three more men jumped him, as Denny Fisher and Chess Dorman sprang to his defense. Soon it was a free-for-all, with tables overturned and food, plates, cutlery and chairs flying in all directions.

Goose ran to the headquarters office for Tommy Daley, but by the time the superintendent arrived with Jeff Nester, his second in command, there wasn't much they could do to halt the fray, short of threatening the rioters with shotguns, which Daley was sure would only add oil to the fire. They watched in dismay but let the ruckus wind down on its own. Daley sent Nester to find Dr. Taylor. The physician, summoned from Mojave yesterday to care for the victims of the cave-in, had remained in camp overnight.

The trouble had started when one of the men, sitting down to a breakfast of steak and eggs, had sniffed at his plate, picked up the slab of meat and tossed it at one of the apron-clad servers. "This is sin-awful grub," he roared. "I ain't paying an extra five cents fer it. I ain't payin nothin fer it!"

"Ain't right to serve this rot to men who just dug out their mates from the ground!" yelled another, hurling his plate against the wall.

That's when Big Joey had taken the matter into his own huge hands. Normally no man was fool enough to stand up to Joey, but this time, some were just too mad to think. The guy who had thrown his plate at Joey now launched his neighbor's plate at the giant. This time Joey ducked, springing up from the crouch with fists fast and furious. His rage caught and flamed across the mess tent. Yesterday's cave-in was like a match on tinder for men worn crackling dry from all the months of hard work under the searing sun. The riot blazed out of control until the tent canvas had been pulled down to the ground and dozens of men, beaten insensible, lay in its tangles. Those still on their feet stumbled away, cursing, holding their bloodied mates up.

When it was over, Dr. Taylor began seeing to cuts, bruises and a few broken bones while Daley organized the cleanup and told Nester to call Chris Bow, who had taken his sister back to Mojave the night before.

"We've got another crew comin off shift in a few hours, and they're gonna need to eat. Most a the cook staff been chased right outta their kitchen. Bow is gonna need to see to it."

Chris was there by noon, flying up the road in the black limo, sending up clouds of sand. His arrival was greeted by shouts of derision and curses from the band of angry workers that had been forming around the camp since the incident. Chris ignored them, heading toward the headquarters office. One word—"Strike!"—ominously rose above the din.

Entering the office, Chris was surprised to see J.B. Lippincott. The assistant chief engineer had just arrived too, having ridden down on horseback from the Jawbone after receiving a call from Daley.

"Where's Mulholland?" Chris heard Lippincott ask division superintendent Daley.

"Rode out this mornin to where they drilled the new shaft yesterday. That cave in was tough luck for young Brecken's crew," explained Daley. "Gonna put them way behind Aston's. The contest is probably over, but the chief went out with him to see if anything could be done. They should be back soon."

"They're talking strike out there," injected Chris.

Lippincott, Daley and Nester all turned toward him, their faces incredulous. "We know that Bow," said Lippincott sardonically. "Why do you think I'm here? I warned you there was trouble coming!"

"And I told you I was fixing it. I've been talking to the railroads about using their icebox cars, like the Harvey Company does, maybe even taking over some of their excess capacity…but I need some time to put it together."

"There isn't any more time," Lippincott snapped. "Your problems, Bow, have given the WFM just the opportunity they've been waiting for."

"But most of the men aren't even union!" protested Nester.

"It don't matter," said Lippincott. "If I'm not mistaken, there's plenty of new members signing up right now, and plenty of others will just follow along even if they aren't members."

They all turned to look out the window at the growing number of men clustering about. The whistle blew for the shift change, and more men came out of the tents, some wearing work boots and helmets, and started gathering in their normal work crews. But as these groups mingled with the agitators and those just milling about, none moved off to the tunnel or to the wagons that would take them into the desert. As wagons arrived with the previous shift's returning crews, these men too became engulfed by the agitated throng.

Lippincott shook his head in disgust. This should never have happened. One of the brilliant strokes of management foresight that he certainly did credit to his boss was the decision not to engage outside contractors to build the aqueduct, companies whose bids were high and workforces largely unionized. Instead Mulholland had argued that the city could hire and manage its own workforce for far less money, which had proved to be true. That made aqueduct workers, technically speaking, civil servants. But Mulholland had also managed to wrangle an exemption for most of his workers, including tunnel crews, carpenters, blacksmiths and muleskinners, from the normal civil service hiring processes, including written tests. Even in his present grim mood, Lippincott had to chuckle at the thought of some of the aqueduct's toughest and crudest workers sitting down to take a civil service examination!

In Lippincott's view, this direct engagement of the men, along with steady work, reasonable pay and, originally anyway, good grub had enabled the aqueduct to proceed this far with little or no labor trouble. The Western Federation of Miners had signed some men up, but not enough to exert any real influence. Until now—now it seemed that Bow's incompetence may have opened the door for them.

There he was: Mulholland had just ridden up with Jed Brecken, and the crowd bent toward them.

"Let's go," said Lippincott, and the management team went out to join their chief. Chris headed the other way, toward the kitchen, which was damaged but still standing. He would find his people and set about putting things right.

Mulholland dismounted and turned calmly to face the crowd. Brecken did the same. His eyes took in the wreckage that had been the mess tent, then scanned the sea of angry faces, which included, he noted, a good number of the men on his own crew.

"Hello boys," said Mulholland. "What's going on?"

"Chief, sir, the men aren't going to put up with these conditions any longer." Carl Ecker, a WFM member, came forward.

"Which conditions would those be Carl?"

"The food! It ain't worth the original fare of 25 cents, and sure ain't worth 30. We demand a pay increase to cover the hike."

Mulholland noted that while a demand might reasonably have been made for a roll back of the fare or an improvement in the food, the union man was steering the situation toward payroll. That's where unions wanted to be negotiating, that's where they built their power base. "The food is adequate," he replied. "It's the same food I eat, same Brecken here eats. Lippincott, Daley and Nester too." The chief paused and shifted his gaze from the spokesman to the crowd behind him. He spoke his next words loudly so that all would hear: "There will be no pay increase, and the price of a meal is 30 cents. That's the end of it."

Mulholland turned aside and walked toward the office, his managers following. Brecken remained where he stood, watching the stunned faces of Ecker and the rest of the men.

Carl turned to him. "Brecken, why didn't you say nothin? Don't we deserve decent food?"

"Yes, we all deserve it, but I reckon this isn't the worst you've had to put up with. Sure ain't the worst I've had." Brecken walked into the crowd, which made way for him to pass, and headed up the hill to his tent. He wasn't going to get drawn into a debate with Ecker, whom he knew to be a serious, clever fellow, not above a devious ploy now and then for the good of the cause. He'd talk to his men later and see what he could do to calm things down.

Meanwhile in the office, Mulholland's staff was near as stunned as the men outside. The chief had been unusually intractable, choosing not even to acknowledge the severity of the food problem. This was surely going to make matters even worse, worried Daley.

"Wouldn't it make sense, Chief, to maybe roll back the meal fare until Bow gets the problems under control?" Daley suggested.

"No, it wouldn't."

"We're likely to have a strike on our hands," said Lippincott.

"Let them strike." Mulholland dropped into Daley's chair and swung his boots up onto the superintendent's desk. He pulled a cigar from his pocket, bit the tip and spat it off. They waited as he lit it and puffed. When Mulholland looked up at them, exhaling slowly, his eyes were twinkling behind the veil of smoke. "In fact," he winked, "a strike might just be quite convenient. We've run up against a delay getting the next round of bond financing underway. So the truth is, without a strike, the money was gonna peter out. We'd of had to lay off workers anyhow. This way, we can shut down most of the operations for a couple of months until the money frees up. And besides, having the camp in San Francisquito Canyon emptied out for a spell will give us a chance to do some test drilling on the east embankment there. See if it's stable and if the canyon is as good a site for a reservoir, as I suspect."

They stared at him. Mulholland smoked calmly, watching them absorb the information and struggle to make sense of it.

Lippincott was first to speak. "Isn't this awfully risky Chief? What if we can't hire enough men back and gear up fast enough when we wanna get started again?"

"Oh, I reckon that won't be a problem," responded Mulholland. "Because when we start up again, we'll expand the bonus system from just the tunneling crews to the whole workforce. Any man who does more work than his daily quota will be able to earn more. That should attract plenty of workers and squelch the bellyaching about an extra nickel for grub."

"What about the extra cost of payin those bonuses?" asked Daley. "How will we keep on-budget?"

Lippincott had already seen it—that Daley wasn't too quick, he thought.

Mulholland answered patiently. "Well, I've had W.B. Matthews, our attorney, look into it. He says we'll be able go a long way toward covering the bonuses from the shutdown savings alone. And when they come back, the men will work faster to earn their bonuses, which will bring us in under time and budget."

He saw they were suitably impressed. Sometimes, Mulholland reflected, problems can turn out to be advantages in disguise. This had proved to be the case already once that day. In the morning, examining the auxiliary tunnel shaft with Brecken, he'd immediately seen an opportunity. Brecken was resourceful and determined, but he was still young, and he'd been near to throwing his hands up in despair after this latest cave-in. His team had been stopped in its tracks; how could they ever catch up with Aston's?

"That cave-in brought down a whole lot of loose rock," Mulholland had observed, as they squatted together peering down through the auxiliary shaft into tunnel. "What if we enlarged this shaft so you could get some of your crew down through it? You put some men to mucking out the debris from this side of the rock fall at the same time as the rest of your teams keep boring through from the other side of it. Might be you'll soon be yards ahead of Aston."

Mulholland had been gratified to see Brecken's eyes fire and the young crew boss's usual aggressive determination vanquish the uncharacteristic spell of doubt. Of course now, with a strike imminent, this new plan of attack would be on hold. But Aston's crew would suffer the same delay. And when work started up again, the two teams would be like pit bulls straining to be unleashed. "Which is exactly how I want them," Mulholland congratulated himself. He smiled and smoked. The day was working out quite well indeed.

The train puffed into the station, its short rhythmic exhalations punctuated by two piercing whistle bursts of steam. It was a Southern Pacific train, come from Chicago by way of St. Louis and Los Angeles, now bound for San Francisco. Janey Bow, watching its arrival through the Harvey House lunch room's sparkling clean windows, knew this because she'd studied the schedule of arrivals and departures in the Mojave depot lounge. She tried to imagine herself inside one of the passenger cars, arriving at these fabled destinations. As Janey sat at the lunch room counter, she'd found herself doing this each time a train arrived. Two had stopped at the depot, and three had passed through without stopping.

If she had to be stranded like a leaf in the eddy of a stream, then at least it was diverting to have all this activity around her. Since yesterday, when he had received the call about the riot, Chris had essentially deserted her. Janey knew her brother had plenty of troubles and responsibilities to see to, but it wasn't right to leave her with nothing to do like this, and only one day left of her visit. Tomorrow she was to return home to Owens Valley.

At first Janey had tried to make the best of the situation. She had stayed in Lesley's room and set herself to writing a story about the cave-in at the Elizabeth Tunnel. Again, she was troubled about how to start and, on top of that, having been kept corralled with the ladies most of that tense day, she now felt ill-equipped with the necessary details about the rescue work and drilling of the auxiliary shaft one would need to write a proper article.

Drifting, she had found herself picturing how Mulholland had looked pacing back and forth in front of the tunnel opening. Always people described the chief in such big terms: To some folks in the valley, he was a monster; to Chris and some of the workers and their families here, he was a hero, and that's how they talked about him too in the Los Angeles newspapers Mr. Chalfant had shown her. To her eyes, Mulholland had been a surprisingly ordinary man in front of that tunnel. He'd seemed normal, like her Pa. And with his worried face, he could have been a Pa, the Pa of all those men trapped down there.

What was that tale someone had told her about Mulholland lecturing on the proper methods for diapering a baby? Janey's mind began to sort through the rag bag of stories and opinions she had collected as she had sat with the women and children the long of that afternoon and afterward as she'd overheard snatches of conversations among the workmen gathered around the rescued crew. Unlike numbers and facts, which she never managed to recall, such tales came back easily.

She started jotting them down. Gradually she began to weave the bits together into some kind of story. But would Chalfant print a story about what folks thought about the chief of the aqueduct and even what sort of man he might actually be? Maybe he'd think it too girlish in nature?

Still, Janey, reading back what she had written, was pleased enough with it. And Lesley, looking at it the previous evening, had thought it of some value. "It's not exactly like what real reporters write, Janey, but it's real interestin!"

Today, however, Janey wasn't so sure. She'd read and re-read the story, between train arrivals and departures, and she was afraid Chalfant would find it silly. She closed her notebook, took a sip of her Coca-Cola and glanced out the window again. The passengers were disembarking from the train. A gong sounded to notify the lunch room staff of their imminent arrival.

This was Janey's favorite moment. As the hungry passengers swarmed into the lunch room and took seats at the counter, the cadre of Harvey Girls stood at attention by their stations. Orders had been taken on the train and wired ahead, so the Harvey Girls were able to begin serving meals immediately—roast beef with mashed potatoes and gravy, Janey observed, was a heavy favorite over the pork with apple sauce. Two "drink girls" circulated around with coffee, milk and tea. They knew exactly which beverage to pour for each customer by how the waitress had positioned the cup in the place setting: up for coffee, down for milk, on its side for tea. As folks wiped up the last smear of gravy with homemade rolls, plates with thick wedges of apple or cherry pie arrived along with a refill of their cup.

All of this took place in the space of half an hour, from disembarking to reloading. It seemed much longer though, and, indeed, the passengers seemed to have plenty of time to savor their meal. Janey supposed that because everything was ready, little of the half hour was taken up waiting for service; nearly all of it was available for eating. She also noticed that the Harvey Girls, though they were trained to use every second efficiently, acted in a relaxed manner—giving the impression that they had all the time in the world to lavish attention on their customers. As Janey watched the satisfied passengers being ushered courteously back out to the train, she felt she was beginning to understand why Chris had been so impressed with this company.

When the lunch room was nearly empty again, Katie Poling, who was one of the servers on duty, came up to Janey and offered her another Coca-Cola. "Don't you want a nice piece a pie to go with that, Janey? You haven't eaten hardly anything all afternoon!"

"No thanks, just the soda." Seeing all that food flooding out of the kitchen with each wave of passengers had taken away Janey's appetite.

"Fine, suit yerself." Katie sidled over to another of the few remaining customers. Two chairs away, Janey hadn't even noticed him until the room emptied. He was smiling at Katie and accepting the offered pie. She watched him surreptitiously. Tall and broad shouldered with black hair, bronze skin and blue eyes, he was reading a book—she thought the title might be *Call of the Wild*—as he sipped his coffee and chewed slowly through the wedge of pie.

Janey opened her notebook again and pretended to be reading as well. She watched him under her lashes. When he had finished, he put his fork down, wiped his napkin across his mouth and swung around on his stool to look out the window. There was little activity on the depot platform at the moment. The young man turned back around and, as he did, caught sight of Janey.

"Hello miss," he said. "May I inquire what you're readin there?"

"Oh, nothing, not really…um…" She was deeply startled that he had spoken to her like that, without any kind of proper introduction, and too embarrassed to tell him she'd been reading her own writing. Janey was even more stunned when he got up with his coffee and moved over to the seat next to her. Katie, she noticed, was watching them from the back of the room, where she was cleaning and reloading the massive coffee urn. All of the Harvey Girls were busy straightening and polishing their stations, and pitching in on other tasks to prepare for the next arrival.

"Looks like more than nothing to me." He was peering at her handwritten text.

She closed the notebook and placed her hands over it. Janey ought to have been alarmed, but she realized, surprised, she wasn't. His smile and eyes were kind, even if they were laughing at her just a bit. And he looked and smelled very clean compared to most of the men she'd seen in town. "Well, it's just something I wrote, or anyway I'm trying to write," she replied. "It's an article for the *Inyo Register*."

"What's the *Inyo Register*?"

"It's a newspaper, in Bishop, the newspaper for the Owens Valley."

He cocked his head slightly and studied her. "Is that where you're from then? What's your name young miss from Owens Valley?"

"Yes, it's where I'm from," she mumbled, looking down at her notebook. It was forward of him to ask her name when he hadn't even given his. But the silence as he waited for her reply was too embarrassing for her to let it go on. She raised her eyes and thrust her chin forward. "My name is Miss Jane Hazeltine Bow, and I am the sister of Mr. Christopher Bow. Who might you be sir?"

It was his turn to feel embarrassed, realizing he'd been rude. "I beg your pardon Miss Bow. The name's Jed Brecken. I'm the northern crew boss on the Elizabeth Tunnel."

It was all she could do not to stare at him, so she dropped her eyes again to the cover of her notebook. He couldn't possibly be the man she'd seen day before yesterday covered head to foot in grime. But she knew he was; the eyes were the same.

Brecken was thinking she didn't look at all like her brother. Chris Bow, fair, big-boned, ruddy faced; she, honey brown and colt slender. He realized he was studying her impertinently and quickly took a sip of coffee.

"Wouldn't normally impose myself on you like this, miss, but I'm in unusual need of company. In fact, I find myself this afternoon in the very odd circumstance of having nothing whatsoever to do."

She looked up sharply, finding him forward again. But the smile that met hers was so warm, and he truly did seem to be seeking just a little conversation. Besides, a man who had been near buried alive just two days ago deserved her consideration.

"You're not imposing Mr. Brecken. As it happens, I've little to occupy myself with either at the moment. My brother is busy with his business."

"Forgive me, miss, for saying so," he said, winking at her, "but your brother had something to do with my present state of lassitude. It therefore seems equitable that I should enjoy a few moment's distraction in the company of his charming sister."

Janey noticed his hair was not black but dark brown with reddish glints. Ignoring the reference to Chris as well as the compliment, she asked, "Your crew has joined the strike then Mr. Brecken?"

He sighed. "Not at first, they didn't. They're a pretty tough bunch, not much given to complaining. But more and more crews up and down the line, in every division, got riled up after Mulholland refused to increase their pay. Lotsa fellas, like my guys, finally joined them, in sympathy, or to avoid being roughed up."

"Oh my," she winced. "What's going to happen now? Is everybody just up and leaving?" She was wondering what would happen to Chris's business if there weren't any more men left to feed.

"Everybody's pretty much gone or going. Except me. I'm staying."

"Why? What can you do here?"

"I can dig. We had a big cave-in the other day, brought lotsa loose rock down. Somebody's got to clear it out."

"By yourself?"

"Sure. Better than doin nothin, like today." He smiled, "Although, this afternoon's sure turned out to be more agreeable than I'd thought."

She flushed, sought for something she could say, something to deflect the compliment. "Do you think Mr. Mulholland was right to refuse the increase in pay?"

He thought about it awhile, and then he said, "I don't see much justice in insisting men pay more for food that's getting worse every day— no offense to your brother. But, on the other hand, I don't imagine it's easy keeping food fresh in the middle of the desert. If it had been me deciding instead of the chief, I would have lowered the meal fare. But I know him to be a fair-minded man, a man who considers all of the facts before making a decision. So I'm sure he had a good reason for what he did; I just don't know what it is yet."

"I wrote about him." Janey tapped her notebook lightly with her index finger, then immediately colored, wondering why in the world she was telling this stranger about the story she wasn't even sure she'd ever show to Chalfant.

Brecken was interested. "What did you say about him?"

"Oh, it's more about what other people say of him. During the tunnel cave-in—I was there," she said shyly. "Chris left me waiting with the women, and they had quite a bit to say about Superintendent Mulholland. I just listened to what they were saying to each other. Tried to ask a few questions too, like a reporter ought."

"What kinds of things did they say?"

"Well, most folks here seem to hold him in high esteem, but not all." She was looking at Brecken's arm, extended across the counter as he ran a finger absently around the rim of his cup. From the well-formed, almost slender wrist it broadened into a muscular forearm that rippled slightly with the movement. He had rolled up the cuffs of his white cotton shirt; below it, the suntanned skin was lightly stroked with dark hair.

"Course not, that's not the way of folks, to be in agreement," he was saying. She pulled her eyes away from his arm, focusing them back on her notebook.

"Can I read it then?" He made a slight gesture toward the volume.

She grabbed it up and hugged it to her chest, shaking her head. "It's not ready yet."

"How did you learn to be a writer—in school?"

"I'm not really a writer, yet. I guess I learned some of how to do it in school. And some from Mr. Chalfant—he's the editor of the *Inyo Register*. I help him sometimes and study the stories he's getting ready to print. He told me that if I saw something worth writing about during my visit here with Chris that I could try giving him an article for the paper. I don't know if he'll want this one," she said, embarrassed, looking down at her notebook.

"I bet he will," said Brecken.

She frowned, surprised again by the familiarity of his remark, and said stiffly, "You don't even know me, Mr. Brecken. You don't even know if I can write a proper sentence."

"It's true I don't know you, Miss Bow, but I do seem to know that about you." He thought for a minute. "Maybe it was how you were watching the waitresses going about the business of serving all those passengers their lunch. You were studying them, as I imagine you were studying everything that happened the day you were waiting at the cave-in," he chuckled, "everything including me, I reckon!"

"Only at the end, when you came out covered in mud!"

They both laughed, but Janey felt her face was becoming permanently flushed. She picked up a safer thread from the conversation.

"I think I learned most, though, from this lady writer who used to live in the valley. I used to spend a lot of time with her. We'd go on rambles into the canyons, up what she called the 'backstreets of the mountains.' She was good with words like that."

"Who is she? Might I have read any of her books?" asked Brecken.

"Mary Austin is her name. I doubt you've heard of her, except if you've read some of her magazine stories in *Out West*, the *Atlantic*, *Scribner's* and such. They're about the Paiute, the Mexican sheepherders and other western folk. She also wrote a novel, called *Isidro*, about life in the old Spanish missions—it was serialized in the *Atlantic Monthly*, and my Ma gave me my own copy for, I think it was, my ninth birthday. That was after Mrs. Austin left the Owens Valley. But my favorite is her first book, which is called *The Land of Little Rain*. She wrote it about the valley while she still lived there. It's about people too, but mostly about the land, the plants and trees that grow on it and the wild creatures that live there."

"Hmmm, wouldn't mind reading that. I reckon my Ma might be able to find a copy for me in Denver—Denver, Colorado, that's where I'm from."

Janey longed to ask him to tell her all about Denver, about himself, but she felt she had stayed talking to the young man too long for propriety. "Excuse me, I'll be needing to be off now and pack for my journey home."

"When are you leaving miss?"

"Tomorrow morning." She rose, and he did too. "Thank you Mr. Brecken for a very interesting conversation."

"Miss Bow." He placed a hand lightly on her wrist. He felt her tense, but she did not pull her arm away. "Once I've read the book, may I write you a letter telling you my opinion of it?"

"I suppose so…" Janey was disturbed, and thrilled. Having never entertained a proposal of the kind from a young man, she hadn't the slightest notion of whether she ought accept it. She wanted to accept it very much.

"If you would be so kind as to write down your address in the Owens Valley…" he gave her an encouraging smile and nodded toward her notebook.

"Yes, certainly." Janey fumbled open the cover and, gripping her pen to stop her hand from shaking, wrote her name and address. She tore off the strip of paper, chastising herself for the lack of decorum, and handed it to him, quickly withdrawing her hand and hugging her notebook.

"Good afternoon Mr. Brecken."

"Good afternoon Miss Bow, and thank you."

She turned and walked out of the lunch room, her face burning at the thought he might be watching.

That night Janey Bow was again the center of attention in the Harvey Company dormitory. Katie had let it be known that Jed Brecken had been in the lunch room—and had sat for near 40 minutes talking with Janey! More than a dozen Harvey Girls crammed into Lesley's room, demanding to hear all the details she could muster about what he'd said and done. She told them everything she could remember, leaving out only the discussion of her article and the request for her address. As with the previous time she'd been called on to recount her day's adventure, Janey was nervous, but this time she was careful with her mode of expression. In any case, no one seemed inclined to laugh at what she had to say.

"Jed Brecken," said Helen dreamily, with undisguised envy.

"Drat, why wasn't I on lunch duty today?" Olive Mason, a homely girl with a slow way of speaking, pointed a lazy finger at Katie. "At least you got to serve him up a wedge a pie."

"I sure wouldn't mind givin that one a piece of *my pie*," said Melissa, tossing her loosened hair back, hands at her thick waist.

"Get in line behind me," responded Nora, extending a long leg to push the other girl over with a black-stockinged foot.

"Now stop that girls! Janey here's still a youngster and shouldn't be a party to such talk." Lesley was only half-joking. Like her coworkers, she was wondering why Jed Brecken had paid the time of day to a skinny little girl with hardly any bosom at all. Maybe he had felt sorry for Janey, being alone there in the lunch room. Sure, that was probably it, the older girl reassured herself as they lay in the twin beds later, talking sleepily.

"Janey," Lesley asked, "how tall is he?" But this last night, it was Janey who had drifted off first.

# Chapter 11

Jed Brecken had guessed right about Chalfant. The *Inyo Register* editor did decide to print Janey's story, though not without misgivings.

The article started well, he judged, with the drama of the cave-in, but it veered off into a piece focused on Chief Engineer Mulholland. And even at that, rather than being rooted in the reporter's interviews and observations, it was a pastiche of the views of many different sources. This collection of stories and opinions about Mulholland was far from the article Chalfant had expected when he had told his young office helper that if she could come up with something on the aqueduct, he "might consider" printing it. Still, he had to admit, the piece had plenty of interesting things to say about the man. Some of it was bad, but most of it was good—Janey had portrayed the man considered a "monster" by many in the valley as quite human. Likely to be a bit controversial, he thought, and that was what decided him in favor of printing it. Sells papers.

Yet even Chalfant was flabbergasted by how much attention the article, which appeared on the second page of the Monday morning edition, actually attracted. Up and down the streets of Bishop folks were reading, discussing and arguing over it—he heard the same about Independence and Lone Pine. And Chalfant sure hadn't expected major dailies in Los Angeles, San Francisco, Denver, Boston and New York to pick up the story, referring to it in their own stories covering the worker's strike, which had made the aqueduct a nationally newsworthy subject again. A couple of the papers even featured long quotes lifted straight from Janey's article, which Chalfant had printed with the byline J. Bow.

The editor was amused: "I wonder if the major dailies would have been so quick to jump on the story if they'd known it had been written by a 15-year-old girl!" he remarked to Mark Watterson during one of their morning conversations in the *Register* office. The younger of the two banker brothers had always been Chalfant's favorite, and last year, when Mark had married Chalfant's cousin Elsie, he had also become family.

Leaving church the following Sunday, the Watterson party approached the Bows, who had been the object of many disapproving looks and whispers as they had entered and left the service. Chalfant, watching from where he stood chatting with the minister, saw the Wattersons step forward. As usual, he thought, rely on those two to set an example of community solidarity and cordiality.

Wilfred Watterson remarked to Alice on the fine day and excellent sermon, and held his hand out first to Ben and then to Chris. The young man, after accompanying Janey back home, had remained in the valley for a brief visit. Then Wilfred turned and offered congratulations to Janey.

"A very good article about a difficult subject," the banker said, smiling warmly. "Don't you worry about what some folks are saying, miss. The reason we have newspapers is so that we have a chance to read all points of view."

"Good job, Janey," agreed Elsie, leaning heavily on Mark Watterson's arm. She was preparing for her own debut, as a mother. "The first time for anything is a little bit scary, isn't it?"

"Yes, yes it is, thank you" was all Janey could manage. She was so unused to being singled out for attention and uncomfortable in the presence of her Ma, Pa and brother at being so.

"Excuse me," said Janey, "Mrs. Bellamy seems to need to speak with me." She indicated Nellie Bellamy, who was beckoning her.

Alice Bow nodded, granting permission from long habit though it had not been requested. "She's still very shy," Alice said, attempting to explain Janey's abrupt departure to the Watterson party, who nodded as if they understood. Alice was thinking that even she didn't understand her daughter very well these days. Bold enough to insist on the trip to visit Chris, and then to come home with a newspaper article, but intimidated by a simple conversation with adults. Though, Alice noticed, she seemed well enough at ease over there with Nellie.

Janey was smiling up at the plump, red-headed woman, who had placed an arm about her shoulders. "I sure enjoyed that sermon this mornin, but not half as much as reading your article!" gushed Mrs. Bellamy. "My, my wouldn't Mrs. Austin be proud of her little friend!" She gave Janey a squeeze. "But I guess you're not so little anymore are you?"

"No, I suppose not," agreed Janey, a bit sadly. For just a moment in Mrs. Bellamy's embrace, she had almost heard Ruth Austin trilling "Belle, Belle!" for her favorite babysitter. Where was Ruth now? Was she all right? Janey wondered it for the thousandth time. Oh how she longed for those golden mornings of gobbling down pastries with the beautiful little girl and hiking up into the canyons with Mary! Everything had been so bright and easy then, when all that had been required of her was to follow.

---

As if Mrs. Bellamy were clairvoyant, a most astonishing thing happened just a few days later: Janey received two letters, one from Jed Brecken and the other from Mary Austin. Ma, walking back up the road from their mailbox out on the lane, was terrifically curious, but she let Janey take the letters up to her room to read them in private.

Janey settled on the window seat, arranging the two envelopes on a cushion in front of her. She sat for a long time, looking out at the big oak with its spreading, reaching branches, then back down at the envelopes. The one with Mary Austin's name—and a return address of Briar Cottage, Carmel by the Sea, California—was lettered in swirling script on thick, smooth creamy paper. She couldn't believe Mary had finally written to her! And where was Carmel, other than, obviously, by the sea? When she reached out her hand to stroke the paper, her fingers were shaking. She withdrew the hand back to her lap. The other, with a return address to a post office box in Mojave, had been lettered with unslanted, equispaced characters. The pale gray paper was thin; she could see the edges of the folded page inside.

She decided to start with it. Tearing open the flap, she withdrew the thin piece of paper and read:

Dear Miss Bow,

Please accept my thanks, both for your agreeable company in the Harvey House lunch room and for your recommendation of the book by Mrs. Austin. My mother sent it to me from Denver, and it has been a very good companion ever since.

You will recall that we are having a strike here, so my days in the Elizabeth Tunnel are long and solitary. I had the notion of rewarding myself each evening when my labors were finished with a few pages from the little volume. As you may imagine, I was unable to restrain myself, and too quickly arrived at the end. Still finding myself very much under its spell, I began again at the beginning, reading more slowly this time and with more attention to the author's choice of words. I made up a sort of game for myself of waiting for the pictures the words created in my mind to fully appear and then letting myself walk around in these favorite hidden places. So you see, I now feel that I have accompanied you and Mrs. Austin on your walks up into the streets of the mountains and sat with you on the rocky ledges, looking out over your beloved valley.

Certainly this means that when we next meet (which I hope will be soon), we will be friends.

Sincerely yours,

Jed Brecken

Janey read through the letter several times, glowing with pleasure at the warmth of his address, his desire to see her again and the respect accorded her relationship with Mary Austin. She slid the page back into its envelope and placed the envelope back on the cushion, turning her attention to its companion. How remarkable that Mary had elected to contact her at the same moment as Mr. Brecken, and after all these years! Was it simply coincidence or a divine plan at work? Janey took the thick, smooth envelope between fingers, now shaking again, withdrew the two pages and read:

*My dear Janey,*

*No doubt you have hoped for word of me these long years. I must assure you that my silence was not for lack of affection but due to my conviction that you had much growing up to do and needed no distractions from it. I have always planned to re-establish our communication when the day should come that I might be of assistance to you. Now, upon reading an excerpt of your article on Mulholland (appearing in the San Francisco Chronicle), I must conclude*

that this day has come, as you are in great need of
my counsel.

Know this dear child: You have been taken in
by a deceitful, voracious and implacable man. It is
not to your complete discredit, as he has taken in so
many others far older and more experienced in life
and politics than you. My assessment of his character is certain, however, as I have met him face
to face. I never told you that during my visit to
Los Angeles, just prior to quitting the valley, I
sought an audience with Superintendent Mulholland. During this meeting, I accused him of cloaking
in false and misleading assurances his true intentions for the valley, which are none other than to
drain it dry. He, confronted by the truth, could not
deny it.

If you persist on this course you have apparently
embraced, you will learn that a journalist's purpose
is not to report what others say about a matter, but
to discover and relate the truth of it. So much more
is this the mission of all serious authors of literature.
But my dear, I fear that you may have little gift for
the vocation.

An editor once said these words to me, which,
grace of God, proved to be untrue. Perhaps this may
be the case for you as well, though I must warn you
that to set your foot firmly on the path of becoming
a writer of any classification, especially for a married woman, is not an easy life.

In friendship and with sincere best wishes for
your health and happiness,
Mary Austin

Janey laid the letter aside and leaned back against the wall, bewildered and feeling tears pricking the corners of her eyes. Mary disapproved
of her article. Certainly she must be right, as she is a famous author and

even Jed holds her in high esteem. Yet Mr. Chalfant had commended this first effort, and printed the piece—he is well regarded too.

Janey hugged her knees to her chest, pushing her face into the knees of her overalls. Brecken was smart, and he had looked forward to reading, and rereading, Mary's words every night, even finding them a welcome escape from his solitary toil. How wonderful to be able to put words on paper that another person would desire to read so ardently, words that might bring the reader some pleasure or relief from daily toil and troubles. Janey knew she would never arouse such admiration, as surely as she knew she would never look like her mother. Why had Mary written after all this time? And what could she say in reply? She'd have to write back, it would be rude and indecorous not to. Ma would insist. Part of her wished her mentor had not reestablished their friendship, but part of her longed to wander again with Mary—where had she been these eight years and what was she doing in Carmel by the Sea—if even by correspondence.

"Janey!" Ma was calling her to help with supper. She put the pages back into the heavy envelope and took both letters dutifully downstairs. Ma would certainly ask to see them.

It was Chris's last supper at home that night; thus, to Janey's relief, her surprising bonanza of missives from the outside world was not the main topic of discussion. Ma had made fried chicken with whipped potatoes and slender fresh-picked carrots with butter and parsley. A peach cobbler, fragrantly steaming, had just been plucked from the oven and sat on the sideboard.

As Chris was accepting a second helping of cobbler, Alice reached over and placed her hand on his arm, gazing at him fondly.

"Wish you could stay on son," she said wistfully.

"Me too Ma." He smiled back, knowing it wasn't true. "But I've got business to attend to. This here strike is an opportunity to make improvements in my supply and transportation methods."

Ben nodded. "That's the way, son. Do the best job you can every day and keep giving the customer more value." Chris had not shared with his father the role deteriorating food quality had played in the strike. He shifted the conversation to another topic, one he had been waiting to address.

"And you know Pa, to continue to improve, I'm planning on expanding. You see, the more business I do, the better deals I can negotiate with farmers and other suppliers, even with the railroads."

"What sort of expansion are you planning, son?"

"Supplying hotels, mostly in Los Angeles. There's lots of growth there, it's the 17th largest city in the nation now, and they're expanding the port. They've even opened up a moving picture company there."

He noted their surprise at this last comment, and hurtled on. "Anyway, to manage properly I'm going to need to live there. So I'm planning to buy a house…," he said, looking down at his syrup-glazed, crumb-encrusted bowl, "and move to Los Angeles permanently."

He raised his eyes to theirs. Ma's were holding back tears. Pa's were just looking at him, calmly as always, but Janey thought she saw pain in them. She was first to speak. "But it's so far away! When are you going there?!" Her voice squeaked.

"Soon as I can find a house." He reached out to pat Ma's arm. "But I'll be back, same as now, for visits."

"Well, then," Ben spoke quietly, rising from the table. "I guess that's settled then."

Chris didn't know to what his father referred, exactly what had been in question and was now settled. But he was glad he had told them, glad it was over.

Pa didn't seem to be much in a mind for reading after supper, heading out to the barn instead. "Got a few chores to finish up."

Chris thought to follow him there so just the two of them could talk, but he didn't really know what to say. So he stayed in the house and helped Ma and Janey dry the dishes.

Janey watched her brother trying to be helpful, wooing Ma's cheerfulness back with comic tales of kitchen misadventures at the work sites—one story's outcome was 20 dozen burned biscuits.

"They fueled quite a campfire that night!" chortled Chris.

Janey didn't feel like laughing. She felt jostled and bruised by Jed's attentions, Mary's criticism and now Chris's desertion. She had felt so proud to be with Chris in Mojave and at the camps, but she could see that soon as the aqueduct was finished, she would almost never see him anymore. He would move to the city, to a new life. And what would she do?

By then she would have her diploma—just one more year to go—but what would she do with it? Mary had continued on to college, but most women with college degrees just taught school, and Janey found that prospect dull and unappealing. Maybe Mr. Chalfant would hire her on as a reporter for the *Register*? But he already had Bucky and, anyway, maybe Mary was right, maybe she hadn't the talent to be a writer, even for a newspaper. Maybe she could apply to become a Harvey Girl and work in some far-off place. Why, Lesley had told her the Harvey Company even had a big, fancy hotel on the very edge of the Grand Canyon!

This fantasy was quite appealing, and made Janey feel better. That night when she nestled into her bed, she brought it back to mind, imagining herself in a starched black and white uniform, standing at attention as her customers took their seats around a large, oval lunch counter. There he was, at the middle of the table, a tall young man with broad shoulders, dark brown hair and blue eyes awaiting her attentions.

# Chapter 12

Mary Austin had not given more than a fleeting thought to young Janey Bow since watching the girl walk out the yard of the little brown house on the day of Mary's liberation from Wallace and the doomed valley. Nor did she consider the girl much eight years later, on the day she got the notion to write her a letter.

That day had begun as usual: Mary passed the morning working, as was her settled habit and generally that of the other members of the budding artist's colony at Carmel. Weather allowing, she preferred to write in her "wickiup," a platform she had constructed in the spreading arms of a giant oak tree in the garden of her house, christening it with the name of a Paiute sacred shelter. Dressed in a flowing Grecian-style robe, her long chestnut hair loose down her back, Mary would mount the rickety ladder and sit at the low desk. Here she felt the spirit in nature around her and the creative inspiration within her.

Just before noon, satisfied with her efforts, she tucked her robe into a riding skirt, donned a light jacket, exchanged sandals for boots and took the trail fringed with dark green ceanothus sprayed with thick purple-blue blossoms to Carmel's scanty main street. Mary had chosen to build her house near the village rather than out on the point among the wind-swept pines so as to be close to conveniences that would enable her to avoid the burden of cooking. She thus took most of her meals at the Pine Inn, where the *San Francisco Chronicle* was available in the lobby and hearty fare served up in the dining room for a mere 20 cents. The special that day was a thick chowder of local abalone, which Mary sopped up with sourdough bread as she scanned the paper. Her attention was snagged by an article about a strike at the Los Angeles aqueduct, which the reporter said could be "ruinous" to the city—a pleasurable prospect indeed to this reader.

Glancing at some boxed text, set off by scrolling line art from the rest of the article, she realized the subject was Mulholland, the man she had long ago confronted in his office in Los Angeles. She was about to move on—after all, what interest did he hold for her anymore—when she saw the credit. The text in the box was credited to J. Bow, special to the *Inyo Register*.

J. Bow could be none other than Janey. How old would the girl be now? Certainly not old enough to have completed college yet. "Special" meant that she wasn't a regular reporter, but had been given a specific assignment. This couldn't have been a very important story, she couldn't imagine why Chalfant had even printed it. How odd the *Chronicle* had picked it up.

"Well really," complained Mary to her cup of coffee. "The girl has no business dabbling in this way. If she's set her cap on becoming a reporter, she ought to undergo some proper training." Mary reread the two paragraphs that had been reprinted from the *Register*. She found the author too favorable toward her subject. Clearly Janey was in need of guidance, and there was no one there in the valley, save Chalfant, to provide it. "He," Mary said aloud, "seems to be losing his judgment."

It was up to her then, so Mary pulled a sheet of her carefully select-ed personal stationery from her bag and promptly composed a letter. She would mail it and pick up her own correspondence at the little communi-ty's post office on her way back home.

When Mary arrived home, she took a short nap to prepare for the rest of her day. In the afternoons, she and most of the other writers and painters of the colony abandoned their labors and shook off their solitary obsessions through vigorous exertion in such activities as hiking, swimming and, above all, conversation. Back in sandals, with robe and hair flowing freely, Mary headed toward George Sterling's cottage, the community's unofficial gathering place.

Sterling and his wife Carrie had been first to accept the offer of a free lot for "any artist who will build"—the real estate developer's grand design for inducing the general public to pay high prices for lots once Carmel became fashionable as an artist's colony. George, scion of a wealthy family from Sag Harbor on Long Island, New York, had arrived in Carmel with the financial resources to build both a fine redwood house and a cabin, originally intended for Nora May French, a friend and fellow poet. Now George, whose own work, though largely dismissed by eastern literary critics, had been lauded in western circles as having "Keatsian promise," used the cabin to write and hold court among companions and admirers who had dubbed him the "uncrowned king of bohemians."

To reach the Sterling house, Mary walked a narrow, winding path through a thick forest of pines and cypress, across a wooden footbridge and down into a ravine. Climbing back up the other side, the path proceeded among majestic oaks where the ground was carpeted with yerba buena, its green leaves and small white flowers both edible. Mary stopped to pick some of it, filling the deep pockets of her robe. Farther along her way, in a sunny thicket, she searched for wild strawberries, popping two of the red buttons, exuberant with flavor, into her mouth.

Soon she was approaching the one-acre Sterling homestead, situated on a pine-covered hillside with a far-reaching vista on its less wooded side out to the Mission San Carlos Borromeo de Carmelo and beyond it to the Santa Lucia Mountains. Below, a flower-studded meadow stretched down to the sea. Mary stood for a moment, taking in the spectacular view, then veered off of the path and strode down the grassy slope toward the narrow strip of beach.

This was where she expected to find George this time of day. Her anticipation was not disappointed, as she immediately made out two figures stretched out on their backs, sunbathing in the golden sand. One of them, who was certainly George, his slender, boyish body clad only in white underwear briefs, was stretching his arms toward the sun. Mary halted her march again, this time to gaze just at him, feeling her body tingle beneath the silky fabric and marveling at what another friend, also a writer, had described as George's "strange mingling of grace and vigor." He had magical, almost mythic qualities, which drew other beautiful and talented folk, both male and female, to him. She knew she was no different, but between them, she believed, was something more extraordinary than this: they were mated in artistic soul and nature's spirit.

Mary stiffened as she recognized the man next to Sterling. Robust physique in dark swimming trunks, arms folded behind a head of tousled, curly dark gold hair, broad chest expanding with deep breaths. This was Jack London, celebrated author of *The Call of the Wild*, *The Sea-Wolf* and *White Fang*, who had recently returned from the East Coast, sailing around Cape Horn with his wife Charmaine on their four-masted barque, the Dirigo. Home for the couple was a ranch house, which Sterling had named "Wolf House," at Glen Ellen in the Sonoma Valley, north of San Francisco.

London and Sterling were great friends, but Mary had found her interactions with the novelist during his frequent visits to Carmel rather prickly. One thorn was that she was skeptical of Jack's passionate commitment to unionism and socialism. It was said to be on full view in an upcoming book, his 36th, *Valley of the Moon*, soon to be serialized in *Cosmopolitan*. This was reputedly the story of a working-class couple who became involved in violent strikes before leaving the city for Sonoma and friendship with the artists of Carmel. London, for his part, found Mary's belief in Spiritualism trivial and amusing. He also took great enjoyment in poking fun at her country background and what he saw as her provincial and prudish ways. Indeed, when she was around him, Mary often felt the awkward country bumpkin, devoid of social graces, worldly sophistication and physical beauty.

Mary straightened her shoulders and stoked her courage. She strode toward them, calling out a cheerful greeting. The two men lazily plopped over onto their stomachs, displaying sand-caked backs. They squinted up at her.

"Well hello, there, Missus Mary. Care to disrobe and come for a dip?" drawled London. His large, shining eyes were strafing her like searchlights. Mary suppressed a shiver; the damned man fairly radiated virility and intelligence. She waved the invitation off with her hand and sat down heavily in the sand.

"Shall we continue with our story?" she asked Sterling.

She and Sterling had recently been playing a treasure hunting game, around which they had begun to craft a collaborative story. Several cohorts had joined in this latest diversion, but London had abstained. Now he responded to her suggestion by rolling his eyes and turning over onto his back again. Damn that woman is a pest, he was thinking. So pretentious in that robe or her other favorite garb, the leather dress of an Indian princess! She actually thinks George could give a fig—she's the least attractive female in the colony and only a mediocre writer if that.

Sterling raised himself onto his forearms and drew his legs up to sit "injun-style," agile as a wood sprite. With his boyish physique and aquiline facial features, he was to Mary's eyes as handsome as a Roman faun in a tale of enchantment and as youthful as Shakespeare's Puck. Yet this romantic, playful poet nearly always carried a vial of cyanide, which he had once referred to as "the key to a prison door." She didn't imagine he had it with him now, however, clad as he was in those scanty briefs.

Here was the man of genius she had once hoped to find in her husband Wallace. In her opinion, Sterling took himself too lightly in this respect. His was not a competitive nature and, having briefly dipped his toe into the seething New York literary sea, he had quickly retreated to gentler waters in the West. He seemed quite satisfied with a renown he characterized as "local and rather tenuous," saying that fame was a bore and having more of it would, no doubt, be a torment.

Her own fame, such as it was, certainly owed more than a little to Sterling, who had been her entrée into the luminous social circle to which she now belonged. Mary smiled with pleasure at the thought of their first meeting in San Francisco.

He had taken her to Coppa's, a favorite haunt of San Francisco's young intellectuals, writers and artists. Entering the long, narrow room on Sterling's arm, Mary had gasped—never had she been anywhere like this. On three sides of the room, the bottom half of the walls was brilliant crimson, which Sterling described as "Dago red," the exact hue of the wine they were soon to imbibe. On the top half was an immense chalk-drawn mural, its various scenes including a five-foot high lobster with nude figures on an island labeled "Bohemia." There were also lewd scenes of men and women drinking and smoking at tables in a room where the printing on the window read "Coppa's" backward, as if viewed from inside the establishment. One woman in the picture, her back to the viewer, snuggled in the arms of her companion while holding hands behind his back with another man. This visual feast had been created through now-and-then contributions by the restaurant's regulars, including Porter Garnett, a calligrapher and printer, and Mexican painter and printmaker Xavier Martinez. Above the mural ran a band of scrollwork plaques, where the names of other favorite clientele, including Sterling and Jack London, mixed with those of greats like Aristotle and Dante. And above that there rose a frieze, painted by Martinez, of black cats crouching below the cornice, watching the viewer with gleaming eyes—his salute to the legendary Paris cabaret Le Chat Noir.

What a delight for Mary's own eyes, but even more a balm for her parched, solitary soul. Sterling brought her to a table where Martinez sat, a flowing red scarf tied at his collar, next to writer Jimmy Hopper, a man with the rough face of a sailor or a boxer, surrounded by a halo of golden curls like one of Fra Angelico's angels. Others joined the party, and the conversation, about literature, art and ideas of all nature, was ambrosial. As they talked, they drank red, fruity wine and ate heaping platefuls of fresh shrimp, sand-dabs that melted in her mouth and a profusion of crisp salads and tender fresh artichokes and zucchini, trucked in that morning by the Tuscan and Genoese farmers who had settled along the San Francisco Peninsula. To finish, there were deep, flaky pies and crumbly almond tartlets filled with whipped cream.

The next day, Sterling had taken her to see the monument to Robert Louis Stevenson at Portsmouth Square, and they had regaled themselves with tea and kumquats in a small Chinese restaurant. She had fancied they might be lovers, but they had become closer than that. Later, at Carmel, Sterling had not only helped her settle, he had also enthusiastically lent his boundless energy and enthusiasm to the task of researching the historical details of a novel she had decided to write about early life at the Carmel mission. As more and more artists gravitated to the little colony and around George, he always made it a point to include her in their excursions and festivities: wagon rides into the Carmel Valley, hikes up the rocky slopes at Point Lobos, walks along Pebble Beach, impromptu theatricals, moonlight picnics.

Today, Sterling informed her, he and Jack had a hankering for a mussel roast, so the afternoon would be devoted to gathering shellfish from the rocks bordering the small beach, laying driftwood fires and mixing up the requisite huge pitcher of the Sterlings' special punch, a mix of bourbon, soda and sliced pineapple with mint from the meadow below the house. Sterling and London got started on the mussel harvest, and Mary began collecting driftwood in a desultory fashion. But before long, Carrie Sterling joined her, as did Clark Ashton Smith, a budding poet and another of George's protégés. Henry Anderson Lafler, assistant editor of the *Argonaut*, a San Francisco literary journal, and Jimmy Hopper arrived along the piney path, each carrying a wicker-covered jug of the spicy, golden local muscatel wine. Soon the merry party of revelers also included two other Carmelites, writers Harry Leon Wilson and his wife Helen.

And so the day ripened, as so many others, into irresistible fruit. Tasting its congenial, earthy pleasures, Mary felt self-consciousness loosen, heaviness dissolve. She wondered at how easily she took part in every frivolity, scampering across the grassy slope, hair floating in the tangy breeze. Here the strictures of society also seemed to loosen, allowing men and women to play together without heed. It brought to her mind the memory of the Owens Valley boys and girls running beneath the trees at the evening social. Yes, for the first time in my life, she thought, I am as joyful as those carefree children.

But her pleasure was even more profound, because here communion of spirit was deepened by a communion of mind. After dusk, gazing into the glowing fire pit, bellies full of fleshy pink mussels, bourbon and wine, they spoke of everything important, including Willa Cather's scandalous new novel *Alexander's Bridge* about a successful engineer's simultaneous relationships with two women, and Ezra Pound's publication of the first English work by the Calcuttan poet Rabindranath Tagore, now on a lecture tour of America. They argued about Joseph Conrad's *Under Western Eyes*, a new novel with a cynical view of the historical failures of revolutionary movements and ideals, thought by some to be a challenge to Dostoyevsky's *Crime and Punishment*. They cheered the rebellious young Association of American Painters and Sculptors, which was mounting a challenge to the stodgy National Academy of Design by organizing its own exhibition of modern European art, including cubist paintings by Picasso, Brecht and Duchamp, for New York City next year. They jeered Teddy Roosevelt, who, when shown a photograph of French painter Marcel Duchamp's *Nude Descending a Staircase, No. 2*, was said to have declared "That's not art!"

But in almost the same breath, they cheered the former president, who was campaigning for re-election. Teddy had recently survived an assassination attempt by the graces of a steel spectacle case and a folded 50-page speech carried in his coat pocket, which had slowed a bullet aimed at close range for his heart.

"Let's drink to the power of the pen and poor eyesight!" Lafler proposed the toast, and they all raised their glasses because it was difficult, even for bohemians, not to like the president, though he be regrettably old-fashioned in his views about art.

Generally, the more sauced the revelers became during these moonlight fests, the more bawdy their talk. Jack, she observed, however, was drinking but little tonight. He had let it be known that he was currently at work on an autobiographical book that would reveal his struggle with alcohol, which had culminated in a particularly black binge during the trip east. He had promised Charmaine never to let it happen again. London's other appetites seemed intact, however, as he told a lusty story about a poet and his naked muse, winking at George.

Mary sighed, growing quiet as the conversation degraded, feeling awkward and ugly. Gorgeous females, enthusiastically applying for the position of muse, threw themselves at London, she knew, and George was known to have had a string of love affairs with beautiful women as well. She would never receive such attentions from them, not even from George, she now realized. But, then, was this hankering after the physical not a weakness, a weakness common to many male writers? Was this need to experience exaggerated sensation before their artistic powers could find outlet in creative expression not a crutch to be pitied? George had once admitted to her that he required an hour's exertion—swimming, splitting logs, pounding abalone or copulating—before his poetic juices would flow.

"Ah, the disapproving frown on our Greek goddess!" Jack flung ironic words at Mary. She fought down the old tide of embarrassment, peering at him with narrowed eyes and raised chin. "I never needed a drink or a love affair to release the subconscious in me. I have no need for such artificial assistance," she stated stifly.

"Ohhh!" Jack hooted. "She wants no prodding from Prometheus!"

"No lubrication from lady luck!" sang out Lafler.

"No dallying with doctor devil!" shrieked Helen Cooke.

Mary stiffened and deflected their merriment with a serious riposte. "It's my observation that women, when given relief from domestic encumbrances, settle themselves far more easily than men to their artistic endeavors."

This assertion was given drunken consideration. Sterling raised his glass and dribbled its contents down his throat before saying with a char- acteristically self-deprecating, slightly sardonic smile. "Probably the trouble is that with me my art is entirely secondary. To live and be happy are my only real concerns."

Helen put her arm around George and planted a loud, wet smack on the side of his chin. "Ah, there," she said, "not all women artists are above the need for such stimulation." She winked at her husband. "Think of me." Then, looking down at the fire, she whispered, "Think of Nora."

Nothing was heard for quite a while then but the crackling of salty wood in flame. Nora May French, the poet Mary had first met at El Alisal, the Lummis home near Los Angeles, had been involved in a series of tem- pestuous love affairs upon moving to northern California, including one with the married Harry Lafler, who now lay on this back, looking up at the stars, perhaps remembering.

"There was a worm in that bud," said Carrie from curled lips. "Reading her poetry was so much more enjoyable than having her company."

"Nora had great gifts," Mary countered quietly.

She felt the need to defend the woman she had once hoped would become her close friend. Carrie, after all, was ill-equipped to pass judg- ment on a poet—she had been but a secretary at Sterling's uncle's real estate firm, where George had been employed for some years, when they married. Still, she knew Carrie was in some sense right. Nora had been dazzling—in those intermittent moments when she hadn't been distraught over a love affair or financial troubles. Mary, well acquainted with the challenges of earning a living as a female writer, felt she could have been a source of sympathy and support, but Nora had turned more often to George, who had probably been one of her lovers. He had even built her a cabin on the Sterling homestead, the one he now used for his studio. It was as Mary had suspected upon her first meeting with Nora—the girl had been accustomed to plying her physical endowments for advancement.

How Carrie Sterling fit into the picture, Mary couldn't fathom. She knew George's wife had for years tolerated his many dalliances, although recently, Carrie seemed less complacent, and she and George were more at odds. Bizarrely, Nora had died from a self-administered dose of cyanide in the main house of the Sterling compound, lying in bed with Carrie sleeping peacefully beside her.

This act, mourned by the poet's friends, was also respected. Some in the circle insisted that by one's own hand was the only proper way for an artist to die. Hence, it had become fashionable among some of them to carry their own vial of cyanide. Mary didn't approve of the notion, though she had decided to assign such an end to one of the characters in her new book, a tragedy about a frustrated woman trapped in a loveless marriage.

Nora's was indeed a tragic story. But Mary wondered if her own wasn't just as woeful. All her life she had been seeking a deeply passionate union of body and soul. Frustrated in that quest, should she not piece together her romantic life from slighter, more transient affairs, as the evanescent Nora had? Would she not have more joy and less suffering this way? But alas, she was too well trained from an early age to forsake this aspect of conventionality.

George Sterling was observing Carrie and Mary. He guessed they were both still thinking, like him, of Nora. His golden girl—he still kept a lock of that golden hair, which she had given him two days before her death, when she had shot if off of her head during a first attempt at suicide. This gorgeous, radiant creature who wrote crystalline poems had once said to him "All sensible people will ultimately be damned."

Was this true? he wondered. Mary, for example, lived in quite a sensible way for an artist, although she styled herself as more of an exotic these days than when he had first met her in San Francisco. He remembered the night when he had taken her to Coppa's for dinner with some of the other members of the city's bohemian circle. She had been so awkward, squat and ill-dressed, but how her eyes had shone when they had entered the restaurant, how gay she had become as the evening progressed. Her composure would have been quite altered, he thought, if she'd known what had actually been going on. It was the tradition of this company when a new person was introduced to take a secret vote—through hand and foot signals beneath the table—about whether or not to admit them into the inner circle of camaraderie. Mary had been roundly voted down, since although her writing was beautiful, her person was not. The result had been different when Nora had been introduced.

Feeling sympathy and a certain liking for Mary, Sterling had taken pains the next day to show her about the city and escort her to tea. Later, he'd helped her find a house site in Carmel. As a resident and a known, though not highly celebrated, writer, Mary had eventually gained membership of a sort in the social circle. But some of the men resented her presence. Jimmy Hopper often complained that she was always pretending love affairs, and there was a rumor that when Lincoln Steffens suddenly left on a trip to Mexico it was because he was fleeing Mary's advances.

Sterling knew his friend longed for love of an intemperate, engulfing nature, but he very much doubted she would find it here in Carmel. He doubted she would find it anywhere. Neither would Mary ever be truly accepted into the inner circle as one of its favored, its beloved, never would she blaze at the very heart of it as Nora during her brief tenure had done.

---

*I did finally write back to Mary, and I know this to have been a brave act. It took courage to thank her for taking an interest in me and entreat her to offer further guidance if she were so inclined—never revealing how wounding her criticism had been. Or maybe I wrote back because I still felt so keenly the void left by our parting, and that hurt was the one in greatest need of repair. Also, I desperately wanted to know how Ruth was faring, a question to which Mary responded shortly: "She's doing well at the school."*

*In any case, this was the beginning of an intermittent correspondence, through which we resumed our mentor-student relationship. It was a lopsided exchange, as it had been before: In return for my scant details and timid questions, she wrote volumes, describing her latest book or stories, lecturing me about life and work, and regaling me with tales of her exciting new life.*

*For Mary seemed to have finally found a place where she fit in.*
*She told me that Carmel was a colony of writers, painters, photographers*
*and other artists, and that here she had made a home and true friends.*
*She even sent me a photograph of her sitting on the beach, engaged in*
*earnest discussion with three men she identified as George Stirling,*
*Jack London and James Hopper—I knew only of London. She wrote*
*as if she were in love with Sterling, who was, she said, a famous poet.*

*Alas, despite this contentment, Mary sometimes seemed to be at war*
*with the rest of the world. She complained of being overworked from*
*having to earn her living producing stories and sketches for magazines.*
*She implied she was put in this difficult circumstance, one that prevented*
*her talent from fully blossoming, because her publisher, Houghton-Mifflin*
*failed to offer sufficient financial and moral encouragement. She com-*
*plained of readers who expressed longing for another* Land of Little Rain
*and of the* New York Times *critic who wrote in his review of her novel*
Santa Lucia, *that although her character depictions were "delightful" and*
*evocation of nature "exquisitely beautiful," "one grieves to note a falling off*
*in that distinction of style which has marked her previous work."*

*I never told Mary, of course, but I thought the critic was right.*
*Though Ma had deemed the subject matter of* Santa Lucia *unsuitable for*
*me, I had managed to borrow a copy from a girlfriend and read it.*
*The tale, about unhappiness in marriage, unreliable and feckless husbands,*
*the temptations of adultery, despair—one of her characters even commit-*
*ted suicide with a vial of poison she carried in the folds of her wedding*
*gown!—was titillating and disturbing. But the language was dull and*
*unremarkable. I started wondering if Mary had somehow left her musical*
*words behind when she quitted the valley.*

*She hadn't. Several years later she relented and wrote a book—for*
*a new publisher, Harper and Brothers this time—which returned to the*
*themes and had some of the magic of her first one. In* Lost Borders, *she*
*again told of desert landscapes and their inhabitants. This book mixed*
*in more stories, presented as having been told to the narrator by Indians,*
*sheepherders, pocket hunters and the like. Several pertained to the trials of*
*strong women coupled to weak men. In fact, some of the observations of the*
*narrator made me feel as if I were back on a canyon ledge, looking out at*
*the blue arch of sky and listening to Mary's words again. Being much older*

*by then, I had some notion of what she was trying to say when she wrote, "Mind you, it is men who go mostly into the desert, who love it past all reasonableness, slack their ambitions, cast off old usages, neglect their families because of the pulse and heat of a life laid bare to its thews and sinews."*

*Reading such words, I felt a little sorry for Mary again, that she carried so much bitterness in her breast. Yet, there was no doubt she had become a successful writer. And, though complaining of penury, she'd proved herself capable of living independently, earning her daily bread with her pen. She was the only woman I yet knew to have accomplished this feat, and it was of interest to me. I was already quite sure I would not end up living the settled family life my mother enjoyed.*

---

During the rest of the spring, Janey was more attentive to her English lessons at school, and when summer came, she stayed as often as possible with Aunt Maggie so that she could spend time in the *Inyo Register* office. She gladly performed whatever tasks Chalfant needed doing, including setting type, cleaning ink trays and sweeping floors, but she also took to reading all of the articles headed for print very carefully, especially those penned by the editor himself.

For those written by Bucky Porter or Chalfant's stringers in other California cities, she studied both the original copy and the edits Chalfant had made to it, trying to understand why he had changed this or cut that. The stories from the stringers had the fewest marks, those from Bucky were covered with them. When Chalfant was in a congenial mood, and not rushing to print or occupied by visitors dropping into the office, she asked him questions, and sometimes understood his answers.

Eventually, Janey began trying to have a look at Bucky's stories before they went to Chalfant's desk. She asked herself how she would change the copy, if she were the editor, to more clearly communicate the essential information, as Chalfant had taught her. He had even written out a poem by Rudyard Kipling to help her remember to give equal weight to all the key facts:

I keep six honest serving-men
(They taught me all I knew);
Their names are What and Why and When
And How and Where and Who

She also tried to follow Chalfant's prescription for challenging each sentence, and even, time allowing, each word, with the question: Does this make the story better? If the answer was no or not much, she mentally removed it, imagining her pen striking out the unhelpful text with one of the looping marks Chalfant used for deletion.

The problem, she decided, was in the word "better." What makes a story better? Chalfant said a better story was one that communicated the "essential facts" as clearly and succinctly as possible. But often, it seemed to Janey, after reading the *Register*, she was still left wondering about what had happened.

For instance, there was an article about the government's decision to create a reservation near Big Pine for the Owens Valley Paiute and move the Death Valley Shoshone there too. Chalfant had quoted the federal Indian agent for the region and several valley residents about why this was a good thing for everyone. But Janey knew that Juan and Rosie's parents felt quite differently. Their Mexican ancestors had been among the first to fight the Indians for a piece of the valley, establishing themselves at Las Uvas near Lone Pine and later homesteading a scatter of ranches in Independence and other parts. They thought everyone should be left alone to live side by side like they'd always done. Janey wondered what Sally John, the Paiute who had now and then kept house for Mary, thought about being told to pack up and go live on the reservation. What about Seyavi the basket maker? None of that was in the article.

And here was an article Chalfant had written about Mr. Fred Eaton and his new chicken farm. The facts, as related in the story, did nothing to help Janey understand the strange Mr. Eaton. He was the man who had come to the valley with Mulholland. They were good friends, folks had said. They'd both had a hand in stealing the water, and everyone in the valley knew Eaton had nearly been lynched the day word of the deal had come out.

But then, just about the time Mary had up and left the valley, Mr. Eaton and his wife had moved into the Rickey ranch in Long Valley. Word was he longed to become a cattle baron like Rickey and that he and Mulholland had had a big falling out and weren't friends anymore. After that, Chalfant and the Watterson brothers, who used to talk like they hated Eaton, had started becoming real friendly with the man, inviting him to sit and smoke with them in front of the *Register* office. The *Big Pine Citizen*, a small local competitor of the *Register*, had even printed a front-page profile of Eaton, declaring: "If we had a few more Fred Eatons in the Owens Valley and the people would work with them instead of against them, this valley would grow by leaps and bounds."

And now, according to this article, Eaton had suddenly bought 60,000 chickens. He was keeping them in a chicken farm, which was really more of a factory, with dozens of chicken houses enclosed by steel fences, and feed coming in by electric box cars over rail tracks. In the article Chalfant wrote about this new enterprise, Eaton was quoted as saying this modern "systematic and scientific" method was the future of agriculture and ideally suited to "the favorable climate and conditions of this valley." With that, Eaton became even more popular, some folk flocking about when he came into town and talking enviously about whether they too ought to consider modern farming methods, and wasn't this an opportunity to "get into something"? But other folks laughed at him behind his back, saying he'd failed as a cattle baron and now aimed to be the chicken baron!

Mary had once told her that valley men were forever trying to do that—"get into something." She'd said the landscape was to blame, its mysterious beauty tricking them into believing fortune was always just over the horizon. Maybe Mr. Eaton had fallen victim to its charms too. Janey's face flushed as she remembered the day she and Mary had spied on him swimming with that other man in the hollow, and how Eaton had been so young and beautiful then, and how he'd moved as if a charmed spirit of the wood. The man she saw on the streets of Bishop occasionally these days stood a little less tall and straight, moved with more heaviness, and his face had become lined and a bit hollow-cheeked, but his eyes were still clear-blue and steady.

Whatever the truth was about this strange man, it certainly wasn't in the "essential facts." They would never explain how Mr. Frederick Eaton of Los Angeles had become one of the Owens Valley's foremost citizens and head of one of its ditch associations. But Jane kept this thinking to herself, since she didn't want to be shamed by her ignorance of proper newspaper methods and she was ever careful of irritating Chalfant lest he tell her to stop coming by. She kept quiet, while keeping her eyes and ears open, and tried to learn.

# Chapter 13

In August, just before Janey was to return to school, her final year, she arrived at the *Register* office to find Chalfant writing an article about the end of the aqueduct strike. The men were going back to work, and the city was looking to hire plenty more. Chalfant was running an advertisement from the city offering steady work and bonus pay to all who signed up.

Janey was glad to know that Jed Brecken would no longer be working alone in his tunnel. There'd been no word from him since that first short letter, but just as well, she thought. If he had written again, she wouldn't have known how to reply—she'd already related the only piece of information about her life that could possibly interest him, her past association with a real writer.

Then one Saturday afternoon in September, Jemmie Shaw brought Chalfant a telegram from his stringer in Los Angeles. Janey watched him open and read it. She was setting type for an article asking valley women-folk to volunteer their efforts for the upcoming Second Annual Harvest Festival. The chairwoman of the event, Mrs. Mark Watterson, promised attendees "a day of jollification" and celebration in "the Owens Valley, the land of plenty."

"They're about to break through!" announced Chalfant. "The Elizabeth Tunnel—they're days, no more than a week, from breaking through to the center!"

Janey's head jerked up from her work, her eyes wide. Chalfant studied his young apprentice across the work table for a moment, then he said, smiling slyly, "It's big news so there's gonna be more reporters out there than June bugs on a porch light. Might just be a good idea for me to send a butterfly instead."

He saw she hadn't an inkling of his meaning. "When there's plenty of competition, Janey, there's usually an advantage in taking a different approach. If I gave you the assignment, do you think you could write another story like the other one, not about Mulholland this time, but about the tunnelers, the team that wins? None of that bull and mush in the dime novels, but the real story?"

Janey could hardly breathe. She'd been trying all summer to learn how to write articles Chalfant's way, and now he was giving her an assignment to do one in what he seemed to think of as her way—an article that would more than likely be about Jed! She tried to compose herself, took a sip of air and let it out slowly with the words, "Yes, sir, I think I can."

"Well, if you can, I'll even pay you to do it. We'll speak to your Pa when he comes in to fetch you then."

Chalfant broached the subject when Ben pulled the buckboard up in front of the office later that afternoon. Janey was silent, letting Chalfant make the entreaty, watching her Pa listening. When Chalfant finished, Ben nodded to the editor, then regarded Janey appraisingly. She dropped her eyes under his probing gaze. "It's up to Janey," he said. "Look at me honey." When she raised her eyes, he asked gently, "Is this what you want to do?"

She wasn't sure if he was asking her about this particular assignment or something more significant, but she said "Yes Pa!" Janey wanted him to think she was grown up enough to know. Inside she felt scared, though, knowing she was substituting enthusiasm for conviction, like the time she'd taken up Juan's dare to swing from a high branch out over the river.

Ben said all right, then it was settled. The following week was the beginning of the school break to let students help their folks with the harvest, so Janey's studies needn't suffer. He would send a telegram to Chris. Janey suggested to her Pa, looking to Chalfant for concurrence, that she would be able to perform the assignment more efficiently if she could stay at the Elizabeth Division camp rather than at Mojave. Mrs. Daley, the wife of the camp supervisor, had told her she could come and stay with them any time she liked. If Chris could arrange that, he needn't be diverted from his own endeavors and she'd be well chaperoned.

A few days later, Janey arrived for the second time at the Mojave depot. Lesley was on the platform to greet her, as Janey had scheduled her travel plans to coincide with her friend's afternoon off. Chris, occupied with business, had arranged for one of his drivers to take his sister out to the work camp, but that would not be for a couple of hours yet. The two girls sat on a depot bench, talking and giggling as they waited the requisite half hour for the passengers who had disembarked from the train and gone into the Harvey House for lunch to return and reboard. When the train had pulled out of the depot, taking its satisfied passengers on to their next destination, the girls went into the lunch room, took seats at the counter, ordered ice cream sodas and continued talking.

"You wouldn't believe all the reporters who've been around here," said Lesley, waving a long-handled spoon around the still-populated room, much busier between trains than when Janey had spent the afternoon observing it.

"All because of the Elizabeth Tunnel?" asked Janey.

"Mostly, but that's not all. Lot of folks started coming around soon as they heard about Whistling Dick."

"What about him?"

"You don't know?! Chris didn't write to tell you? Well, he's dead, that's what!"

"What? How? What happened?"

"He fell off his wagon. Got crushed flat as a pancake under those steel wheels. Squashed his guts right out on the ground, they say."

"Oh no!" The picture in Janey's head was ghastly. "But how did it happen? Was he drunk?"

"Pshaw, muleskinners are always drunk. Haven't heard tell he was any more liquored up that day than any other. Maybe there was a wasp under his saddle, or maybe he just made a mistake."

"But how could he, seeing he was the best and had so much experience driving big teams?"

"I dunno, it's possible. Or maybe his heart just gave out...he was real old." Lesley moved the straw around in her glass to capture the last bit of ice cream. She sucked it up quietly, as befitting a Harvey Girl, then changed the subject.

"That's just dilly, you getting the assignment from Chalfant to write about the tunnel!" She tossed her head in mock anger. "And about Jed Brecken! Boy, now that's a swell job!"

"Well, it might not be about him. The other team might win."

"Oh, that's just crackpot! The hero always wins, don't ya know that? And when he does, he's going to want someone to celebrate with." Lesley thumbed her chest and spun around on her stool. "Here I am darling Jed!"

"Has he been in here much?" Janey tried to make her voice matter-of-fact. She hadn't told Lesley about the letter from Brecken.

"Not a single time since the strike ended. Now that they've plenty of men wantin work again, both teams have been runnin back-to-back crews, just blasting their way right through that rock. Some folks who've been out there say they're getting close to the breakthrough point, and that Brecken's in that tunnel day and night, not even stoppin to eat, just livin on coffee and whiskey."

Janey felt a thrill swell up from her abdomen to her throat. She had to get out there soon and write the story! But her stomach also clutched a bit. Wasn't what they were doing awfully dangerous, especially after that cave-in? Wouldn't it be dangerous for Jed to be handling dynamite with no sleep?

"Do you think it's very dangerous? I mean, the dynamite when the men are so tired?" She was hoping her friend would reassure her, but Lesley wasn't of a mind to be serious.

"Sure, course it is." Lesley leaned her head toward Janey and tapped her friend's forehead with her own. "Use your noodle snookums! That's what makes this a great story for you to write! And anyway, the hero never dies! I told you, the hero always wins!"

Early that evening, Janey was deposited at Dolly Daley's door, where she was greeted by her hostess with a hug and by her daughters Myrtle and Pearl with shouts, songs and giggles. In truth, Jane felt nearly as irrepressible as the little girls. She'd hardly been able to sit still in the back seat of the big automobile that had picked her up in Mojave. Now the girls were dancing her into the spare bedroom—the modular houses put up for supervisors generally had four or five rooms—and helping her unpack. They wanted to know what a reporter was, and she told them it was a person who was paid to write stories about real people.

"People like me?" Pearl asked.

"Could be, someday," Janey answered.

"That's what I'm gonna be when I grow up, a 'porter!" the little girl sang out.

"Then you best learn how to spell!" Myrtle teased her sister. Pearl ran out of the room and came back with a small slate and stick of chalk. Flopping on Janey's bed, she started drawing looping lines.

"See, I can write words!"

"That's not a word! What word is it?!" retorted Myrtle.

"It's my name!"

"You think that says Pearl?" Myrtle chortled.

"It does, it does say Pearl!" The younger girl glared at her tormentor, then advanced on her, chalk held high. "I'm going to write it on you!" Myrtle, screaming, maneuvered away, ducking behind Janey and peeking around her skirt.

"That's enough you savage little injuns, no getting war paint all over yerselves today! Now let Miss Bow get settled." Dolly Daley shepherded them out. "Mr. Daley will be home for supper about seven. You might want to take a little rest from your journey until then."

Janey tried to rest, but mind and muscles were abuzz. Sleep was just as elusive that night, when after a hearty, congenial family meal, Janey lay down in her nightgown under the quilted coverlet, hugging Glenda, one of Pearl's favorite dolls, to her chest. The little rag companion's owner had placed her solemnly on Janey's pillow and told her to "watch over and protect the 'porter."

How generous children are, Janey mused, her thoughts drifting to Ruth Austin, offering up a sticky wedge of cake, wondering if Mary had ever retrieved Ruth from the school in Santa Clara and taken her daughter to live with her in that place she'd written on the envelope, Carmel?

This was only the second time Janey had ever slept away from home, and, again, unfamiliar noises outside pricked her restlessness. It was much, much quieter than Mojave, but still, there were folks about in the night. She could hear footsteps and voices outside, and occasionally the far-off pops of explosions. The tunneling crews were working round the clock. Maybe it was even Jed walking past her window.

---

The next morning, Janey rose early with the Daley household. After helping Dolly finish the breakfast clean up, she stood before a small mirror, neatening her plaited hair and pinching her cheeks, hoping she didn't look as nervous as she felt. Then, carrying her bonnet in one hand and a notebook and pencil in the other, she stepped outside, determined to finally earn her due as a paid reporter.

Jed was nowhere in sight, probably in the tunnel, but there were plenty of other men around, some workers and some in city clothes, whom she took to be fellow reporters. Most of them were just milling around, talking to each other on the slope between the camp offices and the tunnel, waiting for someone to go in or out of the portal. Whenever that happened they bunched up around their quarry, all shouting questions at once.

Janey didn't know exactly how to start reporting, so she tried to copy what the men were doing. This approach didn't work very well for her, however. When she tried to introduce herself to another reporter, her new acquaintance would either be amused and dismissive of her claim to the profession—"Well ain't that nice, miss. Now you shouldn't be out here in the sun on your pretty little feet; let me find you a camp chair and place it under that tree there in the shade"—or be taken aback by her forwardness, growing flustered and quickly taking his leave. One man, however, became quite bold, and it was Janey who made excuses to cut their conversation short.

Eventually, she discovered that instead of trying to insert herself into their midst, she could gather more information by hovering at the edge of a group of reporters and listening unobtrusively to their conversations. When a worker crossed to or from the tunnel or someone of note emerged from the office, the horde of reporters was on them in an instant. Janey, having no hope of getting close enough to ask a question or hear the responses, waited until the bristling bunch fell apart into small groups again. Then she sidled up and eavesdropped on their conversations, thereby gathering the essential facts of what had occurred.

In this way she had passed the first day, accomplishing, to her mind, very little. The news to be had was scant, and there were long periods of waiting for it, punctuated by the "pop, pop, pop" of dynamite going off every hour or so. For Janey, this tedium was relieved once or twice when she caught a glimpse of Jed. She always knew it was him, even before she could see him, as the ferocity of the reporters increased and their shouted entreaties became louder.

On her second day, Janey decided to seek out the camp wives she'd met during her previous visit and, as before, found them to be a reliable source of information. After all, they had been listening to their husbands speculate about the impending breakthrough for months now. Talking with the wives added to her small store of information and pleasantly filled the long hours.

The male reporters had other distractions. They were incessantly calculating the distances gained by the northern and southern crews, and taking bets on which would break through first. Some of them took turns driving back and forth between the two portals in an attempt to stay abreast of both sides of the story. This was a substantial diversion from boredom, as the trip was about a dozen miles each way, though the portal distance itself was little more than five miles, since the tunnel was a straight shot through the mountain.

Each day when evening came, though the work on the tunnel continued, the reporters retired to the ad-hoc tent village that had sprung up under the trees just beyond the lines of tents for aqueduct workers. Those willing to pay the dollar fare Chris charged such visitors joined the lines heading into the mess tent when the cook's triangle sounded. There, in addition to the food, they sought the "inside scoop" from the workers.

"That's likely to add plenty of salt and fat to their news stories. Our work crews aren't religious about stickin to the facts!" Tommy Daley, the camp supervisor chuckled at his own supper table, where Janey sat in the warmth of the family circle, grateful for the good company and good humor that relieved her of the day's frustrations. "You're better off not being there, Jane, as some of those men like nothing better than to pull a reporter's leg with a tale or two. If they aren't careful they're gonna end up wastin their time writin a load of hogwash!"

The girls burst into giggles—they loved that word! Said it, sang it, trilled it!

"Well I can't see that most newspaper editors have any objection to printing...*hogwash*!" Dolly emphasized the word, smiling broadly and curling up her nose as she enjoyed another fountain of laughter from her girls.

Janey hoped he was right. In any case, she hadn't a choice, as Chris had expressly forbidden her from entering the mess tent. And Mr. Daley, seeming to understand her predicament, made an effort each night to apprise her of all the facts he knew about the tunnel work. She thus had an inside source none of the other reporters were privy to.

---

*I can't say that being a newspaper reporter was something I'd dreamt about as a child—I doubt my dreams were that articulate. And I wasn't a born writer, not someone, like Mary, who wrote in a journal from an early age. My "calling" was more something I fell into because I was pretty good at writing and because opportunities opened up for me.*

*I got started at a time when female reporting was confined to the society and women's pages. Beyond these islands of propriety, journalism was a raging sea of testosterone. Titans like Harrison Gray Otis and William Randolph Hearst were like admirals, leading their men into the daily battle for circulation and political influence, ramming each other's ships, offering no quarter. Hearst, in fact, had first gone to war against Joseph Pulitzer in New York before using the same tactics with his California papers to challenge the dominance of Otis's* Los Angeles Times. *Their weapons were sensational headlines, exaggeration, scandal-mongering and belligerent positions on the events and issues of the day. Looking back, it's shocking to realize there was no statement so biased and vitriolic a newspaper wouldn't print it in the era of what became known as "yellow journalism."*

*Yet unusual good fortune found me, or I stumbled over it. Chalfant was a good teacher, and, lacking a better male alternative, he gave me a chance to write about the aqueduct, a decidedly unfeminine, newsworthy and historically unprecedented event. And though his editorial sympathies were clearly with the Owens Valley, and his headlines sometimes inflammatory, he tried to be fair to the facts.*

*Later, when I worked in Los Angeles, my editor there did too. He was one of the early reformers, crusading against biased reporting. And he made a difference. His way became the way for a good long time. Until in the '60s, young reporters covering anti-war demonstrations started crusading against what they saw as the profession's stodgy "Establishment." They said the insistence on facts was a straitjacket holding them back from the truth. The path to truth and glory was in getting beneath the facts to understand why events occurred and the motivations and feelings of the protagonists and antagonists. I was long retired by then, and so not susceptible to their derision.*

*But I must admit that I took some pleasure in observing that these young broncos were fairly quickly put out to pasture too, criticized for trying to play the sociologist and psychoanalyst, for becoming too personally involved in their stories, for writing fiction instead of news. Ah well, we each have our time. And we are so very unaware of how quickly it passes. Something from their era and mine too is still here, in today's penchant for investigative journalism, which I admire, and for celebrity interviews, which I do not.*

---

"We'll be face-to-face tomorrow."

Jed Brecken was dancing from foot to foot as he brought the long-awaited news to his boss that his team and Aston's were close to breaking through. Mulholland glanced up from the blueprints spread across his makeshift desk in a corner of the Elizabeth Division office. Superintendent Daley had offered his own quarters, but Mulholland didn't stand on ceremony; working in the main office with the rest of the engineers would serve just fine.

The chief smiled and nodded. Finally, after nearly four years of unrelenting labor, the two teams were within spitting distance of each other. He tapped his forefinger on the top blueprint. "By my calculations, you're less than a few dozen feet from the center. Good work son."

Mulholland felt a deep sense of satisfaction and vindication. The Los Angeles Board of Engineers had estimated it would take almost six years to complete the Elizabeth Tunnel, but Mulholland had been sure they could do it in less, given the incentive of the bonus system. Now they were nearly there. The crews had beaten the deadline by more than 20 months and, despite the bonus payout, they were under-budget as well.

The chief puffed on his cigar and regarded the tough, capable young man in front of him. That was the way to accomplish great things: Choose the right man for the job, then let him do it, without too much interference. Even so, he had to voice a word of caution.

"I know you're careful of your men's safety, Jed, but now the two teams are so close together, we can't afford any mistakes. Make sure you know exactly what you're doing with every charge, and let Aston know before you fire it." He was advising Jed to use the recently installed telephone line. Running over Elizabeth Mountain and down on either side into both the north and south portals, it enabled the two teams to communicate with each other.

"Yessir," Brecken agreed. "Best be getting back to it then."

"Good luck."

Brecken headed toward the door, then turned back, motioning with his hat-carrying hand toward the buzzing room full of engineers and clerks. "They taking odds?" he asked with a sly smile.

"Even money" was Mulholland's reply. Personally, he favored Jed's team as most likely to break through first, but no sense filling the young man's head with thoughts of victory before the fact.

Jed's smile widened, he liked the inherent challenge in his boss's response. He strode out the door and pushed through the crowd of reporters who jostled him and called out "How close are you Jed?!" "Is it going to be tonight?!" "Think you gonna win?!" He ducked their questions and back-patting arms, but waved to a few of the camp children who called "Jed! Jed! Blast 'er to bits Jed!" and entered the tunnel.

Fishboy, waiting just inside, handed him a mug of coffee. Brecken held it out as his mate added a dollop of whiskey from a flask drawn from his coat pocket. The man had days of black stubble across the lower part of his face and deep black circles under bleary, red-rimmed eyes—Brecken knew he looked the same.

"Thank God this is a drillin contest and not a beauty contest."
He clinked Fishboy's grimy mug with his own, and they both laughed,
then took long swallows.

The muckers had just emptied one of the electric boxcars, so
Brecken and Fisher rode it back to the blasting wall. Powderface, Goose,
Big George and a half dozen new recruits had just about finished cleaning
up debris from the previous blast. Brecken meticulously measured the
footage gained: nearly 18 inches.

He had calculated the next round carefully. When Fisher picked
up his drill gun, Brecken held out a hand. "We're gonna do something
different this time. Fifteen holes, here, like this," he indicated the pattern
he wanted for a denser setting of explosive. When the holes had all been
drilled to sufficient depth, they slid a dynamite stick into each one, tamped
it into place, inserted the fuse and crimped the base of the mercury fulmi-
nate primer cap around it. Then they backed out of the tunnel, unwinding
the fuse to a safe length, where the rest of the team awaited them, and
attached it to the electric detonator. Jed crouched down and motioned to
the men to cover their ears.

"This is gonna be a big one!" He hit it.

"Boom, boom, boom" came the blasts, followed by a thunder of
falling rock deep in the tunnel.

As the muckers headed back in to clear the rubble, Brecken felt the
floor of the tunnel rumbling—Aston had just set off another blast at his
end. He smiled, enjoying the hard contest against a worthy opponent.
This was going to be neck and neck right down to the wire. Mulholland,
he knew, would not be pleased if aware they had not telephoned each other
before these blasts. We will, he pledged silently, when we get a little closer.
For now, he knew, there was no need, they were safe enough. He and
Aston were like dancers, able to anticipate each other's moves.

Brecken marked the progress: more than 26 inches. He and Fisher
leaned against the wall and waited for the muckers to clear the way for the
next round. The crew boss lit a cigarette, inhaled and closed his eyes. His
mind drifted pleasantly to what it might be like when they won. This was
the biggest thing of its kind ever undertaken. The Gunnison Tunnel was
longer, but not as big and nowhere near as difficult. Yes, this would be a
historical achievement, and a thumb up the nose of Mulholland's critics

in Los Angeles and elsewhere who had said it was insanity, said it could never be done. Well, it would be done, and very soon now. The chief was already in the camp, and Lippincott was expected to come down from the Jawbone tomorrow to witness the event. There'd be the Daleys and camp families, and another too—he'd caught a glimpse of her in the crowd of reporters—all here to celebrate the hard-won victory.

He squashed the thought of Janey and told himself sternly: You haven't won yet. And the only way you ever will is with single-minded, total effort. You can bet Aston isn't thinking about girls!

---

Janey thought he had seen her, as he'd made his way through the swarm of reporters to the tunnel entrance. Under these heady circumstances, the newspapermen gave no quarter to females; she'd been jostled and pushed back to the fringes. Still she thought he had seen her, as he must have seen her several times before over the past couple of days since she'd been at the Elizabeth Division camp. There'd been no signal of recognition from him, however, not even a wave. Maybe he was annoyed to see her at the camp. After all, when he'd talked to her before he'd been on a day off with nothing to do, so bored he had found even her interesting. That wasn't the case now. He was in a head-to-head contest, pushing toward the finish, and there were plenty of folks here anxious to talk with him.

This trip had been discouraging so far, on both a personal and professional level. How excited she'd been when she'd first arrived at the prospect of seeing Jed and of being a real reporter. But neither of these things had happened. No one, save the Daley family, seemed to pay her much mind.

That evening, when he came to the table, Mr. Daley had at first little to say about the tunnel. But as he ate, a glimmer of a smile kept rising on his lips. When they had finished, he put his hand on Dolly's arm before she could rise to fetch dessert. Looking around the table with a wide grin, he announced: "They'll see daylight tomorrow, probably by noon! Jed told the chief this evening, and then the same word came from Aston. Lippincott is coming down from the Jawbone, and I've telephoned your brother, Janey. He'll be here tomorrow morning to oversee preparations for the celebration. Now what do you all think of that?!"

They told him what they thought with whoops and clapping, Myrtle and Pearl clanking their spoons together, and baby Tom-Tom pounding his on the table. Dolly, knowing how important this breakthrough was to the aqueduct and to her husband, hugged the little drummer, snatching the spoon from his tiny fist and twirling it in front of him until his huge, shiny eyes grew enormous. She smiled at them all, enormously liking her husband, her dear children and her visitor, then jumped up and called out: "Who wants rice pudding?!"

---

Denny Fisher saw his crew boss couldn't stand still. It wasn't just that they had to keep moving to avoid succumbing to the knee-deep frigid mountain water that had gushed into the tunnel from the last blast. And it wasn't that Brecken was shivering from cold—the man, as usual, seemed impervious to any adverse condition they found themselves in. But Brecken was twitching all over, with energy and excitement he just couldn't contain, as he measured how far they had pushed the granite wall forward and did his calculations.

"I figure there's less than four feet between us and Aston," he told his crew.

"Do we drill or do we blast?" Goose voiced the question in all of their minds. They waited, silent, near breathless for Brecken's reply.

He didn't answer immediately. The outcome of the contest, of four years of single-minded effort, could depend on this decision. Dynamite would be faster and more efficient than trying to drill through the remaining granite core. His calculations indicated that two more precisely set blasts would break through to the other side. The risk was that if they undershot the mark, they'd make it easy for Aston's team to drill through. Still, instinct and experience told him to put his confidence in the efficiency of dynamite.

"We blast," he said firmly. "Fishboy, we've got to set two more rounds of charges. Goose, get on the telephone and let Aston know when we're about to blow the first one."

He headed to the wall with his drill gun, and Fisher did the same. They were boring the holes now in the customary pattern of four cut holes at the center, a half dozen black holes around the sides and top, and four lifter holes at the bottom. They finished drilling, placed the charges, caps and fuses using a reduced, carefully calculated quantity of powder, and backed away from the blasting wall.

"Boom, boom, boom." Fisher was thinking that after all these months of hearing that sound, this could be one of the last times. The muckers moved forward and started clearing the debris. Brecken didn't wait for them this time, scrambling atop a pile of broken rock, leaning his long frame out precariously toward the side wall of the tunnel to measure the distance gained.

Suddenly, there was a sound like a balloon bursting, and Powderface Kelly ducked and yelled. Brecken turned round, still bracing his body with one arm against the wall. It was the point of a drill bit, pushing through the wall, and it had just missed Kelly's head. They all stared at the bit for a few seconds as it grew longer and longer, then looked at each other. They knew the contest was lost. A few seconds more, and the wall shattered at its center, the beast of granite they had battled for years, now falling to the earth like fragments of glass, leaving a 20-foot-high opening. Aston stepped through, as water that had been holed up in the north portal side sloshed over his boots into the south portal side. His dirty face was stretched into an ear-to-ear grin.

"Hello, there, you north portal!"

"Hello, yourself, south portal. Congratulations!" Brecken was quick to shake his competitor's hand, and his crew did the same with Aston's men. They had been bested, but still felt elated and, in some sense, victorious. They had accomplished a gargantuan feat, which some outsiders had said could never be done. They had done it.

The two crew chiefs went over to inspect the granite edges framing the ragged opening in the wall. Brecken shook his head; he had overestimated the distance remaining between them. After his last blast, when he thought they had been at about two feet, there had actually been a mere six inches of rock curtain between them. Still, he was pleased with what he saw. They'd be able to measure more precisely once the rest of the wall and debris were cleared away, but it seemed to him that the sides of the north and south ends of the tunnel met quite closely, perhaps being off on the sides by only a few inches, and the levels of the tunnel floors were nearly flush.

Aston let out a long, low whistle. He too knew that what they were looking at was remarkable. All those years of labor by two separate crews, all the problems encountered and surmounted, especially on the northern end, and still there was so little variation at the meeting. Mulholland's engineering plans had been correct and precise, and he and Brecken had kept their crews true to plan over the long haul.

"By God, she's well done, boys! Well done!"

It was Mulholland, who had come running in with Lippincott and Daley the moment word of the breakthrough had reached them. The chief congratulated Aston and his crew for their victory, slapped both crew chiefs on the back and shook hands all around with the workers. Then Mulholland moved to inspect the edges of the broken wall, as Brecken and Aston had done. He peered intently at where the two tunnel ends joined, leaning into the sheared rock and nodding in deep satisfaction. After a while he straightened up and motioned them all toward the northern portal. "Come on men, it's time to celebrate your victory!"

At the entrance, the line of workers Daley had charged with keeping the crowd back, drew apart to let them pass. After so many sleepless hours in the tunnel depths, Brecken felt the brilliant sun and blaring cheers pierce his brain, and he closed his eyes against them. Someone thrust a bottle of champagne into his hands. Easing an eye open, he saw it was Fishboy. "Here boss, drink up!"

Brecken bent his head back to take a swig, but the stuff inflamed rather than cooled his tongue and throat. He searched around for water and saw Janey Bow. She was standing hesitantly under the trees near the empty camp chairs where the women and children had been waiting all morning. Now they were all celebrating with their men, but Janey had held back, uncertain of what to do. He made his way over to her, undeterred by the reporters who flocked around Aston.

"Hello!" he called out when he'd covered half the distance.

"Hello," she returned his greeting shyly. "You've finished!"

"Yes, it's a victory in any case."

She liked that he said that and that he didn't seem distressed by the loss of the contest. In fact, he seemed quite happy and relaxed, she thought, though exhausted.

"What are you doing here?" he asked, a bit shy himself now, as he was suddenly aware of holding the champagne bottle in his hand and being covered head to toe with grime.

"I'm here to write a story, about the break-through, as a reporter… for the *Inyo Register*," she answered proudly.

"That's great!"

He seemed impressed, she thought, and how nice it was that a man who had just broken through five miles of solid granite under a mountain should be impressed by her little assignment.

"How long are you staying?" he asked her.

"I'm leaving tomorrow."

"That seems to be a habit with you."

She giggled just a little and smiled a lot. He was just as nice as at the Harvey House lunch room counter.

"Clang, clang, clang, clang, clang" the cook's triangle sounded. Fisher, moving toward the mess tent with the crew, called out, "Brecken! Over here!"

Jed waved and then turned back to her. "I have to go. I'm sorry. I have to be with my men."

"Of course you do. In fact my brother let me know this morning he has arranged quite a party for you! Don't worry about me, Mr. Brecken, I'm invited too. I'll be at the Daley table. I've been staying with them," she explained.

He left her then, seeing Chris Bow heading in their direction to fetch her. Bow slapped him on the back in passing, saying "Tough luck old man." Jed bristled slightly, but nodded and made a slight salute with the champagne bottle.

Inside the packed mess tent, his men shouted and gestured for him to take the place saved in their midst. There were more champagne bottles on every table, and kitchen staff were bringing out trays loaded with plates of steak and fried potatoes. They ate, drank and laughed riotously all afternoon, happy to be together, all the members of all the crews, who generally ate and worked in separate shifts, and happy about the paid week of relaxation due them now they were finished.

Jed enjoyed himself thoroughly, but drank with restraint, and after a time he took himself off for a few hours of sleep. It had been more than a week since he'd laid down on a bed. The moment he was horizontal, his limbs, feeling like sacks of heavy, wet sand, sank into the mattress. Just before he dropped off to oblivion he had a notion about trying to see Janey again before she left.

---

"Seems about time we got the women and children out of here," suggested Tommy Daley. He smiled and winked at Chris Bow. "These men are about to commence some serious celebrating."

Most of the eating was over, but not the drinking, and the noise and merriment levels in the mess tent were starting to rise like fever-driven mercury in a thermometer. Mulholland and Lippincott had already returned to the office, and Daley needed to do the same. Chris had to be off to the Saugus Division camp. The aqueduct, when completed, would terminate near there, delivering Owens River water to a series of reservoirs for storage and managed release.

"Remember, Hazy," Chris said, giving Janey a quick peck on the cheek, "one of my drivers will be here for you tomorrow morning at nine o'clock to take you to the Mojave depot. Make sure you're ready, so you don't miss your train. See you soon sis!"

Janey spent part of the afternoon playing with Myrtle and Pearl, who reveled in her attentions. Eventually, Janey, being mindful she was here on a paid assignment, extracted herself and retired to her room to try to start her story.

Chalfant had told her he wanted something different from what the hordes of other reporters would turn in to newspapers in Los Angeles, San Francisco and Denver, as well as to the eastern papers they fed news to as stringers. Well, what information did she possess that was different?

Janey thought she might have a few details about the tunneling crews other reporters didn't have, information she'd gleaned from talking with the camp wives. For one thing, they'd told her the city's civil service board had urged Mulholland not to hire Aston as crew boss for the south portal, questioning his suitability for the position. Although he had a graduate degree in mining from Ohio State University, they had considered him personally "difficult and unfriendly"—a recommendation the chief had ignored. Maybe she could include some of that to show how mistaken the board had been. Aston's team was the victor in the contest after all.

Another story she'd heard about the man was that once on the job, Aston had trouble getting along with Dr. Taylor. Aston's men kept coming to Taylor complaining about their hands, which were covered in open sores and scabs. Knowing it was tough work they were doing, Taylor hadn't thought much of it at first, but finally, when so many men had the same complaint, the doctor had paid a visit to the south tunnel to see what was going on. Watching how the men grabbed any pick or shovel available, he had begun to suspect that these instruments were passing an infection, probably impetigo, from one to another. Taylor had ordered that the handles of all tools be cleaned with antiseptic at the shift changeover, but found it hard to enforce. Aston had been of little help, making light of the situation, and letting Taylor know his men didn't much like getting orders from an outsider, especially someone they figured didn't know the working end of a pickaxe from a shovel. Finally the infection had become so rampant that Aston had realized the danger it posed to his team's prospect of winning the tunneling contest, and he had personally taken steps to see that the doctor's precautions were followed. After that, according to Janey's informants, the infection cleared up and Aston showed proper respect for Taylor's own expertise.

But how interesting would little bits of information like that be, and besides, she didn't want to write a story saying bad things about Mr. Aston. When Chalfant had said he wanted something different, he was asking for a story with a different angle. In newspaper talk, an "angle," as he had explained it to her, was a particular way of approaching the story, of viewing the essential facts of an event.

"Look here," he had said, pointing to the rotary printing press at the rear of the *Register* office. "Walk around it. What you see changes, don't it? That's what you need to decide as a reporter, which side to write from. Most reporters take the straight-on view without even thinking. But once in a while it might just be more interesting to walk around the thing to see if the view from a side or the back might be more illuminating."

Okay, pondered Janey, how could she look at this story from a different angle? What was the front side of the "printing press" in this situation? Well, of course, it was the break-through at the center line by the south portal team. She felt she was actually ill-equipped to write about that, since she had hesitated to join the mob of reporters that had surrounded

Aston and his men when they emerged victorious from the tunnel. She'd held back, and then Jed had come, and so she hadn't gotten any good quotes from the victorious team, although she had picked up plenty of hearsay during the celebratory lunch that followed.

But if I walk around to the other side of the story, what would I find there? She posed the question to herself. And then she knew: On the other side of the victors were the losers. That was a story the other reporters were unlikely to tell. But it could be interesting, and not just because it would be about Jed, though that would certainly add to the appeal, for her anyway. She'd found out something from Mr. Daley that she could use: "Win or lose," he'd said, "Brecken will be known as the best tunnel man on the aqueduct because of all the problems the north portal team overcame. Nobody in the world has ever accomplished anything like it."

She had some information about the problems Daley was referring to. She'd been here during one cave-in, but the camp wives had shared stories of many others. Maybe that could be her different angle: the valiant struggle against unfair odds that brought them, nevertheless, so close to victory, only to lose by six inches of granite.

By the time Dolly called her for supper, Janey had begun assembling facts and notes for the story, and had also packed her trunk for the morrow. It was a subdued meal, as everyone was tired from the day's excitements. Pearl could hardly keep her sleepy eyes open, so her Ma said it was time the girls went to bed.

"Oh please, please Ma, can Miss Janey put us to bed and read us a story?" Myrtle sprang out of her chair and jumped up and down next to their guest. "Please, please Ma?!"

"Yes, please, I'd so love to," Janey assured Dolly, putting an arm around Myrtle.

"All right then." Dolly, amused, waved them all away from the table.

Janey gathered up Pearl and, holding Myrtle by the hand, headed toward their small room in the back of the cottage. Snug in their beds, the girls engaged in a brief scuffle about the book to be read. Pearl wanted *Alice's Adventures in Wonderland*, which Myrtle complained she asked for every night. She wanted a new book, a present from her Pa on her last birthday, *Peter Pan*.

"What does it matter, you're going to be asleep in five minutes anyway," insisted Myrtle.

"Will not! I always listen to the whole thing."

"She doesn't, Miss Janey. Besides, she's heard *Alice* twenty-hundred times!"

"Shall I sing you a song to start?" asked Janey. Receiving unanimous approval, she began "Come to the Ball," and Pearl soon drifted off with visions of Cinderella. Janey gave her a kiss, then moved over to sit on Myrtle's bed.

"That was nice," purred the little girl, cuddling up against her. "Can you read *Peter Pan* now?" she asked, pushing the book into Janey's hand. But as Janey opened it to the first page, instead of settling back to listen, Myrtle raised herself up so she could whisper in her ear: "I have a secret for you!"

"A secret?! Oh my, are you going to tell me?"

"No...show you." Myrtle reached under her pillow and withdrew a folded sheet of paper. "He told me to give it to you." She opened the palm of her little hand and raised the paper up under Janey's chin. "Here it is. He said not to tell nobody but you. It's a secret!"

"Who said, Myrtle?"

"Mr. Jed."

Janey gazed at the packet of grayish paper, unable to say a word, she was so amazed.

"Open it!"

She did, with trembling fingers, and read:

Dear Miss Bow,

Please forgive me for this unconventional communication, but when I recovered from my exhaustion this evening, I realized there was one thing I wanted to do to celebrate the long-fought, hard-lost battle, and that there was only one person I wanted by my side in the doing of it. I hope you will forgive the forwardness of this invitation, but would you care to share a small adventure tonight? I can guarantee you an insight into the Elizabeth Tunnel no other reporter can match.

If you are agreed, please meet me at midnight under the
trees where I found you this morning.
Yours most sincerely,
Jed Brecken

"What does it say?!"

"It says, it…says 'hello,' and gives me some information to help me
write my newspaper story." Janey tucked the note deep into the pocket of
her skirt.

"Oh," Myrtle was unimpressed and tired. She pleaded, "Can you
read *Peter Pan* now?"

Janey did, though she scarcely comprehended her own words as she
pronounced them. Myrtle lasted through nearly three chapters. When she
was asleep, Janey laid the book aside, kissed the girl and left the room.
Dolly and Tommy glanced up from where they sat on the parlor divan, she
in the crook of his arm. Janey, feeling the intruder and anxious to be alone
to reflect on the extraordinary communication from Jed Brecken, said a
hasty goodnight.

In her own room, she closed the door and withdrew the note
from her pocket. She read it again, and then again. What could he have
planned? He must know that to meet him at that hour she would have to
sneak out of the house after the Daleys had retired. Chris had snuck out
once at home and made so much racket, he'd been caught by Pa and punished with extra chores. He'd never tried it again or, at least, never been so
loud about it as to get caught again. But she'd done it, two or three times
of a summer's evening for a moonlight scamper or swim with Emma, Juan
and Rosie. Her parents had never caught her thanks to the near-soundless
route she'd found, out her window to the old oak tree, reaching hands
and feet from one spreading branch to the other, then sliding down on the
swing rope to the ground.

This was different, of course. This was alone with a boy, a young
man. Ma would think it improper, but she so wanted to see Jed, and this
would probably be her only chance. She knew he meant her no harm, and
besides, he'd promised her something none of the reporters would have.
This was the something different Chalfant wanted. She had a professional
responsibility as his reporter to find out what it was.

The clock on the wall ticked 11:56 when Janey slid the guest room door open just enough to ease her narrow form through and felt her way to the front door. Fortunately, the Daley's parlor was sparsely furnished and, on this clear night, plentiful moonlight guided her around obstacles. Outside the air was still unseasonably mild, so she hardly needed her shawl, but she wrapped it tight nevertheless to still her shakiness. It was very quiet.

She looked about the deserted camp. On the slope leading to the tunnel entrance, off to the side under a canopy of leaves fluttering in the warm breeze like captive butterflies, she saw a figure leaning against a tree. From the way he was eased back against it, long and relaxed, and the way he came forward when he saw her, as if in one smooth, unhurried movement, she knew it was Brecken.

"Hello. You came!" he whispered, smiling at her so happily with his eyes and mouth, she couldn't help but smile back. She glanced about nervously.

"There's nobody out," he reassured her. "The men are either in their tents sleeping off the party or continuing it in Mojave."

"Oh." Janey could just imagine the noise coming through the Harvey House windows, and was glad she wasn't staying there.

"Come on," he said, reaching out to lightly touch her elbow. "We're going to be the first to do something everybody else is gonna want to do."

He led her up the slope to the tunnel portal, where she was surprised to see an automobile standing just inside the entrance. Jed reached into his pocket and withdrew a key.

"How would you like to drive right through the tunnel, in one side and out the other? Nobody else has done it yet! They cleared it all up so Mulholland and Lippincott can drive through tomorrow, Aston too, kind of his victory lap. But we're gonna do it first!"

Janey's eyes grew wide and she nodded. He helped her into the driver's seat, leaving the door open. "Can you steer?" he asked. "So we don't wake up the camp, I'm gonna push the car for a bit before I crank up the engine."

She put her hands nervously on the wheel. She wasn't sure. She'd never done this before, even on a road, and the tunnel walls were so close. What if she steered the motor car right into them?

"It'll be easy. I'll be right here next to you."

He reached in beside her legs, and Janey jumped. "Pardon me. It's okay, I have to release the brake and turn on the headlamps," he explained. "There, that's it."

Two cones of yellow mist sprang out into the dark throat of the tunnel. Jed leaned forward and pushed with his legs, one hand against the open door and the other above her, near the top of the vehicle. They were rolling into the tunnel, silently but for the soft crunch of gravel beneath the wheels.

As the vehicle moved away from the moonlit entrance, the side walls of the tunnel became invisible. She knew they were close, could feel their damp, cool presence. Up ahead where the lamp beams spread out and dissolved, she caught fleeting glimpses of rough rock, timber beams and strung wire, but as Jed pushed the vehicle forward, these shadowy forms moved out of the gray illumination into the black beside and behind her.

"Oh no!" Suddenly both beams of light were on the right-hand wall, and it was coming toward them. Janey's fists froze around the wheel.

"Turn left, toward me!" Jed yelled. She jerked the wheel and the car veered left. "Not so much, just a touch." He placed his hand over hers, easing the vehicle back toward the center of the tunnel. "You'll learn, don't worry. I guess that's far enough. Can you move over?" Janey slid to the other side of the bench.

"This is Dr. Taylor's Franklin. It's got a six cylinder engine and can run at over 50 miles per hour!" he said as he went forward to crank the engine.

"How did you get it?" Janey yelled over the sputtering of the machine, which soon smoothed to a loud purr.

"He lent it to me," Jed answered, swinging himself up into the driver's seat. "I told him I wanted to christen the tunnel...I just didn't tell him I wasn't going to be alone. That's our little secret." He turned to her and beamed. "Ready?!"

She nodded, thrilled and terrified.

"Hold onto your skirts!"

He started the automobile forward. She felt the wheels revolving slowly beneath her, bumping over uneven ground, then a little faster, then much faster until all she felt was steady vibration, like on the train. Gray forms on the side walls now rushed through brief, dim illumination into black. Damp air fled by her head and shoulders. Ahead, all was dark except for the two cones of light.

Faster and faster they went, flying through the darkness. She couldn't see Jed's face, but could just make out his hands on the wheel, where, to her amazement, they lay so very lightly. If he was turning the wheel, like he'd shown her, to keep them on course, she couldn't see it. It was as if he were simply a passenger like her, and they were being pulled smoothly as a thread through a buttonhole by a giant hand on the other side.

She turned her eyes back to the cones of light, trying to see deeper into their reach. She felt they were becoming her eyes, beams shooting out of her eyes now and she could see farther and farther, deeper and deeper into the darkness she was being pulled into, flying faster and faster.

A strange silver square now began to form and bounce between the golden orbs. Janey watched, fascinated as it grew larger and larger until the orbs were inside it, and then, as the square continued to grow, the golden orbs faded into it. Jed slowed the car, as they emerged into the silver, leaving the blackness behind them. They stopped.

"Whooooe!" Jed stood up in the car, throwing his arms up and head back.

Janey shivered, feeling she was waking from a dream. She gulped. The Franklin seemed to be on some kind of ledge. In the silvery moonlight she could see that the ground dropped away maybe 50 feet out. To either side, were steep, rocky slopes, reaching down into darkness, which was pierced by a small cluster of lights way below.

"This is San Francisquito Canyon, and those lights down there are Aston's camp," said Jed pointing. "Don't worry, the ledge is stable, and there's plenty of room here to turn the Franklin around. Isn't it gorgeous?!" he asked, waving his arm in an arc like a circus impresario.

It was. He was right, it certainly was. Jane sat back and gazed up at the scatter of stars, closed her eyes and breathed. The cool, damp air of the tunnel had been supplanted by a warm, sweet breeze, and the pine boughs of a tree near the mouth of the tunnel were swaying, releasing aromatic bundles of spicy perfume over their heads.

Janey opened her eyes and looked around, still feeling as though she were waking from a dream. She knew she hadn't really dreamt, but the ride through the tunnel had felt like it. Her mind had taken its own course, taken her somewhere strange and wonderful…they had been flying…her favorite dreams as a child had been flying dreams, and she now felt a little of the disenchantment that had always come with waking from one. Until she felt him pulling her to her feet beside him and catching her up in his arms.

"Hooray! We did it!" Jed shouted.

He hugged her against his chest, hard and warm, and she felt the dream flood back. In her trance, she never thought about the impropriety of being there pressed up against him. They were someplace so far from where she'd been and what she'd known that the rules for young ladies and gentlemen didn't apply.

"Hooray!" she joined in the whooping. He set her down and they just stood there for a moment, grinning at each other. Then he helped her to settle back down in her seat. They put their heads back and looked up at the star-strewn sky, taking deep breaths of sweet, spicy air.

There was no one about, but when he next spoke to her he whispered. Perhaps he too, she thought, felt himself in a dream and feared to rouse from it.

"No one has ever done that before…Janey." He used her Christian name a little shyly. "You and I are the first."

"Thank you…Jed. It was wonderful!"

"You were wonderful to come with me."

"Have you driven through other tunnels you've mined?"

"No, never thought to do it before. Automobiles didn't used to go up to such high speeds—could've probably run through faster by foot than ridin some of them. Can't race a horse through either, they get spooked in the dark. I dunno, it just came to me to do it when I heard the chief was driving through tomorrow—well, I reckon now it's today. Thought I'd sneak my own ride in first. Never worked so hard on so big a job as the Elizabeth. Now she's finished, I said to myself, 'Jed, boy, you deserve a little reward,' especially since I lost the contest."

"But you're still the best tunnel man on the aqueduct."

He laughed his easy laugh, "Where'd you hear that, little miss reporter?"

"Everywhere, everyone says so, even though you're younger than Aston. How did you learn to do it?"

"Oh, I guess I've always known some of it. Mine's a Denver mining family, going back generations. My grandpa was a manager and owner of the Matchless silver mine in Leadville, which was pretty much the center of mining at the time and the start of Colorado." Jed smiled and shook his head. "Gramps had so many stories…He liked to tell how Oscar Wilde came to give a lecture at the opera house they'd built there in the middle of the wilderness. Gramps took him on a tour of the mine, and then they got drunk together at one of the town's saloons. Wilde was impressed by a sign hanging over the piano that said 'Please do not shoot the pianist. He is doing his best.' Later when Wilde wrote about it, he said it was the only rational method of art criticism he'd ever come across!"

Janey laughed, but asked, embarrassed, "Who is Oscar Wilde?"

"He was a scandalous English playwright," Jed told her, chuckling.

"Oh." She dropped her eyes, but then realized he wasn't laughing at her ignorance, but at the unlikely picture of the English playwright in the rough and ready western saloon. Jed went on with his easy talk.

"My Pa was superintendent of the Coronado Mine. But it was different then from the old days when most of the mines were owned by men, like my Gramps, who had discovered them and even worked them alongside their crews. Pa had a small stake in it, but most of the mine was owned by a syndicate of business men from the East. The unions had also signed up most of the men in mines right across the state. So one day they called a strike, and the owners wanted to bring in replacements outside of the union. Pa warned them the miners wouldn't stand for it, but they wouldn't listen. And he was right: The union men attacked the 'scabs,' which is what they call the nonunion workers. It ended in a riot that killed four miners and a fireman."

"Is that why you didn't join the aqueduct strike?"

"I guess." He took a steadying breath, inhaling and exhaling slowly. "I figure the men have a right to say if they're gonna work or not based on the pay and conditions offered them. But I have the same right, and no one's gonna tell me not to work just because others are goin off the job."

He smiled over at her then, his face clearing, the easy grin resurfacing. "Enough of that. Tell me something about the Owens Valley."

So she told him about "Oppapago," the Paiute name for Lone Pine Peak that meant "the Weeper," and how in the springtime "tears" of melt from the Sierra snows ran down its face. And about hiding watermelons in the tall grass by the river to feast on in the hot afternoons with Juan, Rosie and Emma. And about Juan riding bareback, his fingers threaded through the Appaloosa stallion's mane. And about the hollow where the Sierra creeks had carved a swimming hole.

While she talked, he sat in the corner of the Franklin, against the driver's side door, facing her with his arms outstretched along the top of the bench seat. After a while, he tilted his head back and regarded the stars again, a soft smile curving his lips. She stopped talking, afraid she had said too much. But he brought his head back down, looked over at her and said, "Owens Valley seems a magical place. I'd like to visit you there someday."

Janey mumbled in happy confusion something about him being welcome. He stretched out his arm until a finger touched her shoulder.

"Let's go back in!" He ran the finger lightly down her arm. "I just have to turn the Franklin around."

Seeing her pleasure at the idea, or at his touch, he smiled mischievously. "I'll make a bet with you that I can stop at the halfway point! You'll be the first reporter to see where the breakthrough happened!"

"Yes, let's go back in!" Janey clapped her hands. "But I can't see how you could find the exact point in the dark. What shall we bet?!"

"A kiss if I win."

She gazed up at him, but didn't blush. "What if you lose?"

"I won't."

"Yes, a kiss then."

Jed handled the car skillfully and carefully, going forward and backward several times to complete the multipoint turn. Then they dived back into the tunnel.

Janey again felt mesmerized by the flight into darkness with the golden lights pointing the way and the shadows and damp air rushing by.

But she also felt oddly and wonderfully alert, every nerve tingling, aware of herself sitting just a few inches from Jed. The smells of his shirt and skin were still in her nostrils. It seemed they had been in the tunnel but a short time when he slowed and brought the Franklin to a stop. He left the engine running.

"This is it. The halfway point!" Just ahead on the left, where the headlight beams diffused to gray and the sidewall was barely evident in the shadows, she saw a glimmer of white. Leaning forward, peering into the dimness, Janey could make out that it was a huge X, which appeared to have been written in chalk on the wall. "Oooh, that's it?!" She asked, looking toward him in delight, though she couldn't see him well in the dark.

"X marks the spot!" he shouted, "I put it there this afternoon. I win the bet!"

Janey felt his hand down near her legs again, and heard him yank a couple of levers. Then his arms were pulling her across the bench seat, up against him. One of his hands touched the crown of her head and moved slowly up and over her head, halting where her hair was loosely plaited at back. The hand slid under the plait and onto her neck, sending a shiver down her spine. It pulled her head forward until her lips were against his, which he began moving warm and slow on hers. It was a dream again, another dream she didn't want to wake from, so as his arm slid down from her neck to her waist, and pulled her closer still, she reached her arms forward and up onto his back, laying her hands against the hard muscles. His shirt was damp from sweat or the moist tunnel air.

There seemed to be nothing here deep inside the mountain but his mouth and hands. He kept one hand at her waist and brought the other around from her back to the front of her dress, his fingers spreading across her small breast. No boy had ever touched her there. He kissed her more deeply, pushing his lips and tongue between her lips, and she felt the hand moving down from her bodice, along her corsetless side and onto her hip. In a few quick movements he gathered up her skirt and then his hand was underneath her petticoat, on her thigh. It was so strange to feel his hand there, where only the thin fabric of her drawers was between him and her skin, but she let the dream go on, and he moved his hand up over her stomach, his fingers reaching up into the opening between her drawers and camisole, then slipping inside her drawers and onto her bare stomach and

down to her little patch of hair. The dream went on, his fingers
reaching lower, touching her private part, gliding over it because it was
wet, and then she felt him slowly push one of his fingers up inside of her.
Her insides were glowing or screaming or both, and then he must have
released the brake with a third hand or a foot or something, because the
motor car was going. As it rumbled forward, he kept his finger inside of
her and he whispered in her ear, "Feel the movement." In the dream she
tried to do what he said. The motor car was moving and he was pumping
his finger and she felt so much there that she thought she must scream or
faint. Then she felt the rush inside her, and she must have finally screamed
a little, but there was no one here to hear her except Jed, who wouldn't
mind because they were in the dark and in the dream.

The car stopped, and he gently withdrew his finger and ran it up
along her belly, leaving a trail of something warm and slimy to her navel.
He brought his arm out from under her skirt and cupped her cheek with
his hand, bringing her lips to his again. His hand smelled odd, kind of
fishy. He released her and said "Don't move." In the dark, she felt him turn
and reach for something in the trundle seat behind them, then ease back
in his seat, moving away from her. She heard him unbuckle his belt and
exhale in sharp, fast bursts, then groan and exhale again, this time long
and deeply. After a minute, she heard him rebuckling his trousers.
He extended his hands forward, to where they were dimly visible, and
she saw he was wiping them on his handkerchief. Then he put it away and
took her hand, brought it to his lips, turned it over and kissed her palm.

Jed drove very slowly the rest of the way out, and Janey happily
understood that he was trying to delay their awakening. When they could
see the silvery square of the north portal up ahead, her happiness was
replaced with panic. He slowed and stopped the Franklin. Taking her
hand and smiling with his mouth and eyes again—she could see his countenance clearly now—he asked, "Ready?"

Janey grasped his arm and whispered in a panicky voice, "No, wait…
wait Jed, please. Was it bad…what we did?!"

"No, it wasn't bad. That was just something I learned, along with
a few other tricks…from Tansy," his voice went warm with remembrance and affection. "She was a few years older than me, I guess I must
have been about 12 or 13. Me and my pals used to get in all kinds of

mischief—what we liked best was to hop freight trains back and forth down the line. And Tansy, she was great, really really wild! She was a tomboy, always wearing boy's clothes and talkin tough, and she could punch if she'd a notion to. But one time it was just me and her out for a lark, and we caught a ride, and she showed me how to do that—she made me do it to her with the box car door wide open to the countryside! She said that's what made it fun, that and the movement of the wheels...probably works better on a train..." His voice trailed off.

"Is that what you think I am—wild?" Janey was aghast.

"No, no, not at all!" He shook off the memory, took her hand and regarded her earnestly. "You're not wild, Janey, but you do have a way of going right at things. That's something I noticed the first time I saw you, something I like a lot. Maybe," he said, his voice conspiratorial, "because I'm like that."

"But also...," he said, studying her face with curiosity, "there seems to be another part of you that's different, kind of up in the clouds...I don't know...a part I don't really understand, that's nothing like me, or anyone I've ever met...and I like that too."

She didn't know what to say. No boy had ever said or done such things to her. He placed his other hand over hers.

"Janey Bow, believe me when I tell you that what we did in the tunnel wasn't bad. It was *perfect*. In fact, it's possible we may both remember this as the one perfect night of our lives."

Her stomach, which had begun to tense and knot, now relaxed into a warmth that spread to her heart and throat. She dared not speak, but just smiled back at him with trembling lips.

"But I hope not. I hope it's not the only perfect memory we share Janey...I hope it's just the first."

He kissed her, lightly this time, and drove them out of the tunnel and down the slope to the "paddock" where they kept the "horseless carriages"—a camp joke. It was still dark as he handed her out of the Franklin and they walked back under the trees, to where they had begun their night's adventure.

They stood a couple of feet away from each other, eyes fixed on each other's faces. "You're leaving today," he said flatly.

"Yes."

She could see the muscles in his fine, square jaw clenching, but then he gave her the pleasure of his wide, open grin once more and said, "You're as sweet as a peach Miss Bow. I'll write to you if I may."

She was clasping her hands tightly in front of her, and she raised them now from the elbows so that she held them as if in prayer in front of her lips, and her eyes shone out at him, telling him yes. Then Janey turned away and, on shaky legs, tried to walk gracefully toward the Daley house. She knew, hoped he was watching.

# Chapter 14

"It's a good story," said Chalfant, putting down the pages he'd been reading and looking up through bushy white eyebrows at the girl. "Unconventional, but good."

"You asked for something different, you said something from another angle."

He glanced up, surprised at young Miss Bow, who was standing before him, her posture straighter and her voice more confident than he had ever noticed of her before.

"Yes, yes I did…hmmm…" Chalfant returned his eyes to the pages written in Janey Bow's untidy script. He had wanted a story that would stand apart from all the others being written about the Elizabeth Tunnel breakthrough, but even so, he was surprised by what she had turned in. It would never have occurred to him to waste ink on the losing team of tunnelers, yet the story Janey had written about them was enthralling.

She had painted a picture of a tightly bonded group of tough, idiosyncratic men pitting themselves against a worthy opponent in an epic contest. She had shown how the tunneling was not only a feat of engineering and physical prowess, but a game of nerve and skill, especially in the figuring of when, where and how to set the blasts. And she had made the players of this game human. Unlike the dime novels chronicling the daring-dos of Jed Brecken with outlandish bravado and suspect veracity, Janey's story was rooted in details that had the ring of truth.

She'd written about Brecken growing up in Leadville, Colorado, the son of the son of a mining man, about Fisher's days hammering spikes on the railroad and about Big Joey's misadventures searching for Yukon gold. And there were short, funny bits about how Powderface Kelly and Goose had earned their monikers. She had woven all of that, rather expertly, he thought, for a debutante reporter, into a piece that made the crew boss and his men seem like they could be ordinary fellows from next door. That made the story of how they had hurled themselves into this contest, expending every last ounce of will and strength to win—*and still lost*— absolutely gripping.

"We'll print it," Chalfant said. And then simply, "Good job." It wouldn't do, he thought, to let a youngster know quite how well she had done, wouldn't do to let Miss Bow be getting ahead of herself.

This time when the article by J. Bow appeared in the *Inyo Register*, it stirred up less controversy and was received with more appreciation. A good number of Owens Valley ranches were gaining a portion of their livelihood supplying aqueduct work crews with food stuffs, and even those who weren't had benefited from rising prices spurred by aqueduct-created market demand. So *Register* readers were naturally inclined to take an interest in an article about the Elizabeth Tunnel breakthrough. Moreover, Janey's emphasis on the losers of the contest seemed to resonate among many valley folk, still struggling to "get into something," but often feeling themselves coming out the underdog in the contest of life.

Ma and Pa were complimentary and clearly proud when the *San Francisco Chronicle* and *Los Angeles Examiner* both quoted pieces of her story in their respective coverage. Chris told her she should have written about the winners instead, this comment included casually at the end of a letter to the family about other matters. Mary Austin said essentially the same thing, although she put it differently, remarking in a letter full of self-praise for her own current writing project, that the subject of the failure of men should best be left until Janey had more life experience with it.

Jed offered no opinion. He did write, as promised, but never mentioned the article. Perhaps he hadn't seen it or didn't care to read a story about himself. Still Jed's occasional letters were gusts of fresh air that sent her soaring like the hawks and eagles, her emotions looping and criss-crossing like their avian tracks in the sky. There was nothing untoward about them—he never mentioned their night in the tunnel—but they were intimate in the sense that he confided in her what he was thinking and feeling. With nothing remaining at the Elizabeth Tunnel but cement work, he had moved on to the Jawbone, where he was helping with the siphon and some smaller tunnels. He owned that the work wasn't quite challenging enough to suit his tastes, but that he would stay on to the end. He was excited at the prospect of completing the mammoth project. Word was it would take about another year. Her letters, he told Janey, would help to sustain him.

His letters, and the promise of them, equally sustained her during this last year of school, through the winter months. In the spring, when wild almond blossoms flamed out across the fields, she pressed a handful between the pages of one of her replies. By then, with completion of the aqueduct nearing, Jed had begun to talk of returning to Colorado, for a time anyway, and there came a letter that said he'd like to take her with him.

Janey was awash with joy. He wanted her! But she was in agony as well: Did this mean he was asking her to marry him? He hadn't exactly said so. She hoped it to be true, but was she not too young to be married? She daren't ask Ma for advice, as she had never told her the truth about Jed. She'd made up a fib that he was a young engineer, introduced to her by Mrs. Daley, and that she was exchanging letters with him in order to stay informed about the progress on the aqueduct—just a cordial association in fulfillment of a professional duty.

Nor did she dare ask Lesley, knowing the bonfire of interest any word of her relationship with Jed would set ablaze in the Harvey House dormitory. So Janey discussed the situation with Emma, who was herself preparing for marriage to a young farmer whose family owned a large apple orchard down in Lone Pine. In fact, Emma—no one was to know it but her sister Rosie and Janey—was with child by the boy. Emma suggested she might ask Jed his meaning in her next letter, but Janey was embarrassed by that prospect. Jed has his own way, she explained to her friend, and always seemed to know what he was doing. He wasn't a man to be prodded. So instead she simply wrote back that she was anxious for the aqueduct to be finished so she could see him again, and would certainly love to see Colorado someday.

The letters she received from Jed over the summer didn't broach the subject again. Maybe for him something had been settled, or maybe he had forgotten he'd ever mentioned going to Colorado together. Janey wondered and stewed, as she continued to help out at the *Inyo Register*. Chalfant assigned her a few small stories about local events, such as the Fourth of July church picnic. Bucky Porter gave her a sour look when he heard of it; he wasn't entirely a fool, having made out the signs that Chalfant might be grooming a replacement for him.

Then one day in early October, as the mornings were becoming frosty, Janey entered the *Register* office to find Chalfant waiting for her.

"That's it. The work is over on the aqueduct," he announced. "The opening ceremony is set for November 5th. I want you to go to Los Angeles and cover it for me."

"What…Los Angeles?!" Janey put her hand against the work table to steady herself.

"Well, not really Los Angeles, north of the city in the San Fernando Valley…a place where the water comes out the end of the aqueduct and gets stored in reservoirs. It's about 20 miles northeast of a new town they've built called 'Owensmouth.'"

---

*CK doesn't need to know all the details about Jed. Discretion is called for not only by difference in gender, but difference in age as well. Young people hate to hear that their elders once reveled in sensuality. And these younger generations, from the hippie love-child era onward, they think they invented having sex for fun rather than for procreation. They'd be stupefied to learn how even in the Victorian era, many people lived secretly uninhibited lives—writers and artists not even that secretly.*

*In my day, the conventions of the old era were already breaking down. Women were straining to burst out of their corsets and men to be loosed from the conventions of polite society—they were raring to mix it up in a fight. Soon they'd have it, in the war that would rip the past to shreds. Jed and I would come together in a new world striding forth from that wreckage, and we'd feel like we owned it and could do anything!*

"Honk! honk! Move aside!" Rex leaned out the window, cursing under his breath, as he tried to clear a way among horse-drawn carriages, buckboards and other automobiles for the big black Mitchell limousine.

"Gad, 20 more miles of this!" complained Chris Bow to his driver. "There must be thousands of them, all headin to the celebration." It was going to be a long, slow drive, and the freshness of the clear, bright morning was already dissipating in the unseasonable heat.

"You gonna be okay sis?" He regarded Janey, who bobbed her head in affirmation.

Chris was amused. Far from being wilted and bothered, she appeared to be aglow with excitement and taking keen interest in everything around her. The previous day, he and Rex had collected her at the Southern Pacific's Arcade Depot in the eastern outskirts of the city.

Rex had whisked them off downtown to Chris's house in the city's fashionable Bunker Hill neighborhood, where Janey's big brother had enjoyed seeing her awed appreciation as he toured her through the elegant 12-room Victorian. Later, she'd been like the happy child he remembered from their valley days when he took her for a ride on the Angels Flight funicular, which ran up and down the steep slope between Bunker Hill's quiet, shaded streets and the busy commercial district below.

Now she was seated next to him in the cushiony back seat of the limo, attired in a manner that was, for Hazy, impeccable. She wore a high-waisted frock of plum-colored cotton that flowed gently around her slim frame. It was accented at the shawl collar and elbow-length cuffed sleeves by crisp cream-colored lacework in a simple dotted pattern, which showed her honeyed skin to advantage. She had tied her loose plait up into a chignon that approximated Ma's example, despite being slightly crooked and marred by unruly strands Alice Bow would never have abided. In her lap, Janey held a wide brimmed straw hat, onto which she had tied yellow silk roses and ribbon. She was a long way from being smart and modern, like the tailored girls of the city, but Chris thought she looked fine.

Janey had, in fact, expended extraordinary effort, compared to her custom, worrying about and planning her appearance. Not only was she determined to dress in a manner befitting the professional reporter she was, attested to by the small notebook and pencil in her beige lace bag, but for the first time in her life she also intended to be pretty. Soon, very soon, after all these months of letters, she would see Jed again, and be seen by him. He had let her know that he and the other crew chiefs and engineers would all be present at the opening day celebration. He was even trying to wrangle some of his workers to come along, though most of the stakemen had already moved on to other employment. "I'll find you," he'd written.

But here, amidst the sea of Angelenos flowing toward the event site, she wondered how he would manage it. What if he couldn't find her and they missed each other altogether? Now, calm down, she reassured herself. He'll do it. He is, after all, Jed Brecken.

William Mulholland also sat in the back of a black limousine, juggling elation and worry. Today's ceremony would honor his greatest achievement, a glorious end to what had often seemed like endless labor and trouble—but his dear Lillie was not there to share it with him.

For months, he had carried the double burden of the aqueduct and his wife's illness. Only his closest associates knew Lillie Mulholland suffered from uterine cancer. They had orders to find him, day or night, wherever he was along the aqueduct, if her condition worsened. Bravely she had endured, intent on being at her husband's side for this crowning event, and it had appeared her indomitable spirit would have its way. But just days ago, Lillie had collapsed. Rushed to the hospital in Los Angeles for resuscitation and surgery, she had rallied sufficiently to insist on an early return home, still hoping to be able to accompany him to the celebration. But finally she had been too weak, and the journey too long, even in the police-escorted motorcade that had left the city in advance of the throngs of sightseers taking to the road.

Dozens of city officials and distinguished guests rode with him in one of the motorcade's 40 black Model Ts. They included the state's governor and two senators, the mayors of Los Angeles, San Francisco and San Diego, and a representative from newly elected President Woodrow Wilson. There were also publishers of the city's leading newspapers as well as members of the syndicate of businessmen who had bought up San Fernando Valley land before the aqueduct had even been announced. They were about to reap immense fortunes now that Owens Valley water was coming here. Harrison Gray Otis, publisher of the *Los Angeles Times*, a central figure in this real estate cabal, was thus attending in both capacities.

Mulholland glanced over at W.B. Matthews, seated next to him. The dapper city attorney, who had become special counsel for the aqueduct and would soon assume a similar position for the Department of Water and Power, had proved invaluable. Throughout the five years since they had broken ground on the vast project, Matthews had steered him flawlessly through myriad legal, financial and public relations quagmires. This morning Mulholland had joked to the mayor, "I did the work, but Matthews kept me out of jail!"

But there was one more person who certainly should be here and wasn't: Fred Eaton. It was nine years since they had hatched what many had regarded as a crazy scheme to bring Owens River water to Los Angeles. Now it was accomplished, and praised by all and sundry. Yet his former friend, more and more embittered over the years about the city's refusal to pay one million dollars for the reservoir site in Long Valley, had flatly refused to take his rightful place in the ceremony. Mulholland had to admit to holding a bit of a grudge against Eaton, but nevertheless he intended to praise his adversary this afternoon. Near the end of a short prepared speech, he planned to say: "I am sorry that the man whom I consider the father of the aqueduct is not here, former Mayor Eaton. To him all honor is due. He planned it—we simply put together the bricks and the mortar."

Since Fred had removed himself and his second wife to the Owens Valley, the two old friends had seen each other but a few times. On each occasion, Fred had harangued him on why the city must reconsider its decision and pay his full price for the remaining land necessary to build a large dam and reservoir in Long Valley. Once, Fred had arrived at the aqueduct office in Mojave in a seething rage. "You've deprived me of my rightful profits!" he had shouted. Mulholland had tried to calm him, fearing they would come to blows, but Fred had stormed out, slamming the screen door nearly off of its hinges. At this point, Mulholland had begun to fear for the mental health of his one-time mentor. Untempered resentment, wounded pride and self-imposed isolation seemed to have unbalanced his mind. And this was a concern for Mulholland on more than a personal basis, for he was well aware that Eaton had become one of the foremost citizens of Owens Valley, recently even taking on the chairman-ship of one of the ditch associations. If Eaton were losing his reason, there could be real trouble ahead.

"Looks like we've arrived," said Matthews, as the motorcade approached the little town of San Fernando. The tiny depot there was overflowing with travelers, disembarking in their Sunday clothes and setting out, some carrying picnic baskets, along the four mile road to the so-called "Grand Cascade," the curving cement canal that would bring the water surging down into the San Fernando Valley reservoir once it was released. There was a natural limestone amphitheater at this place, making it an ideal location for the ceremony, and at its base, a rough wooden grandstand had been constructed for dignitaries and speakers. A large flagpole was mounted atop it.

Mulholland hadn't replied. Matthews studied him, wincing at the fatigue and worry evident on his boss's face. The face was also deeply lined and leathered by years of exposure to harsh field conditions. And Matthews noticed an occasional involuntary twitch of the man's facial muscles. "You need a rest Bill," he said gently. "You designed and built an engineering marvel that rivals the Panama Canal, but the effort has near finished you."

The chief smiled wanly. Not being an engineer, his companion was unaware of the fact that some credit was due him for that project as well. Hydraulic methods invented by Mulholland had been used in the con-struction of the Panama Canal, and had been essential to solving two of its most difficult engineering challenges.

No need to tell him. Today is for celebrating the aqueduct, and he'd be receiving his full shared of credit. "I guess it was the Irish in me made me take on this job," Mulholland responded congenially. "T'was a fair fight with nature, and I wasn't about to back off."

"Yes, and you won. To victory!" Matthews pulled a silver flask from his coat pocket and offered it to Mulholland, who took a couple of swigs of the whiskey, passing the flask back so Matthews could do the same. As the limousine came to a stop in the secluded area where the motorcade participants would be regaled with champagne as they awaited the start of the ceremony, the lawyer was relieved to see Mulholland's face relax and the twitching subside. He said a silent prayer: Let the man have this day of glory. Let him have one day's relief from his troubles.

---

As the dignitaries were privately feted, the river of buggies and automobiles from Los Angeles continued to disgorge, and the trains to arrive and empty. Before noon tens of thousands of celebrants had gathered around the grandstand and were lining the edges of the Grand Cascade.

Chris shepherded Janey through the crowds and onto the grandstand, where seats had been reserved for them in recognition of his service to the aqueduct. "Hello!" "Hello there, how are you this fine day?!" "Yes, good day to you!" he called out in response to the many voices that greeted him. It was too crowded and noisy for him to introduce her, but Janey was pleased to see how well liked Chris seemed to be among these fancy-dressed city folk.

"Oh Mr. Bow, Mr. Bow…over here if you please! Sit here, next to me!" An attractive young brunette in a belted coat with ruffled collar, wide fedora and dangling earrings reached out to tap his arm. She had broad, glowing cheeks and a generous rouged mouth.

"Why hello Miss Lucille, and thank you, it would be my pleasure. May I introduce my sister Janey Bow? Janey, this is Lucille Mulholland, one of the chief engineer's beautiful daughters. And here…hello there Miss Rose…is the other."

Rose, dressed in a conservative suit, had lighter hair, a longer face, and prominent chin and teeth. She smiled a warm hello at Janey and Chris. With their mother unable to attend, they had been driven here by private car to stand in her stead by their father's side. Despite concern over their mother—a complication of which Chris and most of the other celebrants around them were quite unaware—the girls couldn't help but feel elated. It was a gorgeous day, everyone on the grandstand was in such a festive mood, and their father was the hero of the hour.

Seated beside Chris, who quickly became quite engaged in animated conversation with the vivacious Lucille, Janey scanned the milling crowd for sign of Jed. Now that she was here, among more people than she'd ever even seen in one place—she truly despaired of meeting him. Yet it seemed only minutes had passed when she felt a hand on her shoulder. She glanced up, and there was Jed, sitting just behind her.

"Je…," she caught herself, "…Mr. Brecken! How wonderful to see you!"

Chris, turning around, recognized the lauded tunnel boss despite his uncharacteristic attire in dark suit, starched collar and tie. He thrust out his hand. "Hello there Jed. Big day! Big, big day! Congratulations!"

"Thank you. Yes, it is quite a day. Most of us from the work teams are up there near the gate," he said, gesturing toward where the Grand Cascade's cement canal originated, high on the slope, at a twin-doored portal. The portal had a flat cement roof, upon which, the onlookers could barely make out, several men were standing near large wheels, horizontally mounted on vertical steel poles.

"When they turn those wheels, that will open the spigot and bring the water tumbling down the cascade," explained Jed.

"Where is it now?" asked Lucille, looking the handsome young man up and down. "I'm William Mulholland's daughter Lucille, and I certainly know who you are Mr. Brecken!" She thrust out a soft-gloved hand.

"My pleasure Miss Lucille. Your father is an excellent man." Jed took her hand and pressed it briefly. "The water is stored in two small reservoirs on either side of the Elizabeth Tunnel. Once it's released, it will end up in the San Fernando Reservoir, way over there."

Lucille turned around and called out to the man seated on the other side of her sister, "Mr. Loewenthal, have you met Mr. Jed Brecken? This is the courageous young tunneling boss you newspapermen have been all aflutter about. Mr. Brecken, may I acquaint you with the editor of the *Los Angeles Examiner*, Mr. Henry Loewenthal."

The tall, attractive man, with salt-and-pepper hair and intelligent brown eyes behind spectacles, stood and offered his hand to Brecken. "Yes indeed, I've read of your exploits young man. In fact, there was an article about you and your team at the Elizabeth Tunnel, published in my friend Chalfant's *Inyo Register*, that I very much wished we had written."

Brecken nodded politely. He never paid attention to what was written about him. Loewenthal turned toward Chris and Janey. "Miss Mulholland, would you be so kind as to introduce me to your other friends?"

"Certainly Henry," said Lucille, stretching her arm out over the head of her sister to touch the editor's arm. "May I introduce Mr. Christopher Bow, proprietor of the company that fed all those aqueduct workers, and his sister, Miss Janey Bow."

Loewenthal shook Chris's hand and made a slight bow to Janey, looking at her with ill-disguised curiosity. Then he recovered himself and said simply, "Charmed miss." He then, by necessity, retook his seat, as Rose was attempting to detach him from her sister by reengaging him in conversation. Brecken turned to Chris.

"Would it be all right, Mr. Bow, if I took Miss Bow for a brief tour along the side of the cascade?"

"Certainly, if she likes." Chris was anxious to reengage the lively Lucille in a conversation of his own.

Janey agreed, trying to tether her winging heart, as she took Jed's offered arm and he led her off of the grandstand. Even maintaining the proper inch or two apart, she could smell his skin, and that made her steps a bit shaky. But he held her firm, guiding them through the crowd, dodging vendors hawking pennants, Panama hats and gold-trimmed vials of Owens River water. When they had gone a fair distance from the grandstand and the crowd had thinned out, Jed placed his other hand atop of hers and smiled his smile, the one she loved that started with his mouth and reached up to his eyes, or vice versa.

"It's wonderful to see you Janey!"

"Oh yes, it felt like this day would never come!"

"We haven't much time before they start, and there's something I need to talk with you about."

Janey's heart was in full flight now, brooking no restraint. How so like Jed, to ask her now, just like that, so unconventionally. But it didn't matter because now that she'd seen him again, so tall and strong and handsome, and with that wonderful smile she'd been dreaming about for more than a year, she pushed aside her fears about being too young to marry. She gazed up at him, squinting a little, despite the broad brim of her hat, into the sun.

"I'm going to Barcelona."

What had he said? "Barce...?"

"Barcelona, Spain. Word's gotten around, around the world actually, about the work we did at the Elizabeth. There's a tramway tunnel over there that they've been having problems building, and they asked me to come over and take it on. Maybe bring some of the guys with experience from the aqueduct."

She noticed, in her stunned misery, that his face and voice were alive with excitement. He noticed her frozen countenance and squeezed her hand.

"It will only be a year or two Janey, and I'll be able to come back every six months or so for a visit. I'll come to see you...and then, afterward, I'll take you to Colorado. We'll get married, if you'll have me."

Janey leaned on Jed's arm, feeling her legs go wobbly and her mouth gape. He laughed, and rubbed her hand as if to warm her.

"Buck up there missy, haven't you ever been proposed to before?!"

She hadn't, of course, and hearing the longed-for words mixed with the unexpected and unwelcome news of his departure, she didn't know what to think or feel, and so didn't remember to accept him.

"Well, is it yes then, or are you fixin to break my heart?"

"No...I mean, it's yes, of course!"

He squeezed her hand tightly. "I guess this isn't a proper place to seal the bargain with a kiss."

She felt her face blaze at the memory of what had ensued the last time he had asked for a kiss.

"We'd better head back, they'll be starting soon." He turned them around. "Shall we tell your brother?"

"No, no, not yet. He knows nothing about us, except that I wrote about you." They strolled back, silent for a while. Then she tapped his arm. "I mustn't tell my parents yet either. They wouldn't approve..."

He looked at her, surprised, so she clarified. "Of you, yes, of course, they'll approve of you. But not of the..." she searched for a word that would capture the strange, free nature of what had passed between them, "...the modern way we've gone about this."

Jed gave her his favored smile again. "We'll just keep it our secret then...like the tunnel...for the time being."

She nodded, and they continued their way back to the grandstand. With each step, her hand on his arm, she began to feel a brighter glow of pleasure at the idea of being engaged to this extraordinary man. As they made their way up to the seats, she had to take herself sternly in hand in order to regulate her countenance lest Chris should suspect something untoward. He barely noticed she had arrived, though, so captivated was he by the lovely Lucille.

After seeing her to her seat, Jed made his excuses to the party. "I must be with the rest of the aqueduct teams for the release. I hope to have the pleasure of rejoining you all after the ceremony."

Then he was off, his long legs quickly taking him down the grandstand and off into the crowd. Janey watched him, hoping her state of stupefaction was not evident to any of her companions.

"Miss Bow…" It was the newspaper editor, Mr. Loewenthal, who had apparently detached himself from Rose and was now standing in the aisle next to her. "May I?" he asked, indicating the vacant adjacent seat.

"Of course."

"Please excuse me if this is impertinent, but are you by any chance the J. Bow who wrote the *Inyo Register* article about the losing tunnel team?"

"Why yes, I am."

"And before that, the article about Mulholland?"

"Yes, that was my first attempt."

He nodded, smiling. "Excuse me, Miss Bow, but like everyone else, I had no idea you were a young woman. Now that I've discovered you, however, I must say that I'm not surprised those stories came from a female pen."

Was he about to tell her that they were of little value, Janey wondered. She dared an impertinence. "The pen, Mr. Loewenthal, has no gender."

He laughed. "Yes, of course, you are right. But please allow me to tell you how much I enjoyed reading your stories. They're very good, and very unusual, Miss Bow."

"Thank you," she said. "I am working hard to learn your trade Mr. Loewenthal."

"I'm pleased to hear it. I wonder, Miss Bow, would you consider continuing your apprenticeship in a new location, perhaps in Los Angeles?"

"Los Angeles?!"

"Yes, indeed." He chuckled at her countenance, which was rapt with wonder. "I'm offering you a job, Miss Bow, on the *Los Angeles Examiner*."

"They're starting!" "Are they starting?!" The milling crowd began to settle and hush, spectators on the grandstand leaning forward in their seats to see.

"Shall we talk about this afterward?" he asked. She nodded her head, unable to form words.

Los Angeles! When the police sirens went off to mark the beginning of the ceremony, Janey's head was still reverberating with the new notion that while Jed went to Barcelona she might go to Los Angeles. She needn't be left behind in the Owens Valley. She could become a real reporter for a big-city newspaper!

The sirens continued wailing as the motorcade of 40 black Model Ts, festooned with flag-colored bunting, drove up, honking horns, in front of the stand. The onlookers cheered and waved small American flags as the dignitaries emerged from their automobiles and were led to the front of the grandstand, just below where the Mulholland girls, the Bows and Mr. Loewenthal were seated. Last to emerge was William Mulholland, and seeing him, the crowd went wild. Lucille and Rose joyfully clutched at each other. "There's father, there's father!"

A military band played, and Helen Beach Yah, a favorite performer of Angelenos, sang "California—Hail the Waters!" an anthem she had composed for the occasion. There followed dozens of speeches, every official taking his moment in the sun to associate himself with this great endeavor and to praise the great man who had brought it forth.

Finally "the man who built the aqueduct" was introduced and rose to speak. As Mulholland approached the rostrum, a rifle salute and clashing of symbols rang out. Rose oohed and clasped her hands in front of her chest. He gave a short speech, simpler and more direct than the florid ones that had preceded him. It was a speech that deflected the spotlight of adulation being thrust upon him, giving credit instead to Fred Eaton and to the thousands of aqueduct workers.

"They do so much for so little. I know this type of man from my early life as a sailor. I've worked with them, slept with them and would rather sit around camp with them than be in a circle of lawyers, doctors or bankers." Cheers went up from the clusters of aqueduct workers sprinkled along the cascade and clustered up around the gate. Mulholland waved to them and continued.

"They were a grand lot, they did their work and took their chances in the tunnels and in other dangerous jobs, and they spent their money like sailors ashore and that is the one thing that saddens me today. It has been a close partnership and we have worked together well. Therefore we appear jointly." Mulholland waved again at the cheering men. "And this expression of thanks should be on behalf of us all."

Now the men were throwing their hats and helmets into the air, and the crowd was cheering and waving the little flags in a frenzy. William Kinney, head of the Los Angeles Chamber of Commerce, which had organized the festivities, came forward and presented the chief with a huge silver loving cup, "to be filled with Owens River water!"

Then Mulholland was led to the flagpole, as the band played "America the Beautiful." Drums rolled…he reached out and pulled the lanyard, unfurling the stars and stripes—this was the signal to the men on the portal to begin turning the wheels that would open the spigot and release the water.

Fireworks boomed, people leaned forward for their first sight of Owens Valley water. "I see it!" "Look, do you see it?!"

It came first as a trickle, then surged through the portal, and soon it was roaring down the cement-lined channel in white turbulence toward the crowd, which cheered as the torrent burst by them. Kinney indicated that Mulholland should say something more, but the roar of the cascade and crowd prevented most onlookers from hearing what he said.

Janey heard it though, being seated quite close, and she instantly knew they were words every newspaper in the land would want to print. He had said simply:

"There it is—Take it!"

PART III: 1924-1928

*The Break*

Courtesy Los Angeles Public Library Photo Collection

## Chapter 15

Senior engineer for the Los Angeles Department of Water and Power J.B. Lippincott leaned against the side of his Model T and stretched his long legs. He lit a cigar, and the thin scrawl of rising smoke mingled before his eyes with the soft brightening gray of sunrise on the far horizon of hills. He peered down at the dry creek bed of cracked mud, its surface peeling back in curls, and waited.

"Caw! Caw!" "Caw! Caw! Caw!" came the familiar sound of a band of angry crows. Like black arrows, they darted at a huge hawk circling the top boughs of a tall oak. Lippincott watched, amused, as the raptor finally gave up and flew west, leaving the object of interest, most likely a nest, to its defenders.

Another familiar sound drew his gaze back down to the creek bed in time to see the rush of water fill it. This was Owens River water, and most of it would run down the creek into the Santa Clara River and out to the

sea at Oxnard—wasted, in the middle of the biggest drought
Los Angeles had endured in 30 years!

In March and April of last year, they'd discharged more than
15,000 acre-feet of Owens River water from Power Station No. 1 in the
San Francisquito Canyon into this creek. They were dumping even more
this year, despite knowing full well that a few months from now, at the
height of the summer irrigation season, there wouldn't be enough water to
meet both the domestic consumption needs of the city's population and
the voracious demands of San Fernando Valley agriculture.

Although Superintendent Mulholland had ordered them to be
discrete, making the releases at times of day when few people would be
around to see, rumors of surging creek beds were feeding suspicions. Some
of Mulholland's enemies had accused him of deliberately dumping water
to create public support for further investment in water projects and to
manipulate land prices in the San Fernando Valley for the benefit of the
syndicate of wealthy businessmen who had invested there.

It wasn't true, of course, but nevertheless the perception of wrong
doing was damaging to the reputation of the department. And it wouldn't
be wise to let it be widely known that Mulholland had purchased property
in San Fernando. Hell, Lippincott had bought some land there himself,
and he knew well to keep that a secret too.

"Caw! Caw! Caw!" screamed the crows.

---

*"Bye bye blackbird!" I remember singing along with the vocalist and all
my pals at the table littered with emptied bottles, overflowing ashtrays and
abandoned dinners. The band was playing the tune that had become wildly
popular since the record by Gene Austin had been released. Dancers were
doing the latest faster foxtrot as the words everyone knew by heart rang out
above the hum of conversation and tinkle of glasses and laughter: "Pack up
all my care and woe. Here I go, singing low. Bye bye blackbird."*

*Then the band slid into another hit song by velvet-voiced Gene:
"Yes, Sir, That's My Baby," and my escort tugged me out of my chair, onto
the dance floor to do the latest craze, the Charleston. Some of the couples
already on the floor stayed knotted, others broke apart to do the steps solo.
My partner and I danced separately, but moved in unison, toes tapping,*

*arms and legs swinging in opposite directions, his jacket flapping, my loose*
*sheath swirling around my torso and swinging up above my knees and*
*thighs. All around us other couples were doing the same, but, miraculously,*
*no one got kicked or slipped and broke their keister on the occasional puddle*
*of spilled spirits.*

*Everyone in the place, even those sitting the number out, was moving.*
*Gals were flirting, men were on the make, and I remember it felt so darn*
*good to be there, to be one of them.*

---

Lippincott watched the rush of water awhile, then shoved his hands in
the back pockets of his trousers and walked slowly to the car, shaking
his head. The reason they were having to dump water in the midst of a
drought was, in his judgment, that his boss had made a fundamental
mistake in the design of the aqueduct.

As much as he admired the chief and was grateful for having been
hired on, first for the aqueduct and now at the department, he had to
fault the man for not having built adequate water storage facilities in the
Owens Valley. The handful of small reservoirs at the southern end of the
aqueduct helped to regulate distribution, but they didn't give the department enough control to adjust the volume of water flowing southward
through the aqueduct according to the huge disparity in seasonal demand:
In summer and early fall, agricultural interests could have consumed the
entire 400 cubic feet per second capacity of the aqueduct if they could
have gotten it; in winter and early spring, their needs dropped to just
20 cubic feet per second.

Without adequate storage in the northern part of the valley, above
the aqueduct intake, there was no way to capture the excess water from the
snowmelt and store it for subsequent months of high demand. Without
that capability, the city would forever be at the mercy of California's
cycles of wet and dry periods, which could last for years. Last August,
the gap between current demand and current supply had gotten so bad
Mulholland had been forced to cut off the flow to San Fernando's alfalfa
fields and impose water rationing on other crops. The farmers had been
furious—a situation that made rumors of water dumping this spring even
more dangerous.

Lippincott knew, of course, like everyone else in the department, that Mulholland had balked at paying Fred Eaton's million dollar price for Long Valley, the land in northern Owens Valley where a dam large enough for an adequate reservoir could have been built. He understood why the greediness of a former friend irked the chief—hell, he and Eaton had been friends too! But Lippincott felt that stubborn pride was getting in the way of Mulholland doing what he ought to do, which was to bite the bullet and pay the price of solving the flow control problem once and for all.

Climbing back into the car, Lippincott turned it around and drove slowly back to the city through the San Fernando Valley. After passing the small community of Owensmouth, he stopped on a ridge, overlooking lowlands where the Los Angeles Reservoir spread out like liquid silver to the foot of a jaggedly edged line of low bluish mountains. Although rainfall had been less than half the normal level the past two years, and the Sierra Nevada snowpack also lighter than usual, the spring melt had sent plenty of water charging through the aqueduct's more than 230 miles of canals, tunnels and siphons. This reservoir, the final storage facility, like all the other reservoirs in the system, was full to its brim. They'd had no choice today but to dump more water.

Not all of it would be wasted. Some of it would trickle down through the sand and gravel of the riverbed into the groundwater below the San Fernando Valley, from which sprang the headwaters of the city's only native river. Lippincott chuckled, thinking about how Mulholland often joked that the Los Angeles River "ran upside down," since more of its flow was underground than above ground.

In fact, the San Fernando Valley's unusual hydrologic system of subterranean lakes and rivers, making up a vast aquifer, was the reason the chief had decided to terminate the aqueduct there. While some critics had accused him of colluding with the San Fernando real estate syndicate, Mulholland had always pointed to the natural superiority of the place for underground storage of water, where it was less subject to contamination and evaporation, as the primary justification for his decision. In fact, the chief had even argued that instead of dumping excess water into the ocean, they ought to be pumping it directly into the aquifer.

But the city's board of directors, mayor and business leaders had balked at funding this completely unorthodox, unproven method.

Instead, they'd directed Mulholland to build additional reservoirs in the San Fernando and Los Angeles area. That's what the chief was doing today, Lippincott knew. He was out in San Francisquito Canyon overseeing the construction of the new St. Francis Dam. Another new dam, in Hollywood Canyon, was nearly finished.

This additional southern storage capacity, while helpful, was likely to be too little too late, in Lippincott's opinion, to resolve the volatile situation created by the lack of northern storage and two years of drought. Too little, because the chief's original projections of the city's population growth had been woefully off the mark. Back in 1910, when they were building the aqueduct, Mulholland had figured the city of 200,000 people would continue to grow at about the same rate as it had in the previous decade, which would have put the population at about 390,000 by 1925. The actual rate of growth had been three times that, and today, a year short of that projection, the population of Los Angeles was already over a million.

Mulholland had also been wrong in his estimate of the water consumption of this growing population. He had based his estimate on the presumption that urban and agricultural areas would consume about the same amount of water per acre, and so, even with the annexation of the San Fernando Valley into the city, the aqueduct would have to provide only 90 cubic feet per second of water by 1925.

What had really happened was that the now heavily irrigated San Fernando Valley was consuming far more water per acre than the urban areas—and even they were consuming far more than Mulholland had projected, since people were moving to the city and settling at a much higher density than had been expected. Not only that, but members of the real estate syndicate were now converting huge swaths of San Fernando land from agricultural uses to subdivisions of densely packed houses. Much of the land that remained under cultivation was no longer used for low-water-consumption citrus and other fruit trees, but had been turned over during the war years to more lucrative high-water-consumption cash crops such as beans and potatoes.

The result of all of those miscalculations was that overall water consumption was much higher than Mulholland could have imagined in his wildest dreams—and there was no reason to think that this year it wouldn't continue to climb.

"It's going to be a damn-hot summer again," Lippincott pronounced grimly, looking up at a gauzy, white rainless cloud. And the San Fernando wasn't the only place where tempers were nearing the boiling point.

For nearly a decade, relations between the Owens Valley and the city had been cordial enough, but now they were heating up again. To augment the flow through the aqueduct, Mulholland was drilling ground-water in several places around the valley. When this had first started a few years ago, there had been just a scatter of pumps, mostly in the southern part of the valley, operating for just a month or two a year, and valley folk had taken little notice of it. But with the onset of the drought, Mulholland had ordered more pumps installed, including in the northern valley around Bishop, and extended drilling for a longer period each year. People up there had become alarmed, and some of the farmers above the aqueduct intake had gotten angry enough to start diverting more water into their irrigation canals than they needed, just to prevent it going south to Los Angeles.

"God-damn if that place isn't plumb full of malcontents and trouble-makers!" Lippincott said aloud. If those farmers up there had just learned to irrigate efficiently, none of this would be happening! Since the opening of the aqueduct in 1913, the department had tried to curb the profligate methods of Owens Valley agriculture, but the farmers had been resistant to change and, while precipitation remained at normal or high levels, they'd had little motivation for it.

Today they were still flooding their fields a half-dozen times each irrigation season. Nothing had changed since Jacob Clausen, an engineer for the US Reclamation Service, had first complained to him and Fred Eaton about it, describing the valley's irrigation practices as "disgraceful" and calling the waste from evaporation alone "unfathom-able!" Those words, spoken around the campfire during a camping and fishing trip to the Yosemite almost a quarter century ago, had planted in Eaton's mind the first seeds of the idea of taking Owens River water for Los Angeles—an idea he had later brought to Mulholland.

Mulholland could have done more to change irrigation meth-ods up there if he'd really tried. He'd been too complacent about it, to

Lippincott's way of thinking. When Lippincott had last tried to broach the subject with his boss, Mulholland had simply shrugged and quipped, "If they want to flood their fields instead of irrigating properly, that's fine. The excess water will soak into the ground, and we'll just pump it out and into the aqueduct!"

Lippincott groaned at the thought. Again, Mulholland was making the mistake of not paying attention to public perception. "People don't like the idea of their groundwater being drained right out from under them, even if there's a scientific reason for it," Lippincott now said to himself aloud.

He was thinking that problems like these seemed to be inevitable in the management of large public infrastructures—not a responsibility he hankered for. Nope, far better to build than to manage, and soon, if all went well, he'd be doing just that again. Years ago, Lippincott had surveyed the Colorado River, the great canyon-sculpting torrent that rose in the Rocky Mountains and ran down along the Nevada-Arizona border to Mexico and beyond, for the US Reclamation Service. Mulholland had sent him back to study it again in 1912, and last year, he, the chief and several other engineers from the department had returned to determine if the Colorado—which Mulholland had lauded as "an American Nile awaiting regulation"—could become the next source of water for Los Angeles.

It was already quite clear that the Owens River aqueduct could not keep up with the exploding thirst of Southern California. This would be an immensely bigger project: Legislatures in seven states were in the process of ratifying the Colorado River Compact authorizing the construction of a dam at Boulder Canyon. A new aqueduct would bring a good share of the waters captured by that dam to Los Angeles.

Yessir, this one would make his reputation and earn him back the respect of Reclamation colleagues who had cast aspersions on his integrity and professionalism during the Owens Valley hearings up in Frisco, and were still cool when they chanced to meet him, even after all this time. Even after all this *water under the bridge.* Lippincott smiled at his own cleverness.

Like a gigantic flayed fish with exposed ribs, the winged dike curved around the western ridge of San Francisquito Canyon toward the partially constructed St. Francis Dam. William B. Matthews shaded his eyes with a manicured hand as he watched Bill Mulholland walk the backbone of the dike with two of his workers, through a bristle of vertical steel poles, squatting down to peer at something here, kick or poke something there, to make sure the support form was ready to receive poured concrete.

Matthews found it both amusing and reassuring to watch the Superintendent of the Los Angeles Department of Water and Power, an agency affectionately called the "DWP" by Angelenos, doing what he most liked to do: working with his crews in the field. Having moved from his former position as counsel for the city to counsel for the department, Matthews had continued to work closely with Mulholland, and was amazed that despite the post-aqueduct euphoria that had vaulted the chief to mythic status, the man had taken on few airs. Mulholland still spent as much time as possible out in the field. He still liked to get his hands good and dirty. In recent months, his driver had picked him up at dawn every day from his home in Los Angeles to take him 45 miles northeast to the dam site.

And this rough Irish immigrant, who had never finished school, now held an honorary doctorate from the University of California at Berkeley. He'd been feted and toasted all over town, and the Los Angeles Public Service Commission had insisted, despite the chief's protestations, on renaming the new Hollywood Dam "Mulholland Dam."

Later this year, the city planned to dedicate a new scenic roadway to him in a gala celebration sure to be attended by civic leaders as well as motion picture stars. To be christened "Mulholland Highway," the scenic road would, when completed, wind for more than 30 miles through the Santa Monica Mountains down to the sea. While the chief had had nothing to do with the design or construction of the highway and, Matthews suspected, was a bit skeptical of it, several of his top engineers from the aqueduct were involved, perhaps trying a bit too hard to accomplish something on a grand scale like their former boss. Mulholland had even been urged to run for mayor, to which he had replied with typical brevity, force and color, "I'd rather give birth to a porcupine backwards than be mayor of Los Angeles!"

Mulholland had finished his inspection and was walking toward him. Matthews reached into his breast pocket and removed two Cuban cigars. They had some talking to do on an urgent subject, and the chief wasn't going to like it. "Afternoon Bill." Matthews offered a cigar.

"Afternoon W.B." Mulholland accepted it, bit off the end and spat it out. He leaned forward to meet the lighted match the attorney extended, then stood, legs apart, hands on hips, puffing in short, rapid blasts to get an even burn going. "What brings you all the way out here counselor?"

"There's trouble in the valley, I'm afraid."

"*Which* valley?"

Matthews laughed. "Well, for the moment, I'm talking about the Owens Valley. San Fernando should remain calm, at least until we get into the dregs of summer."

"Hmmph," Mulholland grunted and half turned to look out across the canyon.

"The Owens Valley farmers are getting pretty testy about the groundwater pumping we're doing up there, Bill, and so are the townsfolk in Bishop, Big Pine and Independence. You're aware, I presume, that they're having an even worse drought than we are—the worst on record! Maybe we should lay off the drilling for a while."

"Can't. At least not until we finish this dam and the one in Hollywood Canyon."

The chief was hell-bent on finishing the new dams, Matthews knew, because of the potential for unrest in Owens Valley, as well as the growing water consumption demands of the San Fernando Valley and the rest of Los Angeles. In fact, the St. Francis Dam, which had already been underway, originally planned to operate in conjunction with the two hydroelectric plants in the canyon, Powerhouse 1 north of the dam and Powerhouse 2 south of it, had been hurriedly modified in response to these pressures. To enable the reservoir to hold more water, the dam's height was now being raised from the initial design's 175 feet to 195 feet above the canyon floor, a change that necessitated the addition of the winged dike to prevent water from spilling over the western ridge abutment. The added height would create enough storage capacity, Mulholland insisted, for a full year's supply of domestic water to safeguard the city against drought.

Mulholland had also relayed to Matthews his intention that this largest of the aqueduct's reservoirs should safeguard the water supply against natural disaster. Although it was not widely known outside of engineering circles, the aqueduct's famed Elizabeth Tunnel, extending five miles through the Sierra Madre, intersected the San Andreas Fault, source of the 1906 San Francisco disaster. If such an earthquake were to occur there, the new reservoirs below it would still provide plenty of water for the city until repairs could be made. In placing so much reliance on the St. Francis Dam, Mulholland was basing his thinking on an idea that had first occurred to him more than a decade before, during construction of the Elizabeth Tunnel. That was when he had realized that the topography of San Francisquito Canyon, at the southern end of the tunnel, provided a natural site not only for power generation, but for a large reservoir. That's when he had first conducted test drilling on the canyon embankments to ensure they would provide a sound foundation for a dam.

Matthews knew the chief was now satisfied that he had solved the problem, and once he had solved a problem to his own satisfaction, Mulholland was unlikely to be swayed. The lawyer changed his tact.

"Well then, Bill, you ought to know that our problem isn't just the extra water they've been diverting into some of their ditches. My sources tell me they're organizing again. Those banker brothers, the Wattersons, who hold mortgages on a lot of property up there, are trying to put together an irrigation district that would consolidate land and water rights in the valley. Apparently, members of the Owens River Canal, Bishop Creek Ditch, McNally Ditch and Owens River and Big Pine Canal have all agreed to transfer their rights to the district. Those are the four biggest ditches in the north valley."

Mulholland was silent, but Matthews could tell he was listening. He continued. "Clearly their idea is to gain power from unity. They want to make us negotiate with the district instead of with individual landowners."

"To what aim?"

"As far as I can tell, they're aiming at one of two possible objectives: First, they'll try to get us to guarantee a specific quantity of water for each ditch association according to its needs. If that can't be achieved, they'll try to force us to buy out the entire valley. In that case, they'll push for reparations not only for the farms and ranches, but for the townsfolk too."

"Hell, no irrigation district ever included towns! Irrigation is about agriculture."

"Yes, they do appear to be taking an unusual approach—trying to unite all property owners in the valley, including owners of town lots without water rights. It could work," the lawyer considered. "They're likely to argue the position that the more farmers and ranchers who sell out and leave the valley, the less business they have. So the city is responsible for materially damaging their enterprises. I've tried to head them off by advising that legally I don't believe the city even has the right to pay such compensation."

"Good! No way in hell I'll ever pay a dime in reparations to the townsfolk. Loss of business is just the risk anyone takes when he opens up shop."

Matthews sighed. If Mulholland had changed at all from the avalanche of praise and adulation brought upon him, it was in this increased tendency toward stubbornness and an absolute lack of pity. Matthews admired Mulholland's ambition and boundless energy, but the man could also be, in his observation and opinion, arrogant, self-righteous, ruthless and petty.

"Bill, I think we should try again to reach a settlement on water apportionment," he suggested. Matthews had first tried back in 1913. After the completion of the aqueduct, the chief had sent him up to Bishop to meet with the leaders of the valley's ditch associations. In this and subsequent meetings, they'd gotten close, but never quite reached an agreement. They'd been stuck on how to figure the quantities of water to be apportioned. At one time or another, it would be the ditch representatives or the city representatives delaying the process by calling for more study. Figures submitted at long last by one side would be unacceptable to the other, which would set off another round of calculations and negotiations. Eventually, the effort had withered on the vine, as participants had become caught up in other matters, including the booming wartime market for Owens Valley produce. But with the postwar recession pulling down prices and demand, and the drought adding pressure, the valley folk now wanted to get back to the bargaining table.

"No, it's too late for that. Besides, it's probably not a real threat—that valley has never been able to reach unity on anything!" Mulholland said, his mouth twisting with derision. Then he paused, reconsidering. "How far have they gotten?"

"They've filed articles of incorporation and issued shares to their members. And, of course, they've elected Wilfred Watterson president. They're preparing to issue bonds to raise funds for paying the ditch associations for the transfer of rights."

"How do we stop it?"

Matthews considered while the two men smoked and watched late afternoon shadows deepen in the canyon. "I doubt we can stop it," he said, "but we can delay it. Enough to give us time to take other measures that will make the irrigation district irrelevant. And when that happens, it will fold of its own accord."

Mulholland crossed his arms in front of his chest and raised an eyebrow as he asked, "You working with someone trustworthy up there?"

"Well, I don't know that I would call him trustworthy exactly, more accurate to say he is highly self-interested. The Watterson brothers have an uncle George, whose always been jealous of them. Apparently, he went up against them in business—filed a rival claim on a mining right and tried to set up a bank in the valley—in both cases, coming out the loser. There's also a story that uncle George had his heart set on being first in the valley to have a motor car, but Wilfred beat him to it. When Wilfred drove his Stanley Steamer into Bishop, he was like a movie star, surrounded by an adoring public, and that really got George Watterson's goat.

"Be that as it may," the lawyer continued, "uncle George is an officer of the Bishop Creek Ditch association. He's quite friendly with the president of the McNally Ditch, and with a lawyer who, shall we say, was disappointed in love with one of the Watterson's sisters, Elizabeth, a fine-looking young lady who married a Reclamation Service engineer, friend of Lippincott's, guy by the name of Jacob Clausen. Anyway, we have some levers to work with…if that's what you want to do."

"Do it."

# Chapter 16

When the nice young man hoisted Lesta Parker's carpetbag above her head and settled it onto the shelf above her seat, the lumpy bundle exhaled a cloud of dust and the smell of hard-boiled eggs. Her helper, leaning down to peer at her and ask, "Is there anything else you need, ma'am?" didn't notice or pretended not to.

"No, thank you so much. Thank you," she replied, reaching out to briefly grasp and press his hand with knobby fingers, hoping he wasn't expecting a gratuity.

But he just smiled, straightened up, doffed his cap and headed back down the aisle to the car entrance. She breathed with relief. Turning to look out the window, Lesta saw him swing down from the train onto the platform and stride through the crowd. The sign below the overhang, under which travelers clustered, seeking protection from the searing May sun, read "Williams, Arizona. Westbound trains."

She settled back, placed her handbag and hands in her lap and watched from beneath the brim of her straw hat as the car began to fill with other passengers. New arrivals searched for seats, as many were already occupied by the belongings of those who, traveling through from more eastern points of embarkation, had stepped off the train to stretch their legs and purchase a newspaper or refreshment.

Lesta sniffed and stared. That girl edging down the aisle was balancing a beige leather suitcase on one shoulder, and the loose sleeve on the lifted arm that held it had fallen away so that a person could practically see her armpit and underclothes! The gauzy navy and white stripe dress also exposed most of the girl's slender, shapely legs, which were encased in nearly transparent patterned pale blue stockings. Her hair was cut short, as had become the fashion for young women since the war.

The new arrival slid the suitcase onto the rack and plopped down into the seat across the aisle from Lesta. As she did so, she picked up a newspaper that had been on that seat, perhaps to hold the place for an absent occupant, and tossed it onto the adjacent one next to the window. Lesta continued watching from the corner of her eye as the girl removed her bell-shaped, fitted hat of soft pale blue felt, shoved it between her hip and the armrest, pulled out a notebook and pencil from a beige leather handbag with a tooled design like a fancy saddle, unbuttoned the straps of her beige high-heeled shoes and began to write.

The former occupant of the seat returned, and the girl, looking up at the sandy haired man wearing a bow tie and middle-aged paunch, smiled brightly. "Oh, I beg your pardon sir. I didn't know anyone had this seat. Shall I move over?"

Of course the man, being a gentleman, had to decline. "No, please keep the seat, miss. If you'll just step out for a moment so that I can take the window."

She did as requested, and then settled back to her task. Lesta thought she probably was quite accustomed to wrangling little favors from men. Wearing cosmetics. Probably smoked and drank too like so many wild young ones these days.

How things have changed since I was her age, mused Lesta. We couldn't be more different, this young, confident girl and me. Yet…there was something familiar about her. The honey-colored hair that hung forward along the curve of the jaw line was thick, wavy and a bit unruly. The skin of her bare arm was honey-colored too. Lesta reached out a finger and touched it lightly. "Janey Bow? Is that you?"

Greenish eyes framed by long bronze lashes, snapped up to meet hers, showing surprise, then sudden recognition. A generous smile spread across the red-rouged lips. "Why Mrs. Parker! Yes, yes, it's me, although I go by Jane now—J. Bow in the newspaper actually. I'm a reporter, I guess you know. What a pleasure to see you ma'am. What are you doing here?"

A bit cheeky, thought Lesta, but then that's how young folks talk now, even to their elders. "Well then, I'm on my way home from my brother Herluff's place in Winslow," the older woman replied. "He's postmaster there," she added proudly.

"How nice," replied Jane. "Did you have a pleasant visit?"

"Yes, dear, very pleasant indeed." No sense letting Janey Bow, dressed in those fine clothes with that expensive suitcase, know she'd been forced to go to Winslow to beg a loan from Herluff, spending money she and Cyril didn't have on the train ticket. But it had been nice, despite that bit of business, to spend a week with her brother and his family. They had a fine house, and Winslow was such a big town compared to Bishop. Yes, the visit had been quite nice.

She was sure Janey wouldn't be interested in any of that. Lesta knew she now lived in Los Angeles, by whose standards Winslow was small-fry and Bishop of even less consequence. Mercy, how her heart had ached for Alice Bow when she'd heard the news of Janey's impending departure back in…When was that? Must be going on ten years now. Imagine a young lady like her being allowed to move to that city without her parents—even if she had been fixin to stay in the house of her brother. Imagine her taking on work as a newspaper reporter! The valley had been aflutter with gossip about it.

"What are *you* doing here?" Lesta returned the pert question to show she could be equally modern in her address.

"Oh, I just came in on the Grand Canyon Railway, Mrs. Parker. That's the train that runs from Williams here right up to the canyon rim!"

Jane's eyes gleamed as she declared, "I was at Grand Canyon National Park interviewing Miss Mary Jane Colter. She's the architect who just built Phantom Ranch at the bottom of the canyon! You must have heard of that? We rode mules seven miles down to the ranch, which is just a cluster of little cabins near Bright Angel Creek. And she did buildings at the top of the canyon too: the Hopi House gift shop next to the El Tovar Hotel, and the Hermit's Rest and Lookout Studio along the rim road. You can take a carriage ride along the rim, Mrs. Parker, seeing the whole canyon spread out before you and then stop for tea and sandwiches at the Lookout Studio before riding back. The buildings are quite comfortable inside, with handmade Indian rugs, big stone fireplaces and big windows with gorgeous views, of course, but on the outside you'd never know it! Miss Colter used stone from the canyon itself to make them blend in with nature—Hermit's Rest looks like nothing so much as a tumble down pile of rock!"

"My, my, my," said Lesta, wondering why anyone would want to make a building look like a pile of rock. She was as taken aback by the girl's onslaught of breathless enthusiasm as by the incomprehensible story she was telling.

"Yer headin back to Los Angeles then Janey?"

"No, not right away. In fact, I'm heading the same way as you, I expect, Mrs. Parker, back to Owens Valley. For a visit with my folks before I go home."

She calls Los Angeles home now, Lesta thought. Oh how sad for Alice. She searched for something more to say, picking the thing that had stood out for her most in Janey's flood of words.

"A lady architect, you say?"

"Yes, I was interviewing her for my newspaper, the *Los Angeles Examiner*. Well, she's not precisely a licensed architect—when she went to college, back in the '80s, there weren't many of those. Though there are a few now. But Miss Colter has an arts degree from the California School of Design up in San Francisco, and she works for the Fred Harvey Company now. She's in charge of everything for the structures they're building at the canyon, and most of their finest hotels too all over the Southwest. She just finished the El Navajo Hotel in Gallup, New Mexico, that's the newest Harvey hotel. Perhaps you've heard of that one, Mrs. Parker, since you were near enough to it when you were out at Winslow? It was quite a sensation when it opened—Miss Colter had it decorated with real Navajo sand paintings, and there was a special ceremony of blessing performed by the tribe's medicine men!"

"*Miss* Colter, so she ain't married."

"No, ma'am, she isn't"

"And she travels all over kingdom come by herself, building hotels and such?"

"Well she's a grown woman, after all, probably near my Ma's age."

"How 'bout you *Miss* Bow? Any wedding bells for you?"

"No, Mrs. Parker. Not for the time being." Jane smiled and motioned with her notebook. "Excuse me ma'am, I have a bit of work to finish."

"Of course, dear."

The two women settled back into their seats, and Lesta closed her eyes, pretending to sleep. Well I never…sweet little Janey Bow has up and turned herself into a mighty forward young woman. And what in tarnation is she waiting fer?! She must be…let me think on this now…well, I reckon, near enough 28 years old. In my day, folks would a called her an old maid. But she doesn't look old, and she don't seem ashamed about it. Well, well, well.

Across the aisle, Jane pretended to be reading over her notes, but her mind and emotions were roiling. *Here I am on my way home for my first visit in ever so long and I have to run into old Mrs. Parker before I even set foot in the valley! Before I've even had a moment to prepare myself for seeing Ma and Pa and answering all the questions from neighbors and townsfolk. And, of course, practically the first thing she asks me is if I'm getting married!*

Jane tapped her pencil rapidly against the notebook, matching time with her toe against the footrest. *Well, it's not Mrs. Parker's fault really,* she reflected. *This is probably the first time she's ever even been out of the Owens Valley, maybe the first time she's been on a train even. How can she begin to understand about my life, about how swell it felt to be standing on the rim of the Grand Canyon with the great Mary Colter as she pointed out that the stone she'd chosen for her building's walls mimicked the many-colored layers of the canyon! Colter's naturalistic approach to architecture and interior design are setting the style for buildings in all of the West's national parks, and I, J. Bow, reporter for the* Los Angeles Examiner, *will be the one to tell her story to Angelenos, and maybe to the world! How could Mrs. Parker, with her horizons limited to that narrow valley, understand this?*

*Or anything else about my life now.* Jane stifled a giggle and her countenance warmed as she reflected on what Mrs. Parker might think about her dancing and drinking with her pals into the wee hours of the morning or about the part of her life that involved Jed. In truth, she had expected they'd be married by now. But she wasn't disappointed with how things had worked out. With the completion of the aqueduct, Jed had gone abroad to supervise the construction of a tunnel in Barcelona, Spain, a job that had been followed by another in Hilo, Hawaii. That project had been interrupted for the 19 months Jed had spent in France during the war, building bridges and rail lines for the US Army Corp of Engineers, but he had returned to Hilo after the Armistice in 1918 to complete it. He had recently accepted his third assignment, in the newly independent Kingdom of Egypt, as a manager of construction projects in the Canal Zone, over which the British still maintained control.

In each of these positions, save the Army, Jed's employers had conferred upon him considerable responsibility and lavish pay, the latter providing the means to return to Los Angeles every eight months or so to visit his "old friend" Christopher Bow. That Jed's true objective was his fiancé, Miss Jane Bow, was their secret; the couple had kept their engagement hidden from everyone save Chris.

Jane closed her eyes and hugged her notebook into her chest. Chris was a modern man and a tolerant brother. He had never said anything to Jane about what he surely knew—that for the couple of weeks Jed spent as a guest each time in Chris's Bunker Hill house, he made his way nightly to Jane's bed. Chris had only once said a word about it to Jed, who had related the exchange to Jane.

"He said the only thing he needed to know was that if I got you in a family way, I'd do what's right and honorable by you." Jed had assured Chris he would, and repeated his intention to marry Jane, no matter what her condition, when he returned to the US for good…soon…at the end of the Cairo job.

Until then, thought Jane happily, their love had not suffered, but had continued to grow. They were closely entwined in each other's lives, by grace of letters exchanged weekly. In these missives, they talked about books they were reading, music they had heard, the adventures and challenges of their work and, as the days drew closer to the next visit, what they would do when back again in each other's arms.

This last topic was not only endlessly absorbing, but endlessly unfolding. Jed seemed to have made it his project to gird the bridge of their long engagement by bringing back with him novel ways of making physical love that avoided the obvious risk. He used condoms, but said that since the thin sheaths were unreliable, they should limit the number of times they had intercourse. There were many other ways to give each other joy, Jed explained and demonstrated.

Perhaps these were the exotic customs of the far-away places Jed worked, but how he learned his techniques and acquired the little tools he surprised her with, Jane didn't want to know. She did know, from the comments of her female friends, as over the years they'd proceeded through courtship, marriage and motherhood, that what she and Jed were doing was unorthodox and would likely be considered shocking. Even though this was the 1920s! Even though everyone seemed to be talking about Dr. Freud's theories of sexuality, and beauty advertisements in women's magazines urged readers to increase their "sex appeal"! Even though she knew that her most trusted pal Lucille, the wildest girl in their circle, had had sex before her first marriage as well as between her divorce and second marriage, and was certainly having plenty of it now that the union had been annulled. Still, despite Lucille's hijinks and what seemed to be almost constant talk of sex among people her age and younger, most of the whispered and giggled stories were about pretty conventional love-making. Jane kept the details of her intimate relations with Jed to herself.

Jane sighed, stretched her legs and allowed her thoughts to continue to wander. Of course, she wanted to marry Jed, and someday they'd have children and live a normal life. But for now, she was more immediately attracted to the expanding prospects of what she might do as one of the first women reporters for a major city daily.

The interview with Colter had fired her desire for it. Here was a woman who had succeeded in a man's profession. Jane had seen her acting with easy authority, directing the male builders who worked for her. She'd heard stories of Colter examining a newly completed stone wall, spying something that wasn't quite right or authentic enough in its effect, and commanding quietly, "Take it down. Rebuild it this way." And the work crews did it, just the way she said. Mary Colter, it seemed to Jane, was accorded the same respect from her workers as Jed was from his. She's in command of her buildings the same way Mulholland had been in command of the aqueduct.

And, Jane assured herself, I'm in command of the interviews I do with accomplished people like Colter, and the stories I write from them. It was true that she was sometimes frustrated by the way her editor, Mr. Loewenthal, handed out assignments among his reporters. At least she wasn't confined, like the handful of other female reporters, to the women's pages. But neither was she considered for the top beats in the city, which were the movie, oil and real estate industries as well as the expansion of the port at San Pedro Bay, on its way to becoming an even bigger center for overseas shipping than San Francisco Bay. These were covered by male reporters, not all of them as experienced or talented as she.

Last year when a dockworkers strike had erupted at the port, Loewenthal had fended off her earnest entreaties by saying, "The docks are no place for a woman." She'd had to watch a male colleague file a series of front-page stories on the demonstrators, including the famous novelist Upton Sinclair, author of *The Jungle,* the notorious exposé of the meat-packing industry. Sinclair had attempted to read the Bill of Rights in support of the workers, but had gotten only to the part about free speech. His subsequent arrest and detention had created a scandal that was now leading to calls for investigations of police corruption.

Meanwhile, it seemed to Jane that her editor was still under the spell of her early articles about Mulholland and the aqueduct, as he seemed to have pigeon-holed her as a reporter who wrote about people who build things. While the dock strike raged, she'd been shunted off to interview a Chicago architect, Mr. Frank Lloyd Wright, who had completed the second of two very odd houses in the Hollywood Hills.

From the reading Jane did in preparation for the interview, she learned that Wright had started out working for Louis Sullivan, architect of skyscrapers in the booming midwestern city. But soon he had made his own reputation building houses, new kinds of houses he called "Prairie" style. The designs did away with fussy front parlors and dark, divided interiors, replacing them with spacious rooms open to light and the flow of movement of their occupants. These rooms were oriented around a central fireplace—a hearth about which the family gathered. While the houses could be built affordably, and the plans even purchased from a magazine, Wright had personally built several in the Prairie style for wealthy clients, and on these he had spared no expense, designing and overseeing the construction of all aspects, including every pane of glass and stick of furniture. The architect had also designed a church, called Unity Temple, in Chicago, the Larkin Building in Buffalo, New York, and the Imperial Hotel in Tokyo, which had become famous the year before when an earthquake struck the city, and the hotel was one of the few buildings left standing.

The houses Wright had designed in Los Angeles were altogether different from the ones in the Midwest. Each house must take form from its site, the architect, an imperious man in a white suit, had lectured Jane as they toured "Hollyhock House." This house's site, in the hills overlooking the city and ocean beyond, was, Jane imagined, about as different from the prairie as possibly could be. Water was a key element in the design: The house wrapped around a pool in a central courtyard. Inside, the hearth was set into a shallow pool, a skylight above it flooding the room with rays of sun that played on the surface of the water. The structure was decorated with concrete ornamentation, which though abstract, was meant to represent hollyhock flowers. To Jane, the house look like drawings she'd seen of the ruins of ancient Incan temples in Peru. She had never seen anything of its sort in real life and couldn't imagine what it would be like to live in it.

She'd gotten an inkling by interviewing the owner of the house, Miss Aline Barnsdall. An oil heiress and arts patroness, the woman lived eccentrically and independently with a daughter born out of wedlock. Though professing to still believe in Wright's brilliance, Miss Barnsdall had spent much of the interview with Jane cataloging her disappointments with the house and its designer.

Somehow, toward the end of their conversation, the subject of the arrest of Mr. Sinclair had come up, causing Miss Barnsdall to leap passionately to his defense. It happened that she was a major supporter of the California chapter of the American Civil Liberties Union, which Sinclair had helped to found, and of his so-far unsuccessful runs for congress on the Socialist ticket. This information had given Jane the idea of turning the story inside-out so that it focused on Miss Barnsdall as a keystone of the city's developing artistic and social consciousness. The result was that her article, which would otherwise have appeared in the society pages, ended up on the front page as a sidebar to the dock strike stories.

J. Bow was thereby able to write about the strike after all, and Miss Barnsdall had been quite pleased with the notoriety the coverage earned her.

Nevertheless, Loewenthal had continued to concentrate her assignments on architecture and builders. There'd been the one to interview Mary Colter, and after that would be Julia Morgan. Morgan was the first woman to graduate with a degree in architecture from the École des Beaux-Arts in Paris, and she was a favorite of William Randolph Hearst, the owner of the newspaper. She'd designed the *Examiner* offices where Jane worked. Currently, she was building an estate for Hearst at San Simeon, up on the central coast. Jane had an appointment to interview her there in a few weeks.

Awaking from her reverie, lulled by the rhythm of the train, Jane glanced at Mrs. Parker, who was snoozing, chin tucked against her collar. She's a nice lady, thought Jane, but from a different age. She couldn't possibly imagine my life.

"Lunch stop in half an hour at Barstow!" the conductor informed them.

Southern Pacific passenger trains rarely stopped at Mojave for meals anymore. The town still served nearby mining communities, but with the end of the aqueduct work, its boom years were over. The Harvey House there, where she had spent her first night away from home and relished her first dinner in a restaurant, was now partly closed. The hotel and dining room no longer operated, although the lunch counter—where she had first spoken to Jed—was still open, mostly patronized by locals and freight train engineers.

But at Barstow, the largest and fanciest of the Harvey Houses in Southern California, "Casa del Desierto," had not only a hotel, restaurant and lunch room, but a bowling alley, swimming pool and ballroom! And, as her friend Lesley had written her, it even had its own ice cream plant, producing cool refreshments, which were available at the Harvey House and could also be bought from vendors on the depot platform.

Lesley had long since transformed herself from Harvey Girl to wife, moving with her farmer husband to Fresno, a small town across the Sierra, west of Owens Valley. But she had kept in touch with the girls she had worked with in Mojave as they had dispersed to other Harvey Houses, other jobs or their own homes across the Southwest, and she was a fount of information for Jane.

Jane glanced at Mrs. Parker again. The old lady would probably remember Lesley. I should tell her what's become of her, thought Jane. But Mrs. Parker was still sleeping, so she eased back in her seat and returned to her writing.

Lesta was dozing on and off. The unexpected encounter with Janey Bow had unwound a tight ball of memories. Janey probably thought this was her first time on a train. Little did the girl realize that she, Lesta Parker, then Lesta Hansen, had traveled the entire 3,000-mile length of this great country by train when she was but a slip of a girl at 17. And that was after the long voyage from Copenhagen. Ma had picked her from among six siblings to accompany her brother Herluff, saying, "Lesta, will go. She's the only one of you with a good enough head on her shoulders."

And so the two of them had left home together, perhaps never to return, on a journey that took them first by sea to New York City, then overland to San Francisco, where, it was known, there awaited plenty of jobs. In San Francisco, one could not only find work, but learn about land being given out free to settlers in other parts of California and neighboring Nevada.

Now, lulled by the steady clatter of the wheels, Lesta relived that other train journey. The first part, from New York into the interior of the country is fine, the trains quite comfortable. But, my oh my, how conditions change at Omaha. Trains have been running all the way to San Francisco for only about a year, and the accommodations on this Pacific Railroad, as it is called, are as rough as can be. The fare of $65 brings little comfort on the eight-day ordeal. Meal stops, few and far between, are a mixed blessing for the hungry passengers, who are generally served greasy, stringy meat on cracked dishes at the hands of surly men in dirty, sweat-stained undershirts. At one particularly disgusting stop, Herluff tells her he's heard the "chicken stew" is really prairie dog—the little rodents they've been seeing scampering across barren mounds of dirt and standing on their hind legs to watch the train go past. Lesta leaves it on her plate and sucks on one of the leaden soda biscuits the travelers rightfully call "sinkers." Nights she shivers under a smelly, scratchy blanket on a hard cot in the women's area of one of the establishments that, while generally consisting of nothing but a few shacks, have the pretension to put up the sign "Hotel."

Between these distasteful interruptions, however, the journey is splendid. Lesta spends hour after hour watching through dusty windows, fascinated by all she sees. Especially when, after days of cornfields stretching across flat, horizonless land, the terrain begins to change. The endless upright stalks are now replaced by swirling grasses and small rocky knolls. Lesta spies hawks and eagles winging their way through a sky of the deepest blue she has ever beheld. Groups of spritely little deer with white stripes on their throats and white snouts, rumps and bellies—not deer, but pronghorns, the conductor tells her—spread out across gentle slopes, stepping, pawing, sometimes leaping with what seems to be a playful nature.

The land is becoming browner and rising in mounds like bread loafs, decorated here and there with boulders. Soon they are ascending steep mountain slopes and dipping down again into flatlands.

Days later, looming ahead, cutting through the sky, there's a wall of mountains. "It's the Sierra Nevada," Herluff whispers, as awestruck as she. It seems to Lesta that they are going to run right into it, when somehow the wall of rock parts, allowing the train to enter, and the track climbs abruptly, winding around the steep slopes, hanging onto the edges, until Lesta fears they will fall off. But the train continues to chug up and up, until finally it begins to level off, and the slope to the right of the train becomes more gentle, and the one to the left falls away, and they see, far below, a valley where an immense sapphire lake lays in a bowl of pine-fringed green.

"That's Donner Lake folks," the conductor announces. "That's where the ill-fated Donner Party wagon train tried to cross in the winter of '48. Got blocked by snow and ended up eatin each other, turned into cannibals to survive!" He clearly enjoys startling the newcomers, and is duly rewarded by their exhalations of horror. "There was 81 men, women and children camped by Donner Lake that winter; only 45 of 'em ever left it."

At that point, the train enters a series of tunnels cut deep into the mountainside. As they emerge from one tunnel and head toward the next, the conductor points out the support wall of rough fitted boulders to the right. "That there wall that keeps the mountain from falling down onto the tracks we call the Chinese Wall," he explains. "It were built by thousands of Celestials. That's how railroad folks used to call them Chinamen brought over to work on these tunnels, seein that they called their home the 'Celestial Kingdom.' Reckon it was sort of a joke to their American boss men, but whatever they was called, and sometimes it were werse than that, don't ya know, it never did stop them from building good walls. Made this wall just like that ther Great Wall of China back home, they did."

Once through the longest tunnel at the summit, the tracks begin to drop, more gently on this side of the pass, along the western slope of the Sierra. The train eases down mountain shoulders cloaked in fir and pine. The cool air on this side is soaked with their scent and the fresh, cold spray from rushing, foaming rocky streams. Lesta feels she is in an enchanted land as they make their way into hills of golden grass marked by clusters of purple ceanothus bushes and yellow-orange poppies. "This here country is the Mother Lode," the loquacious conductor informs them. "Land of the Gold Rush! Many a fortune was made in these hills. Most of what's left is big mines run by big companies. But there's still some lonesome miners finding a pocket of it now and then. We call 'em 'pocket hunters.'"

They spend another uncomfortable night, at Newcastle, before arriving the next day at Oakland Long Wharf, the terminus of the Pacific Railroad, on the eastern shore of San Francisco Bay. The last leg of their long journey from Denmark is a ferry ride across the bay. On the boat, the city spreads out, gleaming white before their eyes. It's nestled into the hilly peninsula that forms the southern arm of the famous "Golden Gate" to the Pacific Ocean—the ocean on the other side of the world from where they began.

Now Lesta's mind takes her into the bustling city, which at first appears as a blur of shops, hotels, restaurants, parks and schools. With letters of introduction to other Danish immigrants, they take rooms in a lodging house and begin learning English. Herluff soon finds work at an iron foundry, and Lesta is engaged as a cook for a wealthy family in a big mansion behind a monogrammed wrought-iron gate on the city's exclusive Nob Hill. She works from five in the morning until seven at night, six and a half days a week. With Wednesday afternoons off, Lesta spends this personal time in the public library, reading what books and journals she can to improve her English. Laboriously making her way through the *San Francisco Chronicle*, Lesta learns that her employer, Mr. Torrington, has made his fortune in hydraulic mining engineering, inventing machines, it is said, that lift rivers right from their beds to suck the gold out from under them. Some people in San Francisco and Sierra Nevada towns are angry about this, objecting to the ruination of the rivers and forests, and blaming Torrington for mud-blocked roads, mangled hillsides and flooding across the flatlands. The entrepreneur responds to his critics that he isn't responsible for it, since the bulk of the family's business is no longer in mining, extending now into timber sales, real estate and banking.

Lesta finds her employer and his wife demanding but agreeable enough. As she becomes more adept, the housekeeper and head cook give her greater responsibilities for the frequent, lavish luncheons and dinner parties the family hosts in their gilded, crystal dining room. Elaborate French cuisine is favored, except for two or three times a year when Torrington and his friends go out duck hunting. They plop the warm, soft carcasses on her work table and tell her to pluck and cook them— not more than a few minutes in a very hot oven. "We want them running blood, with plenty of bread to mop it up!" they command. Strange people, Lesta thinks, all the airs of European aristocracy, but underneath as raw as savages.

She's been in service nearly a year when Herluff introduces her to Cyril Parker, a fellow worker at the iron foundry who has a yen for farming. There is still land available for settlers, he tells her, in the Owens Valley, on the eastern side of the Sierra. "It's a magical land," he promises, "plenty of water from snowmelt for irrigating." He likes her fine, he avows, and she doesn't want to spend the whole of her life cooking other people's meals, so she agrees to go with him. They marry in the presence of a few friends and set off the next day.

The Owens Valley. Life here is everything Cyril promised and she had hoped. Not that it is all "milk and honey." Once they put their claim on a homestead, years of work, clearing and planting fields, and building a house and barn begin. For a very long time they live, with two small children, in a simple lean-to fashioned of wood poles with canvas sides. But eventually they construct a comfortable house of respectable size, and by the time their children are up and grown, Cyril feels prosperous enough to take out a mortgage on the farm for the purchase of a tractor to ease his labor and allow him to expand the acreage under cultivation. He's just shaken hands with that nice Mr. Watterson at the bank when he walks down the street to the feed store and hears some neighbor folk talking about a man buying water options all over the valley for a reclamation project—a dam that will triple the valley's farmable land. How elated they are that evening, dreaming of greater prosperity to come!

Something rouses Lesta from the happy memory. She opens her eyes, feeling disoriented. Her conscious mind—it knows that illusion of safety for what it was—is like a hand roughly jostling her shoulder. She's fully awake now and weighted with a feeling of dread.

Everything changed when they discovered what those men were really up to was stealing water for Los Angeles. But confident in the leadership of the Watterson brothers, Mr. Chalfant, the editor of the newspaper, and Mr. Austin, the federal lands register, they added their voices to the outcry of their neighbors. Lesta even wrote a letter to President Roosevelt. A very nice man named Ethan A. Hitchcock, who was Secretary of the Interior for the whole United States, wrote her a long reply explaining why Los Angeles needed the water and how the Owens River produced enough for both the valley and the city to thrive. She and Cyril were uncertain, but others in the valley, even the Wattersons and Mr. Chalfant, seemed to be convinced, so they began to feel better about it too.

And, indeed, for more than a decade, all was well. The city built a standard gauge railway reaching right up into the valley from the south, and the Parkers and their neighbors prospered by selling produce to Los Angeles. They did even better during the war, when prices for crops rose to the sky. But then prices fell with the end of the war, and she and Cyril were forced, like many other farmers in the valley, to take out a mortgage so they could buy feed and enough seed to plant. Then came the drought, and he'd had to reduce the acreage he could irrigate, so now they were having trouble making their mortgage payments. The Wattersons were understanding, giving them extra time, but Lesta couldn't help but set to worrying now and again.

"Barstow, next stop. Barstow!" The conductor swung down the aisle, rousing the car of drowsy passengers. Lesta sat up, startled, then glanced over at Janey.

The girl smiled back at her. "They've just announced Barstow, Mrs. Parker. There's a very fine Harvey House there. It would be ever so nice if you would join me for lunch."

Lesta didn't want to admit to Janey that she couldn't afford to eat in a restaurant, which was why she'd packed the boiled eggs.

Janey, noting her hesitation, said quickly, "I hope you'll be my guest, Mrs. Parker. The newspaper pays for it, and I do so hate to eat alone."

At Barstow, Jane took Mrs. Parker's arm and they walked together into the ornate building of latticed arcades and domed towers decorated with red-and-white brick geometric patterns.

"It looks like a Moorish palace from Spain," whispered Jane. Then she thought maybe Mrs. Parker wouldn't know what that was, so she added, "like a fairytale castle."

Inside they were served their lunch, with reliable Harvey House efficiency and courtesy, within a half hour. Before that much time had passed, Mrs. Parker was smiling, with, Jane noted, crumbs of Apple Brown Betty glistening on her pale lips.

There hadn't been much occasion yet for talking, but now, sipping her coffee, Jane noticed a man across the lunch counter wearing a large red-white-and-blue button that said "Keep Cool with Coolidge!"

The next presidential election, six months away, would be only the second in which women were allowed to vote. She turned to Mrs. Parker. "Did you vote in the last election ma'am?"

"Sure, I did. We needed a 'return to normalcy.'" Lesta nodded her head emphatically as she quoted the campaign slogan of that election's winner, President Harding. The slogan had reflected postwar weariness and tapped into the widespread uncertainty and suspicion over President Wilson's advocacy of the Treaty of Versailles and United States entry into the League of Nations.

Of course, thought Jane. Of course she would have held an opinion and been sure to exercise it at the polls. Jane now remembered that Mrs. Parker had always been rather feisty, and had once even written a letter to President Roosevelt! That thought reminded Jane that they hadn't spoken a word together about Owens Valley. Oddly, their conversation hadn't yet meandered in that direction. "Mrs. Parker, how is it in the valley? With the drought, I mean?" asked Jane.

Her companion peered up at her through narrowed eyes. "Don't yer folks ever tell you how it goes?"

"Well, of course, they say it's dry. Pa says the creek was terribly low last summer."

Mrs. Parker glanced away, out the window at the depot where pas-sengers were moving back onto the train. "Best you ask him if you want to know more about it. Best we get ourselves movin or we'll never git ther at all. And thank you, dear." Mrs. Parker's voice was soft now and, Janey thought, sad. "Thank you so much for the lovely lunch."

---

"Pa! Here, I'm here. Over here Pa!"

The rhythmic four-beat chugging of the steam engine slowed as the train crawled the last few hundred yards into Owenyo station. Jane, who, to Mrs. Parker's astonishment and expressed dismay, had left the seating compartment to perch at the top of the exit stair, leaned out and pumped her arm when she caught sight of Ben Bow on the platform ahead. The brakes clamped down with a long metallic screech, the engine let out a huge belch of steam, and the train stopped. Ben turned and saw her.

"Janey girl!" In several long strides, he covered the distance to where she was descending, reached out for his daughter, pulling her into his familiar bear hug.

"Oh, Pa, how I've missed you!"

"Me too! Your Ma is home baking all your favorites for supper!"

He smiled down at her, his same old wonderful smile, and she marveled at how she could have stayed away so long. It had been more than two years, she was ashamed to admit even to herself.

The last leg of the journey, from Barstow to Owenyo, neither she nor Mrs. Parker had had much to say, both caught up in their own mix of anticipation and apprehension about the arrival. Janey had gazed out at Mojave as the train roared through, and seeing the now-quiet depot had left her feeling melancholy. Lesta had been wondering how to tell Cyril that her brother Herluff had agreed to help them out with a small loan, all he could do but much less than they had hoped.

"Pa, Mrs. Parker's rode with me here on the train, up from Williams."

"Well hello there Lesta." Ben reached up again to the train, this time receiving Lesta from the hands of the conductor who was helping her down the stairs.

"Heard tell you've been to visit your brother. Have a good time did you?" He placed her hand under his right arm and with the other, took the carpetbag the conductor handed him. A sulfurous smell like rotting eggs wafted up to his nostrils. He looked over at Jane quizzically.

His daughter shook her head slightly and suppressed a smile.
"Mrs. Parker was good enough to dine with me in Barstow," she offered
as a partial explanation for the smell of the uneaten, overheated lunch.
No need to say more; Pa would understand and would certainly take pains
to avoid embarrassing the old lady. She gazed at him, adoring his kind,
easy manners, his way of effortlessly doing the right thing.

"How nice of you to take charge of my young'un, Lesta." He beamed
at his neighbor. "May we have the pleasure of returning the favor by
escorting you home?" The Parker ranch was quite a bit north of their own
place, but the offer was made with good cheer and not a trace of hesitation.

"Thank you Ben, but no. Cyril will be here to fetch me...There, there
he is, comin now."

Cyril Parker, a slender, graying man with stooped carriage, wearing
a faded checked shirt and suspenders, was walking slowing toward them.
As he approached, he tipped his hat to Jane and extended his hand to her
father. "Hello my dear," he said to his wife, touching his lips briefly to the
cheek she raised for the greeting.

They talked about the trip and the continuing drought briefly.
Jane thought she noticed something odd, almost surreptitious, in the
looks exchanged by the two men. I must be travel-addled, she shook it off.
Then she was seated by the side of her father in his new Model-T, which
he drove, Janey observed, as calmly and surely as he had the buggy and
wagons of her childhood. How strange, she mused, that no matter how
grown up you become, you still feel like a child when you come home.
A little voice in her head corrected: This isn't home anymore. But it was
immediately submerged beneath her general mood of euphoria.

Jane answered Ben's questions about her trip to the Grand Canyon,
her work in the city and, of course, Chris. It had been even longer since
her brother had been home, and Jane could hear the pain in Pa's voice
when they spoke of him. She tried to turn the subject to him and Ma,
and how the ranch and valley were faring, but he seemed disinclined to
talk about it. He started whistling a tune she remembered, and it brought
her thoughts back to the days when they'd all rode along together in the
wagon singing a popular song.

Gradually the circumference of Jane's attention widened from total absorption in her father to take in the terrain they were driving through. She frowned. "Is this all from the drought?"

"Not all."

It was only late May, yet the south valley looked as pale as the Mojave Desert they'd passed through on the train. As they drove north on the road just east of the Owens River, she was startled to see the drooping, fading cottonwoods that marked its course where luxuriously soft, green trees had once reached for the sky. In the places she could see the river at all, it appeared to be a muddy tangle of reeds and brambles.

Observing her disquiet, Ben placed a hand on Jane's shoulder. "It's better farther north, you'll see. Nothing for you to worry about Janey girl. Besides, you know we're not overly dependent on river water."

It was true that the Bow ranch had the good fortune of being situated right on Independence Creek, an icy stream of snowmelt water running down the eastern slope of the Sierra in a perpendicular direction into the valley, well below the intake to the aqueduct.

"Creek still keeping the cookies cold in the milkhouse?" teased Jane.

"Hold your horses young lady. You'll see soon enough," Pa said, joining in her attempt to lighten their mood.

And she did see. As they approached the ranch, she heard the reassuring sound of water burbling over stones. In the yard, she raised her eyes to the embrace of the big old oak tree, which seemed as strong and friendly as ever, still hosting their childhood rope swing. Then Ma was running toward her, a crisp yellow dress beneath her apron, perfect chignon as usual, though her hair had sparkles of silver now. She gathered Jane into her arms and drew her into the kitchen, which smelled of peaches, butter and vanilla.

"I have a surprise for you after supper," Jane announced as she accepted a second slice of peach pie with Ma's homemade brandy ice cream.

They'd eaten in the kitchen, as it was just the three of them, with Alice serving up roast stuffed chicken, mashed potatoes and green beans directly from the stove. The evening light slanting through the windows burnished the room, adding warmth to faces already glowing with affection. Gradually the light faded, and Alice turned on the electric lamp.

Jane was savoring her dessert, but she was also growing excited at the thought of what she had in her luggage upstairs. When they finished and retired to the parlor, she would bring it down: a beautiful little Crosley radio! She'd bought their smallest model, so as to fit it into her case and so Ma couldn't object to having it on the table in the parlor. But she'd been told it was powerful enough to pick up radio programs from Los Angeles, probably even San Francisco. Everyone in the city was getting them. Now Ma and Pa could not only read in the evenings, but listen to music if they chose.

Ben gazed fondly at his wife and daughter for a moment, then poured a glass of water from the china pitcher, took a long swallow, placed the glass next to his plate and rose from the table. Alice nodded slightly.

"Honey, that surprise is gonna have to wait until tomorrow," he said to Jane. "I need to go out for a little while."

Jane was startled. "What?" Pa almost never left the house in the evening. Maybe some chore left undone because he'd had to pick her up in Owenyo? "If it's chores, Pa, I can help you while Ma does up the dishes. Then we can have the surprise."

He didn't seem to have heard her. Just turned around, took his hat and jacket from the wall pegs and opened the screen door. Her Ma answered in his place. "No, there are no chores sweetie. Just something he needs to do. Leave him be and help me clear this table."

Alice rose, pushing up from the table with her arms in a way that made her look, for the first time to Jane's eyes, tired and old. Jane also got up, gathering her own plate, glass and utensils.

She stood at the sink, peering through the window, trying to see where Pa had gone. She thought she saw him standing, still as a statue, beneath the big oak, but couldn't quite make him out. Then there was the low thrumming of an engine, and a Model-T glided into the yard.

The statue under the tree moved, and she saw it was Pa, getting in on the passenger side. She couldn't see who was driving. The car backed out of the yard and onto the road, where it changed direction and began moving forward. Jane watched in wonder as five or six cars, which must have been parked on the side of the road, fell in behind and, as if participants in a ghostly night parade, drove slowly down the road and out of sight.

"Ma, what is it?" Jane turned to her mother, whose hands were wrist deep in suds.

"Nothing for you to worry about dear. Why don't you go up and unpack now? I'm sure you're tired after that long train journey. Let's just say goodnight now, shall we? You'll see your Pa tomorrow."

The firmness of the quiet voice made Jane feel acutely, for the second time that day, that she was once again a child. She kissed Ma on the cheek and turned away, climbing the stairs to her room, which she found largely unchanged, except for the addition of electric lighting. She walked over to the window and looked out at the yard. In the scant moonlight, her eyes could barely separate the dark branches and leaves of the oak from the night sky.

"This is ridiculous," she fumed to herself. "I'm 28 years old, it's not even nine o'clock, and I'm being sent to bed!"

But she was tired after all, now that the elation of the arrival was wearing off. She snapped open her leather Pullman case, gently removing the radio and placing it on the dresser, then she put on a pair of cotton pajamas, opened her cosmetic case and dabbed a bit of cream around her eyes and on her lips. From her handbag, she reached beneath her notebook and pulled out a book, the new Pulitzer Prize winning novel *So Big* by Edna Ferber. It was the story of a hardworking mother who has to run a farm by herself after her husband dies and struggles to instill in her son the values of education and art over crass business interests. She'd been enjoying the book, but somehow the story made her uncomfortable now. Jane switched off the bedside lamp and tried to sleep. She snuggled her toes down into the cool sheets, but something was wrong. She held her breath to listen better, but there was not a sound from downstairs.

Jane shifted and turned, unable to find a comfortable position. The pillow felt hot under her face. She wondered if Ma had finally come up, she hadn't heard anything. At last, Jane heard the squeak of the screen door, the one that had so often betrayed her own tiptoed entrances and exits. Low voices in the kitchen. She switched on the bedside lamp to look at the table clock: 2:34, then switched it off as she heard two sets of footsteps coming up the stairs. But even after that, she didn't sleep.

---

*As young adults rushing away from home and toward our new lives, we have little care for what our parents go through to endure the changes thrust upon them. And when we return home for visits, we expect not only to be treated like royalty but to find everything much as we left it. If something is profoundly different, in the composure or circumstances of our parents, it can be disturbing. Despite our posture of independence and self-reliance, it is deeply unsettling to have one's roots shaken.*

*CK once told me that the night his grandfather, my brother Chris, was rushed to the hospital with heart pains, he became irrationally frightened, convinced that the home he'd lived in all his life—tended by an army of staff and surrounded by a locked iron gate—was suddenly exposed to danger. He'd asked the butler time and time again if the doors and windows were locked, and listened for the sound of thieves and murderers trying to break in. After the manservant had retired, he'd roamed about the enormous mansion checking for himself throughout most of the night.*

*I felt something of this irrational terror the night my father left in that truck. This behavior was so fundamentally unlike him that I couldn't make sense of it and couldn't, no matter how I reasoned with myself, feel safe enough to shut my eyes. The drowsy net of contentment my parents' voices used to weave, the sound that had charmed me to sleep all the nights of my childhood, had been torn away.*

---

When Jane came down around seven the next morning, her parents had already been about their daily business for a couple of hours. Alice looked up brightly as she entered the kitchen. "Good morning honey. Sleep well?"

Jane nodded, hoping she didn't look as exhausted as she felt. Her Ma was slicing carrots, expertly pumping a knife against the wooden cutting board. To one side, a profusion of bright green carrot tops overhung a silver colander. To the other, a pan of biscuits, just pulled from the oven, lay cooling.

"Chicken pot pie?" asked Jane.

"For tonight. You didn't eat enough last night—not like when Chris comes, though I can't remember now when the last time was. Anyway, no sense wasting half a chicken. And I've picked the first young peas from the garden to put in it too…There's coffee and oatmeal on the stove."

"Thanks Ma," said Jane, coming over to deliver a kiss. She was dressed more conservatively today, in a white shirt tucked into the wide belt of a dark-brown, mid-calf-length skirt. As she filled her cup, she studied her mother's perfect profile, then twirled a couple of fingers in her own cropped, but still unruly locks. It hadn't mattered finally that she never could get her hair into a smooth chignon; today the style was to chop it off just below the chin.

Alice noticed, and said encouragingly, "It's pretty like that, Janey, really. And you don't even need to have your hair marcelled, isn't that what they call it? Yours is already wavy, just naturally."

"Errrgh." Jane tugged on it. "Except that it never waves in the direction I want it to go—just every which way it wants!" She leaned against the counter, crossing her arms in front of her chest, looking down at her feet encased in new cowboy boots. She'd bought them at Hopi House, the gift shop Mary Colter had designed next to the El Tovar Hotel at Grand Canyon. She turned her ankles from side to side, admiring their soft leather sheen. "Shall I help you with your chores Ma? What needs doing?"

"Oh, everything, as usual," Alice replied, laughing. "But I'd much rather you rest today. Take a long walk or visit a friend—you could go see Rosie's new baby. Then we'll have that surprise tonight."

"Will Pa stay home?"

"Of course, Janey, don't be silly. He told you, last night there was something he needed to do."

Jane didn't think she was being silly, and she didn't think her mother's voice sounded right, so cheerily bright and thin. But she did want to see Rosie. She usually stopped by to visit with her childhood friends whenever she was in the valley. Rosie, who had so longed to leave the valley, was now well-settled here, mother of four rambunctious children under the age of eight. She'd married a mining foreman, who was from home for weeks at a time at Cerro Gordo. Emma too was a wife. She'd wed a Lone Pine fruit farmer and had her own brood of kids. Juan, their brother and the fourth of their band of "musketeers," had left home about the time Jane had, working a string of jobs as a ranch hand in Oklahoma, Texas, New Mexico and Nevada, and occasionally picking up extra pay doing bareback bronco riding and steer roping in cowboy shows, "rodeos" some folks called them.

But visits with friends could wait. "Ma, I need to go into Bishop and talk with Mr. Chalfant," she announced. "May I borrow the motor car?"

"You want to drive!?"

"Of course, I told you I can drive Ma. Chris lets me borrow his car whenever I want."

"I thought Chris has a driver."

"He does, but that's just for the limousine. He lets me drive the smaller car, the little Hatfield Coupe." Jane didn't say that she was herself planning to buy a brand new coupe. With Chris building a palatial new home in the outskirts of the city and she about to move into a bungalow with two other gals, she thought she ought to have her own car. But that was something her parents needn't know, at least not yet.

"All right, I suppose. But be careful, won't you?"

"Of course! I'll be back this afternoon in plenty of time to help with supper."

"Wear a hat! You can take one of mine. You know where they are, on the pegs by the door."

Jane groaned, but she obediently selected a straw hat with a wide brim, blew a kiss and hopped down the stairs to the yard. "If I wore this," she said under her breath, "I'd look just like Mary on her mountain jaunts!" She threw the hat onto the back seat.

---

Jane puttered along in the Model T. She'd taken the top down, and now delighted in the late spring sunshine warming her shoulders and settling her spirit. How much easier it was to drive here than in the city, she thought, where some streets were now clogged with automobiles trying to weave their way around each other and the Big Red Car trolleys.
And the air here…the unique Owens Valley fragrance mixing the freshness of snow blown off mountaintops with the perfume of herbs and flowers in heated meadows…like nowhere else! She breathed deeply and leaned her head back to look up.

"Hey there!" Jane called. There in the blue ocean of sky were her favorite flying fish cloud friends, come to greet her homecoming. The oval shapes of white puff were moving across the Sierra crest, and there, ahead in the road, was one of their shadows. "I'll race you to town!" she shouted, and sped up to catch it.

Nearing Bishop's outskirts, Jane slowed, as the density of farms and ranches increased and so did the number of automobiles on the road. Jane turned down Main Street. Though still unpaved, it was a far busier place than what she'd known as a girl. There were now three hotels and a dozen more shops. She pulled up in front of the *Inyo Register*'s still-grimy front window and parked.

Just inside the open front door, a group of men stood talking in low voices, one of them holding open a newspaper. They drew apart and tipped their hats to let her pass. One of them spoke to her. "Why Janey Bow, is that you?"

"Yes, Mr. Bellamy, yes it is. How are you, sir, and how is Mrs. Bellamy?" She had always liked the kind red-headed woman who took care of Ruth when Mary and she ventured out. Remembering her brought the beautiful little girl to mind as well, a sad thought Jane chased away by putting a big smile on her face and offering the man her hand.

"Quite well, generally speaking, miss." Frank Bellamy accepted her hand in a limp, brief shake. "So you're back from the city are you?"

There was something a bit sour in his voice and, she thought, glancing around, in the faces of the other men observing the exchange. There was a tall one she recognized as Mr. Eaton. He seemed little changed, standing erect and self-assured, a charming smile playing on his well-shaped lips and in his blue eyes. Charming, but perhaps not completely sincere? They'd never been introduced, so she felt she needn't directly acknowledge him or any of the other men, who were also not well known to her. She returned her attention to Bellamy.

"Just visiting my family for a few days. Nice to see you sir. Excuse me." She walked past them and headed toward the back of the long, narrow room. They continued to observe her for a moment before resuming their whispered discussion. Normally a young, lithe figure such as hers would have held them under its sway a good deal longer, but today was no ordinary day.

Jane could see it in the countenance of Chalfant, as he peered
out from behind the printing press, recognized her and started forward.
"Hey, you're back! It's been awhile." The hand that took hers and held it
firmly was large and warm. The groves in its knuckles and ridges in its
fingernails displayed permanent black lines, like inked scrimshaw.

"Fine piece on Miss Barnsdall." Chalfant had followed his protégé's
career and usually had a word to say, complementary or critical, on her
latest work. Today, however, the remark seemed cursory. The editor was
distracted by other matters.

"What's happening here Mr. Chalfant?" She placed her hand on his
forearm, bare as always below the rolled up, banded shirtsleeve.
He hesitated before answering. After all, the girl now worked for a
Los Angeles paper—could she be trusted? Hell, this is Janey, he reassured
himself. "There's been an incident at the aqueduct. Someone dynamited a
piece of it."

"Dynamite?! What do you mean? When?" Jane shuddered.

"We don't know much yet," Chalfant replied, reaching over to a side
table to pull a newspaper from the top of an unbound stack. He opened to
an inside page, folded the paper and thrust it at her. "Here, that's all we've
got on it for now. Until we know more, I'm trying not to make too much
of it. Everything round here, people included, is dry as tinder and ready to
blaze. I hope this ain't the spark that does it."

Jane sat down in the armchair covered with leather so worn it was
cracked and shiny. She read the article he had pointed out, which said
little more than that a blast had been heard in the early hours of the morning. Upon inspection, it was found that a hole had been blown in the side
of the canal near the Alabama Gates, one of the points of control on the
aqueduct where flow volume could be adjusted in case of a flood by releasing water down a spillway into the desert. Workers had been dispatched to
patch the hole, and meanwhile the aqueduct was still functioning almost
as usual.

"But why? I know the drought's been bad, it's almost as bad down in
the city, but has it come to this?"

Chalfant regarded her quizzically. "Your folks ain't been tellin you
much have they?"

"Will you tell me? Please, Mr. Chalfant," she pleaded, trying to look confident and steady, though she was starting to feel sick to her stomach.

"I don't have but a few minutes to spare, Janey. The Wattersons are on their way over, and I need to talk with them and the others there." He pointed to the men gathered up front. "But here's a couple of facts you may not know: First, the city has been trying to increase the flow through the aqueduct by pumping our groundwater into it. At first it was just test drilling here and there, but now they're doing it all over the valley, wherever they figure there's a significant aquifer, including a lot round Independence and even near Bishop. That's why you see all those dying cottonwoods. The water table, which took ages to accumulate, is being sucked dry."

Her normally bronze skin paled, making freckles stand out across her nose and checks. He continued in a voice increasingly grim.

"Second thing is they're up to their old tricks again, spreading money and influence around to undercut any kind of defense from the valley, just like back in '04. Watterson brothers have been spearheadin a drive to create an irrigation district, which means everybody who still owns land in the valley turns over their water rights to the district, which then negotiates from a position of power with the city on their behalf. They're all set to issue bonds to pay the landowners for transfer of the rights and for construction of some facilities when the funny business starts.

"Two ranchers, Stu McQueeny and Rory Cartwright, file a suit at the Inyo County Courthouse to stop the sale. Judge throws it out a few days later, but by then the investors the Wattersons had lined up are spooked and the sale has to be delayed. When they finally go ahead, they can't get their asking price, so the $470,000 that does get sold goes for a discount of about 88 cents on the dollar. I think it's pretty strange, this comin from ranchers who don't have the know-how to file a suit, so I do a little investigatin, and what I find is that George Watterson, Wilfred and Mark's uncle, the black sheep of the family and a thorn in their sides, put the ranchers up to it and guaranteed they'd suffer no financial loss because of it. And the only way he could a done that is if Los Angeles was bankrolling him.

"That undercuts but good the district's chances of successfully con-solidating all the water rights. But that's not all. The city is just getting started. Next thing we know, Los Angeles essentially owns the McNally Ditch. It's the oldest major canal on the river, so its water rights take prece-dence over all the later ones. That's a clever move by the city, but this time the buyer isn't Eaton," he said, nodding in the direction of the tall man near the window. "No he's sitting up there in Long Valley, become one of us, so he don't know nothin about it. And he's good and mad at being on the receiving end of the trick this time.

"But George Watterson knows, and his greed must a been as pow-erful as all that stored-up, festering bile against his nephews because he enlisted William Symons, president of the McNally Ditch, and they went around with a lawyer fella name a Hall and in 24 hours they'd bought options at nice fat prices from enough property owners in the ditch asso-ciation to control it. Soon they replaced any of the association officers who wouldn't go along with more amenable folks of their own choosing. From what I can tell, George Watterson and his cohorts spread around about a million dollars of Los Angeles money, with no tellin how much they got paid to do it. Thirty pieces of silver each, I reckon. Folks in the McNally association who still favor the irrigation district are now in the minority, so the new officers can just ignore them. Ultimately most of them have no choice but to sell out too, only the city has no reason to give them a fair price anymore. But the worst of it is, with the loss of the McNally, the irri-gation district makes no sense anymore."

Jane sat, stunned and silent. Chalfant, seeing that Mark Watterson had joined the group in front, moved to finish up. "Point is, Jane, with the only real path to negotiation blocked, folks up here are feeling mighty frustrated and angry. Some are sayin—and I ain't condoning violence—that they have to take a tougher stand."

"Dynamite," mouthed Jane. He nodded.

"Who did it Mr. Chalfant?" she whispered, digging her fingernails into her palms and holding her breath ahead of his answer.

"I couldn't say, and nobody who knows is talking about it. But what I can say is this place is about to be turned upside-down and inside-out with people trying to find out. The sheriff is making his inquiries, of course, but there's also an investigator coming from Los Angeles and an army of reporters and photographers headed this way—in fact, I'll bet your editor has been ringing your Ma's telephone all morning. You best call him."

"Yes, I will, and thank you Mr. Chalfant for telling me."

He nodded, then turned away, walking to the front of the room, where both Watterson brothers had now joined Eaton, Bellamy and the others. Mark Watterson gestured toward Jane, but Chalfant waved his hand and shook his head. Jane assumed he was vouching for her being no threat. She remained still and strained to hear. There were too many now to maintain a whisper, and she was able to catch much of what was said.

"City's posted a $10,000 reward for anyone who comes forward and turns in the guilty parties."

"Nobody's gonna talk."

"Sheriff knows the dynamite came from your storehouses."

"It was stolen. We got no notion at all of who took it."

"Hall's been boastin they cut off the left arm of the irrigation district."

"Yeah, well, he better watch himself. There's some folks talkin about meetin him on the road some night with a rope."

"Look, all we have to do is hold tight and not get hot-headed."

This was Eaton speaking. He tried to convince them. "The truth is we've got Mulholland over a barrel. The city has now wasted a million dollars for the McNally—the very price that would have given them the Long Valley dam site, the only real solution to their problem. Now they've paid the money, but they still don't have a solution. Other farmers will continue diverting water from below the McNally and above the aqueduct intake to protest the groundwater pumping. And I've heard some folks saying, I won't mention names, they're gonna start digging canals to divert water right from the McNally into their own ditches. The city can't stop it—they can't put armed guards along hundreds of miles of ditch!

"With this drought continuing, Mulholland will have no choice. He'll have to pay my price and build a sizeable dam. When that happens, guaranteed delivery to every ditch association of all the water you need will be part of the bargain. His mouth twisted bitterly. "And Los Angeles taxpayers will be fit to be tied—they'll run the great hero out of the city on a rail!"

The nods and murmurs that greeted this speech were respectful but skeptical. "How long do you figure that'll take?" asked Mark Watterson.

"Not long now, not long at all" was Eaton's reply.

---

When the men disbanded, Jane took her leave of Chalfant.

"Remember, when you call your editor," he said, "whatever you just heard, there was not a single fact in it. Just folks blowing off steam about what they think is happening or what they want to happen. There's gonna be a tornado of loose talk around here. Don't get caught up in it. A good reporter sticks to the facts."

"I know, thank you for letting me stay and listen."

"I just thought you ought to have an appreciation for how serious this situation is."

"Yes, I do now. Thank you again. I'll be here a few more days, but I'll come back to see you before I leave, shall I?"

"You better!" he joked, but his smile had faded even before he had released her hand and turned to walk back to the press.

Outside, Jane took a deep breath of fresh air to clear her lungs of the *Register* office's stale, smoky, inky air. She used to love that smell, but today she'd had trouble breathing in the dense atmosphere, and her chest still felt tight. Walking a bit should help with that and give her an opportunity for observation. She headed farther down Main Street, then crossed and came back up the other side, lingering at display windows, building entrances and street corners. For the most part, it was just an ordinary day, with townspeople, ranchers and farmers going about their business. Except that in many of the passing greetings and huddled conversations she overheard there was an unmistakable note of tension and, in a few cases, of excitement too.

Nothing so patent, however, as what she was now hearing taking place down the street, in front of the general store. Mark Watterson and a man she didn't recognize were there, talking earnestly and gesturing to another man, as if trying to convince him of something.

The object of their appeal, standing with arms folded, legs apart, a worn Stetson pushed far back on his forehead, was shaking his head. That's Mr. McQueeney, Jane recognized the rancher a second or two before he began to shout.

"This is all damned nonsense! You wanted us to go into debt to buy something that already belongs to us! The water's fer irrigatin farms and ranches, so why you townsfolk think you oughta have control o'er it I just don't figure! What right you got telling us what to do?!"

McQueeney spun on his heel and crossed the street, getting into another of the ubiquitous black Model-Ts that dotted the valley, this one distinguished by a layer of splattered, clotted mud rising six inches above the running board. He started it up, turned south and headed out of town. Jane had the sudden thought to do the same. She regained her own vehicle and was soon following McQueeney down the road.

He drives like all the ranchers, Jane noticed, amused. Slow, like he's on a horse. Driving like the city girl she now was, Jane soon caught up with McQueeney. He waved an arm to tell her to pass, but when the cars were next to each other, she slowed to his pace and called out, "Mr. McQueeney, hello there. It's Jane Bow, Ben's daughter. Do you remember me?"

"Why, howdy there, Miss Bow, I'd never have recognized you. Nice to see you again. Are you here visiting your folks?"

"Yes, yes sir I am, Mr. McQueeney, thank you. I wonder if I might have a word with you? Could we pull over there?" She indicated the edge of road where overhanging branches of a large oak in the adjacent field might provide them some shade.

"Of course, err, what's this about miss? Everything fine with your Pa and Ma?" He sounded uncertain, but he steered his car over to the side of the road and stopped. Jane pulled hers up behind it, smoothed her hair and skirt before stepping out. He came toward her, clearly puzzled at her extraordinary behavior.

"Mr. McQueeney, I beg your pardon. Everything's fine with my family, and I didn't mean to alarm you. It's just that I happened to over-hear a little of what you were saying to Mr. Watterson and that other man in town, and I wondered if you might be so good as to give me some notion of what's going on in this valley."

"I'll tell it to anyone who'll listen, but I don't rightfully know what good it'll do talkin to you seein as you don't even live here no more."

"No, I live in Los Angeles, where I'm a reporter for the *Examiner*, a big newspaper. And, as I used to write for the *Register* too, I still have the ear of Mr. Chalfant. I may be able to help you be heard."

"What do you want to know?"

"Well, to start with, what were you talking to Mr. Watterson about? What made you so upset?"

"Oh, it's that irrigation district that's been causin a peck of problems—and now this dynamiting too, which is sure to bring more trouble. Wattersons and their cronies talk about representing the whole valley, but truth is, I'm sorry to say, miss, they're more interested in buildin up their own power and profit. It just don't make no sense for townspeople from Bishop to be runnin an organization for irrigatin—what they got to irrigate?"

"Are there other people in the valley who feel like you?"

"Sure, plenty of 'em."

"But Mr. Chalfant says lots of the farmers in the ditch associations support the district."

"Yeah, and all fools, sure enough!"

"I see. Well, thank you Mr. McQueeney. I'll make sure to represent your point of view fairly in anything I write."

"You do that," He tipped his hat to her, turned toward his car, took a few steps, then swung back around. "By the way, miss, isn't your Pa's ranch near the Escobar place?"

"Yes," she responded, surprised. "Yes, we're close enough."

"Do you know that young Mexican feller Juan Escobar?"

"I do indeed, Mr. McQueeney. I used to play with him and his sisters when we were children." She was amused at how older folks insisted on calling people her age "young." Juan was over 30 now!

"Well then, perhaps you can tell me if he's a trustworthy feller. He come to me with a good price on some wild horses he rounded up over in Death Valley. Says he gentled and trained 'em. And I was just wondering if he's a Mexican a man could make a deal with and still sleep peaceful at night."

"Yes, he's certainly trustworthy," she responded, bristling on her friends behalf. "And if there's anyone who can coax the wildness out of a desert horse, it's Juan Escobar."

"Thank you miss." He tipped his hat again. "Good day to you." The rancher nodded and walked back to his car.

Jane climbed back into hers, gladdened by the news that Juan was back in the valley. Why don't I just go over there to see him and Rosie, she thought about it as she watched the rancher drive off at his snail's pace. Later, maybe, I'll have time later. First I have to find out what's going on. Is Pa involved in this? If so, did Ma really know nothing about it? She had to make them talk to her tonight.

---

Jane waited until after supper, and after she had presented them with the surprise. Surprised and delighted, Ma made room for the radio on the side table next to the divan. Pa watched, amazed, as Jane demonstrated how to turn the dial to pick up music programs.

"My goodness!" he exclaimed. "That's really an orchestra playing more than 200 miles away?"

"It really is Pa!"

They experimented, turning the dial back and forth to try to find other programs, adjusting the other knobs to make the scratchy sounds clearer. Finally Jane lowered the volume and took the plunge.

"I expect you both heard about the dynamiting on the canal?"

"Yes, I heard about it," Alice said softly. She stood and placed a hand on Ben's shoulder, smiling at Jane. "I expect you'd better talk to your Pa, Janey. I'm going up to bed. G'night."

Ben reached up a hand and pressed it over Alice's, then stood and gave her a kiss. When she had mounted the stairs, he sat down again and turned toward his daughter. He looks worn out, Jane thought.

She swallowed. "Pa, the other night when you went out after supper..." she looked down at her lap and asked softly, "...you didn't have anything to do with the dynamiting, did you?"

"I won't answer that directly because I don't want you to ever be put in a bad way because of something I might or might not have done."

Jane sucked in a small pocket of air that seemed to lodge halfway down her throat, but her Pa continued evenly. "But I do see that it's only fair to help you understand some of the things going on here in the valley, with which we've been, until now, reluctant to burden you. When you were still little, Janey, it became clear that there was no way to stop the aqueduct from happening. I told myself, and I told you, it would turn out all right. Most other folks here in the valley were doing the same. The city said there would be enough water for everyone, and we wanted to believe them. But now it seems clear that the worst outcome we might have imagined then is facing us today: Los Angeles is trying to drain this valley dry."

"Oh, Pa, it can't be," Jane wailed, leaning forward to put a hand on his arm. "They wouldn't do that, not deliberately…why would they?"

"I expect because they know now there's not going to be enough water to go around. Not with this drought, not for both the valley and the city." He placed his hand over hers. "And they've got their own valley down there where they're using our water for agriculture now, not drinking. They're pumping our groundwater out to make that place into the Garden of Eden that this valley used to be. That's what I hear tell."

"Pa, I'm sure it's not as bad as that. I'm sure they just don't realize the full impact the pumping is having here. I'm sure it's just a matter of adjusting the amounts to make them fair."

"You're sure of all that, are you?" He smiled, in spite of himself, at his daughter's earnestness. "Well, I'll sure be happy to be proved wrong."

"But Pa, even if you're not wrong, the ranch will be fine, won't it? You're not in a ditch association. We've always relied on the creek water, and they're not taking that. Independence Creek is below the aqueduct intake, so there's no way for them to take it."

"They could take it, I suppose, just like the rest of it if they had a mind to. But, yes, for now anyway, I'm grateful we're on the creek. A lot of our neighbors are sure wishing they were as prettily placed."

"Then, why, Pa? Why would you join in with dynamiters? You've always told us to obey the law. Mr. Chalfant says the city's offering a $10,000 reward to catch the men who did it, and they're sending an investigator."

Ben sighed and looked at his hands resting on his knees, then he sat back and gazed somberly at his daughter before responding in a firm, quiet voice. "Janey, just because we're personally all right on this ranch, would you have me desert neighbors and friends who aren't? This valley is a community, it's the place you used to call home, and your Ma and I still do. How could we let other valley folk see their property dried out or bought up by the city and still continue on as if we're unaffected?"

"You're right, Pa. You're right, of course, about that. I'm sorry." She took his hand. "But I still hope it isn't as bad as you say. And I have a notion of how I can find out."

# Chapter 17

"Good afternoon, Miss Bow. How was your trip?"

Chris's driver, Rex, took Jane's luggage in one hand and her elbow in the other to guide her through the throngs of people moving in both directions on the platform of the Southern Pacific Railroad's Central Station in Los Angeles. This disembarkation point was quite different from the picturesque depot that had welcomed Jane on her first trip to the city. The new station was resolutely modern, luxurious and sleek, its marble floors sparkling.

"It was fine." She smiled up at the kindly man, who nevertheless always addressed her at first greeting with professional formality. "How's everything here Rex?"

"Same as usual. The car's just over there. Here we go now."

They crossed the lobby, sun streaming through its tall stacks of windows, and Rex propelled Jane out to the sidewalk and over to the black limousine. Once settled in the back seat, Jane thought better of her careless reply to his inquiry. As the car moved out into the bustling Los Angeles streets, she regarded the back of Rex's head, so reassuring with its thick neck and abundant salt-and-pepper hair.

"Actually, it wasn't fine at all, Rex, and I suppose you know that. You must have heard about the dynamiting up there?"

"It's been in all the papers, miss."

"I'm worried, Rex, worried about Ma and Pa, and all the other folks we know up there."

"Of course you are, miss. These are difficult times for many a family, what with the recession and drought and all."

Jane watched the hectic to-and-fro of Angelenos on the sidewalks and street corners as Rex wove expertly through tangles of cars and trolleys. It was exciting and, although she'd now lived in the city for more than a decade, always a little intimidating to her upon returning after a spell away. Usually on her first day back, she'd get a headache.

"Rex, what do you think about it?" she asked. "Don't the Owens Valley people have a reason to protest? The city's actually pumping groundwater now, not just tapping the river. Is it right to take the water and bring it here, for this?"

"Well, miss, I sure enough sympathize with the valley folk."

"But you don't think dynamiting the canal is a proper response?"

"What I think is that the world has a way of always moving on in a direction no one can stop, and it's best not to let yourself get caught under the wheels."

"Stay ahead of it, like Chris?"

"Well, miss, your brother sure does seem to have the knack of seeing the future and getting himself there in time to meet it."

She laughed. "Yes, you're right about that. Chris has a swell sense of timing." She didn't say anything more, and Rex respected the silence of his passenger during the rest of the journey. When they pulled up to the portico of Chris's house, the door opened and Mrs. Cates, the housekeeper, came out to greet Jane. Rex followed them in, taking her luggage upstairs.

"Will you be dining in tonight, miss?" inquired the always proper but friendly housekeeper. "Mr. Bow will be here."

"Yes, of course, thank you. But I'll be going out afterward. I need to make a telephone call."

"Very good, miss. Shall I ring the number for you?"

"Yes, please. Mr. Simon Clayburgh. He should still be at the *Examiner* office this time of day."

After speaking with her colleague and friend Simon to arrange the evening's plans, Jane retired to her room on the second floor of the spacious Victorian house, where Mrs. Cates had run a hot bath for her. A few minutes before eight, she reemerged to join her brother in the dining room. She was wearing a loose silver sheath dress ending just below her knees, silver stockings and matching high-heeled shoes.

"Wow, you look swell sis!" Chris greeted her in the dining room. "You didn't have to do that for me." It wasn't their custom to dress for dinner, unless Chris was entertaining and required Jane to act as hostess.

"I'm going out after. Simon's coming round to collect me. We're meeting the rest of the crowd at the Montmartre. How are you?" She looked him up and down. His trim form was in business dress, as usual. His thick, straight hair, darker now, was freshly barbered.

He raised an eyebrow at her evening's plans. "Heard from Jed lately?" he teased.

"Yes, and anyway Simon's just a friend." He was, although Jane found him very attractive, and great fun.

"Sure. How are Ma and Pa? I suppose they're upset about the dynamiting?"

"Chris, they're acting so strange about it," she said as they sat together at one end of the large oval dining table where Mrs. Cates had laid out two place settings. She paused as the housekeeper served the soup, then continued. "I'm worried Pa may have had something to do with it."

"Impossible," her brother said at once. "He wouldn't do that in a million years. Pa would never do anything illegal or even unethical."

"Suppose," she said softly, looking up through mascara-covered lashes, "he believed that ethically he was obliged to take illegal actions."

Chris stopped eating and looked at her hard. "What did he say to you?"

"Not much. Only implied that he couldn't stand by and allow neighbors to suffer."

"Now that sounds like him."

Mrs. Cates cleared the soup bowls and brought in the main course of steak frites and corn soufflé. They ate silently. Chris spoke first. "What they really ought to do is just get out of the valley altogether, Ma and Pa. They could come here. There's going to be plenty of room on the estate."

Jane suppressed her amusement at how obviously her brother enjoyed using that word. To tease him, she used another: "How is the *house* coming along?"

"Swell, just swell. They started laying the foundations yesterday."

Chris Bow was building a home in Bel Air Estates, established just two years before by oil magnate Alphonzo Bell. Situated at the western end of the city, the exclusive community, nestled against the foothills of the Santa Monica Mountains, had been laid out by Bell along winding, lushly landscaped lanes. The founder's own 42-room showcase, a villa called Capo Di Monte, Italian for "Top of the Hill," commanded, predictably, the heights. Chris Bow could afford to join this exalted company because at the completion of the aqueduct, when he had shifted his energies to Los Angeles, the young businessman had latched onto the nascent motion picture making industry in Hollywood.

At the time, the Los Angeles citizenry had tended to see the movie business as either shockingly licentious or a land of dreams come true. Chris had seen it as an opportunity. Hollywood studios were beginning to make movies on a grand scale. D.W. Griffith was in the middle of filming *Intolerance* on a monumental set depicting ancient Babylon at the corner of Sunset and Hollywood boulevards. Stars Lillian Gish and Douglas Fairbanks, dozens of supporting actors and more than 15,000 walk-on "extras" had to be fed.

To Chris, the prospect was much less challenging and much more rewarding than feeding the aqueduct workers had been. Bow Enterprises became a supplier of fresh produce and other food stuffs and supplies for Griffith. It also became concessionaire for the Lasky Studio, which expanded in just a few years from a rented barn to a ten-acre facility at the corner of Sunset and Vine, and to Universal City, a 230-acre studio that was now turning out nearly a film a day. When Griffith founded United Artists with Charlie Chaplin, Mary Pickford and Douglas Fairbanks, Bow Enterprises got that account as well. Soon Chris's customers also included Metro Pictures, Goldwyn Pictures and Louis B. Mayer Pictures, which movie theater mogul Marcus Loew had merged last month into a colossal studio to produce a steady stream of films for his growing string of movie houses. The new studio was called Metro-Goldwyn-Mayer, but everyone was already referring to it as just "MGM." To Chris, those three letters meant an immense amount of additional business.

The move to Bel Air had been made necessary, to Chris's mind, not only because it would afford him the opportunity to rub elbows with the city's movie and business elite, but because the once fashionable Bunker Hill neighborhood had declined since he had first moved there in 1913. To Jane's mind, it had become more interesting and exciting, as one after another, the old mansions were sold and subdivided into apartments, attracting flocks of young professionals and office workers who wanted to rent near their downtown places of employment. This house, when Chris sold it, would probably be similarly transformed. Meanwhile, Jane planned to stay in the neighborhood. She would move in with two female colleagues from the paper who were renting a modest single-story house with a big front porch, a gracious but simple style of abode called a "bungalow," just a few streets away from where she presently resided.

They finished dinner without dessert—Chris rarely indulged. He retired to his study while Jane went upstairs to gather her wrap and bag. That estate is going to be mighty empty for a bachelor, she thought. Although recently Chris had let hints slip that he might be considering popping the question to one of the gorgeous fawning Hollywood hopefuls he liked to squire about town. When Jane came down again, Mrs. Cates had just given Simon entry into the hall. His date noticed approvingly the polished dark head, and the stylish, rather rakish hat he held in his hands. Tonight was going to be fun!

"Are you sure she's going to be there?" Jane asked him, as he ushered her out into the warm evening air and into his coupe.

"Said she would be." Simon closed her door then went around and hopped over his own into the driver's seat, without mussing his tuxedo.

"Smoke?" he offered, extending a gleaming silver case.

"Sure." Jane liked Simon, even if he was one of the male reporters always being given the choicest assignments in preference to her. Still, he was one of their gang, and despite the loosening social conventions of city life in the 1920s, she couldn't arrive at the Café Montmartre, the city's first European-style nightclub, unescorted. And it was very important that she go there tonight. Lucille would be there tonight, and she had to talk to her.

When they arrived at the swanky club, advertised as "the center of Hollywood life, where everybody worthwhile goes to see and be seen," there was a line of couples and groups of young people in high spirits stretching from the portico on Hollywood Boulevard around the corner of Highland Avenue. Simon handed the car off to a valet and led Jane to the front of the line. "We're with the Mulholland party," he told the doorman.

Lucille, recently divorced for the second time, was again using her maiden name, and it came in handy. Instantly recognized and universally respected, it was a ticket into any venue she and her crowd desired to patronize.

Strains of a popular tune pulled them up the stairs to the second floor, where they entered the plushy carpeted, chandeliered dining area. On the spacious dance floor, dozens of couples were doing the Black Bottom to music from the orchestra at the far side of the room.

Simon and Jane scanned the tables of revelers talking, eating and drinking alcohol from passed around flasks. It was well known that proprietor Eddie Brandstatter could also supply bootlegged liquor if anyone ran dry. Against the left wall was a buffet of chafing dishes emitting the sumptuous odors of the Montmartre's signature continental cuisine, including, Jane noted appreciatively, though she wasn't at all hungry, its delectable spaghetti Tetrazzini.

"There, they're over there!" Simon pointed to a table on the edge of the dance floor. They wove themselves through the other diners.

"Hey there Simon!" Lucille, resplendent in an intricately patterned and bejeweled scarlet sheath and feathered boa, waved and called them over. Her dark hair was cut short and combed flat and forward, ending with a large curl teasing her cheek on either side.

"Good chap, you've retrieved our JB from the wilderness!"

"The Grand Canyon is hardly a wilderness, Lucille." Jane grinned and kissed her friend. "The El Tovar is really quite elegant. Even you would like it."

"Oh, I'm sure I would, youngster, but I'd never get a wink of sleep there, afraid that the earth would suddenly give way and the whole elegant thing would fall right into the abyss!"

The group guffawed with drunken appreciation. Simon stole a couple of empty chairs from an adjacent table and the others scooted around to make room.

"Well now, at least you're back." Lucille beamed at Jane. "I won't even tell you what you've missed—well maybe just this one little, tiny thing: Valentino danced the Tango here last night with Pola Negri! The way they did it was downright indecent!"

"Lucille, I need to talk to you privately for a minute."

"That's fine, you can accompany me to the Ladies'. I need someone to keep me upright!"

Lucille was certainly tipsy, but she walked on Jane's arm like a queen reviewing her court. As heads turned in a way they hadn't during her own procession through the crowded room, Jane asked herself for the hundredth time since being granted membership in Lucille's inner circle, how does she do it?"

Lucille was beautiful and fetchingly attired, to be sure, but so were hundreds of girls in the room. More attractive than her looks was the sense she exuded of being able to handle anything and of being ready to have a go at anything. This unique combination of social adept and social rebel made Lucille Mulholland quite irresistible. And it was still true after her divorces and countless stormy and sensational love affairs. Lucille's exploits provided constant fodder for gossip columnists, including the formidable Louella Parsons, and were a constant source of embarrassment for her father, who had always attempted to keep the spotlight off of his personal life and family. And, of course, there were those who, on the hunt for a news scoop or a favor, sought out Lucille as a way to get to her father.

Tonight Jane was among them. As they entered the hallway to the powder room, she pulled her friend out of the current of chatting, laughing females and whispered, "Lucille, I need to talk to your father."

"What, another interview? There's hardly a newspaper printed these days without an article or mention about him."

"Not that exactly, but I do so need to talk with him."

"Well, Miss Ames tells me he's hardly to be found in the office anymore, always out at that St. Francis Dam. I don't suppose you want to put on your work boots and follow him out onto a concrete buttress?"

"If I have to, and if he wouldn't be too annoyed to see me there."

"He would be." Lucille smiled and waved back at the frequent greet-ings from passing acquaintances. "Oh, I know!" She lit up with a devilish smile. "Why don't you come out to the ranch this weekend? We're all going up, including father. I'm driving up separately, so you can come with me. And Perry will be so glad to see you!"

"Sure, thanks, I will," agreed Jane. William Perry Mulholland, Lucille's elder brother, as quiet and studious as Lucille was outspoken and fun-loving, was someone Jane knew a little and liked a lot, though not in the way Lucille was implying. Mostly Jane felt sorry for him. Once during a conversation, Perry had told her of his ambitions as a young man to become an engineer or a geologist and of how he had worked with the US Geological Survey for one glorious season before being informed by his father that his future lay elsewhere. Instead of sending him to Stanford University or Harvard, Mulholland had shunted him off to the San Fernando Valley to build and manage a ranch on the 640 acres the chief engineer of the Los Angeles Aqueduct had gradually purchased there beginning in 1912.

This is perfect, thought Jane. A chance to see how Perry is doing and to talk to Superintendent Mulholland quietly in a nonofficial setting, where, she hoped, she would find him in a mood for listening.

But for now, Jane decided, she wouldn't worry anymore. After apply-ing fresh coats of red lipstick, the two girls linked arms and danced their way back to the lights and music.

---

"Jeepers creepers, I swallowed dust for two hours straight on this road going to the aqueduct ceremony!" It was the weekend, and they were off on their trip to the ranch. Lucille was recalling, with emphatic distaste, a previous motor trip to the San Fernando Valley for the celebration of the opening of the aqueduct.

"Me too!" Jane chimed in, smiling at her friend. "I was in the car with Chris. And Rex, his driver, just kept muttering the whole way about the number of people on the road. It was so crowded that we crawled along. Still, it was fun, a lovely day—and the day I met you."

Lucille winked at her under the brim of the red cloche hat fitted low over her ears. When she had collected Jane that morning, the top of the bright red Marmon convertible coupe had already been taken down.

The instant Jane had settled in the passenger seat, her friend had immediately reached below the hem of the boldly patterned red and brown traveling coat she wore, retrieved a gold-toned flask from her garter, and offered it to her. Jane had declined to take a belt of the hooch—"too early for me yet"—but in all other ways had done her best to reflect her friend's buoyant mood. Jane was also stylishly attired this morning in a pleated mauve skirt reaching just below her knees and a long pullover sweater of the same color, decorated with small round silver buttons at the collar and sleeves. Her thick hair was shorter than she'd ever worn it, cut just above the chin. The wind whipped through it as they zipped along. She loved feeling so free.

They drove north out of the city, up into the Hollywood Hills, waving at the huge "Hollywoodland" sign as they passed just west of it. The 50-foot-high sign had been placed on Mount Lee the year before as a real estate advertising gimmick. Jane reported to her friend that the letters were made up of 4,000 light bulbs—working at the *Examiner*, one picked up such facts.

The road climbed to the top of Cahuenga Pass, which bisected the Santa Monica Mountains at their eastern end to link Los Angeles with the San Fernando Valley. Originally an Indian footpath and burial ground, the pass had been used by Spanish and Mexican cattle ranchers, stagecoaches and mule teams. In 1912, the Pacific Electric Railway had completed the route through the pass for its Big Red Cars, all the way to Owensmouth in anticipation of the coming of the aqueduct. And in 1913, tens of thousands of Angelenos had ridden the trolleys, or driven the adjacent unpaved road in buckboards, carriages and automobiles, snaking their way toward the opening ceremonies.

By now the dusty road was mostly paved, and electric wires scalloped along a line of utility poles at its edge. As the Marmon crested the pass, the San Fernando Valley spread out below them, green and inviting. Jane marveled at the transformation of what had been a dry, brown land when she had first glimpsed it from this vantage point more than a decade before.

"No speed limit!" yelled Lucille, stomping her foot on the accelerator. The Marmon hurtled down the steep grade, its driver expertly hugging the curves of the descending road. The opportunity to go at top speed was often highlighted in the advertisements of valley real estate promoters, as an enticement to bring weekend motorists from the city for a day's outing. Once there, they would find, according to advertising copywriters, a promised land of quiet, flower-lined streets amidst citrus groves, just 45 minutes by trolley from the city center. "God made Southern California," they crowed, "and made it on purpose!"

Reaching the valley floor, they headed up Sherman Boulevard. The broad thoroughfare with trolley tracks down the center and parking for motor cars at the edges was, indeed, flower-lined. Developed by H.J. Whitley, who had also played a major role in the creation of Hollywood, it was landscaped with red, white and pink roses and oleander bushes, an abundance of shrubs blooming yellow, purple and crimson, and exotic trees, including magnolias, acacias, deodars and Monterey pines. This avenue into paradise—lavishly irrigated with Owens River water—had been named for Moses Sherman, a member of the syndicate of Los Angeles businessmen who had profited enormously by buying up pre-aqueduct San Fernando Valley real estate. Moses had simultaneously served on the Los Angeles Board of Water Commissioners. Because the syndicate began making its purchases on the very same day the commission was informed of Fred Eaton's success in securing the necessary Owens Valley land and water options, it was widely assumed Sherman had provided insider information to his cronies.

Continuing northeast on Sherman, the young ladies were greeted every few hundred yards by signs and banners announcing such entice-ments as "Rose festival next Sunday, Van Nuys," "Free barbecue Saturday at Owensmouth!" and "Free lunch every weekend!"

"If you're schmuck enough to go for those, you deserve what you get," commented Lucille, "a lousy lunch and a sales pitch!"

All along the road were signs with arrows directing motorists to subdivisions, where, if they acted fast, they could purchase their own little piece of paradise. One of these was at Tarzana Ranch, property that Edgar Rice Burroughs, author of the very popular *Tarzan* stories, had bought from Harrison Gray Otis, publisher of the *Los Angeles Times* and one of the original syndicate investors. Now Burroughs was also subdivid-ing his land and selling plots for housing developments.

Lucille and Jane turned off onto a dirt road, and soon left behind all the marketing and model homes, driving along orchards of citrus, peach, nectarine and plum trees. They passed the tiny hamlet of Zetzah in a blink, then, following a rough-hewn sign "to Chatsworth," continued on several more miles. When they reached a small, carefully lettered sign that said "Mulholland Fruit Ranch," Lucille slowed and turned in. They glided down the drive toward a modest house and barn. Lucille parked the Marmon next to the fence and pointed to the deep verandah wrapping around two sides of the house, where a porch swing and cluster of Adirondack chairs appeared fully occupied.

"They're already here," she said sourly. "Rose drove up with father, of course. Since mother died she's been the stand-in, jumping to for his every demand. She'll never have a life of her own, probably never even leave his house." She sighed deeply, shaking her pretty head. "And Perry too, he just lies down in front of father like a rug…You know how he hates it here."

Jane nodded and placed a sympathetic hand on her friend's arm.

"Oh, well," said Lucille brightly. "Ready to face the General?!"

"Onward to battle!"

Laughing, arm in arm, they walked toward the verandah. Amid the tinkling of glasses, a rough voice called out, "You're late!"

"Yes father, and no doubt you were early," responded Lucille teasingly, rising on tiptoe to kiss the brushy gray mustache on the side of her father's face that did not clench a fat cigar. Watching, Jane appreciated, not for the first time, that although Mulholland could often become blustery and furious with his wayward daughter, he also seemed to enjoy their sparring. She was the only one of his children who stood up to him.

"You remember my friend Jane Bow don't you?" Lucille was saying now. She had chosen not to mention her friend's other role, as reporter for the *Los Angeles Examiner*, though her father probably remembered this, since Jane had already interviewed him once for an article. But you never knew on any given day what his prevailing mood toward the press might be, so best to keep the introduction on more personal grounds.

"Nice to see you again Miss Bow." Mulholland thrust a large, gnarled paw at her. "How is your brother?"

"Very well, sir," she replied. "Thank you for asking." Jane noticed the hand that grasped and pumped hers shook a bit as he withdrew it. Yet Mulholland stood straight-backed, his physique still powerful. He was dressed in his habitual three-piece tweed suit with a plain, dark necktie wrapped and knotted below a winged, starched collar. Jane looked up into a face that was becoming jowly, his cheeks hollowing, she noted. But despite the puffy bags of darkened skin that hung under them, his eyes were as blue and clear, his gaze as direct and penetrating as always.

"Rose, will you do the honors please," Mulholland barked.

Lucille's sister Rose put down the pitcher of lemonade she had been offering around, wiped her hands on the ruffled apron she wore over her pink flowered dress and shook Jane's hand too. Her hair, unlike that of the newcomers, had not been bobbed and was knotted at back in an old-fashioned manner. Her countenance was a little pale, thought Jane, but her smile was warm as she introduced the newcomers to Mr. and Mrs. Maas, a pleasant-looking middle-aged couple, neighbors from a nearby ranch, who were seated on the porch swing. Then she introduced Mr. and Mrs. Matthews, who sat in the Adirondacks to their left. Jane knew Matthews was legal counsel for the DWP, though she had not previously made his acquaintance. The dark-eyed, handsome man was fashionably attired in a beige tweed suit with a diagonally striped tie beneath a folded-down collar. A straw Panama hat rested on the swing beside him. His bobbed-haired wife wore a smart cream-colored, wide-collared linen dress and strapped creamy leather shoes.

Jane was directed to an empty chair. Lucille doffed her coat, revealing a matching sleeveless sheath, draped it over the porch railing and perched beside it. Rose brought them glasses of cold lemonade, frowning at Lucille as she gathered up her sister's coat and took it inside. Jane gratefully swirled the ice cubes in her glass. It was all she could do to keep from gulping as the cool, sweet liquid glided down her parched throat, clearing the aftertaste of the dusty road.

The screen door opened, and Perry came through with a young lady on his arm. "Jane, Lucille, hello! Didn't know you'd arrived. Allow me to introduce Miss Maas. Adeline, this is my sister Lucille and our dear friend Jane Bow."

"Addie, please. Oh I'm so happy to meet you!" the short, slender girl with long curly dark hair, caught with a ribbon at her back, smiled broadly, bouncing a little on her toes. Her well-shaped limbs were shown off in a short-sleeved lemon-yellow shirtwaist dress.

Lucille raised an eyebrow for Jane's benefit. The young man's face was flushed and he acted a bit flustered as he pulled out another chair for Addie. Was there something going on with the girl? Lucille was wondering. Or was it just their father? With Mulholland there, Perry had more of the demeanor of a school boy home for a holiday than of a man nearing 30, the ostensible manager of the ranch and their host.

Jane had also noticed Perry's comportment. But since she was less interested in him than in his father at the moment, she studied the older man as she sipped her lemonade. His hand was indeed shaking as he raised his cigar to and from his lips, but his overall presence was as commanding and charming as always. Before the late arrivals, Mulholland had been regaling the Maases and Matthews with a tale of his days in the British Merchant Marine before coming to America, and he picked up the thread of it now. He was a gifted, witty storyteller, as thousands beyond this privileged company had discovered. Since the opening of the aqueduct, Mulholland had been in great demand as a public speaker. Jane found herself, as usually happened in his company, despite what she knew of him as an overbearing parent and despite her own personal concerns, liking him very much.

Glancing at Matthews and his wife, she thought they've probably heard this story before. Yet they were attentive and gracious. Both of them also held their own against Mulholland when the conversation switched to current matters, such as the United States winning more than double the number of medals as any other country in the Paris Olympic Games, the law President Coolidge had just signed granting US citizenship to American Indians and the recent dynamiting of the aqueduct.

"Took just two days to fix it. Wasn't much of a hole," pronounced Mulholland dismissively.

"The *Times* says it was a Communist agitator, a feller fired from one of yer aqueduct crews?" inquired Mr. Maas.

"Your paper," Lucille said, pointing a manicured finger at Jane, "said it was maniacs, anarchists and unionists."

"I didn't write that. I don't know if that's right," replied Jane.

"More likely some of those ranchers up there who've been diverting and wasting water," asserted Mulholland chomping on his cigar.

"There has been some dissatisfaction in Owens Valley since the drought began," said Matthews judiciously.

"Harrumph! Dissatisfaction is a condition that prevails up there, like foot-and-mouth disease," growled Mulholland.

Jane said nothing. Perry, she noticed, was looking at her, his countenance kind and concerned. He certainly knew how these words might affect her. When he had first been sent on his reluctant exile to the ranch, she had tried to cheer him up by telling him about how much she had loved growing up in the Owens Valley. Lucille and Mulholland also knew of her origins, but had apparently forgotten or chosen to pretend they had.

She also noticed that the Maas family had grown quiet. They were in an odd predicament, reflected Jane. Their ranch is prospering here in this valley because of water from the Owens Valley brought to them by Mulholland. Yet perhaps they feel they can't trust him. He curtailed water to the San Fernando last summer, and some farmers hadn't been able to plant winter crops as a result. He could do it again this year, or worse, and they might find themselves with a bad case of dissatisfaction too.

"Time we got the steaks on, right son?" Mulholland waved his cigar at the others to indicate they should stay seated and slapped an arm over Perry's shoulder as they headed around the back of the house to where a fire pit and grill had been set up. Rose excused herself to the kitchen, and both Jane and Addie followed her inside to help. Soon they were carrying bowls of potato salad, green beans and fresh fruit to a large wooden plank table under an open-sided tent that reminded Jane of the ones she'd seen at Cinco camp during the building of the aqueduct. She went back in to retrieve a pitcher of lemonade, passing Addie laden with place settings. When Jane re-emerged from the house, Matthews was seating the ladies at the table, and Mulholland and Perry were forking sizzling steaks onto large plates.

It was a delicious meal, and the entire company became quite jolly consuming it. When Rose began serving the coffee, Mulholland took a gold-red peach from the bowl at the center of the table and held it up. "Before we brought the water here, all they could grow was hay, barley and beans—and now look at it!" he said, biting into the succulent orb, which squirted juice into his mustache and over his chin. Lucille, seated next to him, rolled her eyes and reached over to dab his mouth with her napkin. Her father roared with laughter and the others joined in, every-one but Janey. She was staring at Mulholland and seeing before her eyes the blue-ribbon-festooned stacks of Lone Pine peaches, which were much bigger than these and had always taken top prize at the county fairs of her childhood. She was wondering if the Lone Pine orchards were still produc-ing these wonders. Could they, with more water being pumped from the ground to bring it here?

After supper, the women headed inside to help Rose clean up, but Lucille touched Jane's arm and motioned for her to follow Mulholland, who was sauntering out toward the orchard for a postprandial stretch of the legs. Jane nodded gratefully and scampered to catch up with him. "Do you mind if I join you on your walk, Mr. Mulholland?" she called.

"Not at all, it's a great pleasure to have such pretty company. Do you know much about growing fruit Miss Bow?"

She stared at him again. It certainly seemed now that he had com-pletely forgotten who she was and where she came from. Jane closed her mouth and tried to put a pleasant smile on it.

"Not much, really. However agriculture is a subject I would like to speak with you about, sir. About agriculture in the Owens Valley actually."

"Oh?" He peered down at her, curious.

"I'm sure you're not fully aware, sir, of how much damage is being done to the Owens Valley by the groundwater pumping. I know you promised that there would be plenty of water for everyone."

He stopped walking and turned to face her. "Is this for a story Miss Bow? Are you muckraking for Loewenthal?"

"I beg your pardon?"

"Is this some scheme of your editor's to sell papers?"

So he did remember she was a reporter. "Mr. Loewenthal knows nothing about this, I assure you. I'm speaking to you out of personal, not professional, interests."

"What personal interest do you have in this Miss Bow?" he asked the question, but Jane could tell the answer was already forming in his brain. He was beginning to recall something he had been told long ago about this inconsequential young friend of his daughter.

"My interest is that I grew up in the Owens Valley, sir, and still have family and friends residing there."

"I see." It now came to his mind, that troublesome valley was where she and her brother came from. But Chris Bow had been an inside member of his aqueduct team and had never mentioned a word in defense of Owens Valley to him. Hell, the young man had good reason to be loyal—he'd taken a chance on him, given him the start he needed for his business. But his sister, well, she might be of a different sort. Mulholland tossed his cigar butt and stamped it out, then reached into his inside breast pocket for another, bit off and spat the tip, then lit the cigar and puffed rapidly. His expression, when he finally looked back at her, was friendly, except for the steely eyes.

"In that case, Miss Bow, I am guessing that you know as well as I do that the dynamiting wasn't the work of any anarchist unionist. It was surely the work of Owens Valley folk, and if you know anything about who did it, you would be very well advised to tell me. If any of your relatives or close acquaintances are involved, or those of your brother, I suggest you warn them they have started down a very dangerous path."

Jane repressed a shudder and held her gaze still in what Chris had taught her was called a poker face. "I know nothing Superintendent Mulholland. And even if I did, my duty would be to relay it only to one person, my editor," she said, reverting despite earlier protestations to her professional capacity.

She forced herself to smile under his now decidedly aggressive gaze. She remarked how low the sun now hung on the horizon, and that it was time she and Lucille started back to the city. He nodded, offering his arm to escort her. She accepted it, as she knew she must, and they began the short walk back to the house.

"Did you know, Miss Bow, that I had proposed back in 1913 to plant hundreds of new trees in the Owens Valley?" Mulholland broke the uncomfortable silence.

"No, sir, I didn't know that."

"Well, for one reason and another, the plan never came off. But I sure wish it had, and do you know why Miss Bow?"

"I'm sure I don't, sir."

"Because if we'd done it, there'd be a lot more trees up there for stringing up agitators who damage city property." He said it in a pleasant conversational tone without stopping or even breaking his stride, but Jane stopped dead upon hearing it, her arm, still under his, moving forward without the rest of her. He felt the tug, and turned to look back at her.

"Excuse me," she said without returning his regard, where she now perceived a malicious gleam, and hurried past him into the house.

He stood awhile smoking. But as Jane and Lucille gathered their things and made their goodbyes, Jane noticed Mulholland motioning Matthews aside into the kitchen.

---

Leaning against the sink, Mulholland chewed on his cigar and pointed with it out the window at the two young women climbing into Lucille's Marmon. "That little gal knows something," he said, nodding grimly. "I tried to shake it loose, but she wouldn't say."

"What of real interest and substance could she possibly know? She lives and works here." Matthews had listened to Mulholland's account of the young Miss Bow and their conversation, but he was skeptical of the conclusions his boss had drawn. "Let me tell you what *we do know*. It's not as much as I'd hoped to come up with by now, but here it is." The attendance of Matthews and his wife at the day's gathering had been prompted as much by the necessity of reporting to the chief as by the privilege of socializing with him and his family. The attorney drew deeply on his own cigar, then cleared his throat and began his account.

"Our investigator says the valley's shut up tight. No one is talking much. He did manage to pry out of a couple of witnesses that they saw a caravan of maybe a dozen cars driving south from Bishop late that night, though they claim not to have recognized any of the vehicles or faces of the drivers. He was also able to track the dynamite to the Watterson's warehouse. When the sheriff questioned the brothers, they said it had been stolen by unknown thieves. That's it, and unless someone comes forward to collect the reward, it may be all we ever find out."

Mulholland glowered and said nothing.

"Now, about the other matter," continued the lawyer, "the illegal diverting of water from the aqueduct has continued. In fact, since we bought the McNally Ditch, it's increased. One morning, a couple of days ago, our men went out to find half a dozen canals had been dug the night before to draw water from the McNally into other ditches. Our crews filled them in, and then some genius decided to give tit for tat by digging some canals to keep water from going into the Big Pine Canal. Not a very helpful tactic. Anyway, they stopped it soon enough because a cadre of Big Pine owners threatened them with picks and shovels. That's the kind of anger brewing up there now."

"Buy up enough property to get control of the Big Pine, just like we did with the McNally."

"All right," said Matthews slowly. "We can do that, but Chief, with this approach, we've already spent more than the million Eaton was asking for the Long Valley reservoir site. Maybe we should just give in. That would solve the problem, ensure enough water for Owens Valley and Los Angeles."

"No, we aren't going to give in, and it wouldn't solve the problem. Not anymore—the city's growing too fast. We're going to need it all."

"Whew, that's going to mean buying out the whole valley?!" Matthews ran fingers through his thick hair, blinking his fine, dark eyes. "It will cost a fortune!"

"No, we buy just the minimum land and water rights we need to out-maneuver our opponents. Buy sparsely but intelligently, W.B. It's a chess game. To win we don't need to own the whole board."

They smoked silently for a time again, and then Mulholland said, "I don't understand that girl. She doesn't seem much like her brother." He shook his head, thinking how different siblings could be—Lucille so wild, Rose and Perry so compliant.

"Did I ever tell you what Dr. Taylor said about Chris Bow?" asked Matthews. "He said he ran across Chris in the city a year or two after the aqueduct was finished. Over a drink, Chris told him he had earned about a quarter of a million dollars supplying food for the work crews."

"Damn profiteer!" Mulholland brought his fist down on the counter. "He made way too much and the doctor made way too little! We built the aqueduct for the enrichment of the public, not of Christopher Bow!"

"Yes, it seemed a bit out of proportion to me too, especially given the way he had pleaded rising costs forced him to raise the price for workers." Matthews did find this offensive, although he found Mulholland's indig-nation somewhat amusing. The tireless service the chief had given to his city for so many years was indisputable, but it was also true that during those years he had, as superintendent of the DWP, drawn a higher salary than the chief of police, district attorney or even the mayor. In addition, Matthews knew Mulholland also maintained lucrative consulting contracts on the side, including with other cities.

"Tell Lippincott not to use Bow on the Colorado," said Mulholland, turning with greater interest to the subject now closer to his heart.

Matthews nodded, though he knew the sanction would have little impact on the young business magnate, whose growing interests in Hollywood were earning him a fortune that made his aqueduct earnings look like a pittance.

---

Jane had been silent during most of the ride back to the city, pretending to listen to Lucille's gay talk of this or that, accepting the flask as it was periodically offered. When Lucille launched into an acerbic critique of her father's highhanded attitude toward Perry, Jane stirred, sensing an opportunity. "Lucille, I want to tell you something about your father."

"Sure, what was so important you had to talk to him about anyway?"

"It was about what he's doing in the Owens Valley. Lucille, they're not just taking water from the river, they're pumping it right out of the ground. There are beautiful, old cottonwood trees dying because of it, and people whose farms may be ruined."

"Well, that's the fault of the drought. Everyone's suffering."

"Did you see anyone suffering in the San Fernando Valley? Did you see those peaches? And your brother's orchard is doing fine."

"It's not that bad—you're exaggerating."

"I'm not. Your father told me in no uncertain terms he'd just as soon see the dynamiters hanged."

"Oh, he was kidding!" Lucille cast her a skeptical sideways glance. "You just don't know him well enough to understand when he's joking."

"He wasn't joking. He was perfectly serious."

"Well if he was, he has a right to be. Did you know he's received dozens of death threats from those lunatics up there? What do you think of that?!" Lucille flashed an angry look, and Jane felt it slash between them like a sword of ice. Then it melted a little, as Lucille rearranged her countenance into a smile. "Ah, come on. Look! Look at the lights of our fair city welcoming us home!"

The Marmon had been climbing steadily as they argued, and now they had reached the crest of the Cahuenga Pass. Below, a breathtaking sea of diamonds spread out below them: the lights of homes, street lamps and automobiles across the vast Los Angeles basin. Down there was not only the city proper, but also dozens of suburbs and contiguous towns, most of which had been annexed into the metropolitan area.

Jane felt a shiver for the second time today. She returned Lucille's smile, but she was thinking: I guess it really is like they say, blood is thicker than water.

Before Lucille dropped her off in Bunker Hill, she had decided what to do.

# Chapter 18

"Is this about the dock strike? I told you why I gave it to Simon and Joe."

"It's not about that, boss. I just need to spend some time with my parents. With the drought, and now all the trouble up there, I feel my place is with them right now."

"Hmmm…" Loewenthal leaned his long frame back in his chair, removed his spectacles and studied Jane Bow as he cleaned them. "You think there's likely to be more trouble then?"

"I hope not. But if so, I'll be in a better position to help my folks being up there."

"You'll also be in a better position to find out what's going on." He replaced the spectacles and considered before speaking.

"All right, I'll put you on leave. But you can still write for me as a stringer. If you get a story worth printing, I'll pay you for it."

"I was hoping you'd say that," Jane responded. "As long as it's fine by you if I also write a few for Mr. Chalfant, if he'll have me."

"That's fine. You know he and I go way back." She nodded, then he asked, "What about the Morgan interview?"

"May I do it under the same arrangement? I'll travel directly from the valley to San Simeon. Miss Morgan needn't know anything has changed."

He was considering again when Bruce, the copy boy, popped his head in. "Boss, they need you in the newsroom."

"Stay put J. Bow," he said, using her pen name. "We'll continue this in a minute."

He followed Bruce out of the room, and Jane wandered over to the window, looking out down the length of Broadway. Since she had first moved to the city, the busy thoroughfare had become a hub not only for business, but for entertainment. Ornate vaudeville and movie palaces were now wedged between tall office buildings on practically every block. Today she had taken a trolley to the office, but often Jane liked to walk to work, making her way from Bunker Hill down the Angels Flight steps to Hill Street, then over one block to Third before turning right at Broadway. On this corner was the Million Dollar Theater, the city's first motion picture house, and Tally's, the Cameo and Loews were farther up the street. Jane loved to look at all the movie posters and show advertisements as she walked. And when she had time and was in the mood, she also lingered in front of the elaborate window displays of the city's leading department stores, the Broadway at Fourth, Bullock's at Seventh and the Hamburger People's Store at Eighth.

Her morning trajectory took her all the way to Eleventh Street, where the *Examiner* building sat at the corner. Jane always found the serene white structure a bit out of place after the hullabaloo of the rest of Broadway. Architect Julia Morgan had designed it in the Mission Revival style, which harkened back to the California missions. The building's chalky white facade, typical of the style, was pierced at ground level by an arcade of wide arches and featuring wrought-iron grillwork, bell towers, cupolas and red clay tile roofing on its upper expanses.

Jane frowned. Angelenos had fallen in love with the romance of mission days long before she was born. In 1884, Helen Hunt Jackson had written the novel *Ramona* about star-crossed lovers in early Mexican-ruled California. Jackson had intended the novel, which exposed the racism and cruelty of white Americans to mixed-race people of Spanish and Indian origins, to be a corrective. She had hoped it would help to change attitudes, as *Uncle Tom's Cabin* had done about slavery.

But readers had been far more taken by her idealized descriptions of mission and rancho life than by her message. Today's Angelenos had adopted the cultural trappings as their own, but not the people who had created them. Los Angeles had been founded by Mexicans, yet their descendants now lived in broken down adobes on unpaved Olvera, Republic and Sanchez streets, next to the old plaza. They were crowded into the slum with a new wave of immigrants who had come north to escape the turmoil of the Mexican Revolution and find jobs, a migration that had given Los Angeles the largest population of Mexicans anywhere in the world except the Mexican capitol.

Of course it wasn't just Angelenos who treated Mexicans badly. Jane reminded herself that the Harvey Company had refused to hire Rosie to serve in their lunch rooms. It was somewhat different in the Owens Valley, where Mexicans were respected for their expertise in mining and had long worked alongside whites in the fields. They were viewed as better than Indians or Chinese. And in Lone Pine, where the largest Mexican community was found, all the town's citizens joined in the Cinco de Mayo fiesta, one of the biggest holidays of the year.

I don't suppose Loewenthal will let me point any of this out in my article about Morgan, mused Jane. Over the past decade, Hearst had become increasingly conservative in his politics, and the paper, established by him as a populist, muckraking counterweight to Otis's rabidly conservative *Times*, was changing. But, fortunately, Hearst could only give so much attention to the *Examiner*. The publishing magnate had many papers across the country now and, being especially taken by his *New York Daily Mirror*, a racy tabloid he'd created to compete with *New York Daily News*, focused the bulk of his attentions eastward. Loewenthal thus had some margin of latitude to steer the paper back toward center.

"Haaazy, wake up!"

Jane turned and made a face at her boss. Once, after an exhausting day, she'd been foolish enough to tell Loewenthal of Chris's childhood nickname for her. Predictably, she'd regretted it ever since.

"Hey, I'm trusting you on the Morgan story," he said, flinging himself onto the davenport and lifting his legs onto the coffee table, "but don't disappoint me!" He waggled a finger at her. "Morgan is Hearst's anointed one, so we can't allow any slip ups that would rub her fur the wrong way."

"You can count on me boss," Jane assured him. She came over and sat in the armchair at the other end of the table and said in a low, confidential voice, "I need to ask you something."

"What, you want something more?" He raised his hands defensively in front of his chest.

"No, not for me. I just need to know what you think about something."

"Shoot."

"Do you think it plausible that Superintendent Mulholland intends to completely dry up the Owens Valley and that he intended to do so from the very start?"

Loewenthal reached for the cigarette case on the table and extended it to her. She shook her head. He withdrew a cigarette for himself, lit it and took a drag, then rested his elbows on his knees, thinking awhile how to answer her.

"Mulholland is a complicated man, Jane. Whatever his attitude may be today, I doubt he was that calculating at the start of this thing. When he promised there would be water enough for everybody, I think, on some level anyway, he believed it, or convinced himself he did."

The editor raised the cigarette to his lips again, then looked down, thinking, tapping it against the edge of the ashtray. He looked up and resumed. "You know, for an imminently pragmatic man, he wasn't thinking very straight. His projections for rates of population growth and water consumption were so far off—though he's not to be faulted for that, no one expected the city to explode like this. But even if it had taken a decade longer for Los Angeles to get this big, we still would have gotten to this point eventually. Even without the drought, there would have come a time when there wouldn't be enough water to go around. I mean, there's an upper limit to how much snow can drop on the mountains and run down into the Owens River. There's no upper limit to how much Los Angeles can grow."

They sat in silence for a while, and then he said, with a twist of a smile on his fine lips, "Did you know Mulholland once proposed planting hundreds of trees in the valley?"

"I know, I was at his ranch with Lucille and the family just yesterday, and he told me he wished he had planted them since there would be more limbs to hang agitators from."

"A joke?"

"I don't think so."

"Ah-huh," Loewenthal sniffed and took another drag on his cigarette. "I think he's changed since this thing started. Maybe all the adulation has made him too sure of himself, or maybe the constant demands for more and more water have shortened his fuse. Maybe both. He always struck me as an impatient man with little tolerance for those who don't see matters his way, but recently he seems to have become even more bullheaded, downright truculent. Here's a story for you…

"About six months ago, I was at a dinner honoring a retiring City Council member, and Mulholland was there. At some point in the evening, I found myself talking with him and indulging in one of his cigars. Now, everyone knows the chief hates those kinds of events, so I was prepared for him to be a bit irascible, but not for what actually occurred. I asked him what he thought about the completion of the dam at Hetch Hetchy Valley, and I guess I was feeling my oats or the effects of the brandy because I reminded him that John Muir had called the San Francisco proponents of the dam 'temple destroyers' for flooding a place reputed to be almost as exquisite as the Yosemite.

"Well, he didn't get angry or anything. He actually smiled quite pleasantly, and then he told me what he thought should be done to ensure the public's enduring right to the majestic beauty of Yosemite. He said that if he were custodian of that national park, he'd hire a dozen of the world's best photographers for one year and let them live in the park without interference from other visitors. Give them a mandate to take photographs of every scenic wonder in every season. Then he'd have all those pictures printed in thousands of books, which he'd send to every library in the country to make sure every American would have access to them. Then, and I remember he leered at me like a wolf as he delivered the punch line, he said he'd build a dam from one side of the valley to the other and— these were his very words—'stop the goddamned waste!'"

Jane's head jerked back, and her eyes popped wide. Loewenthal nodded. "He was laughing, but it was no joke. He was certainly serious. And it wasn't just the arrogance in his voice that chilled me right to the bone, it was the absolutely certainty he was right."

A month later, Jane found herself back in Owens Valley. She had her old room and a new motor car, having splurged on a spiffy light-green Wills Sainte Claire A-68 roadster. In it, she traveled the dirt roads up and down the valley, helping Chalfant try to get a picture of a community that was fragmenting and changing like a kaleidoscope. With some folks quietly selling out and others desperate to stop what they saw as betrayals, the number of visitors dropping into the *Register* for a chat had dropped to a trickle. Neighbors encountered on the streets of Bishop were closed-mouth. With his reliable methods of gathering news drying up, Chalfant was glad to have the unexpected assistance of his old protégé.

Jane's reception in other quarters was mixed. Pa professed to be puzzled about her decision to return for an extended stay and told her he and Ma didn't need any looking after, but Jane knew he too was secretly glad to have her back. Ma was surprised and unabashedly pleased. Some neighbors and townsfolk were cautiously friendly, others overtly suspicious—Tess Beaton, gray-haired now and chubbier than ever, poked the air in front of Jane's face with an accusatory finger. "You a spy for Los Angeles? Which should rightly be called los devils!"

Jane's denial had little effect. People in the valley seemed bent on believing whatever they were holding to, and Jane's confrontation with Tess wasn't the only one to be seen on the streets of Bishop and other valley towns. Yet when Mark Watterson stopped Jane as she was passing the bank, his smile was natural and his manner as gentlemanly as ever.

"Welcome back Miss Bow. We had the pleasure of seeing your mother in the bank yesterday, and she told us you're planning to stay awhile. That's wonderful."

"Thank you Mr. Watterson. Nice to see you too."

"I understand from Chalfant that you're doing some reporting for him, but also continuing to work for a Los Angeles paper?"

"Yes, I'm on a leave from the *Examiner*, but will likely send an occasional story their way as opportunities arise."

"That's fine, fine, even better." Mark's brown eyes engaged hers. "It's important that the truth of what's happening here reaches Los Angeles citizens."

"I'll do my best, but I'm sure you know that the truth is not always easily discovered."

"Yes, surely. But in this case, evidence is all about, just ready to be gathered by a talented newspaperwoman."

Jane waited. She had learned that if she said less, she would often learn more.

"Drive out across the valley, I urge you Miss Bow. Talk to the farmers and ranchers along the Owens River Canal and Bishop Creek Ditch. Folks are scared, becoming desperate, afraid of being left high and dry if their neighbors sell out—like in a children's game where there's no place to sit when the music stops. Except that this is no game, Miss Bow, and even if it were, the city isn't playing fair. They've been buying up property in a checkerboard pattern: This one here, and that one over there, but not the one in-between. So folks who hold out and stand firm with the valley may find that other folks in their ditch association are moving out, and just a handful of them are left burdened with trying to maintain the ditch by themselves.

"City agents and people here in the valley working with them for financial gain, like my uncle George Watterson, are even lying, telling some folks that their neighbors have optioned already so they better too. Then after they sign, heartbroken at the doing of it, they discover from those neighbors that it never was true. But it's too late, they've signed away their farms and strengthened the enemy, and now the pressure is reversed and put on their neighbors. Those kinds of underhanded tactics were used here before, when you were just a child, Miss Bow, and they're the reason you now see the valley rising up again with justifiable anger."

Jane thanked him, and assured him she would talk to everyone she could across the valley.

"Yes, I see you have wheels." He nodded toward her motor car. His mood lightened, as he couldn't help but appreciate the sleek green roadster. Designed by Wills Sainte Claire, who had been Henry Ford's head engineer until 1919, the compact, lightweight vehicle had a powerful engine and was reputed to be graced with especially nimble handling. "How does she drive?" he asked.

Jane offered Mark a test drive, and then took his advice. With Chalfant's encouragement, she traversed the valley, scouring its farms and ranches in pursuit of truth. What she found was far from a united community up in arms against an external aggressor. There were those who told tales of dirty dealing, but Jane also found those who seemed more afraid of their neighbors than of city agents. She even heard of threats being made against anyone who betrayed the valley and sold out. In fact, when Jane talked to George Watterson, the estranged uncle told quite a different story than that of his crusading nephew.

"Don't let Mark and Wilfred fool you," he warned. "Since the recession after the end of the war, they've gotten mortgages on most of the spreads in the valley, and they cooked up this idea of an irrigation district so they could increase their power even more by personally controlling all those water rights."

"But I heard that Big Pine and Bishop citizens voted overwhelmingly in favor of creating the irrigation district. Didn't the owners of the four major north-valley irrigation ditches all agree to transfer their water rights over to the district?"

"Initially that was true, but that was before they understood what a power grab was underway. When the McNally folks saw the thing clearly, they changed their minds."

"And then the Big Pine."

"Yep, that's right."

"Los Angeles now controls both those ditch associations?"

"Look, miss, it's not a matter of the city controlling folks up here, but of a small group of power-hungry, self-proclaimed leaders, led by my nephews, trying to stop folks from making their own decisions about selling options on their land and water rights. I'll tell you what I think, this Eaton fella, who's set himself up like a cattle baron in Long Valley, is in on it too. By convincing folks against selling now for good prices, he's thinkin they'll hold out until their farms and ranches dry up. Then they'll have no choice but to sell to him, for next to nothing! The city will finally give in and buy that dam site and build a big reservoir up there, so he'll have plenty of water for his expanded holdings, and he and my banker nephews will run the entire valley. I've written a letter to the editor of the *Register* exposing the scheme, but that Chalfant is on their side, so he probably won't publish it."

When Jane asked Chalfant about George Watterson's letter, he confirmed receipt of a rambling "paranoid polemic." "No facts," he said. "Not printable."

Indeed, Jane was finding it hard to assemble enough facts of a reliable nature to write a story she could even consider submitting to Loewenthal. Most days when she drove the little green roadster into the ranch yard and parked it beneath the oak, she sat for some minutes in frustration, watching Ma preparing supper in the now-electrically lit kitchen before coming in to help her. Like sand running through my fingers, Jane fumed. Nothing but rumors, viewpoints impossible to reconcile, supposed facts impossible to confirm. I just can't make anything take shape!

---

*My correspondence during those months was of little help in fortifying my resolve. Jed didn't come right out and say it, but I could tell he disapproved. What was it he wrote? Something like "The world keeps moving on, my girl, and we need to move with it." At the time I took it as criticism of me, but now I realize he was simply stating his own convictions, and that his attitude was quite consistent—precisely what it had been during the strike on the aqueduct. Jed hadn't opposed the men's right to strike, he'd even said he understood why they were doing it. But he hadn't joined them, hadn't wanted any of it. He'd returned to the tunnel alone and kept digging.*

*Mary was less delicate. She repeated in her flowing script what she had told me all those years before, our last day in the little brown house: "Do not waste your life in Owens Valley. There is nothing to stay for anymore. You're old enough to understand that now."*

*My mentor had left the valley and, as it became clear, kept on moving. Carmel had not, after all, been the place Mary fit in, for she soon headed to England and the continent, from where she regaled me with tales of rubbing shoulders with such literary luminaries as H.G. Wells, George Bernard Shaw, Henry James, Joseph Conrad and W.B. Yeats. There were some hints that health problems may have been a factor in this uprooting, but also that immersion in such an intellectually stimulating milieu had acted more strongly than the curative waters of any spa and, combined with Mary's own spiritualism, had quite delivered her to good health.*

*Not long after returning, Mary moved to New York City. A play of hers, The Arrow Maker, was to be produced at the New Theatre there, and Mary thought that being in proximity to publishers and periodicals would be of assistance to her career. She wrote that she also meant to make it her mission to argue in person for the literary importance of overlooked western*

*themes and writers. Here too Mary was thrilled to be accepted into the
bosom of the elite, telling of soirées at the home of wealthy socialite
Mabel Dodge, where she conversed with the likes of Willa Cather, another female novelist drawn to western tableaux, journalist Lincoln Steffens,
commentator Walter Lippmann, birth control crusader Margaret Sanger
and political firebrand Emma Goldman.*

*But Mary's letters from the East Coast were marbled with the famil-
iar discontent. Reviews of her play were mixed. One critic denigrated the
dialogue, pointing out that the drama's protagonist, an Indian sorceress,
spoke as if "she had absorbed the slogans of the feminist press" and made
"exclamations straight out of the mass-circulation magazines." And though
Mary had now achieved both a location and a reputation that made it
easier to secure writing contracts, she still bemoaned the disproportionately
small income yielded by her prodigious efforts. In one letter, she wrote bitterly of how a small group of New York men exercised so much power over
what was written and thought in this country. Independence and success
had not brought a cessation to Mary's struggles.*

---

Not every day was difficult. Jane managed to pull herself away from her
quest for a couple of long, lazy afternoons at the Escobar ranch. She sat on
their deeply shaded porch, sipping chilled homemade wine and looking
out beyond the carefully tended vegetable patch of corn, beans, peppers,
tomatoes and chili, to the rows of trellised grape vines.

Rosie still lived here with her parents, but now, her children and
husband Tomas, when he wasn't at Cerro Gordo, shared the rambling old
house. The old folks still worked the land, Mrs. Escobar in her vegetable
garden and Mr. Escobar in his vineyard. Despite Prohibition, no one had
interfered with his tending of the sweet, red uvas. Probably because the
wine Escobar drew from them was so delicious and because he poured it
freely for visitors and friends.

"Emma will be here later," remarked Rosie, as she rocked her young-
est, Maria, to try to lull the girl into an afternoon nap. "Her little ones love
Juan. Ever since he got back, they keep nagging her to bring them here.
He's teaching Alejandro to rope."

Jane looked over to the corral at the other side of the house, where
Juan Escobar had a spirited gray mare on a rope. He was coaxing her to

circle the paddock, the taut rope moving round and round like the hands of a clock. But this was a haywire clock with a spring loose, because every quarter of an hour or so on the clock face she would start shaking her head and stomping her feet in protest. Juan waited until she finished, then continued easing her forward.

"He's good," observed Jane.

"Yes, he is," agreed Rosie. "Your uncle is a fine *vaquero*," she cooed to the silky black head, damp with afternoon heat.

Jane watched Juan begin to draw close to the mare. He was shirtless, and even from where she sat, she could see the muscles standing out in his brown back as he climbed one hand over another on the rope. Suddenly, without Jane quite seeing how he'd done it, Juan was on the horse's back, knees and ankles hugging the surprised animal's torso, fingers braiding themselves through her mane. The furious mare reared and bucked, charging around the corral, trying to throw him off, but he stayed put, moving with her, side to side, up and down, allowing little air to pass between his body and hers. Finally she tired and began to calm. He pulled sharply on the rope bridal to turn her, and they trotted together toward the barn.

"He should get married," said Rosie lazily. Maria had completely collapsed on the shoulder of her mother, who was half-asleep herself. Jane smiled—this wasn't the first time since Jane had begun visiting again that Rosie or one of her parents had expressed the desire to see Juan wed. She knew that, in their eyes, Juan's lack of wife and children at his age was a failing of almost incomprehensible dimension.

The Escobars, and most of the other Mexicans she'd met, loved children. In fact, they seemed to regard them as the very purpose of life. Rosie hadn't always thought this way, Jane reflected. But now, having settled back into the only life that had been allowed her, she seemed contented, and there was even a whiff of superiority about her tone of voice when she addressed her unmarried brother and friend.

Jane leaned back and closed her eyes. The heat and wine were drugging her, and she was longing for Jed. It had been more than four months since she'd last seen him. Too long. And their most recent exchange of letters hadn't been completely satisfactory. His response to her explanations of why she had made the decision to return to Owens Valley for a time was not as encouraging as she had expected. His reproach had been gentle, however, and cushioned by sweet words about their future, about how they'd be married when the job in Cairo was over, which wouldn't be much longer now.

## Chapter 19

Jane's frustration, at least in regard to reporting, was relieved one morning in early November. She had risen from the desk she now shared with Bucky Porter, gathered her coat and hat, and was about to head out to her car, when Chalfant put a hand on her arm.

"Best stay put this morning. And keep an eye out the front window."

"You know something? Something's going to happen?"

"Maybe."

She returned his noncommittal look with pretend annoyance. "Look here," she said, moving to the front window and wiping a hand over the glass in a broad arc. She held the grimy hand out to her editor. "If you want me to do that, you'll have to clean it, say, at least once every five years or so!"

"Very amusing Miss Bow. Why don't you take your coffee outside and sit on the bench awhile. Give me a hey-ho," he said with a wry smile, "if you see anything unusual."

Jane shrugged, did as requested, and was enjoying the late morning sun and crisp fall air when she glanced to her right and saw, from the far northern end of Main Street, a Model-T approaching ahead of a cloud of dust. As the vehicle entered town, she saw that it was actually at the head of a procession of other cars. "Mr. Chalfant!" She leaned back through the door and, without taking her eyes from the parade, called, "You'd better come out here!"

He joined her on the sidewalk and watched, arms folded in front of his chest, hat pushed back on his head. There must have been 50 to 60 vehicles and, as far as Jane could tell, since they had their window shades drawn, a couple of people in each.

"Let's go," commanded Chalfant, waving her to his battered Davis touring car. Jane climbed in beside him, and they followed the line of cars.

Slowly the procession rumbled southward through Big Pine, Aberdeen and Independence, drawing spectators to the sidewalks as it passed and picking up other tag-along vehicles along the way.

South of Independence, the cars turned right, heading west on a narrow rutted road toward the Alabama Hills. This assemblage of reddish broken boulders, eroded into jutting, fantastical shapes, stood out at the foot of the Sierra in sharp contrast to those austere gray peaks.

The area owed its name to a nearby mining claim established by rebel sympathizers during the Civil War in honor of the ship *Alabama*, which had sunk the Union's *Hatteras*. Kearsarge, one of the Sierra peaks looming above the hills, owed its name to a gold mine established by Union supporters in honor of the ship that later sank the *Alabama*.

The caravan snaked through the hills until it reached the Alabama Gates, a place on the aqueduct where weirs enabled water to be released from the main canal, down a spillway to the desert floor. Used during wet seasons to release excess water and reduce the pressure on the siphons taking water southward, the gates hadn't been operated in years now, owing to the drought.

One after another, the cars pulled up near the gatehouse. It was a wood-frame shack built atop a squat cement block structure with a narrow arch at center flanked by two wider ones. Chalfant stopped alongside the other cars, and he and Jane got out and stood with hands over their eyes as shields from the noon-day sun, peering at the assembly of vehicles, motionless as dead beetles. Other spectators, coming in behind them, did the same. Then, as if by silent signal, the doors of the procession vehicles opened, and about a hundred men got out and walked over to the slope. They were unmasked, and Jane recognized the leader, Mark Watterson.

Several of the men, including Watterson, climbed up to the control house and took hold of the huge wheels, turning them to open the gates below. The wheels squealed, and then there was a loud gurgle: A cascade of water surged out of the gatehouse arches, splashing down the spillway and out across the sandy ground, its force carving an impromptu stream bed in the general direction of Owens Lake.

"Hey, get out of there you hooligans! You can't do that!" The gatekeeper darted from the shack.

As he ran to and fro waving his arms, first at this man, then at that one, they ignored him, standing stoically with arms across chests, looking out at the flood of escaping water, faces resolute. The shouts of the gate-keeper turned to sputters. He had probably spent years at his solitary post with only mountain lions, rodents, scorpions and snakes for company— and now this. He slumped, red-faced, sweating and still sputtering onto a boulder. As if the defeat of this little man were a victory indeed, cheers rang out from the onlookers, then people began laughing and clapping, and gradually a roar of approval rose from the crowd.

"This amount of water will fairly cut off the flow to Los Angeles," observed Chalfant. "The city can't let it go on for long, but these men look like they mean to stay awhile. Let's get back to town."

They sped back the way they'd come, Chalfant talking excitedly the whole way. "This is real news, and I wanna be the first to print it, and you oughta get a story ready for Loewenthal just after we go to press. Unless I'm figurin wrong, most of these guys will still be here tomorrow mornin, so unless you hear from me otherwise, you head back here first thing. I'll do the same."

---

When Jane returned to the Bow ranch that evening, Alice was baking bread, a task she usually undertook mornings rather than at supper time. The kitchen windows were steamed up, and the table was covered with a dozen loaf pans of rising dough.

"Your Pa's washin up now, so you best get about it too. We'll have our supper in the other room, just as if it was Sunday noon."

"Ma, what's all this for?"

"For the men at the aqueduct."

"So you know about it! When did you find out?"

"Minty Cartwright was on the telephone to me not an hour after it happened. I expect everyone in the valley knows by now." She nodded at her daughter, a slight smile turning up the corners of her lips. "Minty's boy Joe says he saw you and Mr. Chalfant there." Alice toweled off her floured hands and glanced back at the stove. "Now get on up there and wash up please Janey. Supper's already a might overdone."

At supper, Jane recounted what she had seen at the Alabama Gates. Alice asked a spate of questions about who had been there and what they'd done. Ben listened with interest, but said little.

"Chalfant told me to go back there in the morning. Do you want to come with me?" Janey asked her parents.

"Not me, got chores here to see to," answered her Ma, "but you can take the bread. I was going to give it to Minty, but seeing as you'll be going, that'll save me a trip to her place. The men are asking for meat and whiskey, so Minty and some of the other women plan to take supplies over to them tomorrow."

"I'd be happy to take it. How about you Pa?"

"I don't think they have much need of me at this point, Jane. From what you said, they've already got near a hundred men, and it only took a few to turn the weir gates open. Now they're all standing around waiting for a picnic basket to arrive!"

Ben smiled and winked at his wife. She sniffed in pretended offense and tapped a finger on the table in his direction. "Well now mister, the more women there, the more peaceable the day is likely to go. I don't imagine Los Angeles is going to send men up there with guns if they know ladies are around. And, anyway, Sheriff Collins's wife is likely to be one of those serving up the beans and bacon."

"I suppose you're right my dear." Ben beamed at her, appreciating as always the astounding mix of pluck, beauty and brains that was his darling Alice.

"Pa, it's good, though, isn't it that they're facing up to the city in a peaceable manner?" asked Jane. "It's like what Mr. Thoreau wrote about—you read to us about civil disobedience, remember, from *Harper's* magazine? And now over there in India, Mr. Gandhi is leading people, men and women, just like at the Alabama Gates, to stand their ground and resist peaceably. I mean, isn't it better," she finished her thought quietly, looking down at her plate, "than dynamite?"

"Yes, of course it is, Janey, much better." Ben reached out and placed his hand over his daughter's. "Let's hope that little hole blown in the side of the aqueduct and this peaceful demonstration will be enough to convince the city we've got a right to live and farm our crops up here too."

He patted her hand before withdrawing his to finish his supper.

Jane arrived at the Alabama Gates around half past eight the next morning, laden with two large baskets. The occupied area had been fenced off from the road with barbed wire. A rifle-armed sentry let her through. Several large poles had been erected with spotlights to illuminate the camp and road during the previous night.

Chalfant came over to meet her, lifting the cloth from one of the baskets and poking his head underneath to inhale the yeasty, sweet aroma of fresh-baked bread. He relieved Jane of her burden, shoving a newspaper into her hand instead, talking rapidly as they walked over to a makeshift plank table where two women were serving a line of men from pots of coffee and pans of biscuits baked with thick slices of ham.

One of them was Minty Cartwright, and the other was Nellie Bellamy, a nice neighbor of Mary's who had often taken care of Ruth when Mary went out for her treks into the mountains. Nellie looked quite a bit older and stouter than back then, but she still had curly, mostly red hair. Jane greeted Mrs. Cartwright and received a hug from Mrs. Bellamy, her throat tightening at the kind woman's touch, which brought back memories of the long-ago days when they had brought Ruth to her. Where was little Ruth now?

"What do you think of the headline?" Chalfant tapped the paper in her hand as they moved away from the table. Jane unfolded and held out last evening's edition of the *Inyo Register*:

### AN AMERICAN COMMUNITY DRIVEN TO
### THE DEFENSE OF ITS RIGHTS

"It's good, it's just right." She nodded her approval, scanning the article about the previous day's events.

"Did you get to Loewenthal?" he asked her.

"Yes, I filed a story yesterday afternoon. Mr. Loewenthal said it was a bit different from what they'd been hearing down there—about an armed takeover. I didn't see any guns yesterday, did you Mr. Chalfant?"

"Well, if they have 'em, they're keepin 'em well hidden. The point of this little shindig is to attract sympathy not censure."

All morning people kept arriving, including whole families, lugging baskets of food and piles of blankets. Shopkeepers from Bishop, Big Pine and Independence came with beef, pork and chicken, which were put on stakes over fire pits. By noon, the mouthwatering smell of barbecued meat saturated the crisp fall air, and Chalfant estimated the crowd had grown to well over 500.

Walking among the new arrivals, Chalfant spotted and called out to Reverend Dickey, the Baptist minister from Bishop. "I'm surprised to see you participating in this illegal activity preacher," teased Chalfant.

Dickey smiled and waved a hand toward the clusters of folks milling about and seated on blankets. "I'm here because my entire congregation appears to be here. I don't often get an opportunity on any day but Sunday to corral them together like this."

Jane saw Mrs. Parker walking on the arm of her husband and waved a hello. The old couple returned the greeting and nodded to Chalfant. "I chanced to meet her on the train at Williams," Jane whispered to the editor. "I was on my way here from the Grand Canyon, and she was coming from Winslow. We had a nice conversation."

"Rumor has it she and Cyril are having trouble making the mortgage payments on their farm, and she was out there asking for help from her brother Herluff," said Chalfant. "I sure hate to see folks getting on in years, who've worked their whole lives, hard-pressed for money like that. But that's exactly what's going to happen to more and more homesteaders if this drought doesn't stop and Los Angeles doesn't see reason."

"Is it true the Wattersons hold mortgages on most of the property in the valley? I mean, someone told me that since the end of the war a lot of folks have become indebted to them."

"Well, that's right that with the recession and drought a lot of folks are having trouble making ends meet, but if the person who told you that was implying the Wattersons are taking advantage of the situation, he's dead-wrong. More like they're the only ones extending a lifeline to strugglin folks. Without a firm agreement with Los Angeles guaranteeing enough water will stay in the valley to support agriculture, all the other banks in the county and state have bolted like jackrabbits in tall grass. It's only the Wattersons willing to extend credit. And they've been extending it and extending it. If they weren't, you'd hear tell of a whole lot of foreclosures across this valley."

The crowd stirred, and they looked up the slope, to where Mark Watterson had just climbed atop the gatehouse. When people quieted down, he addressed them in a loud, friendly voice.

"My brother Wilfred extends his greetings to one and all. He isn't with us because he has left the valley for a few days on a mission very much in our interest. I can't tell you about it yet, but I can say that, if we hold steady and firm here, united in our quest for justice, I expect to bring you good news very soon!"

Cheers rang out, and some folks jumped to their feet, waving hats in the air. Then someone yelled, "It's the sheriff!" and someone else, "Sheriff Collins is come!" Everyone turned to see the well-liked, thick-set, ruddy-faced lawman threading his way forward through the crowd.

"Well hello there Sheriff Collins, have you come for the barbecue?" Mark, grinning from ear to ear, swept an arm toward the fire pits.

"Hello there Mark, folks. Now you know I don't want to do this, but it's my duty to serve this notice. His Honor Mr. William D. Dehy, Superior Judge of Inyo County, has granted the city of Los Angeles an injunction that prevents further interference with this aqueduct. Now this here is a temporary restraining order. It means…," he held up a pile of documents, which he began handing out to the crowd, "that you all need to cease and desist, and just go on home now."

Several of the men tore up their copies and threw the scraps into the air. Others grabbed the pile of remaining copies out of the sheriff's hands and tossed it into the spillway. White pages danced for a moment atop tumbling water, then sank and disappeared. Laughter and cheers erupted, as Collins stood there, hands on hips, watching the documents disappear. He was shaking his head, but there was a glimmer of a smile on his face. To show there was no hard feeling, the men who had robbed the sheriff of his documents, now patted him on the shoulder and, guffawing with hilarity, hoisted him up and carried him, as if sitting on a chair, back to his automobile. As the sheriff climbed in and turned the car around to get back on the road, they waved good naturedly, and the rest of the crowd clapped and yelled "Bye now!" "Thanks for coming!"

After that, everything settled down as folks ate and took siestas under blankets that had been laid over ropes to create shade. In the late afternoon, with the sun dipping below the Sierra wall and deep shadows spreading across the valley and eastern mountains, several girls from the Independence high school, wearing khaki band uniforms, carrying brass instruments and dragging a drum, climbed up the slope to just below the gatehouse and began to play "Onward Christian Soldiers." Drowsily, and then with real spirit, their audience joined in.

With dusk descending, campfires popped up all about, mirroring the stars popping up in the dark sky. As Jane took her leave, someone was playing the fiddle.

---

By day three, the eerie lack of further response from Los Angeles was the main topic of discussion at the occupation site. Depending on how folks chose to look at it, the silence was either ominous or encouraging.

What the occupiers of the aqueduct didn't know was that, when informed by the sheriff that the injunction had been ignored, Mulholland had spat a river of expletives, startling even the indomitable Miss Aames, then dispatched Assistant Superintendent Harvey Van Norman and attorney William Matthews, along with two carloads of investigators, to the valley. Matthews had telephoned Sheriff Collins to demand that he and other Inyo County authorities meet their arrival and accompany them to the Alabama Gates.

Instead, Sheriff Collins, warned by townspeople of the potential for violence—"If they try to close the gates, we'll make our own gates with dynamite!"—hurriedly drove south to intercept the Los Angeles party below Lone Pine.

"They've got women and children and newspaper reporters up there, so don't be going and starting any trouble," he advised them.

"They're the ones that started the trouble…," argued Van Norman.

"I think they're more interested in publicity than in trouble," Matthews cut in. "The last thing we want to do is give cause for the newspapers to portray the city as a Goliath to the valley's David. We're going to have to go about this in another way."

They climbed back into their automobiles and returned to the city, where Matthews was at first hard-pressed to subdue and persuade Mulholland. "Chief, you need to talk to the governor," the attorney argued. "If we go up there, the newspapers will say we're the oppressor.

If Governor Richardson sends in state troopers, they'll say he's acting to restore law and order."

The next day Jane was back at the Alabama Gates with another basket, this time packed with a half dozen of Alice's apple pies. Families who had slept out under the stars stood around campfires, shivering with coats pulled tight around them, but waiting cheerfully for hot coffee, flapjacks, eggs and bacon. Some hearty souls squatted by the spillway and reached down into the cascade still rushing out across the desert to scoop up handfuls of icy water for face washing.

The road brought a steady stream of cars, disgorging their passengers, some folks returning after having gone home for the night, others arriving for the first time, to participate or just to gawk. Jane was amazed to see some people unloading wagons carrying wood-burning stoves, tents and beds!

"They mean to camp here, whole families, until the city gives in," concluded Chalfant. He had just arrived too, and was in an unusually excited state. "Practically every store on Main Street is closed! There's a sign on the flagpole at the center of town: 'If I'm not on the job, you can find me at the Aqueduct!'"

"Come on," he continued, gesturing toward the gatehouse. "I've got news for Mark, and you'll want to hear it too."

When they got there, Mark and a couple of the men who'd had a hand in opening the gates, were combing down wet hair. Another man was shaving carefully, having no mirror.

"Look here," Chalfant called, drawing a notebook from an inside coat pocket and waving it at the men, who gathered round, towels and razor in hand. Jane hung back far enough not to seem too forward, but close enough to hear. "The word is out! I've received telephone calls from reporters in San Francisco, Los Angeles, Denver, Chicago, St. Louis, New York and Boston. Newspapers all over the nation are picking up the story, and…" He paused, eyes twinkling. "Telegrams have come in from a paper in Paris and another one in Stockholm." His regard swept the circle of wide-eyed men. "You did it! You've fired the 'shot heard round the world,' just like on old Lexington Green!"

They erupted in hoots and hollers, slapping each other and Chalfant on the back. "Listen to this," the editor continued. "*The Literary Digest* is running a cover story, and here's what they're saying: 'The reputation of Los Angeles for decent dealing throughout the entire country now hangs in the balance.'"

More hoots and back pounding. "We ought to tell everybody here," urged Chalfant. "It'll keep their spirits high."

"Let's wait until this afternoon," suggested Mark. "That way you can bring us another update, Willie, and I expect I'll have some other good news to share by then too."

---

"This armed seizure of a municipal water system by a mob of anarchists violates local and state law. It's interference with a public utility, a more serious matter even than interference with the United States mail, and it must be nipped in the bud!"

Mulholland had the face of a bulldog, Matthews thought, as he delivered this diatribe. They were in the chief's inner office. The superintendent and his attorney sat in a pair of armchairs, with Governor Richardson and his aide in another pair of chairs facing them. By a stroke of luck, the governor had been down from Sacramento, lending his weight to the campaign of a Republican state senator running for re-election in a year when the Progressive Party challenger was nipping at his heels.

"We're requesting that you send in state troopers immediately," Mulholland concluded his appeal.

"Is the city's water supply in danger?" asked the governor.

Matthews observed the portly man with balding pate, yellowish mustache and white eyebrows that spread like wings from the frown lines above his nose. The brown eyes below them were squinting with annoyance. Uh oh, thought Matthews. But Mulholland, insensible to the signals, continued down the war path.

"Damn right it is! We're releasing as much additional water as we can from Haiwee Reservoir, but it's already low because of the drought. If this goes on much longer, the public is going to feel it. Governor, I demand that the leaders of this insurrection be arrested!"

Richardson turned to his aid, a slender young man who perched on the edge of the adjacent chair. "Chester, what do you think?"

"Sir, I've been in touch with Sheriff Collins down there, and he assures me that if two men are indicted, two hundred will step forward to take their place. Judge Dehy, the superior court judge that issued the injunction, has since disqualified himself for reasons of personal interest." The young man peered over his spectacles at Mulholland and Matthews. "He'll be of no more use to you."

"Hmmm," said the governor, and Matthews knew what was coming. The man, who had once been a Progressive, but had gained statewide office as a Republican, had proved to be a deeply conservative governor. Immediately upon taking office, Richardson had embarked on sweeping reforms with the aim of cutting expenditures he deemed wasteful. He'd even proposed closing two universities, saying the state couldn't afford to deplete its coffers on education, an initiative Matthews had been pleased to see defeated. He's going to do nothing, thought Matthews. Doing nothing means he spends nothing, and he risks nothing in negative publicity ahead of the election.

"Let's hold off a bit, shall we," said Richardson, folding his hands over his round middle. "There's no win to be had here through confrontation." He looked over at Mulholland. "I would advise the city to return to the bargaining table to try to work out an equitable arrangement with the valley. I feel certain, gentlemen, that you have not yet exhausted all avenues to a peaceable and amicable settlement of differences."

The governor stood up. "And now we really must be going." His aide bobbed up too as if attached by a string.

Matthews saw them out, past Miss Aames's desk to the door. When they'd left, he turned back toward her and they exchanged tense looks. Augusta Aames knew that the next thing her boss was likely to do was to look at the stack of newspapers she had put on the corner of his desk.

Sure enough, there came the sound of a fist slamming down on wood, and Mulholland stormed out of his office. "Pure hogwash! Traitors, all of them!" he sputtered, waving the morning's edition of the *Times* at Matthews before tossing it into the wastebasket next to Augusta's desk. He strode back into his office and slammed the door.

Matthews didn't have to retrieve the paper from the bin; he knew what it said. Newspapers in Los Angeles and San Francisco that had originally deplored the lawlessness of the rebellion had changed their tune over the past 24 hours. Now they were printing sympathetic human interest stories about the occupiers, portraying the valley as "an oppressed pioneer community" and the event as a "celebration of civic solidarity." And the *Times*, once rabid in its derision of the Owens Valley, had, with its latest editorial, taken the softest line of all.

"I've never seen him so beside himself," said Matthews quietly to Augusta. "He's taking it very personally."

"Well, newspapers are fickle, Mr. Matthews." She looked up at him, her forehead creased with lines. "After all he's done for the city, I really think they ought to support him."

Mulholland roared back out and pointed a finger at Augusta. "Tell Van Norman to double the crews on the dams!"

The chief was thinking, Matthews knew, that the sooner the dams could be finished and their reservoirs filled, the better. If not even the governor would step in to stop interference with the aqueduct up north, the water flow to the city was at risk. They needed to have a reserve down here, enough for at least a year's worth of consumption to ensure the city never went thirsty.

The St. Francis Dam was still months away from providing that. The other dam, to be called the Mulholland, though the chief rarely referred to it that way, was closer to completion. It was located in the hills above the Hollywoodland sign. Mulholland had taken special pride in the design of that dam, which, with its white parapets, balustrades and tower, seemed fitting for its location near the land of fantasy. When the reservoir was filled, it would look like a moat below a castle.

---

At about two in the afternoon, a contingent of Watterson family members arrived at the Alabama Gates. Mark's wife and their three young children came through the crowd, smiling and greeting their neighbors. Old Mrs. Watterson, still walking straight but slowly, came on the arm of her daughter Isabel. Elizabeth, the youngest of her daughters, was also there with her husband and their two children, a boy and a girl, who seemed, to Jane's eye, to be about 10 and 12 years old. Chalfant went over to tip his hat to Elizabeth and shake her husband's hand. They stood talking for a few minutes, then Chalfant returned to where Jane stood.

"That's Jacob Clausen. He's an engineer for Reclamation. Always been on the valley's side, and, I'll tell you this, next to Mulholland, he knows more about dam construction than any man alive!"

Jane made a mental note for future reference, then turned her attention to the gatehouse. Mark Watterson and his lieutenants had climbed atop the structure again, and he was preparing to address the crowd.

"Neighbors and friends, I have encouraging news—and I do mean news!" He held a newspaper high in the air above his head. "Newspapers all over the nation and the world have picked up our story and are calling for Los Angeles to deal with us in a reasonable manner! Even our old enemy, the *Los Angeles Times*, which just two days ago called my brother and me 'mobsters,' and tried to link us with the Ku Klux Klan, has now turned with the tide. Let me read to you from the story that appeared on the front page of that paper this morning:

> **It is to be remembered that these farmers are not anarchists nor bomb-throwers, but in the main, honest, earnest, hard-working American citizens who look upon Los Angeles as an octopus about to strangle out their lives. They have put themselves hopelessly in the wrong by taking the law into their own hands but that is not to say that there has not been a measure of justice on their side of the argument. We call on the Public Service Commission to pay for the suffering its policies have caused. This is not a time to drive the hardest possible bargain. The city can afford to be liberal in its settlement with these pioneers whose work of half a century it will undo."**

He finished and thrust the paper into the air again and again, as cheers came in waves with his movements. Then he gestured for quiet and waited for the moment to deliver the message of victory.

"I can tell you now that Wilfred has been in Los Angeles these past two days meeting with city leaders, including a group of bankers known as the Clearinghouse Association. They have pledged to do everything in their power to see that an equitable settlement is reached with our valley!…Quiet now, quiet…Let me read to you the telegram we have just received from my brother: 'If the object of the crowd at the spillway is to bring their wrongs to the attention of the citizens of Los Angeles, they have done so one hundred percent. The press and minds of the people here will be open from now on and I feel sure that the wrongs done will be remedied. I have the assurance that strong influences here will be brought to bear on the situation to see that justice is done.'"

Unrestrained cheers of elation and relief now broke across the crowd like wild horses bursting out of a corral. Mark no longer tried to hobble them. He beamed and waved, shook the hands of his lieutenants and then gleefully jumped and slid down the hill to join in the celebration with his family and friends.

In the midst of this exuberance, word ricocheted around the crowd that Tom Mix was coming! Strains of music sounded from afar, and many people ran over to the road, straining their necks to see. Indeed, within a few minutes, the movie star, who had been filming in the Alabama Hills nearby, a favorite location for Hollywood directors of Westerns, was disembarking from his limousine.

Mix was closely followed by an entourage of other cars, from which emerged his camera crew and personal staff, as well as by a horse-drawn wagon carrying a mariachi band playing tunes of Old Mexico. This was the signal for a party, which was to go on most of the night.

The next day, the spillway of the Alabama Gates was once again dry, and the victorious citizens of Owens Valley had returned to their usual occupations.

---

"Oh my stars!" Alice brought a flour-dusted hand to her lips as she examined the immense box her daughter had just lugged into the house.

"It's from Chris!" exclaimed Jane. "Look, it says to open now. Where are the scissors, Ma?"

Alice set the bowl of cake batter aside and walked over to the cupboard to retrieve a pair from a drawer. She handed them over, then watched wide-eyed as Janey cut the triple-wrapped, knotted string and pulled apart the box lid layers to reveal a cornucopia of treasures within. Brightly wrapped gifts tied with blossoms of ribbon, a tinned ham, sack of pipe tobacco, huge box of chocolates, bottle of champagne and, inside a lightweight wooden box, bolts of exquisite ecru lace and bobbins of satin ribbon in a rainbow of colors.

"Oh my stars!" said Alice.

The holiday season had a special savor that year for the Bows and their neighbors. With the city reopening negotiations on the equitable distribution of Owens River water, a sense of peace and joy tinted their days like the pink wash of rising sun on the mountain snowfields.

The many gaily wrapped packages from Chris were an extravagance that in some part, Janey believed, was meant to compensate for her brother's lack of support and presence during the struggle. As she knelt by the Christmas tree, disentangling glittery streamers from a velvet box, prying it open to discover a gold and garnet ring, she knew Chris was trying to make amends. They'd had a rare argument just before she'd moved back home. He'd thought she was absolutely wrong to do it, but now, she suspected, he'd changed his mind, now that everything was working out. There was also a cushy, brown fedora for Ben and a carved ivory cameo broach for Alice, gifts which seemed to stun her parents a little.

Yet the most charmed moments, to Jane's mind, and she thought her parents felt the same, were spent reviving simple pleasures from earlier days. Ben popped corn in a pan on the hearth and baked potatoes in the hot ashes while Alice mixed up molasses candy, which she and Jane pulled into fanciful animal shapes. At night the little amber beasts lay in a tray by the window; by morning the frosty air seeping under the sill had crystallized and hardened them.

Jane felt a sweet pull backward vying with the sweet pull forward she had felt since Jed's present had arrived from Cairo. A bright red rectangle of fine silk, embroidered with gold flowers from which hung small, jangling disks of gold. He had sent it to her care of the *Register*, so she hadn't faced the embarrassment of trying to explain the gift to her parents. She could, of course, have claimed it was a large shawl, though she knew—he'd written it on the card—it was to be worn directly over her naked skin.

# Chapter 20

The glow faded in the New Year. Negotiations between the valley sputtered, then stalled. And despite its assurances, the Clearinghouse Association of Los Angeles bankers offered little assistance. Meanwhile, agents for the city had not been idle. They had continued to purchase land options and water rights wherever they could.

In May, with negotiations entirely broken down, the Watterson brothers hosted a dinner at the Bishop Creek Hotel. To Chalfant, it was an echo of another dinner he had attended more than 20 years before when the valley had first mobilized to try to prevent Los Angeles from taking Owens River water. We're back here again, he thought grimly, only now we're struggling to keep the city from destroying the valley altogether.

He glanced around the room. Here were some of the same attendees as back then, including Gus Kispert, a wealthy rancher who'd helped with the citizens' petition the valley had sent to the US Secretary of Interior. The other farmers and ranchers were mostly from the ditch associations that hadn't sold out yet. But agricultural interests were in the minority; most of the men in the room this time were townspeople. While some of the ranchers and farmers who had sold to the city were leasing back their land, without water rights, and staying on, most were abandoning their farms and moving out of the valley. Merchants and other townspeople had become increasingly concerned about the loss of business and community.

"The city isn't offering to buy us out, so what in the hell are we gonna do?!" said Carl Fredeker, owner of the Bishop Creamery, sitting down next to Chalfant.

"I've got some news," advised Chalfant. "Wait to hear it."

As Fredeker and a few more latecomers settled at the table, Chalfant continued to scan the room, looking at the worried faces and thinking, yes, the center of gravity of this thing is shifting away from agriculture to townsfolk. At the back, in a chair against the wall, sat a sole female, Jane Bow, attending in her capacity as Chalfant's reporter. Since returning to the valley, she'd let her wavy bob grow out, and now the cascade of light brown curls was tied carelessly with a cord at the nape of her neck. She held her head high, hazel-green eyes calm and watchful. She's turned into a comely woman, he thought, and though not yet married, was far from the image of an old maid. Then another thought came to him: My God, she couldn't have been more than seven or eight years old when we had that first meeting here. Hell, I'm the one getting old!

Wilfred Watterson finished shaking hands and stood at one end of the table to address the attendees. "Gentlemen, and young lady," he nodded at Jane, "thank you for coming tonight. As you all know by now, the negotiations with Los Angeles are getting us nowhere, and the Los Angeles Clearinghouse Association has reneged on its pledge to help bring about justice for the valley. But we're not finished yet, not by a long shot. Mr. Chalfant has some important news for us," he gave a slight, mock bow to the *Inyo Register* editor, and sat down.

"This will be in tomorrow morning's edition of the *Register*," Chalfant began. "Today, the California State Legislature passed the Reparations Act, which authorizes compensation for…" He pulled a slip of paper from his vest pocket and read, "…'injury, damage, destruction or decrease in value of any such property, business, trade, profession or occupation resulting from or caused by the taking of any such land or waters.'"

Chalfant finished reading, looked up and summarized in his own words. "This basically means that what the DWP's lawyer Matthews told us, that Los Angeles can't legally consider paying reparations to the Owens Valley, that argument no longer holds water!" He sat down with aplomb amid appreciative clapping and shouts.

Wilfred Watterson was back on his feet now, his usually composed face tight with passionate purpose. "This is the valley's last and best stand! We have the tacit support of the state legislature now, and Los Angeles well knows it. If we put forward an aggressive but justifiable proposal for reparations, detailing the damage to as many business and agrarian interests in the valley as possible, there's a good chance the city will balk. It's very likely to force them back to the bargaining table, in good faith this time. And if that doesn't work, at least we won't walk away from this valley and our life's work empty handed!"

He raised his hands to acknowledge and then calm the uproar of agreement. "Now, I propose we create an Owens Valley Reparations Association and get to work. The task ahead is to start putting together the reparations numbers, which I think should be organized into six categories of damages: individual, business, occupational, professional, real property,

personal property and trades. We'll need one or more of you to volunteer
to be responsible for gathering the information in each of these. Go out
and talk to your neighbors, business associates and customers. Get figures
that are supported by documents, bills of sale and so on.

"And this is most important…We've got to stem the tide of people
selling land and water options to city agents. Talk to people before the city
gets to them with an offer. Convince them they'll get a far better deal by
adding their claim to the organized reparations proposal than by going
it alone trying to negotiate with those sharks. The more we stick together
and don't go off making our own deals, the more leverage we'll have to
negotiate the best deal for everybody."

The excitement in the room channeled into industrious energy, as the
work was divided up and the men with assignments broke off and walked
out in small groups, talking in low voices. Chalfant came to Jane after
saying goodbye to the Wattersons. She'd been so quiet, no one but her
editor had remembered her presence.

As he approached, she studied his face. The encouraging expression
he had worn during the meeting now faded. Chalfant slumped down into
the chair beside her.

"Is there something you didn't tell them?" Jane asked in a low voice.

"No, I told them everything, all the facts I know," he answered
glumly, looking at the hands hanging limply in his lap. "It's just a way of
looking at the facts, I suppose." He paused, and then looked up at her.
"It's true there's a good chance the threat of a big reparations bill, endorsed
by the state legislature, could make Los Angles deal squarely with the
valley. But what if it doesn't? Do you realize what that means if it doesn't?
It means we've come to the end, Jane. It means we're taking a hand in
negotiating the death of this valley. Folks here will be picking over the
carcasses of their own dreams."

Jane was stunned. That meaning hadn't been hidden from anyone
in the room, but no one had said it square like that, and if they'd thought
it, they'd kept this sorrow to themselves, as Chalfant had done, until the
business of the meeting was over. Perhaps, like him, they were now talking
quietly, mournfully to one another as they made their way home.

"You know it's funny, but one person knew it from the start."
Chalfant was speaking in a near-whisper again. "As I recall, you knew

her pretty well, didn't you—Mary Austin?" Jane nodded, and he went on. "Well, just about the time we sent the citizens' petition to Washington DC, before we knew which side Roosevelt was gonna come in on, she already believed the valley was done for. She told me she even went down to Los Angeles and told that to Mulholland face to face. Now can you imagine that?"

"I can, as it happens," Jane said quietly. "I was pretty young then, but I remember the day she came back from her trip. That was the day she left Mr. Austin and took Ruth to the school in Santa Clara. She told me before she left that I'd better leave the valley as soon as I could. She said there was nothing here for me."

"Wheeew!" Chalfant let out a long breath. "I sure as shootin hope she was wrong."

"I do too."

After a long pause, Jane spoke. "Mr. Chalfant, have you been in contact with Mrs. Austin these years since she left?"

"Yes, we've exchanged the occasional letter."

"I thought so. Me too. In fact, we renewed our relationship not long after you published my first article in the *Register*. But there are some things I've wondered, things she's not been forthcoming about or I've not felt it my place to press such inquiries."

He observed her, dreading what he knew she was about to ask, waiting for her to gather courage.

"Mr. Chalfant, do you know what became of Mr. Austin and Ruth?"

"Of course, of course, you'd want to know," Chalfant replied softly, studying his hands. "I do have some information for you Janey. Wallace Austin took a job with a company in Death Valley, it might have been mining, I don't know. But I don't think much came of it, and I'm not sure where he is now." He raised his eyes to hers. "I do know that he divorced his wife back in 1914, charged her with willful abandonment without cause. Mary told me he didn't want to do it, always wanted her back, but that she had insisted."

"And Ruth?"

He sighed heavily, forming the words with reluctance. "She's dead, Janey. She died in 1918 at that school in Santa Clara, of spasmodic asthma. Mrs. Austin's recounting seemed a bit confused, so I got in touch with the school physician myself. He told me Ruth's condition had been aggravated by malnutrition. Her body had sort of wasted away, as they had a difficult time getting her to eat."

"But she loved to eat!" Jane broke in. "She adored cakes and pies and muffins!"

"Maybe, when she was at home. Mrs. Austin was a darn fine cook of course. Maybe she was just too lonely at that school...Janey," he put a hand on hers, "Mary Austin never visited Ruth in the 14 years she was there. She said the doctors recommended against it. Better for the children, they said."

Tears gushed from Jane's eyes now, running down her cheeks, and she dug her fingernails into her palms. "I should have gone there, I should have visited her!"

Chalfant put an arm around her and said gently but firmly, "No, you shouldn't have. It wasn't your place, wasn't your burden. You were too young to stop it or fix it. And don't hate Mrs. Austin for it either. I guess she did what she could. We all do what we can in this life, and sometimes it's not enough or maybe it's even the wrong thing, but there's never any going back, and blaming gets in the way of living."

He withdrew his arm and reached into his worn, sagging briefcase. "Did she send you a copy of this yet? It's her latest book, *The Land of Journeys' Ending*." Chalfant handed Jane a thick volume. "It's about New Mexico."

Jane stared at the paper jacket, which had an illustration of horse riders in front of a flat-topped mountain below a deep blue, cloud-spotted sky. "No, she never sends me her books," whispered Jane. "Usually I buy a copy. I read *The Ford* of course."

"Yes, that was an interesting one." Chalfant said pensively. They were speaking of an Austin novel that was a thinly cloaked story of the valley's battle with Los Angeles. Mary had changed the villain to a San Francisco engaged in deceit and double-dealing to steal oil and water from an imaginary rural community. She'd given the novel a happy ending, with the heroine, a young woman who chooses to excel in business instead of love, winning back her family's ranch. But the valley Mary wrote about in this book didn't seem much like the Owens Valley to Jane. Mary's words, which struck her as stiff and mannered, no longer captured the feeling of the place.

Chalfant tapped a finger on the book in Jane's hands. "I read an article in *Literary Review* about this one. The reviewer said it was 'treacherous, waiting to overwhelm with its abundant poetry.' For my part, I must say I find the language somewhat akin to *The Land of Little Rain*—always liked that one, and not just because it's about the valley. This new book is something like it, though now Mrs. Austin writes with much less economy of expression." He chuckled. "Anyway, thought you might like to borrow it."

"Yes," she said, "thank you." So this was the book Mary had been telling her about for months. Though now based in New York, Mary traveled often, crisscrossing the country on lecture tours. During one of these, she'd been invited to New Mexico to stay at the ranch of Mabel Dodge Luhan, a friend who had married a full-blooded Indian from Taos pueblo. The wealthy socialite's power of attraction for the intelligentsia had not dimmed with the relocation and unconventional union. Mary had gushed about meeting writer D.H. Lawrence, painter Georgia O'Keefe and their like at the ranch. And she had told Jane she'd fallen in love with the nearby town of Santa Fe.

"She's planning to move to Santa Fe and build a house there," Jane remarked. "She says she's going to call it *Casa Querida*."

"Well, well, finally headin back to the West," was all the editor had to say about that.

Jane put the book in her satchel and thanked him. They walked together silently out onto the street, where Chalfant handed her into her roadster, waved goodbye and turned up the street toward his office.

---

While the Reparations Association prepared its proposal, daily life in Owens Valley appeared to settle back into a normal state. There was hope for a favorable outcome, and valley folk were by nature prone to see good fortune just ahead.

As summer approached, and the valley remained calm, Jane acquiesced to the reassurances of her parents and the urging of Loewenthal to do the interview with Julia Morgan. The architect had been forced by one urgent demand after another from her employer Hearst to cancel several dates, and Jane, caught up in valley events, had finally not sought to reschedule. Now, however, she requested the meeting again, and Morgan agreed to see her. Jane traveled by train to San Francisco, where she met Morgan in her offices at the Merchants Exchange Building on California Street.

"I'm sorry if you were expecting to tour the ranch," Morgan apologized, and Jane noted she referred to the property by the same name its owner used, though the general public now called it "Hearst Castle." She'd arrived to interview Morgan on a Tuesday, and the architect generally traveled up to San Simeon to supervise work on the Hearst estate only on weekends. That was fine with Jane. Plenty of other Los Angeles reporters, including two from her own paper, had visited the castle in recent years, returning with stories about its ever-expanding size and opulence, and the bevy of movie stars who came for the lavish parties hosted by Hearst and his mistress actress Marion Davies. Jane's objective was to write about the architect.

Morgan, a tiny, energetic woman with fine features and large round spectacles, thrust a bony hand into Jane's and shook it firmly. The woman wore a skirted suit over a crisp white blouse with a bright patterned tie at the collar. Wavy, graying hair was pulled back from the broad forehead in a soft chignon. Jane liked her right away.

They passed an hour together in what, to Jane's thinking, was a fascinating conversation. Morgan had been the first woman to graduate from the University of California with a degree in civil engineering. Later she became the first woman to attend and graduate from the École des Beaux-Arts in Paris, after applying three times. Her first application had been refused on the grounds that she was a woman, her second on the grounds of failing the entrance examination.

"They graded my examination paper much stricter than the others," Morgan intimated to Jane, "to make sure I'd fail."

But Morgan had refused to give up. She'd studied harder and taken the exam again six months later. This time her results had been so outstanding in comparison to the other applicants that it had been impossible to deny her. Morgan had been admitted, and in 1902, at age 28, had earned a Master's Degree in Architecture. Two years later, after working for John Galen Howard on projects for the University of California at Berkeley, she had opened her own office on Montgomery Street.

"Two years after that, it was completely demolished in the earthquake," chuckled Morgan.

Clearly this was a woman undeterred by obstacles, thought Jane. Much like Mary Jane Colter and Mary Austin—and, like those accomplished women, she was unmarried.

Morgan was describing her working relationship with Hearst and how the castle had come to be. "It was originally going to be something quite small and rustic," she confided, amused, enjoying the irony.

The land was a ranch Mr. Hearst had inherited from his father. The son had happy childhood memories of family camping trips on the hill at San Simeon, and had returned there again and again as an adult. "When he came to me," recalled Morgan, "he said he was getting a little too old to keep pitching a tent and wanted the comfort of a modest bungalow. Once we started drawing up plans, his vision expanded a bit." Morgan winked at Jane.

Morgan then went on to tell Jane how she'd started with the guest cottages and just kept on building from there. Hearst liked the Spanish Revival style Morgan had used in the design of the *Examiner* offices in Los Angeles, and he had scoured the Iberian peninsula for authentic sources of inspiration.

The restless newspaper magnate's travels had become, however, a source of additional challenges for the architect. "This is not for publication," she intimated to Jane, who respectfully laid her pencil aside, "but after every trip to Europe, he comes back with more historic architectural styles he wants to incorporate into the buildings and more works of art he needs to house. I endeavor to accommodate all of these requests, but there's a danger we'll end up with more of a hodgepodge warehouse than a home."

And artwork wasn't the only thing Hearst purchased during these travels, Morgan revealed. "He's just bought St. Donat's Castle in Wales as a present for Miss Davies and says I need to start planning the renovations!" Morgan rolled her eyes, but Jane saw she was more than a bit delighted by the prospect.

Jane shook her head in wonder at the diminutive woman's energy and her employer's limitless riches. He was, of course, ultimately, Jane's boss too, but she had rarely thought of the bigger-than-life figure on a personal level. How is it, she mused, that a single individual can amass so much wealth when so many people struggle so long and hard?

It wasn't a question pertinent to her article, however, which ran the next week in the *Examiner*. The story earned a measure of praise from Loewenthal, Simon and several other colleagues.

Not much of a splash, but Jane was pleased with it. She returned to the Owens Valley to check in with Chalfant, see her parents and pack up her things. Then she drove her roadster down to Los Angeles. When she got there, the belongings she'd left in her room at Chris's house on Bunker Hill were packed in boxes. His new house in Bel Air was nearly ready, and he anticipated a move within the next few weeks.

"Are you sure you still want to move in with Katharine and Shirley?" he asked, speaking of the two friends Jane planned to live with. Both worked at the *Examiner* as typists. "There's a room for you in the new house, and we can take all this stuff there directly."

No, she wanted to stay downtown and live with her friends. She wanted to go to nightclubs and picture shows with their crowd, forget about problems and disputes and who was right or wrong and just enjoy being young and busy amidst the buzz and bustle of the city. She certainly didn't want to be stranded out there in the hills at the edge of the city with a bunch of wealthy snobs.

Jane didn't say that, of course, to Chris, who was buzzing with his own excitement at the imminent move and his recent decision to leave off the Hollywood starlets and begin courting Miss Dorothy Bradshaw, a young woman from a prominent family. She just placed a hand on his arm and gave it an affectionate squeeze.

"I'll stay with them for the time being, but I'll be out weekends when I can, if you'll have me."

"Of course. How about Ma and Pa, do you think they'll come for a visit?"

"I don't know, Chris. They seem mighty occupied with the ranch and all. Besides, I don't think they'd be comfortable in Bel Air."

"Ummh. I'm glad things have quieted down up there now." They were still awkward talking about the subject, even months after their disagreement.

"Me too. I hope it stays that way. Chalfant told me just before I left that the Reparations Association has submitted its proposal for compensation."

"What happens now?"

"He says the Public Service Commission will look at the figures and probably come back with a counterproposal. It may take some time. And the City Council has to approve whatever they come up with I guess."

He frowned and shook his head slightly. "I just don't know Hazy, I just don't know if they'll pay reparations."

"Well then, there's still time to come to an agreement on division of water."

"Maybe."

That was all he said, and Jane let the conversation die. She didn't particularly fancy talking about it with him. She'd never told her brother all that had happened, and especially not her concerns that their father had been involved in the dynamiting.

---

Jane celebrated Christmas 1925 in the decidedly modest surroundings of the bungalow on Olive Street. She didn't go to Owens Valley because Jed had timed his visit home to coincide with the holidays. She was ecstatic and proud at the prospect of being on his arm for the season's parties and other festivities, thrilled almost to unbelieving that she would actually be dancing in his arms New Year's Eve.

When they weren't out on the town or making the obligatory visit to tour and exclaim over Chris's Bel Air mansion, they spent long, sweaty, wanton nights in Jane's narrow bed. At the station to meet his train, she'd fallen under a spell at first sight of him swinging his long legs onto the platform. Every minute of the cab ride home, she'd wanted so badly to touch him, to slide her hand up his shirt sleeve and touch his skin. He'd held her hand in the dark car, and she'd drawn it onto her lap. Keeping her expression calm, innocently looking ahead should the driver look back, she'd pushed his hand against her and ground her tailbone into the leather seat, feeling the wet spread between her thighs. Neither Shirley nor Katharine had been home, so there'd been no introductions to keep them from her bedroom. Locking the door, they'd pulled at each other's clothes, and he'd shoved her back near-naked onto the bed, pulling her bloomers down slowly as he watched her, undressing himself, releasing his cock, so stiff it sprung out rod-straight, perpendicular from his belly. She moaned and pulled him into her without giving him time to put on the rubber.

"We'd better not do that again," he'd said afterward. "At least, not for a while yet."

Jane knew he was right, but she wasn't sure she even cared anymore. A part of her wanted it to happen. A part of her still wanted to live this life of freedom and be a journalist on a big-city newspaper, but that other part wanted to just let it all go, and have this every night and every morning, have a baby if it should come, and live a different life with Jed. That part was getting ready for a change.

Jed seemed to be feeling it too. The time was coming for them to get started with their life together, he said on the last night of his visit, cradling her in his arms and playfully tonguing her earlobe. The Cairo project had run into some delays and problems, but when it was over, he promised, they'd get married.

"I won't take on any more jobs as a single man."

---

In April, a month when Los Angeles smelled of ocean and orange blossoms, Jane received a call from Chalfant at her desk at the *Examiner*.

"Someone just blew up one of the city's wells outside Bishop!" he told her. Her fingers lurched for a pencil. "This reparations process is taking too damn long," he continued, "and all the while, the city's been drilling more wells to pump more ground water into the aqueduct. Even though we've had some rain this year, farmers are sayin their fields are drying up cause the water table is falling. Hasn't your Pa told you anything about this? If my sources are anywhere near right, they've doubled the amount of pumping over the past couple of years. You should be able to confirm that down there in the city."

"My Pa doesn't say much, just a hello written at the bottom of Ma's letters, and she doesn't like to dwell on problems. Anyway, I'll see what I can do to check the pumping figures. Do you think this dynamite blast is because of the city's response to the reparations proposal?"

Jane had written a small article about it just two days prior. Instead of accepting or arguing the damage estimates submitted by Owens Valley, the Los Angeles Public Service Commission had finally issued its own proposal. It called for the establishment of a 30,000-acre zone in the valley, in which the city would make no further land or water rights purchases. And the commission also pledged that the city would build a paved road through the valley to encourage tourism, which would help the Inyo County economy. Jane had felt sure, as she'd written the words, that the Wattersons and others wouldn't be impressed. But at least, she had counseled herself, there's communication taking place.

"Course it is," Chalfant answered her question. "I'm not saying, understand, that the Owens Valley Reparations Association had anything to do with the blast, but I know they're not going for the city's terms. They're preparing a counter proposal. The latest word I've got is that they're planning to present the city with a choice of three alternatives: First is, they'll accept the 30,000-acre zone, but they want a reparations payment of about $5 million to property owners, including townspeople for loss of business. If the city can't see its way to that, then the second alternative is for the city to purchase the whole irrigation district for $12 million. If Los Angeles says no to that too, then the valley demands the case be put before a disinterested board of arbitration."

"I see," Jane said dumbly, unable to immediately take in all of what this might mean. "Do you know who was involved in the dynamiting Mr. Chalfant?"

"No, I sure don't. The city's kept on pumping and they've kept on buying land and water rights wherever they can. So even though the drought is over, people are getting real angry and panicky up here. I don't think the Reparations Association is behind the dynamiting, but there are some folks on the edges of it who are real difficult to control." He lowered his voice, and Jane could barely hear the words he spoke next. "We've had night riders on the back roads, Janey. A few ranchers who've talked to city agents woke up to find men with masks and torches threatening them if they sell out. Don't mention that to Loewenthal."

"Oh my God!" Jane felt sick.

"Hold on, hold on…" Chalfant had heard the alarm in her voice. He continued briskly, using her press name. "Now look here J. Bow, no one wants to see that happen, and you can help make sure it doesn't. Since the takeover of the Alabama Gates, newspapers and public opinion have been on our side. But now they're trying to turn it around by publishing a lot of propaganda. Have you seen the pamphlet the DWP printed up?"

"I've seen it. In fact, I have it on my desk."

"Well then, you've read their lies. I can't believe they have the out-right gall to talk about all the benefits the aqueduct has brought to the valley. Here, did you read this…" She heard Chalfant shuffling among papers. "Ah, here it is: 'Never in its history has Owens Valley prospered and increased in wealth as it has in the last 20 years!' Can you believe that? It says any decline in fortunes of Owens Valley farmers is due solely to the drought and the postwar slump in agricultural prices! And here, this is the worst part, it says the hostile reaction of the valley is, and I quote, 'the mental reactions of a pioneer community…uninformed and unaccustomed to the ways of the outside world.' The unmitigated gall!"

"I agree it's extremely biased, but what can I do about it?"

"Just write a piece that examines these claims and refutes them with real facts. You've got most of it from when you were up here, and I'll send you some more. If you want me to clear it with Loewenthal, I will."

"No, he should be fine with it, as long as it's balanced."

"That's all I'm asking."

They said goodbye, and Jane went to talk to Loewenthal, who raised no objections as long as she could fit the extra work in with her other assignments. She would, she assured her editor, and went back to her desk. But she felt jumpy the rest of the day, and that evening Jane waited until Loewenthal and the other reporters had left and then telephoned the Bow ranch.

"Janey, what a treat!" The instant pleasure in her mother's voice twist-ed Jane's heart. She hadn't seen her in so long. "Everything fine dear?"

Jane assured her it was, and they talked about this and that for a moment, then Jane asked after Pa.

"He's right here sweetie. I'll pass the phone over."

"Janey girl!" The greeting was warm, but she thought his voice sounded tired.

"Pa, I miss you! I wish I were there. Pa, what's going on?"

"You mean that well they blew up?"

"Yes. Pa, you weren't…"

"No, honey, don't worry," he stopped her asking. "I wasn't involved. None of us are very pleased with the way things are going with the city over these negotiations, but when an official process like this is underway, you have to let it play out."

She sighed. "Pa, what's going to happen?" asking as a little girl might. But she wasn't little anymore. She reproached herself the moment the words had left her mouth. *He might better ask me, since I'm here with the enemy, and what could I tell him?* She also knew, before he replied, what his answer would be.

"I don't know Janey."

---

The Owens Valley Reparations Association submitted its counter offer. There was no immediate response from the city, and a month later another hole was dynamited in the aqueduct, at about the point where the first blast had occurred two years before.

Jane did her best to confirm the pumping figures, although she found the DWP unwilling to provide details about its operations. It was anything but reticent, however, about sharing its point of view. A steady stream of one-sided pamphlets was distributed over the next several months, including one entitled "The Dynamite Holdup," which depicted the Reparations Association as a bunch of "outlaws" using claims of damages to "milk the people of Los Angeles out of millions of dollars." It claimed they were using the threat of violence to force the city to pay outrageous prices for the remaining land and water rights and that the city had made "every legitimate effort" to "support and increase the material prosperity of the valley" as well as to "establish a system of water development and conservation mutually beneficial to the valley and the city."

In the propaganda war that ensued, the valley gave as good as it got. A wave of pro-valley articles began to appear in various Inyo County, San Francisco and Sacramento newspapers, even a few in Los Angeles papers, with inflammatory language like "The Valley of Broken Hearts," "Land Grabbers Wreck Valley" and "Owens Valley, the pitiful story of an agricultural paradise, created by California pioneers, condemned to desert waste by water looters."

Jane fumed in Loewenthal's office. She, of all these reporters, had reason to care about the fate of Owens Valley, but, well-trained by two excellent newspapermen, she tried very hard to write balanced articles based on facts. "There's so much confusion among the public," she complained to her editor. "No one knows which version of the story is right. The truth, which is somewhere in-between, is being completely fogged out. The press could be helping bring some clarity to the problem so that the public accurately perceives what's happening and the parties understand each other better, and so can come to a fair compromise, but instead they're making it even worse!"

"Welcome to the news world, young reporter" was all Loewenthal had to say. "What took you so long?"

On March 19th, a full-page advertisement from the Owens Valley Reparations Association and its supporters appeared in leading newspapers throughout the state with the headline:

**WE WHO ARE ABOUT TO DIE**

The writer was echoing the translation of a Latin phrase *Ave, Caesar, morituri te salutant*, "Hail, Cesar, those who are about to die salute you," said to have been uttered by captives and criminals forced to fight to the death in combat games. The advertisement appealed to the public, urging readers to insist on fair play from Los Angeles.

The DWP responded by filing a rebuttal with the Los Angeles Public Service Commission, refuting in great detail all of the statements and arguments the Reparations Association had made in its counter-proposal. The commission largely adopted the rebuttal position as its own, and on May 6th, 1927, the Los Angeles City Council unanimously passed a motion denying all claims of damages from Owens Valley.

"What now?" asked Jane, on the telephone with Chalfant.

"I don't know, I just know it's not over," he answered bleakly.

A few weeks later, Jane was working at her desk when Loewenthal came out of his office and stood beside her until she glanced up. "They've blown the aqueduct to bits. You'd better get back up there."

# Chapter 21

Once again Jane reversed in her tracks. She packed a bag and turned the little green Sainte Claire north. That night, too fatigued from the miles and worry to push farther, she stayed at the inn in Olancha. Over breakfast the next morning she heard there'd been another dynamite blast that night as she'd slept. Jane gulped her coffee, paid her bill and sped off north in the roadster, driving straight to the *Inyo Register*, without stopping at the ranch.

All along the way, the valley was browner than typical for May, browner even than when she had come back two years ago and been surprised by the first signs of change. Now the transformation of the valley was plain to see, even from the highway. Cottonwoods and willows stood drooping, some devoid of foliage. The green carpet of irrigated fields had shrunk, reversing the gradual expansion that had marked the years of her childhood. Here and there entire fields, once covered in alfalfa, had been allowed to go fallow, rabbitbrush and saltbush beginning to invade their borders. There was less devastation the farther north she drove, but even the Bishop area now showed signs of decline.

Chalfant looked up from his work table when she came into the office, but his countenance showed no surprise at seeing her after so many months. "You cut your hair again," he observed matter-of-factly.

She didn't reply but walked over to where he sat. "Fill me in?"

"The first blast was the siphon at No Name Canyon, 'bout 11 miles south of Little Lake. That's one of the biggest and most critical siphons on the aqueduct. Someone blew up about 450 feet of pipe. Water gushing out like the Mississippi River. The city had to shut off the flow at Haiwee Reservoir."

"Who did it?"

"No one's sayin, of course. Mouths shut even tighter than before—this here's serious business this time. Story goes the attackers wore masks. Some say there were four, some say more. A couple of them took the two guards and walked them up the canyon while the others set the charge. Before they left, they cut the telephone lines so the guards had to drive into town to report it."

"Here…" He flipped a couple of photographs around and pushed them toward Jane. "I took these yesterday, with that," he said, pointing to the camera anchoring a pile of papers at one corner of the table, the glimmer of smile on his lips relaxing a bit of the tension from his face. It was the first camera she'd ever seen small enough to hold in one hand. "That's my new Leica 35 millimeter."

She lifted the pictures up to examine them. An immense pipe, taller than the man in knee-high work boots who stood next to it, had been squashed, folded over and ripped apart as if a giant had taken it in his fist. Jagged metal edges caught the sun, printing brilliant white in the photograph, sharply contrasting with the black empty guts of the siphon that now lay open like a wounded animal. Two other men in work clothes and one in suit and tie clustered around the gash in solicitous poses as if trying to give medical aid.

Jane laid the pictures down, and Chalfant continued. "The second blast, last night, was at Big Pine Creek. Destroyed 60 feet of pipe at the intake for the city's hydro power plant there. Steel collapsed like a bicycle tire punctured with a nail. Plant's closed down for repair. I'm heading down there now to try to photograph the damage. Don't know if I'll be successful. They let me get close enough yesterday to take these, but from what my sources in the city tell me, after last night, they may not be so accommodating. Half a dozen guards are on their way up here armed with Winchester rifles, tommy guns and orders to shoot-to-kill any suspicious person found around the aqueduct, no questions asked. The city's also dispatched a squad of Pinkerton detectives and offered a $10,000 reward for information leading to conviction of the guilty parties."

"How do you know all that?!" Jane felt she was choking. What about Pa? Chalfant *had* to be mistaken.

"I have my sources, some you know, some you don't."

"But how could it be Mr. Chalfant? This is America! They can't just shoot people!"

"Apparently they can, if those people are on city property and viewed as a material threat to it."

"But that's dreadful! What can we do to stop this?!"

"We can't stop it. But by doing our job of reporting the facts clearly, we may be able to stop some of the rumors and panic that will sure as hell make it worse. Help folks keep their heads, maybe just enough to pull back from lookin over the edge where this kind of violence is thinkable. Get them back to where they can see the wisdom of sitting down at a negotiating table again."

"What can I do?" she asked, placing her palms on his work table and leaning toward him.

"I want you to go over to No Name Canyon. I've got as much chance as a rabbit in a hound's mouth there, but you, with your Los Angeles press credentials, you may be able to get close. Tell them you're there to write about the repair effort—how efficient the DWP is, etcetera—but while you're there, try to find out about the security set up. How many guards are there, where are they being stationed, what kinds of weapons do they have? Getting those fellas to talk to a pretty young thing like you should be as easy as lickin butter off a knife." He winked at her, but there was none of his usual good humor in it.

"All right. I'll leave now."

"Be careful. And get back here this afternoon. I need a story for the evening edition. We'll decide what to run when you get back."

---

No Name Canyon was south of Olancha, so Jane turned the green road-ster around and headed back down the valley again. And once again she passed by Independence without stopping at the ranch. She'd see Ma and Pa that evening. They knew she was coming, she'd telephoned, of course, and they'd been glad at the prospect of seeing her. But there'd been a shade of reluctance in their voices. Had that been concern for her, worries of their own or just fatigue?

A few hot hours of driving later, Jane was on the dusty road into the canyon, looking up at the giant steel snake descending the northern ridge. The blast had been set where the siphon leveled out at the floor of the canyon. It looked like the neck of the snake had been twisted, and a huge gash hung open like a mouth.

Dozens of men were scurrying about, standing atop the pipe just above where it had split open, climbing up and down a ladder propped up against its side, peering and pointing into the yawning breach. A large team was hammering what appeared to be a low wooden scaffold running for about 100 yards along the side of the pipe. Piles of wooden boards and large bobbins of rope and steel cord were strewn around the work area.

"You can't come in here." A big man in denim overalls, his shirt and hat both drenched with sweat, strode over to where Jane had parked the Sainte Claire. He placed a hand on the top of the driver's side door, preventing her from exiting. "Sorry miss, no sightseers."

"Nothing to be sorry about since I'm not one," she said brightly, sliding over to the passenger side and stepping out of the car. She reached into her purse and, taking care to select her *Examiner* badge, walked around the car and held it in her challenger's face. "J. Bow here. I'm a reporter for a Los Angeles newspaper."

"That so?" He sounded skeptical, but he studied the badge, looking at Jane's photograph on it, at her, then back at the photograph. Finally he nodded. "You'd better talk to Mr. Van Norman over there, the one with the necktie." He pointed toward a man wearing a boldly striped tie pulled away from the open neck of his white shirt and flapping limply in the afternoon breeze.

"Mr. Van Norman! Hello sir!" she called.

He turned toward her, surprised, but as she came to him, he politely covered half the ground. "May I help you, miss?"

Jane held up her badge in her left hand and stuck out her right to shake his. He accepted the overture with reserve, the question— *Who are you?*—in his eyes. "Mr. Van Norman. I'm J. Bow, reporter for the *Los Angeles Examiner*. Your man there tells me you're in charge."

He relaxed and smiled. "How do you do Miss Bow. Yes, that's correct. I'm Harvey Van Norman, assistant superintendent of the Los Angeles Department of Water and Power, and the unlucky fella in charge of fixing this mess." He waved an arm toward the injured siphon.

"Indeed! There must have been a lot of dynamite to do that. How long do you think it will take you to fix the damage?"

"A few days to a week at most. We'll have 150 men here by nightfall, and there's already 450 feet of new pipe on its way from Los Angeles."

He explained some of the particulars of the task to her, and she took notes attentively, nodding and smiling encouragingly. "Our readers will be so impressed by the efficiency of your operation Mr. Van Norman!"

Out of the corner of her eye, she'd been watching several other automobiles drive up, disgorging what were sure to be reporters from other newspapers. They too were intercepted by the big man in overalls.

"Mr. Van Norman," she said, placing a hand on his arm and leaning toward him to speak more intimately, "I'd so much like to be able to reassure our readers also that the department is taking security measures to prevent a horrible attack like this from happening again. Can you tell me what you're doing about that?"

He rushed to reassure her that Angelenos needn't worry. "We have armed men stationed at all strategic points on the aqueduct, and we're bringing in more."

"For example…?" She led him with a sweet, eager smile. He responded by rattling off the names of a couple of dozen places, including spillway gates, the Jawbone siphon, power plants and groundwater pumping stations. And Van Norman was happy to oblige when Jane asked him to repeat a few of these locations so that she could make sure to get them all down in her notebook. She thanked him profusely when she had finished and, noticing the phalanx of other reporters approaching, tapped a finger on his arm and said, "Oh, wasn't that one of your men up there on that pipe calling for you?"

"I didn't hear…" He peered over at his workers, hand shielding his eyes. "I better see what's going on." He smiled at her apologetically, tilting his hat in a slight salute. "Hope you got enough information to write your story Miss Bow."

"Indeed I did Mr. Van Norman, thank you so very much. Oh, he's motioning for you again—better get up there! Goodbye now!"

And with that she started walking back to the Sainte Claire, passing the approaching reporters, who, she was amused to see, were now running after Van Norman as he strode away to join his work crew. It might be an hour or two before he'd again detach himself long enough to talk to reporters, she thought cheerfully, and I doubt he'll want to go into all that detail again! J. Bow had learned a thing or two, she congratulated herself, since those days at the Elizabeth Tunnel when the male reporters had confounded her first reporting efforts.

It was dusk before she drove into the Bow ranch yard. It had taken her hours to get back to Bishop, confer with Chalfant and write the story. She'd been triumphant about her trove of information but hesitant about using it. "They're sure going to be sore when they see this in an Owens Valley paper," she'd told the editor. "I'll be persona non grata if I ever see Van Norman again. And what if, by printing the security details, it encourages the attackers?"

"I think it's much more likely to discourage confrontations," countered Chalfant. "If the rebels don't know anything about the security set up, they're likely to get caught in an area that's patrolled by armed guards, and who knows what violence could result. If they know where the guards are stationed, they'll be able to avoid them."

Chalfant's reasoning had made sense to Jane, so she'd set herself to writing the story for the *Register* evening edition. They'd agreed it should be printed without a byline to avoid bringing too much attention to Jane's involvement. When she'd finished, she'd called the *Examiner* office and dictated a shorter story for Loewenthal. This piece focused on the repair effort and avoided the issue of security. Finally, exhausted and still terribly worried, but feeling that she'd at least tried to do something helpful, Jane turned the roadster south again and drove to the ranch.

Van Norman had ticked off quite a few pumping stations in the Independence area, and Janey had held her breath as she'd neared the Bow homestead, hoping not to find it sadly changed. Indeed, it seeme Pa had planted less acreage than usual, but the crops were green enough. In the yard, however, the foliage of her favorite old oak tree looked a bit sparse and perhaps yellow, though she couldn't tell in the waning light.

"Janey, there you are! I've saved you some supper, sweetie. Why don't you put your bags upstairs while I serve it up." Ma's smile and hug were warm as usual. "Your Pa's just finishing up in the barn. He'll be in directly."

Mounting the stairs, Jane realized she was famished—she hadn't taken time to eat since breakfast in Olancha. She deposited her bags, changed into more comfortable shoes, splashed water on her face, tried to run a comb through her wind-matted hair and hurried downstairs with the evening *Register* under her arm.

There, waiting for her, was the familiar comfort of Ma's chicken pot pie, homemade cranberry sauce and mashed potatoes. Jane laid the paper on the sideboard and gratefully sat down at the table, forcing herself not to gobble. "Thanks Ma. It's great, as usual."

Alice poured herself a cup of coffee and sat across from Jane, watching her fondly. Jane looked back at her and around at the kitchen, feeling ridiculously happy to be there. Ma, with her still-mostly-blond chignon, as lovely and neat as ever. But looking closer, Jane noticed purple shadows under her eyes and tension around her mouth—she seemed to be making an effort to hold it in a smile. "You look tired Ma. How are you and Pa?"

"As well as anyone in this valley." Alice stood up and walked over to the window. "Oh, now, here he comes." She turned back to bestow a restored smile on her daughter. "He'll be so pleased to see you, Janey."

He was, wrapping her into his bear hug. But when he had washed up and joined them at the table, Jane saw there was tension in her father's countenance too, which even a bowl of Alice's fragrant lemon pudding cake did nothing to relieve. Jane put down her spoon and reached out to rest a hand on an arm of each parent. "It's bad here, isn't it?"

They said nothing, but Ma looked up at her with eyes that held so much emotion—sorrow, injured pride, worry, but most of all love, love directed at her—that Jane couldn't hold their gaze. She squeezed her mother's arm and looked down at the table.

After a while Jane said, "Pa, they're putting guards all over the aqueduct, and they're armed with Winchesters and tommy guns." She reached over to the newspaper on the sideboard and opened it on the table between them. "We managed to get most of the locations today."

Ben glanced at the paper, then looked up at her with a wry smile that held a hint of pride. He nodded his head. "Good reporting work, Janey girl."

"Pa, whoever is setting those blasts is in danger. Those armed guards change the game!"

"Funny you should say 'game.' Do you know what they're callin the dynamiting now? They call it 'shooting the duck.'"

"Pa, those guards aren't playing, they have orders to shoot to kill!"

Ben's countenance grew stern. "It's not for you to be lecturing me about whether this is a game or not Janey. We know quite well what it is.

We're the ones, your Ma and me and our neighbors, who are living it every day..."

"I'm sorry, I didn't mean..."

"Now you're welcome here as always, and we love to see our daughter, but you aren't to think you should be telling us how to behave."

"No Pa." She dropped her eyes, her face hot with remorse. His voice softened and he reached out to pry one of her hands from the fist in her lap. "Janey girl, this is not your problem to solve." He glanced at Alice, who nodded. He put a hand on his daughter's shoulder. "We don't want you mixed up in this business. Maybe you should go back to the city."

"I can't Pa. Mr. Loewenthal sent me here on assignment. Besides," she added, nodding toward the newspaper on the table, "I'm helping Mr. Chalfant too." She looked from one to the other. "Please let me stay," she entreated them. "I'll leave you be, I promise. But at least I'll be here if you need help." She corrected herself: "If you ask for help, I'll be here."

Alice and Ben exchanged looks again, and he said, "That'll be fine, honey, that'll be just fine." He patted the hand he held and relented. "Just so you won't be worrying yourself awake all night, I didn't have anything to do with either of those blasts."

The relief flooding through Jane surfaced instantly on her face.

"But, I do have sympathy for those who did, and I'm not going to make any promises to you about what I may do tomorrow or the next day. Your Ma and I are figuring this thing and making our choices best we can. Understood?"

"Yes, understood."

"Well, come on then, let's go listen to that radio you've gotten us addicted to!"

It was later than Ben and Alice usually stayed up, and so a rare opportunity to listen to the nine o'clock KFVD broadcast from the Venice Ballroom Orchestra. The station had recently moved from San Pedro harbor to the seaside resort town, and its new slogan had become "The Voice by the Sea." Since opening in 1904, Venice had offered Angelenos and tourists innumerable enticements, including not only 16 miles of canals with gondola rides, but Coney Island-style roller coasters and penny arcades, aviators performing stunts over the beach, a skating rink, an Arabian style bathhouse and even camel rides. It hadn't aged well, however; many of its poorly maintained canals were now clogged with trash and weeds, its attractions dingy and in disrepair.

But the dance hall was more popular than ever before. Young folks packed it nightly to swing to the latest jazz tunes, and people of all ages, all over California tuned in to hum along or "cut a rug" at home. Alice, who had never danced to anything of the sort, adored it.

Despite everything prickling her disposition these days, she couldn't help tapping a foot as she sat in her armchair darning Ben's socks. Oh, how I miss dancing under the stars, she thought, recalling the town picnics of a summer's eve, her composed features revealing nothing of the pining she felt to be back when all was right in the world and Owens Valley was the best place in the world to be!

---

"Well is it Haiwee or St. Francis, damn it?!" Mulholland roared into the telephone receiver. He listened for a minute, slammed the receiver down, charged out the door of his office and barked at Augusta Aames, "Get Lippincott and Matthews in here now!"

Oh my, she thought, he's fit to be tied. The trouble in Owens Valley these past few days had forced the chief to keep to the office instead of venturing out in the field as was his habit and preference. Hour by hour it seemed his anger over the attacks and generally black temper had deepened. She scurried out to perform her task.

"They're on their way to dynamite one of our dams!" Mulholland shouted at the two men the moment they set foot in his office.

"Which one?" asked Lippincott.

"We don't know. About an hour ago, there was an anonymous call to the Los Angeles Sheriff's Department. Said a car of armed men were headed down from Owens Valley to bomb St. Francis Dam. Sheriff calls me, and the moment I hang up from talking with him, in comes a call from one of my detectives up in the valley. This guy tells me there's an attack coming on the Haiwee. Maybe both dams are targets, or maybe someone's trying to confound us, but we can't take any chances."

Lippincott rubbed a thumb and forefinger down across his handlebar mustache, observing grimly, "With the flow shut off for repairs to be made, those reservoirs are the only thing guaranteeing Los Angeles drinking water."

"I want armed men posted all along the ramparts of both dams, and I want them there within the hour!" barked Mulholland.

"Yes Chief! I'm on it," responded Lippincott, turning smartly on his heel and heading out of the office.

"God damn the Owens Valley to hell! A bunch of lawless lunatics every one of them!" Mulholland flew at Matthews. "Call Governor Young. He's not so tight with the purse strings as Richardson was—and besides his predecessor left him with a budget surplus. Let's get him to spend it."

"Yes, I think you're right," said Matthews. "I'll make some calls." He too left the office.

Mulholland emerged and turned his fury on Miss Aames. "Get me the chief of police on the phone!" When the man came on the line, Mulholland, dispensing with formalities, said abruptly, "Jim, I'm in need of your help."

"What is it?" was the equally brief, direct reply. In the four years preceding James E. Davis's appointment in 1926, eight predecessors had come and gone, powerless to make headway in a city that since the onset of Prohibition had become a playground for bootleggers, racketeers, crooked politicians and paid-off judges.

Davis had instituted a get-tough response, increasing firearms training and stressing marksmanship for all of his officers. He'd formed a 50-man gun squad to clean up the streets, warning rum smugglers they'd learn that "murder and gun-toting are most inimical to their best interest." Earning the nickname "Two-Gun Davis," the police chief then announced he would "hold court on gunmen in the Los Angeles streets; I want them brought in dead, not alive and will reprimand any officer who shows the least mercy to a criminal."

Mulholland and Davis spoke for some 20 minutes. When they hung up, it was agreed that Davis would recruit and train an emergency squad of 600 special police "ready to do battle" with the Owens Valley anarchists.

*Some people are like arrows, or a strong-flowing river: they seem to always know what direction to go, and they get right on with it. Others seem to have more trouble finding their way. They struggle to understand and find application for their own good qualities, and to gain the recognition they believe is due.*

*My brother Chris, the Watterson family, Jed, and even my parents were in the first group. Mary Austin was in the second, as am I and my grandnephew CK. I think Mr. Mulholland was in the first group, but not his friend Mr. Eaton. From what I observed and heard, he led a life of struggle, even though folks say he was born to every luxury.*

*People in the second group, we're the ones who spend a good part of our lives pushing against the current or flapping about in eddies off of the mainstream. We watch in wonder as the unencumbered shoot past us... but just because you've been granted a smooth passage doesn't mean you'll like where you end up.*

---

Jane was pressing a cold bottle of root beer against her aching forehead when Bucky Porter poked his head into the drugstore and called, "Chalfant wants ya. Phone call from Los Angeles."

She left change on the soda fountain counter and crossed the street to the *Register* office. Chalfant was talking in a low voice on the telephone at the back of the room. He motioned her to come, and she walked toward him, nearly tripping on the length of cord he'd dragged along the floor.

"That's not possible, where did you get that information?!" Chalfant's face wore a stunned look.

On the other end of the line, Henry Loewenthal responded, "One of my guys wrangled it out of a city clerk."

"I don't believe it," said Chalfant. "The son of a bitch probably just made it up to boast—some folks are always airin their lungs. Or he needed something to earn the fiver your man was slippin him. Anyway, sure as shootin, I'll find out."

"When you do, let me know, will you?"

"Sure. Here's Bow. I'll pass you over." Chalfant held out the telephone base and receiver to Jane. "It's Loewenthal. Says the city is training 600 special police to send up here."

"Oh, no!" She recoiled from the vision. "So many?!"

"That's what he says. Also says he needs to talk to you about one of your city assignments." Chalfant was moving toward the door. "I'm goin over to the bank a few minutes."

She nodded and brought the receiver to her ear. "Hello, Jane here." She listened wide-eyed and with mounting alarm as Loewenthal recounted to her one of the pieces of information he'd just given Chalfant: 600 police were being recruited and trained by Los Angeles. The first detachment of 100 men would be on their way by the end of the week, in a special Southern Pacific train.

"My God!" was all she could muster in response.

"I think the people up there need this information. If they know what's facing them, it might cause some to temper their actions, calming down the mood some. Chalfant thinks likewise."

"Yes, you're probably right, at least I hope you are."

"And there's another piece of information we scoured up, which I'd like you to try to check out up there. And, Jane, keep this one just between us for the moment."

"Of course. What is it?"

"We've gotten wind of a shipment of 58 Winchester carbines from a Los Angeles wholesaler up to Bishop. The recipient is the Watterson brother's hardware store."

"Oh my God! It's like both sides are arming for a war!"

"Right. If it's true, that'll add oil to the fire. And I fear it's true. Since it's not hunting season, seems like a pretty large quantity of arms."

"Yes, yes, it does."

"I need you to find out if the shipment arrived and what's happening with those guns."

"I don't know, Mr. Loewenthal. I'm beginning to feel like some sort of Mata Hari."

Hearing that, Loewenthal felt a momentary flush. The story of the exotic dancer, executed as a double agent by a French firing squad in 1917, was well known. He suspected Jane was unaware, however, that the femme fatale had ended her most infamous dance performances by stripping until she lay on stage bare-bottomed, one thigh discreetly crossed over the other, wearing nothing but a jeweled bra and ornaments on her arms and head.

He briefly enjoyed the image of his reporter in such a state of undress, but pushed it out of his head.

"Nonsense," he strove to reassure her. "The more facts we can dig up and shine a light on, the more chances violent confrontation can be avoided. When both sides know the other is prepared to do battle, some folks are likely to stand down."

"Yes, I guess you're right. Mr. Chalfant's told me the same. I'll try. I'll do what I can."

"Good. Send me a telegram as soon as you find out anything."

Jane agreed and put the receiver down in the cradle, then brought the telephone back to Chalfant's work table, pulling the cord with her, shoving the excess loops of length against the wall. She grabbed her hat and bag, and left the office, walking south down the street, past the women's clothing store with its three-pronged logo for "value, courtesy and service," past the general store with its window advertisement for "Owens Valley, the Home of the Pear," and past the Bishop Theatre with its posters showing John Barrymore in *The Beloved Rogue* and promising "Never less than seven reels!"

When she reached the hardware store, Jane slowed and lingered in front, pretending to study the window display of Millers Falls level tools for "carpentry, masonry and household use." She peered inside. Luckily, there was only one customer, and he soon exited carrying a parcel. She went in and walked to the back of the store where Carl Clarke, the manager, clad in a green work apron, was stocking boxes of nails on the shelf behind the counter.

"Good afternoon Mr. Clarke," she called.

Clarke turned around, surprised. Female customers were rare, and the young woman who stood before him now had never set foot in the store, to his knowledge, though he thought he'd seen her elsewhere in town. "Good afternoon Miss…a, Miss Bow isn't it?"

"Yes, Ben Bow's daughter."

"Well, well. Saw your Pa just last week. Did he forget something from his order?"

"No, sir, I'm here as a reporter for Mr. Chalfant. May I speak with you a moment?"

"I suppose," he agreed reluctantly, casting his eyes about the store. "What about?"

"We were wondering, Mr. Clarke, if you could confirm some information we have received about a shipment of Winchester carbines sent up here from Los Angeles?"

Clarke narrowed his eyes and crossed his arms in front of his chest. "This is a hardware store, miss. We've always sold guns."

"Yes, but this shipment numbered 58 carbines, did it not?"

"Yes, we received a big order," he said slowly. "What about it?"

"That seems to be rather a large quantity, months away from hunting season. Is there any particular demand for them?"

"Could be," he said smirking, "every man in the valley will up and decide he needs a new rifle tonight. A merchandiser has to be prepared for sudden demands from his customers."

"What do you mean *tonight* Mr. Clarke?"

"Just a hypothetical. Look, Miss Bow, tell Chalfant if he wants to know more, to go and talk to the manager, Mark Watterson. They're such great pals, ain't they? Now, if you don't mind, I have work to do." He turned his back and continued stocking the shelf.

The man's behavior was rude, but Jane was becoming used to such treatment. She left the store and retraced her steps along Main Street, thinking about how much the valley had changed from her childhood days. Since she'd arrived back this time, she'd felt a general climate of tension and distrust, which she believed kept some people from acting as cordial as they might otherwise have been inclined.

Oddly, valley folk seemed to have taken it in stride when city-hired Pinkerton detectives had started snooping around. In fact, the "gum-shoes," as they were contemptuously called, had become a source of local amusement. People laughed about the inept detectives eavesdropping under windows and shadowing their prey down streets, thinking their tactics unobserved.

It was ironic, in Jane's thinking, that valley folk seemed to reserve their real suspicions for the actions and motivations of other valley folk. Neighbors suspected neighbors of wanting to sell out or, depending on the situation, of wanting to prevent them from doing so. Some ranchers and farmers suspected townspeople of trying to control and manipulate negotiations with the city for their own financial gain. Some townspeople suspected ranchers and farmers of being susceptible to persuasion from the city and likely to make deals that would leave businesses high and dry without customers or compensation. Phantoms of double dealing were beginning to cast a shadow over all efforts at cooperation.

"Excuse me, miss," a low voice called softly behind her. She turned around and saw Alejandro, Rosie's 12-year-old son.

"Why Alejo," she greeted him. "What are you doing here?"

"I do some stocking chores for Mr. Watterson now, at the hardware and the general store." The skinny, sweet-faced boy tapped his chest proudly. "I'm earning my own money so I can go be a rodeo cowboy like my uncle Juan!"

"I see," responded Jane, thinking of his poor mother, her dear friend. "What can I do for you Alejo? How about if I buy you a root beer?"

"No, miss, thank you. I have to get back to work. But I thought you'd like to know about something Mr. Clarke didn't tell you. He should have told you there's going to be a meeting tonight, in Yaney's field, at midnight."

"Who's going to meet Alejo?"

"The men who bought all those guns that came into the store."

"How do you know this?"

"Oh, you know, miss, they don't pay no mind to Mexicans. They don't think we've got anything to do with their business, or sense enough to understand what they're sayin. We ain't important enough to bother keepin quiet around."

She nodded, placing a hand on his arm. "Thank you Alejo, thank you for telling me." She reached into her bag and withdrew a nickel. "Here, buy yourself a root beer when you finish work. I've got to go see your uncle Juan."

Chalfant climbed the steps to the mezzanine of the bank, where Wilfred Watterson sat behind his desk, talking with a customer seated in the opposite chair.

As Chalfant waited his turn, leaning against the banister, he thought, as he often had in the past, that Wilfred very much enjoyed his role as banker and leading citizen. The eldest Watterson brother had occupied the large walnut desk in the center of the mezzanine since he and his brother Mark had founded this, the first bank in the valley, in 1902. Of course the bank had grown a good deal since then; there were now three other branches. And the Wattersons also owned several other businesses in town, including the hardware and general stores, as well as substantial interests in mining and the soda processing plant at Keeler that reclaimed sodium bicarbonate from saline Owens Lake.

It's a strange thing, mused Chalfant, that the most powerful business enterprise in the valley, which had dominated commerce for more than two decades, was the issue of a couple of sheepherders from the Isle of Man. Old Mr. Watterson, Joseph, deceased nearly a dozen years now, had been a strong, calm man of upright character, whom Chalfant and most everyone else in the valley had admired. His wife Eliza was frail but still regal of posture and sharp of mind. She had started the whole thing long ago by encouraging her sons to open a hardware store and investing a small inheritance of her own as the capital. They had made good the gift, multiplying it into the means for a plentiful, elegant life for their parents and sisters. A happy ending to an intrinsically American story, thought Chalfant. Which was why he was sure that what Loewenthal had just told him couldn't be true.

Watterson stood up and shook the hand of his customer. The man turned and walked toward the stairs, holding his hat against his chest beneath a countenance that revealed both worry and relief. Chalfant now recognized him as Arthur Kinsley, a farmer with a place several miles out of town. They nodded hello. Watterson motioned Chalfant to come over. The banker stuck out his hand in a weary greeting.

"Hello Willie. Another of our customers needing an extension on his mortgage." Wilfred sighed heavily, then sat down and motioned the editor to do the same. "Have you got some news?"

Settling into his chair, Chalfant responded casually, "More like a rumor I need to quash."

"More rumors—what now, then?"

Chalfant chuckled. "Well, it's as plain as red paint this one ain't true, but I gotta check just the same. A source down in Los Angeles claims you've sold the ranch to the city!" He leaned back, expecting his friend to erupt in laughter, going still and wary when Watterson did not.

"We had hoped to keep it under wraps a little longer."

"What?! You pullin my leg?! Whadda ya mean? You've sold out?!"

"We've sold the ranch," Wilfred replied stiffly, "That's all."

"But, by yourself, you mean, without the Reparations Association?" Chalfant leaned forward and whispered incredulously, "How could you sell when you're asking everybody else to hang on and stay united?!"

"Willie, we had no choice." Watterson got up and walked over to the visitor side of the desk, pulling another chair over so he could sit close to Chalfant. "Look man, we have to have money to carry on the valley fight. You saw when you came in here, we've got loans all up and down the valley that people are begging for more time on. The work to put together the irrigation district and the bond issue was expensive, and it all came to naught. Now there's the Reparations Association, and it's an expense too. We've been trying to shoulder as much of the burden as we can so others don't have to. But we need more cash right now."

"But your mother..."

"It's time she moved in with one of us anyway, she can't stay alone anymore. Mary and Gorman are going to take care of her at their place."

"I see." Chalfant didn't know what to think, he was still so flummoxed. "And Mark, is he in favor of this too?"

"You know Mark, he goes along," said Wilfred.

Chalfant nodded, but he was thinking that while Mark clearly adored his older brother, he had a good head on his own shoulders. He was slower to act than the somewhat high-strung Wilfred, but he was decisive. Hadn't he done a great job managing the Alabama Gates takeover, an event that could so easily have turned into a fiasco. He'd held it together until Wilfred had telegrammed to assure the crowd they'd won, that he'd secured from city leaders the pledge of a just outcome, and urged them to return to their shops and homes.

A lot of people in the valley now thought that had been a mistake, and Chalfant was inclined to agree. When they'd given back control over the Alabama Gates, they'd given away the only leverage they had. Without it, the bankers of Los Angeles had been free to renege on their promise and the DWP to return to its intractable ways. And now it had come down to more dynamite as the only hope to force the city to finally negotiate a fair division of water or buy the remaining valley property owners out once and for all. God help us!

Chalfant said nothing of this because Wilfred's burdens were clearly already heavy enough. Recriminations were never of any use. So Chalfant just stared down at his hands as Wilfred continued to try to explain the rationale for why the foremost leaders of the valley rebellion had just made a deal with the devil.

---

When Jane got back to the *Register* office, Chalfant had not yet returned. Bucky Porter was sitting at the desk she and he shared, writing out a story, shoulders slung forward, acne-scarred nose inches from the paper.

"Bucky, can you give Mr. Chalfant a message for me?"

He glanced up and squinted his eyes at her. "What?"

"Please tell him I won't be back today. There's something I need to do. I'll see him in the morning."

"Sure, sure." Shoulders and nose drooped back down.

Can he be trusted, wondered Jane. He's never much liked me. She thought better of it.

"Never mind, I'll leave him a note."

After writing her message out, Jane hurried outside, climbed into the roadster and headed south. The late-afternoon sun was dropping behind the peaks on her right, sending shadows creeping upward across the rounded mountain range on her left. It was all in shadow by the time she turned off the main road and bounced down the dirt track toward the Escobar ranch. Seeing Juan still in the corral, she drove up to it, jumped out and climbed atop a fence rail.

"*Hola* Juanito!" she called, using the affectionate childhood diminutive.

"Hey, it's a Jane!" He was teasing her back, using her name in the generic sense. In recent years, young men had started calling girls "Janes" and unlovely girls "plain Janes." He rode the Appaloosa over to her, and she thought they looked magnificent together: Juan's hair gleaming black, shirt gleaming white; the stallion with black chest, black-and-white spotted rump and flowing black tail.

"Hello Diablo," she patted the beautiful creature's neck as it waved its head, snorted and stomped.

Juan let him dance and display until he settled down. He smiled at Jane. "What brings you here *chica*?"

"I need your help. Can you meet me tonight at the river, the place where we used to swim, at 11? And can you bring a couple of horses?"

"What's this, a midnight ride?"

"Juan, I think there's going to be trouble. A whole lot of Winchester carbines got shipped up here in the past few days, and there's going to be a meeting tonight at Yaney's field—your sharp-eared nephew Alejo overheard some men talking about it at the hardware store. Incidentally, he wants to join you in the rodeo."

He rolled his eyes, and they shared a moment's amusement. She attempted to explain. "I need to go, Juan, and I daren't go alone. Maybe there will be something I can do to try to stop this from getting out of hand. Or, if I can't do that, at least try to make sure the truth gets told about what happens."

He was regarding her skeptically, so she told him the rest, the only part that would make him care enough to come. "And…I want to be there to watch out for my father…I don't know, he won't tell me, but he may be involved."

"I'll be there. *A las once, chica*." He turned Diablo around and rode into the barn. Jane got back into her car and headed home for supper.

---

At supper, Alice had her own news. "There was a letter from Chris today—he's engaged to be married! To Miss Dorothy Bradshaw of Los Angeles. He wants us to come down for the wedding in October. Have you met her Janey?"

"Yes, once. She's very nice. Pretty. High-society, you know."

"Well, all I can say is it's about time. Goodness, your brother's nearly 40 years old!"

"He's only 37 Ma."

"Ben, isn't this good news!" Alice turned to her husband, who'd been listening to their exchange.

"Yes, dear one, it's good news." He patted her hand. "And we sure need some of that, don't we?"

"We sure do." Alice placed her hand over his and they stayed like that for a moment. Janey, watching them, thought they must have been much the same when as a young couple they'd become engaged. Their affection, so constant in all the years she'd observed them, was still in their eyes. But back then their eyes must also have shone with hope, like the eyes of all betrothed, seeing a future of unalloyed happiness. Does anyone ever get that, Jane wondered, her heart twisting with a feeling of wanting to protect her parents mixed with longing for Jed. She swallowed hard.

"You'll go to the wedding, won't you?" Jane asked, directing her question at both of them.

"Of course," said Alice.

"I suppose," said Ben.

They didn't linger long over the radio that evening. All three claimed to be tired and wanting to hit the sack early. In her room, Jane looked around for a way to pass the time until her rendezvous with Juan. She noticed the book Chalfant had lent her on the window seat, where it had lain untouched since she'd unloaded it from her satchel. Now she picked it up, took it over to her bed, removed her shoes, settled back against the pillows, switched on the bedside lamp and began reading.

After a few minutes, Jane put down the book and leaned back against the headboard, eyes closing. Evidently, Mary had indeed found a new place to love. *The Land of Journeys' Ending* was about the southwestern lands between the Colorado River and the Rio Grande, a landscape that appeared to offer many of the same charms of arid beauty and vast horizons as the Owens Valley. It was the kind of place about which Mary had once written, there is a sense of "room enough and time enough."

Yes, the subject of landscape and its inhabitants did recall something of Mary's first work, *The Land of Little Rain* as well as her subsequent *Lost Borders,* although, from what Jane could tell at first glance, this book might also recount more history than either of those. The sometimes poetic language of the new book also echoed the language of its predecessors, but to Jane's mind, it didn't mesmerize like that first, slim volume had, like it continued to do whenever she opened it over the years, longing for remembrance of her long treks with Mary.

Jane rubbed her forehead, the darned headache was back, and glanced at the clock, which said 10:45. She got up and splashed cold water from the basin onto her face, tied her hair back, put on a dark riding skirt and blouse, and tucked her boots under her arm. She eased the door open, checking to see that there was no light under her parents' door and thinking how silly this was, sneaking out like a child. Well, at least she was no longer slipping out the window and sliding down the branches of the big oak tree.

All was dark, so she tiptoed down the stairs, slipped out the kitchen and walked quietly across the yard. She made her way toward the creek and the place where she hoped to see Juan waiting. She was thinking of Jed waiting for her in the moonlight the night he took her driving through the empty aqueduct tunnel. She pushed the still-thrilling memory away. She'd been flirting not only with Jed, but with danger that night—she knew it now even if she'd been only half-conscious of it then. Tonight was no flirtation. There was potential for real danger and, she thought guiltily, I've drawn Juan into it.

Somewhere ahead, Independence Creek, still high in late August from the year's abundant Sierra snowpack, was singing. Soon she saw Juan, crouching next to the rocky stream, a dark spot against a large boulder. The spot unwound and lengthened as he stood to greet her. She heard a soft whinny, and he silently took her hand and led her to where he'd tied up two mares, a dark bay saddled and a black with only blanket and bridle. Juan stood with cupped hands next to the bay, giving Jane a heel up. Then he jumped in one smooth movement onto the other mare and turned her northeast. Janey followed. They cut across the valley toward Yaney's field.

It was nothing but a bit of open pasture, bordered on two sides by lines of cottonwoods, planted long ago as wind breaks, and on another side by the Yaney's farmhouse and barn. Some of the grand old trees were drooping now, their roots forced to reach farther and farther into the ground to find sustaining water, but they still screened the field from being seen by the road.

They heard the faint sound of voices. Juan motioned Jane to dismount, and they tied up the horses to the branches of a fallen tree. Quietly they covered the remaining 200 yards by foot, keeping low behind the cover of bushes. As they drew closer, Jane could see there were 15, maybe 20 men clustered by a stand of live oaks at the northwest corner of the field. Behind them, pulled up onto the field, were a half dozen automobiles that seemed to be mostly Model Ts. In the scant moonlight, they all looked the same to Jane, and she couldn't tell if any of them were her father's. Nor could she make him out in the group of men. They all wore dark clothing with hats pulled down low on their foreheads.

"I can't hear what they're saying, can you?" she asked Juan.

"No, let's move in a little more."

Jane was terrified that every footfall they made sounded like a crescendo of cymbals. Juan reached back to touch her, signaling stop. She strained to hear the men over her own breathing.

One of the men was speaking. "You fellas head for Tuttle Creek while…" The voice, carried by a night breeze, reached her ear then trailed off. The speaker may have turned in the other direction or the wind had shifted.

She couldn't hear the rest, but she saw the group break up and move toward the motor cars. There was some transferring of wooden boxes out of one vehicle and into others. Then the men got into their cars, three or four in each. One man, she thought, was the right size and moved in the deliberate way of her father. The engines started up, and the cars began to move out onto the road.

"What now?" asked Juan.

"Let's get the horses. If I heard right, one of those cars is headed to the aqueduct at Tuttle Creek. Maybe that's the one with my father." At least, Jane reassured herself, Tuttle Creek was not among the places where Van Norman had told her they had stationed armed guards. Perhaps, guided by the list printed in the *Register*, the Owens men had chosen unprotected targets. Perhaps she and Chalfant had prevented violence after all.

When they were again on horseback, Juan headed west. They rode to the far edge of the cultivated land until just below the Sierra wall, then they turned left and headed south toward the Alabama Hills. Here, they could travel faster, unobstructed except for scrub brush and scatterings of broken boulders. Juan glanced back at her, and Jane nodded, trying to muster more courage than she felt. They urged the horses into a gallop. The only light was a sliver of moon, and Jane was terrified of falling or losing Juan. But the big bay was steady footed and hardly seemed in need of direction from her, unerringly following the other horse and its master.

At last Juan slowed. She rode up beside him, and he reached over for the reins of her horse. She could hear the burbling of Tuttle Creek ahead. "Swell riding chica. Thought a city girl might a lost her feel for it," his smile revealed teeth that flashed white.

"I'm sure I will *feel* it but good, tomorrow," Jane groaned. Her body already had sore spots.

They reached the creek, its banks marked by a line of cottonwoods and willows, and turned left, trotting along its course until they could see the long silver ribbon of the aqueduct below them and the mirror of Owens Lake farther south. Leaving the horses tied to trees beside the creek, they crept toward the canal. There seemed to be no one around. A small crane slept on a repair barge near the eastern wall of the channel. There were no lights, apparently no attendants. The night was still except for the sound of flowing water.

"There," said Juan. A single Model T was gliding south on the main road. Its engine had been cut some ways back, its approach now announced only by the crunch of tires on the stony dirt road. It came to a stop, and three men got out, one carrying a wooden box. They knelt by the side of the canal, near where the barge was anchored, and one man switched on a flashlight.

Jane breathed a sigh of relief and whispered to Juan, "He's not there, my father's not there."

Juan nodded, but held a finger to his lips. Two of the men now moved back to their vehicles and crouched by its rear bumper. The third was backing away from the canal, his two extended hands clutching the handles of a bobbin, perhaps six inches in width, from which he was letting out cord like line from a fishing reel. He joined his companions behind the Model T, and again the flashlight revealed their hands and faces. One of the men, Jane thought it might be Carl Fredeker of the Bishop Creamery, cut the line with a knife. While the man who'd unwound the reel held the severed end up, the third man lit a match.

The fuse burst into a starburst of light, like a sparkler on the Fourth of July. It snapped and spat as it flew away from the men back toward the canal. Jane and Juan covered their ears with their hands and ducked low. The explosion ripped through the night, a mass of sound reverberating off of the mountains.

Jane opened her eyes, but in the darkness could see only a storm of smoke and dust. Then she heard the Model T's engine start up. The driver switched on its headlights for no more than 30 seconds, but in that time, she saw that a gash several feet wide had been opened in the canal wall, through which a small stream of water was flowing out onto ground littered with huge chunks of concrete. The barge was listing badly, one side already sinking below the surface.

She watched mesmerized as the crane bent over like a wounded bird, its beak drooping lower and lower, until it toppled into the water. The lights switched off, and the Model T turned east, heading around the northern shore of Owens Lake toward Keeler.

"They're getting off the main road because they know it's going to be swarming with armed guards coming from the north and south," whispered Jane. She put her hand on Juan's arm. "We better get out of here too."

"It's not a good idea to go back the way we came," he advised. "That blast has to have woken up the entire town of Lone Pine and folks for miles in all directions. Every rancher in this part of the valley is going to be out carrying a rifle."

"You're right," she agreed. "The mood is so tense here that no matter which side they're on, folks are likely to shoot first and ask questions later."

"All right, then I say we head north on the road, nice and normal. As long as we're not trying to hide or run, they're not likely to shoot us. If we run into guards, you tell them you're a Los Angeles reporter."

"Out riding around at two in the morning?!"

"Sure, you heard a rumor of an attack on the aqueduct tonight, and you were investigating."

"Hmmm, I guess that'll have to do." As they untied and mounted their horses, Jane saw her hands were shaking. "Juan, I'm sorry I got you into this…but, thank you."

*"De nada chica."* He flashed her a quick, narrow glimmer of white teeth, and then he was turning the black mare around and heading toward the road. Jane followed, nervously, feeling terribly cold for the first time that night. She pushed the collar of her jacket up around her throat.

It couldn't have been more than a few minutes before they saw headlights coming toward them from Lone Pine. As they neared, the lights became blinding, causing Jane's horse to rear. Juan caught hold of its reins and quieted it with a word. They waited as four black sedans surrounded them, stopped and disgorged a dozen men, most in police uniforms, brandishing tommy guns and sawed off shotguns.

"Get off those horses!" one of them barked while others rushed forward to grab hold of the animals' bridles. Someone said "It's a girl and a Mexican!" as Jane and Juan swung their legs over and jumped onto the ground.

"Hold on there!"

Jane recognized the voice, and her heart sank. It was none other than Mr. Van Norman, the assistant superintendent of the DWP. He pushed through the men. He was dressed in a suit and tie, as she'd seen him at the site of the first explosion, but his vest was misbuttoned, as if he been hurriedly roused from bed.

"Well, well, if it isn't Miss Bow?"

"Hello Mr. Van Norman."

"Our supposed reporter for the *Los Angeles Examiner*."

"I am a reporter for the *Examiner* sir."

"Strange then how the list of security stations I gave you ended up in the *Inyo Register* and not in the *Examiner*."

"I sometimes do work for both newspapers, Mr. Van Norman. And if you are a regular reader of the *Examiner*, you know that I did write a story, which, as I promised, made Angelenos aware of the efficient repair efforts of your crew."

"Nothing about security though."

"Mr. Loewenthal, the editor, declined to print that information, sir. I'm sure you understand the news from Owens Valley cannot claim too many columns in a newspaper with many events across a big city to cover."

"Seems it appeared in great detail in the *Register* though, didn't it?"

"Mr. Chalfant, the editor of that paper, found it newsworthy."

He wasn't getting anywhere, so changed his tact. "May I ask what you and your companion," he inquired, gesturing toward Juan, "are doing out on horseback in the middle of the night, miss?"

"I heard a rumor of an attack on the aqueduct, and wanted to investigate. I asked my neighbor Juan Escobar to accompany me for safety's sake."

"A rumor...from who? Who told you that?"

"Just whisperings, nobody in particular."

"Hmmm." He didn't believe her. "Did you see the attack?"

"No, just heard the explosion. We were several miles west when the blast came. We rode along Tuttle Creek as far as the aqueduct, but by the time we arrived, there was no one there. We did see damage to a canal wall and barge. I imagine you'll want to get down there and attend to it."

"James, Terry, take the boys on down." Van Norman waved his arm south, and most of the men climbed back into the vehicles. Idling engines revved, tires spun, and the cars lurched away like jackrabbits. Van Norman and two other men remained.

The assistant chief turned to Juan. "What's your name son?"

"Juan Escobar, sir."

"Where do you live and what is your trade?"

"My family has a place near Independence. I train and sell horses."

"Well, mister horse trainer and miss reporter, Sheriff Collins and I may want to talk to you again once we find out what we're dealing with here. You can go for now. Help the lady up, Mitch."

The man holding Jane's bridle gave her a leg up. Van Norman watched them walk their horses around the remaining motor car, then break into a trot in the direction of Lone Pine. She's not telling the truth, or at least not the whole truth. He knew it but could do nothing about it at present. "Come on boys!" He waved the remaining men toward the car. "Let's get a look at the damage."

Farther down the road, they saw the rest of the cars with their headlights aimed at the aqueduct. An additional half dozen cars, which had apparently driven up from the south, were parked in the other direction, also with headlights blazing. Some 30 men had spread out along the length of the canal, and were sweeping cones of illumination from flashlights onto the surrounding terrain. Van Norman got out of the car and went over to where two men were squatting next to a slash in the cement wall. Water was flowing out, carving a wide, shallow channel in the sandy ground, but it wasn't as bad as he had feared. The crane and barge, however, appeared to be a total loss. "How long?" he asked Baker, his top maintenance engineer.

"A day or two."

"Fine, do what you can to stop it up. I'll get a full crew out to you by 5 a.m."

Van Norman was starting back to the car, to head north to mobilize his workers, when the still, black night broke apart again with an immense boom that shook the ground beneath his feet. "Where is it?!" He spun around, peering south.

"Reckon, several miles, maybe a dozen miles south." Baker was on his feet too. "Could be Cottonwood Creek powerhouse!"

"Damn! Those fools must have all driven up here, leaving it unprotected! Son of a bitch!"

The men came running toward him, and he waved them in and told them all to shut up. "Mitch, take a dozen men with you and guard the canal north of here in five-mile sections. I want you patrolling up and down those sections all night. Dorman, you come south with me." As the men started to head to the cars, he grabbed Dorman's arm roughly. "What did you think you were doing leaving the canal and powerhouse wide open to come up here?"

"But boss, I thought…" the man replied, stupid with sleepiness, intoxication or both.

Van Norman shoved him away and headed to his own car. If I'm not mistaken, he thought anxiously, that last one was a much bigger blast. This one might have been a decoy.

He flattened himself against the side of the canal, hoping the search-lights couldn't reach him and the guard walking a few feet above his head couldn't see him. Ben Bow tried to stuff as much of himself as he could fit into the drainage tunnel where he had just placed a charge in a mound of blasting gelatin. He knew he was trapped.

A couple of hours before, John Dodge and Cal Shaw had driven him from the meeting at Yaney's field and dropped him off at Cottonwood Creek. He'd followed the creek from the road, east to where it was taken into the aqueduct, from which point it paralleled the western shore of Owens Lake. Here, about 12 miles south of Lone Pine, was one of the first hydroelectric plants the city had built to generate power for aqueduct construction.

He'd known the power station had a guard shack, but been unprepared when, a half hour after he had arrived, nearly a dozen heavily armed men had driven up in several cars and begun setting up a searchlight. It now swept the ground in long arcs of illumination as the men patrolled the top of the aqueduct.

Ben knew he'd been lucky to arrive ahead of the security contingent. If he'd come later, it would have been impossible, with all those eyes about, to reach the wall of the canal unobserved. But now he had a different dilemma: He wasn't going to be able to light the fuse. With the men up there, somebody was bound to get hurt. And whether he did or didn't, getting away now seemed hopeless.

Still, Ben stuck with the plan. He set the charge and placed the fuse. Then he tried to stay out of sight while he waited. Thoughts tumbled about in his head. How odd to be here, dug into the dirt at Cottonwood Creek…to have finally become a fighter like Pa.

As a young man, Ben's father, Gilead Bow, had headed west from St. Louis to find his fortune in the gold mines of Colorado. Once there, he'd steered clear of the worst of the Civil War by signing on to drive cattle south to Carson City, Nevada. Eventually the wranglers had brought a herd from there into the Owens Valley, and Gilead had decided to stay.

For a year or two, Gilead fought Indians with the California Cavalry, out of Fort Independence, and was right proud of it. Growing up, Ben had been regaled with tales of how Gilead and his mates had subdued the Paiute, which he avowed to be a cruel, thieving and treacherous race. His Pa several times recounted how they'd chased one band down Cottonwood Creek into Owens Lake, where a strong easterly wind blowing across the water had prevented the Indians from swimming to safety. Not one had escaped.

When a rich deposit of copper was discovered near Fort Independence on the eastern slope of the Sierra Nevada, Gilead caught mining fever again and worked for a time at the Kearsarge Mine. He didn't get rich, but he made enough to stake his future in the valley he'd come to love. In 1865, he filed a claim on a piece of land next to Independence Creek, traveled to Carson City, where he bought an old wooden frame house and married a young woman named Martha, both of which he transported back to Owens Valley. The rest of it—corrals, barn and milkhouse—Gilead built with his own hands. He borrowed a team of two oxen to pull the plow that broke up acres of grassy meadowland and tilled the soil for seed.

The US Homestead Act of 1862 ensured that if he lived for five years on his claim and made improvements, he would earn title to it. By 1870, Gilead Bow owned one of the nicest little ranches in the valley. Over the next decade, with the Indians largely subdued, more settlers poured in, but the best land, along the rushing Sierra creeks and Owens River, was already taken. Still, with the river supplying far more water than anyone could ever use, the newcomers set about digging irrigation canals to bring the water out to their dry homesteads and fields.

Ben and his two sisters, Margaret and Laura, were washed in the first minutes of their lives with water drawn from Independence Creek, and they spent the sweetest hours of their childhoods playing in and along the burbling, singing mountain stream. It had seemed to Ben, though, that these hours were few and that most of his life was spent performing chores under the strict command of his tough, humorless father.

Young Ben was a smart lad and a hard worker, but he knew his father considered him too much of a thinker. Ben was always coming up with odd ideas, like a way to improve the storage life of hay and alfalfa or to change the direction of planting rows to make better use of sun exposure. "Dreaming again instead of workin!" was Gilead's customary response.

By the time Ben was in his early 20s, with Ma and Laura both taken by influenza, Margaret gone to Bishop as schoolmarm and Pa's robust constitution finally given out to a fatal heart attack, the young man was master of the ranch. Gradually, he expanded and improved the house and put his ideas into practice in the fields. Within a few years, he turned one of the first small ranches in the valley into one of its best producers.

But to what end? Ben asked himself, shivering in the dirt by the canal. What my father built, I improved. I made it better and stronger—for what? My own son didn't care enough about it to stay. He cast it off like an old pair of socks not worth the darning. And Jane, she has her life in the city too, a life she would soon return to, whichever way this all turned out.

How had it come to this? He, the son of a man who had built a prosperous ranch from nothing but his own hands, now dug into the dirt here, bent on destruction? The turn of events that had brought him here, after spending his whole life building and improving on his father's legacy, surpassed his comprehension. In truth, Ben could understand how the men who'd built the aqueduct would be proud of what they'd accomplished too—it was a feat often compared to the Panama Canal. But while the aqueduct had at first been like a snake, winding through the valley, disliked but tolerated, it had now become, with all the groundwater pumping, an octopus poking its tentacles into every vein of the community.

A distant "boom!" split the still night, rousing him from his reverie. The guards began shouting at each other and running. "What was that?" "Dynamite, north a here!" "Come on, let's go!" They all piled into the automobiles they'd arrived in.

That's it, that's the signal! Ben held his pocket watch up to his ear and counted out the seconds: 60 of them, then start over and do it 20 more times. By then, the guards would be all the way to Tuttle Creek and it would be time to light the fuse. The searchlight was still on, but it didn't matter, there was no one left to see him. He was beginning to unwind his cramped legs when he heard the steps above him on the canal wall again. His heart sank. At least one of the guards was still there. He wasn't going to be able to do it after all.

There was the sound of an automobile coming north along the road, and the guard ran over to the searchlight. Ben raised himself enough to peek over the side of the canal. The man swung the heavy light in the direction of the car, a large black sedan, which swerved, slowed and came to a halt. A tall man leapt out of the door and yelled, "Turn off that damned light!"

When the bewildered guard hesitated, the man reached into his car, brought out a pistol and pointed it at the searchlight. It exploded in a splintering crash. The guard yelled and scampered away to take cover near the lake. Ben didn't see exactly where he went, as his eyes were adjusting to the darkness, but he did see the man with the gun get back into his car and continue driving north.

As he drove, Fred Eaton stroked his trusty old Belgian FN semi-automatic lying on the passenger seat. He'd bought it back in 1904 for the buckboard trip up to Owens Valley with Mulholland, breaking it in and practicing his marksmanship by blasting "dead soldiers," the whiskey bottles they'd emptied and discarded along the way across the desert. He had dozens of other guns now, but he was still partial to this one. He'd taken it, along with a rifle, down to Mojave to do some business with the slaughterhouse. But his effort to negotiate a better price for his cattle had come to naught and, frustrated, he'd changed his plan to stay at the Harvey House in Barstow, wanting nothing more than to get back to his ranch. So he'd driven through the night alone, and it would probably be morning before he reached Long Valley.

Damned the accursed Mulholland! Eaton fumed. If the man would just see reason and buy the reservoir site, all of this damned nonsense would stop. He will someday, Eaton reassured himself, someday he'll have to.

Ben, watching the sedan move up the road, realized that this strange occurrence had given him what might well be his one and only chance. He quickly unrolled the length of fuse out a hundred feet and knelt behind a pile of boulders along the creek. Then he lit the fuse and watched, hands over ears, while the spark retraced his steps.

"Boom!" He put his head down as the sky rained concrete, ash and sand. When the plume of smoke and debris cleared, Ben drew out the small flashlight he carried in his back pocket and walked over to the canal. About 150 feet of canal wall had been blown out, and water was escaping in all directions. He smiled with satisfaction. They'd have to open the gates of the Alabama spillway to stop the flow enough to make repairs. He had essentially shut down water delivery to Los Angeles.

Ben switched off the flashlight and though little aided by the dim moonlight, made his way by foot across the land he knew so well, back to the Bow ranch. He arrived home just before dawn and crawled into bed, wrapping himself around Alice's back. She took his arms and tucked them tighter about her. They slept, both of them for the first time that night.

Alice got up a couple of hours later, telling Ben to stay in bed a bit longer, she'd start the milking. She closed their bedroom door silently and tiptoed to the stairs. At the other end of the hallway, Janey's door stood open. The thorns of anxiety that had pricked Alice's stomach all of the previous night returned. She hadn't heard Janey leave, but lying awake in the early hours, she'd heard her come in. That had been a good two hours before Ben came home, so she imagined her daughter had been sound asleep by then. Very likely, Alice surmised, Ben didn't know Janey had been out in the night and Janey didn't know Ben had. She intended to keep it that way if she could.

Downstairs there was a note on the kitchen table: "I'm off early to Bishop. See you at supper, Jane."

---

"The president is sending federal agents." W.B. Matthews could finally deliver some good news to his boss. "Governor Young called President Coolidge last night."

"It's about God-damned time!" Mulholland growled on the other end of the telephone line. But Matthews could hear relief wrapped in the complaint. He felt it too, and a cautious anticipation of success, a sense that things might finally be turning definitively their way.

While Governor Richardson had been of no help, he'd been replaced six months ago by the more activist Clement Calhoun Young. The Progressive wing of the Republican party had finally become so frustrated by the overly conservative policies of Richardson, that they had pushed the incumbent out in the primary election, replacing him with Young as their presidential candidate. Victorious in the general election, Young had proved in the first six months of his administration to be quite inclined to action.

When Matthews called, the governor's aide assured him they would be happy to take the matter in hand. A request from a Republican governor would, of course, be entertained by a Republican president.

And Coolidge, who had recently vetoed a bill that would have provided price supports for farmers, declaring agriculture must stand "on an independent business basis," was likely to be receptive to this particular request.

"This should be the end of it then," pronounced Mulholland. "I've heard all I ever want to hear about the Owens Valley. It's been a damned distraction."

"I hope it's over, Bill. I'll keep you posted."

"God willing, I won't have to hear anything more about it." The chief slammed down the phone.

Matthews didn't take it personally. He was used to Mulholland's tempers, and the man's antagonism toward the Owens Valley, whose resistance he'd taken as a personal affront and challenge to his authority, had become venomous and intransigent. Matthews also knew that Mulholland wanted nothing better than to lose himself in what he saw as the final great engineering challenge of his life and culmination of his career: the Colorado River Aqueduct, which would transport an immense quantity of water across Arizona to Southern California.

Perhaps this would finally be the end to all the turmoil. But if it wasn't, Matthews had another idea. It had come to him when Wilfred Watterson had requested an appointment to discuss the possibility of selling the family ranch to the city. Matthews had been hard-pressed to hide his surprise at receiving this call, and unconvinced when Watterson explained that, with his father passed away and his mother ailing, the family had deemed it best to unburden itself of the property.

Matthews suspected the unexpected sale signaled something of greater significance. After talking with Wilfred, he'd called the man's estranged uncle George, who'd expressed a profoundly critical view of his nephews and their enterprises. The man was a weasel, in Matthews's opinion, but what he'd said had given the lawyer an idea. For now, however, he'd keep it in his back pocket and wait to see how events turned.

Within a few days, lower Owens Valley, from the aqueduct intake near Independence to the now increasingly dry Owens Lake, was under siege. Federal agents and city police patrolled the length of the canal, stopping and searching automobiles on the road.

Neither of the Bows dared venture out again, but there were others who did. Within days of each other, there were two new blasts in the Alabama Hills, one ripping out 14 feet of aqueduct wall. Despite the heavy presence of security, somehow the bombers managed to find opportunities to strike.

"There are some clever fellas out there playin cat-and-mouse with the guards," Chalfant told Jane, his voice expressing a certain admiration. "But the situation is getting more dangerous. The organizers have lost control. Even they don't know exactly who's behind these last attacks or when and where the next one will be."

Finally, one hot August morning when W.B. Matthews was yet again fuming over a *Times* front-page story about the latest attack on the aqueduct, he put the paper aside and picked up the phone to make the call. Afterward, he told himself it had been unavoidable. They'd had their chance to see reason. And if people got hurt, well, it was because they were standing in the way of progress.

# Chapter 22

"There's something going on out there." Bucky Porter loped over to the grimy window and peered out at the street. "What in blazes?!" He went to the door and stuck his head out. "Everyone's goin over to the bank, Mr. Chalfant!"

It was noon, and Chalfant had been about to head home for lunch. He joined Porter at the door. "What the hell?! Stay here, Bucky, I'll go see what's up."

Chalfant grabbed his hat and called out "John, what is it?" He intercepted the manager of the Bishop Creek Hotel, who was walking at a rapid pace by the door.

"They say the bank's closed and there's a sign up on the door," said John Burkhardt as Chalfant fell in beside him. A couple of dozen people were milling around the bank's front entrance. Some were trying to peek around drawn window shades to see inside. The two men pushed through them.

"What does it mean Chalfant?" "What's going on here?" People called out to the editor as they let him pass, accustomed as they were to relying on the newspaper for community information. In front of the door, Chalfant stood, stunned, reading the sign:

**We find it necessary to close our banks in the Owens Valley. This result has been brought about by the past four years of destructive work carried on by the city of Los Angeles.**

"This is just temporary, isn't it?" someone asked.

"They've got my money in there!"

"They can't just close the bank like that, can they, without giving us our money back?!"

"They're gonna reopen, right?"

Chalfant turned around and raised his hands to calm the crowd and shield his eyes from the blazing mid-day sun of late summer. "Hold on, hold on folks. I'll get to the bottom of this. Let me just get back to my office for a minute."

They stood aside again to let him pass and watched him run the block and a half to the *Register* and go inside. He went to the telephone and called the bank number. It rang and rang. Chalfant hung up and dialed Mark Watterson's private number. After eight or nine rings, it picked up. "Hello." Chalfant hardly recognized the voice, so devoid was it of his friend's customary cheer.

"Mark, it's Willie Chalfant. What's going on?"

"It's Willie…" Chalfant heard him speak to someone in a muffled voice, as if he'd covered the receiver with his palm. "All right. Willie, you'd better come over here. I'll let you in—but only you, no one else."

Many more people had joined the throng when Chalfant got back to the bank. "Keep calm folks, I'm going to go in and get some information," he told them.

They made way. Delford Morton, the bank guard opened the door a few inches and motioned for Chalfant to come in, saying "Stay back now, folks, stay back!" to those who tried to press in behind the editor as he slipped through the door.

Chalfant glanced around the bank floor. Usually a hive of activity at this time of day, it was dark from the drawn shades and completely empty. Jason Hirsch, the assistant manager, stood behind the counter whispering with the two tellers, Morton Brown and Dave Green, and Wilfred's secretary Daraleen Penny. They watched Chalfant mount the stairs to the mezzanine.

Wilfred was sitting at Mark's desk near the back wall, his countenance pale as ash after a hot fire. Mark, who stood next to him, smiled shakily and extended his hand to his friend. After a moment, Wilfred rose and did the same. He sat back down, and Chalfant and Mark took the two facing chairs.

"Well?" asked Chalfant. "What does that sign mean?"

"It means we're finished," Wilfred answered. "This bank, the four other branches and all of our other enterprises in the valley are bankrupt."

"How can that be, what the hell happened?!"

Wilfred slumped in his chair. "Monday morning, the bank examiner paid us a visit—two months ahead of when his next normal visit should have been." Wilfred cleared his throat and continued. "We hadn't expected him, Willie...and ah, he found a shortfall."

"A shortfall?" echoed the shocked editor. "How much?"

"They say about $800,000, but it's nowhere near that much."

"How did this happen?!" Chalfant repeated his question.

"We had to divert a little money from some accounts to keep the valley going in the fight against Los Angeles. It's just bad timing, Willie. If the examiner hadn't come early, we'd have put it all back by the time he got here." Wilfred continued, his voice and eyes darkening, "And one has to wonder what prompted his early visit."

"The city had something to do with it, we're pretty sure of that!" injected Mark.

Very likely, thought Chalfant. "So just a temporary problem then?"

"Should have been," replied Wilfred. "The bank commissioner gave us five days to restore the funds. I went down to Los Angeles to try to arrange loans from some of the members of the Clearinghouse Association—you remember, the fellows who promised to help when we held the Alabama Gates?" His voice grated with resentment, "Nothing, not a penny."

"I got back last night and we told our families," Wilfred continued. "We came in this morning and told the staff." He gazed up at Chalfant with moist, beseeching eyes. "Our time's up, Willie. Any moment now the bank examiner will be back with Sheriff Collins. We expect to be arrested for embezzlement."

"Oh my God!" Chalfant studied one and then the other of his friends, not comprehending how this could be happening, not knowing what else to say. "My God," he repeated, shaking his head. There was nothing he could say. Chalfant murmured, "I'll wait with you."

He did, as Mark's desk clock ticked through the minutes. There were about 20 ticks before they heard a pounding on the door down below. Mark rose and went to the rail of the mezzanine. "That will be the sheriff, Delford. Let him in."

The bank examiner, a small man in a shapeless brown suit, came up the stairs. Sheriff Collins, towering above him, followed. The examiner was holding the sign from the door, which he had apparently ripped down. He looked at Wilfred, who rose and shook his head.

"Sheriff," the little man said in a grave, sorrowful voice, "please do your duty sir."

Collins stepped forward. "I'm sorry about this boys. Wilfred and Mark Watterson, I'm arresting you on the charge of embezzlement. You'll need to come with me now."

Chalfant walked behind them. The raucous crowd outside had tripled in size, and there were automobiles double-parked along the street. As they stepped onto the sidewalk, the onlookers grew silent, watching in shocked bewilderment as the solemn procession passed through them, continued down the street three blocks, then crossed the street. It wasn't until the grim party had disappeared into the sheriff's office that the spell broke, and the watchers turned back to Chalfant. He had remained standing in front of the bank's door, which had again been closed and locked. Demands for an explanation came at him in a tidal wave. He held up his arms for quiet, and addressed his neighbors.

"Wilfred and Mark Watterson have been arrested for embezzlement." Another wave of sound, this time marked by cries of disbelief.

He motioned for quiet again. "They are accused of it, that's all. In this country, that doesn't make them guilty. I'll be taking up a collection for their bail. A lot of you folks here owe them that much. They've carried this whole valley for years!"

There were a few scattered shouts of agreement and pledges of help. But Carl Fredeker cried out, "How are we supposed to donate to their bail fund if we can't get our money out of their bank?!"

Others joined in. "Yeah, when is the bank gonna reopen?"

"There's still money left in it, isn't there?"

"We're gonna get our money out aren't we?!"

All Chalfant could say was, "I don't know yet. We're going to have to wait a few days for more information. In the meantime, I hope you'll do what you can for the Wattersons. You can drop by the *Register* if you want to make a donation."

---

Some folks did, reaching into their pockets and purses to give what they could. Old Mrs. Parker came in and handed Chalfant a dollar, her hand shaking but her chin firm with resolve. He knew she and Cyril could ill afford it, but he didn't want to dishonor her brave act by refusing.

"Thank you ma'am," he said, feeling her boney fingers beneath the worn glove as he pressed her hand in gratitude. "It will make a difference. I'll tell the Wattersons, let them know there's folks behind them."

"Please do. Thank you kindly, Mr. Chalfant." She nodded, smiled faintly with trembling lips, and left.

Most of the $25,000 bail for each man came from the little valley's bigger fish, however. Within an hour of the arrest, Chalfant was on the telephone to business associates of the Wattersons with holdings in mining, transportation and other commercial interests. By eight o'clock that evening, bail had been posted, and the Wattersons were released to their families. Their trial was set for November.

---

The next few weeks saw the Wattersons come forth with something of their old fighting spirit. The brothers held rallies up and down the valley, in which they attempted to explain their situation. They told attendees that the bank had faltered because of all the frozen loans to people unable to make payments due to recession, drought and the conflict with

Los Angeles. In the Bishop meeting, Jane sat next to Chalfant, marveling as the crowd cheered the Wattersons, cursed Los Angeles and pledged nearly $600,000 to help make up the bank shortfall.

Leaving the assembly hall, a man just behind them shouted, "Bomb the aqueduct to hell!" and several others shouted their approval. Chalfant turned and stopped so abruptly that the inciter almost ran into him. The editor skewered the man with his fierce regard, deliberately speaking in a voice that carried to many around him.

"You know all that's finished now. We all know it." His words, Jane thought, tolled like a funeral bell.

At the Independence meeting, Jane sat next to her parents as they heard much the same appeal from the Wattersons. The audience here was a bit less enthusiastic, and the pledge total was considerably lower. Ben was noncommittal, saying only "We don't know all the facts yet." Jane knew they had always had an account at the bank, but she didn't dare ask how much money was in it. Alice went up at the end of the meeting to offer encouragement and volunteer to be a character witness at the trial.

But by September, the weight of reality was dragging down the Wattersons' momentum. Pledges weren't acted upon, as cash grew scarce. A bank from Bakersfield opened up a branch in Bishop, making credit available again to relieve the commercial stagnation in the towns, where shopkeepers barely had enough cash to make change. But that did nothing to help the many farmers who, with their working capital and, in many cases, life savings tied up in the failed banks, could no longer afford to make purchases from the shopkeepers.

Gradually, enough information seeped out from the criminal investigation against the Wattersons to contradict their message. The brothers, it now seemed, had diverted money from bank accounts for their own speculations in mining, a soda processing business at Keeler on Owens Lake, a resort and mineral water business at Coso Hot Springs and other ventures. When these businesses had faltered, they'd sold securities held by them for customers, and used the proceeds to try to prop up their own enterprises. They'd even falsified reports to the banking commission.

The money was clearly gone. Depositors weren't ever going to get it back. People who'd trusted their life savings to the bank were now penniless. People who had sold their properties to Los Angeles and deposited the payment were doubly hit because now they had neither land nor money. Some of them had opted to lease their land back from the city, less the water rights, and Los Angeles now made a gesture of assistance to these tenants, offering to delay collection of rents.

Those who still owned their land but had mortgages with the Wattersons saw these turned over to a Los Angeles bank. The new lender, having no reason to extend payment terms with the flexibility the brothers had practiced, promptly began foreclosure procedures for anyone who couldn't pay.

Many valley men, accustomed to being breadwinners and masters of their own farms and ranches, swallowed their pride and went to work for Los Angeles as day laborers, drilling the very wells that were sucking their fields dry or constructing the DWP buildings that now popped up throughout the valley. Many families began to pack up and leave the valley for good.

They included the Bows. One evening when Jane returned to the ranch for supper, her parents were waiting for her at the kitchen table. There was no bear hug to greet her. As soon as she came in the door and saw them there, so solemn, she knew. She put her bag on the sideboard and sat down with them.

"Janey, we're going to have to sell the ranch," said Ben. He waited for his words to settle in, saw the pain in her eyes, but no surprise. "We lost a lot of money when the bank went bust. We don't have enough to finish the planting and get through the winter."

"Chris will loan you…"

"I'm not taking charity from my own son," Ben said firmly.

"But Pa…"

"We won't speak of that again." His eyes had gone icy.

"It will be fine, Janey," Alice touched her daughter's arm. "Once we sell the ranch we'll have enough to get started again someplace. And we'll all three of us still go to Chris's wedding next month." She swallowed stiffly. "We've got enough for that."

Jane nodded miserably. She asked her father, "You're going to sell to Los Angeles?"

"Who else is doing any buying in the Owens Valley?" He shrugged, trying to make a joke of it, but there was no humor in his voice.

"I've approached the aqueduct administrator in Bishop," Ben quietly explained. "He said he'd be in touch. I've heard they're still buying property along the creeks—they want to tie up every drop of water they can—so we should get a reasonable bid. Some of our neighbors who depend on irrigation won't be that lucky. The city's bought up enough property along the main irrigation ditches to make it pretty near impossible for the hold-outs to keep the ditches open themselves. I've heard that when those folks go offering to sell, they're getting a pretty cool reception. Probably they'll eventually get something, but it won't be as good a price as the folks who sold earlier."

---

In October, they made the trip south for Chris's wedding, Ben and Alice in the Model T and Jane following in the green roadster. They left before dawn and drove straight through, not wanting to spend money on lodging. There hadn't yet been any word on the sale of the ranch, but they were in good spirits, despite everything, at the prospect of the trip. Along the way, they picnicked on Alice's fried chicken, potato salad, deviled eggs and sugar cookies. In Los Angeles they stopped at a service station to freshen up before driving through the twin vaulted Spanish gates of Bel Air and up the winding roads to Chris's mansion.

Jane had tried to prepare her parents for the house, but saw she'd failed. They were stunned silent by the size and grandeur of the palm-embellished, bougainvillea-draped main house, with towering columns at its entrance, and even more so by the ample single-story guest house that was to be their abode during the visit. Watching them, Jane guessed their son's prosperity, which they'd certainly known about but never fully imagined, cut cruelly in contrast to their own reduced circumstances. And yet, she thought, there must be some pride over what he's accomplished and some reassurance in it. Chris might be negligent with letters and visits, but he would never let his family starve.

And, indeed, Chris Bow lavished comfort and attention on them from the first moment he came bounding down the steps from his front door. "Ma, Pa, it's wonderful to see you, wonderful to have you here!"

Jane saw the mix of emotions playing on her parents' faces as they returned his greeting. She knew they both missed Chris immensely—it had been more than four years, by her accounting, since they'd seen him.

But they must also be feeling, is this our son? Did they find him terribly changed? Jane wondered. She studied her brother: His hair had not only darkened, it had thinned a little at the crown. Brut his face was unlined and he was as fit as ever. He had dressed casually, in navy blue houndstooth trousers and pale blue shirt with rolled-up sleeves.

"Hey there little Hazy!"

"Hello Chris." She stuck her tongue out at him for the nickname as he gave her a hug. Pa started to unpack the luggage, but Chris stopped him. "Peterson will see to those. Come on in, you must be tired and hungry!"

Ben and Alice let their son usher them across the colorful tile foyer, trying not to stare at the dark-suited man who said "Welcome to Los Angeles Mr. and Mrs. Bow," then went outside to take their belongings into the guest house.

It was the beginning of what ought to have been a dreamlike idyll for two people who had spent nearly every day of the past 30 years rising at dawn to shoulder a never-ending cycle of chores and responsibilities. But Jane could see her parents struggling. Ma, a woman used to organizing success in everything she undertook, managed to get through each day's events and interactions with poise and charm. With her refined nature and immaculate grooming, she appeared elegant, even in her simple dresses, next to Chris's chic fiancé Dorothy Bradshaw and her rather fussily attired mother and sisters. Alice entertained their solicitous, if somewhat cold, conversation with her always well-considered, generous responses. Yet Jane could see the effort cost her dearly. At night, finally freed from the requirement to perform, Alice collapsed on her bed, Ben often coming to place a cold washcloth on her forehead.

Pa was less outgoing, though always courteous. He took every occasion that presented itself to embark on long walks, claiming to be taken with the lush planting along the roads that curved up and around the hillsides. No doubt he was partial to it, but Jane thought what he most sought was escape and solitude.

The wedding was an elegant affair, with hundreds of guests arriving in chauffeured cars at the Bel Air Country Club. The bride wore a veil of handmade Italian lace and her dress trailed a 20-foot train. The wedding cake had six layers separated by columns carved in white chocolate, and was topped by bride and groom figurines waltzing beneath a gold-leafed canopy. At the end of the day's festivities the real bride and groom left amid rice and wishes of "bon voyage!" for a month-long honeymoon in Paris, Venice and Rome.

The Bows, at Chris's urging, stayed on in the guest house a little longer. The sale of the ranch was still pending and, he argued, Ben might pursue an agreement more effectively from Los Angeles. Perhaps his son was right, Ben thought. In any case, having missed the winter crop cycle, and with neighbors looking after the livestock, there was little reason to return right away and, Ben hated to admit it, little means of doing so. They settled into a quiet sojourn, declining as many invitations from the Bradshaws as they dared, relieved to be spending most of their time in each other's company or that of the house staff. Alice invaded the kitchen, befriending the initially horrified cook, Mrs. Torrey, with flattery and shared recipes. Ben began coming back from his walks with pocketfuls of cuttings and seeds from exotic plants, and started a small experimental garden at the side of the guest house.

Jane took the occasional assignment from Loewenthal. She saw a few friends, going out to the movies with Simon, visiting Katharine and Shirley in the house she had briefly shared with them on Bunker Hill. She told her parents finally about her engagement to Jed and showed them his picture. He had written to tell her that the job in Cairo was wrapping up, and he'd be back for good by mid-March. Ma, she could tell, was greatly relieved to know her only daughter was not to remain a spinster after all. Pa smiled and kissed her, but she thought he seemed wistful and unhappy.

---

Jane returned to Owens Valley in late October to cover the trial for the *Examiner*. It was held at the Inyo County Courthouse in Independence. With the ranch house closed, she stayed for the trial's duration with Rosie.

On the day the proceeding opened, William Mulholland, with son Perry and new daughter-in-law Addie, set off on a cruise ship to New York via the Panama Canal. The chief would have the opportunity to examine at close hand the engineering feat to which the Los Angeles Aqueduct was so often compared. And when the massive ship passed through the canal docks, Mulholland expected he might rightly feel a sense of accomplishment—in consideration that 50 years ago, before the canal had been built, he and his brother had been forced to walk across the Isthmus of Panama, being too poor to afford passage by boat or train. Meanwhile, the long deadlock with the Owens Valley seemed to have been broken for good with the revelation of the perfidy of those Watterson brothers. On that score too, Mulholland felt a deserved sense of satisfaction.

At Independence, every available seat in the courtroom was occupied by reporters who came from all over the state to cover the scandal and by valley folk who came to watch the somber final act of what many felt to be the end of their way of life. Chalfant, sitting next to Janey, smiled encouragingly at Wilfred and Mark Watterson as they took their places next to defense attorney Philip Carey. Wilfred was thin and drawn. Mark seemed more his old self, smiling at their neighbors and former customers arrayed in the jury box. On the other side of the aisle from the Wattersons sat District Attorney Jess Hession, a lifelong friend, charged with the miserable duty of prosecuting them.

Chalfant scanned the public seating, nodding greetings here and there to the many folks he knew. He stood to reach up over a row of seats, to grasp the proffered hand of Jacob Clausen. Next to the engineer was his wife Elizabeth, her lovely face as pale and strained as that of her eldest brother Wilfred.

"Ladies and gentlemen of the jury," Hession began his opening statement. "We will show that Wilfred and Mark Watterson breached the trust of their customers by deliberately taking money from their accounts and investing it in their own profit-making schemes. We will show that they illegally sold securities belonging to customers and that they falsified two banking reports, overstating assets, to hide these misdeeds. All told, they are charged with 36 counts of embezzlement and grand theft for crimes amounting to $2.3 million."

In his opening statement, defense attorney Carey told the jury that while the Wattersons admitted to diverting the funds, they had used them to work for the valley, always in the best interests of their friends and neighbors. He repeated a key theme from the Wattersons' rallies, that the diversions had been necessary because of all the frozen loans to ranchers and farmers unable to pay during the hard times after the war and during the struggle with Los Angeles. Moreover, the Wattersons had always viewed the funds as loans, intending to restore them once reparations could be secured from the city.

Judge Lambert stopped Carey there. "I won't allow that line of argument. This is a criminal court. I am not trying a case between Inyo County and the city of Los Angeles. The jury will disregard all such references. Mr. Hession, call your first witness."

The prosecutor called the bank examiner, and there began a methodical unrolling of one piece of clear, persuasive evidence after another. Hession showed definitively that the Wattersons' contention that they had been forced to divert funds because of frozen loans was false. The detailed audit conducted immediately after their arrest proved that while they had shown considerable forbearance to customers who couldn't make payments, the bank had nevertheless been profitable due to a majority of loans paid on time and a steady stream of deposits. Hession followed up those revelations by presenting evidence that the Wattersons had, in fact, failed to cancel loans already paid off, keeping them falsely on their books.

On the second day of presenting his case, Hession dropped his bombshells: The Wattersons were unable to account for $33,000 in cash. Also, they had listed $190,000 as on account with the Wells Fargo Bank of San Francisco—an account that did not and had never existed.

"Now if that isn't stealing, I don't know what is!" the prosecutor concluded, letting his grave, sad eyes rest on the defendants.

Most devastating of all to many in the room, the entire amount raised in the Owens Valley Irrigation District bond issue, more than $400,000, was missing! This evidence was so overwhelming that, in making the case for the defense the next day, Carey didn't even try to refute it. Unable to introduce the Los Angeles issue, he could only repeat that although the bankers knew what they had done to be illegal, they felt they had been acting rightly as they'd been forced to these actions in defense of their customers and community. Carey brought forth a string of character witnesses, which did not include Alice Bow. While she had initially pledged to be among them, Jane's mother had found the trip north unaffordable. There were many others, however, who did appear, including some who had lost their life savings to the Wattersons' mismanagement.

When the defense rested its case, Hession rose to make his summation. He acknowledged the testimony of the witnesses to the good character of Wilfred and Mark Watterson. "If I were not prosecuting this case, I would be among them," he told the jury, tears welling up in his eyes. "But in the final accounting, it is their neighbors, whose faith is unbounded, who are the victims of these men."

Judge Lambert gave instructions to the jury, and its members filed out of the room. Jane followed Chalfant out to the corridor, where he slumped on a bench. She went to buy them both a coffee from the stand in the lobby. When she returned, she saw Jacob Clausen had joined him.

"I've taken Elizabeth over to the hotel for a rest. She's about to collapse from nerves," Clausen was saying. He regarded Jane as she approached. "Hello Miss Bow. A wretched day, is it not?"

"Yes it is Mr. Clausen, it surely is. Perhaps this might help?" She offered up a steaming cup.

"No, very kind of you, but no thanks," he declined. Jane sat on the other side of Chalfant and held out a coffee to him. The editor took it, sipped and rubbed two fingers up along the bridge of his nose. "This whole story reads like a Greek tragedy," he observed. "After all those years of struggle, it's over, just like that, not with a bang, but with a whimper."

He pushed the fingers up into his white mop of hair and continued. "It's especially galling to read the moral outrage being expressed by the Los Angeles papers," he nodded at Jane, "the *Examiner* excepted of course. What has it been, a few months, since the Lewis and Berman trial? The pyramid scheme to end all pyramid schemes—$40 million embezzled from 42,000 investors! Now, I'd say that makes the Wattersons' crime look like child's play. But the fact is, the Wattersons are likely to be convicted today while those crooks, because of political pressure and plentiful bribes, were found not guilty. Dozens of others who were up to their eyeballs in the scheme, including, I might add, some of the city's most prominent citizens, probably including District Attorney Keyes, got off free as birds."

The truth and injustice of it weighed down on them. They sat silently until, after a long time, Jacob spoke. "There's one last chance, a long-shot, to be sure, but it could save the valley." Chalfant and Jane turned toward him. He ignored the disbelief in their eyes and continued. "I've heard some talk, through some guys I work with in Reclamation, that there are concerns about the stability of the St. Francis Dam. Seems that…now, mind you, all dams have leaks…but…"

"But the St. Francis might have more than ordinary leakage?" interrupted Chalfant. Clausen nodded.

"What does that have to do with Owens Valley?" Jane asked dully.

"Well, if evidence could be found that Mulholland made mistakes in the design of the St. Francis," Clausen conjectured, "two things might happen: First, they'd probably have to lower the fill level to take pressure off of the structure, and with reduced ability to store water at the southern end of the aqueduct, there'd be renewed pressure for a large reservoir in the north.

"Second, it would shake the unquestioning confidence the city leaders, press and public have in Mulholland, possibly putting pressure on him to take a more conciliatory attitude toward the valley. It's a long shot, as I said, but the end result might well be that the valley ends up with a dam in Long Valley like Reclamation originally planned. And with adequate water storage above the aqueduct intake, there'd be enough water for a fair allocation to the valley farmers who still own their land."

"You mean those who are left," said Jane.

"Yes, those who are left," Clausen agreed gravely.

"Interesting idea, but who's going to find the evidence?" asked Chalfant. "The resistance here in the valley has all but collapsed. Folks don't have the will or means left to fight."

Clausen nodded, and again they sat silently. Finally, Clausen excused himself to see after Elizabeth. Chalfant got heavily to his feet and went off to tend to other business around town. Jane went outside and took a side lane off of Main Street, walking toward the edge of town. At the corner, near the end of the lane, was Mary's little brown house, which had been occupied after her leaving by one or two other families, but was now abandoned. Like our ranch will soon be, thought Jane. She turned her eyes quickly away and gazed up at the triangular hulk of Kearsarge Peak. The sun had dropped below it, spreading an orange glow across the deep turquoise sky. She watched the color deepen for a while, then turned and retraced her steps back to the courthouse.

Not long after Jane's return, six hours after they had commenced deliberating, the jury returned a verdict: guilty on all counts. There was a collective gasp in the courtroom. Not from surprise—the outcome had been almost a foregone conclusion—but from the horrible finality of it. Wilfred stood rigidly. Mark bowed his head slightly and took his brother's arm. Sentencing was set for several days later. Tears streamed down Elizabeth's face as she watched her brothers being led in handcuffs from the room.

Chalfant, his eyes wet like many in the crowd inside and outside the courthouse, drove back with Jane to the *Register* office to write the story for the evening edition. Jane sat down at Bucky's desk to write hers for the *Examiner*. She finished and called the paper to dictate it to a typist. She was almost through when the typist interrupted her, "Uh, hold on a moment, will you Miss Bow? Mr. Loewenthal wants to talk to you." Jane waited as she passed the phone.

"Jane, I've written an editorial to accompany your article, and I wanted you to be aware of it."

"All right," she responded cautiously. "Thank you Mr. Loewenthal."

"You see, a lot of our readers feel our coverage of the Owens Valley conflict has been, ah...a bit too even-handed, shall we say? People here aren't as inclined to see both sides of the issue as they were before the bombings. They want something definitive, a dramatic end to the conflict. That's the way the other papers are going with this, and we need to take a similar stance. Here's how I've started out..." He proceeded to read:

"The Wattersons, supposed champions of right and promoters of progress, proved to be the valley's incubus. With the brothers in prison, which is where they surely will now go, the evil influence is removed. There's no one now to pay dynamiting bills, and no one, so far as anyone can imagine, who wants to blow up the aqueduct. The spirit in the valley is willingness to cooperate with the city in working out problems so that the people there shall prosper. And the spirit here is the desire to cooperate with the valley."

She thought: Those are lies. Even you are printing lies, and you know it. But she said: "Thank you for telling me Mr. Loewenthal."

Jane stayed in the valley for the sentencing. The Watterson brothers asked for no clemency or pardon. They both received terms of ten years in the state penitentiary at San Quentin. Having said goodbye to their families that morning, they were immediately taken outside following the sentencing and put into a police van for transport to the prison. As they walked, heads high but wrists and ankles in restraints, friends and neighbors cried, some tried to reach across the guards to touch them, some called out "God bless you! God protect you!"

In the midst of this outpouring of sympathy, a wad of spittle suddenly hit Wilfred across the cheek. The guards roughly shoved the attacker back, and he stumbled, falling to the ground while almost knocking Jane down as well. Chalfant reached out to help him up. It was Cyril Parker, and he had the smell of whiskey on his breath.

"I trusted those men like they were brothers of mine," said Parker, shaking off the help. "And they stole everything from us. We've got nothing, nothing left! I'm more than 60 years old, and I'm workin like a common laborer just to put food on the table. God damn them!"

Poor Mrs. Parker! Jane's heart twisted at the thought of the misfortune that had befallen the nice old lady, her luncheon companion that day at Barstow. But there was nothing she could do to change what had happened or to help her. The next day, Jane drove the 200 miles back to Los Angeles, glad to be out of the valley. On the long hours through the Mojave, she forced her mind to blankness, her heart to numbness.

It was very late when she arrived in Bel Air, and so she was spared the ordeal of a recounting until the next day. Over breakfast, Alice listened solemnly as her daughter provided a few trial details they hadn't already read in the Los Angeles newspapers. When Jane told about Cyril Parker, Alice broke down into sobs. "Can't their children help?" she asked Jane.

"They're far away, and no better off for money. I don't think they can even take them in," Jane answered forlornly.

Ben shook his head, rubbing one hand across his chin and holding his wife's shaking shoulder with the other. "Don't hardly seem possible that all this has come to pass," he said in a low voice devoid of its usual expression. "It isn't the money I lost so much as my faith in men."

He got up then and went out for one of his walks. When he came back, he had nothing more to say about it, then or ever again.

## Chapter 23

Chris and Dorothy returned from their honeymoon just prior to Thanksgiving, laden with gifts for all. The Bow and Bradshaw families spent an outwardly festive, inwardly desultory holiday season together.

After the New Year, with the sale of the ranch finally achieved, for a price Ben would never disclose to his children, he and Alice prepared to go back for the last time to Owens Valley. They had arranged to lease the ranch for a period of six months while they sold off livestock and what furnishings and equipment they no longer needed or couldn't take to Bakersfield. In this town on the other side of the Sierra, at the far southern tip of the verdant San Joaquin Valley, they planned to purchase a small house with an acre or two of land for growing produce. Ben had read that there was an abundant supply of groundwater there, where the Kern River descends from the western Sierra foothills, spreading out as it moves into the grasslands, with runoff soaking down into the water table.

Alone in the guest house, Jane fell into a pattern of working long hours and spending the rest of her time out on the town with friends. She had decided to stay on in the guest house until Jed's arrival in the spring, when she would take her fiancé up to meet her parents. Still, despite her whirlwind of activity and the prospect of at last starting her life with Jed, Jane felt unsettled and uneasy. In his last letter, Jed had made a point of telling her he was glad she and her folks were finally getting out of the valley for good. He'd said she had to face the fact that there was no future there anymore—words that eerily echoed those Mary had spoken so long ago on her last day in the little brown house.

One morning Jane found herself, for no reason she could fathom, veering off of Sunset Boulevard and, instead of going to the *Examiner* office, heading north through Cahuenga Pass. In a little more than two hours, she had driven across the San Fernando Valley, passing through the small towns of Newhall and Saugus, and was on the rough, twisting road leading up into San Francisquito Canyon.

The road paralleled the largely dry San Francisquito Creek on her left before coming upon Los Angeles Powerhouse 2 on the right. It was a stark, white rectangular block structure, its severity relieved a little by a graceful oak planted to one side. At the northwestern corner of the building, the road crossed over an intake tunnel where water was rushing in from an open cement canal. The road now paralleled the canal, and Jane drove along it for over a mile until she came to a juncture. She took the left branch toward the dam, which she could now see towering above her. Its immense wall, stepped like the face of one of the great pyramids, but with smaller serrations, spanned the canyon.

Soon Jane came upon a small cabin, which she assumed was the damkeeper's. She stopped, climbed out of the green roadster, whose color was by now barely discernible, and knocked at the door. A young woman, thin, brunette with bobbed hair and a baby on her hip, opened it. "Yes?"

"Please excuse me, ma'am, but is this the damkeeper's cottage?"

"It is, but he ain't here. You can find him up on top." She pointed to the west side of the dam. "There's a road about a quarter mile farther that goes right up." She glanced skeptically at Jane's roadster. "It's real steep."

"I'll just park below and walk up," said Jane. She thanked the woman, who quickly disappeared back into the cabin, climbed into her car and continued on until she was just below the dam. There appeared to be no one around. But sure enough, on the western canyon wall there was a road, which began with a hairpin turn before heading steeply up the slope. Jane parked next to it, glanced at her watch—12:35—and began to walk up. Fortunately, she reassured herself, I'm wearing sensible shoes.

Going on foot, instead of trying to manage the road in a car, Jane was able to study her surroundings. She was traversing a scrub-covered slope of grayish rock, which appeared damp where its shoulder met the dam abutment. Halfway up the slope, the rock turned reddish. At this point, she saw a metal pipe, perhaps two inches in diameter, jutting out from the conjunction of dam and mountain, at the base of one of the stepped levels. The pipe reached down, through several angled joints, to the canyon floor. Could that be to drain off water from a leak? she wondered.

Fit as she was and, thanks to Mary, accustomed to walking hilly terrain, Jane soon reached the top. There, she was surprised to see a large black sedan, a chauffeur leaning against the driver's side door smoking.

"Ma'am?" He was as startled as she. "What are you doing here?"

"It's miss...excuse me..." Jane, having expected to see only the dam-keeper, didn't immediately know how to explain herself. Before she could gather her thoughts, there came a deep "Hurrummpf" to her right. She turned and came face to face with William Mulholland.

"Miss Bow, what are you doing here?" Mulholland's dark eyes glowered at her below his black hat.

"Mr. Mulholland, ah, how nice to see you again sir. I…I'm here reporting on the dam of course."

"Of course? And why is that?" He took a step toward her. Playing for time, she looked down. Not far from her feet, she saw a small stream of water cutting across the dirt road and running over the embankment. Like the pipe she had seen on her way up, it seemed to be coming from where the dam and slope met. Another leak? Jane straightened her back and looked him straight in the eye. "There are rumors, sir, that there may be some problems here, cracks in the concrete and leakage." She glanced back down, pointedly, at the rivulet.

"Balderdash!" he said, taking another step so that his bristling gray mustache was not more than a few inches from her forehead. "All dams have leaks, Miss Bow, and all concrete has cracks. That doesn't mean the dam isn't safe and sound."

"I know that, sir, I'd just like to report the facts in order to reassure our readers."

"It's fine, the leak is clear!" came a voice from below. "It's just picking up mud as it goes downhill!" A man was scrambling up the embankment toward them. Jane wondered that she hadn't seen him as she'd walked up. He must have been squatting down to study something or behind a boulder at an angle that hid him from the road. She regarded him curiously as he attained their level. He was wearing a suit, but had removed the jacket. There was something familiar about the brightly striped tie…Oh no, Jane tensed, it's Van Norman. What horrible, unimaginable luck to run into both him and Mulholland here!

The look on Van Norman's face, when he saw her, was equally aghast. "Miss Bow?!"

"Mr. Van Norman." She responded to his question with a statement, keeping her voice calm.

"You know each other?" Mulholland now bore down on the assistant superintendent.

"Yes, I had the pleasure of meeting Miss Bow up in the Owens Valley, when we were fixing the siphon at No Name Canyon. I also ran into her on the road the night they blew out the canal at Cottonwood Creek. If she tells you she's here reporting sir, you might just ask her which paper she's reporting for." Van Norman's voice was steely, and his countenance none too friendly either.

Mulholland's eyes drilled into Jane. "Why, the last time we met, Miss Bow, I believe you were a reporter for the *Los Angeles Examiner*, is that not correct?"

"Yes, but I think you'll find she divides her loyalties with the *Inyo Register*," advised Van Norman, a note of derision in his voice as he said the name of the Owens Valley paper.

"Not anymore." Jane regarded one, then the other, her face as hard and set as theirs. "It's all over in the valley, or hadn't you heard?"

"I think you'd better get back to town Miss Bow," said Mulholland. "You've no business here."

She glared back at them, but said only, "Very well."

They watched her turn and start down the road. Mulholland rubbed his chin thoughtfully. The purported threats to Haiwee and St. Francis last year had never materialized. Maybe the Owens Valley anarchists had gotten wind of the reinforcements he'd ordered to the dams and figured their plan had been compromised. Or maybe there never had been a real threat at all—just hotheads venting steam with bold talk. It was crazy to think that this girl was involved in anything. More likely just an ambitious reporter trying to get a big story. She'll probably nose around until she finds a few malcontents down in the canyon willing to talk about leaks and cracks. Then she'll turn all the mistaken information they give her into a story that will stir everybody up to no purpose at all. Damn nuisance!

When Jane reached the canyon floor, she climbed into her car. Knowing they would watch to make sure she left, she drove out the road the way she'd come. But when she reached the fork, she turned north, heading farther up the canyon toward Powerhouse 1. I'll stay out of sight, Jane decided, then double back when they're gone and try again. Something was definitely wrong; otherwise, why would both the superintendent and assistant superintendent be up here like this? Maybe I can still manage to talk to the damkeeper.

About six miles up the canyon, she reached the other powerhouse. The road passed directly in front of it, another white rectangular building. Jane pulled over to the side of the road and got out of the car. She peered at the base of the powerhouse, where water was gushing through a dozen rounded arched openings.

It was Owens River water, she knew. Having been used here to generate electricity, it was dumped into this open canal, which would guide it into a closed pipe conduit for much of the journey to the second powerhouse, where it would again lend its force to satiate the city's ever-increasing demand for electricity. The water passing through these two hydro plants was one of the reasons that tonight, returning through the Cahuenga Pass, she would marvel at the immense carpet of lights that magically spread wider and wider every year. Just like, as a girl, she had paused with Mary on a Sierra path and marveled at the green carpet spreading farther and farther across the valley. It had seemed unstoppable, but it hadn't been. Now it was shrinking.

Jane peered far up, high on the canyon wall. There it was. At this point, the aqueduct emerged from a five-mile tunnel through the Sierra Madre mountains and dropped in a conduit a thousand feet to this power plant on the canyon floor. The tunnel was the Elizabeth Tunnel, and where this power plant now stood had once been the camp of the tunneling team that had competed with Jed's. Right now she was standing where the lights had been, far below them on the canyon floor, the night they'd sat talking in Dr. Taylor's Franklin after their first headlong rush through the tunnel.

Was I out of my mind that night? She still wondered at the recklessness with which she'd abandoned herself as if spellbound to anything and everything during those charmed and fleeting hours. But the magic had started well before Jed had lured her out into the night. Her visits to the aqueduct, and especially to the Elizabeth Tunnel, had been completely thrilling to her spirit, so ready at that age to take flight. It had all seemed so exciting—the industry and exuberance of the camps, the lean, joking young men dynamiting and drilling through the mountain, racing to be the first to the center, the sheer audaciousness and optimism of the whole endeavor had caught her up. But now she saw where it had all led: to the loss of the ranch for her family, to destitution for the Parkers, to prison and ruin for the Wattersons, to the death of a valley that had once been itself a place of enchantment.

Was I crazy then? Or am I crazy now? What am I doing here?! Why am I way out here neglecting my job and ruining my car and shoes? For what!?

Jane shook herself hard, got back in the dusty roadster and turned it around, heading back down the canyon. She intended to drive straight back to the city, but as she passed the fork to the dam, she swerved right and took it. Again she parked below the steep road traversing the western slope and walked slowly up, cautiously looking about as she approached the top.

The black sedan was gone. Jane walked out onto the winged dike, which extended from the dam like the handle of a spoon, and gazed out at the immense expanse of water. The reservoir was full, within inches of the top of the dam, and a brisk afternoon breeze hurtling down the canyon, stronger up here than it had been down below, was sending lines of waves marching like regiments across the surface. As Jane watched, a gust of wind sent water splashing up over the parapet at the top of the dam, to trickle down its serrated side.

This is Owens River water, she thought miserably. Water that is needed in the valley, water that could have saved Mr. and Mrs. Parker's farm. And they've got so much of it that it's overflowing. They're just wasting it.

A man emerged from the control house at the center of the parapet. After assuring herself it was neither Mulholland nor Van Norman, Jane walked out toward him. He was a young man, dressed in a faded blue denim shirt and a newsboy cap, beneath which fanned out large ears. He saw her and came toward her.

"Hello, there," called Jane, waving casually, adopting a professional voice and manner. "Are you the damkeeper?"

"Yes, miss. Tony Harnischfeger at your service." He was regarding her, Jane thought, with interest rather than alarm. Evidently, her earlier visit had not warranted mention by his superiors.

"I'm J. Bow, Mr. Harnischfeger, a reporter for the *Los Angeles Examiner*." She wasn't sure, but decided to go ahead and take a chance. "I'm also a personal friend of Mr. Mulholland's daughter Lucille."

"Oh, well then, welcome to the St. Francis Dam…" There was a question in his voice. "…*Miss* Bow."

She nodded to indicate he had guessed right, and noticed the light of interest in his eyes turned up a notch or two with the information she wasn't married.

"What can I do for you, miss?" he asked.

"Mr. Harnischfeger, we've heard rumors that there are problems with the dam, some leaks up here and abnormal water flows in the creek down below."

"Awe, those are nothin important, miss. You know how folks talk. People around here are ignorant of engineering science. They think dams are supposed to be water-tight, which none of 'em are."

"So that long pipe I saw running down the dam face over there?" She pointed to the abutment near the road she'd walked up. "Is that normal Mr. Harnischfeger?"

"Sure. Superintendent Mulholland says all dams have leaks like that due to temperature changes and contraction. There's another one over there on the winged dike," he pointed to the spoon. "Mulholland said just to leave it open, as it ain't doin no harm, but we're gonna put in a concrete drain line for the run off. That's why the slope next to the dam looks damp. The drain line will fix that."

"The water level looks awfully high," Jane observed. "Isn't that water there just going to waste?" She indicated the lapping edge.

"Sure, that's why Mr. Mulholland had us turn off the flow into the reservoir five days ago. We've also been drainin some water off at Powerhouse 1 and also at Drinkwater Canyon, down below Powerhouse 2. There's gate valves we can open to divert water from the aqueduct into San Francisquito Creek."

"And where does that water end up?"

"Oh yeah, well eventually it'll join the Santa Clara River and end up in the ocean."

Jane was amazed and a bit sickened that he didn't even try to disguise the waste, but she gave him a bright, appreciative smile and a dose of flattery. "I see, well it sounds like you've got everything under good regulation Mr. Harnischfeger,"

"Sure, miss, nothing for anyone to worry about."

"Still, something special must have brought Mr. Mulholland and Mr. Van Norman up here this morning."

The damkeeper appeared surprised at her mention of their visit, so Jane made up what she thought to be a plausible explanation. "I passed them on the road, and we said hello, but Mr. Mulholland didn't have time to talk, as he was expected back in the city. He said I should ask you to tell me all about it."

Harnischfeger fairly basked in the light of this knowledge that the chief had such confidence in him. He'd received a dressing down recently from his supervisor at the DWP for some jokes he'd made about the dam. "Well, miss, I don't mind tellin ya," he said self-importantly, "I was mighty alarmed early this morning when I was walking below the dam and saw another stream of water coming down on the west side, near where that pipe is. This here was a new leak, not part of that other one, and what scared me was the water looked a might muddy. Now muddy water is serious because it means foundation material is being washed out from under the dam, which could weaken it. So I called my supervisor, and he got Mr. Mulholland and Mr. Van Norman to come directly. They got here around 10:30 this mornin and started investigatin. Mr. Van Norman climbed on the slope, there, following the water to where it was comin out, where the abutment and the slope meet." He pointed. "You can see it if you look real hard. When he come back up, Van Norman was reassured the water was clear at that point, and just picking up mud as it ran down the slope. So that was good news."

"Nothing needs to be done then about the leak?"

"Well, Mr. Van Norman was a might concerned about some fluctuation he saw in the volume of water coming through. It was kind of surging now and then. Mulholland said that's because the water level in the reservoir is so high, and we need to take some corrective measures, but he'd have to do some thinkin on what would be the best way. Meanwhile, he told us to divert more water into the canyon."

"Goodness, that's impressive," cooed Jane. "So your concerns have been answered then, Mr. Harnischfeger?"

"Sure, sure," he laughed, a little nervously, Jane thought. "You know I joke about the dam now and then, but I don't mean nothin by it. Couple a weeks ago, I was at the Saugus Cafe with my buddy Merl to plan a fishin trip. When it was time to go, I said somethin like, 'Well, goodbye Merl, I'll meet you for the trip if the dam don't break!' Guess it got some folks riled up, but I was just pullin his leg."

"I'm sure you were only having a little fun," Jane said, though she was thinking he's an idiot to joke about such things. Nevertheless, she thanked him for talking with her and shook his hand before descending the road once again to her car and heading south out of the canyon.

It was well past three in the afternoon now. Realizing that her stomach was empty and her gas tank nearly so, she decided to stop in Saugus. The service station attendant was gregarious. "I'm the owner," he boasted. "Jack Green's the name. Got another one, my brother Carl runs it for me, over in Castaic Junction."

She asked him if he ever worried about being below the dam.

"Ah, there's a lot of talk, but I don't pay no mind to it. Gotta have power for business, and for that, we gotta have dams."

At the Saugus Cafe, Jane took a seat at the counter and ordered the blue-plate special, chicken fricassee over toast, with coffee. There were a couple of other people at the counter, and one of the tables was occupied. Determined to make use of the time while waiting for her food, Jane smiled over at a man seated two stools away from her. He had weathered brown skin and was dressed in denim and cowboy boots. Lest he think she was being forward, Jane quickly introduced herself. "Hello, I beg your pardon, sir. I'm J. Bow, a reporter for the *Los Angeles Examiner*, and I wonder if I could ask you a few questions about the St. Francis Dam?"

The man appraised her as he finished chewing his mouthful of beef stew. When he'd swallowed it down, he wiped his napkin across his lips and nodded. "How do you do, ma'am. I'm Chester Smith. I'm a rancher up-canyon. What do you want to know about the dam?"

"It's miss, thank you, Mr. Smith. Do you have any concerns about living near it?"

"Well, I do have some." The rancher rubbed a hand over his throat, pulling on the skin over his Adam's apple. "I've been noticing more water running in the creek. Now, I wouldn't normally pay that no mind.

They used to dump water out of the aqueduct all the time, and it'd come roaring down the canyon. But they haven't done it since they finished the dam. So seeing water in the creek again all of a sudden makes me feel a might jumpy."

"I've been told that's just to lower the level since the water in the reservoirs is so high now."

"Could be," Smith replied. "But there's also more and more leaks showing on the west side, and the spur of the mountain where it hugs in on the dam is getting mighty soggy."

"Yeah, I saw a new leak up there yesterday," a sunburned man stood up from an adjacent table, and he and his companion came over to stand next to the counter.

"Excuse me for interruptin, but I couldn't help hearin what you were sayin about the dam. I'm Wallace Denny, from Chatsworth. This is my friend Gary Lawrence. We stopped at the dam yesterday on our way back from a fishing trip, and Gary here pointed out the leaks. This guy who works up there came walking by so we asked him about it."

"Yeah," his friend chimed in, "Wally said something half-jokin like, 'What ya fixin to do, flood us out down below?' and the guy just laughed and said, 'Yeah, we expect this dam to break any minute!'"

"That must have been Tony Harnischfeger, the damkeeper," said Smith. "He's known to pull a leg or two. In fact, I heard his supervisor in Los Angeles put him on notice to stop joking about the dam coming down if he wants to keep his job."

"I can understand why they would," remarked Jane.

"Yeah, but Tony was a guard on the aqueduct up at Jawbone Canyon," remarked Smith, "so they've got enough history with him to cut the man some slack. I don't expect his job's really in danger."

"Sure, that's fine," said Lawrence, "unless they know somethin's wrong and they're just trying to keep him quiet about it."

Jane thought about this comment as she drove home to the city that evening. It was unthinkable that a city agency would ever keep quiet about a dangerous dam, and she felt certain Mulholland, as difficult a man as he was, would never condone such a thing. Doubtless the dam was sound, as Mulholland had stated. But it did seem to her that he was making a grievous mistake underestimating the effect that the appearance of instability was having on the local population. If these people don't have enough understanding of engineering to know that leaks and cracks are normal—and how many people do?—wouldn't it behoove the DWP to educate and reassure them? Instead Mulholland's attitude seemed as arrogant and uncomprehending as it had been toward the Owens Valley.

At a few minutes past midnight, Ray Rising was drifting off to sleep with his wife Louise in the worker's housing next to Powerhouse 2, when he was jerked back to consciousness by a roaring outside. He sprang to the door and opened it in time to see a wall of water, twice as high as the 65-foot-high concrete powerhouse, crush it like an empty eggshell. Screaming to his wife to get their infant from its crib next to the bed, he dived into the next room and scooped up their two older children just as the wall of water fell upon them, fracturing the cabin to matchsticks and sweeping everything inside into a maelstrom. Fighting to stay on the surface, keep hold of his boys and stay free of the surging blocks of concrete and tangles of wire, Ray saw Louise. She was holding onto a log with one arm and with the other raised high, struggling to keep the baby's head above water.

What appeared to be a roof, largely intact, wheeled toward them like a spinning top toy. Ray yelled to the older boy to swim for it and, grasping the three-year-old to his chest, did the same. They made it to the roof and somehow climbed on top. Gripping with all his might, his children pressed beneath his outstretched arms, face pressed against the green planks, Ray realized that what they lay upon must be the roof off of the damkeeper's cottage.

When he had caught his breath enough to raise his head, he saw that they were now downstream of his wife, who was still clinging to the log and trying to hold the baby high. Her face was contorted in the agony of keeping her arm aloft against the force of the torrent. Luck was with them, however, because the roof snagged and slowed, and Ray saw a chance to reach her. He handed the smaller boy to his brother and inched out to the edge of the roof, calling to Louise and stretching his arm out. She saw him and, as the current brought her by the roof, made an immense effort to push off from the log and shove the baby into his hands, then she was swept under.

It had taken only five minutes from the moment the dam broke for the 185-foot wall of Owens River water to travel the mile and a half down canyon to the power station. Behind it, the damkeeper's cottage was gone. Tony Harnischfeger and his baby were never seen again. The body of the small dark-haired woman who, the newspapers would later report, was not Harnischfeger's wife, would be found fully clothed, unusual under such an onslaught, wedged between chunks of wreckage.

About 15 minutes later, the wall of water, now only 140 feet high, slammed into Chester Smith's ranch. After the talk with Miss Bow and the men from Chatsworth, Smith had felt uneasy and so had left the barn door open when he threw his sleeping bag on the pile of hay that night.

This ranch was only one of the cattleman's properties, and he hadn't bothered yet to build a house for himself here. There were two cabins, however, for his ranch hands and their families, one right by the creek and the other a ways up the slope. When the water came, Smith had just enough time to get out the barn door—and only because he'd been awakened 30 seconds earlier by the loud barking of one of his dogs.

Lying in the hay for an instant, cursing the damn dog, he'd heard a sound like thunder followed by trees snapping and power lines popping and sizzling. Then he knew what it was, and leapt to his feet. Outside the barn, Smith saw it coming down the canyon and knew there wasn't time to get to the cabin by the creek. He turned and ran up the slope to the other cabin, shouting. The ranch hand and his wife came running out in their nightclothes, and he waved them up the hill, "The dam's broke! We've got to get to higher ground!"

They scrambled upward, rocks and branches tearing at their bare feet and knuckles, water surging at their ankles, trying to pull them off the hillside, where they clung, shivering and bleeding until the morning light.

It was 12:50 by Raymond Starbard's watch when he heard the rumble. He dropped and put his ear to the ground. The guys he was playing cards with at the Edison Company substation at Saugus laughed and said it was just the midnight freight train from Santa Paula. "That's no train," he protested. "It's water, I'm sure of it!"

Helman, his best buddy, indulged him, and they jumped into Starbard's truck to race to the family housing. They'd covered about

50 yards and were approaching a place where the road ran through a narrow slot between a concrete block structure and a warehouse made of sheets of galvanized metal, when they saw what looked to be a 75-foot wave of water framed in the opening. It crashed through the narrow slot, its force throwing both men out of the truck before tossing the vehicle into the air. Starbard landed on the hill on the Saugus side of the creek bed, snapping his forearm crazily as he fell. Raising himself on the elbow of his good arm, he searched the sea of wood, concrete, poles and wire, calling for Helman. He couldn't see him anywhere, and the truck had disappeared too.

Starbard struggled to his feet and limped up the road toward the Greene gas station, cradling his broken arm and trying not to look at the bone jutting from his shredded shirt. When he got there, he didn't see Greene, so he tried the door and, finding it locked, broke a window. Inside, he picked up the phone and told the operator to connect him with the Edison dispatcher. He told her to contact Los Angeles authorities and get the word out down the Santa Clarita Valley that a flood was coming, then he hung up and asked to be connected to the sheriffs' offices in Newell and Chatsworth, the next towns to the south.

---

By the time Starbard made it to the phone, it was already too late for Castaic Junction. Carl Green stood, rubbing sleepy eyes, watching flares of light going off like fireworks in the eastern sky over by Saugus. He couldn't know that this was the flood snapping power lines or that the mass of water had turned west following the Santa Clara River bed and was now racing down the Santa Clarita Valley toward the ocean. Suddenly the ground beneath his feet began to shake. He glanced up the road at the tourist cabins he and his brother Jack rented to Los Angeles bound motorists too tired to make it all the way. Carl blinked, and blinked again: the cabins were moving, turning, coming toward him!

"Kenny! Clara!" He screamed, lunging toward the house, but it was too late. As the water swept him up, he saw his 8-year-old son Kenny vault out of his bedroom window, with his dog Coyote just behind him. Then a telephone pole, spinning on the water, slammed into his head. Days later, Carl's body, swept out to sea, would wash up on a beach in San Diego, near the Mexican border. His wife Clara would be found impaled by a tree branch. Kenny would be rescued from where he huddled, naked, in a tangle of scrub brush, cradling his matted, shivering, whimpering dog.

About 1:20 a.m., Ed Locke, the night watchman at the Edison work camp at Kemp, heard thunder somewhere off in the eastern hills. He was puzzled, since although there were a few clouds, the sky was mostly clear.

Why, he wasn't sure, but he suddenly had a crystalline sense of danger, and he began running to the tent city strewn out along the river, where 150 men lay sleeping. Before he could rouse them, the rush of water churned down the river channel and engulfed him and the tents. The men inside, trapped under the weight of the heavy water-laden canvas, fought frantically, ripping the nails from their fingers trying to free themselves. Those lucky enough to have closed and secured their tent flaps had a chance. In some cases, air trapped inside the canvas shells floated the tents to the surface, where they bobbed like apples in a Halloween barrel.

Just west of the camp, a line of hills cut into the valley, creating a narrow place, called Blue Cut, through which the river flowed. When the flood waters hit this barrier, they bounced off of it backward, creating a whirlpool that sent some of the tents spinning until they were so heavy with absorbed water, they were sucked down. Floating bodies and swimming survivors were also drawn into the vortex, round and round until they either sank or the terrific centrifugal force threw them free. Just 66 of the 150 men survived. Ed Locke was not among them.

Gradually, through a confused, unplanned web of communications, the word began to reach the people still in the path of the onslaught. Downriver warnings branched out from Starbard's calls at Saugus and from radio messages sent from Powerhouse 1 when operators there, unable to reach their counterparts at Powerhouse 2, had sent a party down to check. People began to be roused and mobilized in Fillmore, Santa Paula, Saticoy and Oxnard.

By the time the flood reached the coast at Oxnard just before dawn, the town had already benefited from three hours of advance warning. The order had gone out for a voluntary evacuation, a caution, it turned out happily, the town didn't need. The water now was moving at only five miles per hour and had spread out to a width of about two miles. It flowed under and over a railroad bridge, debris crashing against the steel supports, but didn't take the bridge down.

In the hills of Ventura, the next town to the northwest, people gathered to watch the wide swath of gray-brown water, with its baggage of mud, debris and corpses, flow into the ocean. The flotsam reached almost to the Channel Islands, more than five miles offshore.

---

Around one in the morning, just about the time when the wall of water was sweeping through Castaic Junction, leaving it, as one reporter would later describe the destruction, "as bare as a pool table," the telephone rang in the upstairs hallway of the Mulholland home at South St. Andrews Place in Los Angeles.

Rose drew on her robe and went to answer it. She switched on the table lamp, but it didn't go on. She fumbled for the phone and lifted the receiver to her ear. "Hello?"

"This is Harvey Van Norman. Is this Miss Mulholland?"

"Yes, yes it's Rose. What is it Mr. Van Norman, what's happened?!"

"Please wake up your father, Miss Mulholland. I'll stay on the phone. The St. Francis Dam has gone out!"

"Oh, no, oh my God! Yes, yes, I'll get him Mr. Van Norman."

Rose entered Mulholland's room and stumbled over to the bed. She gently shook her father's shoulder. He opened his eyes and, seeing her white face, bolted up in bed. "What is it, Rose? Is it Lucille? What's she gone and done this time?"

"No, father, it's Mr. Van Norman on the phone. He says the St. Francis Dam has gone out!"

Mulholland stared, not believing he had heard the words she'd spoken. Then he leapt out of bed and rushed into the hall, stomach clutching, thinking damn, those rogues from Owens Valley finally went through with it! And then, Oh God, please God, don't let people be killed! He picked up the phone. "What happened Harvey? Was it dynamite?!"

"We don't know yet. It went down about an hour ago. It's bad, we just don't know how bad."

"Put armed guards on the aqueduct and Mulholland Dam right now! I'll have my driver pick you up in 30 minutes!" Mulholland hung up and handed the phone to Rose. "Call my driver and tell him to get over here now!" He fled back into his room to dress.

The black sedan raced through the streets of Los Angeles, empty now except for late revelers and night-shift workers. The driver kept a good clip all the way up Cahuenga Pass and through the string of slumbering San Fernando Valley towns, but as they approached Newhall, the road became muddy. In the headlights, they could see muck and debris on the west side of it. Well before Saugus, they were forced to turn onto small secondary roads and dirt fire lanes.

Mulholland fumed in frustration as his driver slowed to negotiate pits and turns. He pulled a flashlight from his pocket and clicked it on briefly: a few minutes before three. Finally, they regained the main road above Powerhouse 1 and headed south. When they approached the building, the driver slowed, but Mulholland waved his hand impatiently. "Go on to the dam!"

From here the road hugged the southeastern edge of the reservoir. All three men flinched as the headlights revealed…nothing. The immense expanse of water that had been there yesterday was almost entirely gone. All that remained was a muddy narrow channel at the bottom.

Then as the road swung down toward the creek bed, Mulholland saw something he couldn't believe: The dam was gone too, except for a narrow section in the middle, which stood like a giant tombstone above the creek. To either side of it, was a huge, yawning gap. Both sides of the dam had collapsed!

"Stop the car!" Mulholland hollered. The three men climbed out, and Mulholland and Van Norman started down the slope, picking their way in the dark by flashlight to the creek bed. From this side, they could see that parts of the east abutment still rested at the foot of the dam in broken slabs. The west abutment had been completely swept away, though the winged dike remained as well as a part of the steep road leading up to it.

Mulholland swept his flashlight south, illuminating swaths of an empty canyon scrubbed clean of trees, brush and boulders. Muck clawed at his boots, and his legs gave way as he slid down on a wedge of broken concrete, thinking about Tony Harnischfeger and his family in their cottage, a quarter mile away, and about Powerhouse 2, a mile and a half below that. Had there been any warning? Had the men and their families had time to get out?

Van Norman sat down beside him to wait for sunrise, both men dreading what they would see when the curtain of darkness lifted.

---

At nine o'clock in the morning, Jane was in the *Examiner* newsroom, teeming with reporters and clerks. She had received her call from Loewenthal's secretary just before six. From that moment, though she'd washed and dressed efficiently by the light of the hurricane lamp the housekeeper had placed in her bedroom, and gone in to the breakfast room to inform Chris of the scant facts known as yet, betraying, she thought, no more than the usual alarm one would expect under such terrible circumstances, she had not been able to stop her body from trembling.

Her brother had been eating by oil lamp, though a thin gray light was now creepin in through the windows. No radio this morning, and nothing about the break in the paper, printed last night.

On her way to the office, Jane was tasked with going to the American Red Cross headquarters, which was in the western part of the city, not far from Bel Air. A fast-talking but calm and methodical supervisor gave Jane her first picture of what had happened. Which towns had been hit the worst and how much destruction had been wrought upon them was difficult to determine, as the areas affected were cut off, their roads and communications down, and the entire metropolitan area, as well as Ventura and Santa Barbara counties to the north, without electricity. Nevertheless, well before dawn, the Newhall Chapter of the organization had been mobilized and was already operating makeshift canteens and hospitals in Saugus and Castaic Junction.

At present, this meager account was one of the only reliable pieces of information to be had. In the newsroom and on the streets, rumors and suppositions abounded. Some people were saying the dam had only partially failed, and when it eventually all came down, there'd be an even larger flood. Others insisted the dam had been built on an unstable foundation, and Mulholland had known it all along. But the most frequently discussed theory was that the dam had been dynamited by those lawless Owens Valley hotheads.

A dozen reporters, including Jane, were now on the jammed telephone lines, calling every lead and source they could come up with to hound out some facts. Loewenthal was sending other reporters out to DWP headquarters on Broadway and Second, to the Southern California Edison headquarters on West Fifth, to city and county offices, and even up and down the streets to find out what ordinary citizens might know. As the reporters headed down the stairs to pursue these assignments, they were jostled by a phalanx of Los Angeles police and detectives pushing their way up.

"Where's Loewenthal?" barked the man in plain clothes at the head of the assault. A reporter, talking on the telephone, pointed to where his boss stood. Loewenthal glanced up, surprised, as they came toward him. "Hello, Jimmy, what's going on?"

"Hello Loewenthal," Detective Jimmy Burnside held out his hand and shook the editor's. "I know this is a tough morning for you, but I'm afraid I'm going to have to make it even tougher. I'm here to arrest one of your reporters, a Miss Jane Bow, on suspicion of sabotaging the St. Francis Dam. Where is she?"

"She's right here," said Loewenthal, pointing to the young woman at his elbow, who was sitting frozen in her chair. "You're not serious…This is a joke, right?" the editor stammered.

"No joke, stand up Miss Bow and put your hands behind your back."

Jane looked beseechingly at her editor. The trembling that had afflicted her throughout the morning now turned into a violent shaking. She knew her legs wouldn't hold her if she tried to rise.

"Hold on, hold on." Loewenthal tried to get between the officers and Jane, but was shoved aside. "Jane, what's going on?"

Two of the officers dragged her to her feet. She tried not to slump against them, tightening her shoulders and thighs to stay erect. "It's a mistake, Mr. Loewenthal." Jane was searching her mind to make sense of what was happening. "I was up at the dam yesterday, investigating some rumors about leaks, just asking questions. They must think I had something to do with the break."

"What makes you so sure it was sabotage, detective?"

"I'm no engineer, Loewenthal. Just doing what I'm told."

"Don't worry Mr. Loewenthal, I'll be fine. Just call Chris, please call Chris!" Jane pleaded over her shoulder as they led her out in handcuffs, past her gaping, incredulous colleagues.

---

"Tell me the truth, little missy, what were you doing up there on top of that dam?!"

The man across the small rectangular table from Jane peered at her with stern dark eyes. He had an aquiline nose, heavy dark brows, which were drawn together at present, and dark wavy hair set back from an ample forehead.

"I've told you, Chief Davis." She tried to keep her voice steady. "I was there investigating rumors of leaks and cracks at the dam."

"And who was your source for this information?"

"No one in particular. It's a common topic of conversation in the area. All one has to do is drop into the Saugus Café to get an earful."

"But you didn't just casually drop into the café by accident, did you?"

"I don't know what you mean."

"Oh, I think you do, Miss Bow. Because you were also at the scene of another dynamite attack, weren't you? The night they blew the aqueduct at…" he glanced down at some papers, "…Cottonwood Creek and… Tuttle Creek."

"I was also investigating that night, sir. I'm a reporter, that's my job."

"Um hmm, I understand that your loyalties in that regard may be somewhat, shall we say, divided?"

Jane tightened her shoulders and tried to explain. "If you are speaking about Mr. Van Norman's accusations that I work for both the *Examiner* and the *Register*, I stand guilty of that charge. But it is not a crime, Police Chief Davis, for a reporter to work for more than one newspaper. In fact, quite a few do."

He wasn't having any of it. Her interrogator leaned far over the table, pushing his face at hers. She tried to hold still. Tried to use a little trick she'd learned to quell fear when, as a journalist, she'd had to interview intimidating persons: find something ridiculous about him and focus on that. The way he poked his nose at her, and the wobbling neck fat above his collar qualified. But as he came closer and closer, her eyes crossed, and she heard the handcuffs that attached her to the hard-backed chair clang against its rails.

"Dammit, tell me! You're in big trouble missy—people died! Now tell me what you did!"

There was a sharp rap on the door. Davis pulled back, a smirk on his lips. Then he rose and went outside, closing the door behind him. He came back in. "Your brother's here. I don't strictly have to allow you to see him, but I'm going to, in hopes he can talk some sense into you. You've got five minutes."

Davis went out, and a uniformed officer opened the door to let Chris enter. He rushed to Jane, knelt beside her chair and put his arms around her. "Are you all right, Janey? They didn't hurt you?" He held her away to look her up and down. She shook her head, but she was crying. The instant she had seen him, her resolve had collapsed. "How could this mix up have happened honey? How could they make such a boneheaded mistake?!"

"Chris, I was just in the wrong place at the wrong time," she blubbered. "I was up on the dam yesterday investigating some rumors of leaks."

"Yeah, but what about in the valley?" His eyes searched hers. He inclined his head toward the closed door and whispered, "They told me you were caught out there by the aqueduct the night those two big blasts happened! You never told me that Janey—what were you doing?!"

"There was nothing to tell, Chris, I swear. I was just riding out to investigate. And I wasn't alone; I persuaded Juan to go with me," she admitted guiltily.

Chris regarded her skeptically. "Is that what really happened, Janey? Was Pa involved in the blasting?"

"Of course not, you know he'd never. Look, Chris, we're wasting time. I had nothing to do with the St. Francis Dam break. I don't know if someone else did or if it came down from structural weaknesses, but I know someone who may know…"

"Jed? I'll call Jed."

"No, you can't reach him. He's on a ship or a train, on his way here. But there's someone else. His name is Jacob Clausen. He's an engineer with the Reclamation Service. Call Mr. Chalfant—he'll know how to contact him."

Chris nodded and placed a hand at the back of Jane's head, kissing her forehead. He rose, in efficient Chris fashion, just as the policeman opened the door to say "Time's up, miss."

---

Jane awoke the next day, stiff from hours of interrogation on the hard chair and dark hours of self-interrogation on the scant mattress of a jail-house cell in the Los Angeles Hall of Justice. Was she responsible for all those deaths? Could she have saved those people?

She prepared herself for a recommencement of the questioning, and was surprised to be left undisturbed for the whole of the morning. She wasn't to know until later that the lull in the interrogation was due to the arrival of Jacob Clausen. Receiving Chalfant's call in Carson City, he had taken the next train to Los Angeles. His haste was prompted by regard for Chalfant and a sense of responsibility for having discussed potential problems at the St. Francis in front of Miss Bow. Did she do something wrong with the information, he wondered briefly. But he couldn't believe it, surely her arrest was just a big mistake.

He called ahead to tell Harvey Van Norman he was coming, and the assistant superintendent met him at the station. Clausen was highly esteemed by engineers within Reclamation and all over the West. Van Norman figured that if anyone could find evidence of sabotage, Clausen was the man.

From the station, Van Norman drove them directly to the St. Francis ruins. They spent more than an hour examining the huge slab of dam that remained in the middle of the channel and the piles of concrete from the broken east abutment. Clausen picked up a small piece and ran his fingernails over it. The outer layer crumbled. "This sometimes happens when there's been an explosion," he remarked, "but it could also be a problem with the concrete mixture."

"There's no problem with the concrete," countered Van Norman.

"At any rate, there's not enough here for us to say conclusively either way," said Clausen.

They continued on. Climbing over first the east and then the west embankment, they found nothing to indicate blasting. But Clausen spent some time looking at the east canyon wall. For about 50 feet above the creek bed, the now-exposed wall consisted of a grayish mica schist formation. The engineer ran his hands over the deep fractures, which sometimes created a cross-hatched pattern, on the face of the rock.

"Was there ever any concern for the stability of this wall?" he asked Van Norman.

"None. Mulholland did test drilling on it way back when he first had the idea of putting a reservoir here, when they were working on the Elizabeth Tunnel."

Descending again to the creek bed, the two men walked the muddy channel downstream, peering into the pools the wave of water had left behind. "There are a lot of dead fish in these pools," observed Clausen.

"Do you think it could have been concussion from an explosion?"

"Possibly." Clausen squatted down and reached into one of the pools with his hand. "There's a good deal of silt in here too," he said, bringing a goo-caked hand up in front of his face. "Fish could have died from that."

Driving back to the city, they agreed there was no solid evidence of sabotage. "You've got to tell the police to let Miss Bow go," advised Clausen. "They don't have enough to prosecute her."

"Yes, yes I suppose you're right," Van Norman concluded reluctantly.

Jane received the good news about two in the afternoon, when she was led back to the interrogation room. Taking a deep breath as she entered, expecting to see the surly, porcine face of Davis bearing down at her again, she was instead met by the smiles of Chris and Jacob Clausen.

"They're letting you go, Janey!" Chris put an arm around her shoulders, "Thanks to Mr. Clausen here!"

The engineer extended his hand. "Nice to see you again Miss Bow, although I would have hoped for that pleasure under more agreeable circumstances." She squeezed his hand and leaned forward to kiss his cheek. "Mr. Clausen, I will be forever grateful. Thank you so much for coming. Does this mean you found out what caused the dam to fail?"

"I don't know for sure," he replied, "but when the investigation is complete, I believe the cause may prove to be more geological than human in nature. I have my suspicions about the stability of the east embankment."

"Mr. Clausen, how many people died?" Jane had to ask, though she was terrified of the answer.

"I don't know that either."

# Chapter 24

No one yet knew how many had died, but the estimate kept climbing. In its evening extra edition of March 13th, the *Examiner*'s headline had read:

**ONE HUNDRED BELIEVED DEAD**
**IN AQUEDUCT DAM BREAK**

The next day, the *Examiner* and newspapers all across the country had upped the count to 274 dead and more than 700 missing. Ultimately, as rotting bodies were dug out of the mud, the number of confirmed dead would rise to over 400, about the same number as had lost their lives in the San Francisco earthquake of 1906. With many bodies never to be found, the number of estimated dead would be much higher still.

The public demanded a reason for a disaster of this magnitude, and a flurry of investigations were launched to find it. Governor Young appointed a commission, and so did the Los Angeles City Council. The Department of Water and Power assigned its own investigators, as did the California Railroad Commission, ostensibly in response to the damage done to its tracks, bridges and equipment. Ventura County sent an investigator, and the Los Angeles County Board of Supervisors hired J.B. Lippincott, who, true to form, saw no conflict of interest in the lucrative contract.

The results from these initiatives were as quick as they were inconclusive. Within a day of appointment to the state commission, one of its engineers announced to the press that the cause of the failure was that the dam had been built on a faulty foundation. The commission's official report, submitted after only five days of study, was more circumspect: It said they had been unable to determine the manner of failure, but that foundation weaknesses at the abutments were suspicious. The report was, however, quite clear in concluding that the state had no liability for the tragedy. The full responsibility lay with the "Los Angeles city engineering authorities who built the dam."

The city council's commission concluded that the cause had been a defective foundation on the western abutment, but could provide no irrefutable proof. J.B. Lippincott took pains in his reports to debunk the theory put forward by a commercial cement manufacturer's association that the culprit was the city's insistence on mixing its own concrete, just like on the aqueduct—an idea of Lippincott's for which Mulholland had received the credit. That was "poppycock," in Lippincott's view, since the aqueduct mixture had been made from local tufa deposits, and the cement used in the St. Francis Dam had been mixed from sand and gravel taken from the floor of San Francisquito Canyon. He sent samples out for analysis by an independent laboratory, which agreed that the cement had been of good quality and could not have been the cause of the disaster.

Meanwhile, newspapers, including the *Examiner*, reported on the widespread suspicion that the dam had been dynamited. "Startling new evidence" included a crude map of the dam found discarded in Hollywood and turned into the police by an anonymous citizen, a piece of rope found tied to a bush on the cliff above the dam and a wooden crate of dynamite recovered from the Santa Clara River wash.

Jane was glad she wasn't among the reporters trying to follow the tangle of accusations and theories. Loewenthal had told her to keep well away from the investigative efforts, saying "You're too close to it. I don't want any more appearance of involvement on your part." He'd assigned her instead to cover the cleanup efforts in the devastated towns, sending Simon with her "to keep you out of trouble" and a photographer to feed what was developing into an insatiable appetite among Angelenos for ghoulish pictures.

They reported on men, women and children rescued from where they clung naked to bushes, logs and the remains of splintered houses, as well as on the less fortunate: muddy corpses piled like firewood until the overwhelmed undertakers could see to them. But they also told stories of heroes: ranch crews, Boy Scout troops and local homemakers who turned up in large numbers to help however they could, merchants who delivered clothing and shoes in truckloads and a policeman who had made a "Paul Revere ride" on his motorcycle through the sleeping streets of Santa Paula to rouse the population ahead of the coming onslaught.

There were telephone operators who had bravely stayed at their posts, calling everyone they could reach, though they themselves were in the path of the waters. This behavior was expected of them, being a part of their code, like a captain pledged to be last off of a sinking ship. Still Jane felt that their unanimous adherence to such a difficult precept was laudable, and she highlighted it in a story that celebrated the heroism of ordinary people. Her little story appeared on a day when the front page was largely devoted to the movie stars, including Gloria Swanson, W.C. Fields, Jack Benny, Laurel and Hardy, Fay Wray and Tom Mix, who had appeared at the midnight gala benefiting flood victims staged by Syd Grauman, whose Grauman's Egyptian and Chinese theaters were becoming emblematic of Hollywood.

But neither the public mood nor Jane's lingering sense of horror and guilt could be soothed by stories of community solidarity, heroism and movie stars. There had to be a reason for so much death and destruction. Blame had to be apportioned. For this, everyone awaited the Los Angeles Coroner's Inquest. Among the many ongoing investigations, it was the only one with the power to bring the weight of potential criminal liability to bear on the question.

---

The inquest was held eight days after the dam break, in the Hall of Justice. Jane had often walked through the white Beaux-Arts-style building's ornate lobby, with its terrazzo floors, marble columns and glittering chandeliers suspended from a carved ceiling. But she would never again be able to do so without thinking of the long hours she'd recently spent in the county jailhouse, which occupied the top five floors of the building. She climbed the iron and brass railed staircase to the second floor and met Jacob Clausen and Mr. Chalfant, who'd come down from Owens Valley for the inquest, outside of the hearing room.

They took their seats early, knowing the limited gallery seating would soon be packed with other journalists and spectators. Superintendent William Mulholland was already there, dressed in black mourning attire, sitting quietly at the large table in the center of the room. Soon he was joined by DWP counsel Matthews. Assistant Superintendent Van Norman sat in a chair against the wall, alongside other associates and expert witnesses. The county coroner entered, in the place of a judge, and nine men were led into the jury box.

The day's proceedings began with the testimony of the autopsy surgeon. The district attorney, Mr. Asa Keyes, called for the bailiffs to bring in the subject of his autopsy. Shocked whispers accompanied the entrance of a gurney with a sheet-covered form on top. The physician was asked to recount his findings, which he did in gruesome detail. The woman had suffered extensive bodily injuries, but the cause of death had been drowning—her lungs were filled with water, and her throat and stomach with silt.

Keyes now called Mr. Ray Rising, a city worker who'd been stationed with his family at Powerhouse 2. When the young man was seated, the district attorney partially pulled back the sheet from the corpse to reveal a dark-haired woman whose pale skin was covered in livid purple cuts and bruises. Keyes asked Mr. Rising if he could identify the body, and the man nodded, saying in a low, broken voice that it was Louise, his wife. Rising then told the story of their terror-filled struggle in the dark to protect their three children, ages 10, 3 and 22 months, as the water had descended on the family. He sobbed as he said he had thought for a moment they might all be spared, holding onto the floating roof from the damkeeper's cottage, but he'd been unable to reach his wife, who had saved their infant by passing the child to him an instant before she was taken by the rushing current.

There was not another sound in the courtroom as Mr. Keyes thanked and dismissed Mr. Rising and declared that Mrs. Rising would, for the purposes of the inquest, represent the 69 other victims who had also been autopsied and determined by the coroner to have died from drowning.

The next witness called was Superintendent William Mulholland. As Jane watched him walk heavily and somewhat unsteadily to the stand, she had a profound sense of déjà vu. Just four months ago she had sat in a similar room watching the trial of the Watterson brothers. Mulholland had, no doubt, been exultant over the outcome. Now here he was being questioned himself. Of course, the difference was that he was a witness and not the accused, in semblance anyway.

Mulholland endured questioning for long periods over the next several days, and was brought back again and again after the testimony of other witnesses. The prosecutor at first concentrated on the appearance of leaks and cracks at the dam, pulling from his briefcase sheaves of signed affidavits from witnesses. The chief explained patiently that such occurrences were normal.

"Like all dams, there are little seeps here and there, and I will say, as to that feature of it, of all the dams I have built and of all the dams I have ever seen, it was the driest for a massive dam of its size I ever saw in my life."

When asked about the appearance of a leak of muddy water the day before the disaster, Mulholland responded in a voice ringing with conviction that he and Assistant Superintendent Van Norman had gone immediately to the dam to check the report, and had found the water issuing from the leak to be entirely clear. But he became somewhat pugnacious after an engineer attested to the propensity for any large slab of concrete to crack under moisture and temperature changes, and the advisability of designing structures with contraction joints to compensate for this tendency.

"It is not the policy of the department to make provision in dam design for contraction joints," insisted Mulholland, "because it is believed to be a better policy to allow cracks to occur where stresses dictate and subsequently close them if necessary."

And when Keyes implied that the department had been aware of the risk represented by the leaking and cracking, Mulholland responded indignantly. "No, no, no! I would have been the first, the very first, sir, to spread the alarm. I would have exerted every effort to get every man, woman and child out of the path of those terrible waters!"

Chalfant leaned toward Jane and whispered, "That Keyes is a damn hypocrite! He should be behind bars himself instead of struttin around down there like a turkey gobbler in a hen pen!"

Keyes shifted his questions to the design of the dam, asking Mulholland to confirm that the St. Francis had incorporated no steel reinforcement into its massive concrete structure.

The superintendent confirmed this information, explaining that it had been designed instead as a gravity arch dam, which requires no such reinforcement since it withstands the immense water pressure through its sheer weight alone. The St. Francis Dam, Mulholland stated, had a gravity section safety factor of approximately three to one—that is, it was three times stronger than the water it contained.

"But isn't it true," Keyes countered, "that most of the other dams in the aqueduct and those you have designed elsewhere for the city are reinforced with steel and that you were using this new approach for the first time at San Francisquito Canyon?"

"No, sir, we used it also at the Mulholland Dam in Hollywood Canyon," the chief corrected, referring to the dam by the name the Public Service Commission had insisted on giving it. "That dam is nearly a duplicate of the St. Francis, in design and in the underlying rock foundations, and it's as sound as sound can be!"

The crowd gasped. Keyes stood back and said nothing, letting the words have their effect. No doubt, thought Jane, Mulholland had spoken them believing they would bolster his claims that the St. Francis had been just as well constructed. Instead, she knew that everyone in the room was now worried about a similar failure at the other dam, which rose like a castle fortress above the busy intersection of Hollywood and Vine streets.

That evening, one of the papers ran a late edition headline:

**FILM CITY IN FEAR OF DAM BREAKING**

The next morning, as they met outside of the courtroom, Loewenthal told Jane and Chalfant that hundreds of frightened, furious Hollywood residents were marching at the dam site, waving signs and shouting slogans. "They want it emptied before it comes down too," he said. "They won't get that, but we just found out Mulholland did order the water level lowered by some 20 feet, and they're going to plant a screen of tall trees in front of the dam, so people won't be afraid looking up at it."

"So, the district attorney's strategy of questioning the overall soundness of the dam is having its effect outside the courtroom as well," remarked Chalfant.

"Yes, the talk on the street is shifting from sabotage to Mulholland," agreed Loewenthal.

"The *Times* ran a photo this morning of a badly damaged house in Santa Paula. There was a painted sign stuck in the front yard that says: 'Kill Mulholland!'"

"Still, I find it strange that the district attorney hasn't introduced any evidence of sabotage, since your papers have reported so much about it," mused Chalfant.

"Yes, it seems to be a deliberate tactic of Mr. Keyes to avoid the subject," remarked Loewenthal. "I can only guess that the powers that be don't want the public thinking the city can't protect itself from—with my apologies to the two of you—a few hotheads from the Owens Valley or perhaps local union anarchists. That might dampen the public's enthusiasm for approving the bonds for the Colorado River Aqueduct. Better to have the cause be engineering mistakes."

"But wouldn't that undermine public confidence as well?" interjected Jane. "I mean, since the engineer who conceived the new aqueduct is the same one who designed the St. Francis Dam!"

"Sure, the strategy could backfire," answered Loewenthal, "but I suspect the district attorney can't resist the opportunity, despite the risk. Keyes is extremely ambitious, ruthlessly so. You both know he was accused of taking a bribe in the Lewis-Berman case, though the prosecutor, because of ineptness or maybe financial motivation of his own, couldn't prove it. But now, by going at Mulholland, pulling a public hero down from his pedestal, Keyes not only whitewashes his tarnished reputation, he also attracts publicity that could help his career."

"Hmmm, he would do well to take a lesson from the mortification he's causing Mulholland," mused Chalfant. "A month ago, the man was a god who could do no wrong. 'Pride goes before destruction, and an haughty spirit before a fall,'" he quoted the familiar admonition from Proverbs.

"My dear Chalfant," responded Loewenthal, "from my many years of observation here, I can tell you that Angelenos are not the sort to take a lesson in wisdom. I have never known a city more hell-bent on getting ahead and more tolerant of every kind of shenanigans and misdeeds in the service of that goal. And if you think I'm joking, let me enlighten you with a few facts: This city leads the nation in number of embezzlements, bank robberies, narcotic addictions and suicides."

"You know, there's another way of looking at this tragedy," Chalfant said dismally. "Some folks up in Owens Valley think it's divine justice. They're saying: The city steals Owens River water, and the stolen water wreaks havoc on the city."

Jane's heart thudded in her chest. She'd been trying not to entertain such thoughts. Chalfant couldn't know how dreadful his words were to her ears. He couldn't know that she'd stood on the parapet of the dam, full to bursting with Owens water, which just hours later would become a force of death and destruction. And now when she remembered how the water had lapped at the parapet edge, gusts of wind sending it trickling down the face of the immense dam, she found herself thinking of

Oppapago, The Weeper, and how the snow melt sent tears tumbling down its world-weary rock face.

As they took their seats, Jane's emotions continued to jump about. There was gladness that the search for blame had shifted away from possible saboteurs. She also felt some satisfaction that Mulholland was being called to answer for his arrogance and, in a sense, for the damage he had done to so many innocent people by changing the course of the Owens River. And yet, she felt sympathy for Mulholland too, seeing him sitting slumped as he did now, again in the witness stand under siege from the relentless Keyes, made her heart ache. She thought of Lucille, Perry, Rose and their other siblings, not one of them at the inquest. The pride of their father, she surmised, and his aversion to exposing his private life to the press, had made their attendance impossible.

Today the district attorney was taking a new tact. He brought forth a parade of geologists, who testified that the dam site had been problematic from the beginning. One of these, an esteemed professor from the University of Southern California, questioned the stability of the mica schist formation on the east embankment. He claimed it was so badly fractured, it would have absorbed water from the reservoir, becoming saturated to the point where it could no longer support the immense dam. Jane leaned over and whispered to Loewenthal that Jacob Clausen, an engineer from the Reclamation Service, had told her that he had examined the mica schist formation as well and had some concerns.

On further questioning, the professor asserted that any competent geologist would have recognized the problem and advised against building a dam there. Keyes asked him if, to his knowledge, such a geologist had been consulted by Mulholland. The man answered no.

Assistant Superintendent Van Norman was then called to the stand. The aim of Keyes's questions for him seemed to be to clearly establish that Mulholland had relied exclusively on his own knowledge and judgment in designing the dam and supervising its construction, eschewing the readily available advice of geologists and other experts even in his own department. Van Norman could do naught but confirm that the chief's mode of management was generally not to seek consultation.

Calling Mulholland once again to the stand, Keyes surprised the onlookers and his witness by asking his next question in a kind, solicitous voice. "You've heard days of testimony sir and you are, without doubt, the one individual most knowledgeable about all aspects of the city's water facilities. What do *you* think was the cause of the failure of the St. Francis Dam?"

The courtroom was silent except for the rustling of jury and spectators leaning forward to hear the reply.

"I have no explanation that could be called an explanation," said Mulholland, looking down at his hands, "but I have a suspicion, and I don't want to divulge it. It is a very serious thing to make a charge." Jane froze as he looked up, straight at her. "To me it is a sacred thing to make a charge, even of the remotest implication." His gaze held her—it must have been for only a moment, as no one else seemed to notice, but it seemed like forever to Jane. Then he dropped his eyes and slumped in his seat.

Keyes closed in for the kill. "Then are the citizens of this county to have no answer for this dreadful tragedy, this night of terror during which the dam you built, sir, unleashed what the *Los Angeles Times*," Keyes proclaimed, waving the newspaper theatrically, "called a 'tide of doom'?"

Clearly, the district attorney's kindness had been short-lived. Mulholland met Keyes's piercing eyes with his own, resolute but weary, then he gazed sadly at the jury. "Fasten it on me. If there was any error of judgment—human judgment—I am that human."

There was shocked silence at what most now took to be an admission of guilt, torn from Mulholland by Keyes at last, after all these days. But Jane doubted the veracity of it. She knew he believed she had done it, or knew who had. Then why had he not insisted? Why had he chosen to fall on his sword? Perhaps it was exhaustion, but more likely pride and a certain valor. He would give the city its answer, the necessary sacrifice it required to move on to greater glory. Despite her anguish for her family and neighbors—and despite the scare he'd given her just now—she couldn't help but feel impressed and dreadfully sorry for the man.

When the jury retired to deliberate, she told Loewenthal and Chalfant she had to get out of the stifling room and would take a walk. Outside, Jane headed south, between the adjacent red sandstone Romanesque-style County Courthouse and a small grassy park. Turning west at the corner of Temple Street, she continued until she stood in front of the gleaming white new Los Angeles City Hall, with its massive square tower at center. Rising up 32 stories, the edifice dwarfed the Continental Building, which had previously been called a "skyscraper."

To reach its unmatched height, the new city hall had been granted special dispensation from the city's 150-foot building limit. Municipal leaders had long been concerned with avoiding the dark "urban canyons" of New York and Chicago, but they had pulled out the stops for this shining monument to the City of Angels. It was the culmination of a recent frenzy of civic improvement: Two years ago, a splendid new public library had opened downtown, and last year the city had broken ground in the western hills, not far from Bel Air, for the campus of the University of California at Los Angeles.

Even grander than those occasions would be the christening of this edifice, scheduled for just two weeks hence, which explained the army of workers rushing about, carrying paint cans, carpentry tools, wood planks and rolls of carpet. There was no question of missing the opening date, as an immense amount of planning and money had already been invested in the celebration, which would include parades, movie stars, dancing Indians, singing Mexicans and elaborately decorated floats. The crescendo was to come in the evening, when President Coolidge would press a golden button, and the huge beacon at the top of the tower, dedicated to aviator Charles Lindbergh, would send the light of Los Angeles beaming out for 120 miles in all directions. The *Examiner* press room, like all the others in the city, had been fully informed of every detail of the planned epic event.

Jane leaned against the fence erected to keep bystanders like her away from the worksite. Today they were bystanders, onlookers, but in a couple of weeks, this magnificent building would belong to them, to Angelenos… like her? Would she ever consider herself to be one of them? It was exciting here, to be sure, fun to be caught up in the optimism and booming growth. But what about the things Loewenthal had said about the character of the city? He had never spoken so bluntly in front of her before, and his words reinforced her own misgivings about this place.

Also, since the Watterson trial, she had been feeling like a traitor being here. After all, it's Owens River water, stolen from the valley by Mulholland, that's making all the growth and glory this new building represents possible! Why should I feel sorry for him?! What about Pa and all he dreamt of and built? Now it's gone, he and Ma were up there selling it away, piece by piece. After all the years of work and struggle, they have to start over in a new place they don't even know at an age when they should be able to take their rest.

I don't want to be a part of this anymore, this rushing forward to grow and grow no matter what it costs! I'm going as far away as I can with Jed! We'll have a new life overseas! Jane made an about-face and walked briskly back to the Hall of Justice. As she turned the corner onto Broadway, heading toward the little park, she saw him, right there, as if her longing had conjured him up. There he was next to a palm tree, near the statue at the center of the park, reading a newspaper.

"Jed! Jed!" she cried.

He turned around, tall, broad-shouldered, blue eyes shining in a face as brown as a berry above the white collar of his shirt. Jane ran toward him, and he caught her up in his arms, bringing her down with a long kiss, all of which attracted a considerable amount of attention from passersby. They laughed at the spectacle they were causing, and he drew her down to sit next to him on a bench.

"I'm so glad to see you!" Jane whispered urgently, gulping the scent of his skin and hair.

"Ready to see me every day?!"

She nodded emphatically, and he squeezed her hand. Her eyes wanted to take him in all at once: dark hair lightened by the sun, tiny lines at the sides of his eyes, which made them even more attractive. "How did you know I was here?" she asked.

"Chris told me. I couldn't wait until tonight to see you. And, I wanted to come by the inquest. How is Mulholland managing? From what I read in here," he said, tapping the newspaper he still held in one hand, "the prosecutor really has it in for him."

"Yes, Keyes has been giving him a tough time," Jane confirmed.

"All of that supposed evidence by the supposed expert geologists is hooey," asserted Jed. "The chief would never have made a mistake like that, not in a million years. It had to be sabotage."

"The prosecutor doesn't seem to think so," Jane responded reluctantly, not wanting to be talking about this with Jed, wanting to let go of it now he was here.

"Why isn't he presenting any of the evidence that's been in the papers, like that crate of dynamite?"

"Perhaps it's not conclusive enough. Jed, how can you be so certain Superintendent Mulholland couldn't have made a mistake?"

"I know him, professionally and personally, that's all. No one is as knowledgeable as he is about this type of construction, and he's too smart and too careful to have done anything dangerous. It's just a lot of small men, fellows he may have had to step on in the past to get things done, trying to drag him down. That's what happens to great men like Mulholland."

"But Jed, he's not infallible. And, besides, it's been almost 15 years since you worked for him. He might have changed."

"There isn't a month that's gone by I haven't written to him or him to me. Hell, Jane, his recommendations got me those jobs, and his advice helped me make a success of them."

Jane stared at him. Her mind and mouth tried to form a question: "You've been corresponding with Mulholland all these years?!"

"Sure…"

"But you never said…"

"Honey, with all that going on in Owens Valley, I thought you might not want to hear about it."

"You were right, I guess," she said in a small voice, dropping her eyes for the first time from his face. Her mind counseled her she was making too much of a small thing, but her heart didn't agree. With all they had shared by letter and by touch, he'd deliberately kept this from her.

"Jane, honey, what does it matter now? What matters now is our future. We're going to get married and settle down." He put a hand under her chin and lifted it, looking side to side before teasingly stealing a quick kiss. "And tonight…" He licked his lips.

She couldn't keep the smile from returning to hers. "You're right, it doesn't matter now."

"On my next job, I'll be a married man. We've been promised a nice little house…"

"Where?!" She felt a little thrill, the dream flowing back into her. "Where is the next bridge or tunnel that can't possibly get built without the famous Mr. Jed Brecken?! Are we going back to the Middle East? Or maybe South America?"

"No, the next one is in Arizona." He paused, she waited, and then he said, "I've been hired to work on the new aqueduct to bring Colorado River water here to the city. I've been hired by Mulholland."

His words slammed into Jane's head like, she later thought, the wall of St. Francis water must have slammed into downstream houses. She stared at him, stunned, breathless, wordless.

"Honey, come on now. It's a great position. This is going to make the Owens aqueduct look like child's play. It's going to be the greatest civil engineering project ever undertaken..."

She struggled to find some way to respond to his entreaty and the warmth of his hand pressing hers, some way to make the happiness and elation she'd been engulfed in just minutes before wrap around her again. The thing that came into her head to say, she knew, would not be helpful.

"How do you know he'll still be chief after today? How do you know he'll even be allowed to build the Colorado River Aqueduct?"

"Oh, he'll get through this, I know he will. Because that's the kind of man he is and because when it comes down to hard tacks, the city needs what only Mulholland can provide. To keep growing, Los Angeles needs the water only he can bring it."

Jane withdrew her hand to her own lap, clutching a handful of skirt, and turned her head to look toward the tower of the new city hall. Jed waited, letting her get used to it, giving her the time. She has a mind of her own, and she always has to think things through her own way. He sat patiently, watching her, loving the bronze curls flitting slightly in the light breeze above her knitted forehead, and the glowing skin of the slender neck, almost the same color as her hair. When she turned back and took his hand, he saw she had worked through it. They'd be fine now. He was entirely unprepared for her words.

"Jed, I'm not going to Arizona with you. And I don't think I can marry you. I release you from our engagement."

"What?! Jane, what are you talking about?! You're joking, aren't you? You can't mean that!"

"I do, I do mean it Jed. I'm sorry." Now there was real alarm in his eyes and a glimmer of tears. She felt tears rising in her own, knew she owed him an explanation, but could only say, "I don't know Jed, it's just that you and I, we're…I don't know, we're just too different after all."

"What do you mean, 'too different?'" he asked woodenly.

"I don't know…I just know it's true. All of a sudden, after all this time, I know it's true." She sat there miserably, unable to meet his eyes.

Finally she said, "You once told me I'm the sort of person who goes right at things, and you loved that because you're that sort of person too. But you also said there's a part of me that doesn't, that holds back to dream and ponder and question, and you loved that too because it's not like you. Well, I think that's the only lie you've ever told me, though you didn't know it to be untrue. That part of me, the part that can't keep moving forward no matter what happens, no matter what the cost, is the part that's saying no to you now. We're too different."

He reached for her hand again. She didn't resist, but let it lie limply in his grasp. Unknowingly, he pressed rough fingernails into her skin. "You just need a little time, honey. You'll change your mind after you've had some time, I know you will. And I'll be waiting for you in Arizona when you're ready."

"I have to get back in, Jed, my editor is waiting for me." They stood up, neither one knowing what to do next. She raised herself on tiptoe to brush his lips with hers. "Goodbye Jed. I know you'll do well in Arizona."

Jane walked across the park to the entrance of the building, forcing herself, as she had their first night together, not to look back to see if he was watching.

---

'It's time." Loewenthal touched Jane's arm but got no response.

For the past hours she had sat blankly staring at the ornate clock that dominated the hallway, without comprehending the movement of its hands. She felt dead inside. What was she doing here, acting as if any of this really mattered? Of course Jed was right, Mulholland would be exonerated and he'd go on to build more aqueducts and dams. Los Angeles would continue expanding.

Loewenthal shook her arm gently. "Come on, J. Bow, the jury's in."

For the second time in six months, Jane found herself in a silent courtroom watching as a jury filed in with somber faces. In this instance there was no accused to stand and face judgment.

The jury foreman rose and read their report. It placed the responsibility for the disaster on the Los Angeles Department of Water and Power, its chief engineer and its board. The report went on to say that, with the great destruction caused by the dam failure and the absence of living eyewitnesses to the actual break, it was impossible to determine with complete accuracy the cause of the disaster, but it was in all probability a failure of the rock formations upon which the dam had been built rather than any error of design and construction. The jury recommended that there be no criminal prosecution by the district attorney, as there was no evidence of a criminal act or intent to do harm on the part of those responsible. Rather, errors of judgment had caused the tragedy.

Jane saw Mulholland stiffen at this pronouncement. He sat rigidly as the jury foreman delivered the report's conclusion: "It was apparent that the entire personnel of the water department had an unusual degree of confidence in Superintendent and Chief Engineer William Mulholland and relied entirely upon his ability, experience and infallibility in matters of engineering judgment. The construction of a municipal dam should never be left to the sole judgment of one man, no matter how eminent."

That was it. The inquest was over, judgment rendered. Jane shook her head and said bitterly, "He's been exonerated, he's not liable for any of it."

"Not liable," agreed Loewenthal, "but there's no doubt who is to blame. That report essentially said it was Mulholland's arrogance and the department's acquiescence to it—that's what killed all those people."

The district attorney and coroner thanked the jury, and people began leaving. As Mulholland stood up to make his way down the aisle, Matthews supported him on one arm. Van Norman came grim-faced behind them. As they emerged into the hallway, reporters swarmed around Mulholland like wasps driven from their nest.

"I'll meet you back at the office," said Loewenthal, rushing off down the stairs. "See if you can get a comment."

But Jane and Chalfant both stood back, unwilling to add their sting to the swarm. Somehow Mulholland and Matthews pushed through the crowd and made their way down the stairs. Jane, watching their progress from above, saw a dark-haired young man step forward and clasp

Mulholland's hand. Jane and Chalfant followed the flow of people outside. By the time they stood on the exterior steps, Mulholland's black Marmon sedan was pulling away and Jed had disappeared.

# The Field

"Did you ever change your mind?"

I look at my interrogator, leaning across the kitchen table on his big-boned arms. Earnest blue eyes, shaggy blond head, ruddy skin. For the thousandth time, I think: CK is so much like Chris.

"No, I never did." I can see by his slightly disapproving expression that he finds the abruptness of my change of heart about Jed difficult to understand. Young people generally find it incredible that anyone could quit the love of their life just like that and then live on for decades without regrets. Well, I didn't say I had no regrets.

I try to explain. "I guess I had been so long without him that the parting didn't come as much of an adjustment, just a letting go of a dream. And I was doing a lot of that by then." What I don't say is that maybe I was just a dream for Jed too. When I think of Jed these days, Mary's words often come to mind about the breed of men addicted to their own vitality, to "the pulse and heat of a life laid bare to its thews and sinews." I suspect Jed was like that, and I suspect he never did settle down to a more conventional way of living.

CK doesn't look convinced, so I elaborate. "Those young adult years, in one's 20s and 30s, they're quite formative, my dear. The way we live then, the patterns we set, they can last a lifetime." I'm thinking that I hope there are exceptions to this rule I'm so loftily pronouncing—hoping CK is an exception.

"What happened to Jed?"

"I don't know. I never saw him again. But I do know that if he went on to build the Colorado River Aqueduct, he didn't do it for Mulholland."

"What happened to him?"

I get up, pushing off with one hand against the table, the other grasping my cup and cane. Over at the counter, I pour myself more strong black coffee. I look out the window at the mountains, as I always do standing here. The sun is still high, but beginning to drop toward the jagged white edge of snow fields. "How about another cup of tea?"

He nods and sits back in the chair to await the tea and my answer. CK is a patient boy—in this he does not resemble his grandfather. I spoon the chamomile leaves into the pot and begin reheating the kettle. My companion does not approve of coffee, computers and other artifacts of the "go-go '80s," as this new gilded age is sometimes called. Born too late to become a bona fide hippie, CK found his calling in the "back to the land" movement of the '70s. Rejecting the business empire passed to him at the death of his unhappy, alcoholic father, he has for the past decade managed a small organic farm in Santa Rosa, a town northeast of San Francisco.

He doesn't own the farm, he just manages it for a guy he knows. CK disapproves of excessive ownership and money, even though he came into a considerable inheritance when he turned 30. For a couple of years now, the funds have percolated in a trust account, growing ever larger from earned interest. My great nephew has never touched a cent, and he's told me several times of his intention to give it all away to charity and be done with it.

The tea kettle whistles. I pour the water into the pot and replace the lid. CK comes over to bring the pot to the table as I make my way behind him with the cane. We sit together silently, sipping our drinks, then he repeats his question. "What happened to him?"

I don't want to talk about Mulholland, but realize I owe CK an answer. He's spent the better part of his three-day visit so far plowing *through a pile of pages covered with handwriting as wobbly as my knees. I had started writing a few things down as a remedy to quiet my nerves and clear my brain, but then found I couldn't stop. Soon I was filling page after page with memories, of my own experiences as well as what I later found out had happened and what I thought might have happened. After all these years of hiding away and telling myself none of it matters a whit anymore, I'd come to the point of needing to explain to someone.*

*"Mulholland's star fell very quickly," I answer CK's question. "Within weeks of the St. Francis Dam inquiry, the city changed the name of Mulholland Dam to the Hollywood Reservoir. Before the end of the year, at almost the same moment the state legislature ratified the Colorado River Compact, Mulholland was retired, and Van Norman took over as superintendent of the DWP."*

*"Pushed aside, just like that?"*

*"Yes, though there must have been some solace for him when just a month after his retirement, the district attorney who had interrogated him, Asa Keyes, was finally convicted for bribery. He was sent to San Quentin alongside the Watterson brothers, although Keyes was pardoned by the governor after less than two years, and they both served half of their ten-year sentences."*

*"What did Mulholland do after he retired?"*

*"Not much. Lucille and I exchanged letters for a time after I came here. She told me that, out of kindness, she supposed, Van Norman hired Mulholland as a consultant and provided an office for him in the department. He went there every day, but what he did, Lucille didn't know. He may have been asked for advice from time to time, but he wasn't in the thick of things anymore. And Lucille told me that some of the engineers who had worked for him for decades shunned him. That hurt worse, she said, than the shift from public adulation to censure. The deepest cuts are personal.*

*"The saddest thing she told me, and maybe the last time she ever spoke to me of him, was about five years after he retired. Lucille said Rose had taken a call for him in the night. It was Fred Eaton's son Burdick, and he was urgently pleading for Mulholland to come. Eaton had suffered a stroke and was failing. After all those years of estrangement, his dying wish was to see his old friend again.*

"Lucille said her sister Rose drove Mulholland over to Burdick's home, somewhere in LA, and waited in the parlor while Mulholland went up alone. She told Lucille their father's face was quivering with sorrow when he came back down the stairs. On the way home, he sat blankly staring out the window for a long time, and then he told Rose how he found it so strange that Eaton had called, as just the night before he had dreamt of his old friend. They had been young and virile, swimming naked in a cold river and laughing, but he'd known, as one sometimes does in dreams, that they were both dead."

"So Mulholland never gave in and paid Eaton the million bucks for the reservoir site in Long Valley?" CK asks.

"No, he never paid Eaton's price. But the city did eventually purchase the land and build a large reservoir up there. The way it finally happened was that Eaton went bankrupt—he had lost a lot of money himself when the Wattersons' bank failed and the rest, I suppose, from mismanagement and bad investments. Anyway, the city paid $650,000 for the land to the bankruptcy court the day before Eaton died. Lucille said her father was devastated because history seemed to have fulfilled a prediction he had once made that he would buy Long Valley over his friend's dead body."

"God, it's like a Greek tragedy!—a lesson in what happens to a man who has everything, but is afflicted with the tragic flaw of greed."

"Yes, maybe Eaton was greedy, but the struggle between him and Mulholland seemed to be about more than money."

"Pride—another tragic flaw," CK almost spits the words. "Two men in a pissing contest, and neither one will back down. Mulholland especially. It sounds like he never backed down about anything. I know guys like that, who always think they're right."

"For a long time, it did seem that Mulholland was right," I say, shaking my head to disperse the still painful pricklings of my last conversation with Jed.

"Auntie Jane, why did you come back here anyway?" asks CK, reaching across to touch my hand.

I have to get up then, subjecting CK to the spectacle of me lurching about the kitchen, picking up here, wiping down there. I stop finally, caught and quieted by the view out the window to my mountains. I turn around, leaning against the sink. "I suppose I thought I needed to be here,

as some kind of witness, I don't know. Ma and Pa were gone—
your grandpa must have told you they died not long after the move to
Bakersfield. Pa of a heart attack. One hot day he just dropped to the
ground in a field he was clearing for planting. Ma passed of pneumonia
the following winter."

I make my way back to the table and sit down. "I know there are
medical reasons for what happened, but I've always felt Pa had given everything he had to our life up here in the valley, and he just didn't have the
heart, when it came right down to it, for starting over somewhere else.
Ma didn't want to stay without him."

CK is trying to be sympathetic, but he never met his great grand-
parents. Still, I suppose he can, as they say now, "relate" to Pa after what
I wrote about him, CK also being a farmer who takes great pride in the
quality of his produce. I continue with my story.

"By that time I had decided I didn't want anything more to do with
Los Angeles. I was living in Bakersfield, helping Ma and Pa as much as I
could. I took occasional assignments for the Examiner to support myself and
try to contribute to the household. When my folks passed away, I didn't
want to stay there anymore either, and I couldn't stomach the thought of
returning to Los Angeles. The only place I felt I belonged was here, and
coming back was a way of finally showing some loyalty.

"Anyway, I guess I invented a reason for myself, this notion of bearing
witness to the destruction of the valley. At least 300, maybe 400 families
packed up and left Owens Valley like mine did, and a lot of these people
were leaving land they had been born on, land their grandfathers had
cleared and fought Indians and ruthless cattle barons to hold. I must have
walked miles of irrigation ditches they'd dug by hand and kept clear all
those years—all drying up and choked with weeds. I made a sort of maca-
bre game of counting the dead tree trunks along what was left of the
Owens River."

I'm enjoying the elegiac tone of my own language—I've so little need
to care for my choice of words these days—so I continue. "I drove through
alleys of gray stumps that had once been promenades of cottonwood trees to
ranch houses, abandoned now, standing forlornly, paint peeling, windows
stripped for salvage, doors banging in the breeze...after a while the city
bulldozers just went in and flattened them. Some of those bulldozers were

*driven by valley men who used to own their own place, now working for a wage. They plowed the lawns and gardens under too, and uprooted the orchards."*

*"You sound like you're reading that," comments my less-than-impressed grandnephew. "Like it's some article you wrote."*

*Busted, as the kids say. I wave a thin-boned, large-veined hand in front of my face, as if shooing away a fly. "You're half-right, they're words I would have written. I tried to write about these things for the* Examiner *or even the* Register, *but nobody wanted to read it. This was the beginning of the Depression and of talking pictures. Folks wanted distraction from reality, they were more taken with movie stars and gangsters. Stories about the suffering of a rural community beaten down by a big city weren't interesting anymore, even to valley folk. They needed to escape what they were living every day."*

*"How did you manage if you weren't a reporter anymore?"*

*"Oh, on a shoestring most of the time!" I laugh, and then admit the truth. "Your grandfather helped out. He never would have let me starve. And when he died, although the bulk of his estate, as you know, went to your father, I received a small inheritance. It's been enough."*

*"You never seemed to be working when I came here," CK recalls. "I thought it was kind of odd."*

*So he hadn't been oblivious, as children usually are, during his annual summer two-week visit. Those were treasured days. During those sojourns, I shared with him the fruits of my real labor, taking him on long rambles up Mary's "streets and alleys of the mountains."*

*For once I got back to Independence, some siren wind whistling down the canyons lured me up onto their rocky slopes again and again. I became, I imagine, something of a comic local figure, a skinny middle-aged woman in denim jeans and shirt, unkempt braid poking from a floppy hat, striding over the valley floor toward the broken boulders at the foot of the Sierra. I spent my days retracing the trails of my youth and pushing beyond them. Sometimes I'd head up Mazourka Canyon to 8,800-foot Badger Flat or follow Independence Creek to its headwaters near Onion Valley, 5,000 feet above the valley floor. Sometimes I'd go on from there another five miles to Kearsarge Pass at nearly 12,000 feet. Other days I'd climb beside Big Pine*

*Creek to a string of icy mountain lakes below Palisade Glacier, largest of the Sierra glaciers.*

*And though I may well have been a comical figure, I eventually became regarded as a local expert on hiking the back country of Owens Valley. For many years, clerks in the sporting goods store in Bishop gave my name and address to those they judged to be serious hikers, and this flotsam of youth, mostly young men with beautiful muscles, dirty clothes and friendly faces, would wash up into my yard several times a month. No need to tell CK all that.*

*I excuse myself and make my way to the bathroom, holding cane and hallway walls for support, my striding days long over. I know I haven't told CK the real truth, the hard rock of truth beneath the idea of witnessing the valley's transformation back into desert, beneath the obsession of climbing every path into the high Sierra.*

*This truth is that once I was back here, what had been in my youth a place of protection gradually became a sort of prison. Rarely venturing outside of the valley, I lost my ability to move about with confidence in the world, especially in cities. The fewer professional assignments I took, the less competent I felt as a journalist. As reckless a young woman as I had once been, I became an adult full of fear—not of rattlesnakes or mountain lions, bears, heights or lightning, but of the world of progress and power. At some point, I figured out that probably the reason I'd come back here was that I simply hadn't been up to it. Not all that different from a young man who quits a doctoral program in biology at the University of California at Davis, complaining of the tyranny of his advisor, a celebrated scientist, the machinations of departmental politicians and the sin of testing on animals. A young man who wiles away the next decade growing vegetables in a field that isn't even his own.*

*When I get back to the kitchen, CK has pushed my pile of scribble aside and is looking again at the newspaper, the one with the front-page story about the car crash that killed that young environmentalist. It's been sitting there on the corner of my table for almost a week, and since CK arrived, we've each reread the story several times. Though the paper is becoming brittle and the type blurred from all the unfolding and refolding, I still can't look at it without feeling fury rise in my throat.*

"What did you mean when you wrote there were two deaths, two Davids against one Goliath?" he asks when I've sat down again across from him.

I take a deep breath, forcing air down my gullet, willing myself to relax. Now, at last, we're on the brink of the conversation I need to be having with him. Still I hesitate, wondering where to begin my strange tale. I begin:

"The first death wasn't actually a David. That was his role, being David to Goliath, but not his name. His name was Father Crowley."

"Like Crowley Lake?"

"Yes, the reservoir in Long Valley—the one Los Angeles finally built on the land they bought from Fred Eaton's bankruptcy court—that was named for Father John Crowley." I smile and shake my head, still amazed at the memory of the small, bespectacled man who had crisscrossed the desert in his Model T, seemingly immune to the searing heat in his black suit and high collar.

"He was a Catholic priest, and a most unlikely hero. His territory, or parish, I guess you would call it, was most of Inyo County. There were about 600 Catholics in these parts, but they were spread out, so Crowley had to cover a circuit. Every month he'd travel, mostly driving but also by train, from Bishop through all the towns of Owens Valley to Barstow and then on to Death Valley and then back again to Bishop. He used to joke that he was an 'ecclesiastical tramp.' Most men would have been exhausted from it, but Crowley had so much heart and energy. He cared about all the people here, not just the Catholics, and he wanted to help the valley."

I judge that CK isn't bored yet, so I continue. "It was a sad time in the '30s when Crowley was here. There had been anger and rebellion in the '20s, but now there was only bitterness and despair. In truth, Los Angeles had done its best to atone for its sins by buying out the rest of the property owners, including townspeople with no water rights at all. They didn't have to do that. Those folks who clung on were mostly leasing their land, houses or shops back from the city. Most of us were hopeless.

"But Crowley didn't see it like that. He organized plays and pageants to bring some enjoyment to valley folk and awaken a sense of pride in our heritage. And he started writing a column called 'Sage and Tumbleweed' about Inyo County for one of their Catholic publications. Pretty soon it got *picked up by lay newspapers, like the* Central California Register *and the* Inyo Independent.

"*He was a natural writer with a down-to-earth sense of humor—
I remember I always got a chuckle from the way he signed his columns, as
'the Inyokel.' People looked forward to reading them because, even though
he acknowledged the problems we faced, he focused on the sunny side of life,
as we used to say back then. He wrote about desert lore and legends, rural
wisdom and the home cooking of country cafes. He was also inclined to
write about movies, like* Gunga Din *and* Charge of the Light Brigade, *that
were being filmed in the Alabama Hills. I remember a hilarious column
once about Gary Cooper and his wife Franchot Tone waiting for an ele-
phant to be trucked in from Los Angeles.*

"*Most of all, though, Crowley loved to write about fishing back
country streams and hiking the trail up to the summit of Mt. Whitney.
One Sunday, he even gave a mass on the summit to attract publicity
because he thought it might encourage tourists to take the drive up the
new Highway 395. That route had just been completed, and it linked
Los Angeles to the 'vacation land' of Owens Valley. In fact, Crowley
knocked on my door one day to ask me to help him promote opportunities
for developing recreational business in the valley. I remember he told me
that Inyo's one inalienable asset was its scenery.*"

"*Did you help him?*"

"*No, I didn't, I'm sorry to say. I was pretty bitter and despairing
myself then. Afraid to hope. Los Angeles had kept buying up land and, by
now, owned, I don't know, about 80 to 90 percent of not only the farms
and ranches, but town property too. Owens Valley had become like a
colonial province or medieval vassal state of the DWP. And I didn't fancy
having a swarm of Angelenos make the Owens Valley a stopover on their
Sierra fishing and hiking trips.*

"*But he wasn't about to let naysayers like me discourage him.
He organized a group called the Inyo Associates—Chalfant joined—
and they set about helping folks around here get into recreation-oriented
businesses. Things like mule-packing, rock climbing and trail guides,
motels, coffee shops. They also had ideas for a whole slew of civic projects.
One of these was to get the county to build a road linking Death Valley
with Mt. Whitney. Crowley liked to say it would 'join the top and bottom*

of the nation!' They were successful in getting it built, and for the opening of the road in 1937, there was a three-day celebration like you've never seen, rivaling any spectacle Cecile B. DeMille or any other Hollywood director could have conjured up."

"What did they do?"

"Well, Crowley christened the event 'The Wedding of the Waters,' and the idea was to take water from Lake Tulainyo, about a mile north of Whitney, which is the highest lake on the continent, and transport it by hand to Bad Water Basin in Death Valley, which is the lowest water not only on the continent, but in the whole western hemisphere. Along the way, the plan was to highlight the proud history and industry of the county. So it started with an Indian runner dipping a gourd into Lake Tulainyo and taking it down the Mt. Whitney Trail to the beginning of the trail head at Whitney Portal. He gave the gourd of water to an actor portraying a Pony Express rider, who rode it down the canyon.

"After that, an old prospector took the gourd by burro part of the way, then there was a nearly 100-year-old covered wagon, then a 20-mule team, then a real stagecoach, then an old-time steam engine pulling a Southern Pacific train, which the governor was riding. The final night, they put on a rodeo in Lone Pine, which my friend Juan directed. The next morning, before dawn, the governor handed the gourd to a champion race car driver in a Lincoln Zephyr. The last handoff was to a pilot who carried the water in a white airplane over Death Valley. The superintendent of Death Valley National Monument was in the plane, and he dumped the water from the gourd over Bad Water."

"Ah ha, that was the 'wedding,' right?" CK makes the connection.

"Yes, but the spectacle didn't end there. When the waiting crowd saw the little shower of water droplets hit the surface and let out a cheer, a troop of Boy Scouts lit a signal fire at the side of the Bad Water pool. More Boy Scouts on the cliffs above saw the sign, and they lit their own fire, and another troop on Telescope Peak saw it and lit theirs. And so it went, with watchers from mountain crest to mountain crest, creating a chain of beacons to pass the word all the way back to Whitney that the waters had been joined. Then a pillar of fire appeared on that greatest of peaks, reaching upward to the stars!"

"Cool!" CK may be immune to Hollywood-style excess, but he's a sucker for the Boy Scout signal beacons.

"All of that may seem frivolous, and I thought it was then, but it turned out to be very important to the survival of the valley. By the time you made your first summer visit here—what was that, 1965?—probably 90 percent of the economy was from recreational businesses of one kind or the other."

"So that's why they named the reservoir for him?"

"Yes, and that's mostly what he's remembered for." I get up and go back over to the coffee pot. He shakes his head when I lift the tea kettle. I'm not finished with my story, and now I must get to the point of it.

"But what is really important to know about Crowley is not that he was a promoter and a brilliant economic mind, but that he was a fighter. He was an Irish immigrant just like Mulholland, and he had the same tough spirit. The Inyo Associates had a Committee on Relations with the city of Los Angeles, and one of the first things they did was help defeat a state assembly bill that would have given the city an even tighter stranglehold on the valley.

"If this bill had passed, the valley would have been forced to get permission from Los Angeles before creating any incorporated cities or public associations aimed at making public improvements. So that would have prevented Big Pine, Lone Pine and Independence from becoming incorporated cities with the power to assess taxes or offer bonds. And it was clear the city also wanted to push Bishop, which was already an incorporated city, toward disincorporation. Anyway, thank goodness the bill didn't pass.

"The next thing they did was to take up the cause of Lone Pine, which was drying out to the point where health hazards and fire danger were issues. Some of the people down there had filed a suit against Los Angeles to restore enough water so that the town and a handful of farmers who still owned property with water rights could survive. Crowley was asked to chair some of the meetings they held with the city to seek an out-of-court settlement, and I heard he was very skillful and organized, and understood legal affairs quite well."

"What happened?" CK lifts his chin, curious.

"Well, it was a long process. There was a lot of maneuvering, including a countersuit by the city. Eventually the committee broadened the effort and submitted what it called a 'six-point program' to the DWP. I'm not going to remember all the points, but they included that the city should sell back any valley property—without water rights, of course—not needed for aqueduct operations, that it finally agree to a maximum amount for its water withdrawals from the Owens River, allowing valley residents to use any excess above that maximum, and that it adjust the rents it was charging business and residential tenants to reflect the depreciation of property values and diminished earning potential in the valley."

"Wow, that's quite a one-two-three punch!"

"Well, it was six points, but the others weren't as important."

"Did they get it?"

"Some of it. The board of commissioners of the DWP agreed to start offering for sale any unneeded lots in all the valley towns, and they followed through. I'd say that within five years, about 50 percent of the town properties held by the city were back in private hands. They also dropped the countersuit."

"That's it? That's all they got?" He's visibly unimpressed. "What about setting a maximum water level?"

I feel my mouth tighten with the old bitterness. "Well, if you recall from that pile of pages, getting Los Angeles to state a maximum was something the valley had been trying to do in one way or another for decades. I'd like to say that Father Crowley achieved it, but he didn't. The valley wouldn't make any headway on that for a very long time, and then it was through legal action—but you know something about that."

"So, Crowley was a David who threw a few stones that bruised Goliath, but he couldn't take the giant down."

"He might have though. Father Crowley was determined and irrepressible. He had so much optimism and, of course, faith that I know he wouldn't have stopped. He'd have kept pushing until he got one more concession from the city, and then another..."

"But he died, right? That stopped him," CK states flatly.

"Yes. He was driving in the early hours of the morning to Death Valley, where he was scheduled to give a 6:30 morning mass. Somewhere just past Mojave, a steer apparently jumped out from the brush onto the highway, and when he swerved to avoid it, his car was hit by a lumber truck. The newspapers said he died instantly, of a fractured skull, broken *neck or both. They made a great deal of his little dog Tray, which had been riding beside him and was thrown clear. The dog sat near Father Crowley's body, guarding it for hours. He wouldn't let anyone come near until another priest the dog recognized as a friend arrived.*

*"At the time I just thought it was Providence, playing tricks on the valley again. Like when the Watterson bank failure happened—a complete and utter disaster, out of the blue."*

*CK is looking at me with a puzzled, critical expression. "But you don't think so now?"*

*"I don't know anymore, CK. But I will tell you that when Crowley died, resistance to Los Angeles just collapsed again, like it had when the Wattersons were sent to prison. And people around here were devastated like before, myself included.*

*"This time, I'd been just a bystander. I hadn't joined Crowley's committee, hadn't volunteered to lick stamps or bake cookies. I'd told myself I'd already gone through those battles before and knew where they would end up, with the city victorious and the valley even more firmly under its heel. But I had still followed their progress—Chalfant had kept me informed— and I was just starting to change my mind, to believe just a little in the possibility things might change, when Father Crowley died. And I was destroyed. We all were. That good man's death set the cause of justice for Owens Valley back to slumbering for more than 30 years. If he'd been here, I know we would have eventually gotten limits, and with those in place, I don't think Los Angeles would have ever been in a position to build the second aqueduct in 1964—they called it the 'second barrel,' like a double-barrel shotgun!"*

*"Well maybe you're right, his death did set the valley back, but what does it have to do with David's death?"*

*CK is talking about David Gaines, the David he knows personally. He met him at UC Davis in the mid '70s when CK took an ecology course from Gaines, who was commuting between lecturing positions at Davis and Stanford. Gaines had a National Science Foundation grant to study the ecology of Mono Lake—what he found there led to the formation of the Mono Lake Committee. They were a small group of young folks dedicated to fighting the environmental damage caused by the extension of the aqueduct north to the Mono Basin.*

At the start, it was a long, lonely legal battle, but recently momentum had seemed to be swinging in their direction. The state legislature had ordered an environmental study, and the National Academy of Sciences had completed a report confirming that excessive diversions of water by Los Angeles threatened the survival of the lake ecosystem and endorsing the idea of establishing a sustainable limit. Trout fishermen bringing a parallel suit had been successful in obtaining a superior court injunction forcing the city to reduce its diversions from the creeks.

The city also seemed to be losing the publicity battle, with favorable press coverage of the "battle for Mono Lake." Bumper stickers and t-shirts with "Save Mono Lake" appeared all across the state. Television stations loved to cover the annual "Bikeathon," where riders dipped canteens in the fountain outside of the DWP's Los Angeles headquarters and then rode more than 300 miles to pour the contents back into Mono Lake.

CK knows all this better than I—he was the one who brought it to my attention. I'd been vaguely aware of the Mono fight, as it had been in the papers, of course. Most valley folk didn't think much of these "hippies" and "agitators" coming in from their universities and "acting like they own the land."

I remained skeptical and inactive, like I had in the Crowley years. But I had reasons for watching the progress of the scrappy little band of environmentalists with some interest, as a fledgling hope had been hatched in the Owens Valley as well. After the second aqueduct and increased groundwater pumping in Owens Valley, Inyo County sued Los Angeles under the California Environmental Quality Act, saying the city had failed to do an environmental impact report. The court forced Los Angeles to file a report, rejecting both its first attempt in 1976 and its second try in 1979, and imposing court-mandated limits on pumping in the meantime.

Since then, there'd been a counter-suit against the county, multiple studies by both sides and on-again, off-again negotiation. Three years ago, the county board of supervisors approved a five-year agreement with Los Angeles on pumping levels. A final environmental impact report and long-term agreement were still to come, but it was a beginning. With it, and the growing prospect of a victory in Mono as well, I had begun to hope again. At least until a week ago, when I picked up the morning paper and read about the crash.

I look at my grandnephew and decide to go for broke. *"Don't you find it strange, CK, that the first time in 30 years the Los Angeles Department of Water and Power is seriously challenged, the first time anyone makes real headway against them, the leader of that movement is also killed in a car crash on a mountain road?"*

*"Yes, it's strange,"* he says slowly, then his eyes widen and he starts to laugh. *"You don't think it could be some kind of conspiracy, do you Auntie? Are you suggesting the two deaths are linked in some way?"*

*"Probably not,"* I drop my head, embarrassed, and pick at a ragged cuticle. *"But it is a possibility."* My throat is closing again, so I take another deep breath and force myself to raise my head and look him straight in the eye. *"But consider the idea from another perspective: Do you think there's any possibility that the assassinations of John F. Kennedy and Martin Luther King could have been a conspiracy, the acts of some kind of organization rather than of single individuals?"*

*"Maybe, maybe especially JFK."*

*"With all the questions that have been asked and investigative articles published over the years, could you in all honesty totally discount the possibility of conspiracy?"*

*"No, no thinking person could totally discount it."*

*"And I hope I qualify for that distinction."* He smiles and bestows a nod. *"CK, I am quite sure that William Mulholland went to his grave believing with the conviction of his soul that I was involved in some way in the dynamiting of the St. Francis Dam."*

*"You didn't have anything to do with it!"*

*"He didn't know that. And he didn't live long enough to be presented with convincing evidence to the contrary. There was a book published in 1963, I think it was, that concluded, based on testimonial and geological evidence that the failure had been caused by a rock slide on the geologically unstable eastern slope. Other studies have pointed to Mulholland's decision to increase the height of the dam by 20 feet after it was already under construction as a contributing factor. At that late date, there was no possibility of widening the base to compensate for the added height, and this may have created destabilizing uplift pressures. Mulholland didn't get to see any of that new information."* I'm drifting, I realize.

"My point is just this: Mulholland was an extremely rational person, and he believed that I and other Owens Valley people were capable of an act of sabotage that was sure to kill many people. That tells me he was quite familiar with the darker deeds of his fellow men. He hadn't spent 40 years in Los Angeles, rubbing elbows with the city's most powerful, ambitious and ruthless citizens, without knowing what they were made of."

"Oh come on, Aunt Jane!" He's laughing at me again. "You're saying there were men like Noah Cross in that movie Chinatown...you know, when he says to Jack Nicholson," CK adopts his best John Huston voice, "Mr. Gittes, 'At the right time in the right place people are capable of anything.'"

But I've gone too far to be intimidated by ridicule now. "Precisely," I say crisply. "In fact, that's one of the only things in that movie that actually rings true." The Roman Polanski movie, which many assume is about the Owens River controversy, is a fine film, but actually corresponds very little with the facts. "CK, you've got to figure that Polanski, having lived so long in Hollywood, was as well acquainted as Mulholland with the dark side of the city. And I'm not just talking about maniacs like Charles Manson, but men in suits!"

He shifts uncomfortably in his seat. "You're starting to creep me out, Auntie Jane."

Well good, I think, now you're starting to hear me. "CK, do you know what they call the rich white men who've always made up the city's board of water commissioners?" He shakes his head.

"They call them the 'Water Buffaloes.' Because they can smell water hundreds of miles away, and once they do, they obstinately plod right toward it, and can't be turned away. Their kingdom is now not only Los Angeles and its Owens Valley vassal, but the whole Metropolitan Water District encompassing Orange County and San Diego County too.

"These men who wield the power of precious water across all that land have always done things pretty much as they see fit, with little or no accountability or oversight from anyone. Many of them are real estate magnates, cut from the same cloth as the syndicates that made fortunes when the original aqueduct brought the Owens River water to the San Fernando Valley. Like those scoundrels, they're committed to the continued growth and development of Los Angeles at all costs, and they'll do whatever is *necessary to get the water to support it. They pushed through the Colorado River Aqueduct and the Mono Basin Extension, the second Owens River Aqueduct and the State Water Project up to the Sacramento River largely by scare tactics and sheer political and economic brute force."*

*"I see what you mean," he says thoughtfully. He's not laughing at me now. "But why would they care so much about Mono Lake?"*

*"Money and power," I answer. "Water from the Mono Basin and Owens Valley costs much less than water from the Colorado or the State Water Project. It's of higher quality, so it also costs less to process for consumption. And both of those other sources involve a lot of political wrangling against other state, county and city entities."*

*"Okay, okay, I get where you're going with this. But, it's only a possibility, not a probability, Auntie Jane. You have to admit it's far more likely that the two deaths, which are weirdly similar, I give you that, are just a bizarre coincidence." He looks worried. "You do see that, don't you?"*

*"Yes, I see that is far more likely. But my theory, it is possible."*

*We've come to the end of it then, as CK has to leave soon to drive up to Lee Vining. There's going to be a memorial and dinner at that little town on the edge of Mono Lake in honor of Gaines. He'll most likely be back very late he tells me.*

*After he leaves, I can't settle down. I pull on my coat and ease myself down the front steps to the street and start walking north. I'm feeling more than restless, I'm feeling angry—furious really because I know it is possible! Maybe not the water commissioners, maybe not anyone I could ever identify by name, but there are such men in that city! Plenty of them there, and here, and everywhere. I'm furious because I know people do commit despicable acts in the name of progress and the future. Elected officials do betray citizens for their own gain or misbegotten principles. Civilization does tolerate wickedness and folly to a degree that doesn't bear scrutiny. People do see their dreams and the hard-won products of their labor crushed to dust.*

*All these years on this earth, and that seems to be one of the only things I really do know. I saw plenty of evidence again during World War II when they shipped all those Japanese Americans here to a dusty piece of ground called Manzanar, near Lone Pine. They actually put them on a reservation, just like they did the Paiute. A few years ago they made it a national* historic landmark, which is fine by me since those poor folks lost everything they had. But there's no monument to the Paiute and none to folks like my parents and Mr. and Mrs. Parker, who lost everything too.

The late afternoon sun is dropping, bringing the canyons, outcroppings and slides of the Sierra rock faces into sharp relief. I never tire of watching the texture and patterns change, but I can't look now because to make sure of placing my cane and feet in the right places, I have to keep my eyes on the ground. Inexplicably, they are stinging with tears.

What a ridiculous sight I must make, an old woman wobbling down the street with her cane, crying like a babe. I'd be hopping mad if I could hop! I'm really feeling quite enraged, not just with the ways of the world, but with my parents! This is even more ludicrous than anyone watching me could possibly guess: a 92-year-old woman enraged with her parents! Especially Pa—the world didn't turn out to be like he told me it was, in this enchanted valley, protected from storms by the Sierra rain shadow.

Most of my life I've kept this fury under wraps and buttoned down, out of sight even to myself. Except once. I did not dynamite the St. Francis Dam, but I did eventually light a fuse.

On September 15, 1976, out of the blue, for the first time in almost 50 years, the aqueduct was once again blown sky high. More accurate to say, a moderate-size hole was blown out of a canal wall near Lone Pine. It took the DWP just a couple of days to fix it, but the blast was so unexpected that it attracted a lot of publicity, which provided a momentary lift to the spirits of valley folk, particularly those in the south end, which was being sucked to the marrow by the second aqueduct and pumping. The DWP and local authorities launched an investigation, but, just like before, no one knew anything or, if they did, they weren't talking. And I feel sure that nobody, not the hardware salesman who sold a nice little old lady blasting gelatin so her "hired man can root out some gophers," and certainly not CK, never CK, suspected it was me. Of course, that was 12 years ago, when I could still drive my car, squat on the ground and walk at a reasonable pace.

A futile, stupid gesture, a feeble scream of frustration, utterly useless— like closing the barn door after the horse has already run out, and not only the horse, but all the cows and chickens too! Sure, I know that well enough. Yet, as I huddled there against the canal that night, carefully placing my equipment and counting through the sequence of memorized instructions,

*I felt such relief to be finally taking some action. And I had a sense of my father's presence, of somehow being close to him again, united in spirit and deed. I had always suspected he had participated in some way in the bombings, though he had never admitted to it.*

*For years after doing it, I've felt much better. But then came this second death, and my mind started bucking again and jumped the corral fence. Now here I am bawling on the street. Thank goodness the few folks out and about seem intent on heading home to supper and take no notice of me.*

*When I arrive at my destination, the tears have stopped but I'm still shaking with fury. I steady myself against the picket fence in front of the little brown house and turn west. I've rarely come here, to Mary's old house, although it's only six blocks from my own. In fact, I used to drive a block or two around just to avoid it.*

*But here I am, and here it is: the field. The one Mary wrote about in* The Land of Little Rain. *Her words in the oft-opened, now shabby slim volume have haunted me all these years.*

*She wrote about this field, her neighbor's field, that God must have meant it to be a field from all time, so admirably suited was it to its existence. She spent hours observing and writing about its busy life, trying to fix the precise moment when the predominant bloom in spring turned from the fire of wild almond to the brilliance of blue lupine. But she also watched the great red-tailed hawks swoop down to take their prey, their keen eyes seeking out what was invisible to hers in the afternoon light: scurrying jackrabbits and cottontails, gophers and mice, doves and small birds.*

*Mary didn't turn away from predators or try to sashay around their ravages. She said that one must force oneself to adopt the view point of the gods on such things, to avoid becoming too pitiful. Maybe so. I watch the field as the sun sinks below the Sierra and, sure enough, in the gathering twilight, an immense hawk comes soaring, seeming to spring from the castle ramparts, circling high above the field, tilting like a puppet strung from the fingers of some cruel master in heaven.*

*Mary said the enchantment of this valley was just that, an illusion. Bewitched by fables, dreaming of treasure, we are blind to the tragedy of our real lives. But Oppapago is not. The sad old rock has looked down on the cavalcade of human endeavor for centuries, and she weeps for us.*

*Standing there, my old bones as rickety as the picket fence they're propped up against, I no longer feel like weeping. Instead I'm surprised to find myself smiling, smiling at the memory of Mary, her tumultuous hair flying around the kitchen, as Ruth dips a spoon into the golden work of art that is Mary's cherry pie.*

*I recently read a biography of Mary, which I judged better than her own autobiography, and more accurate than my own fading sense of her, pieced together from our dwindling exchange of letters. The author said that even after settling permanently in Santa Fe, Mary retained her irascible, cantankerous nature. She wrote cruelly of friends, especially Mabel Dodge Luhan, thinly disguising them as characters in her novels, and she was known to turn her garden hose on visitors she didn't want to entertain. But she was also likely to show up without warning at her neighbors' homes with raspberries picked from her garden or fresh-baked muffins.*

*I gaze over at the little brown house she had inhabited with her larger-than-life spirit. A tragedy of Mary's life was that when she died in 1934, she was still struggling for financial security and still terribly, terribly lonely. In that sense, she had not moved far. And though she was respected by the luminaries of her day—she collaborated with photographer Ansel Adams on a book about Taos pueblo and inspired dances by choreographer Martha Graham—her works are little read now. Except for the first one, which I've always believed to be her best.*

*Another tragedy—for one's first work to be one's best? I suppose so. But now I'm thinking that while Oppapago from her lofty vantage point may find our lives tragic, we're at least down here giving it our all. Longing and clashing and trying to build something to mark our passing. Oppapago must see more than tragedy, perhaps a fragment or two even of heroism, in that.*

*It's become quite dark now, and I must make my way back home. I say goodbye to the field and the little brown house, and start walking south as the stars begin to pierce the deepening cyan of evening sky. Strangely, I feel rather lighthearted. When I reach home, CK has not yet returned. I'm not hungry, so I go to bed, and when, after dropping my head onto the pillow, I first stir, it is, miraculously, to morning light. Like most old folks, I'm accustomed to sleeping in short intervals, but this night I have traveled the whole of the way in a deep child-like slumber.*

*When CK rouses himself from his bed at nearly 11 o'clock in the morning and stumbles into the kitchen, he finds a misshapen but fragrant cherry pie on the table. "You're baking!" he exclaims, amazed at the aunt who won his devotion during summer visits by serving up a steady stream of hot dogs and fried chicken TV dinners.*

*"Yes," I answer nonchalantly, pouring his cup of tea. I had started the kettle when I heard him clomping about.*

*For hours before that, I'd been playing, yes that would be the correct word, playing with flour, sugar, vanilla, butter and cans of sour cherries. In rolling out the dough, I remembered Ma said, one shouldn't touch it more than necessary. Too much handling makes a tough crust. I remembered Mary's beautiful hands, hardly touching the dough at all, flitting like angel wings above it. My hands were shaky and awkward, of course, but not as bad as I had expected. Maybe I was "channeling Mary," as the kids who are "into" Eastern mysticism, say these days.*

*"Can I have a piece after breakfast?" CK is eyeing the pie hungrily.*

*"Why not have it for breakfast?" I say, taking a tablespoon from the drawer, poking it into the crust, and shoving the pie dish toward him.*

*"Really?!" CK can't believe it. "Hey, this is really good!" he exclaims after swallowing an immense mouthful.*

*"When you've finished, I want you to drive me somewhere," I tell him, applying a towel to the bowls and spatulas in the draining rack.*

*"You've got it," he says, chewing enthusiastically.*

*The place I ask him to drive me to is the Eastern Sierra Regional Airport, a couple of miles out of Bishop. CK looks at me quizzically, I haven't packed a bag, and he knows I've nowhere to go.*

*When we get close, I unfold the paper with the notes I've taken over the phone and point to a hangar. In front of it, a long, sleek sailplane lies belly-down on the tarmac, its nose hitched by a cord to the back of a small single-propeller plane.*

*"You want to watch the gliders?" CK tilts his shaggy head side to side like a confused puppy.*

*"No, I want to ride in one!"*

*Oddly enough, it's been discovered that Owens Valley's unique topography—the very features that made it attractive to the Paiute, homesteaders and urban water seekers—also create world-class soaring conditions. There is a phenomenon here called the "Sierra Wave." It's a potent current of air that forms off of the eastern slope of the Sierra Nevada, and it's the reason most of the world's sailplane records have been set over the Owens Valley.*

*I wasn't planning to go for a record, I just wanted to fly with my fish clouds. It turns out that the particular shape of those clouds, which scientists call 'lenticular,' is a sure sign of the formation of the Sierra Wave. They're particularly evident in winter and spring, and present in abundance today.*

*I don't have to explain this to CK, who's been reading about sailplane competitions in Owens Valley since boyhood. I learned the little I know about the Sierra Wave from his magazines. He's even been up in a glider several times, but this is something different. That his great aunt, who never showed the slightest interest in the contraptions, should form such a desire at this advanced age stupefies him. He peers at me as if trying to figure if I've lost my marbles.*

*"This isn't a midway ride at the county fair, Auntie," he lectures. "The wave is strong here, and it can be dangerous. The vertical movement that gives such a powerful lift can also create rotor winds. Planes can get sucked into a vortex of turbulence."*

*"Well," I say, "that would certainly be an exciting way to go!"*

*He stares at me. I've got his full attention, so I tell him the rest. "CK, I want you to go up with me now in the sailplane, and I want you to promise to do one more thing. I won't be around much longer, and it's the last request I'll ever make of you."*

*"What?" he asks cautiously.*

*"Claim your inheritance, don't give it away—and stop hiding away from the world." He starts to protest, but I hold up my hand. "As someone who's done precisely that most of her adult life, I have the right to say this to you: Get out there and mix it up with the forces that be. Use the money to do something! Start your own organic farm, if that's what you care about most, or an environmental research center, or help win the battle once and for all for Mono Lake and Owens Valley."*

*I reach for his hand. "Will you promise to do this for me CK?"*

*He leans over and hugs me, enveloping my bony frame in his fleshy embrace. Then he kisses my cheek and leans back, looking at me with affection.* "*I promise I will think about doing it Auntie Jane. I'll think about it very seriously.*"

*That's all I can ask for, so it will have to do. CK helps me climb down from his Jeep and takes my arm to lead me over to the planes. One of the two young men in matching orange baseball caps and t-shirts emblazoned with a yellow eagle design examines me skeptically. "Ah, excuse my asking ma'am, but how old are you?"*

"*I'm 72,*" *I say without hesitation. Young people, I find, never have any accurate notion of the age of their elders. The man looks at CK for confirmation, and he nods.*

*Fifteen minutes later we've been prepped with safety information and we're tucked into single seats along with the pilot. The tow plane engine starts up and we begin to move down the runway. Gradually, we pick up speed, like a horse going from a walk, to a trot, to a canter and then to a full-out gallop.*

*There's a bump or two as we lift off, and I look down at the ground falling away. There, spreading out below us is my valley, mostly brown, but still green here and there. Cutting through it is the wavy line of the Owens River, its shrunken banks now marked by grass, reeds and tree skeletons, but with an occasional surviving cottonwood, standing proud like a sentinel.*

*Suddenly I see the tow plane circling around and descending—we've been detached! And now, there ahead, are my flying fish. We glide over the waves of air to join them.*

Rebecca Hansen Carrer is a native Californian, and *Rain Shadow*, a work of affection for her beloved home state, is her first novel. Rebecca has been a freelance commercial writer for most of her professional career. She lives in California with her husband Laurent, a transplanted Frenchman who also loves this amazing place, and their two cats.

* 9 7 8 0 9 8 9 9 1 4 8 1 9 *